Marching to Byzantium

Brendan Ray

Deux Voiliers Publishing

Deux Voiliers Publishing
First Edition, December 2011
ISBN 978-0-9879641-5-1

Please note that the three books of *Marching to Byzantium* have also been published in separate volumes as *Sultans, Viziers and Alchemists, Cutting the Throat* and *The Fall of Constantinople*.

*To my wife, Nejla
For her friendship,
love and support*

Forward

Walking the streets of modern Istanbul, there are two faces that will be seen to be portrayed almost everywhere. The first is the stern countenance of Mustafa Kemal, the much beloved founder of the Turkish Republic. The second is that of Fatih Sultan Mehmet. Fatih, The Conqueror, is revered as a Turkish national hero, conquering the unconquerable city when he was still in his late teens. His face and his seal are emblems of the city, and his representations are seen all over. Fatih is the name of one of the largest neighbourhoods within the city walls. Topkapi, meaning Cannonball Gate (referring to the siege,) is the name of the neighbourhood on the opposite side of the walls, not to be confused with Topkapi Sarayi, the old Ottoman palace at the tip of the city's main peninsula. The bridge crossing from Asia to Europe is called the Fatih Sultan Mehmet Koprusu, the Mehmet the Conqueror Bridge, and crosses the line of the Roman and Anatolian Castles, which played such a large part in the original campaign.

This book started to suggest itself when I was first working in Istanbul, in 2003. Some colleagues and I decided to go for a walk along the whole stretch of the ancient Walls of Theodosius in the old city. We took the tramway down to the neighbourhood of Sultanahmet to show some of our new co-workers the touristy highlights, and then took a boat up to Haci Husrev Park and walked southward from the Golden Horne, all the way to the Sea of Marmara. We started in a neighbourhood called Fener, a rough-and-tumble slum area that used to host the imperial palace and adjoining buildings, and was now home to less grandiose inhabitants. From there we continued on past gate after gate until we reached the mesotechion area. The mesotechion is now, much as it always has been, in decay. Where the cannons finally broke down the walls, the walls are still down. The rest of the walls are still in a rather functional state, more than capable of fending off any pre-gunpowder army that would mysteriously show up in the modern city of twelve million. The wall-complex now houses homeless people and animals. The southern half of the wall was in much better shape than its northern counterpart. The gates, walls and moats are all in a restored condition, despite their exposure to the elements. The exception was the Golden Gate, the gate once reserved for imperial triumphs. This gate was boarded up and inaccessible to law-abiding tourists. The final peg in the wall was the so called Marble Tower, which if truth be told, was neither marble nor really a tower.

I found myself acting as the tour-guide/narrator of the group, explaining the events of 1453 to my team, and I was constantly trying to give more and more background to the conflict. Most of my audience was aware of the dynamics of the Western-Islamic conflict through the eyes of their televisions, and were familiar with the crusades, as well as the more modern conflicts in Mesopotamia and the undeservedly named "Holy Land." They were trying to place Istanbul's narrative into that context. I was constantly trying to take the story out of the moralizing politics of victimhood that have dominated the discussion of the field and place it into its own box, a rational conflict where both sides were just and unjust, both sides acted in their own self interest, and both sides were doomed to fight.

In the essay "Why I Write," George Orwell noted that "Writing a book is a horrible, exhausting struggle, like a long bout of some painful illness. One would never undertake such a thing if one were not driven on by some demon whom one can neither resist nor understand." This whole endeavour started out as my way of explaining history as events and interest rather than falling into the nationalist dialogue of retelling the past as teleology for the present, and it took wings of its own.

My original plan was chewed up and spit out in the revision process as Ahmet, Mario, and Ezera wrestled each other for page space. For years, draft after draft emerged. Ongoing researched unearthed new details which had to then push themselves into the story. My experiences changed the characters over the years, until they finally took the form in which they've settled. Before the first draft was done, the demon in the book was writing its own dialogue, the characters were disobeying my wonderfully laid out plan and seemingly had their own motivations, while the historical events took place around them. Some characters flourished, some died off and some escaped to mere survival, reacting the only way they could while the whole world crashed around them.

When writing historical fiction, you run into the problem of history versus fiction. This book is an example of the later. When I was cataloguing the dramatis personae, it became obvious that a cast of thousands with many having very similar foreign sounding names would take away from the readability of the story. Because of this, there are several characters that have been merged into one; Stavros of Brussa is one such character, who is a stand-in for an entire faction of Byzantine society. The Emir of Sinope was a real person, but his character has been merged with that of Hamza-Bey. Mario Orsini is almost wholly fictitious, but inspired by the German physic Paracelsus, who would not come around for another seventy years. There are several minor players identified as Vikings, even though the Viking age ended two centuries prior. The "Vikings" in this story are Germanic peoples from Scandinavia, the Baltic basin, and the rivers of northern and eastern Europe.

The final journey in this saga has been finding the right publisher. I was thrilled when Deux Voiliers Publishing accepted the manuscript. I was equally pleased to learn that my Trilogy, which chronicles the end of the Eastern Roman Empire, would be published at the same time as Stephen Bennett's The Last of the Ninth, a tale of Roman intrigue taking place in many of the same regions as the Trilogy, but also a brisk twelve centuries earlier.

Writing historical fiction, especially on themes that touch on the nationalist nerves of the people of the Middle East and the Balkan Peninsula, is as delicate as un-anesthetised dental surgery on a tiger. You write knowing that there will be some who are bound to be offended by your presence in their temple. This book is an unaffiliated hermit's view into the temples of the past. The view that I try to present is one based on sincere love and respect for the people of the region, their tumultuous shared histories and their living culture. As Terry Pratchet so kindly put it, history's always got a few tricks up its frayed sleeve, it's been around for a long time. I hope that you enjoy my stroll through the old city. I hope that it will delight and entertain, with a few surprises, and if the spark of my enthusiasm for the history of the area is contagious to you, all the better.

Brendan Ray, Toronto – 2012

Book One
Sultans, Viziers and Alchemists

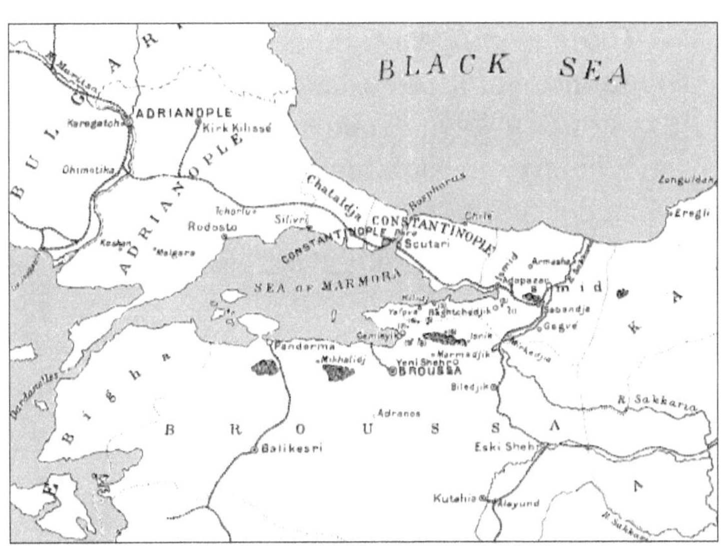

Sailing To Byzantium

Stanza One

That is no country for old men. The young
In one another's arms, birds in the trees
—Those dying generations—at their song,
The salmon-falls, the mackerel-crowded seas,
Fish, flesh, or fowl, commend all summer long
Whatever is begotten, born, and dies.
Caught in that sensual music all neglect
Monuments of unageing intellect.

William Butler Yeats

Chapter 1 - The Call to Mehmet

The killers awoke before dawn and pressed southward into the hills. Their ship had arrived on the coast as the sun had set last night, and the two men set about their task immediately. They quickly learnt that their prey was in the hills south of the city on a hunting expedition with the local governor.

This information was disturbing to the two, as this meant that their target was armed, accompanied and prepared for a fight. Their orders were, however, quite clear and time was pressing. As the sun began to rise along the coast, and onto the hills of black and green, over the wooden houses of the Black Sea port, the two men clad in hunting gear walked past the south guard picket of the town's watch and began their own hunting party.

That day, the sun shone uncharacteristically fair upon the Pontic Mountains, a region famous for its inclement weather. The spring rains had left the forest floor green and the earth rich and fertile. Along the winding path through the maze of rises and runs, trotted two horses carrying two men in hunter's garb. Their road led from the main highway to an old Roman watch tower that was now essentially abandoned for obsolescence in light of the lack of a nearby border to watch. It was now known as *"The Rookery"* and served as the recreational hunting camp of Kazim-bey, the governor of Amaseia Sanjak.

The two figures proceeded up the path nestled between a burgeoning canopy of green above them and blanket of black earth below them. From that earth, grasses, flowers and foliage were pushing their way past the memory of winter to proclaim the long awaited arrival of spring. The slopes of Kale Hill hosted this war of seasons and was crowned with a round crenellated tower.

"Their watch has probably seen us already, and will be sending someone to greet us before we arrive at the tower," said the first hunter. "Don't get worried, we're just messengers, we've come at the behest of the governor's patron, there's no reason for them to be suspicious."

"So you've said," replied the second rider "But it's still a dangerous errand that we're on, so I'll continue to worry, thank you very much."

"Don't talk like that," the first one said, his eyes scanning the forest around them. "We are being observed from the tower for certain, but we don't know if there are any other observers in hiding and underfoot. We'll have to be careful until we get him away from the governor and his guards. The last thing we want is to find ourselves surrounded by an angry clan of hunters, armed to the teeth and looking for blood. Let me do the talking once we meet our hosts."

"*Hosts* implies that they were expecting us…"

"Regardless of what they were expecting this morning, they are expecting us now. I can see some outriders coming towards us now."

"They're armed"

"Of course they're armed! So are we. Smile, and let me do the talking."

They were met by three riders who were not dressed for a hunt. They were clad in light mail armour, greased black so as not to reflect the sun's rays. Their conical helms were black, and plumed with brown horsetails. They each carried a plumed lance, a sword at their side and a bow on their backs. Their large horses were protected by light mail as well, and were fitted with quivers of arrows and an assortment of javelins and smaller melee weapons, to be used at their rider's discretion. The eldest of the three rode in front, flanked by the two younger ones.

"Peace be upon you, travelers," he greeted the two intruders.

"And unto you be peace," replied the first of the two hunters. "We are messengers from Adrianople. We bring urgent tidings for Prince Mehmet, son of Murat. We were told that we could find him on this mountain."

"Then we'll say '*welcome*' to you. Before you receive an audience however, we do need to know a few things. For example, your names and your business," announced the eldest of the three.

"My name is Ohuz, son of Osman, and this is Nuh, son of Ibrahim. We are servants of Sultan Murat, Khan of Khans and Marshall of the Faithful. We are here to accompany the prince back to Adrianople with us."

"You are a long way from Adrianople, Ohuz-bey. We'll bring you to Kazim-bey, son of Attila, and you can make your requests to him. Before we bring you to him, you and your silent friend there must surrender your weapons to my two sons here, and then you can follow me to the camp."

The old horseman pointed angrily at him and Nuh as he spoke.

Nuh looked nervously at Ohuz. Without missing a beat, the spokesman of the two replied that "It is not customary of officers of the imperial court to surrender anything to local tribes; especially when we are on urgent business of the sultan."

The elder rider looked on impatiently and continued in an unintoned cadence. "I don't like to repeat myself, Ohuz-bey, but I will none the less. You are a long way from the capital. I don't recognize your face, your tone is hostile and we're three, while you are two. Please surrender your weapons."

Nuh, who had been silent to this point, saw the two younger horsemen trot sidewise, flanking the two interloping messengers. It was at this point that he decided to abandon his silence. "Of course we can place our arms and our protection in your safekeeping, Gazi. You do your lord fine service, and should be commended for your diligence." He turned to his travelling companion. "Ohuz, we have a job to do that doesn't need any more distractions along the road." Nuh removed his scabbard from his belt and handed it to one of the younger riders. Ohuz met the old rider's gaze and smiled politely. The gesture was not reciprocated. He handed his sword to one the two younger horsemen.

"You travel lightly to carry only one sword apiece," said Hassan, one of the two young riders. His face wore a moustache that didn't yet have the strength of root to fill in completely.

"We are but humble messengers, young one," Ohuz replied with a whisper of unveiled sarcasm.

At this, the young rider smiled slightly as he looked upon the confiscated scabbard. It was wood and steel, covered with silk and inlaid with turquoise and gold filigree, an impressive piece. Not what one would expect from a humble messenger. He turned to his father and nodded.

The old man turned his large charger sidelong. "You two will follow me, side by side. My sons will follow you." The camp is only an hour or so up the hill, and the governor is hunting with his sons and the prince. The road up the hill is treacherous, so pay attention and don't waste your time on idle conversation along the way. Follow me."

Ohuz shot Nuh an angry look, and the party began their assent to the Rookery.

During the hour's ascent, Hassan and his younger brother Ahmet examined their two guests while they rode. The two guests were both lightly armed, hardly prepared to defend themselves. Their cloaks were of fine grey wool; their tunics were green silk, covered with leather jackets. Their leather leggings ended in soft leather boots, more appropriate to a life in the halls of the palace than for trekking cross-country. Their horses were slight but obviously well cared for. They rode in a disciplined manner, but were hardly as '*at home*' on horseback as the two brothers and their father. These two were obviously not '*sons of the steppe*', nor were they mere messengers as they purported to be. Who they were, and what they were doing here would be the prerogative of their master to judge.

The task of observation was shared by the two messengers from the capital. Their three escorts were obviously Turcoman tribesmen in the employ of the local potentate, Kazim-bey. They were coarse and had a casual air of violence about them. It was upon the spears of men such as these that the old sultans in Iconium had created an empire, and upon their bows that the local beyliks maintained their sovereignty against a dwindling Christian empire. Their gazi lifestyle made for swift recruiting during wars against the enemies of the faith, but it hardly made for a culture upon which the new sultans in Adrianople were forging an empire. They had a place in the order of things, but that was dwindling, or so they thought to themselves.

The Rookery loomed over their path and seemed to watch their arrival. The standing round-tower dominated the compound at the hill-top, its walls covered with a combination of moss, lichen, fungus and creeping vine that made it seem to grow out of the forest itself. The compound was fenced in by a stone pile wall, opening at one side to pour out the pathway upon which the five entered. The wall was to keep out animals, and was without any real martial merit.

Within the walls were seven buildings. All were wooden and built into a circle with the tower as the keystone. They opened into a courtyard that hosted a large fire-pit. On the left of the tower was a wooden stabling house that stood next to a small mess hall. On the right was a single floor wooden barrack, and a small prayer room next to it, adjacent to the opening of the compound. On the far side of the compound was the small hut that served as the camp's latrine and in the opposite corner was a covered water reservoir.

The party of five was met at the gate by a footman, also clad in light armour.

"Peace be upon you, Ali." He said to the elder horseman.

"And unto you be peace, Jengiz," he said as he dismounted. "We have two new guests. Tell the cook to prepare them a meal, these two have a *hungry* look to them."

He dismounted and turned to face the two messengers. The two messengers were a little suspicious of the manner in which he had pronounced '*hungry*'.

"You can dismount here. My sons will see that your horses are properly stabled, and that you are properly fed. Kazim-bey should return from the hunt shortly," he handed the reins of his horse to Jengiz the footman and walked to the tower.

Ohuz and Nuh were fed some meat soup, a welcome break from the dry rations that had subsided them for their trek into the hills, and took a seat together at the fire. The two brothers kept an eye on them, and remained alert and armed, but outside of earshot.

"They aren't very hospitable here, are they?" Said Nuh as they sat together at the fire. "I've got a bad feeling about this."

"Don't worry, they're just being cautious. If they suspected us, we'd have been killed on the road," Said Ohuz, as he coiled up next to the fire. "Stay alert, because we may have to get out of here *very* quickly. The walls wouldn't keep us in, but on foot I don't like our odds of escape. We need to get the prince out of here, and into open country, and do it quickly. Remember, there'll be other interested parties behind us."

"What if they get here before we can get the prince? If they're only a day or so behind us, that means that we will probably run into them on the road back. If Kazim-bey's hunting party comes back with us to the port, we'll have a very ugly situation here when we run into them."

"They'll probably take a few days, but you're right, we can't be too cautious. Tonight, when everyone is sleeping, you'll get the horses ready and I'll do the deed. Our horses are two of the fastest in the master's stable, and we're travelling light. We could make it back to the port, and get out of Amaseia before they could catch up with us. Eat your soup; we're going to have a long day."

Ohuz didn't know how right he was. Atop the tower, Ali's old eyes squinted as he saw yet another party enter the valley before the mountain from the north. This one was bigger than the last. He couldn't guess their numbers at this distance, as night was approaching, and he would probably wait until morning to ride out to meet these new guests; the road was dangerous enough in broad day-light. He hoped that Kazim would soon return from the hunt along with the young prince. "We're going to have a long night." He thought to himself, echoing Ohuz's assessment.

The shadows were long, and night was a closing when the hunting party of five men and a half dozen hunting dogs returned to the camp. The first was Kazim, an aging warlord decked out in the trappings expected of a man in his position. Standing little more than five feet off the ground, his rotund presence seemed to take up more space than his stature would allow. Upon his brow was a large dent that seemed to dominate his face. In his youth he had met an axe-wielding footman during those hellish months at Varna, and been cut down and left for dead. His skull mended to a point, though the scar added an aura of menace to man of his surprisingly congenial nature. Behind him strode his three sons, aged fourteen, seventeen and twenty-one. They all shared their father's characteristically short stature and well-fed belly, although seventeen and twenty-one were slightly taller than their father.

The fifth man of the party was slim and tall. At age eighteen, Mehmet, third son of Murat, was an oddity in the camp. He had been educated in the harem, trained by some of the great minds of his day, and was fluent in Turkish, Arabic, Latin and Greek, and functional in Persian and Hebrew. This explained his rather bookish appearance to the rest of the hunting party. Although he was an accomplished rider and a good hunter, the ways of the semi-nomadic populace didn't quite suit him.

Two years ago, he had been sent out by his father, into the provinces to receive what he referred to a "horseback education", and to learn the more traditional aspects of the martial powers that built and maintained the civilized empire that was dreamed of in the halls of power. Although he tried to put a positive face on his predicament, Amaseia was truly an exile for the prince. It was intended as such, and interpreted thusly.

"Peace be upon you, Ali, Jengiz," Kazim said as he entered the compound.

"And unto you be peace, Kazim-bey," the guards greeted him. "We have some guests."

Behind him, Ohuz and Nuh had risen up from their seats around the fire, but were still out of earshot. "They claim to be messengers from Adrianople, with urgent business with young Mehmet." Ali kept eye contact with his patron, and didn't address Mehmet directly. He found the young guest to be a little snobbish and aloof.

"But?" continued the dwarfish chieftain.

"They are from the capital, for certain, but there's something about them that I don't trust," He looked over his shoulder and dropped his voice to little more than a whisper. "There's another party coming from the north. They are camped at the bottom of Kale Hill. I intended to leave at daybreak tomorrow to meet them. They are a large party. I'm not certain how many."

Mehmet looked past Ali at the two messengers in their expensive attire and court-trained comportment. "My father must be dead." He said flatly.

"I believe so, sir." Ali said, turning his gaze to the young prince, and without any intonation continued. "God bless him and God bless you, I'll pray for you both."

"That explains one messenger, but two parties of messengers raises a question." Kazim whispered. "Do our two guests know about the other party?"

"No. They can't be seen from the courtyard, and these two have stayed by the fire since we arrived a few hours ago they should be night-blind by now. Their weapons are in the tower."

"Then let's meet these messengers, and see what they have to say," replied Mehmet. "By your leave, Kazim-bey."

When Mehmet was seven years old, his older brother Abdullah had died. He fell from his horse, under mysterious circumstances. Another older brother was an invalid and a ward of the harem. A few years ago, Mehmet's younger brother Ali had been strangled to death as he slept. His nearest blood cousin, Orhan, was a prisoner in Constantinople. Mehmet was never accused outright of having a hand in Ali's death, but the Latin of

'*Qui Bono?*' would certainly have fate cast a suspicious glance in the young prince's direction. Royal succession was a bloody business, especially since the time of Mehmet's grandfather and namesake, Mehmet the First. It was a business that fine-tuned the suspicions of those involved.

Kazim led the group up to the two emissaries, and kissed them both warmly on each cheek. "Welcome to my home, for this camp is certainly more my home than my house in the city," he said smiling. "I'm told that you have important news for my young friend here."

Mehmet aped his host's greeting by kissing the two guests. "Speak, if your message is so important."

Ohuz and Nuh returned the greeting and the *selams* to Kazim and to Mehmet. "Thank you for your warmth. We have a message that is intended only for the young prince alone. It is by order of his father, Sultan Murat."

"You insult my host," answered Mehmet quickly, but with a smile. "Speak now, and save my friend the insult of speaking behind his back, and save me the chore of repeating everything to him later, as I of course would do, so far as God lifts my memory to accuracy."

"We bring ill news of your father, Prince." Ohuz began. "A week ago, he suffered apoplexy, and two nights ago, he died. We came here as quickly as we could."

"Two nights from Adrianople? Fast that was. I hope that Hassan and Ahmet have been looking after your poor horses!" Kazim said incredulously.

"They have been most hospitable, Kazim-bey," Nuh answered thankfully. "Prince Mehmet is wanted in the capital."

'*I know I'm wanted in the capital!*' Mehmet thought to himself. '*The question is who wants me there and who doesn't. These two chased lightning to arrive here in three days, ahead of someone for sure. Which means that the party in the valley contains the real emissary, and these two junior courtiers see a path to advancement by either my good graces or my elimination.*'

"Your speed is something to be noted, men. You do your duty well. Who sent you?" Kazim asked with a friendly smile on his face. Apparently his thoughts were along the same lines as those of Mehmet.

"We have been sent by your mother, the Valide Sultan."

'*Idiots*' Mehmet thought to himself. "If you have been sent by my mother, then I shall greet you as my brothers!"

'*If they'd been sent by my mother then they'd be angels sent to escort me to the hereafter!*'

With that, he kissed the two men again. Mehmet continued. "Now, we've brought some rabbits with us, so we'll have the cook begin a barbecue, and eat together as one big family. While there is no blood relation between myself and Kazim-bey, I call him my uncle, for he has given more love and guidance than many who are in my immediate family. Tonight, we'll have a family meal, and in the morning, I'll leave you, Uncle, and go with these men. Destiny awaits! Now if you two will excuse us, we must wash up before we sit."

The emissaries bowed and the hunters went to the stable, where they washed prior to the meal, and the two messengers waited at the fire. "What luck, Ohuz! In the morning we'll go, the prince in tow, and no witnesses!"

"Greed is our friend, Nuh. Did you see the way he lit up when he heard that his father was dead? I don't know what Murat did to deserve such a remorseless son, but we'll erase him from the lists of the living, shortly after breakfast tomorrow!"

"Thank God for such a simple delivery!"

The hunting party gathered silently in the stable house as the last light of day hid itself in the west.

"Your mother?" Kazim asked.

"My mother was a slave in my father's harem," replied Mehmet. "She died many years ago, unannounced, as his current wife never cared for her. The new Valide Sultan, my father's *wife*, is alive and well in Adrianople. Last summer, I heard a rumour that she was with child. These men must have been sent by her."

"And the men down in the valley?"

"Probably the real messengers, but I can't be certain."

"In the morning, we'll go and meet them, and see their business. I will have Ali arrest our two guests, and bring them to the city in the morning."

"Thank you, Uncle." Mehmet smiled with genuine affection. Kazim had been a loyal soldier in his father's service and had fought at Varna, a glory and horror still fresh after only eight years. It was there that some Italian mercenary gave him that brutal reminder of service. For his trouble, he was elevated to the title of Sipahi, or knight, and given a non-hereditary fiefdom called a "*Sanjak*" in Amaseia. Killing unarmed men in his camp seemed a little cold-blooded to him, as opposed to killing in the heat of battle, when the other man is armed and in possession of an equally strong urge to kill or be killed. Mehmet was polite about receiving this favour from his host, but a little regretful that Kazim was unwilling to execute the men on site.

To everyone's surprise, it was the usually shy Ahmet, the younger son of Ali who spoke up. "Should we not simply kill them both here tonight? I don't mean to speak out of turn, Sir, but they came here to your home with murder on their mind. Your *home*, Sir."

There was a moment's silence as Kazim-bey considered what was said. He took a deep breath and looked to Mehmet. "You are to be the sultan, and a great sheikh in your own right by the week's end. What does you wisdom tell you?"

Mehmet looked at him wearily. "After the kindness you've shown me for the past year, I would not presume to tell you what to do in your own home, Uncle." His gaze didn't waver.

Kazim half turned to Ahmet. He nodded slightly. Ahmet nodded back. Mehmet rested a hand on Kazim's shoulder in gratitude. "Thank you, Uncle."

Ahmet and his brother Hassan walked past the fire pit where Nuh and Ohuz were quietly plotting and went to the tower to grab their equipment. Ahmet took two javelins, each measuring little more than a foot in length. "Ok, brother… They're both sitting by the fire. I'll lead in. I'll hit the quiet one with the first javelin, and then the talkative one. They won't be able to see that we're armed because of the fire and the darkness. The javelins will wound them, then we'll just put them to the sword. If one escapes, I'll pursue, you join once the other is dealt with. If they both run, I'll chase the chatterbox, you take the other one."

"We should take our armour off. If we chase them through the forest, we don't need to be weighed down. Besides, they're unarmed," added Hassan.

"We didn't properly search them, they might have a knife."

"We've got swords and javelins. They *might* have a knife, Little Brother."

The younger brother nodded, and the two took their mail off, made eye contact for an instant, and went out the door.

Ohuz was sitting in front of the fire, warming himself in the cold spring night. Nuh was next to him playing with one of the hunting dogs. Nuh saw the two brothers approaching the fire out of the corner of his eye. He turned to wave with a smile on his face. As they came into range of the firelight, the smile disappeared from his face.

Ahmet held the first short javelin by the grip at its base, and whipped it over-hand at Nuh as he squatted happily in front of the fire. The javelin's tip dug in his side below his bottom rib and above the tip of his hip bone. He tried to stand at the last minute, but it was more of an involuntary muscle reaction than any serious attempt at escape. He tried to stand but collapsed under his leg and torso's inability to hold him. He crashed into the fire and rolled out just in time to see Hassan's scimitar come down. The dogs jumped from beside the fire and started barking, adding to the panic around the fire.

The dog's barking, and Nuh's flailing was enough of a quick distraction to alert Ohuz to the immediate threat. His hand darted into his boot and withdrew a knife. While he had enough time to draw his weapon, he didn't have enough time to throw it before Ahmet struck.

Flicking the javelin in the same whipping motion that had neutralized Nuh, Ahmet's javelin struck Ohuz's crouched knee just below the patella and slid under his kneecap. In their deaths, as in their lives, Ohuz was much more talkative than Nuh. He screamed in pain and turned to run. The weight of the javelin lodged under his kneecap pulled him down as he turned and brought his right knee with him. The javelin butt hit the ground and Ohuz fell on top of it, pushing the javelin through to the other side. He rolled to his back and tried to scream. His lungs had no force to do so. Ahmet's sword was drawn.

'*Where's my knife?*' Ohuz thought to himself quickly. It was, however, far too late to mount any reasonable defence against the sudden and lethal attack from the sons of Ali. Ahmet's sword came crashing down, and the deed was done.

In the stable, the rest of the hunting party waited and listened. They had agreed not to interfere unless they heard a cry for help. If they had all gone out at the same time, the two would-be assassins would know that something was amiss and run. Ali was against this idea, and wanted to lead the charge, rather than sit back while his sons entered into combat. They had assured him they would call at any sign of trouble. They heard dogs bark, and Ohuz scream, and burst out into the courtyard seven men with swords drawn. When Ali arrived at the fire pit, a few mere seconds after he left the stable house, he saw the deed was finished and his two sons were silhouetted against the firelight.

Hassan looked up first. "We're fine, Baba! Don't worry! It's finished."

"Somebody shut those dogs up!" yelled Kazim, as they were barking at the two corpses, and running around in a general panic.

While the melee had lasted only a few seconds, its evidence was everywhere apparent. The smell of Nuh's burnt hair hung in the air. Blood had pumped from their bodies onto the mud and the grass. It glistened black off the log that was being used as bench in front of the fire, and it caught the firelight on the ground.

"Put the bodies by the latrines, we'll bury them in the morning light. Jengiz, you'll have to clean the fire area before breakfast. Ali, put the dogs in the tower." Kazim instructed. "Let the fire die out, we won't be sitting here telling tall tales tonight, boys."

The two sons of Ali brought the bodies over to the far corner of the Rookery's courtyard. To their surprise, Mehmet helped carry the bodies and spread lime to keep animals away.

"You two children did very well tonight, thank you." The prince said. The Turkish word *Chojuklar – children*, is used to denote friendship here, Ahmet and Hassan were both older than Mehmet, unlike English, the word in Turkish doesn't convey any disrespect.

The two brothers were both a little surprised by Mehmet's show of interest, as it contrasted with his more usual aloofness. "We did our best, Prince."

"You had enough brains to think of a good, if simple, plan, and you had enough fortitude to see it through. It was fairly cold-blooded of you both. Many people couldn't kill two unarmed men blinded in the dark."

They were not sure if that was a compliment.

"I'll be leaving here soon. If either or both of you are interested in joining me in the capital, I will need some strong people who I can trust." He motioned towards the two corpses, lime scattered over top of them. I don't want to be surrounded by the more traditional court appointments.

The two men's blood was still up. Over the space of five minutes, they had become killers of men, and were now being offered the friendship of the man who was heir to the House of Osman and by week's end would become one of the most powerful men in the Mediterranean World.

"Thank you, Prince," the two blurted out almost immediately.

Echoing previous assessments, Mehmet concluded, "Now go get a good night's sleep. Tomorrow's going to be a long day."

In the valley, the emissary camp was on the move shortly after dawn. They were led by a stout man, who maintained a vicious dignity about himself. He wore no armour, simply a felt cassock with a silk undershirt and leggings. Once upon a time, his boots were of very fine quality, but use had weighed heavily upon them, and they bore the marks of many repairs. From out of his silk sleeves came two hands that also bore the marks of heavy use. They were littered with minor cuts, scrapes and burns, healed over many times over the years. He wore a bushy black moustache that wrapped around his hawkish face, from his right ear to his cauliflowered left. Atop his head stood a giant white felt tower of a cap. The cap was one of the primary identifies of this man as a member of the elite Janissary Corps.

Early in the morning, the company of Janissaries numbering what must be close to a hundred men, were met by the hunting party of ten on the road leading to the rookery. Mesut, the commander, was greeted by Kazim.

"Peace be upon you, Janissary," Kazim announced icily.

"And unto you be peace, Sipahi," replied the emissary. There was no love to be found between the Sipahis and Janissaries, there's was a rivalry with long standing. "We have urgent news for Prince Mehmet."

"My father is dead, and I am summoned by the court," said Mehmet.

"My condolences to you. God bless your father, and now you." Mesut paused for a moment. "The news has reached you?"

"Two men came to the camp last night to tell me. They won't be joining us for the trip back," answered the Prince. "These two men, Ahmet and Hassan, the sons of Ali, will be joining us to Adrianople."

"We have a boat in the harbour that will take us to the European shore, and horses from there will take us to the capital."

"Then let's go. We are all on horseback, so if we push we can make town before noon, and set sail in the afternoon." Mehmet turned to the governor. "Kazim-bey, I sincerely thank you for your hospitality in your province for these many months. Your friendship, and that of your family will stay in my heart for all my days."

"The duty given me by your father was a great honour, Mehmet. Peace be upon you."

"And unto you be peace."

They remained on horseback, kissed each other on both cheeks, and then parted company.

Hassan and Ahmet bid farewell to their father, who was beside himself with a father's pride. His two sons were to be companions to the sultan. One day in all likelihood, they would be elevated to Sipahi, like his master, Kazim had been, so many years ago.

The three joined the hundred on the road to town, and the seven returned quietly to their hunting camp.

Chapter 2 – The Ancient Regime

Halil's belly rolled over his towel as he entered the main chamber of the bathhouse. He was approaching his fiftieth year, and most of those had been spent in the luxury of one palace or another. His fleshy appearance showed the legacy of that opulence. His podgy body clipped across the marble room on his little wooden sandals as we walked around the octagonal chamber, looking in each of the four marble side chambers that adjoined the steam filled room. He could relax only once he was sure that he was alone.

Along the eight walls were two doors, one leading to the dry sauna, the other one opposite leading to the outside. Along four of the walls were small marble booths for him to relax and have a private bath, and on the other two walls, running perpendicular to the exits were two long marble benches, where men waited to have their public washing. In the middle of the room, was a large four metre across octagonal marble table, called a *Gobek Tashi,* or Belly-Stone. Under it was the furnace and the hot water that poured out of the eight basins, one on each wall.

"Ooof," he exhaled and sat on one of the stone benches next to a hot water basin. He tensed up again when the wooden door opened on the far wall.

A large bathhouse attendant walked in, wrapped in a towel and wearing the same wooden sandals as Halil. He waved to his guest. "Good morning, Halil-Pasha."

"Good morning, Arto," Halil replied, stealing a quick glance out the door as it opened and closed for a quick moment. "Peace be upon you."

"And unto you be peace." Arto replied. He carried a large copper bowl in one hand and walked over to his guest. "Are you well?"

"I'm busy, but I'm healthy." Halil replied ambivalently.

Arto put the bowl down on the bench next to his honoured client. Out of the bowl came a bar of soap, a large white cloth and a razor blade. Halil noticed it with disapproval. Blades of any kind always seemed tools of ill omen, and his belly-length beard testified to his conviction on that point. Arto turned on the faucet in the basin next to Halil and began to fill it with hot water. "It's a wonderful day today, spring is here."

The attendant kept up his idle conversation as he poured hot water from the basin onto Halil's head, using a copper bowl, and began to wash his hair and beard. Halil listened impassively as the attendant cleaned him. They engaged in the regular chit-chat of weather and innocuous statements that give social cohesion to the service industry.

Then the door opened again.

A stranger walked into the room, dressed in the normal towel and wooden sandals of a Turkish bathhouse, and sat down on a marble bench directly across from Halil and Arto. Halil looked at him suspiciously.

The man across from him was not a local. He had long and unkept hair, and a tight physique, not the sort of urban notable who usually haunted the capital. He looked like some rabble who could ill-afford to visit this bathhouse. The most telling evidence of the man's origins came from the ash tattoos on the man's arms and legs. Tattooing was a traditional Turkic funeral rite, the ash from pyres used as ink and inlaid into the flesh of some honoured mourners. This rite was haram – forbidden by religious law – and practiced only among tribesmen who still secretly practiced the old pagan ways or was kept as part of a convert's legacy. The sight of the man's marked flesh repulsed Halil, and surprised the attendant.

Arto contained his surprise and continued his work. He politely acknowledged the guest and worried more about cleaning his honoured guest. He took the soap and rubbed Halil's short cropped hair vigorously.

'*Who is he? I don't recognise him,*' Halil thought to himself as Arto poured hot water onto his head again to wash the soap from his hair. He tensed up as some of the soap washed into his eyes. He tried not to panic as he tried to keep his eyes open despite the hot soap and Arto poured another bowl full of hot water over him, rinsing his hair again. '*He could be sent for me, attack me, alone and blinded here.*' His thoughts flew to the razor blade beside him.

"Relax, Brother!" Arto told his stiffened client. "Come on, lie down here."

The attendant walked up the giant octagonal stone dais in the middle of the room. He slapped the hard surface loudly. Halil lay down on the belly stone, it was hard and hot under his back. This was normally a very relaxing experience, but today he was anything but relaxed. He kept glancing over at the strange interloper in the room. The attendant washed him, scrubbed him, and massaged his underused muscles. All this time, the unknown man sat on the far side of the chamber silently.

After the massage, Halil sat up on the edge of the marble table. The attendant massaged his back. All during this, Halil listened carefully for any movement on behalf of the man to whom his back was now turned.

"You are very tense, Halil-Pasha," Arto commented once finished. He washed the man's face one last time.

"It comes with the palace, Arto. There is lots of stress. Thank you, I feel great."

"Are you sure? You still seem anxious."

"I'll be fine, thank you."

"Maybe you should go to the mosque and pray? It is Friday, you know. That can help relax your mind."

"Thank you, I'll do that." He looked over his shoulder and saw the same man quietly waiting. Halil walked around the belly stone and left through the large wooden door. The tattooed stranger watched him leave.

When he stepped out of the steam-room, and into the reception area, his skin screamed rebellion against the cold spring air. He had intended to walk straight through the reception room to the dressing area, but stopped dead when he saw the only inhabitant of the reception room was another large man, wearing the same face as the stranger in the steam-room.

"Greetings, Vizier," the stranger said. "I'm glad that you are healthy and safe."

"Why wouldn't I be?" Halil asked looking over his shoulder, to see the towel clad stranger step out of the steam as the door opened behind him.

'*They must be brothers*.' He thought to himself.

"We have been asked to bring you to the palace, Prime Minister." The clothed one continued. "I'm Hassan, and this is my brother, Ahmet. We have been sent by Mehmet, the son of Murat."

Halil's face showed nothing. "Of course. I'll go get dressed, and then we can go."

"Thank you, Pasha," Hassan smiled in a friendly manner that seemed quite genuine. This was oddly enough, even more upsetting to the Grand Vizier than being stalked by these two unknown tribesmen in the bathhouse.

"Indeed."

Halil was the grand vizier, prime minister to Murat and Mehmet Chelebi before him. Halil was so trusted by Murat, that he was given a special task, allowed to no other man. This task was the education of one of the sultan's sons: any of whom could become the future sovereign.

This was no light task. Ali, Abdullah and Mehmet had to be taught languages and mathematics. Culture and philosophy were to be the hallmarks of the boys' education. They would learn the Koran, as though the ink were drawn over their own beating hearts. They were all to be philosopher-princes, pious lords, unspoilt by the corruptions of office and wealth. This was Murat's dream, and so Halil went about it with a grim enthusiasm that would tolerate no faltering. This task he undertook with the full support of the most powerful and pious man in Europe. Murat was a prince of unequalled virtue in both peace and war.

It was a blessing to Halil, because of the opportunity that the charge presented him. Not only could he serve the current sultan, but his position after the eventual death of Murat would be secured. More that secured! More than merely influential! He had the opportunity to create new princes, operating on the blank slate of these children, with whom his lord presented him! Oh, it was a happy day.

There are some who say that the devil is in the details. That would prove to be a grotesque understatement when it came to this opportunity. Halil would find himself praying for deliverance from these devils. These devils transformed children, full of infinite possibilities, into base youths with more privilege than wisdom, and whose star would rise only with their father's fall.

The two brothers brought Halil to a large room in the palace. The walls were grey stone, the floor was covered with a lavish green carpet, and there were cushions along the wall. This waiting chamber was the most bland room in the palace. The austere nature of the chamber was offset by the rather flamboyant appearance of the two inhabitants when

Halil entered.

"Peace be upon you, Brother Halil," said the first one, draped out in red silks. He rushed over to the Prime Minister and kissed him on both cheeks.

"Unto you be peace, Brother Kalid." Halil responded. He saw his two brothers, Musa, the Chief Treasurer in blue, and Kalid, the Administrator of Religious Foundations in red. "Peace be upon you, Brother Musa."

"Unto you be peace, Brother Halil," Musa replied sullenly. "You've been summoned also? I was accosted on the street by a couple of Anatolian goat-herders!"

"As was I," continued Kalid. "They came to my home."

"They found me in the bathhouse near the Tall Mosque," added Halil. "The young prince intends a serious cabinet meeting, I suppose."

"Or to finish what was started two years ago," Kalid answered.

"He sent messengers to Iconium and Brussa. That can't be good for us," added Musa

Halil swallowed nervously. "We're not without options, my brothers. We still have friends and allies, at court and elsewhere…"

"Enough of your constant plotting, Halil!" Kalid snapped. "If we throw ourselves behind him now, and support him wholeheartedly, he may decide to let the past stay in God's memory and out of his own!"

"I agree, Halil," Musa implored the grand vizier. "We don't need to continue your vendetta. We must support the prince as much as possible now. Not like before."

"We were right before!" insisted Halil. "You may think that because today's politics are different, that the past has changed its form. If you pour grape juice from an earthenware cup into a glass goblet it will not become wine! Current forms don't change past content, brothers!"

"Of course, Halil is right! Halil is always right!" Musa replied with disgust. "God help us all if Halil is ever forced to concede bad judgement!"

"My judgement has made me prime minister, Musa. Your judgement would leave you as a fat layabout, but my patronage elevated your importance. Don't forget *that* before you begin comparing our conclusions, Brother."

The two younger brothers looked at each other and conceded, as they usually did, to their older brother's judgement. "Let's just get this sordid affair finished with, I wish we could just erase the last two years." Musa whimpered.

"Don't think like that, little brother." Halil replied quickly. "The last two years have been good to all three of us, and we shouldn't regret them. If Mehmet asks you to recant what we did, don't. It was the right decision, based on the situation. Don't forget that. If he asks you to recant or stand by your decision, you can't take it back! That's a trap. Then he'll know that you're just telling him what he wants to hear."

"The best situation would be if he just retired us all, then and there," Kalid said with a bit of a forced laugh.

Halil turned to his other brother. Halil's eyes seemed to be focussed on something far, far away. "That can't happen." He said slowly. "He will never allow us to retire, because he wouldn't trust us to disappear. He will either keep us close to control us, or get rid of us altogether. There aren't any other options for him."

The younger to brothers looked down at their sandals and mulled over what they had been told. They had nothing to do but continue waiting for their summons.

Two years ago…
"What the hell have you done, boy?" The old man asked angrily.

Mehmet, a slight boy of sixteen, could only remain silent.

"Do you know what I hear? I left this city fifteen months ago, and still I am summoned back! What were you thinking?"

Mehmet looked down, rather than meet his father's angry gaze.

"Answer me!" Murat roared.

The former Sultan reached across the space between them and grabbed Mehmet's chin to push his face up to meet his gaze. "I asked you a question. Don't act like a mute. You're supposed to act like a sovereign."

Mehmet inhaled deeply, as though he were to reply to the charges, but instead chose to hold that breath and steady his jaw. His attempt to seem strong was a dismal failure. His voice broke as he tried to answer "Father, I…"

"Father?" Murat retorted indignantly. "You look like you are about to cry! You are to be a gazi, but you stay at home and cry! Look at you! You are sixteen years old, rather than a warrior who carries the horsetails and sword of our community, you cry! You drink! You share your bed with a damned milk-maid! You've turned into a degenerate! It's no wonder those infernal Janissaries rebelled! They thought that you'd turned the imperial treasury into a whore-monger's account!"

"Father, the duties of Sultan…"

"…Are yours no more, boy!" Murat's face stormed like the sea. "You've spent the last two years debauching yourself with wine and women…"

The old man's face contorted in rage and disgust. There was another charge that entered the conversation before the words made the accusation formal.

Father and son made eye contact for a split second, and father turned his gaze away in sorrowful disgust. News of his son's sexual escapades and drunkenness had reached the elder man's troubled ears all the way across Anatolia.

"Some decisions have been made, my boy." Murat began. "I am to return here to Adrianople permanently, to resume my responsibilities as Sultan. You are not capable of leading our armies against the Bulgars, nor are you fit to carry the banner of the prophet. You've squandered enough money on your lechery and tribute to your own soldiers."

Mehmet's face turned red as his sorrow fermented into a hateful rage. The only redeeming grace of this humiliation was that there were none here to see it. "Yes, Father."

"Second…" He continued. "Zaganos-Pasha will be sent back to Iconium."

"Please, Father, he's been a good advisor to me…"

"He has given you very bad advice, Mehmet. His influence has dragged you into conflicts in Europe and Asia, not only against the unbelievers, but against the faithful as well. You would do well to avoid the convert's zeal. The fire of faith can warm a heart, but with a man like that all it will do is burn. He's being sent home, and forbidden to leave the city. I pray that he has a nice quiet life for the rest of his days."

"Yes, Father."

"Third, *that girl* will be moved to your cousin's service in Brussa."

The rage in Mehmet's eyes picked up as he met his father's gaze. Murat looked at his son and wondered if that was a step too far. "Don't worry. She will be forbidden to any man. I'll extract that promise from my cousin, Ziya, but you are not to see her again."

"I love her, father, and we want to marry."

"Of course you do, that's why you are finished. You will marry for political expedience. You'll take on the sister or daughter of a king or other great man to seal an important alliance, at some future date. You are not going to take on a slave girl as your first bride. I'll find someone for you within the year, but Aynur is officially forbidden, from this day forward. Do you understand?"

"I do." Mehmet looked at his father with an assertive anger for the first time. "Fine then, Father. If you're the sultan, if you never relinquished your command in retirement, then by all means, lead! If this was an unlawful exercise by that corrupt minister and those treacherous Janissaries, and I am the true and honest sultan, as I believe to be the case, then I order you as my servant to come back and play the role of sultan. It bores me!"

Murat paid no mind to his son's furious posturing.

"What's more, you are to be sent away. You're off to Amaseia. You will stay with an old servant of mine, Kazim-bey. He will take over the remainder of your education."

"You mean exile."

Murat looked at his son. "I wish that it could have been different, Son."

"So do I."

"Now then," Murat said sitting back down. "You have many tasks before you, as do I. I suggest that you go about them quickly."

"I will then. Good night then, Father."

Without any discernible expressions, Mehmet bowed to his father, took five steps backwards and left the room.

Sitting in the waiting room, outside of the Sultan's meeting room, Mehmet saw his teacher with a collection of scrolls and ledgers waiting for the returning Sultan's attention. The Prime Minister was surprised to see that his defrocked prodigy was still in attendance. His eyes showed his surprise.

"Mehmet, I didn't realize that you were still with your father." Halil tried to cover his surprise.

"Well, I was," Mehmet continued his exit from the palace wing, and then as an afterthought, turned to continue his conversation with his mentor. "Oh, and thank you very much, Teacher."

Halil, who was about to step into the private meeting chamber of the Sultan, looked quixotically at his apprentice. "You're welcome, Mehmet... but whatever for?"

"For calling me by my name, rather than the honorific due the sultan. It was very thoughtful of you, to save me the trouble of explaining recent events. I guess that you were privy to that information."

Halil was quiet for a moment.

"Don't worry, Teacher. I'm off to the eastern provinces in the morning, and I won't forget all that you've done for me."

"Prince..."

"Don't!" Mehmet raised an angry arm and pointed his finger at his most honoured of teachers. "Don't you dare play innocent! There will be a time when I come back. And there will be an accounting of everyone's actions on the Day of Judgment, but for you, you jackal, it will come sooner than that!"

"Young one! This is hardly the time or place for this sort of thing, remember your place, Prince. You are the youngest former Sultan in our history. Many men triple your age before their lives ground to such an ignominious halt. You are my biggest heartbreak, Mehmet, my saddest disappointment. Mine and your fathers."

"Despite all this, I love my father very much, and respect him as the great sultan that he is. I pray for his long life and success, I suggest that you pray even harder than I, for when his liveliness fails, as it does for every man, I will see you again, and our meeting will be sweet for me."

"Don't you understand, Child? You're done. Your life is effectively finished today. Your legacy to future generations will be as a warning. Parents will tell their children to work hard and not to drink or fornicate, otherwise they will end up like Sultan Mehmet the Second – the forgotten, the expended and in the end the quietly exiled by his own father." Halil looked at his failed protégé with sadness and shame. "I don't suspect I'll ever see you again, but I will pray that God finds good use for you. Peace be upon you, Mehmet."

"Damn you!" Those words were unsophisticated and lacked the verbal finesse that either of the two men would have liked, but they nonetheless carried the precise emotions that Mehmet intended to get across to his teacher. The deposed Sultan walked back to his private apartment in order to prepare his things.

Today

Through the door and into the drab waiting room stepped the two sons of Ali. The big tribesmen looked horrifically out of place in the chambers of the Sultan's palace, but they were both given public favour by the young sultan, and accordingly shown respect by the moneyed notables that vied for standing in the corridors of power. Hassan and Ahmet looked at the three sons of Turjan Chandarli, all ministers of the divan – the cabinet, and smiled in their cheerful rural deportment.

"Halil, Kalid and Musa Chandarli, the Sultan wishes to see you now," announced Ahmet.

"Let's go!" seconded the equally cheerful Ahmet. He lightly poked Musa's large belly. "We could go quickly if you'd like. It seems that some of us need some exercise."

Musa looked angrily at the unwashed barbarian. "It's customary to take a more formal tone with members of the court, young man."

The smile never left Ahmet's face as he replied in his cheerful voice. "I'll try to remember that, Big Man," he then nodded his head towards the door. "This way, Uncle Kalid."

"I'm Musa, he's Kalid."

"As you like."

There was something carnivorous about the faux politeness of the two young men that made the three older men nervous. "We know the way." Halil said, and let his brothers out of the stone cell where they had been forced to wait for the past three hours.

Down the corridors, the three brothers walked, followed by their two escorts. Musa, the third in line felt as though he were being followed by wolves, having the two Anatolian strangers behind him, nipping at his heels.

Finally, the party of five entered the grand audience chamber of the Sultan of Adrianople. It was a huge granite cavern, crowded with supplicants and polluted with the noises of pious fealty.

At the entrance to the chamber they were met by a negro, tall and thin, and wearing a bright green silk robe. His face was marked with ritual scarification in a design particular from his tribe from the Upper Nile region, and he stood head and shoulders above anyone else in city. "Peace be upon you, Halil-Pasha, and to you all, Kalid-Pasha, Musa-Pasha."

"Peace be upon you, Kabira," Halil responded by rote. "We are here to see the new Sultan."

Kabira easily looked over the heads of the three ministers and saw the two men who had brought them to the audience chamber. "Thank you, men. I'll take them from here."

The two brothers made no attempt to hide their disgust of the negro. Kabira was a eunuch. Every time the brothers saw him, they thought that somewhere in those robes of his was a silver case, which held a long straw-like instrument that helped the mule to urinate. To a couple of young men from a tribal world, where masculine virtue is praised as an ultimate goal for anyone, the thought of the giant negro with his giant weakness was simply disgusting. The two men didn't wear their characteristic smiles when they spoke to the him. The simply dropped off the three ministers and went into the chamber themselves.

The chamber was huge, and full of the normal collection of courtiers and courtesans, as well as other assistants and general hangers-on. At the centre of it all was a handsome young man, scarcely past his eighteenth birthday. Mehmet was the only man in the room who was clean-shaven, he had decided that it was more dignified to shave rather than to wear a beard and moustache that couldn't quite fill in. He wore red and green silks under a white caftan and a white turban was tightly wrapped around his head. He sat down at a raised dais, so as to be able to see everyone in the room without standing. Everyone was eagerly awaiting their opportunity to speak to the new man. Mehmet displayed no eagerness to meet them.

The three brothers sat together at the back of the chamber and talked amongst themselves. It was Kalid who first broke their awkward silence.

"He seems better suited for the job this time around," He commented absently.

"I don't think he's seen us at the back here." Added Musa.

"He's seen us, boys," Halil said. "Don't worry about that. He's just making us wait here, like he made us wait in the other room. So that we remember how important he is, and how unimportant we are."

"Look, he's getting up," Musa said with interest.

At the front of the chamber, Mehmet stood up, and the room fell silent. Mehmet snapped his finger at Kabira and motioned to the three brothers in the back.

The entire room seemed to pause, and the air became heavy as everyone turned to the back to see what the Sultan was concerned about. The three brothers looked at each other and Kabira came to them.

"Come," ordered the eunuch.

The three of them were escorted to the front of the room, to stand before the Sultan. Behind him they could see the two Anatolian guards smirking at them, as though they were privy to a secret denied to the senior cabinet.

"Thank you, Kabira, but normally you should bring these three viziers to me directly. They are the prime minister, the secretary of the treasury and the secretary of religious foundations. They are three important men, whose voices should be here, and not in some distant corner."

"I am sorry, Your Majesty."

"Why did you take a seat so far away, uncles?" Mehmet asked coolly.

Halil looked at the young man's face for any sign of emotion. No anger, no resentment, no pleasure at the opportunity for vengeance. No nothing. "We were unsure about your intentions, Your Majesty," Halil offered.

"You have all served my father well in your respective offices, and I see no reason to remove you from them. Do you wish to be removed from your offices?"

"No, Your Majesty," replied Halil.

"And what of your brothers?" Mehmet's gaze travelled to the two younger siblings. "Do you wish to remain here, or do you with to seek out other responsibilities in your older age?"

Kalid and Musa assured the Sultan that they were honoured to continue serving him.

"Then you may all take your places over there, with my other counsellors." Mehmet motioned to his right, where his father's cabinet was assembled intact. Everyone else was already there, and they eyed the last three in attendance with a mix of suspicion and relief.

"Now let's continue on with our business," said Mehmet. He didn't even make eye contact with any members of the cabinet again that day. When all of the meetings of the new administration were finished, and everyone had presented their gifts and fealty to the new sultan, Mehmet stood up and left through his own private door, leaving the cabinet where they were, feeling a little useless.

"What does this mean?" Musa asked.

"It means that he's not strong enough to come down on us yet," Kalid answered. "We've got until he feels strong enough to make him our friend again."

"He's waiting for something," Halil conceded. "He doesn't want to change anything and make people feel nervous just yet, but the time will come. He hasn't forgotten anything."

"So what should we do, then?" Musa asked.

"Avoid him." Kalid said. "We have to keep our distance, and keep to our duties right now. Give him no reason to expel us. We'll come at him from a different direction, make ourselves indispensable and then we can pressure him if need be."

"He's planning something. He doesn't want any problems right now, but he's avoiding us so that he can carry about his own agenda," Halil assessed. "Let's be friendly to whatever agenda that is, but not so friendly as to give him the opportunity to move on to other things. When does his woman arrive from Brussa?"

"In a month's time," Musa answered.

"Good. We'll start there."

Chapter 3 – A Blank Slate

Late afternoon in the springtime of Thrace is a beautiful time and place. Green sour plumbs are plump and pulling heavily on the branches of their trees. Fields are green and the sun is warm. It is like a beautiful summer day, though the sun isn't hot enough yet to burn or exhaust anyone, and the insects haven't hatched out of their holes yet. For these reasons and so many more, it was a glorious day.

The villa of the grand vizier was a celebration of spring. Rather than marble austerity, the walls around the garden where built out of a soft red brick, and capped with earthy terraces, currently undergoing a spring renovation. The green grass inside the compound was divided by grey flagstones, to allow for walking paths through a garden that seemed almost like a miniature forest, and in the middle of this fantasy forest was a gathering of women.

They were forbidden public gatherings by custom, so they arrived, escorted of course, to places like this where the female servants would bring them fresh juice and sweets, and the women of the court could let their hair down, both literally and figuratively. The bulky head coverings that were worn in public in order to make pious women invisible to the men of the city were cast aside in the reception room of the house. The women wore brightly coloured silk and wool dresses, and decorated themselves with henna, and sang traditional songs about love and family.

The world of women was a world that was largely invisible to the world of men, though both were irrevocably intertwined, even at the level of state. What men do to other men was influenced by their women and vice versa, and how the women interacted in their ruthless games of posturing was largely dependent on the statuses of their respective husbands. The amount of influence that was peddled among these women was enormous. The daughters of even the most influential men were subject to the whims of the Mother of the Harem, as to which potential man she could presented to. Seating arrangements, as to who would sit by whom, who would sit near the Sultan' wives and who would sit alone, was a carefully guarded rite. That right was constantly and viciously contested by everyone, but Ayshe guarded it jealously.

One of the few men who truly understood this, was the grand vizier, Halil-Pasha. Halil had been blessed by God in many special ways. He was of noble birth and led a great family, he had a sharp wit and a well-noted innate sense of deception, but it could never be overlooked that he had a brilliant wife.

Ayshe was no longer a beautiful woman, though she had been so in past years. She was what Turks refer to impolitely as *"At Gibbi – like a horse"*. She was tall and broadly built, her face was long and her hands were larger than her husbands. She wasn't unattractive to everybody, but not every man is attracted to a large-boned horse-like woman.

Her physical presence certainly helped her to lord over the shy young girls of the court. The wee ones would come to the larger than life Ayshe-Teze (Aunt Ayshe) and try to impress her. With wit, charm, beauty, or piety, they would try to show their worth, because they knew that a favourable opinion of the Prime Minister's wife would allow for the infrastructure of a proper marriage, an appropriate husband, a favourable appointment for a son, and even some times, for an illicit affair to be arranged. The flip side of the wondrous social bounty offered by Ayshe's favour was the crippling isolation of her disfavour. While this woman was forbidden a place at court, her role in the machinations of the state was an important one.

Ayshe looked out at the assembled ladies in her garden, playing with their young children (boys under the age of seven were permitted at such gatherings) and wondered how long it could all last. Her influence was strong while her husband was the grand vizier, but Mehmet's return put that into the air. If the new sultan came down hard on her husband, her position and those of her friends and *'sisters'* would follow that lead. It was a precarious situation that they were in now.

The Mother of the Harem looked to her right side at Fatma. Only twenty-five years old, the poor girl. Fatma was the most recent wife of the Sultan Murat. In her young and frail arms was the diminutive figure of Kareem, the Sultan's last seed to take fruit. "How is the boy, Fatma?"

"He's hungry!" Fatma laughed as she nursed the infant. "He will grow to be big and strong like his father."

"If God wills it," Ayshe said robotically. She gazed over at the young mother and her baby. That baby could be the next Sultan. So Mehmet would have to act. He could expel mother and child, kill them both, or take his step-mother on as a resident of the official harem. The last option was the most unlikely of the three, the first being to most probable, and the middle one being more of a nightmare scenario. Ayshe knew that she would have to do her best to bring about harmony between Fatma and her estranged step-son. "Have you met him?"

"Who? Oh, yes, Mehmet," Fatma didn't really seem to understand the seriousness of her predicament. "Twice, when we came back to Adrianople two years ago."

"Have you met him since he came to the palace and took on your husband's diadem?" Ayshe prodded.

"No, not yet. He hasn't summoned me. Do you know when he will?"

"I'll see what I can do, Dear," Ayshe was not pleased at all with the new Sultan. He had arrived only a few weeks ago, and took over like a thief in the night. He didn't keep close council to any of the traditional influences of court, but kept company with barbarians and crowded the palace with tribesmen; what was worse, was inviting strangers into the safety of the harem. Nulifer and Aynur were both on their way to the capital. Nulifer was Mehmet's chaste wife, whom he never touched. She was useless unless her husband took interest in her, or she took an interest in another man. Aynur was a house slave, with whom Mehmet was infamously attached. She had no family to manipulate because of her exceptionally low status. There was no value to her other than what her womb could produce. Once she had a son, Ayshe could start to work on her, but until things changed with Mehmet and his women, the highest office in the land was cut off from the tendrils of the harem.

"I hope to see my step-son soon." Fatma continued on with a smile on her face. "I'm sure that he would love to meet his new step-brother."

'Where did old Murat pick this village turnip?' Ayshe wondered to herself. "Of course he would."

The gossip filled luncheon received a special guest after the ladies of Adrianople had finished eating. That guest was the only man who was allowed to enter a garden full of unveiled women. The chief eunuch of the palace, Kabira, emerged out of the walled forest and into the clearing to stand before his long-time friend, Ayshe. Some of the women catcalled him as he entered, joking at his diminished capacity.

"Peace be upon you, Ayshe-Hanim."

"And unto you be peace, Kabira-Bey," she replied in a friendly manner.

Some of the women in attendance were a little put off by the negro's presence. They were unused to a male presence seeing them when they were relaxing. Some tried to hide their faces from view, others giggled and others watched as their centaur-like matron made casual conversation with the tall African.

"I've come on an important errand, Ayshe," Kabira began. "The Sultan of Adrianople, commander of the faithful and defender of the shrines of his forefathers has asked me to summon his step-mother from your home."

The gracious demeanor that typified both Ayshe and Kabira never faltered, but the two of them had to carry on a heavily sub-text conversation with their eyes, as they were both well aware of how many were watching them.

"Of course, Kabira. She is right here by my side and will join you as soon as she gets ready. May I ask about the nature of the meeting?"

"The Sultan wishes to see his father's wife. Family is important to our new ruler."

'*He needs to verify the succession.*' Ayshe understood. "If you'd like, the ladies here would love to look after the baby while the mother's gone. I'm sure that the young Sultan does not want his home disturbed by the crying of an infant."

"That would be wonderful. Thank you, Ayshe-teze," the eunuch bowed gracefully. Kabira was grateful that Ayshe understood that the baby needed her protection right now. He deeply regretted the role that had to play in the forthcoming drama, but he accepted that obedience was the most important virtue for him to possess.

Kabira was in many ways, the quintessential opposite of Ayshe, and that was probably why their friendship was so strong. Kabira was cold and understood the tempers of those around him; Ayshe was like a fire, controlling the emotions of men and women to her own needs. She had never been able to manipulate the chief eunuch, and after several years, she simply stopped trying. Both of them saw the potential of Kareem, if the current holder of the Sword of Osman should prove to be inappropriate for the tasks given. Unfortunately, they were well aware that Mehmet saw this potential also, and in not quite so positive a light.

Ayshe excused herself from her own party and brought Fatma out of the garden and into the palace. She helped her get ready for her audience with the Sultan. She changed her clothes quickly and was ready to leave almost immediately. Ayshe looked into Fatma's eyes, and tried to explain the situation to her as precisely as possible.

"Fatma, you have to understand what this *boy* wants. He is the new Sultan, he has no real friends or allies in the capital, only people who want to either manipulate him or replace him. Your baby is key in that. Do you understand this?"

"What do you mean?"

"I mean that the sultan's life would be much easier if both you and your baby were not in existence. You have to convince him that this is not the case."

Fatma silently took in that assessment. "What can I do?"

"When you meet Mehmet, always defer to him, don't treat him like a child, but remind him that you are his father's widow. Remind him of his commitment to protect you. He has a responsibility to maintain public piety, and that is a great opportunity to do so. You have to be of some helpful service to him, otherwise both you and your baby are in great danger."

The younger woman's eyes were starting to turn red.

"He'd never…"

"Knock that off!" Ayshe snapped. This was the first time Fatma had ever seen Ayshe angry. "You can't be emotional at this time, or you will be thrown into the gutter. Be strong."

Ayshe straightened Fatma's shoulders.

"Be strong, and impress Mehmet. Be loyal to your step-son as he is the continuance of your husband's house, and we'll all find a place for you in the order of things, Fatma. But remember, if you lose your head and start crying, then God protect you, because nobody else here will."

"I will, Ayshe-Teze," Fatma said in her strongest voice. "But what if he doesn't believe me?"

"You're still young and beautiful, girl. And Mehmet is renown for his voracious sexual appetites, that's a possibility," Ayshe said as an afterthought. "But let's hope it doesn't come to that."

Fatma's face lost a bit of its colour, but she merely nodded her head. "Whatever it takes."

"Good. Now follow me to the entrance room."

The two women, covered from head to toe in robes, Ayshe in brown and Fatma in red, walked to the antechamber of the grand vizier's palace. There, they were met by the tall eunuch and two muscular brutes. The two young men looked unwashed and out of place, as though they had just finished marauding the countryside, but neither seemed to feel self-conscious about the discrepancies in attire.

Ayshe thought they were both handsome and rugged in their furs and leathers, with unbejewelled swords at their sides, but she was more concerned about her immediate task at hand.

"Be strong," she said as she and Fatma kissed goodbye.

"Thank you for everything, Teze."

And with that, Fatma followed the three men out into the street. They brought her to the palace, and the two guards left her for other, related business.

"Night's here," Hassan announced as he looked out the gate of the tea garden down the road from Halil Pasha's palace. "We should go soon."

"When we see the first star," Ahmet concurred.

The two brothers from Amaseia were sitting under a canopy of vines at a small table, only a few centimeters off the floor. They themselves sat on carpets thrown onto the grass. The tea that they were drinking was from their home province on the Black Sea.

"What do you think about this, Hassan?" The younger brother asked hesitantly. "I mean, it's not exactly what I thought we'd be doing when we came to the capital."

"Me neither, but it's what we have to do," the elder answered. "Are you going to be okay?"

"Yes, I suppose it'll be like those two men that came after Mehmet back home," suggested Ahmet.

"Yeah," Hassan said unconvincingly. He blinked and looked away, he didn't want his brother to see that tears were trying to make their way out

of his eyes. He looked up and saw Mars sparkling near the horizon-line.
"Here we go."

"Here we go."

The sleepy baby looked up at the giant dark eyes of Ayshe and smiled. Ayshe had never been blessed with any affinity for children, and was one of the few women in the imperial harem who genuinely disliked children intrinsically. They were merely vessels of authority to be fought over, but this one seemed friendly enough; all the world's potential was in his face.

Baby Kareem clenched his tiny fist around Ayshe's large pinky finger and gave a gassy giggle. Ayshe smiled back and brushed the regurgitated milk from the infant's mouth.

Paths not taken can lead only to regret, and Ayshe allowed herself none of that particular self-indulgence. Ayshe had been pregnant once, when she and her husband were newly wed. The baby died *in utero* and they'd been unable to conceive again. She was not the type to allow herself to wallow in her own tears, but those paths untrodden are never covered completely by the grass of years.

In an instant, the smile left her face and her head cocked up and her ears seemed to spring out like a fox's. Footsteps, two pairs of men's footsteps. She stood up and pulled her head covering back to give her ears greater access to the silence being intruded upon. She walked to the doorway and looked down the corridor.

'*God protect us*,' she thought to herself.

The personal audience chamber of the Sultan had been designed to the specifics of Murat. It was as opulent as any office of its kind. Gold filigree lay upon the red walls of the large room, and large gold rimmed windows allowed sunlight to pour in and light the office during the day. Now, as the sun was setting, the room was lit by a series of lanterns, but it had a comfortable ambience. On the floor was a lush, red and black woollen carpet, and there were cushions of the same design along the floor and walls. Mehmet was standing by one of the windows, holding a purple flower he had picked from the garden and he looked out into the night. He was wearing a fine silk shirt and tunic. On his head was a white silk turban, held in place by a bronze pin bearing his newly designed *Tugra* – an emblem with his name in stylised calligraphy.

He was thinking about how wasteful the room was with all its decoration. He decided to alter it, make it seem austere to the point of simplicity. There should be nothing in a room of this purpose save for the implements of a clerk's office.

Kabira's voice came into the room. He coughed to get his master's attention.

"Your step-mother, Sultan."

"Welcome," he said quietly, still looking out the window. "I hope you weren't waiting too long."

"Thank you, my son." She replied. "It wasn't a problem."

Mehmet turned his head, his face wore a sad expression, but he said nothing for an instant. His step mother was only a few years older than himself. She hardly looked like a manipulator of state affairs, just a simple girl who caught the attention of a great man, to the detriment of her own destiny.

"I hear that congratulations are in order." He said dryly.

"Thank you…" She almost called him *'my son'* again, but decided against it. He was clearly in no mood for family reconciliation.

There was a silence that held itself in the room.

"You are my father's wife. You had little patience for my mother during her lifetime, and little interest in your husband's other sons until his death. Then you found an interest in me. We received your message, even so far in the mountains."

Neither of their faces betrayed the slightest emotion, only well honed politeness. Mehmet continued.

"I am a very busy man now, and I don't really want spend the evening reminiscing about past times, or complaining about things that can't be changed, so I will speak to you quite bluntly, I'm afraid. I realize that you must be used to the harem, where everyone says one thing and means something else, but please take what I am about to tell you at face value, because I don't intend to repeat myself, or speak to you again. Do you understand that?"

Fatma nodded.

"Because of your years of love and loyalty to my father, which I do not doubt..." He began. "...you are to be allowed to stay here in Adrianople, if you choose, or return to your father's home, if that suits you more. You may keep your place in the harem if you wish. You have lived most of your life under my father's protection, and you may continue to live so under mine."

"Thank you. May God remember and return your mercy on the Day of Judgment."

"Who sent the two messengers?"

She was silent for a moment.

"I need to know if it was you, sneaking out of the harem, or if you had an accomplice in this crime." Mehmet's face betrayed no emotions, but his eyes held hers and let her know that no half answers or lies within truth or truth within lies were to be tolerated. "You sent the men, or you know who did. I want a name."

She nodded carefully and took a deep breath. "Sadullah, son of Saleh arranged the two."

"Hmmm. Sadulah is here under the patronage of Halil, my father's prime minister. Was Halil aware of this?"

"I don't know."

"Did you speak to Halil?"

"No."

"His wife?"

"No, not about this."

Mehmet looked into her eyes carefully. He saw that she was afraid, but that she had resigned herself to honesty as the only way to emerge on the other side of this conflict.

"Very well, then. You may stay here in the harem, if you wish. Your son may not."

"He's an infant."

"Now, yes. Boys grow."

"You can't exile a baby, tear him from his mother's bosom!"

He met her gaze coolly. She gradually realized why she had been taken away from the protection of Halil Pasha's palace.

"You are becoming an old woman at a very young age, Fatma-Teze. Concern yourself with other things." Mehmet turned back to the window, to the garden beyond it, and to the shadow of the Macedonian Tower beyond that. Night was descending and tears began to swell in Fatma's eyes and fall over her cheeks. If she could examine her stepson's face more closely, she would notice the same tears begin to swell there, if only for an instant, though they were fought off by a young boy trying to be as hard as possible.

Mehmet crooked his head, but didn't look back at her; he couldn't allow her to see any weakening in those eyes of his. "You may go now." He said nonchalantly.

Fatma ran out into the street.

Hassan and Ahmet crept down the hall to the nursery. Breaking into the home had been surprisingly simple. There were tens of workmen and laborers working hard all day to build latticing around the Grand Vizier's palace. The two brothers innocuously grabbed one ladder from the unguarded construction site and used it to cross the fence wall. Onto the wall, they brought up the ladder and rested it along the top, out of sight. After that, they hopped in a window, and in less than a minute they went from the street into the private home of one of the most prominent citizens of the Ottoman state.

They had been shown a map of the inside of the villa, and knew exactly where they were going. Rather than creeping suspiciously they walked quietly but boldly, as though they walked these halls every night. Down the hall they went, then left, and into the first door. Ahmet almost knocked on the door to be polite, but suppressed the habit.

Into a very comfortable room they walked, there was still enough light from the outdoor twilight to see little more than vague shadows and forms. The walls were stucco with periodic wood paneling and a carpeted floor; medieval soundproofing for the nursery. There was a large window on the north wall, a solitary chair, a dressing screen and a crib. On the shelves were blankets, towels, a water basin and a full jug of water.

'What a dismal and lonely room for a baby.' Both men thought to themselves. In their more traditional lifestyle, the babies were always around their mother's necks, always with the extended family, never stowed away like this.

"Do you smell something burning?" Ahmet asked.

"Someone must have just been in here, I smell burnt wax." Hassan answered. He put his hand above the extinguished lantern. "It's still hot."

"Don't wake the little guy," Ahmet said as he looked down at the baby. "Don't disturb him, I should say, he's wide awake."

Hassan didn't answer with words. He stepped quietly over to the bench, and began solemnly to fill the water basin with water.

Behind the dressing screen, Ayshe didn't move a muscle. She hid as she listened to the two men prepare their grizzly task.

'*I must act,*' she thought to herself. '*To quietly wait here is disgusting. I'll never be able to live with myself. The baby is under my protection. These two will flee as soon as they realize that they aren't alone. I have to act.*'

Then her mind was invaded by that most cruel seduction of reasoning. Reasoning allowed the good to do nothing and allow evil, it allowed the strong to ignore the wicked and it helped corruption find tolerance. Of all the intellectual sins we allow ourselves, none are more atrocious than reason.

'*The child must die anyway, that's been decided already. If I try to stop them here, they will just kill me as a witness. Then I'll be dead along with that silly girl's baby.*'

All these clockworks of the mind moved their cogs and widgets in the confines of Ayshe's perfectly still body, and behind her wood-like face, no movement, no untimely breath, nothing happened to reveal her location or presence, as she listened to such a heinous act.

She heard the two brothers, though she could not guess their identities, work in tandem. She heard them place a ceramic bowl be placed on the bench. She heard the water pour itself into that bowl, getting quieter and quieter as the bowl filled. And she heard the baby's sounds as it was brought over.

There was the gentle splash of water as the babe entered the basin, which was followed by a wail of protest against such a baptism. The wail was cut short as the infant was submerged. Water was ineffectively kicked out onto the floor. No baby could defend itself against such an assault.

She allowed herself no movement, breath, nor even blinking, but as she head the infant Kareem's last muffled sounds in the water. A soundless tear evaporated from her eye before it could ever fall. Thank God for small miracles.

Chapter Four - Late One Night

The mansion of the Prime Minister was a beautiful building, encased in red-brick and green vine. The wall prevented dogs, cats and other animals from wandering into the property, but it was hardly designed to keep people out. Adrianople was a very safe city. The wall wasn't really designed to keep people out, but it would do that job. As to keeping people in, well, that was a task for which no one had considered.

Neither brother needed to set up the ladder in order to scale down the wall. They both jumped down the three metres and rolled on the soft lawn at the base of the wall. Ahmet went first and landed like a cat. Hassan, on the other hand, bounced like an overfilled wineskin.

"Are you ok?" Ahmet asked.

"Fine, you?" replied Hassan. "It's just a scratch."

Hassan was lying. His ankle rolled over itself once he hit the ground, and the socket felt like grinding sand between stones. The proud tribesman would of course never admit that it hurt, so he chose to suffer the injury in silence and pretend that nothing was wrong.

"Good. Lets get out of here now. I'll see you back home in the morning." Ahmet could tell that his brother was lying, but it would disgrace his brother to point this out, so he too remained silent about the obviously near-incapacitating injury.

"God protect you, Ahmet."

"God protect you, Hassan."

And with that, the two split up. Hassan went south to follow the river road, and his younger brother went uphill towards the tower. They were both planning to lie low until sunrise, they had been told not to return to the palace until that time.

Unbeknownst to either of them, a single pair of eyes watched them from the shadows. Those eyes had seen the brothers as they set up the ladder and entered the house. Hidden in the darkness of the plaza construction site, they watched the brothers jump off the wall and regroup on the ground. The two brothers split up and their observer watched both of their movements.

'*The southward one,*' he thought to himself. '*I'll follow him; he's limping.'*

A man's silhouette poured out of the umbra of hiding and followed Hassan in the direction of the river.

One of the wonderful things about clay or earthenware ceramics is that they simply won't burn or melt, almost regardless of the temperatures to which they are exposed. For this reason, clay was used for such myriad purposes as holding liquid steel during the smelting process before it is reconstituted in a new shape and holding burning substances as they change their qualities before a chemist's eye. The most common use of this remarkably useful quality of clay would have to be the innocuous but important role of holding the heater in a water pipe.

Into the clay bowl, speckled with air holes to allow for flow into the base water-bowl was placed a burning ember of charcoal, no longer than the last bending of a grown man's thumb. And onto that burning ember was placed a gooey mixture of herbal mulch, followed by a small rounded ball of hard black, tar-like substance that seemed to dampen as soon as it was added to the heat. That substance was as religiously forbidden as it was practically available in the capital city. That dark, syrupy substance had travelled all the way from a seed in the Persian plateau to a flower in the summer sun, then into the black clay blob on the fire; a long way to be certain.

Fire from the ember now burned. That burning produced more change within the substance itself, for that basic flame started a process that scientist would call pyrolyis. From that process, enzymes and compounds were torn out of that little black ball, poisonous materials that were best left hidden from daylight. Some of them stayed in the prison of the burning coal, and some escaped in a slowly lingering cloud of smoke. This cloud of smoke crept out the back door of the water-pipe, through the holes in the clay bowl and through the pipes into the water-bowl. Feeling trapped in a watery grave at the bottom of some strangers pipe in a faraway land, the smoke then tried to escape through the only other opening left to it, and out it went; through the long hose and past the lips of a young man eager to forget about his horrible deeds earlier in the evening.

Ahmet leaned back into the cushions that had been set out by the proprietor of the store. During the daylight hours, this dark room was a part of a warehouse for the city's artists and men of letters. It was a depot for inks and dyes from along the fabled Silk Road, the trade route that went from Anatolia all the way to the gates of China. Along this route, various other trinkets were acquired in places like Persia and Bactria, making their way both East and West.

What had made its way west, and eventually poured itself like liquid euphoria into the consciousness of a semi-nomadic Turkish tribesman from the Black Sea was form of slavery to many. Ahmet knew that potential when he was first taught about it from one his uncles. Unfortunately for him, his uncle's warnings were quickly forgotten like a puff of smoke in the wind.

There were a handful of other men in the room, sharing bowls of smoky relief, some alone, some were sharing, but all were equally oblivious to those around them.

Ahmet breathed in the vaporous numbing and relaxed. He could watch the images of warriors of old, and dragons and other stories unfold in images that swirled in and out of the smoke in his own mind. As he watched this, the memories of his own recent and excruciating sin disappeared behind this veil. In the years to come, he would deeply regret this night for the sin he committed earlier, the one he was indulging in now, and the one that was still yet to come.

Hassan was aware almost immediately of the man following him. The elder of the two brothers saw himself as having two basic options; the first would be to lose the shadow in the crowds of the city centre, but that would be wise only if he could be sure that he knew the city better than his pursuer. Hassan had only been in the city for a couple of months.

Instead, he obeyed his second option and continued along south to the Merich River. During the day, the busy river was home to many of the more elaborate gardens and parks that previous sultans had deemed necessary for a capital. At night, the north bank, where Hassan lured his hunter was abandoned by citizens and guards alike; only the owls, cats and rats seemed to find a home there after sunset.

The main road of the area where Hassan brought his unknown guest was not made of the cobblestones of the city proper, but a trampled earth road, the mud baked dry by the sun and stamped flat by thousands of bustling townsfolk. To the sides of this main road were grassy meadows, small stature trees and tea gardens next to fruit orchards and herb gardens that poured their aromas into the night air. The humidity of the spring night couldn't quite raise a fog out of the river, but it pulled up enough moisture to muffle any sounds that originated more than a few metres away, even the river was barely audible.

'*Here is as fine a place as any to make a stand.*' Hassan thought to himself. The tribesman was all alone, save for the mysterious figure behind him, a figure that had been slowly closing the gap between them since they entered the suburbs of the unwalled capital.

Hassan was hardly the type to engage in a test of wits, or patter about with slanted words. He didn't know who his follower was, nor did it particularly matter. Anyone following him tonight of all nights was privy to his sin. So now, it was in Hassan's utmost best interest to remove the man from the face of the earth. He closed his eyes gently in order to proximate where the other man was, he reached under his linen shirt and took out the only weapon that he could carry on the street without raising suspicion, a hand-made iron dagger. The blade was elaborately decorated with poorly worked images of two hawks fighting. He had made the dagger himself many years ago, when he was twelve or so. The design was poorly worked, but the blade was still sharp enough to be effective. It was short, so Hassan knew that he would have to get in close and fast to use it.

The dagger quickly found its old home in the grown-up child's hand, and the young tribesman spun around quickly and walked directly at his pursuer. There was no one within ear shot, so he didn't need to worry about any witnesses out here, and he didn't want to worry about losing his breath in a melee by running into things. This was to be task which called for deliberate action. He prayed to God to guide his hand, but his conscience suggested that it would be perhaps in his best interest if God ignored him completely for this evening.

The closing figure didn't miss a beat himself. Without speaking a word, he produced a blade of his own and matched pace to close in on his prey. The attacker was stocky and tightly built. He reminded Hassan of Kazim, his father's patron in Amaseia. He was bald and his bony brow cast shadows over any features that would normally be recognizable in the moonlight. He had a shirt of hardened leather.

'*Damn.*' Hassan thought to himself as they closed in on each other. The armour looked strong enough to deflect his little dagger. On top of that, a stocky opponent with a short blade presented a dangerous condition to a melee. They both had short blades and needed to get in close to use them effectively. On the inside range, the nameless attacker's short arms would be more nimble than the gangly Hassan. The tribesman needed a longer blade, and then he could strike and withdraw, and then strike again. From years of experience sparring with the similarly built Kazim-bey, he knew that he would do best fighting this man from the outside. On the inside, this was going to be ugly and messy. His twisted ankle was not ready to allow him much manoeuvring speed to stay on the outside.

'*I wish I'd brought my scimitar,*' he thought uselessly.

The smaller man had apparently made similar calculations. As soon as they came within a few metres of each other, the compact attacker quickly closed the gap between them. He intended to set the range quickly and keep it there. Attack, attack, attack, if he chose to defend, dodge, counter or parry, he would lose his initiative and quite possibly find himself in a rough position. His enemy needed to lose time, if he gave up his aggressor's initiative, then the taller man would cut him down immediately.

Understanding this, Hassan forced tempo to set range. He took a defensive stand against the oncoming man and prepared to try a manner of defence that would play to his strengths. Hassan's longer arms and legs were to give him more mobility, and, if God willed it, the ability to determine the range, rather allow his enemy to do so. In frustration, he damned his injured ankle which would limit his ability to do so. Perhaps splitting up after the deed wasn't one of the sultan's brighter plans.

The stout attacker picked up to a sprint as they closed in. Holding his dagger in his back right hand, Hassan first let his open hand fly. A quick left jab was intended not to harm anyone, but to force momentum away from the bald-headed mystery man. The light fist found its target and the attacker stopped to try to defend, surrendering what Hassan wanted right away. The man raised his long dagger to try to strike at Hassan's striking hand, yielding the tempo without damage.

From behind, almost too far for a quick enough strike, came Hassan's old home-made dagger, straight at the other man's hand. Fair enough, if he moved his hand, his face was right behind it, which would be an even better prize for a second strike. Nonetheless, the dagger missed the flesh of the hand and slid over the man's exposed knuckles, cutting two, and slicing deep into the flesh of the third.

The man yelped out like a wounded dog and dropped his only weapon. That was to be his last mistake of the altercation.

Hassan's elation was short lived, because before he could continue his work with the knife, he felt a sharp pain as the smaller man's knee collided sharply with Hassan's exposed belly. It hurt to breathe and Hassan's brain didn't properly record anything from when he was hit until he hit the ground, though his mind sprang back to life right away afterwards. The man with the bleeding hand used this second to roll over the dagger and kick it away.

Hassan tried to roll the smaller man off of him, but to no avail, the stranger immobilized him with one arm, and with his free arm reached into his boot to draw another dagger.

"God have mercy on your soul, Son of Ali." The man whispered against the back of Hassan's head. "You have done a great service."

The dagger slid between two of Hassan's upper ribs. Hassan could no longer voluntarily control his breathing as his lung deflated into his chest. Twice more it slid through his ribcage, and then a third time.

"Ahmet..." he whispered, afraid for the fate that would soon come for his brother. "Run..."

Ahmet was too far away to hear this plea, of course, and in no condition to do anything about it, had he heard it.

Halil's night had been terribly busy. The sultan's step-mother, Fatma, had arrived alone and unescorted demanding to see her baby. They found the babe drowned, and Ayshe spent the rest of the night trying to console the poor woman. As terrible as it seemed, this was actually good news to Halil. If the sultan was sending assassins to his home, and was not the target, then perhaps Mehmet's offer to continue his father's governance was a genuine one. Kareem had to die, there was no question on that matter. The old sultan had seven sons, and now only two were left, and one was a mentally incompetent infant of twenty-seven. Mehmet would never be secure as long as there was a potential pretender floating around the palace. There was only one other remaining cousin: Orhan, a guest of the emperor of Constantinople, where he'd been for most of his life. Orhan represented considerations for a later date, and Halil's mind returned to the conditions at hand. In the mind of Halil he was a potential, in the eyes of Mehmet he was a threat that cost three hundred thousand akches of silver a year to maintain in foreign luxury.

"With the babe removed, does the sultan intend to continue a purge, or does he have other plans in mind?" he whispered into the air.

The Grand Vizier quickly drew up messages to be couriered to his two brothers, letting them know what had transpired. Halil instructed his servants to deliver them only to Musa and Kadir, and to verify that they were alright. He sent another message to the palace of the Sultan, asking to meet with the monarch as soon as possible. The message was returned within an hour requesting the immediate council of the Grand Vizier.

The message came with a little more speed and enthusiasm than he'd hoped.

Halil-Pasha sat in the cold and dark of waiting room. The room was lit by a few candles and oil lamps, but still had a cold feel. The old prime minister was tired, and leaned against the wall, letting his eyes rest ever so slightly. His mind snapped back to alertness when the negro eunuch walked in to summon him.

"This way, Pasha." Kabira said dutifully, although obviously a little tired. The shadows from the candles seemed to make the decorative scars on the man's face stand out more than usual.

"Thank you, Kabira-Bey." He answered as they walked into the sultan's private office.

Sitting in the middle of the room, at a low table covered with papers, were two cross-legged men in the middle of a discussion. The Sultan stood up and greeted his minister.

"Peace be upon you, Halil-Pasha. I trust that you remember Zaganos-Pasha. My old councillor has returned from Iconium."

"Unto you be peace, Sultan. Of course I remember Zaganos-Pasha. Welcome back to the capital," Halil and Zaganos kissed each other on the cheek as a welcome. Halil would prefer to have a tooth extracted than to share the company of the Greek convert who held such a destructive sway over the Sultan. The man was short but densely built, his head, face and body were completely hairless, and had been so since the day he was wrenched from his mother's womb. Wrapped around his right hand was a bandage. "Did you hurt yourself, Brother?"

"Yes, but it doesn't matter," Zaganos answered in heavily accented Turkish. "I arrived here a few hours ago, Prime Minister, and presented myself to the sublime personage of the Sultan. To say how proud I was of his return, to wish him good luck, and to repeat my oaths of loyalty that I had kept in my heart for all these years. To my delight, he has accepted my good wishes.

"But I also came to him with a request," the Greek continued. "I asked to visit you, and to make amends for any bad blood that had existed between us, you and I."

Halil's face was the picture of politeness. "Oh?"

"Prime Minister, I went to your home, earlier this night, and I saw two suspicious men. I decided to follow one of them, to see what had happened. I learned of a horrible, sinful crime that they had committed in your home. Under duress, the one I followed told me of a murder most foul, and then proclaimed that I would suffer the same fate as the child. We know why you are here, of course, about our sultan's beloved brother. His heart is heavy, but he knows that you provided the best protection possible for the poor child."

Halil's mind was in a controlled race to understand what had happened.

"I am truly sorry, your majesty," he said, bowing low to the Sultan, who lowered his head slightly to return the grace. "Who was the assassin and where is he?"

"He is dead." Zaganos spoke in the Sultan's stead. "I killed him after he gloated of his crime. He was a Turcoman from the East who hid himself in the palace retinue."

"Not the two brothers that came to gather my brothers and I, Your Majesty?"

"The same, I'm sorry to say," Mehmet replied evenly. "They must be spies for the Romans. One is dead, the other is still in hiding, I hope that my men will recover him soon."

"As do I, Your Majesty," Halil replied. This was a ridiculous lie of course. Halil knew that they had acted on the Sultan's behest to kill the boy, and were now to be killed in natural order. They would have had no idea about the machination, they were both mindless thugs, brought to the capital for this purpose and no other. The Sultan would put both their corpses on display on the Stone of Judgment outside of the palace and be done with it. "I pray that your men find the villain as soon as possible, Sultan."

"Thank you, Minister."

Zaganos walked up to the aging vizier and looked him in the eye. "Halil-Pasha, I bear you no ill will. Despite all that happened, those years ago, I look to you as a brother in faith, and ask you to return the favour."

Halil looked into the eyes of Zaganos. He saw the passion of a convert, but also the drive of a dangerously ambitious man who sought to re-establish his influence over an impressionable boy, and captain a ship of state. But there was also something else there. Not any genuine hope to make amends, but… could it be… a bit of crushed pride? Had the Sultan forced him to do this? Zaganos wants nothing more that to cut off the vizier's bollocks and carry them on a spear. The sultan is making him play nice for now. Perhaps the boy's become a little more assertive than history would show. Halil decided that while Zaganos was to remain an enemy and an obstacle, if he didn't publicly make a show of friendship, then he would incur the wrath of the sultan. The Greek must also have made this assessment. Yes… the boy is stronger than he used to be. I wonder if his former puppet master feels worried about lost influence? There will be trouble between these two eventually. For now, it is wise to remain friends with everyone.

"My brother," Halil proclaimed and kissed Zaganos on his cheek. "Let nothing but friendship and loyalty make a home in both our hearts."

Halil could swear that he heard Zaganos' teeth grinding.

"May I be excused, your Majesty? I would like to comfort my wife, as she is quite distressed, and your step-mother is also at my home.”

“Please...” the sultan answered with dispassionate politeness. “Extend my sympathies as well.”

Halil bowed deeply and left the office.

Outside the office was the tall chief eunuch.

“Walk with me, old friend,” Halil said.

Kabira walked with Halil to the gate of the palace.

“What is the other brother’s name?”

“Ahmet,” he replied efficiently.

“If he comes back here, you send him to me, do you understand that?”

“Pasha?” Kabira asked gently. “Are you sure?”

“My friend, if he comes here, expecting a warm welcome, he will be murdered by that little Greek barbarian.” Halil said with disgust. “I want to save the life of an innocent Muslim from that jackal.”

Kabira of course knew that to be an outright lie, but accepted it for what it was.

“This new sultan... I am afraid he won’t tolerate the same kind of vendettas as are normally practiced here...”

“You owe me, Kabira!” Halil kept his voice down. “And I don’t care what he wants to tolerate. We have two hundred years of tradition to keep, and an important mission to bring Islam to the world. I’m not going to let that all be risked by some unpredictable teenager. Murat is dead, but some of us stay loyal beyond the man’s natural life. He was a great man, and that greatness does not end when God brings the man home. Can you understand that?”

“Yes, Pasha.”

“If the barbarian comes, warn him, send him to me.”

“Yes, Pasha.”

Halil was woken up by his chamberlain before the sun rose. He was informed that a certain expected guest had just arrived. He quickly prepared himself, put on his robe and went to the garden. Sitting on one of the stone benches under green-plum tree was a tall long-haired man of frightening build and humble clothing. The minister sat down next to him.

“Arc you okay?

"My brother is dead," the stranger half-sobbed.

Halil was always made uncomfortable by such shows of honest emotion. Among his peers in the council and court, everyone's emotions were carefully measured postures. This man's honest, heart-wrenching sorrow brought a constriction to his throat. He put an arm on the big man's shoulder.

"Yes," he confirmed. "He was killed by a man named Zaganos-Pasha, at the behest of the Sultan, Mehmet the Second. He needed you both executed for murdering his baby brother earlier tonight."

Ahmet looked up at him incredulously. "Mehmet is our friend, he brought us here to help him! We are like cousins."

"Why would the Sultan of Adrianople, Lord of the Horizons, need two tribesmen from Amaseia Sanjak? What makes you special or qualified to do anything special except one task, to be cast aside afterwards?" Halil asked rhetorically. "Did you think that your brains or cunning were something special? I'm sorry, but this was why he befriended you and your brother. This is why he brought you both here. To send you on a grisly mission, and then wash you both away."

"I'll kill them both," the barbarian said, his blood rising.

"No, not yet." Halil counselled. "You know about my history with Mehmet and Zaganos, I presume?"

Ahmet nodded. He'd heard rumours, but not details.

"I'm going to argue for your freedom, I'll say that you've accepted the ways of the world…"

"Accepted?"

"Not important," Halil snapped at the young man. "You understand what's happened and why, you will ask for mercy from the Sultan, and apologize on behalf of your brother."

"I'll put a knife in his belly before I do anything…"

"Then I'm sure that you will die quite bravely, young man," he assured him. "Make no mistake, there are men out in the city hunting you as we speak. I'm taking a very dangerous risk having you here, for a second time tonight, I might add."

Ahmet's eyes burned at the vizier with a visceral hatred.

"Boy, you can't just charge into the palace and execute the Sultan and his advisor. Regardless of how angry you feel, a crafty hunter can kill a mighty lion. Mehmet is a very crafty hunter, and you are a very ferocious lion right now, wild and destructive, but ultimately doomed if you continue."

Ahmet didn't even blink.

"If we can arrange your pardon, you will join my house, and we can go about our shared task, Ahmet."

"And what task would that be?"

"Vengeance, my boy. The destruction of Zaganos and Mehmet. Alliances will come and go, but if you can control yourself, you'll live to see these men destroyed. I've been watching my enemies destroyed for over half a century. I've been the chief counsellor for three sultans. You need some sleep, you look terrible. I'll go and speak to the sultan in a few hours."

"And why should you help me for this, Pasha?" Ahmet asked suspiciously.

Halil smiled.

"I'd like you to think about that, and answer the question tomorrow."

"I don't understand politics."

"Don't worry, you will." Halil stood up and put a hand on Ahmet's shoulder. "I'll have one of the servants make you a bed."

Chapter Five - The Guests

"What do you mean, staying here?" Ayshe asked incredulously. Halil could see that his wife was in the process of working herself up to a dramatic outburst.

"I mean that he will be a guest of our house for the next little while, Wife. I'll explain all of what's going on after I get back from the palace. In the meantime, ignore him. Have the servants deal with him. I'll be back before mid-day prayers."

Ayshe's expression didn't change.

"Need I remind you that Fatma is upstairs? She was hysterical last night, we needed some opiates to simply control her and put her to sleep!" Ayshe stabbed her husband with that last accusation, reminding him of how far gone his sense of morality was when it came to political expedience. "This man is the man responsible for all this. What are you thinking!?"

Halil chewed his tongue, knowing that he was in the wrong, from her perspective. From his perspective of course, Fatma was a naïve young woman whose usefulness expired in a bowl of bathwater. It was unusual of his wife to get so attached.

"Mehmet is the man responsible for all this. You don't blame a dagger for a murder. As for taking him as a guest, you're right, of course, my love. Don't tell the poor girl." He spoke as if the two guests were feuding children, incapable of playing nicely. "She'll stay in the harem part of the house, he'll stay in the hall for a few hours. There shouldn't be any danger of them bumping into each other and engaging in any awkward conversations."

"He broke into our home and you treat him like a guest!"

"Quiet, Woman. I don't want that poor girl to hear you. I have to speak to my old pupil and make some peace between him and this other man. That boy out in the hall didn't kill out of malice or evil. He was commanded by the sultan. He thinks he's an obedient soldier. He feels betrayed."

"I don't care how he feels! How many soldiers do what he did?"

"A surprisingly large number do worse, Darling.

"Don't be so dramatic!"

Halil took a deep breath and looked at his wife in an effort to calm her down. "One of us is being dramatic enough for us both. Now I'll explain things to you this afternoon, you know I'll want your help for this. Right now we control two of the most important players in Mehmet's most atrocious sin. We can't squander that in order to be nice to a harem-girl that you've made friends with."

"What about the other one who was with him?"

"Dead."

"Who killed him?"

"Zaganos."

Ayshe exhaled angrily through her nose. "He's back?"

Halil nodded.

"What about Nulifer?"

"I haven't seen her, but I presume that she'll come in her own good time." Halil pulled his fingers through his beard. "If they are here, they won't make any public appearances until this is over."

Neither Ayshe's face nor her body made any movements, but in her eyes, Halil could see her brain sprinting along different avenues, trying to ascertain exactly what angles were at play. His eyes smiled, though his mouth didn't let it creep out. He was one of the few men in the divan who had only one wife, and that was because he was lucky enough to have one capable enough to keep him vigilant. She had a huntress' look in her eyes when a course of action was decided upon. As arranged marriages go, he was blessed by God when his mother picked Ayshe for him.

"Ayshe," Halil kissed his wife on the cheek, "I'd like you to see to Fatma. Help her through this horrible ordeal. Be there for her. Let her always remember your mercy and kindness. She's lost now, but maybe not permanently. She can remarry. I'm going to do the same for Ahmet, that's the man in the hall. Then we can deal with our murderous young sultan."

He raised her hands to his mouth, kissed them both, and raised his face with a wry grin. Ayshe smiled back and kissed her husband on the cheek. When she thought of the perverts and buffoons that some of the women of the harem were stuck with, she thanked God and her mother for choosing Halil for her. Her husband went out the door and she set about her own tasks, most of which were to coincide with her husband's ideas.

"He's plotting something, you know," Zaganos assured the sultan in his most reassuring voice. "He's jealous of you. He always has been, and I'm afraid it won't stop until his own family sits on the throne."

"Then I suppose I should be glad his wife's borne him no sons. When my days finish, Adrianople will be a shadow of my greatness. If Halil wants wind and shadows, he can have them." Mehmet said as he fell onto one of the giant pillows that adorned his opulent sitting room. He smiled as he leaned back and enjoyed the luxury for an instant, then, getting bored of it, hopped up energetically. He found it very difficult to sit still these days. "I've asked you to give him the benefit of an opportunity, Minister. If he can put the past behind him, thank God. If he can't, that's a different case, but I don't want that fate for either of you, you have to forgive and forget as well. I don't want a return to the bitter back-biting that crippled us last time."

The two edged nature of that response wasn't lost on Zaganos. "Whether you want it or not, you've got it, Your Majesty," Zaganos assured him. "This is the capital, that's how things are done here, and if you expect the best from everyone, you will end up with nothing but an expensive state funeral. The best and most brutal player of this game is your grand vizier, he's been doing this for years. And it grieves me to say so, but he's not on our side!"

"All the more reason not to play that game anymore. I've got more important plans than pissing on everything like a new dog in the house, putting my scent on everything."

He looked out the window of the palace built by his grandfather Mehmet I, and into the gardens that his father had built to honour his older brother's birth. Murat was now buried beside the body of his favorite son, Ali, in far off Brussa. "I truly hate this city. I don't intend to stay a prisoner of the palace forever. I won't die here, and I won't be buried in these gardens."

"With all due respect, your majesty, Adrianople is your home now. The only way out of it will be when you move on to that higher capital with God. There is no third try at the sultanate, and any move that you're considering is useless unless you have the unwavering support of the entire capital."

"We'll never have unqualified support from everyone here. The divan is a nest of vipers that we'll have to intimidate by constant crisis. If they feel secure, they'll just go back to their plotting."

The eighteen-year-old sultan looked at his advisor. Zaganos was twenty years older than him, but Mehmet rose a half a head higher above the ground than the second minister. Because of the fact that they had shared a failure and dishonour together two years ago, Mehmet refused to break faith with those who showed him such loyalty. Some would see that to be politically unwise, but loyalty was to be the benchmark by which he judged others. After his betrayal by some members of the divan and their Janissary allies, Zaganos had accepted exile rather than denounce the expelled sultan. That precedent gave the counselor more breathing room than any other members of the divan.

It was perhaps this veneration of loyalty that made the boy so uncomfortable with the situation of the sons of Ali. Kareem had to die. His killers must then die in turn. This was a necessity, but that didn't make it palatable. It simply had to be done.

Then Ahmet disappeared. Hassan was no longer an issue, but Ahmet was a living, breathing man who had been betrayed by the sultan. Mehmet's conscience about this whole ugly affair was far from clear. He understood the importance of what was going on, but the look on his step-mother's face last night had been soul-crushing. He had already made arrangements to return the woman to her father's home in Karaman. He prayed that he would never need to see her face again.

The Sultan felt terrible.

The Sultan hid that broken conscience very well.

"I don't want any trouble from the old guard, Zaganos. Soon, our eyes will turn to the east, but for now, I just want this unpleasantness dealt with."

Zaganos stood next to his young friend and gave him a pat on the back. "You behaved correctly, Sultan. Please don't punish yourself."

He could sense a surge of emotion in the Sultan, which he mistook for sorrow over his horrible crime. In reality, it was Mehmet cursing himself for showing weakness. Anger replaced guilt for a moment, and Mehmet resisted to the immediate impulse to berate his counselor for seeing through him.

"No," Mehmet mumbled "I punished the two men who obeyed me loyally."

"Do you think that they are innocent of any crime then?" Zaganos asked rhetorically. "Are the charges false?"

"Ha ha. That's very witty,." Mehmet answered sardonically. He immediately took a tight rein on his anger.

"So why then do you think that Halil-Pasha wants to see you? Other than the obvious, of course."

"Don't start."

"He's planning something."

"I know. Don't you start planning."

"Sire, I…"

"I have my own plans," Mehmet said with an air of finality.

"Yes, Sire."

Ahmet scratched his head as he paced the room. The room was beautiful and luxurious by any standards, but the aesthetic of the capital had never really appealed to him. Artistic decorations among the Turkic tribes of Anatolia were limited to weapons, carpets and children's crafts. His filigree bow and inlaid sword, the horsetails on his spear, these were the only artistic flairs that he carried. Hanging a patterned tapestry on a wooden wall for years on end was just ostentatious.

His mind raced around the previous night. He and his beloved brother had lost everything. They had been promised money, women, a place at court, a life they would have never dreamt of a few years ago. Now, they had lost it all, and Hassan had lost his life, and Ahmet his dearest flesh and blood.

They had been betrayed by a man to whom they had been loyal, then told to split up so they could each be killed in turn. When his brother needed him most, he was not at his side. He was in an opium haze in one of the subterranean halls north of the city centre. Rage and sorrow wrestled each other for prominence in his heart, but eventually settled on a delicate draw.

Into that delicate truce stepped a handsome woman. She was much older than Ahmet, and maybe a little taller than him also, which was far from usual. 'Built like a horse with eyes like a donkey,' he thought to himself, recalling the local compliments.

'Eyes like a donkey' means big, black and beautiful with long eyelashes. *'Built like a horse'* means large body features with a long face and big hands. Most men found horse-like women to be intimidating, but Ahmet had always fostered a certain restrained attraction for that type of woman.

She had a graceful demeanor that made Ahmet stand up when she entered the room.

"Are you Ahmet, the son of Ali?" She asked in a deep and slightly sorrowed voice.

"I am," he answered. "And you, Madam?"

In the capital, it was very strange for a woman to meet a strange man unescorted by another. In the village, social decorum had a different etiquette, but Ahmet intrinsically knew that there was a taboo nature to the conversation. She was bold to the point that she even held eye contact when she spoke.

"My name is Ayshe, I am the lady of the house, and you are a guest of my husband."

"Thank you to you and your husband," Ahmet tried not to bite his tongue in disappointment. He wanted to seem grateful and sincere, but he had been cooped up in this sitting room for two hours, and he was too frantic to sit still much longer. "I appreciate all that you've done for me, but I need to be able to move around. I'm afraid I'll go mad if I have to stay here for much longer."

"The mother of the child that you murdered last night is also in this home. You have to stay in here so that you don't accidentally meet."

Ahmet almost vomited. All his anger at Mehmet, and guilt at himself, and sorrow for his brother was forgotten in an instant as he forced himself to think of the two completely innocent victims, the baby and his mother.

"No. You can't meet her to apologize." The woman of the house answered his unasked question. "I'm sure that you realize just how much she would not appreciate that right now."

Ahmet wasn't sure what to say.

Ayshe looked at his face and summarized him. *'This idiot can't hide anything.'* She thought to herself. *'Handsome but foolish. How can a man who just did what he did appear so innocent?'*

"Please just wait for a few more hours. I'll have the servants bring you something to eat."

Despite all of his racing emotions, Ahmet couldn't find it in him to refuse the woman. He admonished himself for thinking this way about a married woman, especially when he should be thinking of other more important things. "Yes, Madam."

'Experience can kill foolishness, I hope that happens before his face ages.' Ayshe thought to herself. "Thank you."

Ayshe was preparing to go, when Ahmet opened his mouth to ask something. Unfortunately for him, the words simply couldn't make it past his lips.

"Is there anything else?" Ayshe asked him.

Ahmet gave up at that point, and simply answered "No, Madam."

Ayshe quietly nodded and left the room. *'Beautiful but foolish. If only he were a mute.'*

"His Excellency, the Grand Vizier Halil Chandarli," Kabira announced.

"Thank you, Kabira," Mehmet said absently. He looked at some of the papers on his table, and then turned to Zaganos. "We can talk about these things later, minister."

Zaganos was unhappy with being cast aside and felt as though his counsel were being marginalized. "Sire, he is…"

"I know," Mehmet was growing impatient. "I'll explain this to you one last time. I'm trying to mend bridges, and I know he doesn't believe me yet, but he will. If he is the first to break this peace, then don't worry, you'll be there when his head is hoisted on the Stone of Judgment outside the palace. You can make a day of it. In the meantime, don't assume my naiveté."

"I'm sorry, Sire. I was out of place," Zaganos was not happy at all. "I'll try to remember that in the future."

"Don't worry about your place. I have an important task for you for later, but making peace with our old enemy is important for now," the sultan disliked being curt with his friend, but he disliked how he tried to reassure him also. It shouldn't matter what one advisor thinks; he was the sultan. So much of politics went against his grain, but he would have to learn, or die trying.

Zaganos left the room by one of the side entrances, and Mehmet commanded Kabira to escort Halil into the chamber. Halil arrived with a long black robe, a globe of a white turban upon his head and a grey beard straightened to the point that it could almost reach his waist.

The prime minister stepped across the hall and bowed deeply in front of his old apprentice. "Your Majesty."

"Hello, my teacher," Mehmet rose to his feet and kissed the old man on both cheeks. "Welcome. Peace be upon you."

"And unto you be peace. I hope you are well."

"I am fine, but you know of the sorrow that fills my heart at the loss of my brother."

"I do, your majesty, which is why I have come."

Mehmet motioned for the old man to sit and the sultan abandoned his own seat to sit next to him. "Your condolences are appreciated. How is my step-mother?"

"As to be expected, Sire," he shrugged. "But I also have another guest, a surprise visitor. That is why I need to speak to you, Sire."

"Oh?" Mehmet asked. *'Here it comes.'*

"Ahmet, the son of Ali came to my home in the middle of the night last night. He is there now, and you can arrest him there."

Mehmet didn't move a muscle, but his eyes burned their way into Halil's head. "Why is he in your home?"

"He feared for his life, and he came to me for help. He's afraid to meet the same fate as his brother."

"He is a murderer of a prince, there is little question about what is proper justice." Mehmet tried to contain his rage and disappointment. *'Zaganos would be thrilled when he learned about this. Maybe I should just send the guards to the prime minister's home, arrest the assassin and the family that harbored him. No, this has to be done quietly. Everyone will know, but as long as the divan doesn't really know, they can ignore my fratricide. Once I start arresting people, people will talk.'*

"Sire, he is an assassin, and he begs your mercy for his egregious crime. He says that if you forgive him, he will seek out the man who is truly responsible for this evil." Halil took a deep breath. "And that would be Sadullah-Pasha, the vizier of the Divan."

Mehmet's brain tripped over itself. Sadullah was the man who organised the two men to meet him in Amaseia. He was the *Bashdefterdar*, or guardian of the purse strings and official representative of the cabinet. Fatma had laid the blame for the assassination attempt at his feet. Now, Halil was offering him a chance to rid himself of that traitor. The gambit that Halil was offering to Mehmet was thus: let an assassin go, and you can get rid of a traitor. But the gambit was that there would be a man in the empire who knew everything of Mehmet's crime. Perhaps that was not such a bad thing, as it would remind other would-be-assassins of what happens to the enemies of the Sultan. He could start devising a way to get rid of Ahmet later. Sadullah was a more valuable prey.

"What should be done with my cousin Ahmet after this other act is finished?"

Just as Mehmet needed to dispose of his dagger in the form of Ahmet, Halil needed to do the same in the form of Sadullah.

"That would of course be your decision, Sire," Halil said. Throughout this conversation, Halil's gaze had been securely fixed on the ground in front of him. By not making eye-contact, he allowed himself time to think. He knew the right decisions would come to the Sultan. "Although he has asked me if he may be of service to my house, your majesty. I have need of a new body-guard for when I travel outside of the city and such."

Mehmet thought for a moment. *'Ahmet doesn't really know anything. His defection wouldn't be a serious blow to my cause and faction, but the elimination of Sadullah most certainly would be a great boon. How did Halil know that Sadullah was a traitor? Why can't this man just be loyal? Does Ahmet pose any real danger to me other than a man out for vengeance?.'*

"You may tell your guest that I accept his offer," he answered after some deliberation. Halil knew that he would, of course. "Halil, I would like this finished as soon as possible."

From his seated position, Halil bowed deeply. "Of course your majesty."

Halil kissed his wife on the nape of the neck. "Are you alright?"

"Yes," she replied. "I've been with Fatma for the past few hours. She slips between catatonic and hysterical without much warning."

She hugged her husband as he sat down next to her.

"I've spoken to the sultan."

"Was Zaganos there?"

"No, but I suspect he was in the next room listening."

"What did little Mehmet have to say?"

"I'm going to keep the young man from the tribes around as a body guard." He said while playing with Ayshe's dark hair. "He will have to do a task for Mehmet. Sadullah. In exchange for that, he'll get a pardon."

"So he'll be a part of our house?" she avoided eye contact by bringing her husband's head to her shoulder.

"He will. It won't be a big problem once Fatma is sent back to her father's home in Karaman."

"She's so young to be a spent force."

"We can't afford to be sentimental, darling," the vizier absently scratched his beard and kissed Ayshe's shoulder. "We've got a new member of the house, and we must say goodbye to the girl. Then, we've got bigger problems lurking on the horizon. The Janissaries are marching home."

"How will that go?"

"Well, I hope. If he pays them off, then we won't have to worry about any grandstanding adventuring on his part, we can keep things quiet in the capital, and keep him under control. If he doesn't pay them off, then there'll be a revolt, and we've got enough to pay them off on his behalf. That debt would also keep the young boy in his place."

"We might hope for the latter, then we could have more clout outside the capital."

"Come on, darling. The former is a much cheaper option for us, and the money saved can buy different influences." He kissed her shoulder again. "I've got to get ready for prayers."

"I'll go see how Fatma's doing."

Halil and Ahmet sat on a bench in the garden. The exchanged selams, and the normal pleasantries of 'how are you?' and whatnot before turning to the task at hand.

"Your life has been spared, Young One." Halil opened. "You can breathe easily now."

"My safety hasn't been my major concern, sir. I have been wronged, as has my brother. My brother has been murdered."

"I know, I know," the old man repeated. "But if you go out for vengeance without a plan, and you try to storm the palace, there are a thousand guards ready to cut you down in the process. We will have to isolate him."

"Do you mean, lure him out into the garden?"

Halil tried not to show exasperation at the foolish suggestion. "No. If we did that, then rest of the court would just hunt us down like common criminals. You killed a boy yesterday, and there have been no reprisals. The reason for that is that powers that be in the capital believe that it was necessary. We have to change the circumstances among those same powers, so that they see the Sultan the same way, as an impediment to their order and their own power."

"But he's the Sultan."

"He is a new sultan, to be more accurate, Ahmet. He has to let everyone know that he is in charge, or they'll walk all over him. The first reactions of the Janissaries and the nobles will be one of resentment, because he is infringing on their own sovereignties and powers. Then, eventually they will accept him as their lord, and either accept the infringements or be granted new powers by their lord's grace. Do you understand that?"

"I believe so."

"Over the next month or two, resentment of the Sultan at court will be at its highest. On top of that, the Janissaries are marching back home. It was they who forced his removal from office last time. They refused to recognize a boy on the throne and emptied the treasury through extortion. We have to keep that resentment burning. The nobles and the army will unite against him."

“And then my job must be done?”

“Exactly.” Halil was glad that the tribesman seemed to understand what was going on. “Now I have some questions about the palace for you.”

“Anyway that I can help.”

“Do you know the names Nulifer or Aynur?”

“Yes, they sound familiar. They are coming to the palace. Who are they?”

“The Sultan’s wife and mistress. Do you know when they will be arriving?”

Ahmet was surprised to hear that Mehmet had either woman. For two years in Amaseia, he shared nothing of that side of his personality. “Soon. I don’t know any more than that. I’m sorry.”

“That’s alright, Kabira can help me with that.”

“Kabira, the bastard’s negro? Will he help you?”

“How did you know to come here?”

Ahmet remembered the eunuch stopping him at the palace gate, quickly explaining what had happened and sending him here. Apparently he was a servant of two masters. All of this plotting spun Ahmet’s head. “So, what should I do in the meantime?”

Halil grinned severely. “Do you know the minister, Sadullah?”

“Yes, my brother and I gathered him the same morning that we found you in the bathhouse.”

“I’ve got a special task for you…”

Chapter Six - Old Business

The meeting of the Divan finished well before sundown. The secretary of the cabinet had intended to stay in the palace later than he did, but he wasn't able to arrange a meeting with the grand vizier. He was a little fearful of a cold shoulder from anyone these days, and from an old friend like Halil especially. The succession of a new Sultan would of course make anyone nervous, especially when the personal bonds and relationships with Murat were not as strong as those with his son and heir.

Many in the Divan were afraid of Mehmet. They had supported the Grand Vizier and the Janissaries when he was removed from power two years ago, and now found themselves sitting across the table from someone with legitimate grounds to hate them all. This was especially a problem for the vizier Sadullah, who had followed Halil's orders and arranged for a special messenger to be sent to Amaseia, once the new Sultan was nominated. Sadullah found it to be an abomination that the religious council, the Ulema, had agreed to invite that lecherous degenerate back into the capital, let alone give him his father's throne.

Mehmet retained his father's divan, and was incredibly magnanimous in public. Even in private conversations, he expressed his strong desire for reconciliation with some of the old conspirators. Some in the counsel believed him, and some, like Sadullah and Halil wanted no part of it. Most of them were biding their time and waiting to see where everyone was standing before they committed to anything. Sadullah believed that Mehmet needed revenge. How could he not? He was disgraced in the capital, for the entire empire to see. His own father rebuked him, for God's sake! No, there would be no reconciliation. No *"sorry, won't do it again!"* This would end in blood and in no other way. Sadullah believed himself to be the only one who understood this.

He thought angrily about his predicament as he walked home along the streets, accompanied by his entourage of assistants, accountants and bodyguards. The spectacle made Ahmet's task easier. It was hard to miss the tall thin man with his army of supplicants. He looked like a carnation with his big white flower of a turban capping his green cloaked stem of a body. Ahmet counted the guards as he followed the procession through the ordered grid streets of the old Roman town.

Of Sadullah's four guards, only two seemed potentially dangerous to Ahmet. Of the other two, one was too young to pose any real threat to anyone other than himself, and the other seemed practically old enough to remember the capture of Adrianople, a little over a century ago. The other two were young and strong,

'Like Hassan and I,' he thought to himself.

They were both members of Sadullah's family, but didn't seem to hold themselves with enough sense of danger to intimidate any but the most girlish of schoolboys. Ahmet reminded himself that just because they looked and acted like catamites didn't mean that wouldn't fight like lions to defend their family patriarch. *'Gay lions…'* so the saying went *'are still lions.'*

He followed the group to a villa in the middle of the residential district, just north of the Merich River.

The manse was a three-storey story wooden block of a house. Unlike Halil's palatial villa, which had two sets of stone walls, extensive green spaces and a walled garden, this home had an unadorned wooden façade, revealing nothing on the outside that would identify it as the home to one of the empire's more prominent citizens. The house was as unostentatious as Sadullah himself. Even its size wasn't as impressive as others in the district. Most of the divan lived in small compounds of a few buildings surrounded by protective walls, like little villages within the city. Sadullah lived more modestly as a part of the urban landscape. That made his home a little more vulnerable than the compounds, in that there were so few natural defences.

Ahmet didn't like all of the pedestrian traffic. When he and Hassan went into Halil's home, there was no one around, they assumed. Wrongly, as that turned out. Here, there were people just milling about, and shops doing business. Ahmet walked around the building.

There were no windows on the first floor and there were only two doors, one that opened onto the street, and another that opened to an alley behind the house for the servants to use.

Ahmet decided to wait until nightfall, when Sadullah and the men of his family would leave for evening prayers. He walked down the main road a few hundred metres to the river bank, where all of the nicest tea houses were, and prepared to while away the next couple of hours. He had no way of knowing, but just outside of the tea garden where he sat was the exact place where Zaganos, the sultan's counselor, who was coincidentally Sadullah's cousin's husband, had killed his brother.

"Your Majesty, Lady Nulifer is here to see you." Kabira announced as the Sultan drank his rose tea. He was trying to ward off slumber after a long meeting of the divan. Meetings of the cabinet were still subdued, as no one really wanted to stand strongly in favour or against anything in counsel just yet. Everyone was more interested in ascertaining where they stood in the new order of things. As a result, one man would make a modest general proposal, which everyone else would tepidly note the good and bad variations, and then wait for Mehmet to respond with an opinion which everyone would quickly adopt as their own. The Sultan grew bored. The unexpected arrival of his wife in the capital this afternoon was at least something interesting.

"Send her in." he told the eunuch as he mentally kicked himself awake.

Nulifer had a face that only a mother could love, love and secretly mourn. When she stepped into the room, she kept her veil, even in front of members of her own extended house. She dressed like some desert Arab with a thin black abaya covering a colourful dress, and with the veil drawn over her face, covering everything but her big brown eyes. Her marriage to the Sultan was political. Her father was the Emir of Sinope and Kastomonu, one of the three most important lords of Anatolia. Attached to this girl was a dowry that could have bought an empire from the Great Khan himself. Their marriage secured peace in Anatolia as well as the succession of the Ottoman dynasty. The only problem was that Mehmet found her physically repulsive. Nevertheless, Mehmet rose when her party arrived.

"Hello, My Darling," he said as she came before him. The divan had gone home, but there were still many servants and functionaries milling about. Zaganos was sitting next to the Sultan discussing plans for a campaign the following spring. "Please sit down. You must be very tired."

"Thank you, husband," she replied formally and took a seat across the carpet from him.

Zaganos watched her without mercy or regret. He saw only an opportunity. As long as the sultan had such a wife, he would be led around by his libido. He would have to wander and take on new wives, since he'd never be able to be happy with this one. He cursed Halil's control of the harem.

"Everyone!" Mehmet called out to the room. "I wish to speak to my wife. You are all excused!"

Zaganos looked at Mehmet who nodded towards the door. Zaganos nodded humbly, stood up and left the Sultan to his wife.

Nulifer of Kastomonu took off her veil once everyone had left. She had dark skin and dark eyes that were too widely spaced. Her eyebrows seemed to creep dangerously close to one another and her teeth poked out of her mouth like pieces of straw plugging a water pipe. Mehmet had married her because his father needed the dowry to finance a campaign against the Hungarians, leaving Mehmet to keep paying for that war in his own way. Truth being told, Murat saw her father as a brother, and Mehmet saw him as an uncle. The only burden on the happy family being Tolga's unspeakably shrewish daughter, who became Mehmet's unspeakably shrewish wife. Mehmet imagined that his father-in-law danced for joy when he rid himself of such a daughter.

"Welcome to your new home, wife. I wasn't expecting to see you until the morning, you must have so much to attend to."

"That's what your negro servant told me," Nulifer replied indignantly. "I wanted to speak to you right away. You've put that girl in as a servant in the harem. My home! Do you think that I don't have any pride left? You summoned me away from my family's house for this? What do you take me for?"

Mehmet hated the sound of the woman's voice, but he had to placate for now. A public divorce and return of the dowry was completely out of the question. He decided that the best way to deal with her would be to honestly explain the realities of the predicament to her. Mehmet was too young to understand that a relationship between a man and woman based on honesty was a tower built on quicksand.

"Nulifer, we are both here as prisoners of our fathers' politics. I have promised to care for you beyond any possible dream of an ordinary woman. You can rule your own roost as one of the most powerful women in the House of Peace, and you come to me angry. Look at what you have, and we can both be happy, what do you want?"

"A husband!" She screamed back at him.

'*Oh God, why have I been saddled with such a person?*' he cursed himself. Women from the Black Sea are as emotionally turbulent as the sea next to which they were raised.

"You have as much of a husband as you'll ever need." He answered her without thinking. "You are completely independent in the harem, you can meet with the other women of court, I'm sure you can have a grand life here. Just don't worry about my habits."

"You bastard! If you won't send that Jewish whore back to Gallipoli, or whatever Thracian dung-heap she comes from, I'll go back to my father tonight! I'll say that you won't leave your concubine…"

Mehmet exhaled, this woman was just working herself up into a frenzy, and everyone in the palace would hear it. Mehmet was well aware that several of the servants were willing to sell information about his private life, and if these troubles got out, many offers would find their way to him and he would be a commodity for the city's women to barter over again. None of that was desirable. He tried to tame what men who have the singular honour to find themselves with women from her region call '*Black Sea Storm.*'

"Darling, Darling. You're right. Of course you're right," he lied. "It was a bad decision. Aynur and I are finished from this point on. I promise."

"Oh you promise, do you? That's wonderful!"

"It's true! Look at me, my sweet." Mehmet tried to build his most sympathetic face. "Let's just forget about all this unpleasantness and start afresh. We've been separated for two years. I know how hard that was on you. It was hard on me, too."

She looked like she was about to start storming again, but Mehmet didn't give her a chance. "I took comfort where I could. I'm sorry." He kissed her on her forehead. "Now, let's stop fighting and start worrying about…succession."

He smiled playfully.

She did not.

"That girl goes tomorrow."

Mehmet bit his tongue and tired to think quickly. "I took her from her father's house and I can't just send her back."

"Then you're sending me back." she readjusted her veil and prepared to storm out.

"Wait, wait, wait," he said quickly. "She's yours now. She has to stay here, but I won't enter the harem. The harem is yours. She's your servant now."

Nulifer was too angry to be tearful right now, she thought about compromise.

"She's mine, you will never speak to her, or of her, again?"

"I swear before God almighty."

The storm was starting to dissipate.

"We'll see."

"Thank you, darling."

"We'll see."

Ahmet followed Sadullah to the mosque for evening prayers. There were so many people there, that Ahmet couldn't possibly do anything. He kept close to the minister but tried his best not to be noticed.

Sadullah was a social man and tarried around the mosque, performing his ablutions in a leisurely way with his neighbours, chatting about the day's events. Ahmet was afraid that the man would never leave the mosque. It took Ahmet a minute to realize how lucky he was, as everybody else was going home to sleep, and the old man was dithering about. It was well into the night when the minister and a young man, presumably his son, started to walk back home.

The streets had emptied by this time and were left to the dogs and cats to try to find what food they could. Ahmet followed the two up the hill to their house.

'They must know that I'm following them now, there's no one else on the street.' He thought to himself. Ahmet knew that he wasn't exactly inconspicuous. He was probably the tallest man in the city (after Kabira the palace eunuch) had a large frame, and by his *'fresh from the steppe attire'* was obviously not a local. That boy could probably identify him. *'Damn it.'*

He walked quickly enough to catch up with the duo before reached their home.

"Excuse me, Vizier!" he called out as he grew closer. The street was quiet and empty, but the wooden houses and the humidity in the spring air seemed to muffle his words.

The two stopped and turned. "Yes?" The tall man in green asked.

Ahmet kept walking quickly up he began to speak. "Vizier, I need to speak to you. I've been sent by Halil-Pasha to…"

Sadullah gasped as he recognized Ahmet as the tribesman that he'd heard so much gossip recently.

"Assassin," he breathed. "Run, boy!"

The boy froze for an instant, not knowing what to do. Ahmet had intended to tell the boy to wait, and ask to speak to Sadullah alone for a minute. His plan never would have worked, but he couldn't help but feel insulted to be thought of as an assassin.

Sadullah raised his hands in front of his chest to ward off his assailant and took a deep breath.

'I can't let him call out.' Ahmet jumped the gap between them, and in a single motion drew his knife from its satchel and buried it in Sadullah's belly. The boy turned and ran.

Ahmet left the knife in Sadullah's belly and tried to push him down to the ground, and pursue the boy, but Sadullah grabbed onto Ahmet's arms. The knife in the belly would eventually take the man's life, and for now, it prevented him from calling for help, but he was going to use what little remaining strength he had to give time to his son.

Unfortunately for him, his strength failed him. Ahmet ripped his arms free from the dying man's grip and let him fall. Sadullah tried to grab at his legs from the ground, but Ahmet stepped over his grasping hands and ran after the boy.

The boy was running in a panic. He was trying to scream out but he couldn't make enough noise and was quickly out of breath. Ahmet's long legs threw him faster along the road and he was quickly on the boy. With a leap, he tackled the son of Sadullah to the ground and was swiftly atop him.

The boy struggled, much more than his father, but Ahmet was too big and too strong for the thirteen-year-old to stop. Ahmet reached both arms around the boy's head and jerked back with all his considerable might. The boy's neck snapped with a muffled sound like two rocks being smashed together underwater.

Ahmet rolled back off him quickly and ran to Sadullah. The Vizier had a panicked look in his eye and was trying to make noise, or do something about the knife stuck in his abdomen, but his muscles weren't responding to his will.

Ahmet slid the knife out of his belly and made a sliding cut along Sadullah's throat. A lifetime's experience as a glorified shepherd paid off and death came swiftly. He wiped the knife on Sadullah's robe once, stood up and walked away as quickly as possible.

'Walk quickly, don't run.' He thought to himself as he made his way through the city's residential district and up to the marketplace. He couldn't go back to his master's home just yet, in case someone saw him. Who couldn't see him? He had killed a minister of the empire a hundred metres from his house in the capital, and left him and his dead son in the middle of the street. This was awful. Ahmet cursed himself.

'Halil will be furious at me for this, and look what a mess I've made.' Ahmet's heart sunk as he arrived at the paper merchant's warehouse and set up a bowl. *'I've made a mess of everything! My brother is dead! I've lost my family, and I can't go back home. Everything is shit! Now I've killed children! What the hell am I doing? How has it all gone so wrong?'*

He pulled back on the pipe and let the clouds of smoke fill his mind, and obfuscate the terrible realities of what he'd done. At least he had that.

At the same moment as Ahmet let his mind go, Mehmet's was just making its return to earth. He rolled out of Aynur's embrace and onto his back to catch his breath. His mistress snuggled over his chest as it rose and fell until it returned to its normal rhythm.

"I'm going to miss that," she said minutely.

"Don't worry, darling. We can still do that. We can arrange something, we'll just need to plan." Mehmet kissed her head tenderly.

"But not all the time."

Mehmet shrugged impatiently. If he couldn't have relaxing, non-dramatic sex with Aynur, he might have to find someone else. There was a time when he couldn't imagine being without her; they'd been together since he was fourteen, and she eighteen. She could coax him in certain ways that no one else could, and Mehmet resented being manipulated, but he couldn't stay angry at her.

But that power of hers over the young Sultan was waning. In the past, he had always thought that she was '*the one*,' even when he was exploring different sexual adventures. Then, she was perfect when she was around, but out of mind when out of sight. Now, he was losing patience with her as soon as the sex was over. After his climax, what next?

Mehmet's two years of exile in the east were a period of self-imposed celibacy. When he had been given sexual dominion as a young sultan, it was lust that ruled him. Two years of guilt-racked chastity cured him of that. He would forever be slightly intimidated by sex, and the power it could have over him, and he would never again allow one woman to hold such sway over him that he lost focus.

Aynur was aware of her declining influence over the Sultan, and was getting worried about her place now. She knew that Nulifer had demanded her expulsion, which was a good break for her. Mehmet could never yield to her first demand, or he would be a light man for the rest of his years of marriage. Nulifer's demand secured Aynur's place in the palace. But what if Mehmet decided to honour his promise to his wife? Aynur knew that Mehmet was not the type to stay loyal to one woman forever. He needed constant change, or he would grow bored and frustrated. Much to Aynur's dismay, Mehmet needed a woman as tumultuous as his wife to keep his attention. It was a good thing the new queen was so ugly. There was nothing for her to do now but to try to imagine some new diversions for her thrall.

Ahmet lumbered back to Halil's villa in the middle of the night. He expected Halil to be at the door waiting for him, waiting for news of the marginally successful, although horrifically public, job. To his relief it was Ayshe who let him in through the servant's entrance.

"Come in quickly," she whispered. "Are you alright? You look terrible. What's wrong?"

The shape of her face peaked its way out of the clouds in Ahmet's mind.

"I'm fine. I'm fine." He answered quickly. "It's done."

"And?"

"Sadullah is dead, so is one of his sons. Damn. The child was there. I couldn't get him out of the way. I tried, but he knew me. I don't know him. I didn't know him, I guess."

"Did you do it in his house?"

"No, on the street outside his house."

Ayshe's face blanched. "Did anyone see you?"

"No. I left there quickly, and I've been keeping busy ever since."

"Did you leave them on the street?" Her voice was urgent, but not worried.

"Yes. I left them to the dogs and cats."

"Okay, don't worry." She hooked her hand onto his neck in a comforting way. "The local Janissary cohort will find the bodies and clean it up tonight. The sultan, the grand vizier and the Janissaries all wanted this done. They'll make certain that you're safe."

"I won't trust the sultan's good will…"

"Do," she was so rational that her tone made Ahmet nervous. "This was something that everyone knew about. I suppose even Sadullah must have known it was coming."

Ahmet thought to the vizier's instant recognition of who Ahmet was and why he was there.

"You're safe here," Ayshe continued. "Don't worry about any reprisals, but don't leave the grounds for a while. Do you understand that?"

Ahmet nodded.

"Now, come with me."

The mistress of the house led him across the house to the guest rooms where he was staying, and brought him to his door. Ahmet thought that was a little inappropriate, all the more so because his digestive system was beginning to rebel at its neglect, but it was her house and she could do as she liked there. Then to Ahmet's bewilderment, she opened his door and walked in.

Ahmet froze in confusion. Was he having some bad reaction to the opium?

"Oh, don't be daft!" she scolded him. "Come in here."

Ahmet obeyed, and felt embarrassed for thinking that her intentions were less than honourable. There must be some other good reason that she is here. Maybe she wants to tell him something.

Ahmet walked in and Ayshe closed the door behind him, before walking into his arms and kissing him rather forcefully.

She pushed him back onto the wall before releasing him. After releasing the kiss, she walked over to the bed and removed her headscarf as though there were no one else in the room. She looked up at him and motioned with her face for him to come to bed. She seemed quite impatient about his lolly-gagging.

"Is there a problem, Ahmet?" she motioned towards his crotch area under his tunic and skirt, and raised a questioning eyebrow.

"No, Madam," he replied obediently out of an opium induced apathy. "No problem."

Chapter Seven - The Gathering Storm

Several wagons trains beat paths along the old Roman roads, towards the city of Hadrian. On the north side of Adrianople, near the Macedonian Tower, was the Aslanhane, or *'Lion's Den.'* This was a bit of a misnomer in that the lions contained therein were soldiers, recruited from all over the empire. Encased within a wooden palisade was a compound of over a dozen buildings, making a destination for the martial pilgrims coming from their march around the Balkan Peninsula.

The Lion's Den was the beacon home of the Janissary Corps. There were smaller versions of such a compound in the provinces, but here in the capital, it was an almost mythic centre of power. It was a Mecca for pilgrims of war. It was home to the Sixth, Seventh, Eighth and Ninth Ortas, and among them none stood taller than the Eighth.

Ironically, most of the people in the capital were only marginally aware of its existence. To them, it was just an army barracks. The locals here in the capital were largely Muslims and hence not levied into Janissary ranks as were Christian children. They were also largely urbanites, and not fit to act as Sipahis, who were rural governors like Kazim-bey in Amaseia. The denizens of the capital were largely ignorant of this important fortress. They enjoyed the protection it gave them, and paid no mind to what was within it.

Within these walls, the compound had its own wells and vegetable gardens. It had barracks enough for almost two thousand men and enough provisions to keep them until Judgment Day. It had one of the largest caches of weapons in the Islamic world or Europe, collected for the sole purpose of uniting the two. There was also a large mosque complex and a rather luxurious dining hall.

The mosque complex consisted of the temple itself, a bathhouse and a tekke. There was also a hospital and a small library. A tekke is a study hall associated with Sufi orders. The Janissaries were heretics against normative Islam. They were Bektashis, but that heresy was tolerated in light of their military prowess. They had a more ecumenical and mystic slant than the majority Hanafi Muslims in Anatolia and the Balkans.

The most important institution in the Lion's Den was the school.

Every few years, Christian boys would be levied from around the empire and be readied for military service in the corps. On their first day, they would be told that they were now adherents to the Bektashi sect of Islam, get circumcised and have their unit number tattooed on their arm; 'Welcome to the corps, *boys*.' The average recruit was between seven and ten years old.

Every member of the corps went to a similar school. They spent ten years learning religion, weaponry, languages, reading, writing and arithmetic. The four orta-regiments attached to the capital studied here, at the most prestigious school but the were many like it in the provinces, for their own local branches of the corps.

Every member of the corps studied to be a soldier. The brighter students are selected as class leaders, these leaders became officers. Mesut gradually followed the *corsus honorum* from an eight-year-old class leader to a twenty year old junior officer, to become a thirty-year-old adjutant. At thirty seven, he had one of the most coveted commands in the empire.

As his orta marched into the world contained by the wooden walls of the Aslanhane, the entire population was mustered on the mainground. The children, dressed in their misshapen red cloaks and lopsided white caps, were watching in awe as their future walked past, colours flying, standards unfurled, mud and their boots and clothes caked in dust and gunpowder residue. The children saw their own glorious destiny marching home.

Mesut was unimpressed with the haphazardly dressed students. They seemed to be getting more and more slovenly every year. Things were so much stricter in his day. In reality, of course, discipline was still strong and had changed very little. Mesut's standards had simply ossified after twenty years of controlled violence.

It was with an elaborate ceremony that the regimental cauldron, scepter and banner were placed into the great hall of the school. The orta mustered to the delight of the children. Drums boomed and trumpets blew. The regimental cauldron was a soup pot, and the scepter was but a soup ladle. This was the curious symbol of authority within the orta. The commander's official title was Chorbachi, or "Soup-maker."

After a brief ceremony, the regiment was dismissed to its quarters. The students were terribly excited, because tomorrow, they would have guests in their classes to tell them about life on the frontier, fighting a holy war against innumerable legions of armour-clad Christians in the mountains of the Balkans. They would hear of exotic places, and some would hear about their own forgotten homelands. It was an exciting time for them.

It was also an exciting time for the returning Janissaries. They were back home, to peace and quiet, or bar and brothel if they so chose. Most would choose both. They would tell atrocious lies to the young ones tomorrow about how each of them personally killed a hundred Christian knights before breakfast, and single-handedly saved the day a hundred times over. The students would hang on their every word, as every scar and injury would get explained in its most dramatic, if not always honest, tones.

Mesut wouldn't be indulging in any of these vices of pride or flesh. He had business to attend to. The Grand Vizier had summoned him to the capital. Little Mehmet had returned to the throne and Mesut's old Janissary comrade was the counselor at his side. On top of his curiosity of the political situation, Mesut was looking forward to seeing the new Sultan again. When the other three regiments of Janissaries rebelled and demanded more pay, Mesut brought his regiment, the Eighth Orta to the palace to defend the boy king. Mesut didn't see himself as being any more or less loyal than any of his comrades and friends in the other Ortas, he saw himself as being the only one who knew that there would be a reckoning for what happened on that night, and he was determined to be on the side of the next winner, which he knew wouldn't be the grand vizier. He was looking forward to seeing the hopefully grateful boy king again.

Ahmet felt caged in the soft bed of his mistress. The boredom of living in luxury was making his skin crawl and his veins itch. He missed the forest, hills and general greenery of home, along with his family and friends. The stone grey and brown earth from the farms of Adrianople was a poor substitute, to say nothing of his adoptive clan. He was going mad thinking about his brother and of retribution delayed. He hadn't even had a chance to send a messenger home to Amaseia to tell his family about what had happened, though Halil had said that he would take care of it.

Despite his claustrophobia and betrayal, Ahmet felt very grateful to the Grand Vizier. He had given Ahmet an unsolicited favour, and one which he truly believed would pay off highly in the end. The tribesman was simple, though not stupid. He knew that Halil was playing his own angles on this drama, but he couldn't understand what they were.

The only things that Ahmet brought to the stage for his new patron were the matters of character. Halil was an urban noble, and needed to have a stronger connection with the tribes, for political purposes. Having a wild-eyed and loyal 'son of the steppe' as his body guard was a showy piece of political fashion, but one that he decided to wear with pride. The second attribute that Ahmet held was a willingness to dirty himself. No one with political ambitions could have done what he had done. No political animal could make a partnership with such a man. When the lion lies down with the lamb, it is the lion who sleeps well.

It was this second task to which Ahmet seemed most suited. He and his brother had killed two assassins and an infant at the behest of the new sultan. Six nights past, Ahmet had killed a prominent member of the cabinet and his son, and left them both dead on the street. He couldn't help but think of how much his life had changed from a year ago.

Ahmet didn't like to think too much. It turned otherwise strong men into brooding, self-indulgent philosophers and degenerates. But, trapped in his room as he was, he had little else to do but contemplate his circumstances. His bed needed to be changed, it was filthy with sweat, sex and luxury.

It has been said that the best kept secrets are the ones that everyone knows about. Great Aunt Petunia likes the occasional glass of sherry to keep her spirits up; Of course a Member of Parliament's salary can pay for such a nice house with a pool; I'm sure Cousin Johnny simply hasn't met the right girl just yet. The lie that everyone in the prime minister's villa had decided to adopt was to believe that the lady had meetings and political friendships with a slew of handsome young men over the course of her long and house-bound marriage.

All of the servants know the nature of her "special friendships" and none were surprised when the Vizier's handsome new bodyguard was burdened with some additional extra duties with regards to the Lady

Ayshe. Most of the house was aware of this well before Ahmet was. Many of them also thought that Halil was at least partially aware of this. He must be, for it was so brazen for everyone else. Denial and self-delusion, as it turns out, would eventually punch a hole through Halil's fortified wall of speculation until such a point that he could no longer plausibly pretend he didn't know. That time was fast approaching, but it wasn't there quite yet.

In the afterglow of a morning's lust, conversation between the two was forced only by circumstances.

"So…" Ahmet began awkwardly. "…when will your husband come back?"

She lay over his chest and listened to the sound of his lungs breathing and heart beating. They were strong and regular, not old and diseased like those of her husband.

"In about an hour or so, after morning prayers are over."

Ahmet absently brushed her hair with his hand. He felt guilty, after all the kindness shown him by the grand vizier. Lately it seemed that he'd developed a talent for ignoring his conscience. Ever since that night in the mountains back home, when Ahmet and Hassan had killed those two men, things had gone further and further away from home physically and spiritually. Ahmet thought about the baby Kareem all the time now, even more than he thought about his dead brother. Only a week ago, he'd killed a man for no reason other than his master's instructions, and of that he felt nothing. And now here he was, in bed with the wife of his beloved master, a man who'd shown him such kindness.

In addition to all this, he was finding himself in the market's opium den at least twice a week now, and his dependence seemed to be increasing. His lust for the opiate was becoming even stronger than his lust for flesh, in which he was also over-indulging. Maybe someday it would eclipse his lust for revenge. He hoped not, but he feared so.

"Who am I supposed to meet this afternoon?" He asked her.

"An important man. His name is Mesut," she sat up, allowing her full but fallen breasts to hang freely. She was still very attractive, but when her brain was working, there was no room in the conversation for anything but her machinations. She became instantly de-sexualized as she explained the situation to him.

"Don't speak unless you are spoken to, and don't answer without thinking. Mesut is not a nice man, and he won't care much for tribals like you. He's a Janissary, they don't care about anyone from outside their precious corps."

Ahmet grinned at that, but she glanced at him and her eyes carried the full force of a strong slap.

"Don't get too proud, Ahmet. For now, you are a guest at the table of two important men. Don't forget your place. Halil has other plans for you, as do I." She smiled coyly at that last bit but then reverted to her serious tone in a rather jarring shift. "Learn to understand these people, before anything else. What do they think? What do they want? For themselves, their friends and their enemies? You have to assess them first, and then move towards their goals. When you're strong enough to control their goals, you can move them. When you can move them, you can control them. But for now, just do what you're told. Observe."

Ahmet took a deep breath. This wasn't what he had thought he'd be doing when he left home.

Mesut was warmly received into the villa of the grand vizier. Halil himself welcomed him at the door and brought the man through his home into his famed walled garden. Halil and Mesut lay down on cushioned recliners in the fruit and herb arboretum of which Halil was so proud. They were served frozen sorbet from the cellars and fresh green plums from the orchard.

Sitting behind Halil was Ahmet, stewing in his thoughts of the day and hating himself for brooding so much. Mesut's body guard had a similar position behind his master, and he wasn't terribly impressed by the introspective looking tribesman. Ahmet's counterpart was a Janissary, fresh from the front, and armed to the teeth under his big red robe. The guard noted that Ahmet was so lost in his own thoughts that he had only one sword, which was rigged for secure transport rather than swift access. Still, he was a big barbarian, and his obvious emotional instability didn't make him seem anywhere near *un-dangerous*.

Mesut motioned his head towards Halil's bodyguard.

"I recognize your friend. I brought him and his brother to the capital, along with the sultan."

Ahmet opened his mouth to speak but was quickly interrupted by Halil.

"He's in my household now, he helps to keep my person safe. Unfortunately, his brother, peace be upon him, was called to God recently."

"I heard about your brother. He was a big strong lad. My condolences."

"God's will, Sir," Ahmet answered reflexively.

"I've heard a fair bit about him and his brother." Mesut commented returning his conversation to Halil. "There seems to be lot of strange businesses in the capital. How safe do you really feel now, Pasha?"

All the extra thoughts floating around his head cleared the way for the entrance of icy rage. Mesut's guard clutched the hilt of the sword under his tunic and looked at the unshaven tribesman with his huge shoulders and un-kept hair. He was an intimidating sight to any man, and his eyes somehow made him seem explosive. There are a million different attributes that can be shown in a man's eyes and none of those on display in Ahmet's seemed friendly.

"I feel very safe, Chorbachi," Halil repeated with a smile. "My young friend's tale is probably worth repeating, but I don't have the inclination to do so right now. Have you spoken to the Sultan?"

"You know very well that I haven't!" Mesut knew that Halil controlled, or was at least aware of, all the protocol issues of the divan. I've an audience this evening."

"He can't afford an accession gift for the corps, you know. After Murat's expedition in Serbia, his disposable income is a little threadbare."

"You've invited me to your home to tell me things that I already know, Vizier. It seems that perhaps we have both wasted our time."

"I would like to know your plans, Mesut, and those of your fellows."

"You want to know what will happen if the corps isn't paid its due? You know perfectly well the answer to that, older brother. Don't forget that my voice is stronger today than it was those years ago."

"Of course, that would never happen. In an emergency, my family would of course be able to provide your well-deserved gift. You can assure your fellows of this."

Mesut smiled. That smile made Ahmet feel uncomfortable.

"And what would we owe for this adequacy masquerading as beneficence?"

"Only that you be aware of the current economic problems, and know that the empire cannot afford any extravagant campaigns in the immediate future." Halil answered. "Hungary has paid tribute, as have Serbia and Wallachia. Even the Christian Emperor in Constantinople sends tribute to the banner of the Prophet. All I want is peace with our neighbours."

"You want a sultan who won't squander your wealth on far flung adventures and holy wars," Mesut considered that. "That's a noble goal, your eminence. But it does cut against the grain. For two hundred years the sword of Osman has been wielded against the enemies of the faith. If this emperor sheathes that sword, what's left?"

"Peace and prosperity?" Halil suggested, trying to restrain his sarcasm.

"Our Muslim allies would abandon us in favour of fighting amongst themselves. The tribal levies would go home. The gazis, the holy-warriors, would sail to Al-Andalus and fight the infidels there. We would weaken. Our enemies would then turn on us and destroy us. Don't forget, that we are beset on all sides by enemies: Christians in Europe and aspiring beyliks in Anatolia, who would love the opportunity to champion a war against the infidel. Without a good war, we would wither and die."

"I'm sorry, I underestimated your selfless patriotism, brother Mesut. Or perhaps overestimating your confidence in the House of Peace," Halil answered. "I suppose in light of your new found warrior fervour, you will be fighting for God and Sultan and won't need any regular pay, and certainly no bonus! I also look forward to seeing the new Sultan again, as he will be thrilled to hear this news. You only need God to keep your purse heavy."

Mesut's smile never lost its carnivorous quality. "I'll give you some time to think about what is to be done in the near future. And about the more distant future. You will have to excuse me, I must meet with the other commanders of the other regiments, they should be arriving any time now. I also look forward to meeting our new sultan. I hear many things about the man, I'm curious to know what an audience will reveal."

"He's a man like you or me."

"Not like me, Vizier. I am well aware of the young man's past disgrace, having played a minor part in it. I can only hope that my role is remembered accurately by the returning sultan. I suppose that you'll have to pray for lapses in memory, because of your role in the escapade. Were he like me, no priority would precede vengeance. It would appear that the boy possesses either the quality of forgiveness or patience. Which do you believe secures your person, Vizier?"

"There is another possibility to those two virtues that I would add, noble Janissary. That is not a virtue, but a vice. That vice is weakness. We are both aware of how much a man, any man, would want to settle old scores if ever they had the power. The Sultan's son has all the power he will ever have, and it will never be enough to stand up to great men. The power of the Sultanate in Thrace rests not on the brow of some teenager, but in the minds and will of the divan. The sultan is a boy who will act according to our will."

"And where would your will guide the community, Pasha?"

"It would protect peace and commerce. It would allow the House of Peace to enjoy the fruits of God's earth and flourish in our own time. All of our neighbours already pay us tribute, Janissary. Now is the time to sheath thy swords and enjoy our bounty."

"We have an obligation, Pasha. To spread the faith and defend the faith. We can't be complacent in this. In Thrace and in Anatolia, the Sultanate protects the faithful among the heathens, the Sea of Marmora is now but a Muslim lake. But in the middle of this House of Peace, there is a danger. The Christians will always look to Constantinople as a capital. The source of their longing is in the heart of our peace. That city is free from our laws and civilization. Its ships sail freely from the infidel republics and monarchies of the West, to the khanates and emirates of the East. This is a dagger poised above our heart, and the new Sultan has let it be known that he appreciates this threat."

"Constantinople is a wounded beast and Rome is a defeated empire, Mesut! What's worse, it is an impossible dream that our Sultan nurses. If we ignore the beast, it will simply bleed to death. If we attack it, she will fight most viciously. Were you there with Sultan Murat's soldiers?"

Mesut nodded. "It was my first year as a soldier, they pushed my class through the Lion's Den early, so that we could all join the battle."

"Then you know how strong the walls are! You were there when the mighty strength of the Janissaries proved insufficient to the task! Are you so desperate for another stab at suicide?"

"Vizier, in my house there is an expectation of death on the field. The corps considers itself to be ever victorious. By accepting the impregnability of Constantinople's walls, we concede defeat. We were not defeated by force of arms, those many years ago. We were defeated because our alliance failed. Our Christian allies made a separate peace, and refused to pay our Muslim brethren to continue the fight. The Janissaries were betrayed by the weak policies of the divan. We don't concede Constantinople as a loss. It was a setback and we pray that this new Sultan will continue the war against the infidel."

"You would sacrifice our peace in order to carry on a spurious campaign of defeat?"

Mesut looked at the grand vizier without expression. "You don't understand, Pasha. There is no peace. There is only active warfare and temporary truce. This will be the situation until the banner of the prophet leads all of God's creation as one. Ours is an eternal task, given to us by an eternal God. I understand that you would like to peacefully enjoy your later years, but the affairs of empires won't stop for one old man's mood."

Mesut stood up to leave, and Halil followed suit. As they walked to the door, Halil reassured him.

"Don't worry about the gifts, they will be delivered in an appropriate capacity, and I ask no price in return from you or any of your noble brethren. Make certain to pass the message on."

Mesut looked as though he were about to say something, and then declined.

"Peace be upon you, Halil-Pasha. And you, too, Ahmet. Again I am sorry to hear of your brother."

"Unto you be peace. Thank you, Mesut-Bey."

No sooner had the door closed behind the Janissary commander and his companion than Halil turned to his bodyguard.

"Damn it, Man! What's wrong with you? You looked terrible just now. You can never show weakness in front of a man like that!"

"I'm sorry, sir…"

"Sorry! That won't do, damn it!"

Just then Ayshe walked into the vestibule where the two men were talking. She was covered in normative modesty for when a man from outside the family was present. "Are you both alright?" she asked delicately.

"I am!" Halil answered "But this man can't keep anything to himself. Look at him blushing now. His emotions are all over his face."

Neither Ayshe's heart rate nor her breathing increased in the slightest. Her cheeks did not blush, nor did she show any discerning interests.

"I suppose I should be grateful that you didn't say much." Halil continued berating his new servant. "But you have to learn to bury things within. Reveal nothing!"

"Yes sir, I'm sorry for that," Ahmet felt even worse having Ayshe here for this. "But sir…"

"Yes?"

"I think that you've read Mesut wrong. Money isn't what speaks to him."

"He's a Janissary, Ahmet. All they care about is wealth."

"He cares about it, for sure," Ahmet conceded. "But he's more concerned with what he can do. Where he can go, with his men and for them, and for the empire. For Islam."

"Ahmet, I believe that you have a good heart, but leave the thinking to me. He'd prostitute his own daughter rather than support anyone or anything out of conviction. You weren't here two years ago when they rebelled. When these people are not fighting their enemies, they're fighting their friends. They're just parasites that need to be handled properly."

"Yes, Sir," Ahmet tired to sound convinced.

Ayshe looked at the two men and wondered how the experienced politician assessed those around him so poorly. He had been slipping for many years, and Ayshe could not always be there to correct his instincts.

The women of the capital arrived in a timely manner to the Prime Minister's villa. Every Friday in the spring and summer, they would all sit together in the closed garden, enjoy the sun, eat fresh fruit and put on their most polite smiles as they jockeyed for positions based on how successful their husbands and sons were, and tried to arrange some aggrandizing marriages for their unmarried children. There were close to a hundred women around the garden, about a third of whom were pregnant after the long winter. The number of children under the age of seven was almost impossible to guess. The women were all discussing the news of week.

And the news of the month was the talk of the town: the absence of Fatma, the wife of the departed Sultan Murat II, the arrival of Nulifer, the wife of the newly installed Sultan Mehmet II, and the murder of Sadullah. Rumours swam in a sea of curiosity among these garden women. When she finally arrived, the women could scarcely believe what they saw.

Nulifer, dressed in a blue and white cloak under her black abaya, was a humble sight to see. She was beneath bland. Many of the older women allowed themselves a secret smile as they planned to position their more attractive single daughters as ladies in waiting, servants or whatnot in the imperial court, and maybe they would be able to give birth to a future Sultan. There was no way that a young man, especially one with Mehmet's reputation would be satisfied with this homely face. Many options began to take flight in people's minds.

Despite Nulifer's humble appearance, she held herself in high decorum. She was the daughter of an important Emir, and the wife of the Sultan of Adrianople. She could visit a room with dignity, and used her refined charm in a way that would even make the revered Ayshe seem socially awkward at times. Ayshe and Nulifer exchanged selams.

Ayshe stood up and warmly returned the pleasantries. She then gave the young daughter of Kastomonu a warm embrace, and a kiss on both cheeks. Nulifer barely came up to Ayshe's shoulders, and the older woman's hands were large enough that they both completely encircled Nulifer's arms when they hugged.

"Thank you for inviting me, Lady Ayshe," her voice was surprising strong, for a woman of such small stature. "I'm new to the capital, as you know."

"Well, don't fret, little one. You have many new friends here now," Ayshe tried to seem as motherly as possible to the new lady of the harem. "I'm going to introduce you to everyone here, but I'm afraid you'll find it a little dizzying at first, there are so many guests."

"I'll try to remember as many as possible, Aunty."

In the Turkish language, there are two ways to properly address a woman older than yourself. The first, Abla, means older sister. Many friends will informally call each other abla. Teyze, on the other hand, means maternal aunt, and is much more formal and respectful. Many women start to feel old when children begin to address them as Teyze, rather than Abla. Ayshe liked being addressed as Teyze. She knew that she was not a little girl anymore, though her adventures kept her spirit from aging. She wore the title of "auntie" with a certain matriarchal pride. That was how she related to all the women of society, she was everybody's auntie. Despite that, she couldn't help but feel a certain intimidation at its usage here. Ayshe had to wonder if this little girl honestly intended to make herself the new *grande damme* of the capital.

Ayshe dutifully introduced her new '*daughter*' around. '*Kizim*,' my daughter, is a term of endearment used to a woman younger than yourself. Some grown women hate it and find it condescending when addressed with it, but Nulifer let it slide. Nulifer was the very picture of decorum when she met every woman who was anyone at the party.

After a round of introductions, she sat next to her hostess to chat.

"What's wrong with that poor woman over there? Her eyes swell, I think her name is Hazal."

"Yes it is." Ayshe tensed for a moment, but didn't let it show. "Her husband died recently, she is in mourning. God protect her here and her husband in Paradise."

"Oh no, I didn't realise. I'm so sorry."

'*Does she not know about Sadullah?*' Ayshe wondered to herself. "Her husband, Sadullah, was the secretary of the divan."

"That's horrible. God bless them both."

'*Interesting*.' Ayshe thought to herself. '*The Sultan has decided not to take this woman into his confidences, she's a political necessity. Bad move on his part, she's smart enough to be formidable, and far too homely and ambitious to be a display flower. If she's outside of the Sultan's interests, then his home is still open, and with Kabira's favour for sale to the highest bidder, every woman here will be sending their daughters to the palace for one reason or another. Perhaps finding the right son to pluck this flower is the best way to proceed.*'

She sat back and continued plotting.

'I won't need to do that, of course. Here's my agent, right here. This poor ugly girl will be so happy that I respect her, and listen to her, and can advise her how to reconcile with her husband. Loyalty and friendship, sisterhood. I'll be her new mother, and grand-mother to the next sultan, if God wills it.'

"Make yourself comfortable, kizim." Ayshe said and rubbed Nulifer's shoulder.

"Thank you, Teyze. You are very gracious."

"No, daughter, thank you for honouring my house so."

At the end of the party, the servants of the important ladies gathered in the cloak room to collect the outdoor garments of their ladies. They gossiped inconsequentially amongst themselves about the mundane tasks of housework and other such these in the great homes of the Adrianople.

One of the house's guards was helping the women organize their things.

"… and that's for you," finished Ahmet with a sigh of relief as he gave the last of the garments to Aynur.

Most people took no notice of the serving girl who attended Nulifer, though some knew of her past and possibly present role. Aynur was dressed in a plain brown dress. Her hair was covered. Everything about her appearance was designed not to attract anyone's attention.

"Thank you very much, Sir," Aynur said dutifully. "May I ask you a question?"

"Yes?"

"Where are you from? I can't place your accent."

"I'm from around Amaseia-sanjak, I'm from the Orguz clan. My name is Ahmet, son of Ali."

"Oh," Aynur hid her surprise. She had heard all about this man. Mehmet felt terrible about what he'd done to him, but with time, the Sultan would learn to kill feelings toward insignificant men such as this. "How do you like living in the city? It must be quite different."

Ahmet nodded his head and his eyes refocused for an instant. "Different it is."

"Do you like it?"

"The grand vizier and his family are very kind to me."

'There's something underneath that,' Aynur thought. Aynur was blessed with a sharp eye for human dynamism, and Ahmet was cursed with a complete inability to hide what he was thinking. "Lady Ayshe seems remarkably gracious."

"She is quite a lady."

"Is she as friendly normally as she seems here?" Aynur asked playfully.

The unsuspecting tribesman smiled and answered that "She's a very good woman, I can't say anything bad about her… or her husband."

'God protect him! This ignorant pumpkin can't hide anything. He's with the prime minister's wife. Mehmet will have to hear this,' She smiled. "You're lucky to have such masters then. It's nice to meet you."

"Wait," Ahmet started. "What's your name?"

"Aynur."

"That means *'Moonlight.'* It's very beautiful."

Aynur smiled coyly, remembering that she had to pretend to be a simple and coy serving girl. "Thank you, Ahmet-bey. Bye now."

"Good bye." Ahmet smiled to himself as she left. *'What a nice girl,'* he thought to himself. He felt better than he had in weeks.

Chapter Eight - The Path before Us

After a meeting of the divan, Mehmet was tired. He then held court for three hours, where every local farmer with a dispute about the price of watermelons was free to petition a redress to him. Then public prayers with the mufti and a banquet with the emissaries from the Christian vassals. Through all of this, Mehmet was forbidden to yawn. He had to appear to be neither bored nor interested, only dutiful and pious. Zaganos was constantly encouraging him, and while the advice was welcome, even that was beginning to grate on the young Sultan's patience.

At the end of the day, he went to the royal bath to relax. It was a small room with a small belly-stone, that Kabira had warmed up an hour earlier. Mehmet was looking forward to a hot bath on the hot marble, a massage, and then bed. Tonight he had the patience for neither Nulifer's nor Aynur's affections, and certainly lacked the motivation to select a new playmate.

He stepped into the room, lit by a dozen beeswax candles and sat on the marble table. He looked up, expecting to see the ebony Kabira ready to give him his bath, but instead saw Aynur, wearing only a towel to show an iota of decency.

"Hello, Darling," Mehmet said wearily. He was not entirely surprised.

"Sit back, I need to talk to you," she said.

Mehmet sat back against the hard stone. "What do you need to talk to me about?"

"Your wife and I went to Lady Ayshe's luncheon today."

Mehmet grunted as a signal for her to go on.

Aynur wetted the cloth in the basin of hot water and began to wet Mehmet's head and shoulders.

"She's a formidable politician, that old Teyze. Did you know that?" she asked.

"Darling, I am very tired. Is there something that you'd like to tell me so I can relax and enjoy my bath?"

"She has a lover."

Mehmet's eyes jumped out of their torpor and he looked at her with new energy. He smiled.

"How do you know?"

"He's one of the servants."

"You can't trust servant's rumours."

"He didn't say. He tried to hide his feelings, but he wasn't very good at it." She leaned over to whisper in his ear, exposing her ample cleavage to her former thrall. "You may remember that I can always tell when someone's lying to me."

Mehmet let his cheek drag along hers as her face withdrew from his. His cheek was tight with a smile. "So, the prime minister is a cuckold to one of his own servants. That's great. Zaganos will be thrilled to hear of it."

Aynur continued to wash him as his mind plotted. "Would you like to know who the man in question is?"

"Telling me his name won't help much, I don't know any of his servants. Tell me his job. Is it the gardener? The cook? Oh no! The stable boy!" Mehmet laughed.

"You know one of his servants."

Mehmet looked at her without understanding for a second, and then comprehension landed like an eagle into its nest. "You don't mean..."

"Ahmet, son of Ali."

Mehmet laughed out loud at that revelation. "Ahmet, you bastard! Ha ha! I'm glad I didn't keep him around after all!"

"I'm glad you're so happy." Aynur smiled as she soaped Mehmet's back.

"Who else knows about this?"

"I do, and probably every servant in Halil's house is aware of it, he's not a subtle man."

"That he's not." Mehmet's back tensed as he thought about the ramifications.

"What are you going to do?"

"I want you to tell this to Nulifer," he answered. "Tell her that she should pass this information on to her husband, you both know how important it could be."

"What?"

"I want to see if she actually would pass it on or try to play her own games. Also, it would help the two of you get along better."

She stopped washing him.

"For now, you have to be a friend to her, and she to you. Just do what you're told."

She didn't move or speak for a second.

"I didn't tell you to stop, Darling." Mehmet said. "You're not done your job here yet."

Aynur averted her gaze and started washing the young Sultan again. The boy she knew those years ago never would have spoken to her like that. He would have hung on her every word, bought her beautiful jewels, and spend the next month thanking her and expressing his undying love. This man just put her back to work without so much as a hint of gratitude.

Aynur was not pleased with the unexpected direction of their conversation.

Mehmet, on the other hand, felt revitalised.

A few days later, in the middle of the night, intruders came again to the villa of the grand vizier. There was no stealth or mystery to their approach, for the intruders were not burglars or assassins, but soldiers. The commotion was loud enough to wake the grand vizier on the second floor. From the top of the stairs, he listened. Someone was shouting at Ahmet, and Ahmet was shouting back. Halil couldn't make out exactly what was being said.

He quickly threw his robe on and was going to go downstairs to investigate, when a stranger appeared coming up the staircase. Halil's mind began to panic and he ran back to his bedchamber. He opened the window and began to look for something that he could use as rope. He was too old to scale the eaves or anything so dramatic, so he quickly changed his mind and looked around for something with which to defend himself. The door opened and the stranger stood at the door, squinting against the night.

Although the room was dark, Halil was standing in front of the starlit window looking for a weapon. The intruders easily saw his silhouette and yelled out. "Grand Vizier Halil! Stay where you are!"

Halil froze and turned to the man. There was no light to recognise a face, but the bulky tunic and folded back felt hat were as unmistakable as a face would be incidental. They were Janissaries. Halil took a deep breath. "Who are you to come into my house?" He tried to use his status to sound intimidating, but his voice fell flat.

"Come with me, Sir." The Janissary instructed as he closed in on the old man. He grabbed his arm and brought him to the stairs. At the bottom of the stairs, the only light in the antechamber was coming in from torches outside. He could make out the shapes of half a dozen Janissaries, and could see Ahmet pressed hard against the wall by two of them. One of the Janissaries was bleeding through what looked to be a broken nose.

"What is the meaning of this!?" Halil cried out.

"I'd have thought that a clever man like you would have figured this out by now," answered Mesut's voice. "The Sultan has made a most urgent request for your presence."

The hard face of the Janissary commander looked grim.

"Like this?"

"Like this."

Halil nodded and walked up to Ahmet. His thoughts went to the assassination of Sadullah. He felt sorry, knowing that he would now face the same fate as Ahmet and Hassan, for the same reasons. This had always been a possibility.

"Ahmet, my boy. Tell the Lady Ayshe that I love her very much. Don't blame yourself for all this." He patted him on the shoulder and went with the guards. He was determined to give no satisfaction of showing his fear to any of these beasts arresting him.

A white hood was placed over Halil's head and he was made to stumble along the streets for what seemed like half the night. He fell many times but the soldiers would simply pick him up and throw him back on his feet again.

After an amount of time that was thoroughly immeasurable to the hooded minister, they arrived at the gates of a building. Halil mentally prayed that it was the palace and not the Lion's Den. If he was truly summoned to Mehmet, he could talk his way out of things, no matter how bad they were. If it were the Lion's Den, he'd be tortured. If they were going to kill him and be done with it, they would have taken him out to the forest, or the Stone of Judgment.

His guards roughly handled him through large echoing rooms and down narrow muffled corridors. Eventually they made him stop. He could hear people leave the room. A hand grabbed his head roughly and pulled off his hood.

The hand belonged to the arm of Mesut, who stepped back from him right away. They were in a room in the palace, thank God. The floor was stone and the walls were stone bricks, covered with kilims and assorted ceremonial weaponry. In the middle of the room was a large table, covered with papers. Sitting on the carpeted floor in front of the table were Zaganos and the Sultan.

"Don't step on the carpet," Mesut said flatly. "Your feet are bleeding."

Halil looked down and saw that his feet were cut and bruised from tumbling along the stone roads on the walk over here.

The young sultan raised his eyes to his old teacher and Zaganos began to speak for him.

"Do you know why you're here?" he asked through his heavy Greek accent. "Why we brought you before your sultan at this hour and in this manner?"

"I think so."

"Do you?" Zaganos asked.

At this point, Halil threw his manicured decorum to the wind.

"Your Majesty!" he cried, throwing himself onto the floor. "Please, after all that I've done! I've done it all for loyalty! To you and your father's legacy! I gave my life to loyal service to your grandfather Mehmet and your father Murat! Please don't break this faith that has been so freely given! Accept any gift that I may provide for you!"

The Sultan made neither sound nor motion for a full minute. Zaganos and Mesut both averted their eye-contact from the captive vizier. Mehmet made no such discretion. Halil took a deep breath and tried to swallow his absent spittle.

"Mesut-Pasha, Zaganos-Pasha. Please leave us for a moment," the sultan ordered without raising or intoning his voice. "We will be having a conversation, which out of respect shouldn't be heard by others."

Zaganos stood up and bowed, Mesut did likewise and the two of them left the room quickly and quietly. It was only because of the other that neither Zaganos nor Mesut would listen at the door.

Mehmet glared at Halil. The sultan's jaw and stare were immobile when set against their target. Halil on the other hand wore a corpulent face that hung off his skull, and from those fleshy hangings peered two eyes, whose long extinguished fire was starting to kindle again.

"Loyalty, teacher?" Mehmet asked softly at first. "Loyalty and duty are powerful words."

"They are powerful feelings, Sultan."

"Yet you've been plotting against my succession for the past three years. Before my first reign."

"Your Majesty, I…"

"You'll be quiet until I am finished," Mehmet dropped his voice to a whisper when he uttered those words. "You wanted my brother Ali as Sultan. You found him more malleable than me. That's understandable. My father would have preferred him as well. But after he died, you should have put that behind you. Instead, you kept fighting that cause, long after it was beyond redemption. You destabilized the house of my ancestors with your plotting."

Halil wisely remained silent.

"When I returned as the new Sultan, I offered you peace. Unconditionally. To let past rage be forgotten and past sins be forgiven. I've kept Zaganos in line, and I haven't pursued any of my own rights of vengeance against you or your family. And how do you return the favour of this amnesty? Plotting and scheming still. The rest of the Divan is avoiding you now because it's obvious to everyone what you're doing, and what I will eventually be forced to do because of it. When did you cease to be the loyal Cerberus to my father's house and degrade yourself into an obstinate old fool?"

Halil looked at him and wasn't certain if this was a wise time to answer or not. Mehmet made that decision for him and continued on with his own diatribe.

"That was how you wasted your second chance. I won't throw mine away so easily. I'll use it to its full potential! A chance to start afresh with no strings attached, my accession gift to you was polite mercy. Now, where has that mercy gone? It's gone to those who've shown me loyalty.

From your house I see none. Your two fool brothers are afraid of their own shadows and can't speak in counsel without looking at you first. What good are they? How should I return this disrespect, teacher? Honestly, how would you advise me?"

"I believe that the time when you listened to my advice has long since passed, My Son."

"I'm not your son. You give me no loyalty and you'll receive none in return. Not from your Sultan, not from even from your own wife and servants do you enjoy loyalty. You are aware of that nasty rumour aren't you? How can you continue as the leader of my council when everyone says that you are a cuckold to your own bodyguard. You've destroyed your position." Quietly and deliberately, Mehmet let that accusation float.

Halil's face was as stone as the granite slab on which he stood. The sultan's words confirmed his own suspicions of past weeks, and his heart sunk. There was an ember in his eye that had not quite been extinguished, but remained hidden from view. He didn't know what to say.

"Anything, teacher?" Mehmet prodded. "Can you not now, with your keen mind and honed philosophy, say anything in defence of your name, your house, your very life? Are you now, with such a long path before us, be it ever dangerous and impossibly difficult, now silent?"

"Sire...I am aware of this." he began slowly. "It pains me that you take such pleasure in my disgrace."

Mehmet looked at his listless prime minister and pitied him. He hated that he would still allow pity into his heart after all this, but there it was nonetheless. He needed to steel himself against his own conscience, for mercy is a weakness to princes.

"I gave you a second chance, in a world that tolerates no fools. There is no pleasure in my heart tonight."

"Thank you, Sire. I wish that I'd possessed the good sense to take advantage of it."

In Mehmet's mind, the Vizier seemed to honestly understand what was being told to him, but there was creeping fear that he was only telling Mehmet what he wanted to hear. Halil wanted to end this conversation quickly, go home and take the honourable way out after visiting wrath on his wife. A part of Mehmet realised that this would probably be to everyone's benefit, and bring the little drama between the Sultan and

Vizier to a definite end.

"As do I."

"May I leave your sight?"

Mehmet looked away and scratched his head under his ill-fitting turban. He could see the abject sorrow of a broken man who had tried his best to destroy him. There was a voice in his conscious mind, telling him to revel in his victory and in the destruction of his enemy. And yet he couldn't bring himself to feel joy at his victory. He didn't have the hate in his heart to send Halil home to open his veins. He still had love and respect for his teacher, even though it was diluted with hate and vengeance. Oh, if only he could accept friendship and loyalty.

"Sit down."

"Sire, my feet..."

"Sit down before you fall down."

Halil carefully curled into a robed heap on the ground.

"I will give you a third chance, Teacher. To you and no other," Mehmet couldn't look at him while he spoke. He was disgusted at himself for what he was doing. "I'll forgive your brooding and plotting. I'll forgive your rather extensive relationships with the Christians. I'll forgive your disloyalty and your slander this time but never again. You, in exchange for this kindness, will become the greatest champion of my will. My plans and ambitions are the foremost causes in your heart from this night forward. Any man, Janissary, Sipahi, Ulema or Divan, who libels or slanders my person or office is your personal nemesis. Your family will also personally finance the ascension gifts to the Janissary corps."

Halil felt dizzy. He had been brutally knocked down and then caringly picked back up again. Was this politics to gain his obedience? And his wealth? Was this Mehmet's attempt at the '*hot then cold*' approach to breaking someone down? Or was it genuine kindness and mercy on the part of his old student?

"Can you live with those conditions, Halil?" Mehmet asked slowly.

Halil blinked. If this was an elaborate deception on the part of his protégé in order to pay off the Janissaries, then it was best to go along with it. If it was an honest attempt at reconciliation, it was best to go along with it.

"Thank you for your kindness, Sultan," Halil wiped away a bead of sweat that was forming on his brow. "It honours me to serve you, Sultan Mehmet."

"Your service honours me, My Teacher," the eighteen-year-old insisted sorrowfully. Halil found it hard to believe this was the same boy before him as he tutored for so many years. "Now cast your gaze at the table and you'll see exactly what we desire. What we work towards, plan for and plot at, dream of and breathe in. It is our Mecca, Medina and Jerusalem, until such a day as we may behold it."

Halil knew what it was before he looked on the table. Halil looked and saw an elaborate map of a city. The city was a triangle of land surrounded on two sides by the sea and on the third side by an infamously strong wall. Halil recognised it instantly.

Constantinople.

"I was there when your grandfather was forced to swallow his pride and abandon the siege," the old vizier said.

"You'll be there when I ride through the gates."

Halil looked at the map. He looked at the impregnable western walls, upon which so many of the old sultan's soldiers crashed like waves against a cliff. He looked at the sea walls that prevented any attack on the city's flanks. He looked at the harbour of the Golden Horne, accessible to the sea and constant reinforcements. Across that harbour was the Genoese colony of Galata, where the Muslim traders could purchase goods from all over Christendom, and had done so for over a century.

"You have two obsessions now, Prime Minister. The first is this. The second is to keep any aspiring king-makers afraid and in check."

Halil nodded as he looked at the map and thought.

"Go home. I would like to have breakfast tomorrow with you and Zaganos-Pasha. We have much to discuss."

"It would be my pleasure," Halil said, accepting the offer. "Your Majesty, what is to happen to my house? With regards to that part of my disgrace?"

"It's your house, Teacher. I wouldn't presume to tell you what to do there. But don't put too much stock in unsubstantiated rumours," Mehmet put a hand on Halil's shoulder. "If anyone spreads libel against you, I'll strike at them with my wrath and fury. My vigour will burn through your enemies, as your experience will cripple mine."

"Thank you, my most successful pupil. Thank you for your faith, which is strong indeed."

Mehmet closed his eyes as he nodded. "I'll see you after morning prayers."

Halil bowed and left.

Halil made his way home and found all of his servants and his wife in the kitchen. They were all greatly relieved to see him at the door. The questions started to fly. What happened? What did they want? What's going on? Is the Sultan angry at you? What happened to your feet?"

"Everyone, everyone! Don't worry." He called out over the din of mild panic. "I'm fine, you're all fine, everyone's fine here. The Sultan needed to speak to me to settle some things, which are now settled. You can all go back to sleep now. Go back to your beds and try to forget about this troublesome night. Good night, everyone."

There was some general milling about, the cook gave Halil many great kisses on the cheeks to welcome him back, and many of the house servants were obviously worried. Halil took this as a compliment. It is nice to be reminded that some people care about your welfare, not just because of self-interest. The last to leave the kitchen were Ahmet and Halil.

"Come with me, boy. I'll need your help with something." Halil and grabbed a lamp.

"Of course, Sir." Ahmet dutifully followed Halil out through the garden and into the reservoir house where the rainwater was stored. At Halil's request, he filled a basin of water while the Prime Minister lit the lamp so that they both could see plainly. Halil showed his feet to the Ahmet, who immediately started cleaning them for his pained master.

"How are you, Ahmet?"

"I'm fine, Sir," Ahmet answered as he picked pebbles out of cut flesh. "What did they do to you, Master?"

"They led me down a winding path in bare feet, in the dark. I suppose I should be grateful that nothing was broken."

"We'll get revenge on that goat," Ahmet promised Halil. "There will be a time extract payment for what he's done."

"What he's done certainly calls out for vengeance," Halil conceded. "We've all done things that would demand the same however. If the family of Sadullah sent someone like you to try to abate their feelings, Ahmet, would they be just?"

"It grieves me, but I think they would."

There was a moment of silence.

"Would you resist a man who tried to visit righteous retribution upon you?"

"Anyone who would try to damage me, or someone care about, I would strike them down with all my might, Pasha – justice or not."

"Even if they were just?" Halil winced as flaps of flesh were cleaned of dirt and debris.

"If they were just, I wouldn't hate them for what they were doing. But I would still defend myself, of course." Ahmet didn't like philosophical arguments like these. "Why do you ask me these questions? Am I in danger?"

"Yes, but not immediately. You'll have to remember that there are people who feel that you've wronged them, and many of them are correct in that assumption."

"I'll remember that."

"You've done some ugly things since you came here. I've asked you to do some of them." Halil was vague as to whether he meant the villa or the capital by the term '*here.*'

"Yes, Sir."

"Do you think that I've forced any evil into you? Into your heart?"

"No, Sir!" Ahmet looked confused. "You've treated me very well, and I'm grateful for your kindness."

"Are you now?" Halil leaned forward. "Ahmet. Is there anything you would like to say to me? Anything to appease a guilty conscience perhaps?"

Ahmet looked very nervous as Halil looked straight into his eyes.

"No, Sir," he lied.

"Is there anything you'd like to tell me about someone else in my house?"

For the first time in his life, the normally hot-blooded Ahmet felt his veins chill. He pushed all his feelings of anger, sorrow and guilt out of his heart, met his master's eye, and lied without blinking. "No, Sir."

Halil held the gaze for the length of a few breaths.

"I believe you, Boy."

Mehmet climbed into his bed, exhausted.

"Good night, Darling," he said from the verge of slumber.

Nulifer, unfortunately, was wide awake. She kissed him on the cheek.

"Husband, I have interesting news." She said slyly.

"Huh?" After a day such as this, Mehmet was having difficulty with long words.

"I have news about someone."

Mehmet's brain peaked back into the world of the living, though his body was almost too far gone. "What kind of news, Darling?"

"A salacious affair for one of the wives of the divan. You'll never guess who!"

Mehmet smiled and kissed her forehead. "Just tell me, my darling. You know I'm bad at guessing games."

Chapter Nine - Venice

Mario took in a deep breath about a hundred yards from the house. At the age of twenty-seven, he was not the kind of man, who by either class or predilection, would normally find himself in this area of town. Nevertheless, here he was on a fair spring night, seeking out ill business in a house of ill repute.

He looked at the establishment in question, which was adjacent to two stone roads. It was far from the canals, churches and palaces that had made the city so famous for so long. In the backstreets of the Lagoon City, Mario bowed his head down low and hoped that no one would recognize him on his way to the old house. He walked as quick as his legs would allow him.

The Silk Palace Inn was a great grey building surrounded by trees. It could easily access two roads, and had adjoining stables to shelter any coaches that might come knocking. It was site built for opulence and anonymity, as well as swift access and quick exits. These were the house's only redeeming features in the mind this particular special guest tonight. He ducked off the street and into the shadows of the trees and breathed freely only once the darkness surrounded him. He climbed the stone steps to the elevated door and knocked nervously. He looked around in the frantic hope that no one would see him here.

Mario waited by the door for what seemed like an eternity to him. He brought the collar of his coat as high as it would go to hide his identity, but he still feared that he would be recognized. Mario was a fairly nondescript looking man, with average height, weight, build, hair and clothes. His curse was his eyes. They advertised a mind that was a sea, it was both vast and motile under the surface of the lenses. He wasn't comfortable around other people, and his brain was always lost in the nebula of his work, rather than the earthly reality of the world around him. People remembered his aggressively wandering eyes, and they made him uncomfortably conspicuous.

A man opened the door. Tall, fat and mustachioed, he ushered the young gentleman into the house. Mario reflexively cast his gaze away from the open door, lest the light from the house illuminate his face to draw attention from a passer-by.

"Welcome!" the big man announced as Mario stumbled quickly into the house. "I don't believe that I've ever seen you here before. If you follow me, I'll sit you down. Is there anything specific that you're looking for?"

"No, uh… I've never been here before," Mario said trying not to seem so damn conspicuous. "I'm here to meet someone."

"Well, I must say that you've found a great place to meet someone," the door man chuckled. "My name's Nicolo, and if you see a woman that you'd like to meet, you tell me, or my friend Enzo at the bar, and we'll arrange everything for you. Now doesn't that sound nice and easy?"

"Could you tell me where I could find a man," Mario blushed in horror as he realised how that sounded, and then adjusted his desires quickly. "His name is Ezera, he's expecting me."

"Ah," the big man sighed, knowingly and then added with some sly enthusiasm "Captain Ezera is upstairs with Ophelia. I'll let him know that you're waiting for him."

"Thank you."

The big man seemed friendly enough, but Mario couldn't even make eye-contact. Such was his self-consciousness at being in a place like this.

The inn was a tinderbox of dry wood that should have been cast away rather than used for constructing. This wood was covered with silk drapery, whose pastel tones seemed to absorb what little light the copious candles and lamps actually provided. Apparently here you were not meant to get that good a look at the women who rushed up the stairs, down the stairs, into the lounge and through the hall. The silk and wood combination muffled light and sound, but they also held tight the unmistakable smell of the place. This left no room for confusion as to what primary trade was practiced there.

The main room was a sitting room, with women dressed up in a presenting manner all around, their breasts bare for all Christendom to see as they gallivanted about. In the next room over, there was a harpsichordist playing and some voices from men and women keeping pace together, singing a bawdy song about a lusty sailor going to market. Mario could hear an ungodly commotion upstairs, and could see the lazier, more full-figured ladies loafing in wait for new clients. There were some men chatting away with some of these ladies, discussing whatever they may. The women would throw their well-rehearsed natural-sounding laughs at all of the men's jokes. Mario looked at these men and his heart shamed himself again. He didn't want to be like them. He was pious, he had taken vows of temperance and chastity, and all around him was indulgence and lust. The very thought of someone recognising him here and thinking that he came to enjoy the sundries of the flesh that were sold here like so many common wares repulsed him and made his skin crawl. He blushed reflexively.

"Can I get you a drink, Sir?" asked a buxom maid, dressed in bright red and blue scarves, shirt and blouse. Her dubious taste in fashion made her a pain for him to look at.

"No, thank you."

"Something else?" her eyelids crept over the orbs of her eyes for an instant in a manner to suggest her services.

"I'm waiting to meet someone."

The woman dropped all pretence of niceties at that. She could see the shame and embarrassment on his face and played to that by raising her voice. "This isn't a free lounge, you know!"

Her raised voice tripped a panic instinct in Mario. People across the room looked over at his table. Was there anyone he knew? Were he recognized here, his career would be finished! His life would be over!

"Here!" he said throwing some coins on the table. "Get me a drink."

"Right away, Sir," she said, lowering her voice back to a normal level and smiling as she skirted off.

Just as quickly as their interest had raised, it fled. The rest of the house's patrons returned to their own conversations and the horrified Mario returned to his thoughts. These thoughts were disturbed by a tap on the shoulder. Nicolo the doorman bent over to his ear.

"This way, Sir," he whispered to the young man. "The captain would see you now."

"About time," Mario said, quietly standing. There was no point in waiting for the drink that the serving girl had already extorted from him.

He followed Nicolo up the stairs to the inn's chamber-rooms. The halls were bustling with activity. Men were coming and going, women were pushing them out and pulling them into rooms. Above the sound of men chatting as they waited their turns, he could still hear the music from downstairs. Mario focussed on Nicolo's shoulders as he followed them around the patrons and up a second flight of stairs. Mario made eye contact with no one as he followed the broad shoulders up the stairs.

The third floor was quieter and less public than the first or second. There was the thick smell of incense covering up various other smells. The residue of sweat and sex filled in the void between the walls. There were only four doors on this floor, and Nicolo knocked on the third.

A surprisingly tall woman opened the door. She was taller than Mario and almost as broad at the shoulders, but her face was small and sweet. She had curly brown hair and eyes that held an obvious cunning. Everything about her was both enticing and intimidating to Mario. She smiled slyly at him.

"I haven't seen you here before."

"No, and I hesitate to say that you shan't see me here again, Madam. I am here to speak to a man named Ezera. Is he here?"

She held his intimidated eyes and smiled knowingly. "Of course. Come on in."

The room was exactly as Mario imagined it would be. Hot, humid, reeking of spent lust, marked by the corruption of over-ripe flowers. Lying the bed was a huge dark-skinned man with long hair, a beard and moustache, and little else. The naked man noted his guest's arrival sleepily greeted him.

"Good evening, Friend! You must be Antonio's man."

"I am that. You are Ezera, I presume?"

"That I am. The great Captain Ezera, in the flesh."

"I'd noticed," Mario looked around the boudoir. The big-boned woman sat down in the bed next to her client and observed Mario, who pretended to take no notice. "I have money."

"And I have your rocks. They're in a bag over there, on my delightful Ophelia's dressing table."

Mario took a small merchant's scale out of his coat and walked over to the desk. Black velvet cloves also emerged from his pockets and found their way to his hand. He didn't want to handle his prize with any exposed flesh. He took the black pouch and emptied its contents onto the tabletop. Four small red stones fell out. They were ore deposits, and ranging in size from the size of a thumbnail to the full thumb. Mario weighed them each accordingly.

"Are those rubies?" the wide-eyed Ophelia asked, suddenly losing interest in the two men conversing in her bedchamber.

"Heavens, no. They're an ore, rubies are a crystal. They're called cinnabar, and in time these stones will look very much like rubies, but their value comes from a much different sense," Mario answered.

"Cinnabar, from the slave mines of Morocco," the faux-maiden's bed-mate answered. "The Sultan of Tangiers would execute anyone possessing this, let alone stealing it out of the country. The local authorities don't much care for lay figures possessing them either, or so's my understanding. Not that they know what they are or where they came from. The Papal legates in town wouldn't much care for an impressionable young man like you, playing God with these four little rocks."

Ophelia was ignoring him and looking at the stones, and the purse that Mario placed on her night table that chinked of coin when it rested down.

"The papal champions here in Venice wouldn't know iron from day-old bread," Mario retorted with a bit of offence. "They think that anyone examining the larger world is questioning Father, Son, Holy Ghost and their representatives down here. Not all of us are so narrow-minded. Your money is on the table, Captain."

Mario motioned towards the purse. "Are you going to count it?"

"Not just yet." Ezera said, standing up and getting dressed. "I'd never willfully double-cross your Antonio, and I'm sure he'll be true to me under ideal circumstances. We have a respect based on mutual distrust, you see. It keeps us both honest."

Mario gave a look of annoyance at the naked man's nonsense and grunted a dismissive response.

"Well, I'm going. I've got things to do elsewhere," the captain announced and hopped out of bed. "If you'd like to spend the next hour with Ophelia here, I can think of worse ways to spend my time. Tell you what, lad – my treat."

Mario's face turned beet red.

"No, thank you," he answered testily.

"I find myself unsurprised," Ezera chuckled, now fully dressed in a coarse shirt and breaches. The man's presence seemed to effortlessly dominate the room, leaving other sights and smells to mere details. "Give my regards to the esteemed Don Antonio."

"I will," Mario nodded. Despite the discomfort of the place, this captain seemed to make him relax and feel at ease. "Good luck with your… other things."

As Ezera made for the door, there was a knock and the Captain opened the door for Nicolo to enter. The doorman whispered something to the captain who nodded and took in a deep breath. He collected his thoughts before speaking. "Whatever your name is, it would appear that one of us has been followed, and we both now have a problem.

"Nicolo, make sure that no one comes up this floor," Ezera looked at Ophelia and Mario before turning back to the guard. "Do you know this man?" He asked, pointing at Mario.

"I've never seen him before in my life, Captain," Nicolo answered truthfully.

Ezera's once sleepy eyes were wide awake and burned at Mario.

"You, Boy! What is the name of Antonio's sister?" he quizzed Mario.

Mario's mind blanked for a second.

"Rebecca," he answered once the name arrived.

Ezera nodded.

"Good," he had no way of verifying that. He didn't even know that Antonio had a sister, but the look of fear on the boy's face was that of an honest man afraid at being falsely accused. Ezera walked past him and looked out the window.

"Who's watching us, Nicolo?"

"We count two constables hiding in the shadows across the road, Captain. There are another pair on the main floor."

"I see them. The two of them shouldn't be too much trouble for me. Why are they waiting?"

"They're waiting for Balias," Nicolo answered delicately.

"Who in hell and creation is Balias?" the Captain demanded.

Mario's head started to spin. "He is the castellan of the city's constabulary."

"Why would some sergeant-at-arms be looking for us? Or more likely, for you?"

"Because his brother is a priest of immodest ambition here in the republic," Mario shot back. "There is a standing disagreement between him and my master, Antonio. Is that a good enough reason for you?"

"Isaac?" Ezera asked, much to Mario's surprise.

"You've met?"

"That we have," Ezera looked around the chamber. "Now, you don't strike me as the kind of chap who can talk his way around a gang of angry constables, if you don't mind me saying so."

"No offence taken. Who does?"

"I'll tell you a story some time," Ezera smirked. "In the meantime, we'll have to get you out of here somehow. Maybe a disguise…"

With that, he started to search Ophelia's cupboard.

"What about you?" Mario asked.

"Me? I'll simply walk out the door the same way I came in. You're the one they want, not me. I'm just a sailor in a brothel. No offence intended, Ophelia."

"No offence taken," she answered.

Ezera looked out of the window at the two spies in the shadows.

"Where is the stabling house?"

"That way," Ophelia pointed through the wall of her room.

"Come with me, boy," he jumped through Ophelia's door and then into the neighbouring chamber.

"Excuse me!" He shouted as he entered, Mario shortly behind him. "Continue on as you were. We'll be just a minute. Evening, Sarah."

What Mario saw in the room was a scene of fleshy indulgence. A rather angry man in his thirties had apparently been in mid-coitus, when he'd been so rudely interrupted by Ezera's entrance. He quickly rolled away from his purchased service and stood up to protest his most foul interruption. Ezera for his part, was more concerned to look out the north-facing window than worry about some stranger's sexual adventures.

Mario watched on in horror as the furious naked man stood up and reached for his sword under a pile of his clothes at the foot of the bed. Ezera was on him in a flash. He led in with a striding foot, landing atop said pile of clothes, snapping the sword back to the ground where it came from. The naked man had bent over to pick up the sword and Ezera lurched above him. The captain quickly whipped his over-sized head down on the back of the naked man's skull, knocking him to the ground, face first onto the wooden floor boards with his snapped head-butt.

"Alright, Boy! Come here!" He hollered, rubbing his head as he opened the windows. "You're going to have to jump."

"What?" Mario was still in shock at the unconscious stranger.

"Come on, look. The stable is only two meters across the chasm and a fall of two metres down. You jump that, then run across the roof, stay on this side of the peak, you don't want the constables to see you, until you get to the far corner. Once there, you can just hop on that tree, climb down, get a horse and ride away."

"Mario was shocked at the entire situation. "I can't do that! I'm a physician, not an acrobat! This is completely irrational!"

"Boy, if you're arrested in a brothel with alchemical supplies, you'll be a circus performer to an audience of prisoners in the local dungeon soon enough. Doing what I just told you to do is perfectly rational. Waiting for The Inquisition to arrive is the act of a madman," Ezera grabbed the sword from the ground and inspected it before throwing it back onto its unconscious owner. "It's cheap steel. Mine would have cut right through it. I suggest you get going before our friend wakes up, because his cheap steel is still good enough to pierce your poor clay, just as sure as the arrival of the constables will put you in a pillory."

"What if the men try to stop you?"

Ezera motioned to the unconscious man on the floor. "I'll worry about that if the situation arises."

Mario looked out the window to the stable. It was about fifteen metres straight down out of the window, and two meters across the alley to the stable. The stable roof was only thirteen meters above the ground. *'Two out and two down. The roof has I mild slope. I can do this if I must. Oh! God protect me for once!'*

"Oh, by the way, lad!" Ezera called before he left. "What's your name?"

"Mario Orsini."

"Nice to meet you, Don Mario. Good Luck! Maybe we'll cross paths again," He said with a wave goodbye.

"Thank you. You too!" Mario answered, doubting the possibility very much.

'What now?' Mario pondered. Before him, he saw a perilous drop and probable death. Behind him, he saw an unconscious naked stranger and two barely clothed prostitutes who were watching him to see what he'd do. *'This is insane.'*

"Is he actually going to jump?" Sarah asked Ophelia.

'If I'm caught here, I'll have to spend the rest of my days in a place like this. Treating the broken bones and infections of these girls and removing unintended pregnancies. Either that or hire myself as a veterinarian to the local cavalry corps. Damnation!'

"I think he will," Ophelia answered optimistically. "Don Mario, if you don't want to do this, we could get you a drink and you could wait for The Inquisition to arrive."

"They know the place!" Sarah joked and the two girls shared a giggle.

He looked at the two whores, who were coaxing him on. He'd prior to this considered places like this to be mere sources of sexual gratification, an annex to the self-abuse he lectured against at the university. Although he was denied the release by the vows of his position, he understood the strength of lust to drive a man here. But he never understood why a married man would come. It was watching these two brazen women watch him that brought that conundrum into clarity. It wasn't just sex. Simple men came here to feel like great men. To be called great lovers by women who couldn't possibly be impressed, and to play the part for an hour or so.

"I won't wait, but thank you very much for the offer," he replied politely.

"He's going to do it," Sarah said excitedly.

"God protect me," Mario whispered as he put one foot upon the window sill, then another.

He refused to look down the chasm between the buildings. He focussed on the spot of the stable roof where he intended to land. He crouched. He took in a deep breath, and with all the might his legs could command, he sprung out from the safety of the window ledge and into the night air.

The landing was far less graceful than Mario's rather spontaneous attempt at flight, but by God's good grace it was on the desired target. Mario landed feet first, knees second, pelvis third, followed by his belly, torso, and finally a good jar on the chin. He rolled over on himself, but thankfully not to the edge.

Shocked by what he had just done, he stood up grinning. Grinning and bleeding. Oblivious to the pain and quite real possibility of internal damage. He looked back at the window to see the two girls watching him, mouths agape. Sarah clapped her hands and Ophelia smiled broadly and blew Mario a kiss. Mario, through the adrenaline rush and pain of landing, felt like a great man for the first time in his life.

"He'll be back," Ophelia reassured Sarah.

A proud Mario strutted across the rooftop to the Blue Cyprus that hung over the corner. He easily manoeuvred his way down to the ground. It was less dramatic, though also less harrowing than his leap from the third floor window a moment ago. He slipped into the stable-room, where twelve cages were lit by a single lamp on the middle of a table where two men were playing cards. Standing above them was the doorman, Nicolo, who had apparently taken the more conventional way down.

"You got out, that's great. Did they see you?"

"I came around the side, they couldn't have seen me."

"We don't have a side entrance," Nicolo said, looking confused.

"I need a horse," Mario said, changing the subject.

"You can take this one, Sir. We'll send someone around to pick her up, along with a fare for her use."

"Thank you, Nicolo." Mario gushed.

"No problem, but bring her back tomorrow. You don't want me to go looking for you, Doctor."

"Tomorrow, thanks again." Mario confirmed. His blood turned to ice at the mention of his title, as he realized that the staff knew exactly who he was. His precious anonymity was lost.

He mounted the horse and bolted onto the streets and away into the night. The two men guarding the garden of the Silk Palace Inn were forced to flee back into the shadows to avoid being run down as their target galloped past them.

114

Chapter Ten - The Captivity

Mario laughed out loud despite himself as he galloped across cobbled streets and masoned bridges. The physician, stuffy and conservative before his years and still shy as a schoolboy, had received his own epiphany. He felt stronger than Samson in the temple and strutted atop his horse as he clipped onto the university compound like Caesar re-entering Rome.

As quickly as his newfound confidence had been delivered, it was taken from him when he realized that he was not alone on the campus square. All around him were soldiers, wearing helmets and breastplates, and the white cross on a field of black that identified them as soldiers of the Inquisition. A dozen or so of these men milled about the green, carrying pikes, halberds and harquebuses. His horse whinnied her discontent as the men circled them.

"Mario Orsini!" a senior guard called out. "Step down from the steed!"

Mario was gripped by fear as he looked out at the soldiers before him, and the fearful cross born on their standard. He obeyed the armoured soldier and sallied down from the borrowed steed.

"What's going on here?" he asked.

As if to issue a clearer answer than words would allow, another group of soldiers came out of the Grand Academy of Philosophy and Medicine, in a procession of unholy grandeur. Among the guards were two unarmoured men whose faces Mario knew. One was thin, sallow faced and wearing a great black cape. The hair on his head was trimmed back in a tonsure and exposed the whiteness of his scalp; it was as though someone had placed an egg atop a pile of gunpowder and painted a face on it. This was the imposing figure of Balias, the Lord Constable for the Republic of Venice.

The other man, fat, tall and red-faced, was Mario's beloved mentor, Antonio di Padua. He was being marched out in chains, but his aloof presence made the accusers seem all the more vulgar.

"Don Antonio!" Mario called out.

Antonio blinked his eyes and made a resting motion with his hand, to tell Mario to stay calm and say nothing.

"He just arrived, Sir," the senior guard told his commander.

"Good, that saves us the trouble of finding him," Balias answered. "Does he have anything of interest on his possession?"

The soldier motioned to one of the neck-less thugs who helped enforce order in the city, who began to search Mario's person. He unearthed a merchant's scale, some incidental coinage and a silver medallion with the letters 'A' and 'M.' on either side of a cross. Although Albert Magnus (Albert the Great) would not be properly beatified for another two centuries, he still enjoyed tremendous respect among philosophers and physicians, particularly those interested in experimentation as a pathway to hidden knowledge. Balias' eyes narrowed when he saw the medallion, but he said nothing until he saw the heavy pouch.

The guard looked in the pouch and brought it over to the bald man.

"And what will I find in this pouch, Physician?"

Mario looked over to Antonio for advice, but none was coming.

Balias reached into the bag and removed one of the four red stones and held it up to the torchlight.

"Ahhh, cinnabar," he grinned. "Tell me, young man, are you intending to distill vermilion from this and pursue a career as a miniaturist? Is that why you would go to such lengths to procure such materials, or did you have some other plan in mind?"

"I'd not go to such lengths were it more freely available to students and teachers at the university, Constable."

"Oh, I see. You are correct, young one," the glorified jailor began. "In the past, this material was mined but a few miles from here, but now no. Do you know why that is?"

Mario tried to look defiant, but his fear showed through in the torchlight.

"It is because some men used it for black magic," he continued. "Cunning men, wizards and warlocks, who intended to pull at the loose threads of God's great tapestry in a slow attempt to unthread this great work. That is why Pope Nicholas has decreed that certain materials be banned, and those that pursue them be punished."

"God leaves no loose threads, Good Sir," Mario stated simply. It was quite uncharacteristic of him argue with anyone in authority, but his blood was still up from his adventures earlier in the night.

At this point, Antonio could hold his tongue no more and spoke up for the first time since Mario's arrival. He had a booming voice that made some of the soldiers jump.

"This is asinine! Stones are no more evil than plants and animals! They are made in God's world and function within God's parameters! Trying to control them with your brutality is like trying to ban clouds from spoiling a sunny day. God's will supersedes your preferences, *Balias*!"

"You are in a position from where it is most unwise to mock the agents of God's justice, Doctor Antonio."

"The agents of God are angels and prophets, Balias di Napoli! You are neither!" Antonio called back in righteous anger.

Mario's heart sunk, knowing as he did what the inevitable result of such an outburst would be. If only his master were more capable of arresting his passions.

Balias straightened himself and stared into the defiant Antonio's eyes. "Antonio of Padua, you are under arrest for committing yourself to the Devil's handicrafts and degrading and destroying God's work through the vulgar practice of alchemy."

"And what else would you charge me with, Pilate?"

"And for seeking unholy knowledge," he added. "Men, bring him to the courthouse. We'll have his trial after Terce."

"Your Grace!" interjected the senior guard. "What about his servant?"

"Oh, yes," Balias examined Mario's face. The inquisitor's face contorted as he planned to put the lad to the test. "Tell me, boy, which element is said to be the enemy of copper?"

"Sulphur, Sir!" Mario answered quickly.

"Very good, My Boy. You obviously have some expertise in the infernal arts. You may join your master."

"What? I..."

"Arrest him, too."

The fat man paced about his unlit cell in the town jail. The rage burning in his belly prevented any sleep from entering his night, but also prevented even a moment of weakness from entering his thoughts. Plots circled plans to block counters and prevent ideas that led to conspiracy. All of these thoughts stalked his mind in order to save him from what cards fate had dealt earlier in the night.

Those thoughts and plans always found form in his ordered mind by a certain order. Assess, plan, act, at least, they usually found that order. The burning vitriol in his stomach pained him as dawn crept closer, but worse than the acidic pain in his belly was the fact that he knew it was clouding his judgment. He wanted to act out. He wanted to throw his fat hands around the neck of that self-pontificating thug Balias, and squeeze until he was guilty of a crime serious enough to justly land him in his current cell. It was circular reasoning, but he allowed it of himself.

Balias was, however, merely a jailor and a brute. He never would have arrested the rector of the university without specific instructions from his brother. Balias' brother was the dangerous offender behind the curtain. Isaac was the Bishop of Venice and the overseer of religious authorities in the republic. Because Antonio and Mario were being charged with religious crimes, nonsense of demonic knowledge and whatnot, the judging authority would be handed over to the Bishop and the ecclesiastic courts, rather the Doge's office which dealt with secular matters such as smuggling, a crime of which Antonio was, in fact, guilty of abetting.

'*Balias arrested me to feed me to his brother,*' he assessed. '*His brother wants to throw me to the stockades.*'

'*No! That can't be right! I've no serious conflict with the Bishop. He would gain nothing by all of this save for a completely unnecessary conflict! What is it he wants?*'

Antonio scratched the bloody psoriasis on the back of his hand. It would act up whenever he was stressed.

'*Why me? Why Mario?*' he thought.

As if to answer '*Why not?*' the tumblers to his locked cage started to click and clack and prepare the door for opening.

'*If it's a guard, I'll demand Balias. If it's Balias, I'll demand to speak to Isaac. If it's Isaac, we can talk.*' He reasoned. '*If it's Mario, then they've turned him against me and sent him here to weaken me.*'

His second instinct proved true as Balias walked into the cell, his black robe hanging off his frame, revealing only his pale face to the light. "Good morning, Doctor."

"I have nothing to say to you. You've charged me with variations of heresy. You have no authority to do anything here anymore. Where is that brother of yours?" Antonio tried to crane his neck around Balias' frame. "I can't see your puppeteer, but I know he's here, pulling your strings. Oh, how he makes you dance for the entertainment of everyone around. Maybe some good can come out of you, if only to give an audience a bit of a chuckle, like some gypsy juggler."

A rare grin pulled at the corner of Balias' skeletal like maw. "He's here. I'm simply here to remind you to be on your best behaviour when you speak to the bishop. If you raised a hand against him, you can imagine the situation in which that would place me, can't you?"

"My God! You are such a lifelike boy, Pinnochio. If I didn't know any better, I'd swear that you were a real man, capable of his own thoughts and imagination. It's a good thing that I know better, isn't it?"

Balias looked on at the fat man's psoriasis-ridden face with a touch of self-amusement. "Some of my guards can explain the rules to you for proper behaviour in a prison, Doctor Antonio. Feel free to call out if you consider their behaviour inappropriate to a man of your standing."

"Now, now, Brother!" came a serpentine lisp from the darkness beyond the cell. "I'm sure that the good doctor will behave himself without any excesses of your guards."

To Antonio's surprise, a look of rage, similar to his own, made its presence known in Balias' gaze. "Of course, Brother."

A man wearing the fineries of papal palaces stepped out from the shadows of the stone cell gate and into the dreary chamber. His jewelled fingers hanging from his hands like over-ripe fruit from a tree, and his arms in turn hanging from his frame like weighed down branches; only his torso had any strength to it.

"If you need any assistance, Brother, just call out. We're right outside the door."

"Thank you, Brother," the elder whispered. "I don't think that I'll need any help. The doctor is a very smart man, and I don't believe that he intends to sacrifice that character trait just yet, regardless of how he feels right now. Am I correct, Doctor? Is that famous brain of yours still at capacity, or has a night's incarceration turned you into one of the screaming lunatics of the basement?"

"I'm just fine, Your Grace," Antonio's mind was heavily laden with the task of assessment. Vengeance could come later.

"Good," Isaac put his hand on his brother's shoulder. "If I need you, I'll call for you, but I'm sure that Doctor Antonio will be reasonable."

"Brother, I…"

"Don't worry. I'll be fine," he smiled until his brother closed the door behind him.

"Why do you do this, Isaac?" Antonio demanded as soon as Balias had left the room.

"You would do well to address me as '*Your Grace*', or '*Bishop*'. Let us both remind each other that I am no common prison-hand and you are no common criminal, *Doctor*."

"Fine, you're special. I'm special. We're both bloody special. Now why have you done this?"

"I wanted to ask you some questions. Who's that boy of yours who was arrested with you?"

"What?" Antonio was a direct man who disliked circular conversations, but he didn't really have much option other than to play along for now. "He's my apprentice and a lecturer at the university. Mario Orsini. He's a fine physician, are you ill, *Bishop*? Is that why you've summoned us in these unorthodox circumstances? A rather nasty case of gout mayhap? Maybe some rot on your member from a visit to the cathouse?"

"Sarcasm will get you nowhere, Doctor. Is he a practitioner of dark arts, by any chance? A conjuror of Satan?"

"What kind of foolish question is that? Of course not!"

"Just checking," the bishop dismissed Antonio's answer. "Now that that's settled, we can move on. Do you have a family, Doctor Antonio?"

"No. Children and family is forbidden by our vows. Doctors must take on a life of celibacy when we choose our trade, as you must know."

"Yes, of course, don't we all," Isaac was showing little interest. "There are some in the clergy that say that your university is housing Hussites and Cathars. Did you know that?"

"Impossible! There haven't been any Cathars for over a hundred years, and as for Hussites, in case you were unaware, my own father died during those wars to re-Christianize Bohemia! I'd be less tolerant to any of those heretics than you ever would!"

"… Your Grace," the cheerful Isaac tacked on to the Doctor's statement.

"*Your Grace*," Antonio spat.

"Remember your manners. We're not savages," he chided. "Now, no one wants here what happened in Prague, so there are many who believe that the officers of the university should all be appointed directly by the clergy. I'm inclined to agree with them, in order to keep our social cohesion together."

"You can't do that! A theologian doesn't know anything about humours and sciences! How can we train without expertise? You'll throw the Republic into a scientific backwater!"

"Hmmm," Isaac pretended to consider Antonio's point and pondered. "I believe you're right. I believe that the correct solution to our problem here, would be for me to appoint only good men of science to the positions in the university. Men like yourself. You'd have a religious appointment, and the proper knowledge and skill for the position. Everyone's happy. Isn't that so?"

"What is this about, *Your Grace*?"

"I have a candidate. He's eighteen and I've looked after him since he was an infant. He's like a son to me. I would like him to be trained by you personally, to be your replacement in ten years time or so."

Antonio looked at the Bishop and realised what this was all about. "I can see how seriously we both take our vows, Your Grace. Is he truly *like* your son?"

"Ha ha! You are a clever man, Doctor. That's why I want you to teach him. Teach him everything. Surely you don't think you'll still want to be a teacher when age weighs down your bones. Thirty-ish would be a good age for him to take over the rectorship of the university."

"You could have simply asked for all this without this elaborate charade of heresies and smuggling, Your Grace."

"You're correct, I could have come to you as an equal, looking for an ally. But you see, I'm not," the Bishop's eyes narrowed and he stepped closer to the much larger of the two. "I didn't consider the wet-nurse who weaned my son to be my ally, nor the tutors who educated him, nor the soldiers who guarded him. They were all servants, who did their job diligently, knowing what failure meant to them. I wanted to let you know how I felt about this task being given to you, and where exactly we both stand with regards to each other."

"Do you think that I will make myself your loyal toady after all of this? If so, you've sadly misinterpreted the situation. Very sadly indeed!"

"I know that you are indeed a proud man, Doctor Antonio. But if you refuse me here, you'll be tried as a heretic and banned from any office in Venice. You'll have to go back home to Padua, where I understand that your charming personality has ensured that you still have some enemies. After which, I'll simply replace you with someone more affable. Please do yourself the favour of reigning in that infamous temper of yours, and consider your options carefully."

"It's my prayer that you find yourself in a cage someday, just like this one. Don't worry, I'm sure that there'll be many who'd want to come and visit you."

"Tut tut, Doctor. 'I pray about some cage, *Your Grace*.' I'll be back in an hour for your answer."

Antonio spat on the floor as the bishop left.

Unlike his master, Mario didn't pace about his cell like a caged animal. He understood that he was imprisoned and that no yelling or complaining would remedy that situation any time soon. If he could speak to Antonio, his master would think of something. Otherwise, the university would surely put some gold in the right hand to pull him out of harm's way, and he would be indebted to whomsoever paid his bail. Or not. The end result of Mario's reasoning was that after a night that started with his awkward trip to the brothel, continued along with jumping from an open window onto another building, galloping away from the constabulary and ended with his arrest, he was finally ready for a good night's sleep. And sleep he did.

Shortly after dawn, Balias entered his cell to rattle the prisoner's chain, the jailor was shocked to find him sprawled out in slumber.

"Wake up!"

"Huh?" Mario sprawled off of the tiny wooden cot and fell onto the hard stone floor before propping himself up against the wall.

"Good morning, Doctor Mario!" Balias taunted him. "I hope that you slept well, I don't think you'll get many more quiet nights where you're going."

"Where am I going?" Mario asked politely.

"You'll spend the rest of your days with cut-purses and cut-throats. You'll never have your own room like this, so you better give a good long prayer of thanksgiving before we send you off."

"You can't do that! I've done nothing wrong! The university will pay my bond! I'm sure of it!"

"No one wants anything to do with you, my boy! You are a heretic who gets himself arrested after leaving a cat-house!" Balias saw the look of panic on Mario's face and knew that this was the place where he should drive his nails. "You naughty little bastard, you. Everyone knows your dirty little secrets now. You trade with whores and pirates. You send your gold to heathen Sultans. You are supposed to be the one teaching Christians to heal each other. Physician, heal thyself! No one else will help you in that endeavour now. You're finished here, and your name is a curse to everyone."

"What?" the young doctor whispered in disbelief.

"That's right, to *everyone*. Your sins are very public, you've shamed your house and your academy for generations, you have," Balias shook his head and tisked. "Even the Senate knows about you and your master's black arts."

"That's not true! We did no such things!" Mario insisted.

"Really? Then explain what you were doing?"

"We were studying mercury! That's all! We can't find any here, so we asked the captain to procure some when he went to Morocco. That's all!"

"That's not how it seems to me, Doctor Mario," came a slithering voice from beyond the cell's door.

Balias stood at attention as his brother, the bishop of Venice entered the cell.

"Do you know who I am?"

Mario nodded.

"Good, that means we needn't doddle about with introductions and whatnot." The tall man smiled at the shaking figure of the imprisoned doctor.

"You may leave us, Balias." he said over his shoulder.

"Yes, Your Grace," Balias gave a curt bow and left the room.

Isaac looked over the slight figure before him, who had so recently awoken from sleep. He then reached into his robes and took out one of the red stones that Mario had bought from the pirate Ezera. He held it up to the new morn's sunlight that was sneaking around the bars to the room's window.

"What exactly is this?" the bishop asked. "I can recite all the gospels and the Acts of the Apostles from memory, but an aptitude for science was never among the gifts graced to me by God."

Mario regained his breath from the panic that Balias had put him through. It took a minute to recognize that he'd been asked a question.

"This." Isaac repeated. "What is it?"

"That?" Mario's mind quickly returned to him. "That's cinnabar ore, Your Grace. You shouldn't handle it with your bare hands. It's dangerous."

Isaac was hardly one to take orders from anyone, so he held it up to the sunlight of the window and inspected it, rather than obey Mario's commands. This was extraordinarily unwise on his part.

"It's pretty, I suppose. It looks like red silver. Is it expensive?"

"To have it brought over from Morocco, yes. In past years, it was mined near Padua."

"I understand that it has value to you, beyond simply a pleasant appearance, of course. What good is it?"

"It's a source of mercury, Your Grace," Mario answered. He felt immediately comforted by returning to his teaching persona. "We melt down the ore in a furnace, and mercury seeps out of the cinnabar. We use mercury in experiments and chemical studies for medicine. What's left of the ore turns into a red crystal."

"Mercury is dangerous, is it not?" Matthias asked.

"Yes, that's why we have to be so careful. Pure mercury isn't dangerous at all, of course. Every metal in creation, from gold to iron has at least some mercury in it."

"Really?" the bishop was amused by this revelation.

"Yes sir. Mercury and sulfur. These two metals, in different proportions, make up all the different metals of the world."

"Then why do you take such a great chance by sending away for this, and at such an expense?"

"Because we needed pure mercury, or red mercury. With pure mercury, we can seep it in and out of other metals, and hopefully upset the balance of sulfur by doing so. As the balance of the two prime materials change, so will their composition. Like alternating water and flour to turn bread into the right consistency."

"To what end?"

"To turn iron into bronze, bronze into steel…"

"Lead into gold?" Isaac asked with a dirty look.

"If you wanted to enrich yourself, you could do such a thing. Yes," Mario conceded. "But we were only seeking knowledge, Your Grace. We don't know how to transmute gold… that is to say, we don't know the practical methodology of that."

"Yet."

"Yet," Mario nodded his head. "But that's really not what we were doing."

"I see. Do you think it responsible to try to unmake metals that God has created in a certain form? Do you think that God made an error when he produced iron in the ground, in lieu of… oh, say… tin?"

"Do you think that God erred when he grew grain in a field, in lieu of in the form of loaves of bread? We transform grain into bread in order to feed ourselves, this is no different."

"An interesting point, I must concede," the Neapolitan native straightened his back. "But what does all this have to do with you? Why have you been brought here today?"

"I don't know, Your Grace. This whole situation seems frightful to me. I believe that someone has born false witness against me to say that I've acted against God. I need to speak to the master of my university. Don Antonio can explain the situation with more grace than I."

"Antonio has confessed." Mattias hissed gently.

"Huh? Confessed to what?"

"He's confessed that a succubus, a harlot demon, came to him in the night and seduced him to seek unholy knowledge. With that knowledge he would try to unmake God's world, and she promised him her unholy favours." Isaac had the gift that he could lie without batting an eyelid.

"My God!" Mario looked like he'd been slapped. "That's impossible, he'd never do such a thing."

"Men are capable of many things when they are led by demons."

"No, not that," Mario almost laughed. "Confess. Of course he'd never be seduced by a demon but even if he were, he'd never confess it. At least not to you, your grace. He doesn't trust clergymen outside the university."

The cleric raised his eyebrows in a knowing manner, and Mario's heart sunk.

"You tortured him. You couldn't have. You tortured one of the city's most prominent citizens. You … you…"

"Now calm down, we didn't torture him. He broke down when I arrived. He confessed his sins and received holy sacraments. He's fine. He claims that you knew nothing of his sins, and that you were simply his unknowing assistant. Because of this, we're going to let you go after your confession."

"He received sacraments?" Mario stared into the cleric's eyes. "This doesn't make sense."

"Perhaps not to you, but it doesn't need to find reason in your mind. All you need to do is confess to me, in front of two witnesses, I'll simply summon two of the guards here, that it was doctor Antonio of Padua, also known as Antonio the Wise, who ordered you to perform the experiments, procure the equipment, and taught you your arcane knowledge. After that, you are free to go."

"No… You're lying. You want me to bear false witness against my mentor."

"But he did teach you. He did order you in your experiments, and it was he that ordered you to procure these little red rocks from the land of the infidel. There is no false witness here, unless you intend to feign total innocence on behalf of yourself as well as your master."

"I don't know what you're plotting, but you will have to do it without my help, Your Grace. I won't speak any evil of Antonio."

"Then you can wait in this tiny room until you choose to change your

opinion. Or until such time as my brother decides to send you downstairs.
One way or another. I'll bid you good day then." With surprising grace,
he turned on his heel and slid out of the cell. Behind him, the door closed
and the lock clicked and clacked its way to fortification.

"Have you made a decision?" The bishop asked upon entering the
first cell.

"Has it already been an hour?" Antonio asked sullenly.

"No, but I concluded my conversation with your apprentice and I
don't intend to wait about the city jail making small talk with the guards
while you try to justify a decision that you've already made," Isaac
answered. "I know your decision, Doctor. You are an intelligent man.
You're called Antonio the Wise, the Solomon of the lagoon! You hardly
need time to consider yourself. Are you prepared to take on a new
apprentice and show more support for my family in the city and with your
senator friends, or are you honestly intending to fall upon your sword?"

Antonio glared out the window.

"I didn't think so. Still, I'd like to hear the words come out of your
mouth."

"I'll train your son, Your Grace."

"For formality's sake, he's my ward," Isaac corrected him

"Yes, of course," Antonio snarled

"Now, as to the charges against you," the bishop pulled his skeletal
hands up, as he were about to perform an ablution. "I believe that you
were unaware of the unscrupulous experiments of your rogue assistant. If
you'll just confess to that, we can send you back to your school in time for
a late breakfast."

"Mario's just a boy. He bore no sin but obedience."

"He's almost thirty, Doctor. You do him no favour by coddling him
so." Isaac closed in on his captive. "If you confess that the sins were his,
then he'll be sentenced to exile in the colonies. We can't exactly set him
free, now can we? None of the other cities of Italy will house a heretic
like him as a doctor. You'll find a nice post for him where he can do no
harm."

"He'll not confess to something he didn't do. He's an honest man."

"An honest man has no role to play in the affairs of our world, Doctor. He's the lamb to be sacrificed on the altar of Saint Mark," Isaac concluded. "All things considered, he was the best choice. It would be a great loss to the city to have someone as esteemed as yourself face a ruined career, and I can think of no one better to train the next great scientific mind of Venice."

"Why don't you have your ward trained to be your own replacement, Your Grace?"

"Given our respective positions, Doctor, I'm hardly inclined to listen to your suggestions as to how to manage my house," the bishop answered without losing a tempo. "You'll be the one to convince the boy to confess his sins, and I'll have preparations made for his expulsion. My brother Balias here, will escort you to his cell in just a moment. Please, enjoy the rest of the day, and I'll introduce you to your newest, grandest pupil in a few days, after your boy is taken care of."

Antonio's face was grim.

"I believe that the word for which you search is '*Yes*," Isaac suggested.

"Yes," Antonio said stoically.

"Yes, Your Grace?" Isaac prompted.

"Yes, Your Grace."

"Good, good!" Isaac clapped his hands. "Don't worry, it will come more easily in time. It'll eventually be second nature. You won't even need to think before you defer to my will and show proper deference. Doesn't that sound wonderful?"

"Yes, Your Grace," Antonio spoke through grinding teeth.

"Don't forget that. Balias will fetch you in a moment."

"Pardon me, again!" announced Isaac as he entered Mario's cell.

"What do you want now?" Mario asked.

"Out of Christian charity, I'll give you a chance to change your mind. Confess the truth of Antonio's crimes, and you can go free this very moment."

"Then I'm afraid you've wasted your valuable time, Your Grace," Mario answered.

"Oh, come now boy! That's twice you've denied me what I asked for, and I am a man who doesn't care to be denied by those of such as you, Doctor."

"I shall not bear false witness against any man. Let alone Don Antonio."

"A noble value to hold, but I'm afraid that it isn't terrible practical in this world of ours, my boy," Isaac put a hand on Mario's shoulder. "Do you believe that your master would return the favour of loyalty, which you've shown so admirably this morning?"

"I do."

"Then you, my boy, are a fool," Isaac's hawk-like face leaned close to the ear of the young doctor. "Please, my boy. He's betrayed you. He's told me that it was you who were acting without his knowledge. You were arranging for smuggling, speaking to pirates, seeking unholy knowledge of spirits. He claims that he is innocent of every crime save negligence. He neglected to observe you as duly as he should have. Please, tell me that he knew about what was happening. Tell me what I already know. Just confess the truth!"

"I will speak no ill of my master, whether it be true or false, your grace."

"You are a loyal servant and an honest man, Mario Orsini," Isaac said with finality. "…and for these graces, your career is finished. You may no longer teach medicine in the university. You may no longer claim the right of priesthood. You may no longer claim citizenship in the Republic of Venice, nor may you flee its borders. You will be banished to one of the colonies, under military guard, to eke out a living as best you may. If you are caught trying to escape from our lands, your life will be forfeit. News of your heresy will prevent you from finding another teaching position anywhere in the civilized world."

Mario started to deflate against the wall, but Isaac stepped to him and held him up in a sideways embrace.

"There is a way out of all this. Just tell me about your master. Deny me not three times! The sun's risen already, Boy!"

Mario raised his moist eyes and spoke very slowly. "I cannot do this."

The two were very still for an instant, and there was a knock on the cell door. The constable poked his head in. "It's time, Your Grace."

"That, dear boy, was the rooster crowing. Three times you've denied me. May God bless you, for your friends and masters here on this poor shadow of creation will certainly not do it at their Lord's behest."

"I'm sorry to let you down, Your Grace."

"Not yet, you aren't. When you are old and your bones ache, and your belly swells from a lifetime of hunger and poverty, and you think back to your youth, and how you squandered this opportunity to live out your days in comfort, then you'll be sorry. You'll play this conversation in your mind's eye a thousand times, each time wondering what would have happened had you been just a little more reasonable."

"That is possible, Your Grace."

Isaac shook his head as he walked out. Before he crossed the threshold out of the cell, he called back. "Your master is here, he'll explain the ways of the world to you before you exile. I'll pray that you listen to him, for he doesn't make the same foolish mistakes as you!"

And with that, he stormed out of the prison. The bishop was partially right, for years to come Mario would think back on that day and wonder what would have happened if he'd told the bishop what he wanted to hear. However, Mario never, ever, thought back on it with regret.

Chapter Eleven - The Expulsion

The University of Venice was a series of small buildings, locked in by a thick wall, and surrounded on all sides by canals, making it an artificial island within the city. There were four bridges that connected the campus to the rest of the city. Inside the walled island were a series of specialized buildings catering to the university's needs. There were cottages to house the staff, dormitories to house the students, a lecture hall for class, a dining hall for… well… dining, and of course a chapel for even the most benign ceremony of education. The staff cottages were irregularly placed across the small campus, some faced onto the medial square of the community, some were cornered onto the walls, and some were attached to larger buildings.

Antonio looked out the window of his office and saw his young apprentice walking briskly across the cobblestone campus towards him. He opened the cabinet next to his bookshelf and took out two small ivory plated cups and a bottle of a clear liquid. He was pouring the anisette when Mario knocked on the door.

"Come!" Antonio called.

Mario stepped into his mentor's cottage that had been his second home for many years. "Are you alright, Antonio?"

"Yes, yes. I'm fine. Does it still hurt?" the elder noted the scrapes on Mario's chin and hands. Residue from his apprentice's first flirtation with heroics.

"No, they're better now, thanks. I told them what you told me to say, they noted it down and let me go."

"You were limping across the campus."

"That was from a fall I took earlier in the night, getting the damned ore in the first place.

Antonio handed one of the anisette-filled cups to Mario. "I'm so sorry for all this, My Boy. It was never to have happened like this."

"I know. There's no apology necessary."

"Ten years ago, we could simply import with a trading license from the Doge's office, now we have to cater to the ignorant superstition of credulous fools like this filthy bishop! He thinks that he can make the university follow his shepherd's staff like the rest of the village sheep. He'll learn soon enough that there are those who aren't quite as willing to be humble servants as the rest of the dross in this world."

"I'm glad to hear that you're still fighting." Mario said with a hard-earned reverence for his master's rage. "The bishop told me that you turned me in to save your own skin."

"Never!" Antonio reassured him with an arm over his shoulder. "But we must act carefully for now. Isaac's won this little battle, so we need to force his gambit to pay higher."

"What exactly has he won?" Mario asked. "He told me that I was to be exiled. Is this so?"

"You'll have to see that as a temporary setback," the giant fat man blustered.

Mario's face blushed red as he only now realized that the bishop's threats were more than fanciful. "What can I do?"

"We're going to speak to a friend of mine tonight, an important man, and we'll see what we can arrange for you. You're too good of a physician to become a vagrant, don't worry. I don't want you slinking around Venice while lesser men walk with their heads high. We'll find a position for you within the republic, just away from the city itself. Maybe we can send you to Crete or somewhere else where you'll be safe."

"To what end? If I'm to be banned from Venice, why should I linger in obscurity in the colonies? Florence, Sienna and Milan all need physicians, I can start there…"

"This is a temporary setback, Mario. Don't go thinking it's permanent. Within a year, Isaac'll either be dead, reassigned or brought under the thumb of the Senate. Fools like him try to throw their girth around, only to find out that no one wants to carry their weight. His thuggery is making him enemies."

"Why did he arrest us? I still don't understand," Mario protested.

"He wants to subordinate the university to his person, rather than the offices of the senate. He'll hope to join our merchant republic closer to the pope, but no one here will stand for it. I'll have to give him his tithes for now, but each coin of silver, each lie-soaked word of respect with which I'm forced to part will weigh him down until he can move no more, and then he'll be through. I'm not like him, I don't seek to play with my prey,

I'll cut off his bollocks and send him back to Rome as a late-in-life castrati."

Mario smiled. His blood never ceased to boil when Antonio's rage was lit. Over the years, Antonio had made more enemies than Mario had thought possible, and they had all fallen to the wayside in his wake. The wrathful and uncompromising nature of his mentor was what attracted him to the master's table. Mario lamented that his own nature was too soft and malleable. Antonio's knowledge of the secrets of alchemy, medicine and natural science was second to none (with the exception of Albert the Great or maybe even Galen himself), but it was the lit rage that Mario wished above all to learn, and to add to his own person. So many people feared Antonio based only the danger of his angry words.

"I'm glad you're on my side, Antonio," Mario saluted with his anisette and took a sip. "Isaac's got no chance. How long will I have to be away?"

"Probably no more than a season or two, by next year, that priest will be gone, his oafish brother will have disappeared behind him and I should be sitting in the senate as the representative of the city's physicians and the university. In a year's time we'll be princes in our own city!"

'*Princes in our own city, again*,' Mario thought to himself. Five years ago he had heard this phrase fly out of Antonio's mouth for the first time. Along with his promise to himself that he'd sit in the senate in a year's time. The fat man was a force of nature, and anyone was well advised to stay clear of his path when angered, but so often his reach exceeded his grasp.

"This time for sure," Mario tried to sound hopeful.

"You're damned right, this time! This time there's no Luchesi or Ibullia or Pietro, or war with Milan and Florence to stop us!" he said, rhyming off a litany of rivals, former and fallen. "Next to those obstacles, what is this priest? We've fought bigger battles and won before! Who does he think he's dealing with? I tell you this, he'll spend the rest of his days on this earth cursing the day he crossed me! As for his son? He'll share his father's shame! He'll find a nice street corner from which to beg, and I'll pass him every day, and maybe on Christmas or Easter, I'll give him enough for a bowl of soup at some rat-hole inn!"

"Antonio, Antonio. This is wonderful and true. But what about me?" Mario interjected. "For the immediate future, I'll have to flee. Who is this friend of yours who can help us?"

"Oh yes," Antonio said composing himself. "Senator Raphael Avruham. We'll meet him tonight. He can be a bit religious, so play the part, but don't worry, he has no love for the Bishop."

"Sounds promising."

"Don Raphael, Don Antonio is here to see you," the servant announced.

Raphael Avraham looked up from his book and his eyes strained to focus against the light pouring in from the door. "Is he alone?"

"No, Sir. There is a younger man with him."

Raphael's eyes re-adjusted through their spectacles. "Give me a minute, and then send him in. Oh! And bring a bowl of grapes."

"Sir," the doorman bowed curtly and left.

Raphael looked around his office. It was a dreary chamber, to be sure. The brown walls were dotted with black book cases and the floor was decorated with a red and green carpet. In ways of furniture he kept a small collection of unused chairs placed around a small table in front of his desk, where he organised his legers and books. The only decoration adorning the walls was a giant map that took up most of the southern surface. The map depicted Venice as the centre of the world, and from there illustrations abounded of the Venetian mercantile reach. There were images of the Pyramids of Giza, the Church of the Holy Sepulchre in Jerusalem, the Cathedral of Holy Wisdom in Constantinople, the Rock of Gibraltar, the Plains of Zama and Papal Palace of Rome; all the wealth of the Mediterranean world.

Everything in the office seemed to absorb what little light was given it by the lamp on Raphael's desk, so he walked to the room's single floor-to-ceiling window and pulled back the velvet curtains to allow some proper light into his office. Raphael was mildly surprised to see that the promise of a new day had again yielded to night, and the window didn't seem to help light the room. Raphael went about lighting lamps around the room.

There was a knock on the door to announce the arrival of his guest, and Paulo, the servant, opened the door.

"Doctor Antonio Antonius of Padua, and his assistant, Doctor Mario Orsini of Venice."

"Yes, yes. Come in my old friend," Raphael greeted Antonio warmly. "It is good to see you again, I hope that you are well. Your skin seems healthier than the last time we met."

"It is. Thank you," Antonio said cheerfully. "And you, how is your knee?"

"Good, thank you," Raphael chuckled politely. "And who is your assistant?"

"Ah, yes. May I present to you, Mario Orsini, one of the finest physicians in Venice!"

"A pleasure to meet you, Young Orsini. Are you related to Clemente Orsini, by any chance?"

"I am, Don Raphael. He was my father."

"Your father was a fine magistrate, and must have been very proud to have a son so young become such a reputable doctor. His death was a great loss to the city."

"Yes, Senator. A great loss to me as well," it had only been a year since his father had died, and while Mario was generally over the loss, he had become frustrated by constantly accepting delayed messages of condolence over the past year. He didn't let that nuisance show, of course. "He spoke very highly of you, too."

Raphael smiled serenely and nodded.

"Please sit down," he offered. "I've got some grapes here, if you're hungry I can have Paulo bring you some stew."

"That won't be necessary," Antonio assured him. "We've come for some help that I hoped you'd be able to provide."

"Anything in my power, of course."

"It seems that the university has made an enemy," Antonio began.

Raphael held back the question as to whether it was the university or Antonio personally who'd made the enemy, and allowed the doctor to continue.

"And I find myself in a bit of a bind," he continued.

"Antonio, you've never needed my help to deal with your enemies in the past." Raphael said. "Who seems to be giving you such problems?"

"Isaac, the bishop of Venice."

Raphael's face was unmoving as he heard the name.

"He arrested Mario and myself last night, and is trying to subordinate me to his service," he resumed. "Which is laying down brick for his own prison, but he started his attack very strongly."

"How strongly?" Raphael asked.

"I'm to be banished from the city," Mario announced.

Antonio neglected to make eye-contact with his young friend. "So I've come here for your assistance, Don Raphael."

"You want me to pick up the sword against the bishop? I'm afraid you've come to the wrong house for that!" Raphael said testily. "My mother became Christian and married my father, but there are many in the city who would still believe me to be a Jew, despite a lifetime of uncircumcised Christianity. If I'm seen to do anything against that self-enriching hucksterish fraud, I may as well lay my own pyre now."

"Oh, no, my Friend!" Antonio reassured him. "I don't need anyone's help to send Pilate to hell. I need help protecting Mario here."

"Oh, yes," Raphael looked back to the boy. "An exile you say?"

"Don Antonio tells me that you have many friends in the world outside of Venice," Mario noted hopefully. "Perhaps you could assist me in finding a position at a university or hospital."

"What kind of baggage will the boy be carrying?" the aging senator asked Antonio before turning back to the boy. "Have you been charged with a crime to merit an expulsion, or simply told to leave?"

"He called me a heretic, but I've had no trial to that effect, Senator."

"For any other crime you'd need a trial to merit an expulsion. Heresy is unfortunately an indictable offence and bishops are empowered to simply announce a punishment for it. Without an appeal from the Senate, you have no right to a trial and he has no responsibility to give you one. I'm sorry, but I'll not give you that appeal. As for assistance, I think that I can manage that."

Raphael leant back in his chair and touched his curly hair as he thought. "Isaac will spread word of your heresy, be it true or otherwise, to anywhere you go, so you may well have to step outside of his influence. The eastern rite churches would care little for the opinion of a western rite clergy officer, so you'll probably have to head east in order to keep a prestigious position. If you stay in the west you would have to take work as a surgeon or barber in Italy. God help you if you find yourself north of the Alps."

Antonio shuddered at the thought of sending Mario off to live among the trans-alpine barbarians of the Holy Roman Empire, which Voltaire would eventually properly describe as being neither holy, Roman, nor an empire. He, like most Italians of the renaissance, considered their northern neighbours to be barbarous on the best of days and monstrous on the worst.

Mario nodded and listened carefully.

"I have a friend, Giovanni Cardillo. He's the governor of the Venetian colony in Constantinople. I can write you a letter of introduction, and once you're there, you could make a comfortable living. I'm sure that Antonio could also write a letter of introduction for you as well, testifying as to your experience and ability as a physician."

"Thank you! I guess that I'm to be away then, to the east." Mario sounded rather upbeat. "I've read very much about the first Christian capital."

Antonio looked at the floor and thought while his apprentice spoke. His world was the university, and he'd dedicated so much of his life to the institution and his life there. He was embarrassed to lose a loyalist like Mario. His only reprieve from shame was that Mario was trying his best to seem enthusiastic about leaving. Antonio wouldn't be able to show the same kind of cheer, were the situation reversed.

"Second, Doctor," Raphael corrected him. "Far into the east, it was the ancient kingdom of Armenia which first accepted Our Lord. Armenia was a great Christian bastion for over a thousand years.

"Unfortunately, it's now completely subordinated to the marauding armies of the Turks, the Arabs and the Persians. Remember that there is always a threat in the east; the barbarous armies of the infidels are always on the move, and always looking westward. You shouldn't seem so pleased about the prospect of a new adventure. The three of us are now conspiring to send you to the great bulwark of civilization and Christendom against the raw and unsheathed sword of Mohammed. Constantinople is as vulnerable as it is valuable to the unresting horde."

"You're right, Senator. But I thank you none the less."

"So be it." Raphael conceded. "I'm pleased to help a physician, a man of God and a son of Clemente Orsisi in any way possible. I will wish you good luck and God's speed on your journey. I'll write the letter tonight, and I'll have my servant bring it to your chambers at the university."

"Thank you, Sir," Mario said.

"You're welcome. May God protect you, Young One."

"I pray for this as well, Senator."

Turning to Antonio, Raphael continued his farewell. "And the same goes to you, old friend, for I think that you'll need my prayers and wishes of safety even more than the boy will."

Antonio was forced to laugh at that.

"Thank you! I'll accept them, but it's always been my enemies who found God's graces lacking rather than I."

"I'll give them none the less," Raphael repeated kindly.

The Porto Vacca resounded with songs sung to a bawdy drone. The crew of the Nineveh was not yet sick with wine, women and song, but they were well on their way there. All thirty men of the crew had flagon in one hand and most had a semi-clad house girl within arm's reach. The eldest of the crew, an old oarsman from Valencia named Pere, carried the tune with an old ten-stringed guitar.

Ezera enjoyed listening to his crew sing, but he didn't give himself over to their indulgences tonight. He had declined the services of the young (and some not so young) women of the house. He also drank very sparingly. Tonight, he was on his hind legs in preparation for a disaster. Ever since last night's arrest of Mario and Antonio, he'd kept his mind clear and his focus on the exits to the room at all times.

"Are you alright, Captain?" Gaspar the coxswain asked him. "You've been strange these past few days."

"I'll be fine soon," Ezera assured him. "As soon as we finish off with our business here, I'll be happy to leave. Tomorrow morning, we'll set sail east."

"Any last minute packages?"

Ezera shrugged. One of the temptations of Venice was its harbour. Hundreds of ships and warehouses were full of the wealth of the world, and it was his for the taking if he didn't mind the prospect of never returning to the Lagoon City.

"I'm sure we can pick something up on our trip south," Ezera finally answered.

"We could find plenty right here, captain."

"Ay, we could at that. But I've already picked up something better than any load we could steal here this week. Also, we wouldn't have to worry about fighting our way out of the Adriatic."

"Yes, everyone's quite curious about your meetings since we arrived in town," concurred his second in command.

"I'll explain that when we're at sea," Ezera leaned back into his creaking wooden chair. "In the meantime, enjoy your time in the city. But don't wander off. We might run into some trouble later on."

"What kind of trouble?" Gaspar leaned in close to hear the answer above the din of the musical bar.

Ezera's face darkened more than God's dose of pigment had already done as a figure entered the Porto Vacca. "This kind."

Into the bar stepped a dark-clad and rotund figure. Black robes hung off his girth, the only flesh that appeared was pale and pock-marked with visible blood marks and scabbing covering all surfaces of the man's face and hands. From behind droopy and diseased eyelids, the man's steely blue eyes searched the room and narrowed in on Ezera's table.

"Give us a moment, but be ready," Ezera whispered to Gaspar, who did so immediately.

"Hello, Doctor," Ezera greeted Antonio with an even voice. "I'm glad you managed to find us!"

Antonio stormed up to the pirate, cursing half at him and half to himself.

"You son of a bitch! Judas!" he roared. "I followed the stench of betrayal!"

Pere stopped playing his guitar and the crew stopped singing. The girls looked about to find the men who normally keep order in the house, the three of which looked at each other and then at the thirty-man crew whom they feared were about to get unruly.

"You filthy, lying, prolapse of a man!" Antonio threw his raised finger in front of Ezera's face. "You betrayed me! And you'll pay for that! I don't accept apologies from liars, nor do I forgive traitors!"

"That's fine by me, Don Antonio, as I'm not offering an apology. Now calm yourself."

"You stabbed me in the back! You sold me to the bishop! What did Caiaphas promise you? Thirty pieces of silver? You'll get paid in full, but you know how that story ends!"

Everyone was quiet and watching the shouting match between the two, though Antonio was the only one shouting. Most of the Nineveh's crew was quietly grabbing cudgels and daggers. Luis, the lead oarsman, grabbed his tankard as he had always maintained that glassware, flying and jagged, was a good opening to a brawl.

"First of all, I don't stab people in the back. I stab them in the belly. They always see me coming and they know why I'm there. Second, no one insults me in front of my men. Even as old a friend as you."

"Friend?" Antonio snarled in response.

"I'm glad to see that you're unharmed, Antonio. Not many men can go through your ordeal so unscathed. Don't press your luck."

"You have no idea what I've been through."

"The priest promised me you wouldn't be hurt. I hope that he didn't lie. You seem alright from here."

"You sold me, you dog-faced pirate!"

Ezera raised his hands in mock-surrender. "Of course I did! And I got a good deal out of it! What do you expect, old man? I did my best to help your little friend."

"You've forgotten who I am?"

"No, you're the one who seems to have forgotten. You're a buyer of rare items, and a good customer," Ezera's natural confidence was unshakeable. "But your charming temper makes you more enemies than it does friends, Doctor. And the Bishop's pockets are deeper than yours."

Antonio was aware of the crowd watching and the violence of which they were capable. For a second time in as many days, his fear was thwarting his rage. Behind him, Antonio could hear the Nineveh's crew assembling.

"Now... I offer no apologies for my sins; either God will punish me in the hereafter, or he won't. I'm glad to see that you're unhurt," Ezera added in hopes of making an opening for Antonio to save face without bloodshed. "How is your apprentice?"

"Banished." Antonio said from behind gritted teeth.

"Oh," the captain wasn't quite ready to let the light close on that last opening. "Where will he go?"

"Constantinople."

At that, the crew tensed and Ezera laughed out loud.

"Is something funny, *Captain*?" Antonio asked.

"It so happens that we set sail in the morning for the eastern capital." Ezera promised. "Your friend the bishop gave me the choice between a Republic-wide license or a pillory and I chose the former!"

"I'm happy for your windfall," the fat professor said sarcastically.

"The situation left us little option, and I'll not judge you by whatever deal you were forced to make in order to secure yourself," Ezera stepped out from behind his table to approach the doctor's orbit. "Although I'm sorry that you couldn't secure such a gentle deal for your poor assistant."

Antonio's eyes darted venom.

"Remember where we both are, Doctor."

The blue globes of the doctor's eyes lost none of their intensity.

"I'll give you my sympathies, good man. We've both faced a rather torrential storm of troubles of late. I took my chances and picked a winning side, so I came out ahead. You tried to wrestle the storm and now find yourself in a tough bind. I'm offering to help you out, so much as I can. If you keep following your path of rage, you'll just find yourself buried further and further under a mountain of shit." Ezera took a deep breath. "I can help you. I'll take to boy to Constantinople personally, and keep him safe, as far as I'm able."

"Your neck will guarantee his safety," Antonio threatened.

Ezera was in no more mood for the old man's obstinate posturing.

"You've lost all authority to threaten anyone, Don Antonio," Ezera replied. "I'll try to help the boy, to appease my own guilty honour, but you're not the man you thought you were. You haven't been for a long time. Time's dulled your razor, sir. The sooner you can accept that reality, the better for everyone, including your friends."

"You self-righteous pirate! You don't dismiss me like that! I'll have you and your filthy crew thrown out of the city! Banned from the damned republic! You look at me, Look at me! I still hold sway here," Antonio snapped his fingers for dramatic effect. "I've had a surprise setback, but it's a long way from over. This war's just begun!"

"Men rarely get surprises like that more than once, and wars are always just beginning, Doctor. But not yours. I'll get the boy to the east for you," Ezera's grin had dissolved into a condescending smirk. "You should leave now."

The Nineveh's crew stood back and made a gap, through which the doctor could find his exit.

"This isn't over."

Ezera's face was as unchanging as a wooden statue. Antonio looked at him for one last time in disgust, and then stormed out of the bar. Once the place fell silent again, it was Gaspar who first spoke.

"Captain, what should we do now?"

"Find the boy, offer him affordable and immediate passage to Constantinople."

"And the old man?"

"Fuck him," Ezera answered quickly. "We don't need to worry about people who've outlived their usefulness."

'Constantinople!' Mario thought to himself as he re-read Don Raphael's letter of introduction. *'It might as well be Araby or Hindustan!'*

He marched up and down his office, placing his notebooks carefully into a pile. Seven in all, he looked at the collected folios and decided that this was the base of what would eventually become the largest alchemical library in eastern Christendom. Atop the pile of seven books sat two letters of introduction, addressed to the governor of the Venetian colony in Constantinople, one by the Senator Raphael Avruham and the other by the current rector of the University of Venice, Antonio. Mario placed the books and letters into a pack.

Mario didn't believe for an instant that the exile was temporary. For the last few months, Antonio had been slipping more and more into the bottle, and his control over his own domain had been slipping from him.

It would have been an understatement to describe Mario's emotions as mixed. He felt betrayed by his master, who cast him aside to keep his own job. Antonio said he'd keep fighting against the bishop, and Mario knew this to be true. Antonio would fight with all his hate and that keen mind of his. On a rational level, Mario understood that the removal of his person was because of Isaac's success, rather than Antonio's failing. No, he wasn't betrayed. He had freely given his patronage, not to someone who would betray and rebuff him. The failing was that Mario's master wasn't up to the task. His mentor had brought him into a fight that he couldn't win. When knights fight, the grass gets trampled, and that was what happened to Mario. It's a sad feeling to know that someone who'd given him so much, was now going through a such a personal failure. Antonio was probably as upset as Mario about all this. Mario couldn't hate his patron, even now.

For eight years now, Antonio had taught him medicine, then taken him on as a personal prodigy; the youngest teacher at the university. In secret, Mario's mentor taught him the subtleties of alchemy and of the experimentation techniques from which all knowledge was to come. Servants of the holy fire of God, they followed in the footsteps of Albertus Magnus, Roger Bacon and Alexander of Hales, but they also investigated the Greek writings of the Andalusian Arab, Averroes, and the Persian Avicenna. They believed that the basic elements of the physical world were malleable to man's designs. This basic building blocks could be changed. If corruption could turn grapes into wine, and lead become gold when lit by the torch of wisdom, then certainly dust could become enough bread to feed the hungry, spears could become plough shares and the sinful world could be made in a closer image to the promised City of God.

In the end however, it was the more blunted world of politics and power that cut short their investigation into the fine-tuning of creation. Blunter still was the force that opened his cottage door and interrupted his moping.

"Good evening, Doctor. You can imagine my surprise to find you here tonight, when I distinctly recall my honoured brother telling you to leave," Balias announced as he stepped past the threshold of Mario's humble cottage.

Mario gestured to the packed trunk and traveller's bag near the door. "I'm sorry for my timeliness, Constable. You can probably guess how much I despise inconveniencing others, it's a crippling social phobia, count yourself lucky that you obviously don't suffer it.

"Ha ha ha." the brawny soldier laughed sarcastically. He entered the one wooden room of the building which consisted of nothing but a bed, a series of pegs hidden by black robes from the university and a seemingly unending collection of scrolls, quills and ink stains. Behind him stepped two other guards. The tiny cottage had never held four people before, and the walls seemed to groan in protest of the overcrowding.

"What do you want?" Mario asked nervously. "I've no money, you must know that. I'll leave in the morning, I just wanted to say goodbye to someone."

"That time's finished, young man," Balias answered and slowly curled a tense arm around Mario's neck. The friendly gesture had a decidedly unfriendly tone. "You see, we're here to make sure that you don't return to Venice."

Mario's face went white.

"No, no! Don't worry, we're not here to kill you!" Balias protested, seeing the panic in Mario's eyes. "Though you may think that's our purpose before the night is through. We just want to make sure that you understand exactly what the future holds for you if you decide to make another stand here in our city."

Mario's eyes darted about the room, and quickly inspected Balias and his two henchmen. He was a surprised to see them unarmed.

One of the goons chuckled, understanding what Mario was looking for.

"We don't need weapons for this job, boy," he said through a half repressed laugh. "I can't imagine you weigh more than my left testicle, and I doubt that you'll even bother to try resisting us. Isn't that right, Doctor?"

Mario was silent.

"I said…" the constable repeated. "… that you know how weak you are, and you already accept that your best course of action is to take your beating and hope that we get tired and bored. Isn't that right?"

The silence continued.

"Damn fool must be deaf, boys!" the falsely exasperated constable announced to his henchmen. "I'll try again."

"Don't bother," came a cheerful sounding voice from the doorway. "We're here for the boy, and we'll take him with us now, if you please."

Four sets of eyes looked at the door. Leaning his brow against the cross-top of the small frame was an imposing figure dressed in overly worn clothes, and clasping his hands behind his back.

"Are you packed, Don Mario?"

Mario recognized the pirate from the brothel the previous night. He nodded and motioned to the trunk and pack by the door.

"Good," Ezera stepped back out of the cottage's light and two crewmen stepped out from the shadows. Gaspar grabbed the pack and one end of the trunk, while Luis grabbed the other end, and they took it out without much fuss. The constables still held Mario, but were silent. "Now, now, Constable. I overheard your little conversation earlier, and now it's your turn to quietly accept this little loss. You know what would happen if the three of you tried to resist me and my boys out here. Thirty on three? That would be an even more violent party than the one you were planning for our doctor friend."

"Pirate!" Balias swore, but accepted the logic. Once the luggage was removed, and there was a bit more breathing room in the cottage, Ezera stepped in.

"Yes, Constable?" the Catalan captain's figure seemed to make everyone in the room uncomfortable. Ignoring the fact that Ezera was tall and broad, his features, his face, his hands and shoulders simply seemed bigger than they really were, he took up more space than a man of his size should, he was an invading presence wherever he went. "Will there be anything else?"

"What are you doing here?"

"I'm sailing away in the morning, and I thought to take this man on as a passenger. He'll work his fare as our ship's doctor. I'm sure you can understand that my crew and I could make good use of him."

"Do you all need a doctor?" Balias accused. "Is your crew so sickly after their whoring that you need to kidnap doctors?"

"Yes, from time to time," he answered truthfully. "We don't usually find ourselves outnumbering a little piece of prey by three to one, but we sometimes do. Oh, and we always bring whiskey and weapons to such a brawl. You don't seem quite so well prepared."

"Did Antonio send you?" Mario interrupted.

"Something like that," Ezera didn't break gaze with Balias. "We're going to take the Doctor now, and we'll leave at first light. Good evening, gentlemen."

"You'll hear from us again, Captain." Balias promised.

"No, I don't think so. I know that your first instinct will be to gather all your men and hit the harbour, but the harbour guard would never allow that, and if you did get past them, the rowdy, drunken crews of a hundred ships just like mine would clamour for a fight. When you tell your brother about this, he'll agree, and tell you to forget about it. Besides, you're not about to do anything without his approval, are you now? Are you ready, Doctor?"

"Oh yes." Mario rushed past Ezera into the night without ever looking back.

"Gentlemen," Ezera bowed his head and backed out of the cabin, and then took his crew and his passenger towards the harbour.

On their way to the harbour, Mario turned to Ezera. "I need to say good-bye to Antonio. I'll meet you at the harbour."

Ezera grabbed the doctor by the arm. "Sorry, Boy. Not tonight. A great many things are unsafe now for that kind of sentimentalism."

"But…"

"Don't worry, you'll see him again."

Chapter Twelve - City by the Sea

Three weeks after his imprisonment, Mario was aboard the Nineveh as it glided through the Hellespont and into the Sea of Marmara without event. The famous water way that burrowed its way between the hills of Anatolia and Thrace seemed to Mario's eyes to be but a river that flowed into the Aegean Sea, albeit one overcrowded with jellyfish and seabirds. But that river was deep bottomed and ran a kilometer through the hills before emerging into a whole new sea, prophylactically separated from the Aegean. The Sea of Marmara was a darker blue than the comfortable azure Aegean waters, harsher and the waves cut louder and higher. It also seemed noticeably colder.

After a half a day's sailing on this new sea, Ezera called Mario to the foredeck. Mario emerged into the blazing midday and saw the rolling hills of Thrace on the port side of the ship, to the south he could see hills over the water in the far distance. Ezera motioned cheerfully to a small fishing village coming up along the irregular northern shore. "Do you see that? That's Studion. It's where the fishmongers collect their day's catch to bring into Constantinople. We'll approach the city soon. There are six harbours in Constantinople proper, and one in Galata, on the north side of the Golden Horn. Their mooring fees are too expensive for these fishermen, so they collect here, and bring their catches in to the city by cart."

"Poor buggers," Mario assessed. "What's wrong with them that they can't afford their trade?"

"They're refugees. The Turks keep spreading across the Balkans. Some people stay and endure, while others flee to the capital. These men fled in hopes of joining a Crusade to retake their homelands," Ezera let silence step onto the deck and into their conversation for a second before continuing. "The last crusade wasn't the roaring success that the old emperor had hoped for. Seven years ago, the armies of the west – Poles, Hungarians, Serbs, Italians, Bohemians, Germans, Croatians, Lithuanians and mercenaries from everywhere, myself included – tried to push the Turks out of Europe, and were destroyed. They'd tried to reclaim Christian land, and all they did was entrench the Muslims even more,

More death, more poverty, more refugees for everyone. Wars don't make peace.

"Just remember, you could end up like them if you're not careful." He added.

Above the small harbour of Studion there was a cloud of seagulls scrounging for their meals. There were about a dozen fishing boats in the harbour, two leaving, and one on its way home. Mario considered his future carefully for the ensuing ride.

"What's the capital like?" he asked.

"I haven't been to the city in... oh.... Five years or so, but it's a strange place. There are some of the most beautiful cathedrals in Christendom there, many prestigious academies and schools as well. The noble ladies show wealth like the Empire was still aglow with the unerring favour of God. Then, there are the majority of the locals who live in conditions that would make Sicily look like Venice. They might not have food every day, but at least they can see the beauty that their tithes pay for!" Ezera smiled as his gaze focused on the horizon. "Here it comes, the Crossroads of the Universe."

City walls began to emerge on the horizon. The first sight was a marble tower that speckled the horizon. This tower marked the cornerstone of where the land walls and the seawalls met. The giant curtain of land walls cascaded north off of this tower. A moat, followed by the stout outer wall standing before the towering inner wall, snaked northward over the hills of Constantinople. The land walls marked the western periphery of the capital, and the sea-walls along the Marmara and northern harbour marked the second and third sides of the defensive triangle. The sea walls were not as large as the land walls, but they made any landing into the city completely impossible except through one of the city's main harbours. There were only ten metres between the sea walls and the shore itself. And on that stretch of land, skirting the sea-walls were more fishmongers, leatherworkers, boat-wrights and smithies. Between the walls and the sea seemed busier than the inside.

The city itself could be seen on hills above the walls. Being surrounded by water for so many years seemed to have taken a lasting effect on the city's geography. Inside the walls, the famous seven hills of New Rome (although realistically more like forty) seemed to rise and crest like the waves of the sea.

Ezera pointed to the tower and shouted above the crash of the waves, the crew and the seabirds. "From the tower, the walls go north for four miles, and east for five. The land wall turns south-east when it hits the harbour, and then meets the seawalls three miles later at Acropolis point. That's twelve miles of stone and mortar. Certainly enough for you to feel safe inside."

"It's impressive," replied Mario, looking at the dreary hills of the city. "It looks empty in there."

"A lot of it is! The city is mostly still ahead of us. One of the old emperors built these walls in the hopes that the city would keep on expanding and eventually fill in. It never seemed to quite live up to his ambitions. The far tip of the city, around Acropolis Point is where we'll find the Venetian Quarter. We'll moor there, we have a special dispensation so we won't have to bleed through the teeth when we pay the harbourmaster, unlike those poor fishermen. On the other side of the Golden Horn, is Galata. It's a fortified little Genoese colony. They have their own harbour, they use their own currency, and their own soldiers. Venice's much more integrated into the city than Genoa. It's also more popular with the locals, but at the end of the day these Greek bastards still hate anyone from the *barbarian* west."

"And then there's the Bosporus." Continued Mario, trying to focus on the geography with which he was familiar, if only from books.

"That's right. It goes from where the Golden Horne meets the Marmara, to the north. It leads up to the Black Sea, to the Golden Horde, to the emptying of the great rivers of Europe, the Don, the Dneiper and the Danube. Everything from Munich to Kiev comes through this little waterway, and the Emperor gets his cut."

"How free will I be within the city?"

"The Venetian Quarter is semi-separate from the rest of the city. It's cordoned off by a series of stockades and fences. I know one of the officers in the Venetian Quarter who should be able to help you get set up. You don't want to stray too far from the Quarter after dark. Things get pretty dangerous in the main part of the city. They're poor, the locals are, and you're rich. The dregs know this. Most of the beautiful parts of the city are in the Quarter anyways, you can stay in the quarter, unless you're curious as to how the slums are built. The Church of Holy Wisdom, St. Sofia, is right next to the Venetian merchant district."

"You seem to know this city pretty well."

"I do! I spent a year and a half here, but that was before Varna. It was a long time ago. That hill there on the horizon is Acropolis Point. It marks the apex of the city, and right below are the ruins Bucholeon palace. That's a pretty dangerous area," he joined his hands together to make a pointing triangular figure. "We'll sail around it. You can look up the Bosporus, but it's too winding to see all the way to the Black Sea. We'll moor the Nineveh in Proshorianus Harbour, one of the three Venetian harbours in town, and enter the quarter directly. Acropolis Point gives quite a view."

Mario watched the red brick palace of Bucholeon as they passed. At one time, it had its own harbour that opened onto the Sea of Marmara, guarded by red walls capped with white marble towers. Atop the palace were famed gardens built to shame those of Babylon, but they were now invisible to the eyes of the living. Behind the walls and towers was where the emperors of old had lived and held court. Archways bobbed and weaved along the sea walls of the palace and wrestled with the green ivies that wrapped around them as snakes around Laocoön and his brood.

The ship slowly sailed around the hill that marked the tip of Constantinople. At the top of the hill, Mario could see the famous Church of Holy Wisdom. From its perch it had dominated the skyline of the Imperial city for almost a thousand years. He listened to Ezera as he continued his introduction to the city.

"Those islands over there to our south are still in Imperial possession, or at least they were last time I was here. Over there, you can see the Asian shore of the Marmara," He pointed to the land to the east of them. "Those two settlements over there are Scutari and Chalcedon. They're both in the hands of the Turk now."

Mario turned quickly.

"What?! Those two towns?" he couldn't make out the figures of people, but he could definitely make out buildings and ships as they continued eastwards. "They're so close."

"I know. Five times a day you can here the call to prayer from Scutari. Holy Wisdom's bells usually drown it out."

“Sweet Jesus.”

“It gets better, Mario!” Ezera said, as always with a smile on his face. The ship heaved its northwards arch to circle around Acropolis Point. “Do you see that over there?” He pointed at the giant estuary next to the point.

“That is the Golden Horne, and that…” Moving his hand to point at a fortified encampment on the north shore “… is Galata.”

Galata was a small town built up where one of the hundreds of hills met the sea. It was surrounded by walls, and at its northern extreme was a stout round tower, looming over its little encampment. The local harbour seemed to be very busy indeed.

“The Genoese trade with the Turks, and they’ve been known to attack Imperial possessions along the Marmara and in the Black Sea when they don’t get the kind of concessions they want. As I said, they are not extraordinarily popular with the locals.”

“It seems that the city is in a pretty precarious position,” Mario stated incredulously.

“Make no mistake, Mario. This is a pretty dubious exile, and it’s not a pretty place. I wouldn’t trust the permanence of this place, if I were you. The glitter has worn off the crown.”

“It’s been around for a long time,” Mario countered.

“My grandfather was around for a long time. Long life does not make someone immune to death. I’ll introduce you to a few people, and leave you to settle yourself.”

“Thank you, Captain. You’ve given me so much help in your actions and advice.”

“Don’t thank me yet, Doctor. We’ve a long way to go until you’re sorted.”

Upon their arrival in harbour, Ezera paid a messenger boy to bring a message to an officer in the Venetian Quarter’s garrison. The message was delivered, and as the ship was being inspected by the harbourmaster and his staff, a detachment of twelve guards arrived on the dock to greet the captain and crew of the Nineveh.

An officer dressed in a fine brown robe and a shining breastplate underneath it came to greet them. He was tall and broad, and had a look of such casual violence in his squinting eyes that Mario wanted to get back on the boat. The officer in question greeted Ezera at the dock.

"Welcome back, Captain!" The officer said as he embraced the pirate.

"Thank you, Captain!" Ezera replied with a smile. "It's been a long time."

"It has indeed. Four or five years, I'm a captain no more, I'm now the commander of the Venetian Garrison."

Ezera blinked.

"Plague and mercenary rules can promote a man quickly these days." The commander said with a smile.

"I'm glad that you needn't wait around for something as frustrating as seniority." Ezera joked in return. "My Lord, the empire's been good to you!"

"The republic, not the empire! I'm still in the employ of Venice, but I do stand at court in Blachernae."

Ezera looked at his old comrade. His face couldn't be any older than thirty five, though his eyes could place him older than that. He had light brown hair, cropped short, and tight facial features which seemed to refuse to move in unison. When he spoke, his mouth moved, but his eyes, nose cheeks and ears stayed perfectly still as though they were resting.

Ezera turned to Mario. "This is Mario Orsini. A physician of some repute from the academy of Science and Philosophy in Venice, he is here to ply his trade as profitably as God allows."

"Really? Welcome to Constantinople, Master Orsini," the commander leaned over to Ezera. "Who is he, to get sent here? A grave robber? Pedophile?"

"Of course not! He's a great and noble man. And this…" Ezera said, continuing his dockside introductions "is Vincent DiCastillo, formerly a captain in the Catalan guards, and now commander of the whole bloody garrison, I'm pleased to say."

"A pleasure to welcome you."

"A pleasure to be welcomed, Commander."

"Where will the two of you be staying?"

Ezera smiled broadly.

DiCastillo smiled back having already guessed the favour he'd be asked. "The two of you are of course welcome to stay in my home. Your crew will have to find their own accommodations, as our barracks are pretty full. I have a villa in the middle of the Quarter, near the Forum of

Constantine, and I happen to have a few guest rooms, which my servants keep ready for some such as you. We'll dine together tonight and we'll see what we can do to get Master Orsini settled here."

"A villa? The times have been good to you!" Ezera said smiling.

Vincent nodded his head sideways in a quixotic sort of way. "The times are strange here. We can talk about these things at dinner. For now, I do have thing to attend to, so I'll bid you goodbye for now. I'll have one of my men come to gather you here in three hours, how does that sound?"

"It sounds wonderful, Commander. Thank you for offering a stranger so much hospitality," Mario answered.

"It's no trouble. Ezera is an old friend. You are a new one. I bid you welcome again, and must take my leave. I'll see you both for dinner. Goodbye."

Vincent walked off the pier and went through the gate and into the walled city.

"He seemed very friendly." Mario remarked.

"Yes, he did," Ezera said under his breath once his friend had left the dock. "That could have gone a lot worse than it did. Tonight, keep your wits about you. Don't drink. He'll offer lots, but he won't drink himself. I'll drink, but don't you do it! It might be nothing, but I've got a tricky feeling."

"You mean he's not to be trusted?"

Ezera looked at the walls for a minute and then at Mario. He seemed to be searching for the correct words.

"He's… self-interested. Of course you can trust him, it's just a question of what he can be trusted with."

"I understand," Mario nodded, giving him a sly look.

"No, you don't. He's a good man, and his offer of friendship is probably quite sincere, but you don't want to be in his thrall. Make sure he's your friend, but not your master. Because that's what he'll try to do. He's cut-throat and ruthless, but he's still a good man, I love him to bits, he's very much like a subtle version of Antonio. Just remember, with men like Vincent DiCastillo, you're one of three things, a vassal, an ally or an enemy. Just keep your wits about you, be strong, and don't show any weakness."

"I understand."

"And when I say 'be strong', don't be domineering, because he'll cut you down fast."

"I got it."

"And if you show weakness and *then* try to be stronger to cover it up, he'll think that you're impetuous and put you in your place, which is not where you want to be."

"Alright."

"And quit agreeing with everything I say, it makes you seem malleable."

Mario stopped for a minute and wondered how to respond to that last one.

"Just don't drink." Ezera surmised.

Mario walked around the harbour and ventured into the city. He promised Ezera that he would return in two hours, so that they could be escorted to Vincent's villa. Ezera insisted on sending two guards with him, to which Mario conceded to take Lorenzo and Luis, two rather large oarsmen, with him. What he saw in the Venetian quarter came as no small surprise to him.

Walking around, he could see shop-signs in Piedmontese Italian. He could see men and women walking about in the Venetian fashions of more than ten years ago. He could see wooden houses, based on the designs of the stone and mortar houses of his home. He wandered into some of the local churches, and breathed in the incense that lingered in the air. The art that adorned these houses of God was traditional, and simply not as sophisticated as what was being done back home. It was as though the colony was a miniature version of Venice, that didn't get it quite right – like a hastily constructed set for a play.

He heard the bells of Holy Wisdom, clanging overhead but decided that he would go there only when he had the time to properly see the church. He had read so much about it, he wanted to see it properly. He mentally began to schedule a viewing for himself.

After an hour of exploring the area around Eugenius Gate, near where the Nineveh was moored, he decided to walk along the sea walls up the Golden Horne. Using the walls as a location marker, he planned to walk for a half hour, then return on time to meet Ezera and the escorts.

Stretching along the city walls, the colony went. The area next to the two Venetian harbours, along the Golden Horne, predictably didn't attract the best crowd. Mario was glad that he had taken the two brutish-looking pirates with him for protection. After they passed by three sea gates, the Venetian colony narrowed into a panhandle. Measuring only fifty metres across from sea wall to wooden palisade, the three walked along the elongated district, and noted how much of a change there was in their environs.

Next to the harbour gates, the area was poor and run-down. In the panhandle, however, it was starting to get more settled, in a way. On the street, there was rubbish all about, with open and unmanaged sewage, but the buildings themselves seemed somehow cleaner. As long as he closed his nose and didn't look down, it was quite attractive. Then he heard a very strange sound. It resembled the howling of a wolf, crying out in pain. Yet it seemed also to be a vaguely human language. He took his guards and went to investigate.

At the end of the panhandle, the saw a small building, a single story, nestled between several larger buildings. I would have been quite easy to miss. It had a steeple rising above it, and men were bumbling about, in and out of the front door.

"What's that?" Mario asked one of his guards.

"It looks like a mosque. It's a Mohammedan church," Luis answered suspiciously. "There're one or two in the city."

"How? This is the capital of the greatest Christian empire in the world?"

His two bodyguards shrugged.

"Can I see it?"

"That's a bad idea." Lorenzo said. "We're three, and there's a lot more of them."

"Yes." Mario squinted at the small building, and looked around. Many of the people here seemed to be neither Greek nor Italian. "We should go."

They turned around to leave, and they saw a minor procession coming down the crowded dirty road towards them. Riding towards them were a dozen men, trotting in three ranks. They were led by strange spectacle of a man.

Their leader seemed to embody every fantastical image Mario had of the orient. He wore flowing silk robes that seemed to create a multi-coloured cloud atop his horse. Running behind him was a servant boy, trying to steady an elongated umbrella, keeping the burning sun out of the horseman's face. The horseman wore a giant bushy moustache that had been brushed and waxed to stick out from his face at hard angles, and resembled horns coming out of his cheeks. His eyebrows were groomed outward in a similarly aggressive style.

As the entourage passed by Mario and his two guards, the oriental man didn't even bother to look down at them. They simply proceeded to the mosque, dismounted and the men began to cluster around them and pay homage as they entered the building. Everyone wanted to speak to him and kiss him on the hand or cheek.

"Who, or what, was that?" Mario asked rhetorically.

"Don Mario," Lorenzo said. "We must get back to the Nineveh soon. You're expected."

"I suppose." He looked back at the spectacle that had just ridden past him and shook his head. "Let's go."

Chapter Thirteen - Dinner

The three arrived at the docks just as their escort did to bring them to their host's home. They were brought along a single cobblestone thoroughfare up to an open crossroads lined with shops, workshops and cedar wood homes. They turned left, in the direction of Holy Wisdom and continued to a large round forum in the Roman style. Their pathway seemed to always venture uphill, and Mario began to pant more heavily than a man of his youth should from the walking. Mario wondered if they were taking an uphill and longer route intentionally. The Forum of Constantine was centered round a giant square column made of marble blocks. Past it, they could see more such obelisks. They turned right again, and after a short circling walk back in the direction of the harbour, they found themselves at the stuccoed gate of a rather large villa.

Mario was used to the city of Venice, where every neighbourhood was administered by guilds and patrons, and was decorated according to the tastes of the day. Constantinople, on the other hand, was decorated rather randomly. The forums were built with precision and care, but the neighbourhoods were a random collection of mud streets and paved roads. Itinerant shacks would sit beside mansions and homeless masses slept outside of palaces. The grand houses themselves were cut off from the city. They had huge walls on the outside, blocking out the city around them, and faced inward courtyards. Even the home of a great patron of the arts would look like a red brick box from the outside, its beauty invisible to passers-by until you stepped into the inner sanctum and saw the beautiful life hidden inside.

That's what made Vincent's villa so special. The villa was a three story ziggurat of marble, cedar and stucco. In the brilliance of the setting sun, the compound seemed to exude its own source of stored sunlight. The roof was terracotta and the garden was flowered with herbs and well manicured flowers. Within the villa compound was a stone table outside the main building with wooden latticework that held a creeping grape vine sheltering it from sky. The compound's walls that seemed so severe from the outside, that they seemed to be a serene border to the civilized enclosure against the harsh world outside. It seemed to be a thousand years out of time, from a period when it would serve as the home of a Roman patrician. The guard at the gate nodded to the escort and ushered them in. From out of the front entrance of the villa stepped Vincent, clad in fine brightly coloured robes, rather than the vulgar armour in which he was seen earlier in the day. Around his neck was an ornate, silver cross. Following behind him was a bearded cleric, dressed in many layers of uncomfortable-looking black.

"Hello again, Captain!" he greeted Ezera warmly. "Welcome to my home, and a warm welcome to you, too, Doctor Mario!"

He embraced them both warmly.

"Thank you, Vincent! We are both quite glad that you've opened your home to us after such a long absence," Ezera said, his smile resting comfortably on his face. "Young Mario here's walked around the quarter a bit this afternoon, and has been quite impressed with your little ward!"

"I have indeed! I haven't had a chance to see Holy Wisdom yet. I was hoping to see it tomorrow."

"I can take you there, Doctor. I've business there in the early morning," the clergyman said cordially. "It's especially beautiful in the mornings, when the sun is in the east. I like to go there for morning prayers."

"Thank you very much!"

"It's no trouble." He replied.

Vincent turned to his friend and then back to his two guests. "I'd like to introduce you both to an important friend of mine, Isodore of Philipi."

"Father." Mario gave an unenthusiastic greeting.

"Please, I'm only a lowly monk. I don't merit any honorifics," he replied in nearly perfect Piedmontese Italian. "I lived in Venice for seven years and fell in love with your city. When Don Vincent told me that he was accepting a guest from my adoptive Eden, I invited myself."

Mario seemed puzzled by the stranger. "I was told that the Greek priesthood didn't care for their Latin brothers."

"That's unfortunately true, in the main," Isodore acknowledged. "I saw art and beauty where my countrymen saw only graven images and heresy. We're the poorer for it, I dare say."

"Now, all of you come inside," Vincent announced. "My house is your home!"

"Thank you for your hospitality, Commander," Mario said with false bravado.

"Please, you're in my home now, call me Vincent."

"Thank you, Don Vincent."

The commander brought them into his villa through the sliding wood doors of the main entrance. The inside of the home was lavish, and well decorated with silks, marble busts, and rich carpets. It smelled of a warm fire, incense and wildflowers. The entrance room also had a large wooden dining table, and recliners along the walls. There was a large granite fireplace on the north end of the room, seasonally alight with aromatic woods. There were four doors leading out of the room, one to a kitchen, the other doors were closed. There was also a polished wooden staircase leading up at the east wall.

"You have a beautiful home, Don Vincent."

"The city has been good to me," he replied to Mario. "I hope that it will be as good to you, someday. Please come in, and be comfortable. Take a seat. My family will be down shortly. Can I offer you some wine?"

"Thank you, but I've promised my brother that I would abstain from hard alcohol until I can toast his wedding on the tenth of next month. I look forward to that day."

'Good call, let's hope he doesn't smell the ship's rum on your clothes,' Ezera thought to himself as the three of them sat down in the recliners. "I'll have some wine!"

"I'll drink to your brother's impending nuptials for you, then. I'll have one of my servants bring you some fruit juice," he called to the kitchen and spoke in Greek. "The fruit here in Constantinople is excellent. Our colonies on the Black Sea bring us apricots, pears, peaches, strawberries, pomegranates, apples, oranges, nuts, any thing under the sun according to the season. It keeps our kitchens well stocked."

"It's a noble oath, dear Venetian," Isodore concurred while collecting his own half-filled goblet. "Though my own oaths have different weights, the fruit of the vine is permitted only for religious feasts. God be praised, every day of the calendar is dedicated to a different saint. I'll toast your brother, and Saint Alexius the Confessor, whose feast day is today. Cheers!"

The monk bottomed up his goblet.

"You both honour a stranger and I thank you both." Mario said humbly.

A servant brought some wine for Ezera and Isodore, and some fresh apricot nectar for Vincent and Mario.

"On the subject of a well stocked kitchen, we'll be dining on fish tonight," Vincent continued. "The Bosporus Strait to the north of us flows two ways. The top the current flows fresh water south from the great rivers of Europe, and the bottom current flows north with the salt water from the Aegean. Depending on how deep the fishermen set their lines, there are fresh water or salt water fish."

"That sounds like a tricky waterway."

"It is! It's the source of the city's wealth and frustrations," Isodore sank deeply into his recliner.

"It certainly seems like quite a city."

"It is. It's inclement and changeable, and so are the people," continued Vincent. "That's part of why I like it here so much. I married a local girl. Are you married, Mario?"

"Not yet," replied Mario politely.

"Don't marry a Greek girl!" He said looking up the stairs to see if his wife was in earshot. "They're as emotional as the sea here."

"Roman! Roman!" Isodore joked. "We like to pretend we're the true heirs of Romulus and Remus over here."

"I'll keep that in mind, Sirs," Mario smiled in spite of himself. He really liked the warmth of his reception here, and after so long at sea, it was especially well received. He caught that relaxation of his mind and reminded himself of Ezera's warning.

"Who is that?" Mario asked pointing at the marble bust on the far wall.

"That is the Roman Emperor Constantine the Eleventh. He is the current Emperor of New Rome, here in Constantinople. You must remember that while you're here. If you call Constantinople the Greek Empire, they will take offence. It's the Roman Empire, even though they don't much care for Rome around here."

"And well we shouldn't," came a voice descending the stairs. Two women in their early twenties, dressed in silk dresses came down to the meeting hall.

"And may I present my family to you both," Vincent said standing. "This is my lovely wife Daria." He said introducing an olive skinned woman in a green dress. Mario suspected that she may be with child, but decided not to mention this in case fate would have it that she was merely girthy. She curtsied formally.

"And this is my sister, Ella." Vincent introduced a stunning hazel-haired woman in a yellow dress. Her skin was fair, and her eyes a deep blue that seemed to be speckled with green light. She was a round girl in all the best ways to Mario's eyes. Her eyes, her cheeks, her breasts and her hips, without being fat *per se*, she had a voluptuousness to her appearance. She also curtsied, more politely and less formally than her sister-in-law.

Ezera, who had been conspicuously quiet for most of the introductions, spoke up. "You have been truly blessed by God to share a home with two of the loveliest women in Christendom."

Mario wanted to roll his eyes as Ezera made his way over to the two ladies and extravagantly kissed both their hands.

Vincent smiled before turning to the two young women. "Captain Ezera here is an old friend, and the other one here is Doctor Mario Orsini, a new friend. They've both arrived today from Venice."

While Daria didn't seem amused at all by Ezera's characteristic attempt at charm, Ella seemed to find it amusing and smiled at Mario when Ezera kissed her hand, as if to say '*Where did you find this mad man?*' Her smile hit Mario like a thunderbolt, but he tried his best to keep that to himself. He smiled back and nodded politely as if to say '*He's my semi-adle-brained cousin and I have to look out for him, but he's harmless,*' She smiled back at him with a light laugh.

The four men talked for hours around the dinner table and the table was lit by a series of candles and oil lamps after the light of day took its rest. The women were polite. They always smiled. They laughed appropriately when a joke was told. Though their interest dwindled in the third hour of a conversation on trade, medicine, alchemy and rumours of a renewed war with the Turks, the two women never let it show.

Mario was resolute in his attention to the discussion with Vincent. He stuck to the topic at hand, never wavering, he spoke about medicine and field hospitals, and about the wars in Northern Italy between the ever changing alliances between Florence, Pisa, Genoa and Venice. He did his best not to let his gaze wander to Ella. He couldn't help but thinking of how he would love to talk only to her. Direct avoidance of the girl was in his best interests right now, the best he could do was talk to everyone but her. He decided to turn his attention away from Vincent delicately and involve the rest of the table.

"So, Daria… Are you from Constantinople?"

"I am. I was born a mile from here, near the Arcadius Forum. My parents still live there."

"Were you and Don Vincent married in the Greek or Latin rite?"

Vincent's eyes froze when those words were vomited onto the table. Daria smiled elegantly. "We were married in an orthodox Christian rite church, Master Orsini," she answered with a polite, if aloof, air; the way one would correct a child who misspoke a minor lesson.

"You're stepping on dangerous grounds, in this city, when you speak of religion, Mario," Isodore the monk cautioned him. "I find it wise to avoid the issue altogether."

"I'm sorry… I didn't mean to cause any offence."

"Why should any be taken?" Daria responded quickly.

Ella brought her napkin to her face to cover her smile, knowing full well the line of conversation onto which her sister-in-law was about to embark.

"This city is the capital of the Christian world, you see," Daria began. "It is in Western Europe that men have degenerated into local heresies. The rules of God are universal. As you know, the Roman churches have opted to allow local rituals and variances on this. They've put local traditions above divine rule and are happy with that. We've maintained the rule of the first churches here, until God decides in his own good time to tell us any different."

"What my charming wife is trying to explain to you," Vincent continued, after a quick glance at Daria, "…is that the Patriarch of Constantinople claims direct authority from Saint Peter, and through him back to Christ. In my opinion, the Bishop of Rome owes his allegiance to whichever Italian family bought him the office, as opposed to here, where he owes the Emperors patronage. They'll just claim God's patronage after their appointment is fait accompli. What do you think, Doctor?" "

Mario didn't want to appear rude to his hosts, but also remembered Ezera's warning about not seeming too malleable. He decided to politely challenge that, but he knew he was best to also play this a little close to hand and not over-extend himself. It was best to seem curious, but not ardent. "The Bishop of Rome makes the same claim. He…"

"He is appointed by local Italians, taking into account the balance of power in Italy as it now stands," Daria was also being cautious. "At least that's my understanding. Maybe I'm wrong. Is the Pope truly a spiritual figure above local and dynastic politics?"

Mario decided it was best to end this line there. "I wouldn't go that far, Milady. I apologise if I've caused any offence."

"No apology is needed." She answered with the same elegant smile that she started with.

"Fair enough," answered Mario. He took a breath and his eyes squinted as he tried to focus on the correct words for his next inquiry. "But I do have a question, not that I want to open another dangerous topic, but today I explored a bit of the Quarter here. It is quite lovely. But I saw I strange sight here. Near the harbour walls, I saw a Mohammedan building. And riding to it, I saw a rather curious spectacle. There was a horse entourage going there, led by the most peculiar looking man…"

"That would be Prince Orhan," Vincent interrupted. "He is the nephew of old Mohammedan Sultan, the cousin of the new one. He surrendered after their failed siege twenty years ago and has been a prisoner here ever since."

"He seemed to gallivant around quite freely, hardly the way a prisoner is treated in Venice," Mario had the suspicious voice of recent experience when he said that.

"He is relatively free here in the Venetian Quarter. This is one of those political concessions that are so abhorred among the faithful here; that's why he's in the Quarter. He won't run away, his cousin would murder him if he could reach over the walls. Turks don't suffer competition or rogue heirs to flourish. So we give him a free run in the Quarter. There are a few hundred Turks here, mercenaries mostly. They are technically supposed to be Christian Turks, like the Avars or the Alans, you'll see many of them in the Imperial Armies, but in practice, they're allowed here because Orhan is a pretender to the throne, and it never hurts to have one of those in your custody."

"That seems very reasonable." Mario concluded.

"There are many among the faithful who'd disagree," Ella chimed into the conversation. "Generally speaking, you'll do much better here if you avoid any knowledge of such politics altogether."

'*My God, her voice is beautiful,*' Mario kept his face as stone-like as he could. "I think that's good advice, thank you."

Their eyes met for a brief instant, and then Mario turned immediately to Vincent. "I've learnt a great deal about life in this city tonight."

Vincent looked at him with a polite severity. It reminded him of the way that Balias the Inquisitor had looked upon him. '*Oh, God! Did he see that? I'm such a fool!*'

He was thankfully saved by Ezera, who was by now a little drunk. "I'm sorry, my old, dear friend, but I think I've pressed your grapes too hard tonight." He was leaning on the table. I've always respected your generosity with these things, you know."

The commander's politely severe gaze turned gradually to Ezera. "You've always tested my generosity, Captain." He joked.

Ezera put his cup down very gently, smiled at his old friend and opened his arms. "I've always given you the opportunity to show kindness, Vincent. God likes that sort of thing, you know. Is that not so, priest?"

Isodore the semi-drunk monk laughed at that. "That's right, Vincent! You're like Jesus curing the lepers, only you're feeding us wine." He smiled at his host's wife who kept her elegant composure unscathed, though it was obvious that she didn't approve of the comparison, especially by a drunken man of the cloth.

Vincent turned his gaze back to Mario and opened his mouth as if to say something, and then looked back at Ezera. "I've had our servants ready a room for the two of you, I'll show you there myself. My wife and sister appear ready to sleep as well, so it's time to adjourn."

"Thank you for the meal. It was wonderful," Mario tried to show as much polite gratitude as was appropriate.

Vincent crooked his head to Mario and kept the same dangerous looking smile that flooded recent memories back to the young doctor.

"It was my pleasure," despite the different face worn by the man, it carried the same predatory expression as Venetian constable who'd arrested him almost month ago.

"I thank you as well," acknowledged Isodore, who then stood up precariously. "Don Mario, I'll gather you here, shortly after dawn tomorrow."

"I look forward to it."

Isodore was seen out, then Mario and Ezera said goodnight to the ladies and Vincent took a lamp and brought them up the stairs.

"This is our extra bedroom," he said leading them in. "Both beds have been lain, the window faces the west, so you can sleep past sunrise, don't worry. I think you may need some extra time in the morning, Ezera."

"I'll be fine." Ezera said falling into his bed.

"It was nice to meet you, Mario," Vincent shook Mario's hand.

He's got a very strong grip,' Mario thought to himself, trying to show genuine appreciation for the hospitality, and not any sign of intimidation. "Thank you, Commander. It was nice to meet you, too. I look forward to seeing Holy Wisdom tomorrow."

"Yes." Vincent answered. "See you tomorrow. Good night, gentlemen."

And he left them alone.

In the darkness, Mario sat next to Ezera's bed. "Are you awake?"

"What?" asked Ezera through the darkness of the room and his own mental haze.

"How do you think that went?"

Ezera grumbled and turned to his side. "I think it basically went well. You stood your ground with his stubborn wife, and handled yourself well talking about different things. But you should be careful."

"Careful about what?"

Ezera rolled over and looked at him with a gaze that stabbed through Mario's defences. Mario could barely make out the look on his friend's face through the darkness but he could guess what it looked like.

"What?" Mario repeated.

"She is very beautiful, but you need to be careful."

Mario was about to deny all knowledge of what Ezera was hinting at, and then conceded. "You're right. On both counts."

"She seemed interested also, but be careful. You don't want to make any enemies you don't have to."

"Do you think Vincent noticed?"

Ezera's voice chuckled.

Mario exhaled and started to think.

"Just be careful."

"But she's so beautiful. I want to go across the hall and tell her this."

"Don't," Ezera advised. "She's a problem waiting to happen. Worry about getting yourself set up here, and start planning on new options. If you start paying attention to something like that, you can squander your money and any influence you hope to get. Remember that."

"I've never seen anyone like her. I want to go across the hall and ask her to marry me tonight!"

Ezera's eyes narrowed as he squinted to try to make out Mario's face. "You're a virgin, aren't you?"

Mario returned the gaze in frustration. "What?"

"I know your oaths, and I've seen the way you turn your nose up at the crew when the talk about going to the cat-houses, and to me when we first met. You're an unmarried prude, you are."

"You're drunk. Go to sleep. Those oaths finished when I left the university, I understand all about the more vulgar side of manliness."

"Maybe she should be careful," he laughed

"Goodnight," Mario jumped into his bed and turned away.

"Maybe we should all be careful!" Ezera laughed and the young doctor's predicament.

"Goodnight!"

Chapter Fourteen - Holy Wisdom

Isodore of Philipi arrived at the villa of Vincent DiCastillo shortly after sunrise, and was met at the door by a giddy Mario Orsini.

"Good morning, Doctor Mario," he said in truncated, but grammatically correct Piedmontese Italian. Sobriety challenged his fluency.

"Good morning to you, Brother Isodore," Mario replied in well-studied Greek.

"Your pronunciation is wonderful, Doctor," Isodore laughed. "But I'm sorry to tell you that the average vendor on the street will have no understanding of what you just said."

"What do you mean?" Mario fell back into Italian.

"There are three Greek languages. There's the language of the street and market, which is a combination of Greek, Armenian, Georgian and Latin, there is the language of the educated classes and then there is the dead language of antiquity in which you're so fluent. Unfortunately, they are all pretty incomprehensible to each other."

"That's too bad," responded the crestfallen Mario. "I've learned the language of Homer."

"And in the event of The Rapture, you will be able to speak to all the Greek Classicists in their own tongue. Don't worry, all educated people will speak and understand Ancient Greek, they'll just find your speaking a wee amusing."

"I'm glad to hear that," Mario said, sounding a little more upbeat and returning back to the original language of ancient Hellas. "Shall we see the great Cathedral?"

"We shall indeed, Doctor. I'm sure that your diction in the ancient tongue will endear you to some of the elderly and more scholastically inclined citizens of the city."

"I'll remember that," Mario said with fair optimism. "Is this the way to the Cathedral?"

"It is. It's just straight up this hill."

"Of course," Mario was surprised at how incongruously everything in the city seemed to be uphill from everything else.

Their cobbled road led from Vincent's villa, up the hill to the Forum of Constantine, a circular forum with a large column and two wide roads heading east and west. To Mario's relief, the major streets seemed to follow the spine of a hill, and the east-bound road took them on a leisurely stride for a few hundred meters. Out of a silhouette caused by the still rising sun, rose the incredible figure of the city's famed Hippodrome.

An ovoid shape track, larger than the coliseum of Rome, emerged. At first glance, Mario thought that it was smaller than he'd imagined, but he then realised that it was downhill from the spinal road upon which he was walking. The road crested as they came nearer, and Mario's jaw dropped as he gazed down the length of the huge construct.

"That's where horses race," Isodore pointed out. There are four teams: the glorious Reds and the honourless Blues are the major players, but the Greens and the Whites also compete, but nobody really supports them except your friend Vincent."

"Who does Vincent support?"

"He supports the Greens. They haven't won a race in nearly five years. He says that he supports them because of their tenacity, but I think he just enjoys the look of shock on people's faces when they learn for whom he cheers."

"They sound like a bad team to support."

"They are, but if someone is too vocal in supporting the Reds or the Blues, blood's been known to spill in some neighbourhoods. Most people will just roll their eyes if you support the greens or whites."

"Can we see a race?" Mario asked.

"On Saturday, there are usually races but there haven't been any lately because fear of a riot, but that should abate once the new patriarch's appointed. We'll get you a nice red tunic and you can watch a grand spectacle."

"I take it you don't support the Blues?"

A serious shadow descended on the monk's face, and his voice lowered. "Many years ago, when I first came here, I wanted to cheer for the Blues," he took a deep breath. "But then, the Blue supporters found out that my parents were married and I couldn't join their number."

Mario paused for a second to understand what he'd been told.

"That was a joke, Doctor."

"Sorry, it's a little early in the morning."

"Of course," the monk smiled once they arrived at the plaza outside of the Hippodrome. He turned to the North-east and motioned for Mario to do the same. "This, Don Mario Orsini, is the Cathedral of Holy Wisdom."

For the second time that morning, words failed Mario. From the outside, Holy Wisdom was the quintessential opposite of Renaissance Italy and Gothic Germany. The airy flow of flying buttresses and giant windows was instead replaced by giant stalwart pillars holding up a dome, and then sub-domes and semi-domes, demi-spheres and curtain walls seemed to pour out from the font of that giant dome. It seemed like a fresh water spring coming out of a solid rock, both vibrant and flowing, but also hard and immoveable at the same time.

"Good God."

"*Solomon, I have outdone thee*," Isodore announced. "That's what the Emperor Theodosius said when he first entered."

"Justinian."

"Doctor?"

"It was the Emperor Justinian. Theodosius built the walls," Mario said as he inspected the architecture. "Although, to be fair, it was an army of conscript labourers who built it, not the Emperor himself, he simply takes the credit."

"Did the Hebrews build the Pyramids or did Pharaoh?" Isodore asked, mildly irritated at having been corrected.

"You're a priest, surely you believe that God built it all and merely selected human hands to act as his proxies."

"I do, of course. But I'll suggest you avoid the topic of religious discussions, especially when we're inside."

"Will people accuse me of heresy and throw me in jail?"

"Heavens, no!" the idea seemed ridiculous to Isodore – the very idea seemed incorrigibly rude. "They'll talk your ear off as to why you're wrong, and we'll never get anything done."

"I'll hold back my tongue, in that case," he answered

"Especially around him," Isodore motioned to an elderly priest trotting awkwardly up the Cathedral steps like some black crab who had accidentally washed ashore. "He's someone best avoided."

"Who is he?"

"That would be the priest, Father Gennadios. A worse representative of human piety you'd be hard pressed to find, I don't mind telling you. Shames me as a man of God. I know that it must be difficult for you to believe, but there are some men who are attracted to the religious orders, not by obedience and love of God, but out of ambition here on earth."

"I've met men like him before." Mario made a mental note of the priest's name and appearance and watched him hobble past the giant doors of the church.

"Some say that he'll be the next patriarch. I pray that either God or the synods choose someone more deserving."

"Do you think an ambitious politician of a clergyman could sneak one past God or Synod?"

"Nothing happens against the will of God," Isodore agreed. "But at some times, the holy wisdom of Our Father is easier to see than at others."

"On the subject of seeing Holy Wisdom…" Mario motioned to the church.

"Ah yes, of course." Isodore tried to turn his attention away from politics for a short time.

The monk guided the doctor through the main doors and into the marble-floored reception hall of the Cathedral. The narthex was large enough to house a handful of small chapels if possible, its ceiling soaring high above its narrow length.

"I'm afraid that you've probably lived closer to the capital's greatest works of art than anyone else in this city," Isodore said sullenly. "Two centuries ago, knights from Venice sacked Constantinople and set up a short lived Latin Kingdom here. Most anything that wasn't nailed down found its way back home with the knights."

"It's impressive, nonetheless," Mario nodded.

High above their heads was a gold embossed ceiling with beautiful mosaics, too high for knights to scrape off. The side walls were naked save for polished stone in sedimentary patterns. The mosaics that had been placed there had long ago been scraped off and sold for their gold components. The simplicity of the naked stone, offset by the complex beauty of the ceiling mosaic held a certain beauty, and the bare walls seemed to catch every sound of breath or footfall.

They then proceeded into the main body of the cathedral. The nave of the church shocked Mario. For almost five hundred years, this room had been the largest enclosed space in the world. There were a handful of women at the front, veiled in black cloth, waiting for a blessing from the priest that Isodore had pointed out at the altar. They looked like little ants scurrying about, such was the dwarfing effect of the chamber. Giant pillars swept up, surrounded by the bubbling walls of the Cathedral, into a crown dome at the top that seemed to hover on stone stilts. Again, the simplicity of the walls was crowned by golden mosaics of Christ and angels above them, safely out of ladder's reach.

"I think he may have indeed outdone wise Solomon," Mario breathed.

"It seems hard to believe that anyone could have done better," Isodore grinned with pride. While it would be ridiculous for him to claim any personal authorship of the church, as he felt great pride when foreigners were notably impressed with his adoptive city. Despite the glowing pride, Mario suspected that something was amiss with the monk, as he was constantly looking over his shoulder and his eyes couldn't sit still for more than an instant. "That dais over there is where the Emperor Constantine Paleologus sits during mass."

A wooden throne seemed to erupt directly from the marble floor. It seemed so small, though it was undoubtedly the largest chair Mario had ever seen. It was in front of the altar and to the left hand side of the central plan. To the right hand side was another throne, this one smaller and covered, more of a palanquin than a throne.

"That's where the patriarch sits," Isodore answered, and then turned around. "And up there is where you'll find the empress during a high mass."

Prior to having the balconies pointed out to him, Mario had not looked so far up to see them. He felt like a village bumpkin with a slack-jawed awe of his surrounding, but he couldn't help it. Galleries surrounded them, soaring high above their heads. Isodore was pointing to the gallery above the narthex from which they had entered.

"I'm at a loss for words, Isodore," Mario held up his hands. "This is one of the most impressive building I've ever seen."

"Yes," Isodore said, but he seemed distracted. "Do you see that balcony, up over there? Do you see the men there?"

Mario squinted and made out sever figures milling about. It seemed as though some kind of meeting was going on. The men at which Isodore was pointing were heavily built and lightly armoured men. They were obviously guards of some kind.

"Whose balcony is that?" Mario asked.

"No one's. That's the synod chamber. Those guards look like Adam Karian's men."

"Who brings guards to a church?"

"Four Emperors have died on this floor, doctor," Isodore kept his head looking up and pointed at the marble floor. "Let's go up."

"What?"

"Come on, I'm continuing your tour," the monk motioned for this guest to follow.

"Who's Adam Karian?" Mario asked as he caught up with the monk.

At the north end of the narthex was a gateway, through which Mario followed his host. Through the gateway was a ramp that climbed in a rectangular pattern up and up the church. Large enough for the two men to stand upright and abreast, the twisting corridor was lit by a series of widows, the sunlight reflecting off the stonework, polished by thousands of footsteps over the years.

"He's the general of the Imperial Legions, which is to say that he's the head of the local police force," Isodore replied as they entered a winding ramp that twisted about a dark passageway up to the galleries and started the long climb. "But he has the Emperor's ear and he's still one of the most important men in Constantinople. I wonder why he's here?"

"To pray?" Mario huffed behind him

"No, he's Armenian. They pray in their own churches," the monk was panting from the long and winding path up to the balconies. "He's here to either meet with Gennadios or with someone else. Noah's probably there as well."

"Who's that? Why are you so interested in who's meeting whom?"

"Vincent asked me to see what I could see. We're a little late; I thought they'd be arriving after us."

They finally arrived at the top of the long twisting ramp, and Isodore had to stop and put his hand on a pillar to regain his breath.

"Sorry, I suppose that I've spent too much time in an incense-filled monastery."

"Are you alright?" Mario looked appraisingly at the monk.

"Fine, I'll be fine," Isodore waived off Mario's interest. "You certainly seem healthy enough! Now come with me."

They continued across the main gallery, past the Empress' kiosk to the far Synod balcony. Across the sun lit gallery between the balconies, was a large marble wall, rising three metres from the marble floor of the gallery and reaching nowhere near the ceiling soaring above them. The door had been permanently removed by Constantine the Fifth as his way of saying that the Synods were to be open to all, rather than just loyalists. In practice that just meant that his successors would simply post a guard.

There was no guard there right now.

Isodore scrambled quickly across the open gallery to the open gateway in the marble wall. Just as he arrived, a broad-chested guard stepped out through the gateway and stopped the monk in his tracks. The monk almost tripped over his robes.

"Ah!" the Bulgarian native said in mild surprise, and he began to speak in the archaic Greek for which he'd chastised Mario for using earlier. "Do you understand what I'm saying?"

"No understand," the guard replied in stunted accent. "No enter."

The guard was a stump of a man, squat, broad, and sporting spiked hair and a spiked beard. His disposition was that of a blunt force instrument, and not someone looking to verbally spar with the talkative monk.

"Ah, I see," Isodore raised a hand to silence Mario.

The guard shifted his weight and blocked the entrance to the marble gate more completely.

"Varangian," Isodore said before reverting to the dead tongue of Herodotus. "Come with me, Doctor."

Mario was guided far along the gallery to the other side of the long ramp. Isodore hid the two of them into a darkened hollow between one of the giant pillars and a support wall.

"That oafish brute is a Varangian, they're mercenaries hired among the river-men, Rus, Danes, Saxons and that. They're bodyguards for the emperor and some of his ministers. They're a dangerous bunch, and completely above the law. They'd kill you in front of a constable and a priest and then think nothing of it, no one can touch them," Isodore explained. "We'll wait over here."

"What are you doing?" Mario whispered.

"Nothing. I just want to see who comes out of the meeting. They'll have to take the ramp, you see, it's the only way out of here."

"Why?" Mario's patience was wearing thin at this point.

"Because Vincent asked me to. He wants to know who's meeting here. I told him that I'd find out."

"Are you really a monk?" Mario asked accusingly.

"Of course!" Isodore smiled. "But even monks have to pay attention to such things. So do doctors, incidentally."

Mario suppressed his instinct to simply walk away at this point, and instead voiced his objection by giving out a long sigh.

"Shh. Here they come."

Then the procession entered their view. Everyone seemed to wear the same clothes, a black long-coat, thin but still climatically inappropriate for such a warm day as today. Over that, they wore white waistcoats. Mario had no way of knowing, but this was the standard dress of the court of the eastern empire.

The first out of the gallery and down into the black hole of the exit ramp were two body guards, followed by a bearded man wearing a purple sash.

"That's Adam Karian." Isodore whispered. "Behind him, with the blond hair and blue tassels on his waistcoat, that's Noah, he's a priest friendly to union. He's a friend of ours."

"Who's us?"

"Shh," Isodore was ignoring Mario's rising tone of anger. "That's an unexpected face."

"Who is?"

"The last in the procession. That's Hectore Pazzi," the monk's voice was barely audible. "That's interesting indeed."

"Who's Hectore Pazzi?" Mario asked.

"He's the commander of the Galata garrison. He's taken on his own enrichment as a quest given by God, and he drags too many good men into that mission. Holy Wisdom is probably the only place where the three of them can meet without weeks of planning and protocol."

"So they just had a friendly meeting?"

"No, they just had an emergency meeting. One that was hastily prepared."

"Why?"

"That's a good question. Let's get back to Vincent." Isodore suggested.

"That sounds like a good suggestion."

Turning, turning, turning, they descended the stone spire back to the narthex of the cathedral. At the bottom of the stairs stood an elder priest, dressed in his black hassock, waiting for their arrival. The old man's craggy and stubborn looking face seemed to hold both of their gazes before focussing on Isodore.

"Good morning, Brother. I haven't seen you or your ilk venture into this house of God for some time. I take it that the occasion isn't to celebrate your reversion to the true faith?"

"A guest in our city wanted to witness with his own eyes the famed wonder of Holy Wisdom, Father," Isodore said with a formalised bow. "As for conversions and reversions, my faith has never strayed from the true faith of Christ, nor from the holy communion between shepherd and flock."

"You represent a heretical order – a cancer that is not welcome in the body of the faithful. I pray that you take Christ into that ruined palace of yours and into your heart, but please, don't ask others to respect your depravity. You must leave this place until God sees fit to bring you to Him."

Isodore's eyes strained. He wanted to argue and debate the truths that were obvious for all to see, but he still needed to leave in a swift manner. In the end, his intellectual pride demanded a parting word.

"There are still those in the House of Christ who believe in communion of all the faithful, Father. I pray that someday you may join that table and sup with your co-religionists from Assyria to Eire. It is a big table indeed. Your communion table is a bit too restrictive for my tastes. One wonders if you'd find room for a master and twelve followers to sit in such an exclusive company."

"There is always room for the just, young brother. We don't, however, break bread with transgressors, informants, traitors or spies. If you recall, Our Lord's table was one seat too inclusive."

Sensing that the two men were involved in an argument of some kind in one of the incompressible dialects of Greek of which Isodore had warned him about, Mario spoke up in his own verbose antiquated language skills.

"Pardon me, but I'm a stranger here and cannot understand your argument. I must bid you both the peace of God and make my way, if you'll both excuse me."

"Of course." Isodore joined him in Attic Greek. "I'll guide you."

Gennadios the Priest stared at the newcomer. "Peace be with you then, stranger."

"And also with you," replied Mario. He then motioned to the monk that it was time to go; Isodore smiled at Mario and then uttered a few words of farewell in Greek.

As they left the gate that housed Holy Wisdom, a haunting echo snuck over the Sea of Marmara. Echoing over the water and creeping like waves onto the hills and sea walls of Constantinople came the lilting whisper of the Arabic call to prayer:

Allah-hu Akhbar! Ash-hadu allah ilaha ill-allah! Ash-hadu anna Muhammadan rasulullah! Haya alas salat! Haya alal felah! Ash -shalātu khayru min an-naum! Allah-hu Akhbar! La ilaha illallah!

The call was distant enough to easily have gone unnoticed, but Mario froze when he heard it and looked out to the sea. A scant distance across the Sea of Marmara, was the ancient Christian city of Chalcedon, home to the famous synods of Chalcedon, where much of the early Christian theological dictums were established. It was now captured and held by the Turks, and from there, they observed their heathen rites. As the sound reached Mario's ear, it passed over him and into the pan-handle of the Venetian colony, where it was heard by the clan of Mohammedans surrounding the crown-Prince Orhan. The call was returned. Mario turned around in near panic as he heard the Arabic prayers besiege Holy Wisdom.

"Relax," Isodore told him. "We keep a delicate balance here in the capital. Orhan and his brood are allowed to practice their heresy, but if they proselytize, then they'll be expelled. As for the call coming over the water, there isn't much we can do about that."

"It's horrifying."

"Really? I find it kind of relaxing. Certainly more melodic than bells.”

“You’re a priest!”

“I’m a monk, not a priest, and that makes no preclusion as to my opinions with regards to music.”

“I suppose,” Mario said incredulously. “We’re going the wrong way. Don Vincent’s Villa is this way.”

“He’ll be at the garrison, and that’s this way. Follow me,” Isodore corrected him. “We’ll be there shortly.”

The Venetian Garrison headquarters was a squat round tower near the Forum of Theodosius. Adjoining the main tower were a few barracks and sundry buildings, and around those developed an impromptu marketplace, making it a bit of a chore to find the entrance to the garrison. Near the forum, a wooden palisade wall stretched off along a north-south axis in order to keep the Italian concession separated from the rabble of Constantinople proper. Every day, thousands of Greek-speaking so-called-Romans would trundle through the gates to work in the Quarter.

The guard at the door recognised Isodore and quietly motioned him through the front door of the tower. Inside the tower there was a spiral staircase stretching up to the top of the tower.

‘Wonderful, I’ve found a city of hills, ramps and stairs. My legs will fall off before I ever see Venice again,’ Mario thought to himself as he and the monk climbed up to the very top.

At the cappa of the tower stood Vincent and a half dozen soldiers and constables, supposedly on guard, but it seemed more as though they were milling about and discussing next week’s chariot and horse races.

“Hello, Boys.” Vincent’s coarse voice called over upon their arrival. “How was the cathedral?”

“A true work of God’s art,” Mario proclaimed.

“That’s wonderful,” Vincent said tersely before focussing on Isodore. “Iso?”

“There was a meeting there, as you said, between Adam Karian, Noah, followed lastly by your friend Hectore Pazzi.”

“Pazzi?” Vincent considered the last name. “He and Karian are rarely up to any good together. How long were they meeting?”

"They met before our arrival, unfortunately we arrived as they were preparing to leave, but I'd guess not long."

"Good," Vincent's face lost expression as he considered what the meeting meant, and then reset himself when he turned back to Mario.

"I'm sorry to involve you in that little bit of reconnaissance, but I'm sure that you'll understand. Things in the Capital aren't quite stable right now."

"I had noticed," Mario testified.

"The Turks are raising a new horde. So we have to keep abreast of who knows what."

"Do you think that there will be another war soon?" Mario asked.

"Of course!" Vincent answered quickly. "Right now, you see, this city is a house divided. On one side of this fence here, there is the remains of the Roman Empire. It's old, corrupt, poor and putrid. On this side, you find the invigorated Republic of Venice, earnest to defend civilization, but put off by the obstinacy and closed nature of the Greek mystics. On the other side of the Golden Horne, just over that hill, you find Genoa, hoarding merchant trade from Constantinople and Venice, and doing little but enriching itself at the expense of fellow Christians. They also trade rather freely with the Muslims. If the Turkish Horde didn't realise that now was the right time to attack and scatter the last Christian outpost in the East, they would be foolish. And after spending the better part of twenty years here, I've witnessed the reigns of four Sultans, two Emperors, five Patriarchs and three Popes. I've learnt that the Muslims are no more fools than their Christian counterparts, which is more-or-less a compliment."

"This is my second day here," Mario reminded everyone.

Isodore smiled and made as though to laugh, but Vincent remained serious.

"Well may I welcome you again to the world centre of Christianity," Vincent said. "We'll have some lunch, and remember that your second day isn't finished yet. This afternoon I'll be bringing you to meet Giovanni Cardillo, the governor of the Venetian colony. I can only imagine what you'll think of our adoptive home after you've been here a week!"

"I find it quite stimulating, I assure you."

The governor's manse was downhill from the Hippodrome, but facing the Sphendoneh, the curving far end of the structure. Still, the random nature of the city's urban planning only managed to puzzle Mario as he walked past slums and masions. Perhaps there actually was an order to it all, but Mario's perceptive nature couldn't yet seem to find it.

The seat of Venetian authority looked like a granite brick prison. Four undecorated walls on each side, keeping the outside world out and the inner world in. There were not distinguishing markers on the building to identify it as opposed to any of the dozen or so other similar buildings.

Once Vincent and Mario were ushered in the door, Mario was very impressed with what he saw. White marble statuary, standing out against the red of the brick walls seemed to dare the outside world to try and penetrate. Inside the walls of the manse was a large and well maintained garden, with fruit trees, herbs and flower beds. A peacock was sunning itself on the grass; a little taste of a walled-in Eden.

Giovanni Cardillo's character seemed the exact opposite of his home. He came out of the upper chambers of the villa to greet his guests, and Mario was surprised at his ostentatious dress. He wore a red silk coat over his black shirt, and he was the first man wearing trousers that Mario had seen in the city. He also wore no hat, in a city where everyone else wore caps, helmets, czapkas or scull-caps. Everything to his appearance seemed to say that this was an explosive personality and free-spirit with an inner fire, similar to Don Antonio or the sea captain Ezera.

Everything but his eyes.

His eyes were a cold black and held no detectable emotions. When he greeted Mario, there was no warmth or friendliness to his greeting, only simple, rehearsed spontaneity. His personality seemed to be the antithesis of what Mario supposed it to be by his appearance.

"Welcome to Constantinople, Doctor," he said in measured tones. "Commander DiCastillo tells me that you've got letters of introduction from my old friend, Raphael Avruham."

"I do, Governor. He was kind enough to write them for me before I came," he handed over the letter, which Cardillo then read quietly in its entirety.

"Are you a Jew, sir?" the governor asked at length.

"No, Sir. I'm a Christian and always have been," Mario answered.

"Who is your father?"

"Clemente Orsini. He was a magistrate. Also a Christian, in case that's your next question."

"It's good for you, as only Christians can work at the hospitals in the Empire. That's why I ask," Giovanni continued. "I have neither love nor hate for the children of Isaac, mind you, but it does affect politics here. Their cousins, the sons of Ishmael are our problem. Why have you come to Constantinople?"

"I finished my extended stay at the university and because of the ongoing war with Florence tapping the coffers of the Republic, I found myself obliged to seek work abroad," Mario lied.

The governor's eyes seemed to observe everything and reflect absolutely nothing of his own inner thoughts. The stare made Mario uncomfortable.

"There is a hospital down the road from here, I'll have my factor assure you a position there." He said after a time. "Have you any experience as a martial surgeon?"

"I'm not a surgeon, Sir," Mario blushed. "I'm a physician."

Physicians were students of the body's humours and God's compositions of life. They would rarely see their patients, they would delicately look at a vial of urine and diagnose an ailment. Surgeons were one part butcher and one part folk healer. Calling a physician a surgeon was roughly analogous to calling an architect a builder.

"Pity. We'll be needing surgeons soon enough," he replied dryly before turning to Vincent. "And the meeting?"

"As you suspected, Karian, Noah and also Pazzi," Vincent answered. "It's a good bet that they've confirmed the project to our north. It's possible they know more than us, Genoese spies have always had further access into the Sultan's court than ours."

"And what about the priest?"

"He's still there. If you want, we could remedy that this afternoon."

"No, that would be too vulgar for their sentiments. The Emperor has promised to replace him with our man, but he's put off that obligation for too long. He's allowed him to poison the mob against union, and against us. I'll remind our friends that he needs to be removed as soon as possible."

"Yes, Sir," Vincent answered.

"There certainly are a great many priests and monks here," Mario joked.

"Yes, there are," the governor answered instantly. "Do you have any particularly strong religious convictions, Doctor?"

"I seek truth, where it may be found, but I'm not dogmatic," Mario answered delicately.

"Good. This city will burn while its residents discuss dual-nature and triple-aspect theology," Cardillo showed a touch of emotion for the first time in the meeting. "Is there anything else that we need to discuss, Commander?"

"No, Governor."

"Good. You may go then. Doctor, stay."

Vincent bowed and left them.

"Come with me, Doctor," the governor instructed Mario.

Mario obeyed and followed him into the garden.

"I have a problem, Doctor," Cardillo seemed about as though he were not nervous, but uncomfortable to admit something to a stranger. "I feel tired. Not only at night, and not only when I wake up, but all day. I don't trust the doctors here, they're mystics, not men of science."

"I see." Mario listened intently. "Are you sleeping at night?"

"Yes, if it was a lack of sleep, I'd understand, but this seems like there might be something wrong with me, medically," he answered the foolishly mundane question.

"You look pale, do you eat enough meat?" Mario's face contorted in thought as he questioned his new patient.

"I believe so."

"Galen and Aristotle both teach us that good health comes from keeping the four humours of blood, phlegm, black and yellow bile in harmonious levels. When those balances are upset, illness ensues. I think that you probably have over-abundance of phlegm and yellow bile, and a lack of clean blood," Mario announced. "Tell your cook that you need to eat lightly cooked meat, at breakfast, lunch and dinner. I'll bring over a compound to help your body clear itself of phlegm. It will purge your stomach and bowels, so you should drink it in a tea an hour or so before every meal."

"Thank you, Doctor. I hope that helps."

"It certainly should. If it doesn't help after a week, I'd like to examine your urine. I have a crystal bottle that can help with that."

"Thank you, Doctor. I'm sure that it won't be necessary," Don Giovanni said with a note of closure. "Now, I must excuse myself. As I said earlier, my factor will make an arrangement for you at the hospital near here, and when he's made such an arrangement, he'll find you staying at Commander DiCastillo's villa."

"Thank you for your patronage, Don Giovanni."

"It's my pleasure to help any friend of Raphael Avruham."

"I'm deeply indebted to you both then."

Chapter Fifteen - The Riot

Light flowed in through the long and tall windows and under the floating dome of the Cathedral of Holy Wisdom. The sanctuary of the cathedral was uncharacteristically packed for this special occasion. Today was neither Easter nor Christmas, Epiphany nor Pentecost; today was the final service of a priest beloved by the city. The details surrounding his early retirement were sketchy to most of those in attendance, but between the stone walls and floating alongside the burning incense was an unshakeable faith in God, and in the man who had led the flock of Constantinople for the last fifteen years. He had rallied the city through civil strife and through a siege that many believed was the arrival of the anti-Christ.

The aging cleric stood before the altar and looked out over the masses in attendance.

'*The moment of truth,*' he thought to himself as readied himself for what was to be the most important sermon of his life. It was to be short and to the point

"My friends," he began slowly and quietly. "Today, the faithful are again besieged by the tyranny of the faithless. We have no valour of David, nor wisdom of Solomon enthroned to protect us. Instead, we are ruled by Herod, who breaks bread with the Romans and oppresses his own countrymen."

He let the magnitude of his opening remark sneak in alongside the sunshine and settle among those in bulging attendance.

"We all know that to the north of us, the legions of the anti-Christ muster and prepare once again to wage their unending war against those who refuse to break faith with God. We also know that Herod has paid ransom and tribute to them, and allowed them to settle in lands where the cross has been carried for over a millenium. We know that Christians have given ground for centuries to the advancing horde and fled in the face of their idolatrous tyranny.

"But we see not only sorrow, but hope among us as well. And hope can sustain the mightiest empire or the humblest man. For within the walls of our city, we have always kept the faith," the walls seemed to close off the wilderness so that all that existed was the present communion of the faithful. "We have always honoured the covenant between God and humanity. God promised Abraham that if he kept the faith, his seed would prosper. God promised Noah that he and his family would survive if they remained true. God promised Moses redemption to a sinful tribe and through Jesus, the redemption and protection of all humanity. That hope kept us.

"Jesus promised to humanity salvation for those who refused to waver. From Jesus that promise went to Peter, and from Peter, the bishops of Rome and then of the New Rome. We pray to God in thanksgiving for this patronage and protection, and we thank every man in this city for never wavering, even when the most voracious barbarians came to our gates. It has been because of this unyielding loyalty to God, that God has been unyieldingly loyal to us."

"But now that loyalty is under attack. And from this attack, no Legion, *tagmata* or *stratiotes* can defend us. There are those here, who believe that we can be saved by abandoning our unbroken loyalty. That by accepting western heresies as our equals, we will receive their favours. This temptation, my friends, is folly. Union is now as sinful as when it was first proposed," Gennadios took a deep breath. "For their faith is false, and it is they that must amend their ways. We should not abandon our brothers and sisters to hellfire, but that doesn't mean that we should join them in sin. When we abandon correct thought, we abandon our walls, our armour, our swords and our spears. We will do the Turk's job for him if we bend!"

At the back of the mass, a cowled monk observed with loathing and apprehension what he knew was about to transpire. The crowd was getting rambunctious, this pleased the demagoguerous cleric immensely.

"It is no secret that the mass today is to be my last. Because of my opposition to the faithless, Herod has ordered my execution." This was not actually true, as the Emperor had ordered him into a soft exile in Athens. "We think of the sacrifices made by the early church fathers. And we wonder if the time came, would we be able to stand against the tyranny of oppression and say '*do your worst, kill me if you must, but my faith will remain standing!*' My heart is strengthened today, for I know that there are some in this city who will say this! Who will not abandon their faith, who will not abandon their walls, who will not abandon their swords and spears! There are those who say *'Come what may, I will not abandon you, O God, and I know that you will not abandon me!*

"As you leave this cathedral this morning, I ask you to look at the agents of Herod in our midst. I ask you to look in your hearts and I ask you remember the martyrs. Remember all those who have died for over fourteen hundred years, to preserve us. I pray that my service to God has been beneficial, and I pray that my service to you has been strong, and that you keep the faith that has preserved you for so long. As you leave this cathedral of stone, I ask you to remember that the cathedrals of your heart, in all of you, is more unshakeable than stone, and stronger than the whims of Caesars. This I truly pray, in Jesus' name, Amen."

Isodore could sense the potential for violence that had been raised by the priest's farewell address. The monk was the first man out of the cathedral and he went straight to the local Venetian garrison.

Blachernae Palace faced the Sea of Marmara and was home to the Roman Emperor. It was also home and office to a staff of six hundred servants, dozens upon dozens of courtiers, and their staffs. A curious thing about many of the elite courtiers of the all but conquered empire was that they possessed ranks without lands. The proconsul of Brussa, for example, was a man named Stavros. Stavros was quite proud of title of *Anthypatos*, even though Brussa itself had been conquered by the Turks in 1326, almost a century before his birth. Despite this, the proconsul was a respected noble at court and he looked at the sight of foreign interlopers in their midst as a necessary evil.

The men of the court at Blachernae glanced uneasily at the unusual sight of Giovanni Cardillo. The governor of the Venetian Quarter stood among those gathered that morning and garnered the attention and whispers of all by his appearance. All the nobles of the court dressed in the traditional black coats and white coverings of the Empire. They wore undyed cloth tunics, hanging colourlessly under their black coats – hardly practical summer-wear. Cardillo dressed in the fashion of Renaissance Italy, with a flourished collection of tassels, scarves, ribbons and pendants adorning his clothes. Instead of the traditional black hat of the court, his head was covered only by his brown hair.

Despite his audacious appearance, he was typically the most silent member of the court. His silence today was brought on not by his natural stoicism, but by an earthly malady that had afflicted him ever since the doctor first gave him that compound a month ago. Since then, he'd been sleeping fine, but he was constantly in a state where he was discharging copious amounts of unwanted matter. While none of the gathered harpies could see his discomfort, his belly groaned in protest to every movement

Today, he arrived on a summons from Emperor Constantine, and waited outside the Emperor's private office with the other noblemen of the court. They looked at him. They pointed and whispered. They giggled at his strange appearance and bizarre manners. Cardillo could only smile at their attitude. *'This empire is collapsing, and handful of modern cities divide the capital and now play king-maker. Yet they still believe that they are the centre of the civilized world and I'm the barbarian in their midst.'* The governor shook his head in smiling frustration.

A guard crossed the floor of the audience chamber and approached the oddly dressed foreigner. "The emperor summons you, Don Giovanni."

Giovanni Cardillo nodded but said nothing. The assembled elites looked on in suspicion, even the proconsul of Brussa. The thought of some provincial yokel being given a private audience was a shameful thing in his eyes. Giovanni followed the guard out of the audience chamber while the other notables watched on in envy. He said nothing as he walked out of the hall, down the red-stone corridor, and into the centre of the universe, the private meeting room of Constantine the eleventh, the emperor of Rome.

"Ambassador," the proconsul nodded as Giovanni passed by. He had a nose that seemed built for staring down at people with.

"Proconsul," Cardillo answered back. He was meticulous about using the proper titles, as it amused him greatly, how seriously they took their empty titles.

The room was made of the same red-brick as the rest of the palace. It was dominated by a giant oaken table and golden icons covered the walls. A huge window of rose tinted glass gave a feeling of perpetual dusk to the room. Two men dressed in the fashion of the court were speaking to each other as the governor entered.

The Emperor had been a strongly built man in his youth and his frame kept its size, but his physical mass had turned to waste. His kindly eyes and temperate nature made him beloved by the average Constantinopolitan, but did nothing to impress the shark-like Italian.

"Hello, Your Majesty," the governor said bowing formally. "I pray you are well."

"Thanks to God I am," replied the elder of the two men. "You remember Adam Karian, commander of the legions."

Adam Karian was a man of slightly above average height, though he had a slightly overweight face that incongruously managed to make him seem shorter than he really was. He had a full head of curly black hair and he wore the black coat and white waistcoat of the court. The only thing to distinguish his rank was the purple sash that ran over his right shoulder and down to his left hip. This alone identified him as the *strateogos*, the supreme commander of the non-existent legions.

"I do, it's good to see you again so soon, General. I wish the circumstances were different."

Adam's serious face nodded gravely in acknowledgement.

"I've summoned you here to discuss the current state of things." The emperor began. "You've heard, I presume, that the Mohammedans are mustering an army in Adrianople, and a fleet at Thessalonica?"

"I have, Your Majesty. I've also heard of a fleet at Varna, on the Black Sea, and a regiment of Janissaries along the northern Bosporus."

"It is about this that I want to speak to you today."

"That's what I imagined."

"The sultan has rallied an army of about fifty thousand men, including Janissaries and mercenaries, as well as local and tribal allies and levies from Anatolia," Adam stated.

"Really? Our spies put it a little higher than that, General," the governor replied. "This *Mehmet* has sent agents all over Anatolia, Sire. And not just to nobles and chieftains. They send dervishes and spies to recruit from Sufi lodges and local garrisons all over Asia Minor and the Balkans. They're recruiting and conscripting not just Turkish tribesmen and townsmen. They are drawing also upon the subject kingdoms Serbia, Macedonia and Bulgaria. They'll field more Christians than you at their current rate. We believe that they'll attack the city in a year's time. When the snows are gone, and the mud has dried. We anticipate next spring."

"No Christians will attack this city. They will suffer martyrdom before forced into such vulgar servitude," the emperor looked across the table. "How many men do you think they will be able to call to force?"

"My informants suggest anywhere between eighty and a hundred and fifty thousand men, Sire. It's impossible to guess accurately as to how well the recruiting will go over the summer and into the winter."

"They could never get so many! The tribes would never put everything they have behind a child!" Adam retorted.

"General, I believe that there's more to this child than his years would tell," was the only answer that the governor could think to say. He sniffled and wiped his face before he could continue. "Emperor, they intend to uproot the tree of Rome once and for all."

"They'll find a surprise when they hit these walls," Constantine said looking out the window of his private chamber.

"Yes, Sire, and that surprise will be about three thousand Italian mercenaries, one thousand local militia and two thousand support troops, if you decide to continue our stay. A pleasant surprise that would be to such an overwhelming oceanic tide of an army. Have you had any luck recruiting any more mercenaries, or training locals?"

"That costs money," the emperor looked a little embarrassed. "Right now, we've taxed the populace beyond its maintenance. Our tariffs aren't what they once were because of those *pimps* in Galata eating up our trade. We've scraped the gold off of almost every icon left in the city to pay for the defences that we do have. Have you spoken to the doge?"

"I have."

"And?"

"Venice will underwrite your loans until you can repay them, Sire, but you know the condition."

"I've met your condition! We have agreed to recognize the western churches!"

"You haven't recognised the Holy Father, Emperor."

"You press us too hard, Cardillo! I've alienated the clergy enough to get as far as we have already!" Constantine had to fight himself not to yell. "We carry more than fourteen centuries of traditions in our liturgies and our prayers, and you would have us forsake this for blood money from the west in our time of need! What you ask is extortion, do you hear me!? Extortion!"

"Sire, please… if our offer causes you so much offence, then it would sadden me to take it off the table, but the Senate of Venice will never finance the Eastern Empire as long as it remains…" Cardillo quickly thought of a word to replace *'heretical'*. "…independent of the See of Rome."

"We *are* the See of Rome! We inherit the redemption! Not them!"

"Yet you allow Rome to be publicly ridiculed and disparaged in the streets of Constantinople, and by the Metropolitan thereof in the solemn Cathedral of Holy Wisdom!"

Constantine's blood stayed up. "This is not Italy, Don Giovanni. I cannot simply remove the patriarch from office without repercussions. These things move slowly."

"There are ways to speed that sort of thing up."

"Again, I say, this is not Italy. I can't have him killed in the middle of the night. Thank you for the reminder of our differing religious traditions," the emperor regained his composure. "I have removed Gennadios from his office. Tomorrow he will go into exile, and his replacement will take over. Noah's much more affable and will do as he's commanded."

"A good lamb indeed, but one who's not preaching today. This is an invitation to a disaster."

"He understands what's going on, he won't cause much trouble."

Adam cringed to himself as the words came out of the emperor's mouth. The silent regret was not lost on the Venetian envoy. Karian's distaste and distrust of the Metropolitan had become far too public for the taste of many at court. It was known and documented outside the court as well, as every street-cleaner and olive-presser knew that the general hated the priest.

"You disagree with the emperor, General?" Cardillo asked, bringing the gesticulation to Constantine's attention.

"The Emperor knows how I feel about the metropolitan," Adam answered. "What he's asking of you is whether or not Venice can contribute to the defence of Christendom once the Turks attack."

"Sire," he began, turning his attention back to the Emperor, "We will support our brother Christians, as long as you support union. With gold and with blood, but we fear that this city may be a lost cause, unless you tie your banner to our standard."

At this Adam had to protest.

"You were not here when they attacked last time! Fifty thousand of them charged these walls, with all their rage and hate and lust, but we held for true. Where are the walls now? They're where they've always been. Where are we? We're still here? Where are the hordes? They went back home to cry to their mothers that the heartless Christians wouldn't roll over and allow themselves to be buried alive! Lost causes in the eyes of some men are not always lost causes in the eyes of God!"

"That's true, I came here after the siege was lifted," the governor admitted. "But you may also recall that they lifted the siege when your kinsman, *Your Majesty*, capitulated on behalf of the attackers. They were here as mercenaries in a local war of succession, and their numbers were much smaller then. Now they come to topple Christendom, as they see it. They believe this city is lined with gold ready for the plunder, and that every infidel that climbs over those grand walls will find paradise in this world or the next when they get to the others side."

There was a knock at the door and the room fell silent. A guard was allowed in and whispered into the emperor's ear. The emperor took a deep breath upon receiving the message.

"I'm sorry, but there seems to be a situation in the Venetian Quarter," his eyes narrowed. "It seems that a riot of all things is breaking out."

Cardillo blinked. "May I be excused, Your Majesty?"

"You may."

Giovanni walked quickly out of the palace, feeling even worse than before.

Two footmen walked along the concourse to the hippodrome. It hadn't been repaired for several seasons, and suffered from the wear and tear of the elements and the earthquakes to which the city had always been exposed. The soldiers walked northwards towards Holy Wisdom on that beautiful Sunday morning, enjoying the sun and the birds in the trees on their rather routine patrol of the Quarter. Ahead of them, they could see the crowd coming out of the building after the mass.

By the time they turned the corner eastward around the elongated rectangle of the hippodrome, they could see that the crowd was definitely in an angry mood.

"What do you think is wrong with them?" Marco asked Primo.

"I don't know, but they don't look happy," Primo answered.

They kept about their rounds as the men of the crowd started to draw closer. Marco waved politely and smiled at the crowd, trying to appear friendly. "Keep walking." He said under his breath. "We should tell the boss that the locals seem to be a little worked up today."

"Try not to seem nervous," Primo replied.

The crowd closed in on the two Venetian mercenaries on their patrol. Some of them blocked the soldier's pathway, some clustered behind them, and the majority was to their northern flank, coming out of their church, the soldier's southern flank was blocked by one of the hippodrome's imperfectly preserved walls.

"What seems to be the trouble?" Primo called out.

"*Eh, Kariolis!*" one of the crowd shouted at the guards. "*Pare mu ena tsibuki!*"

"How's your Greek?" Marco asked Primo.

"Good enough to know that's not their way of saying '*hello*'."

"What do we do now?"

"Do you see that archway into the hippodrome? We'll step into there, and keep them at a bottleneck. I'll fire my harquebus, which should summon more of the guards. We can't exactly disperse this group ourselves."

"Sounds fine to me."

The guard's walkway graced the entrance to the hippodrome. The red-stone flat wall of the base stretched high into the sky and wide along the road. Decorating the front wall were soaring archways and states of saints and emperors. The sight was impressive, but was doing little to intimidate the crowd, who was growing more and more restless.

More catcalls came from the angry crowd. Enzo recognised the look in the eyes of the rioters. They were trying to psyche themselves up to attack. Even though they were over a hundred, and the guards were only two, they were still afraid but didn't want to let that show. With no leaders as of yet, they would be slow to move, but once it started, they would be difficult to stop.

Once the two guards were in front of the stone archway, Primo unslung his harquebus. A harquebus is a long-barrelled hand cannon, brutal at short range, and intended to punch holes in a crowd or enemy company. It had only one shot in it, and it would seem wasteful to discharge it into the air, especially as an act of retreat, so Primo quickly turned around at looked for the biggest man in the crowd.

Powooooooooosh! The hand-cannon fired, a man dropped, and the two soldiers drove into the deep archway. Their rear protected, they each drew a sword in their left hands and top-heavy clubs in their rights. The crowd could only come into the gateway three abreast at a time, and the two guards were more than capable of handling two-on-three-odds against an unarmed Sunday mob. They just had to keep the mob at bay until the rest of their company arrived.

The swords and clubs kept the mass away for a minute, but it wasn't to last. There were some children in the crowd who had the brilliant idea of picking up rocks from the ground, and throwing them at the two. The guards threw commands at the crowd to disperse and the crowd began throwing rocks in return.

The throwing of rocks gave an anonymity to their attack. No one could tell where the small projectiles were coming from, only that they were coming.

"We've got to fall back, come on Marco!" Primo said. The two ran back through the deep archway into the sandy hippodrome.

Inside the grand stadium were antique monuments and derelict men. The centre was a wide open space with two obelisks marking the curving ends of the horse track. The building also served as a sleeping spot for the drunks and homeless of the city. Old men, young children and a few stray dogs looked up sleepily at the melee that entered the floor. Marco couldn't help but think that the spectacle bore a certain similarity to the days of the old Roman Empire, with the crowds watching a gladiator show of a different sort.

The crowd rushed in behind the retreating guards. One boy, he couldn't have been much older that twelve, rushed to the front of the crowd and charged Marco. The guard swung his club faster than most people could see and the boy fell with the violence of a roughly shattered amphora. The guards kept retreating.

"Should we run to the far exit?"

"Don't drop your weapons, we'll still need them, RUN!" The two guards turned and bolted, weapons in hand, to the far exit at the other end of the raceway.

Into the fading glories of the forum charged the Greek urban mass. It felt like a scene out of antiquity. The triumphal mob felt the blood of Plataea in their veins, driving off the invaders once again. The broken down stands stole back their lustre and the lethargic drunks in the stands were transformed into the nobility of the grand days of old. The mob cheered. Their gladiators were victorious. The banners of the reds, the whites, the greens and the blues could be imagined by all, hoisting their glory for an empire whose glory could never die. The invaders run, they always do! The Persians! The Bulgars! The Serbs! The Turks were turned back before, and they would be turned back again! Now the Italians flee!

This glorious euphoria lasted for twenty minutes of songs and slogans. After which time, the Venetian guard mustered in front of the Hippodrome, and charged what was left of the ancient complex. Seventeen rioters were killed, and almost a hundred injured. The rest fled into the Quarter. They would be unable to escape back to Greek Constantinople, as Vincent had ordered the stockades and gates closed to all locals.

News of the riot and massacre spread quickly over the city, and by mid-afternoon, the city was in an uproar. Kill the foreigners! The Roman idolaters have no place in the house of God! Bring back our father! Our priest is loyal to God and the people! No to Union! We don't accept heresy as orthodoxy, nor heretics as brothers! The city shut all its gates and harbours, and tried to contain the riot underway.

Vincent ran into his villa in the Venetian Quarter. He found Ella and Daria in the reclining chairs of the sitting room, where he expected them to be. To his surprise, he found his houseguest there chatting with them. Mario saw the commander enter the room and stood up immediately. He had a very guilty look on his face. Vincent ignored him at first.

"Girls, go and pack quickly. A riot has broken out. Quickly get whatever you absolutely need, and let's go. I've spoken to Ezera, he's going to bring you two across to Galata."

The girls looked shocked, and seemed about to question him, but a quick glance told them to hurry up. When the girls went upstairs, Vincent turned his attention quickly to Mario.

"The ship is open to you as well, if you need it. I'll give you this purse, you'll need money. Don't leave the harbour, wait there. It's too dangerous to leave the protection of the capital.

"Thank you, Don Vincent," Mario felt like a child who'd been caught with his hand in the cookie jar and hoped that Vincent didn't suspect his motives towards Ella.

"Spare me the honorifics. Your hospital is near Contoscalion Harbour on the Marmara, we're going the opposite direction, you can't collect any of your goods, and you're going to the Genoese district. I don't want any surprises, only obedience, do you understand?"

Mario nodded.

"Good," Vincent jogged over to the stairs and yelled up. "Girls! Now! This isn't a holiday!"

The girls came rushing down the stairs with a hastily packed bag apiece. Vincent and five of his guards took them to Proshorianus Harbour, where Mario first arrived a short month ago, and left them at the city gate.

"Mario, you know where the Nineveh is, get them on board, and light a fire under Ezera to make sure he's quick about it. Go!"

"Yes, Sir. Thanks again."

Vincent didn't glance to return Mario's thanks. Instead, he kissed his wife and his sister goodbye and turned back into the city to set about the task of returning order to the Quarter.

Vincent and five of his guards kicked down the door to the rectory next to Holy Wisdom and poured in like the wind. Immediately behind the door was a rather shocked nun.

"Where is he?" shouted Vincent. "Where is that motherless dog who calls himself a priest?"

The nun turned to run but was cut down immediately by Vincent's boot colliding with the small of her back. Before she could get back up, he was atop her. He pressed her head against the marble floor and leant over her and Vincent repeated himself.

"Where is he?"

The nun began frantically praying in Greek.

"He's in the study!" came Isodore's unseen voice from behind the soldiers.

Vincent hopped over the sprawled nun and his guards followed him to the back. There he found a small chapel with wooden walls and a small altar. The priest was there instructing two young aspirants in the cosmogony of life.

A startled priest looked up from a conversation with two younger priests. "What's the meaning of this?"

Vincent paid no attention to his words and stormed up to the enraged cleric.

'*A simple man, to be dissuaded by simple words*,' the metropolitain thought to himself. "You will control yourself right now! This is a house of God!"

Without stopping, Vincent quickened his pace towards Gennadios. Once he was close enough to the old man, he raised his hands slightly to his side, as if to attack him. The priest flinched his own hands to the side, and Vincent head-butted strait upon his brow. The old man fell back into a bookcase.

"Arrest those two!" Vincent said, pointing at the two shocked younger priests. "Take them out of here, now!"

Gennadios tried to stand but Vincent kicked him in the side as he tried. Vincent's shin collided with the priest's rib-cage, and the sixty-year-old felt his breath escape his body. The priest found himself on the floor again, inhaling hurt.

Vincent grabbed the prone man's wrist and rolled him over, lifting his arm. He put his foot behind Gennadios' shoulder and levered his arm, forcing Gennadios onto his aching belly. The attacker leaned over his victim, putting all his weight on the foot above Gennadios shoulder blade, pressuring his arm at the joint. "Now, the only reason that I won't kill you is because you are going to tell all of your angry little followers to stop their little riot and accept the way things are. If you don't, you will spend the remainder of your rapidly shortening life-span in the kind of excruciating pain you've since only read about."

"I'm prepared to die!"

"Good!" Vincent pressured the priest's shoulder in its socket by simply shifting his weight. "Now, we're going to take you to my friend in the tower, and he's going to show you some hot things. And sharp things. And hot sharp things."

Gennadios grimaced in pain, but refused to scream. Vincent landed a backhanded fist onto the clergyman's ear. His eyes seemed dizzy, but he refused to cry out. Vincent did it again and the man lost consciousness.

It was a nervous Gennadios who found himself in the private audience chamber of Emperor Constantine XI, facing not the Emperor of Rome, but his lieutenant. An angry and dark man with curly hair and a purple sash over his shoulder..

"I'm glad to hear that you weren't mistreated, Metropolitan," Adam said with a sneering smile.

Gennadios looked up at the general. Water dripped from his left eye. He wasn't crying, but his tear duct had ruptured during his arrest and hadn't stopped flowing for almost an hour – dehydration had long since set in. He glared at the Armenian through his bloodshot eyes.

"What do you want?" the old man asked.

"We want you to call off the insurrection," the general said without intonation.

"I don't see what I can do about it."

"You started this debacle, and you're going to end it, before more people get killed," he ordered.

"They aren't rioting because I told them to, Adam Karian." Gennadios insisted. "They are upset because of the state of affairs among the faithful!"

"The state of the faithful is a dismal one!" answered the general angrily. "We are besieged from the north, east, south and west. We cannot muster enough soldiers to enforce our own horizons! Without help from the west, the empire will fall! Is that what you want? The Muslim call to prayer echoing from Holy Wisdom, convents will be turned into brothels, palaces into stables and churches into mosques! Is this what you hope to accomplish? Because if it is, then bravo, priest! Your aspirations for the Church of Christ are obviously incompatible with my own.”

“Obviously, Sir,” he wiped some water painfully from his bruised cheek. “I hope that someday they will be compatible.”

“What do you want?” demanded Adam.

“What do I want?” asked the priest incredulously. “What I want is irrelevant. What God wants is what is relevant, and those desires are quite vividly spelt out in the scriptures. Compromise with heretics for political convenience is not mentioned.”

“But subjugation to infidels features prominently?”

“There are, regrettably, many precedents for that,” he sadly conceded.

“I suppose you would consider the Paeleologi to be the new Hasmoneans?”

“I don’t presume to guess God’s plan for me, Soldier,” he answered back with an obvious show of disgust. “The only way this city will stop rioting, is by the return of God’s rules over those of some petty earthly viceroy.”

“You mean by your own interpretation of God’s will!” shouted Karian.

“I have the advantage of siding with God, General,” the priest replied with contempt. “It is you who chooses to find yourself standing in opposition to that authority.”

“Shepherd, I am ordering you to call off the civil unrest personally. You will have to walk around the afflicted areas, proclaiming the restoration of order, and telling the hooligans to go home.”

“I can do that on behalf of the church, only if concordance is restored. I need to hear that from the Emperor’s lips, not yours.”

“And how would that happen, may I ask?” Karian replied with veiled sarcasm. “By purchasing a new cathedral, your restoration to the court?”

“It can happen only with the death of union,” the priest answered. “If we are no longer a Christian city, then it is not worth defending, General. I can think of nothing that would encourage the Muslims more, than what we are doing right now. They are sitting by the harbours in Scutari and Chalcedon, and watching the city tear itself apart. I beg you, Karian, convince the emperor, commit to the restoration of order with honour, and I will do everything in my power to help him."

"And give up any hope of assistance from the West?"

"They will never help. You know this. Their words are always sweet, but they trade with the Turk, they dine with the Turk, the Sultan of the Turks was educated by Italians in the City of Hadrian. Constantinople is the standard bearer of Christ, and we will stand or fall on our own. Our friends will give us generosity only in their promises. You are trading the blood and bodies of the faithful, for the promises of heretics. No merchant would tip the scales at such a one-sided deal! Why do you think I would do so, then!"

General Karian was silent as he mulled over the potential consequences.

Seeing the opening, Gennadios pressed his case. "General, I promise to do everything I can to support His Majesty personally. We have had our differences over the past three years: since he was crowned illegally in Mystra by the Morean despot and you both support Noah over myself, but this is in the past. Please, Adam, I beg you as a Christian, if we abandon union, and if he takes the sword of our ancestors, I will personally replace the crown upon his head in the belly of the Cathedral of Holy Wisdom and have every priest in every church, cathedral, chapel and shrine tell every man who's even close to fighting age to take up arms. Not just here in the city, and not across a conquered empire, but across the Christian world, from Greece to Russia and from Egypt to Syria, to Armenia and Serbia. I implore you, General, pick up the spear that pierced our lord and wield it against his enemies. Our relationship has been a terribly destructive one for the empire, but if you steel yourself and his majesty to this cause, I promise you, our friendship can send this horde back to Asia and the heretics back to Italy. I promise you!"

"Everyone's got lots of promises these days."

In a far off corner of the Emperor's office, a curtain drew back slightly, and the face of the emperor Constantine could be discerned by Adam's eyes. Constantine nodded to inform his general that he was to accept the priest's offer, and then he disappeared again behind the curtain. Karian made no movement to acknowledge what he'd witnessed. All he needed to do was obey.

"You've nothing left to lose," Gennadios insisted.

Adam eyed the stubborn cleric in front of him. He nodded slowly, then turned his gaze to the window.

"The emperor accepts your offer for now."

The words squeezed joylessly out of his mouth.

"That's all I needed to hear."

Chapter Sixteen - The Island

"**W**elcome aboard the Nineveh, ladies," Ezera greeted Ella and Daria as Mario guided them through the crowds of the harbour. "Welcome back, Don Mario."

"Thank you, Captain Ezera," Daria answered as the she navigated the slats to climb onto the Galley. Her awkward canter was reinforced by what was now the obvious fact of her pregnancy. She held her globular belly as she staggered up the runner onto the boat with far more dexterity than would be expected.

"Yes, thank you very much," added Ella as she did the same but with an un-pregnant grace.

"Hello again, Captain," Mario greeted the Catalan with a smile. He would call Ezera by his first name on land, but aboard his ship, calling him anything but Captain was an invitation to disaster. "We need to get out of here as quickly as possible, the Quarter is erupting."

"I know, we got back this morning and everything was peaceful. Everything seems to have happened in the past couple hours or so," Ezera noted fairly apathetically. "Don't worry, Doctor, Ladies. You're all aboard the great ship Nineveh, we just got back from the Crimea and arrived just in time for the show. How've you been?"

"Good," Mario felt a little strange stepping back onto the boat that had been his home for so many weeks. "It feels heavier."

"It is, we're hauling timber!" Ezera answered. "We didn't have time to unload or find a buyer, so it's still weighing down our hold. We'll be a little unwieldy crossing the harbour to Galata, but it's nothing we can't handle."

"It's good to see you again," Mario slapped Ezera on the back. "What can I do?"

"Help the ladies downstairs into your old cabin. We don't want them getting in the way, then come on back up here. We'll need some help spotting."

"I won't be a minute."

Mario carefully navigated Ella and Daria down the step ladder to the quarters and put them both in his old room.

"It smells awful!" Ella complained.

"Well, that's true, but there isn't much that can be done to fix that just yet. If you both just wait here, we should be able to moor the ship in the Galata harbour and then find an inn or someplace within an hour or so." Mario assured her. "We'll be out of this as soon as we can."

The two ladies acquiesced, no small feat for Daria, who was quite unused to having her fate outside of her own hands. When they were within their acceptable limits of comfort, Mario excused himself and joined the crew that was preparing to row across the harbour. On his way up the ladder the ship rocked and Mario lost his footing. There was a thunderous hammer sound that echoed in the ship.

'*We've hit something*,' Mario thought to himself, and he could hear swearing on the foredeck.

When he was back on deck, he could see the crew of the Nineveh shouting at the crew of a sailing ship next to them. The other ship had been pulling off of the dock and collided with the Nineveh while she was still tied to the dock. The crews of the respective ships were casting out swears at each other trying to assign blame.

"Bloody Vikings!" Ezera shouted at them. "Stick to the rivers and leave seas and harbour to those who know how to sail them!"

Mario trembled at the sight of the brawny northerners in the guilty ship and wasn't so sure that the Nineveh's crew was wise to risk provoking a fight with them.

Ezera and a handful of oarsmen charged over and struck side of the offending ship with long prods and hit the other ship like a phalanx, pushing it away from them, and the Norse river ship did the same, all the while cursing at each other.

"Take one of those gaffs!" Ezera called out to Mario. "I want your help on this! This is going to be a rough sea day."

"The what?" Mario called over the hurly burly of the collision.

"The gaff-pole – the God-damned stick! Take one of those sticks!"

Mario helped and the Viking Longship was pushed out into the harbour to follow her own course. It was only now that Mario looked out at the Golden Horne, and realised just how busy it was. All of the ships that had been anchored on the Constantinople side were now fleeing into the much smaller, and already more full, harbour of Galata.

"How are we going to cross this?" Mario asked himself. The harbour wasn't very wide, but it was crowded, there was limited space on the other side, and the Nineveh was weighted down past the point where it was still capable of aqua-batics.

Ezera eventually got the ship far enough away from the dock to turn her around and make for the far side. They kept their sails unfurled and navigated by oar to secure a spot at the harbour. This was, of course, a fool's errand. There was nowhere near enough room for all of the ships that were looking for safe mooring.

"Shouldn't we cast down the anchor and wait for a ferryman to take us to shore?" Mario asked Ezera.

"No," the Catalan bit tongue and tied back his unkept hair. "We'll be waiting here for days if we do that, and I don't want to wait until the smoke clears. We'll sail up the Bosporus a bit."

"What?" Mario asked nervously and then gained momentum. "There's a Turkish castle on the Northern Bosporus. I know this because you told me so! Vincent told me to be protective of the girls!"

"We won't go anywhere that far north, just up to Diplokion. It's a small fishing village at the opening of the strait. We can anchor there and head ashore."

"Wouldn't it be safer to wait here?"

"No, it wouldn't," Ezera answered quickly. "We're at the entrance of the harbour, most exposed to the elements. Everyone is going to leave the harbour, because they'll want to escape from this over-crowding, so everyone'll be trying to get past us. We'll be hit, rammed and jigged by almost every ship on its way out, and the Nineveh is a tough old girl, but she's too heavy to deal with that today."

Ezera stood on the forecastle and started yelling at his crew in Catalan, a language of which neither Mario, Ella nor Daria had much knowledge. And with that, the Nineveh turned to the north-east and began the long row past Galata.

"Look, Mario. A nice quiet fishing village. What a nice place to spend an afternoon." Ezera joked as the sight of Diplokion finally emerged round the hub past Galata's walls.

"Captain!" Gaspar the coxswain called in Catalan.

"I see!" Ezera yelled back, his voice drawing to whisper. "Curse our cargo.”

“What’s wrong?” Mario asked.

“Over there, coming out of the strait.” Ezera pointed at the watery opening between the hills of Thrace and the corresponding hills of Bithynia. “It’s a Fustae.”

“A what?”

“A scout ship, small and lightly armed. Their usually messengers.” Ezera answered back. “Damn that cargo! If we were lighter we could take her!”

“Is it a Turkish ship?”

“Yes, they’re usually weighed down only with gold and a crew readied for diplomacy and courier service rather than fighting. A grand prize if you catch one. What’s it doing this close to the city?”

“It’s heading to Chalcedon,” Mario observed. “Maybe you could unload us and the lumber at Diplokion and try to catch them on their way home.”

“That’s a fine idea, but impractical. Damn the riot! Oh well. If there’d been no riot, I’d be trying to sell the cargo right now. We wouldn’t have been able to catch him anyway. I…”

“Captain!” Gaspar hollered back.

Mario, Ezera, Gaspar and the crew of the Nineveh looked on as another ship emerged from the strait, and then another, and another.

“Three more ships… Fustae you called them?” Mario noted.

“Fustae?” Gaspar asked sarcastically, and then began yammering in his own tongue.

“What the distinguished Don Gaspar means to say is that those are not scout ships, Doctor. Those are triremes – three-galley warships.” Ezera then started barking orders in the ship’s native language and everyone responded immediately by manning the oars and turning the ship. Others began to ready the sails and others still began to mount the crow’s nests.

“Damn that cargo, we’re too heavy!” Ezera cursed to himself.

“Can we outrun them?”

“Not indefinitely, but they probably won’t pursue us, three ships wouldn’t give any consideration to the folly of attacking so near the Capital, there are hundreds of ships there ready for war,” Ezera answered. “If we weren’t bogged down with cargo and guests, we’d be attacking them now. Take the four ships back in tow to the Golden Horne."

"Your ship would attack four?" Mario questioned dubiously.

"Don't abandon trust just yet, Doctor. Those ships are captained by men whose only qualifications to sea are that they have the wealth to have ships built. Their sailors are tribesmen who've probably never been off land in their lives. The Nineveh's captured twelve ships in seven battles over the years, and have been paid a good bounty for each. Certainly much more than the pay we'll get for the lumber or passengers.

"There's no real comparison between our seamanship and theirs, Mario," he continued. "Look at how weighted down they are, even with our holds full, our deck would still be above theirs. Their crow's-nests are too small to store arrows and javelins for martial purposes. Even now, when we're too laid down to properly maneuver, and though we'd be horrifically outnumbered, we'd still expect a victory. Turks fear the sea, any place they can't ride a horse. They'd probably try to outrun us."

"So how are you enjoying the life of an honest trader, Captain?" Mario asked. "Do you miss a pirate's life, yet?"

"What are those ships doing in the Marmara?" Ezera asked again. "They'll be torn to bits if they sneak out of Chalcedon."

The captain inhaled slowly as realisation dawned on him.

"It's starting."

"What's starting?" Mario asked.

"The Turks wouldn't have any ships in the Marmara without a safe harbour, and they can't have one so close to the Capital," Ezera answered. "They must be building up somewhere near the Bosporus. They'll try to close it off, cut off access between the Black Sea and the Aegean."

"Where?"

"Probably at Anatolian Castle. It's a castle that they built forty years or so ago. It guards the narrows of the Bosporus. We saw them preparing something there this morning as we passed by. By treaty, they aren't allowed to block it, and the Emperor pays the Sultan personally to keep it open and allow access for Roman and Italian ships." Ezera growled in frustration. "Damn the cargo! If we were free enough, we'd be capturing ships, investigating the strait and making a king's ransom while doing so! Mario, my friend, this honest trader's business is going to be the death of me!"

"I'm sorry to hear that," Mario wasn't entirely sure how to respond. "Don't worry; I'm sure it won't shackle you forever. Where to now?"

"We can't harbour here, the warships might decide to raid the village. We'll have to head to Principios, it's an island just south of the Asian shore."

"Is it safe?"

"Safe enough for now, but safety is turning into a relative term."

There are many islands in the Sea of Marmara, but in the environs of Constantinople, the most famous is Principios. Rising up from the sea, the island was home to wild horses and monastery prisons that had housed numerous former emperors, would-be-emperors, their relatives and other important characters.

At the base of the great hill of Principios Island was a minor fishing community, with only one dock, barely large enough to house the Nineveh, once Mario paid all of the fishermen to move their own boats to the beaches. There was also an inn, where the travellers found refuge.

To no one's surprise, Daria complained incessantly that Mario was over-paying the lazy islanders for food and board.

After the boat was safely fastened to the dock, the only inn in the village was completely rented to the crew of the Nineveh. Everyone hoped that no strong wind would come along and dislodge their ship from its humble mooring. The village itself consisted of twelve permanent buildings and no one was pleased to see a crew of foreign cut-throats arrive, gold or no gold. Catalans were a particularly distrusted nation in the empire, as they had made up the bulk of the mercenary army that rebelled against the empire in a previous century, and caused so much damage to the stability of life within the sphere of the New Rome.

Captain Ezera hosted his passengers to a dinner on the ship's deck before they retired to the inn. Not surprisingly, fish was on the menu.

"I'm sure that everything will be under control again soon, and we'll be able to go back home in no time," Mario said enthusiastically.

"I'm not so certain," Daria answered before Ella could get a word in. "This has been a long time coming. A lot of people resent the foreigners in the city, and hate the idea of union."

"I don't see why they should," Mario answered matter-of-factly. "Most of the city's wealth comes from the two Italian concessions, as well as about two-thirds of the army. Without the foreigners in the city, it would have fallen to the Turks years ago."

Ella and Ezera looked apprehensive about this topic.

Daria remained undaunted.

"Most of the city's wealth *goes* to the two Italian concessions as well, Mario. The foreigners come here, make their money and move on. They contribute nothing and take everything they can. They're like locusts. While here, they are allowed to practice their heresies, and they treat the men and women of the capital as servants. In case you haven't yet ventured out of the Venetian Quarter, most of the city is quite poor, most of the foreigners are quite rich."

"I know, the emperor loots his own city with impunity, and squanders the money on trophies for his palace," Mario added.

"No, the emperor loots his own city, and uses the money to pay for foreign mercenaries and arms, in order to keep the city free from the Mohammedans. I suppose it would be easier to simply ignore the giant horde that perennially attacks us, at least until they sack the city and kill every living man, woman and child."

"Every city and empire has to pay for its army…"

"And our city has to fend off an organized horde. You have to understand that. The rest of Christendom doesn't look over here, they fight among themselves, one prince wins a battle, another loses, it doesn't make much of a difference who the prince of the day is, but here, if our soldiers win a battle, we go on fighting, because they keep on coming. If we loose a battle, our civilization will end. Christianity falls with Constantinople. They will kill everyone and empty the city. The rich city-states of Italy don't care because they don't think that this is their problem, but it will be, for once we fall, the Turk will turn his attention to the West. The city walls of Constantinople guard Christian civilization; if they fall, then the apocalypse will be upon us all."

"Excuse me," Ezera inserted himself. "I'm sure that it's been a stressful day for all of you, I'm sure you would be happier to discuss a lighter topic over our delicious meal."

Ella giggled. Mario tensed as his body that was suddenly piqued with jealousy. *'I should be the one making her laugh.'*

"You're right, of course," he returned to Daria. "I'm sorry if I've offended you again, Milady."

"You seem to think that I offend easily, Don Mario," Daria responded. Mario could see a wall coming up.

"What my beloved sister means to say, is that we are happy to be friendly, and it's probably a good idea to change the topic."

Daria looked like she was about to remind all that she was more than capable of answering for herself, but a pleading look from Ella convinced her to acquiesce. "Exactly."

"So, Mario, I understand that you're setting yourself up in the Quarter," Ella began.

"I am. I've found a house, though it's obviously not quite as beautiful as your brother's. It's next to the hospital, near where the Corso meets Contoscalion Harbour. It will be large enough to build a small forge and a laboratory, and it's quite comfortable, so things are going quite well, thank you."

"That's an awfully hilly area, isn't it?" Daria asked.

"I need a hilly area, I need to build a forge that will go underground, my workshop has to be built onto a rock surface. Without a hard rock surface, the weight of the forge would gradually sink into the earth."

"I'm sure you'll be looking at a long line of local boys looking to be taken on as apprentices," Ezera said optimistically, though Mario could detect a very miniscule implication of sarcasm. "It isn't very often that a *bona fide* doctor from Italy sets up shop."

"I hope to take on some apprentices. I hope to actually take on my own sons someday."

An ominous silence sat like a smiling troll on the table as Daria resisted the urge to make any further inquiry into his family plans.

"We'll wish you luck on that, but in the meantime, Ella and I must adjourn for the night." Daria said in a lightning-paced stacatto

Ezera leaned back in his chair and smiled as if enjoying some private joke.

"It's early, Daria," Ella insisted.

"Not too early for prayers, Ella!"

"But…"

Daria face remained resolute.

"Now."

"Yes, sister."

They exchanged the pleasantries of saying goodnight. The men kissed the women's hands, as was only appropriate for people of their standing (Ezera notwithstanding). When Mario kissed Ella's hand, she smiled.

'*She smiled*,' Mario thought to himself happily. '*She smiled!*'

Mario and Ezera sat on the wooden wall that surrounded the jetty and looked across the Sea of Marmara at the sleeping city of Constantinople on the European mainland. To their right, they could also see the smaller city of Chalcedon. A warm breeze crept over the dark sea, reminding everyone that summer was on its way. Ezera passed Mario a skin of wine that he had picked up in the Crimea.

"I think I want to marry Ella," Mario said over a minor stupor.

"She's definitely interested, but you should be careful, Daria might be a bit of a problem."

"She doesn't like me at all."

"She's Greek, if she didn't like you, she'd say so. She's just a little hostile. It could be much worse," Ezera stopped to think for an instant. "You've got to be stronger around her. She thinks that you're weak, and she won't let you near her sister-in-law because the thinks you're a western effete. Be more assertive."

"I know," Mario conceded with odd humour. "But you forget, She's not Greek, she's Roman!"

"Yeah, you should be careful with things like that."

"Your friend Vincent must have his hands full with a woman like that. I imagine she keeps him well behaved," said the inebriated doctor.

"Don't be so sure about that, Vincent would never tolerate her speaking to him the way she speaks to you. She likes you, you give her a chance to be bossy."

"Do you think Ella would marry me?"

"You need to be more assertive, Mario," Ezera again counselled his friend. "Your shyness and your loneliness go together. Lose them both, or keep them both. You're gambling with nothing worth keeping."

Mario shrugged.

"I know."

"You Italians are supposed to be famous for your skill in the romantic arts!"

"I know, but I took vows at the university. I'm free of those for the first time."

"We won't be on this island forever, Mario."

"I know."

Ezera tried a different approach. "She is beautiful, I give you that," he leaned over to hold eye contact with the Mario. "Maybe I should try my luck."

Mario glared at him.

Ezera raised an eyebrow and continued. "Move quickly, Mario. A beautiful girl of marrying age doesn't stay available forever."

Mario exhaled loudly, and was about to speak, but Ezera cut him off. "And don't say '*I know*'."

Mario swallowed the words before they past his lips.

"But I do," he insisted.

"I know," answered the smiling briggand.

"Wake up, Mario!" Ezera kicked Mario in the thigh.

"Ow! What!"

"Look out the window. Come on!"

Mario's eyes adjusted as he looked out the poorly made glass of the second floor of the inn. He saw Ella walking along the wooden fence where he and Ezera had been drinking last night.

"She's alone, go!"

Mario groaned in resistance, but Ezera would have none of it. He threw clothes onto Mario and pushed him out the door. Consciousness was still in the process of arrival by the time he found the young DiCastillo girl alone and enjoying the salt air.

"Good morning, Ella," he said once he had made it as far as the footpath. "It's a beautiful day, isn't it?"

Ella smiled and looked at the weather. It was overcast and humid.

"I suppose."

"How are you doing?"

"I'm fine, but my sister tells me to be careful talking to men alone," she looked back towards the inn. "Will you walk with me?"

"It would be my honour, Ella."

The two walked along the breezy seaside for a bit. Mario gave a silent thanks to God for providing a wind strong enough to bring the sweet smell of the sea, rather than allow the smell of a day's haul to dwindle.

"So, how long have you been in Constantinople?"

"For about seven years now. When my parents died, I went to live with my brother. I hadn't seen him for many years at that point, it was a very difficult time."

"Ahh," there was a moment of silence. Mario was determined to not lose what could well be the only chance he had to speak to her alone by wasting in on his own shyness. "May I ask you a personal question? You can refuse, I won't take any offence."

She looked at him slyly. "You seem very anxious to ask me a personal question, so I won't stand in your way."

"Well, it's just that, you are a beautiful woman, Ella, and… you come from a well-positioned family… and you're smart and cultured…"

"Is this a question?"

"Why aren't you married yet?" Mario blurted out.

"That is a personal question," she confirmed and looked over at the village again. "Because most men in Constantinople are too afraid of my brother. Those who aren't afraid of him want me for some political arrangement. My brother won't marry me off to a Greek family in the Capital; he doesn't approve of eastern men. So, I stay in the house and occupy my time with music, needlework and helping my sister-in-law get ready for the baby. What about you? You're rich, your family is rich, you're educated, and you're quite charming. Yet you seem to live like a monk."

"I'm not that rich, and I've lived like a monk for many years. However, I'm waiting for someone special."

"Really?" she was playing with him now. "Do you have anyone in mind?"

"Don't laugh, Ella," Mario said with a mild blush, which

unsuccessfully tried to hide behind a false laugh of his own. "It could be you someday."

She was confused. "What does that mean?"

Mario blushed scarlet.

'*Be strong*.' He could hear echoing in his head. "I mean that, it is a difficult situation to be in, when I see such a beautiful and good-natured girl, and I want nothing more than to tell you this every time I see you."

Mario tried to look into her eyes, but she looked away. It was her turn to blush. Their eyes met for no more than an instant. She looked so sad. She inhaled a short breath and looked away again.

"No," she said sadly.

She turned away and walked quickly to her sister-in-law at the inn. It was all over.

Mario did not deflate. In fact, much to Mario's surprise, he didn't feel crushed, or depressed, or ruined in the slightest. All his life, he'd controlled his behaviour in order to be proper, and he had lived a very dull life to this point. Always alone, always the serious one. This morning, he acted on his heart for the first time he could remember. It didn't end the way he wanted it to, but he learnt that he could surprise himself. He knew that he could choose to change his habits and behaviour when the need called for it, and if he could do that, she couldn't resist him for long. It was a strangely cathartic feeling that her rejection gave him.

He smiled all the way back to the barrack room that he was sharing with Ezera. Ezera took one look at him and laughed.

"Oh my goodness! You look like a man who just inherited the world!"

"I feel like that."

"What happened?" Ezera was beaming with pride at his young friend. "Come on!"

"She refused me," Mario said smiling. He forced his lips to hide the smile, but his eyes still carried it.

Ezera looked at him doubtfully.

"If she said no, you wouldn't be this happy."

"One would think," Mario had to surrender to that logic. "When it's safe to go back to the city, it will be an awkward trip back, but I feel fantastic."

"You're a strange one, Doctor Mario," Ezera surmised. "And I think you're lying to me."

"I never lie, Captain. But if wanted to, I'm sure I could," he smiled again. "Self-transformation is the alchemist's greatest ambition."

Lunch at the inn was a tense meal. Ella was tense. Daria could see that Ella was tense, which made her tense. Ezera was observing them with his keen eyes, which made him seem tense. This in turn only exacerbated their condition when they realised that he realised how tense they were. Only Mario seemed relaxed.

"It looks like the city has calmed down," he announced cheerfully. "Tomorrow morning, we should all go back home, I believe."

"Let's hope so," Daria said, resting a hand on her swelling belly. "If I wanted to live in a village, I would have married a farmer."

Ezera guffawed at that. Daria stared at him to silence him, but it didn't seem to work. "I couldn't agree more, Madam. I'm not terribly picky about my dining habits, but this public house is not much for entertainment."

"Then why don't you go back to your ship?" Daria asked acidly.

"I intend to. I'm going to go back after lunch, actually. We'll take the ship to the city and come back tomorrow. If everything is fine, we'll take you three back home. If it's not, we'll wait."

"Thank you."

Ezera smiled warmly at her. She responded politely, but no one would describe her smile as warm.

"I like it here," Mario added. "I want to go back home, I have a great deal of work before me, but it's peaceful here. Back in the city, not so much."

"Ah yes, you must get back to your laboratory," Daria meant the comment to sound a little condescending towards his academic pursuits, but much to her surprise, Mario didn't accept.

"Yes, how's your... ah..." he smiled. "... your home?" the implication was that she had little else in the world of which to be proud.

'Don't even try it, boy,' she thought. "It's big, and cleaned and maintained by my large staff of maids and servants."

Mario laughed and raised a hand as to calm a child.

"As I find myself saying in many of our conversations, I meant no offence."

"And as I've said in many of our conversations, Master Orsini, why would any be taken?"

Mario smiled at her. His mouth began to twist into what could easily transform into a laugh. Much to his surprise, Daria lifted her normally cold appearance and smiled back, as if she found him quite amusing.

"I don't know why God sent you two here to keep us company," she said in exasperation.

Mario quickly caught Ella's eye and smiled before returning his attention to Daria.

"I've often been asked this question with regards to my company, I'm still waiting for an answer."

"Maybe you've been given an answer," Ella spoke for the first time.

"Then perhaps I'll wait for a different one," Mario tensed at his own atypical assertiveness.

"I guess we'll all have to wait together, Mario," Ella replied. She met Mario's eyes for just an instant. Daria looked from Ella to Mario and the smile left her face. Ezera caught her gaze and grinned. She was not amused. Ezera, on the other hand, was quite amused.

"Well!" Ezera said as he clapped his hands on his legs. "Off I go. Mario, do you want to come with me?"

"I'm fine, thank you," Mario answered. "I'll stay here and wait."

"If you're sure of that, then I bid you all farewell, and I hope to see you again tonight."

Ezera chuckled to himself as he made his way down the quay to the harbour.

Book Two:
Cutting the Throat

Sailing To Byzantium

Stanza Two

An aged man is but a paltry thing,
A tattered coat upon a stick, unless
Soul clap its hands and sing, and louder sing
For every tatter in its mortal dress,
Nor is there singing school but studying
Monuments of its own magnificence;
And therefore I have sailed the seas and come
To the holy city of Byzantium.

William Butler Yeats

Chapter Seventeen - Galata

Isodore clamoured back to the inn after spending the entire afternoon on and about the docks, waiting for the Nineveh to arrive. He'd been charged by Vincent to help look after Daria and Ella, but their ship never came in. He spoke to longshoremen at all of the docks and shipyards and assured them of gold if they let him know when the ship in question arrived.

One hauler claimed that he saw the Nineveh break from the crowd at midday and head towards the strait, and that it could have been bound for Diplokion, a nearby village, in order to find a place to lay aground. The hauler was given a dirham for his observations, as was the stable boy Isodore sent out to the fishing community.

The boy returned shortly before nightfall with news that the docks of Diplokion were filled with galleys and other ships, but none of which matched the description of the Nineveh. The Galata ferrymen cast further hopelessness on Isodore's charge by telling him that there was no ship named Nineveh anchored in their harbour or awaiting mooring.

The monk quickly ate a dinner of harbour-caught bonito-fish wrapped in leaven-less flatbread and thought about his predicament. Certainly he was not responsible for the non-appearance of the ladies—that blame would go to the pirate, but rationality was not always the trump with Vincent that it was with other men, especially when family was concerned. Vincent may well choose to blame Isodore if something drastic happened to the two girls. Isodore glumly returned to the public house where he had rented out two rooms for himself and the two ladies.

On his way up the Corso Arno, where he planned to retire for the evening and start his search again in the morning, he saw a surprising sight. He was pushed off the road by a convoy of guards escorting a black carriage up the hill towards Saint Catherine's Gate. The windows were covered with canvas, and the guards were fully armed and armoured. What was strange was that Hectore Pazzi, the captain of the guard, was atop the carriage, and dressed in clean robes. The convoy ignored Isadore and pushed rudely past, almost crushing him under the advance of horse and wagon.

After his first instinct of outrage at the rudeness of the those who passed over him, his natural curiosity (a most unwelcome characteristic for a monk) began to poke questions into the back of his brain. It took very little prodding to make him acquiesce to his inquisitive side and Isodore continued along the Corso, following the carriage in a most nondescript manner.

The carriage settled in preparation of gathering their guests, outside the city gate, and Isodore walked past them as nonchalantly as possible. He counted five guards in addition to Hectore. Across the clearing in front of the gate, were a series of shops, closed for the night, and a workman's eatery. The monk entered the eatery and took a seat in the shadows, with a good view of the entourage waiting at the gate. He ordered some wine and bread, and nursed the meal for over an hour, until there was some action at the gate.

The city walls of Galata cascade down from the top of Pera Hill towards the Golden Horne to cradle the Genoese Colony in a stone half moon. South across the Horne was the Capital of Eastern Christendom, and to the north were a thousand trails criss-crossing the hills of Thrace.

Traversing over and around those hills one night in the late summer of 1452 were two innocuous-looking horsemen. The first was a lean and strong young man. Like his master behind him, he was cowled in order to hide his appearance. While this effort was rewarded by properly disguising his identity, the sword at his side, the bow on his back and the armour that chinked with his every movement did little to disguise his role. Ahmet, son of Ali, was there to guard his master on his business.

The second figure was an old man, bent over with age, and unlike his guard, he was obviously not used to life atop a horse. He held onto the reigns as tightly as he could, and tried to focus only upon the horse in front of him to lead him safely through the night. He coughed as they travelled and his eyes darted around at every sound from the lightly forested hills around him. This humble figure was the Prime Minister for one of the strongest states in Europe.

The two horsemen clip-clopped past Saint George's Hill, around Resurrection Hill to the Valley of the Springs, and made their way to the land-side wall of Galata.

At night, the city was closed up, and especially after a day's rioting on the south side of the harbour, security was tight. All of the doors and gates were manned, and on full alert. Saint Catherine's Gate, normally manned by two town guards, was guarded instead by five Genoese crossbowmen and the captain of the town guard. It was to this gate that the two travellers directed themselves. Upon the small wooden door that was the centrepiece of the giant stone archway, the horsemen knocked.

"Who's there?" called out a voice from inside the city.

"Pilgrims from the West," answered a finely piqued voice, speaking the Greek of the upper classes.

Pazzi motioned that the door be opened, and his men hurried out to meet the two. They helped Halil down from his horse and offered temporary stabling Ahmet dismounted independently with speed and grace. He was taller but more lightly built than the Genoese soldiers, and his wild-haired steppe appearance made the guards puff their chests and wear their coldest stares in an unsuccessful effort to seem extra intimidating.

"Please come with me, Your Excellency," the captain said with a bow.

The guards took the horses and Halil and Ahmet followed their host in through the gate. On the inside of the gate house was a black coach. The coachbox had covered windows and room for more than just the two guests, but there were only two intended passengers on this ride. Ahmet and Halil entered the closeted transport and the guards followed behind as the coachman snapped the horses to a trot down the roughshod and slanted streets of Galata.

"I take it that this is your first view of a Christian city, Ahmet."

"It is, Uncle," Ahmet answered. In recent months, the Prime Minister had unofficially adopted the tribesman and was grooming him for a higher responsibility later in life, provided they both survived the upcoming travails. Ahmet had begun to address the Grand Vizier as *"uncle." Amja* or *Ineshte* meaning paternal and maternal uncles respectively are words that are not only applied to family members, but are meant to convey love, loyalty and deference. All three of these virtues Ahmet gave freely and willingly to Halil, though his heart weighed heavy whenever they were in the company of Halil's wife *'Ayshe-teze'*. Ahmet was pleased to join Halil on a trip away from the capital.

"This city is a small one," Halil said, looking out the curtained window as they jostled along in the carriage. "But one with which we keep on friendly terms. It's the city across the harbour that causes us so much trouble. It tempts our Sultan's eye, and like Eve in the Garden, he's drawn to that apple."

"Then it's here where he'll over-reach."

"Correct," Halil nodded with approval. "We'll need to keep the other Christians neutral, remember. If little Mehmet insists on war, we'll have to make certain that it's a small one. Left to his own devices, he'd drag us into a war with all of Italy, and the Holy Roman Empire to the north. All for the fate of a corner of land!"

"If the Venetians and Genoese are kept happy, then Adrianople will control All of South-east Europe, south of the Danube, in addition to large tracts of Anatolia," Ahmet concluded. "But there's something I don't understand about your plan."

Halil raised his eyebrows to pry the question from his apprentice.

"If Mehmet starts and loses a war, dying in the process, won't all of the subject kingdoms rebel? They'll think that Adrianople is weak, and the Sword of Osman without an heir."

"That is an excellent point, Ahmet," Halil jostled as the wagon clamoured through a pothole. "But there is an heir: Prince Orhan."

"Who?"

"The Sultan's cousin. He's a prisoner of the Roman Emperor in Constantinople. He has a retinue of a few hundred loyalists and guards. They live in the Venetian colony in the capital. That's yet another reason why we have to stay on good terms with these foreigners."

"That kind or ransom won't come cheaply, Uncle."

"No," Halil acknowledged. "But it will come nonetheless. A new branch of the Ottoman dynasty, with you and I as two of the senior power-arbiters, my boy! We stand at the cusp of a brilliant new age for the Ottoman state, and for all of Islam. What we do here, will have our names called out among the most honoured on the Day of Judgement. A brilliant day will soon be upon us, Ahmet. Smile."

"I'll smile when that bastard lies at my feet," Ahmet answered. "But I'll smile here for politeness sake, nonetheless."

When the two horsemen had arrived at the gate, they were quickly ushered through the gate and directly placed into the carriage. It all happened so fast that Isodore barely got a good look at the two men. His swift view was good enough to identify their faces as those of Turks, the enemies of Christendom. The first was a simple soldier. His demeanour and appearance were those that Isodore had seen a hundred times on a hundred different faces, right away he dismissed him as a guard without importance.

The second man was a different story, however. Old and frail, he had the eyes of a thinker and the decorum of a courtier. The two of them got into the carriage and settled out of sight. Two guards stayed at the gate to hold the horses, and the rest of the group prepared to make way along the road.

The carriage set itself onto the arterial road heading east, as Isodore knew it would. To the east of the gate was the tower. Galata Tower was a century old round-cone that was visible from everywhere in the colony and around the Horne. Rather than risk following the carriage, the observant monk ran quickly through back and side-streets to the base of the tower. By taking his more direct route, he got there before the carriage did on its up and down ride along the hillside.

Isodore comforted himself into the shadows of a nearby alleyway and waited for the events to unfold.

'I hope this makes up for the temporary setback with the girls. Vincent's going to want to hear about this,' he thought to himself.

The carriage halted in the stone plaza outside the tower. The guards who'd been running alongside the carriage as it made its way through the city had an opportunity to catch their breath and the guards who'd ridden on top the carriage descended to open their transport and allow their guests out into the open air.

Ahmet hopped out with claustrophobic exuberance. He was glad to be outside of the rolling coffin and pleased by the night breeze. From the hillside plaza outside the tower where they stood, Ahmet looked downhill towards the Golden Horne, a gibbous moon's reflection breezing over the rippling water, and across there he laid eyes on Constantinople for the first time. The hilly peninsula stabbed across the horizon, and hooked the Horne away from the sea.

And those walls. Even in the darkness of night, the sea walls were visible across the water, the moon capping their brims. Following the walls along the harbour, the land walls jutted out as the lit-up palace cornered the earth and water. Blachcrnae Palace, the grand palace, was a solidly square fortification that in the night revealed none of the day's beauty. No arches or mosaics or frescos could be discerned, only the squat toughness of the fortress, like a sleeping tortoise. And again, the walls upon walls. They looked like layers of an onion, one after another pushing back against each other. That was the killing ground that Halil remembered so ominously. That was where Mehmet planned to crash wave after wave of his countrymen until the house of Islam was emptied of all its bravest warriors. That was the killing ground where Mehmet would be sacrificed at an altar of his own ambition.

Behind him, Halil exited with far less grace than his guardian. Ahmet called himself away from his land-gazing to help the Grand Vizier out of the wooden beast.

"Anna kwayiss. Ben iyim," he said in a soup of Arabic and Turkish.

'I'm fine.'

"This way, Sir," the guard captain motioned for the two men to follow him while he spoke in Greek.

"Thank you," Halil reciprocated the Helene tongue before continuing his conversation with Ahmet in Turkish. "A beautiful view, isn't it?"

"It looks impressive from up here," Ahmet agreed. "I've never been too inclined towards cities and crowds. But I'd like to see the inside of that big one."

"I'm sure you will." Halil smiled to himself. "The only question is in what capacity."

"As a ghazi! I'm not sure if I'll ever hold a merchant's scales or a diplomat's tongue, so I think the only way I'll cross those walls is with sword in hand," Ahmet smiled back. "I can't imagine doing so any other way."

"We'll see what we can make of you. Now come and pay attention. Watch how we speak to each other, the Count and I. See how our conversation unfolds, it doesn't matter if you don't understand the language. The way we act, and the things that we don't say are just as important," Halil touched Ahmet's arm and motioned towards the waiting guard. "Now let's meet this Count."

"Selam-u Alaikum," the picturesque figure of Count Dominic Trebianno greeted the envoy as they entered the reception chamber of the tower. *'Peace be upon you.'*

"Wa Alaikum As-salaam," Halil returned the greeting with the standard form. *'And unto you be peace.'*

Dominic Trebianus was an archetypal renaissance figure, with shoulder length hair and an equine nose. His eyes betrayed a rapacious intellect that was barely kept in check by those around him. He wore the minimalist long black gown and white waist-coat of the court and unto that minimum standard he threw flairs and tassels, stripes and tails of coloured cloth. At first glance he would seem to be a sort of clown, mimicking and parroting the court, but his face overshadowed the appearance of those clothes with grace and an explosive personality.

"I'm glad to see you again, my old friend!" Dominic kissed Halil on both cheeks as he spoke his words in Aristocratic Greek.

"Politics have kept us apart for too long," Halil responded in kind. "The ruminations of popes and sultans keep our houses apart. It is a heavy heart that brings me here tonight, to try and avert a disaster."

"I'm glad that you came, Prime Minister," the warmth of the Italian's face belied the machinations that formed just below the surface. "There are storm clouds to the north of us. I pray that it's not yet too late to avoid the tempest?"

"A tempest comes as an act of God. The catastrophe on the horizon is one made by the fallible hands of fallible men. Unfortunately for all of us, the great Sultan of Adrianople, heir to the sword of Osman, was taken unto God before his time, and before he could secure an heir, and now the kingdom is without a head to lead it," the vizier mourned.

"What of the new boy-king of whom we've heard so much?"

"He's nothing," Halil scoffed. "He's but a pretender to the throne, and an insult to his father's memory. His father's seed would have been better spent had it been cast to the ground, rather than form into that tree."

"That's why I love speaking with you, Halil Pasha," Trebianno laughed. "You leave so little room for ambiguity as to your opinion!"

"The Seed of Osman is without a just heir right now. Despite the boy playing with his father's trappings, there is no leader in the capital."

"Is he of so little potential?"

"No, he's smart, but arrogant. He doesn't want to accept guidance from those who have knowledge of such things as governance and leadership. He is stubborn and he thinks that he can alienate the old alliances without causing troubles for those around him. He'll fall soon enough, but I fear that he's aggressive enough that when he falls the chaos in his wake will be to everyone's detriment."

"So you're concerned about the possibility of a new heir," Dominic suggested.

"That's one thing."

"And what about the north of us?" Dominic asked. "It seems that a small army is mustering, only a few hours up the Bosporus."

"That is the first stage of a larger plan. The boy has it in his head to fortify the strait. He's stationed a construction battalion there, alongside an entire regiment of Janissaries in the Anatolian Castle."

"Does he intend to block the strait? That's a tough bill to pay, even with a sizeable naval presence," The Count suggested.

"He's got a new playmate. Some years ago, he brought his friend Zaganos into the divan to help him. Things went from bad to worse, and eventually led to his removal. Now, his new grand hope lies in a Hungarian charlatan and illusionist who insists that he can make the strait impassable." Halil said dismissively. "That's his character: He places all his hopes in one man, or one argument, and hopes for the best. A man like him is doomed to a lifetime of disappointments."

"I know of this new playmate, a gunsmith named Orban."

"A self-described gunsmith who claims to be able to build the impossible!"

"I was impressed with him when we met." Trebianus stated. "He tried selling his services to the empire at about this time last year, Adam Karian, the minister of the army believed him, but they couldn't hold his hire. Cardillo, the governor of the Venetian colony, and myself were both interested, but he was asking for too much gold. He claimed he could make guns big enough to knock down the Walls of Jericho and Solomon's Temple. A moot promise as those walls had been knocked down without the aid of such a cannon."

"Your emperor was wise to cast him out!"

"My emperor is Frederick the Third, of the house of Hapsburg," Dominic corrected. "So where does that leave you?"

"I'm now effectively a prisoner in the Anatolian Castle. We're supposed to oversee the construction of a new and improved fortress on the European side of the Bosporus."

"Who's we?"

"Myself, the Greek mongrel Zaganos, and the boy."

"The Sultan is there?"

"The sultan is dead, my friend. Mehmet is there," Halil answered. "Can you approach Prince Orhan for me? Keep him out of harm's way?"

"I'll offer him sanctuary on the Genoese side," Dominic offered. "And I'll also send some emissaries north. In the event of a war between the Greeks and your Kingdom, my city has no stake. We won't involve ourselves."

"And what do you think of Venice?"

"What I think of Venice would make a sailor blush, Vizier!" the governor laughed. "But they are a merchant state, like Genoa. You can come to an understanding with them, they know that their alliance with the Greeks is not a suicide pact."

"Then, in exchange for leaving Galata unmolested, would you be willing to promise your neutrality?"

"I would, and in addition to that, I would also require the rights of ships flying the flag of the city of Genoa to trade in ports under the suzerainty of Adrianople. In exchange for that, I'll keep your future liege safely away from the upcoming violence."

"If you can deliver Orhan, we have an agreement," the vizier smiled.

"Consider it done."

And with that they shook hands, kissed cheeks, and Halil and Ahmet returned to the carriage to be escorted away.

The Sea of Marmora was choppy on the way back to the mainland the next morning. Mario enjoyed the ride from the forecastle of the ship and took his first real day-time view of the shining domes of Constantinople since his arrival a couple of months ago. He also saw the villages on the Asian shore. They weren't really so different from fishing villages like Diplokion or Pricipios, save for a few minarets stabbing out of the countryside.

The sun was warm, but the wind cooled his skin; unbeknownst to Mario this was a recipe for a sunburn, but he contemplated other things as he watched the Turkish villagers ashore carry about their day-to-day lives. They loaded fishing boats by the harbour. Were they truly so different? Fishing the same seas and dining on the same bounty as their Christian neighbours who lived only a short stretch of water away? Was war really so inevitable, that armies must crash against each other to determine their own mastery, before those fishing ships can go back to their fishing and the farmers go back to their fields? Those fishermen certainly needed neither Emperor nor Sultan to set their nets and sell their haul. For centuries in either direction, their lot was the same, under either Cross or Crescent.

Without any regard needed for the name or religion of any given Caesar, the relationship between sailors and the sea, farmers and the land and soldiers and their generals was ostensibly the same. Was it so timelessly the same between men and women, or was each coupling new and unique? Mario smiled as he thought about Ella.

'She'll come to me,' He thought to himself.

He had no real experience to base this upon, save stories told by friends or from vulgar tales told by mouth or pen. But in his heart he knew this to be the case. There had been something at motion in him for some time now. His lifetime had been spent in dutiful study and obedience, but something seems to have happened to him. On one night, a few short months ago, he was forced to act outside of his usual walls and go to a baudyhouse. Since then, the borders of his own world had been thrown into flux and things seemed ready to find their new regium. A year ago, he could never have spoken so bluntly to Ella. He could never have left Venice, he would sooner have taken his own life. Not sooner, as it turned out. He certainly would never have leapt out that window. All his adult life, his world had ossified around him comfortably and then all of a sudden their world burnt down on him. What was emerging out of the ashes was surprising him.

Upon their re-arrival at the public docks of the Venetian Quarter, they took a sigh of relief that everything appeared to have returned to normal after a day's unlawful insurrection. Guards were out and about in the dockyard and along the walls and townspeople nervously glanced at anyone who seemed to be either armed or foreign. While order seemed to have returned to the city, it was obvious that things were not comfortably so. There was a palpable chill in the air, beyond the morning breeze from the Horne.

Mario and Ezera said their goodbyes in a minimalist fashion, without tears or exuberance, and Ezera made a show of epic swashbuckling grandiosity while bidding farewell to the two ladies, with a kissing of hands, bowing and applause from the crew, which in turn caused the crews of two ships docked nearby to join in with cheers. Mario escorted the two blushing girls from the docks back to the villa.

Up Acropolis Hill they trekked until they reached the front courtyard of Vincent's home.

"I'm glad to have had the opportunity to enjoy the company of you two beautiful ladies, so thank you again for the pleasure," Mario said as a farewell.

"Thank you for your company as well, Doctor," Ella said in a voice that would freeze summer dew.

"Yes," Daria said dismissively as Vincent emerged from the manse to meet his family.

He embraced his wife and sister warmly, kissing each of them on the cheek and holding them tightly.

"I'm glad to see you both so well!" he announced after the pleasantries of greeting were carried out. "Mario, how are you faring?"

"Wonderfully, Don Vincent."

"You certainly seem cheerful for a man whose just returned from exile."

"What?" Mario asked incredulously.

"From exile," Vincent nodded his head in the direction of the dockyard from which they came. "You're back in Constantinople."

"Oh yes," Mario's brain caught up with the conversation. "I just was thinking of... here. Pardon me, I'm rambling. "

"Would you care to come in for a cup of wine?" the officer offered.

"I'm sure that your girls are in no condition to entertain now, and that they would prefer to settle themselves rather than continue to play host to the likes of me, but thank you Commander."

"So be it then," Vincent accepted his refusal and prepared to bring the girls into the house.

"It's no trouble," came a strong voice from Daria DiCastillo.

Ella turned with a quiet rage, but Daria didn't bother registering it.

"We would love to extend our shared company." She made a gesture to her sister-in-law of widening her eyes.

"Of course, Don Mario," Ella added, though the emotions behind the words were hard for Mario to approximate.

Mario tried to hide his surprise at Daria's offer before turning to Ella. "If you're certain it's no trouble."

"None at all," Ella replied without her earlier coldness.

Mario was silent and held her eye contact for an instant.

"It's no trouble, now come along," Daria instructed everyone into the house. Vincent entered first, asking Mario about their trip, followed by Ella, with an outwardly serene Daria pushing her from behind.

Chapter Eighteen - Sofia

Peotre and Marten looked down from their camp in the Rila Mountains south of Sophia. They could see their city, encased in a vaguely octagonal-ish block of wooden palisades, nestled among the Balkan highlands. To the south-east of the city, they could see an infidel army on the march towards it.

Marten turned to Peotre. "Well, those sure aren't local Sipahis."

"I can see that. They're bloody Janissaries," Peotre looked at the regiment that came marching toward the city. They couldn't make out any of the signs or insignia of the cohort in any great detail, but the sight was unmistakable. Marching five abreast, stomping their way over the dried roads of early summer, came the daunting sight of a Janissary Orta. Their cymbals were clashing, their drums beating and their trumpets announcing their arrival.

"I knew this would end poorly," Peotre mumbled to himself.

"Don't be so pessimistic," came a voice from behind them. A fat man in his early forties seemed to appear right out of the thin mountain air behind them. "We knew that there would be repercussions to what we did. You two go scout out our uninvited guests. Come back at tell me what you see."

"Yes, Bojidar!" Peotre said. "There sure are a lot of them, though."

"We can all see that," echoed the rotund chieftain with a touch of nuissance. "Tell me how many. Tell me how they're armed. Tell me about guns and horses, but don't tell me that you're afraid! We knew that they would come sooner or later."

"Yes, Uncle," Peotre said. He and his cousin Marten went off down the hill and ran into the city.

They watched the procession of the Janissaries enter the city and followed the spectacle as it snaked through the city streets. The arrival of a Janissary Orta was always a cause for worry. They marched in step, even the horses seemed to obey their rules of drill and meter. The soldiers all wore the same long red coats and white felt hats back over their heads like Egyptian Pharaohs. They carried scimitars at their sides and bows on their backs. Some marched with halberds and spears, and some with muskets, harquebusses and hand-cannons.

There were about twenty men on horseback, the rest of them, probably about six hundred soldiers in all, were on foot. Unlike Uncle Bojidar's band, these were professional soldiers. At the head of the procession were two horse-back standard bearers, one carrying the horsetails and tugra (a stylised signature-emblem) of the Sultan, the other carrying a red flag with a two-pointed sword that looked like a snake's tongue flying out of the pommel. The two-pronged sword of Ali was the standard of this particular regiment: The Eighth Orta. Behind these was a third horseman, tall on his horse, with a stern face and harsh eyes, this would be the commander of the company; Mesut, son of Abdullah. Behind him was the regimental band, playing the obtuse tunes of Turkic army music. Next was the infantry. They were the core of the corp. Kidnapped, bought or forced into slavery from Christian families in the Balkan Mountains, and raised on Islam and war until they reached fighting age. Some could pass for locals, others (Serbs, Magyars, Croats or Albanians) had been forcefully recruited from other territories on this unhappy European peninsula.

Pulling up the rear of the military procession was about fifty men of the Kopekji, the mastiff trainers; each one of whom held four of the bulky hell-hounds on a leash. They seemed to lack the cadenced discipline of the rest of the regiment, their clothes were cleaner and their faces wilder. They marched separately from the main force.

The dogs make for a terrifying sight when angry, but many of these dogs seemed almost friendly as they entered a new town, so much to see and smell. Peotre smiled and waved at one who passed by, sniffing the new smells of the town. Marten cast a disapproving glance at his cousin's display of affection for the dogs of war. Peotre shrugged at the rebuking glance. One orta was probably not enough to put down a sanjak in open revolt, but it was certainly enough to dissuade a city from going down that path.

Behind the fighting force came the support. Mule trains of supplies, and wagons, carrying food, silver, presumably there were also some of the *'traVeling women'* that always accompanied soldiers around the world.

The procession marched down the dirt streets of the frontier city, their music alerting everyone of their presence. The young and old, women and children all came to see what was going on, and shuddered in fear as the soldiers passed by. No one needed to be reminded that for over a century, no army had stood to face the Janissaries and held their ground. Those that stood, fell. Eight years ago, Varna had proven that. Only those who hid, survived. Even when Constantinople refused to fall, twenty years ago, they had still extracted a usurious tribute from the current emperor's late brother. Any man could be harsh and ruthless, but the organization, and single-mindedness of these foreign trained footmen was what put them a step beyond being merely harsh thugs, and turned them into the iron fist that held the Sword of Osman. They were wisely feared by all rational men.

Peotre and Marten followed the soldiers through the city. They counted their numbers and shuddered. They knew that in the mountains, they had commanded a certain respect from the local authorities, and within limits were even an authority unto themselves. But they still only numbered a hundred brigands and twice that in sympathisers. Many of them were good with a sword and fast with a bow, but the sight before them was simply out of their league. They looked at each other and tried to avoid the feelings of pessimism that their uncle, Bojidar had warned them against.

When the parade arrived in the town square, they were met by the local notables. There were two aging Sipahi tribesmen, raised on horseback, ready to meet the arriving force with about two hundred armed guards, dressed in mail with pointed steel helmets. Along with the Turkish noblemen, there was the local bishop, dressed in his *'Sunday-best'* as it were.

The commander of the orta rode out past his standard bearers to meet the dignitaries.

Like most Janissaries (almost all, but there were a handful of exceptions), Mesut had been sold into slavery at age seven. The corps bought him from his Christian parents, renamed him, converted him to Islam and began his formal education in the arts of war. He was taught drill, archery, swordsmanship, and the care and maintenance of the tools of his trade. He also learned the basics of ballistics for artillery purposes, seamanship in the Aegean and basic medical care in the barracks of his adoptive family. He studied the Qur'an, calligraphy and could read and write Turkish, Arabic and Persian along with his native tongue. He was familiar with literature, poetry and philosophy in all these languages.

The Janissaries were all slaves; even those masters of high rank were still owned men. They were the direct property of the Sultan, and every day they worked harder than any agrarian peasant or freeman would. They rose and trained, and fought and served, all for the honour of the Sultan, who owned them, and in a sense loved them as a father would love his obedient sons. The eighth had a reputation for doing so with more enthusiasm and genuine loyalty than any other orta.

"Peace be upon you, brothers," Mesut greeted the two horse-mounted sipahis.

"Unto you be peace," the free-born nobles both responded. They shook hands on horseback and welcomed their guest.

"My name is Yusuf son of Mustafa, and this is Jenket son of Burak," the elder said. "Thank you for coming so far from the capital."

"It isn't that far, and I had business here anyways," replied the commander coldly. "We can discuss your problems when my men are barracked. I trust you've made the proper preparations."

"We've set a pasture aside for your tents, Janissary."

Mesut looked at them and blinked before returning to his more diplomatic stance. "A pasture? For tents? We have much to discuss, the three of us, but that can wait for now."

He looked down at the bishop, who was waiting uncomfortably. Mesut quickly poured off his horse and stepped up to the elderly cleric, greeting him in fluent Bulgarian.

"Peace be upon you, Christian."

"Thank you, Muslim. I hope peace stays upon you and all in the city for the duration of your stay here."

"That is a nice sentiment, but the peace has already been broken. Some of your local flock have murdered their lord. Sanjak-Pasha Jem, is not here to greet me because he was so egregiously murdered by some irreligious rabble who have no fear of God."

The bishop looked down. "It was none of my flock, My Lord. We wish to live peacefully until God's plans are made more clear to us."

"Since you've chosen not to submit to God's will by accepting Islam, that seems quite unlikely, Bishop. You are allowed to practice and live in peace, with the condition of obedience. What do you think should happen now, that your concord has been breached by some of your own? Is our commitment to protect your holy places, your peasantry and most of your lands now void?"

"No, Sir. It's just that some men, young men, foolish with hot blood, have been unable to accept some of the harsher demands of the Turks..."

"We are Muslims, priest, not Turks. We carry God's permanency for all races of humanity. The House of Peace is the governance for all the world, not unique to Anatolian tribes. Your deposed king was the tsar of the Bulgars, a petty local potentate. You should rejoice that you've been liberated from an isolated fiefdom and brought into world civilization."

"Of course, I'm sorry," the bishop tried to recover, but was cut off again by Mesut.

"You've been allowed to retain your status here unmolested, bishop. As long as the city doesn't rebel, and pays its taxes, you are welcome to keep your local superstitions. That was part of the terms of surrender, I remember when they were last renewed. Your duty is to minister to those who ignorantly keep the old ways, and to help keep the peace. We'll meet tonight and discuss ways in which you can better do your job. In the meantime, I should address this cheerful looking crowd."

The military procession stood and silently looked on as Mesut took a place on a raised platform in the middle of the square, set up for the occasion.

"People of Sofia!" He yelled in their own local dialect, only slightly accented by the rust of disuse. "My name is Mesut-bey! I bring greetings from your new sultan, the trustee of God's revelations, deputy of the world's law, khan of khans, Mehmet the second! He wishes you peace and prosperity! A bountiful harvest! And an opportunity to see your families prosper unmolested by raiders from the north, the west and the east! I am sure that your tribute in this season of harvest will warm his heart to you even more than it has already! On our master's behalf, I thank you!"

Musut could see the fear and general lack of enthusiasm in the eyes of the locals as his words echoed off the wooden houses.

"It is with a heavy heart that he learned of the fate of our beloved cousin, Veli-Jem! We know that your hearts must also mourn his loss! But fear not! My men and I shall not leave this region until his killers are brought to justice, and face God's law from this very square," the two-sided threat of the comment was not lost on his audience.

"I am here to make a promise to anyone who helps in this endeavour. I will promise twenty silver akches to anyone who leads us directly to the murderous rebels, and a hundred for anyone who brings me the head of their leader!"

There was a murmur about the square. Anyone who made more than twenty silver akches a year was considered quite well-to-do in these hills. Mesut wondered to himself if the irony of twenty pieces of silver was noticed by anyone other than the bishop... and if then.

Mesut turned to Yusuf. "Take us to this... *pasture land.*"

They were escorted by the local militia to a field, where they set up their tents and prepared a base for what they hoped to be a short campaign. Mesut left his officers in charge of setting up the minutia, and rode to Yusuf-bey's house were he was to dine tonight.

One of Yusuf's guards escorted him to the large wooden building on the outskirts of the city. He was welcomed at the door by the noble family and brought into a large room, with a table set on the floor. There were rich pile carpets on the floor and kilims on the walls. The only other decorations were a wooden short bow and a collection of swords and spears on display along the far wall. Mesut took a seat with Yusuf, Jenkat, and their elder sons. The women were sent away to carry out their female responsibilities.

"Thank you for your hospitality, Yusuf-bey," Mesut said formally after they had been served a dinner of early-harvest vegetables and fish from the Vladaiska River. "I usually eat soup for breakfast and dinner, this is a delicious reprieve, my sincere appreciation goes to your wife and daughters for this wonderful meal."

"You honour my house, Mesut-bey."

"I need to discuss things with the two of you, and I'll ask that your guards and sons be excused."

Neither Jenkat nor Yusuf liked the sound of that. It would be rude for a guest to insult his hosts, and nigh unthinkable to do so in front of their servants and family, which would be the only reason that he would ask that they be excused. Yusuf motioned with his right hand and their entourages departed from them, leaving them to their own conversations.

"You are from Eskishehir, aren't you, Yusuf-bey?" Mesut asked once they were alone.

"We both are," replied Jenkat.

"I can tell, by the decoration on that kilim, for example; local and tribal. Tell me, do you have anything in your home that would place this house in the Sofia region, rather than Eskishehir?"

"We've chosen not to imitate the non-believers, as the Prophet has commanded all good Muslims."

"Fair enough. That's true, they should imitate our ways," said Mesut with polite acknowledgement. "Yet, I haven't seen any evidence of this, either. No mosque, no medrassa, no bathhouse. I understand that the church here still maintains the responsibility for educating the children of the city. I trust they do a good job?"

"We've been here a short time…" started Yusuf.

"We've been here for thirty years!" Mesut answered quickly. Anyone listening at the doors could surely have heard his change of tone. "You two have personally been here for four! You mind your own affairs here and let them mind there own in the city. You've made yourselves ignorable!"

"You forget your place, Slave," Jenkat said angrily. His blood ran hot at the prospect of a rebellious slave, regardless of rank.

"My place is beside the Sultan, one of the most powerful lords in the House of Islam! Your place is in a quiet mountain town were it was thought you could do no harm. Yet here I am, doing the job at which you've proven to be incompetent!" Mesut saw that his hosts were preparing to protest, but he didn't allow them the opportunity.

"Get that arrogant look off your face, Old Man!" he held Jenkat's gaze with the violence of a shepherd wrestling a sheep on shearing day. "Your position here is dependent on the good graces of the Sultan, which are maintained in two ways. The first is that you administer a quiet province that needs no special attention from the capital. At that, you have failed miserably. The second is that you expand the faith. You can't even expand the faith in a city that capitulated and begged for mercy without so much as a drawn sword, thirty years ago!"

"Mesut-bey, you are out of order!" yelled Yusuf angrily.

"If these words were my own, you would be correct to protest, but they are not. They come from the second vizier Zaganos, son of Abdullah, and were given to me in front of his majesty the Sultan. Most of the blame for this situation falls on the hands of Veli-Jem, who invited disaster into his own house by his whoring and corruption, and for that has been called to God with the assistance of the local rebels, but if you two continue in this manner, I will be back in the spring, with more than a single orta, and intent on hunting more than simple brigands, a task which should be done by local sipahi, someone capable of this simple task!" Mesut kept them locked in his hard gaze. "I will meet with this bishop, if he can direct me to the rebels, good. If not, then he can hang with them."

"He won't be much help to you, they hate us here," consigned Yusuf.

"Of course they hate us! We conquered their country, we killed their livestock, we kidnapped their children, scurried their kinsmen and executed their king! To walk from that history to one of friendly co-existence is impossible. You have chosen the path of *'ignore them and hope they warm up to us'* which is an impossible crop to harvest. They must be reminded every day that they were conquered them because of their weakness! Because of their decadent culture! Because of their false religion! Because of their corrupt customs! We conquered because of our faith and piety, because of our organization and because of our will to act as God's sword on earth! They have to see this every day! They have to be taught this as children, and be reminded of it in old age! They are a conquered people, and the time of their traditions is past. They can convert and join the future, or remain bogged down in superstition and poverty, but there is no half-way! They hate us! We welcome their hatred! We are here to destroy their past and give them a future, yet they will suckle the dead teat of their own ignorance if we let them! What else could they possibly do but hate us! Grind their past into the mountains, build up a future here for the faithful until the new generation knows nothing but God's grace!"

There was silence where a reply should have been.

"I thank you again for your hospitality," said Mesut as he recomposed himself. "Do you have any idea where we can find these rebels?"

"We think they're somewhere in the mountains, south of the city."

"You think? Somewhere in the mountains?" Mesut looked around the sitting room. "I suggest you start preparing some proper barracks for when my men and I return. Peace be upon you," he said standing.

"And unto you be peace," the two Sipahis replied sullenly as the Janissary stormed out of the door.

Later that night, Mesut silently rode out of the camp. He was wearing riding clothes, still too well dressed to pass for a peasant, but not immediately identifiable as an officer in the precinct's unpopular army of occupation. Rather than going directly into town, where he might be seen, he skirted around the stockade, and rode the rise up into the western hills.

Though the moon only half-full in the sky, it still shone enough light to lead Mesut along the well marked path that led up to one of the thousands of nameless farms that dot the landscape of Eastern Europe. The farm consisted of a few acres of marginal land, some nearby forest that was held in community possession, the remains of a summer crop of barley, a budding autumn wheat field and a donkey. The farmhouse itself was a single story hovel, with a few asymmetrical attachments added on. It looked like a wart protruding from the face of the hill. A dog ran out of the house and started to bark at Mesut as his horse drew near.

An old man came out of the house to greet the guest.

"Thomas?" The old man asked.

Mesut hopped off his horse to greet the old man. "Hello, Father."

The two men who hadn't met in many years hugged each other strongly.

"Come inside, your mother is waiting for you." The old man said trying vainly to hold back a giant grin. "We've missed you very much, Son."

"I've missed you, Papa."

The farmhouse door opened into a room that served as a kitchen, dining room and sitting room. An old woman dressed in old, faded clothes beamed when she saw her son enter the room. "Thomas!" She said excitedly.

"Hello, Mama," Mesut said as he hugged his mother. "You look wonderful! The winters fall off your face like water off a duck's back."

"Oh, oh, oh you stop that! I'm as old as the mountains now! You look very healthy, Thomas! They must feed you well!"

"Of course they do, Mama," he lied, looking across the room. There was a thin man in his late twenties standing behind the kitchen table. "My God! You've grown, Pavel! It's good to see you again!"

Mesut hugged his little brother. Pavel was reluctant at first, but returned the hug once it was upon him. "Hello, Thomas. I saw you in the city today. I recognized you right away."

"I didn't see you in the crowd, Pavel. How are you doing? I hear that you're twice a father now!"

"I am, little Marc is five and a half now. He's still growing every day. Tatyana is eight, and Sophia is pregnant again. We're praying for another boy."

"That's good, Brother. I'll pray for you this as well. Are they here?"

"They are up the road, at Sophia's family's home."

"The last time I saw her she was pregnant, it's hard to believe that lump in her belly is now an eight year old girl."

"Time moves on."

"Sit down, sit down." interrupted Maria (the matriarch of the family). "I'll get you a cup of wine."

"Thank you, Mama," Mesut said patiently. "That'd be grand. Let's talk about you. How are thing here? I've been away for so long, and I'm curious how you are doing."

"I thought that you people didn't drink wine," Pavel said with casual malice.

"Some do, some don't. How are you doing, brother?" Mesut asked.

"Things are hard," Pavel answered. "Taxes are hard, life is hard. I don't think that your friend Jem will be missed very much around these parts."

The others were a bit off-turned by this comment. Maria gave her younger son a *you-be-quiet* look.

"Probably not," Mesut replied. "But he'll be replaced. With someone hopefully a little bit brighter than Jem. Time goes on, as you said."

"And sometimes stands still, especially when you live under tyranny."

"That's enough of that, your brother Thomas has come a long way..." interjected their father, Vasili, trying to put out a little fire before it grew.

"I'm sorry Thoma... wait, what is your new name? I'm sorry my memory sometimes fades," Pavel's apology hardly seemed sincere. "Something, Son of something?"

"My name is Mesut, called the son of Abdullah. When I was seven, I was given that name, along with an education, and an opportunity to see much of the world. Abdullah was the commander of the regiment when I joined, a quarter of the men in the regiment are called the son of Abdullah. How is your pig farm doing, little brother?"

"Boys, let's not fight this fight again…" Maria tried to step in.

"No, Mama. Pavel had a good point," Mesut said with the same aggressive monotony he used to address Yusuf and Jenkat earlier. "He said how bad things are for people who live under tyranny. I just want to say that he's right. Absolutely right! We're brothers, it's good when we agree. Amen and halleluiah, Brother! Some years ago, I was in Wallachia, and *there* is a land in tyranny. The local Christian Voyvod, he's called '*The Dragon Prince*', he butchers Christians more than any Muslim could. There is some tyranny for you, Pavel! You don't think about that! You think that because the religion of the law here now is Islam, that it must be tyrannical, because living under a Christian potentate would be so wonderful! Good governance requires no church," Mesut tried for a moment to catch himself. He hadn't intended to get worked up.

"That's an easy justification for you, isn't it Mesut," the name fell out his mouth like a tooth after a heinous brawl. "You're just happy because you're at the Emperor's table. Well, your country's on that table, Brother."

"Think that one over, Pavel. As long as you *peasants*…" In his later years, he would really regret using that term derisively in front of his parents "…pay your taxes, and don't riot, you are free. You are free to pray like a Latin, like a Greek, even like a Jew if you want, in the peace of the House of Islam! Do you think that the same is true on the other side of the Danube? Do you think that the Princes of the Germans, or Wallachia or Italy or Hungary would give you that freedom? They murder each other over any difference of faith! This land is conquered. It has been since before you were born, and will stay that way long after we are both dead! You were born free, rebellion gives you chains!"

"That's enough! Both of you," Vasili said. "This should be happy day…"

"The prodigal son returning to the family farm?" spat Pavel.

"The prodigal son is unrepentant!" boiled Mesut.

"That'senough," retorted Pavel. "I'm sorry, Papa, but I must go. I don't want to keep company with this *Turk*."

"Why don't you run to the hills, then? That's where I'm heading tomorrow. Your so-called loyal countrymen have sold out their would-be-liberators for a pittance. You hear that? A pittance!"

Pavel looked away as he stormed out of the farm.

Silence hung in the air.

"I'm sorry, Papa, Mama. I shouldn't have come."

Maria was weeping now. Vasili tried to comfort her.

"For what it's worth, I brought this," Mesut said as he put a purse on the table. Coins jingled as the purse rested. "I know times are difficult. This can help. I love you both."

Mesut embraced his parents and returned to his camp.

He and the Janissary Orta set out early the next morning.

Bojidar looked out as his motley band of rebels. They numbered only a hundred, and were sorely outclassed against the soldiers from Adrianople. His men were nervous and he could tell that many were considering the timely option of desertion. Marten raised an eyebrow and looked questioningly at his uncle.

"Maybe we could temporarily disband? No one for them to fight, they'll just go home."

The chieftain looked at the sheltered horizons of the valley where they were held up. "They won't leave. Your cousin Peotre said that they're moving south. They know about the monastery, that's where they're headed. If they can't find us, they'll just start killing to make an example, and wait until our countrymen give us up, one by one."

"If we know where they're going, we could ambush them."

"No. We can't win a fight. We can't surprise them, you saw their dogs. That's even if we could catch up with them. They move fast on the roads, we'd make better time over open country, but we're traVeling through mountains here. They're ahead of us, and they'll get to the monastery long before us."

"We could hit them at the monastery?" Peotre suggested

"Wait 'till they're fortified? Behind the stockade of our own base? Think clearly or don't think, Nephew."

"Have you made any decisions, uncle?" He asked.

"We can't back down, and we can't fight them, so our options are limited," Bojidar confessed.

"I'd like to have five minutes alone with that traitor." Marten said with disgust. "Without the army, we could show him the fibre of our mountains."

Bojidar turned to him inquisitively. "Really? What at would you do to him?"

"Whoever he was, I'd put this sabre in his belly. Let his blood spill upon the land he betrayed," and then Marten turned a little more quixotic. "Where did that commander come from? He speaks like one of us."

"He's a Janissary. Janissaries are kidnapped from Christian families and turned into slaves and male prostitutes in the harems of the Sultans, and they get convinced that if they do a good job brutalizing their own people, they'll have a spot in heaven, serving Mohammed in the afterlife. Even in their dreams they're slaves. He might well be from around here, originally, but he's one of us no more."

"They steal our women and our children and wonder why we hate them so much," Peotre spat with disgust.

"What if we did kill him?" Marten asked rhetorically. "We killed Veli-Jem. We went to his ranch, killed him, his guards and his family."

"That was justice," replied Bojidar. "One of his guards dishonoured one of the village girls. Then he gloated about it."

"You don't think worse is going to happen now? Hundreds of armed soldiers are looking through the hills for blood," Peotre argued. "When they get to the monastery, they will barrack there as a headquarters. They know that our supplies are there. They know that we need to get back there or disappear. The can use it as a base, and hunt in the surrounding hills, they'll get us eventually."

"What can we do about that?"

"It's hard to sneak into the monastery, but it shouldn't be too hard to walk in the front door. Dressed as a monk back from a pilgrimage. The monks there would help back up the story, they hate the Mohammedans, but won't take up arms themselves."

"I'll do it, uncle!" Marten said without hesitating.

"It won't be too hard to get in. It will be difficult to get to the commander. They all sleep together, he won't be isolated with guards. He'll be surrounded by the other soldiers."

"No, he won't, Uncle," Marten was excited now. "They'll have to stay in the northern barracks. It's narrow, there will only be about seventy men to a floor..."

"Seventy men, Marten! That's better than a thousand, but not much!" Bojidar protested.

"Listen, Uncle! The building is designed to house pilgrims. All of the rooms are small. There are enough beds for everyone, there are three beds to a room. I could find him surrounded by three men, not a thousand, not seventy!”

“Three professional killers, Marten! In case you’ve forgotten, you almost cried when we killed the lamb for Easter dinner!”

“That was a very long time ago, Uncle Boji! That was before Veli-Jem,” Marten implored his uncle. “I can do this. The monks won’t raise arms against the Turks, but they’ll help me. They can tell me which room is the commander’s. They can help keep the others who stay in the room busy. I can find him alone.”

“He’s still a more experienced fighter, and he can call for help,” Peotre reasoned.

“I can find him asleep.”

Peotre laughed out loud. “When did you become so ruthless, little cousin? Do you suppose you can simply walk up to a sleeping warlord and slit his throat?”

“I became this ruthless when you weakened!” his gaze forced Peotre down before turning back to his uncle. “I don’t want to fight him, Uncle. I know I can’t win. But I can poison him. I can strangle him in his sleep. I can’t bring a weapon to slit his throat like a pig. A way can be found. I’m a weapon. Steel and poison are just tools.”

The rotund chieftain looked hard at his nephew and decided to burden him with this responsibility. “Fine, we’ll dress you up as a monk, and send you away. In three days, we’ll meet you at Widow’s Cave. Don’t act if you might get caught. Find out what you can about them, and report back to us. If the opportunity presents itself, kill him. If it’s not possible, such is the way of things, we’ll think of something else. Come back to us safely. Do you understand that?”

“I do, Uncle.”

“Good,” Peotre came to his nephew and kissed him on his cheek. “Come back safely.”

Martin’s plan went beautifully. He was received at the door by the abbot himself, who insisted to the newly arrived Turkish garrison that he was one of the local friars returning from Phillipopolis, and was rushed past the guards at the wooden walls. The monastery had been abandoned thirty years ago, when the Turks first invaded, but had been reoccupied quickly as the territory’s administration became stable once again. There were only about thirty monks there, maintaining the chapel as an important religious pilgrimage site, and room to house hundreds in the barracks. The cramped housing facilities went along the wooden stockade walls, circling four buildings: the kitchen and dining hall, the rectory, and of course the chapel itself. The courtyard was large enough to act as a muster field for the force that had arrived unexpectedly. Surrounding the fortified monastery were steep mountains on three sides, and a road that led out of the valley.

The monks had allowed Bojidar's band to hide there from the patrols of the local sipahis, but were now afraid to allow any overt assistance with the arrival of the more serious force. Despite that, there were still monks who would do what they could, and were excited when Marten arrived on their doorstep. When he arrived, he was taken into the seclusion of the rectory and told all about the housing situation of the Janissaries by one of the junior monks.

"They are all housed along the northern wall," he told Marten, confirming his original assessment. "On the third floor, you'll find the commander. He is polite and courteous, he speaks our language, but you must be careful. He smiles like a hungry wolf."

"How many people share his quarters?"

"None, he's alone."

"Good."

"If you do what you plan, Brother Martin, then the rest of them will tear down this abbey, and kill us all."

"There is a way out, isn't there, Brother Monk?" Marten asked knowingly.

"There is a passage under the kitchen. We can move enough provisions there for us for a few days. We can send someone out of the monastery for a few days, who can come and get us after the Turks have left. If we simply flee out the other end of the tunnel, their hounds will hunt us down."

"What if they burn the monastery down?"

"Then we are in God's hands."

"There is too much wealth here for them to do that, I hope. They'll loot the icons and the treasury for gold, and come back later. This place makes too good a fortress for them to destroy it. I hope."

"I pray this, also."

"If you all go into hiding, then they'll know that you were all privy to the assassination. You can't claim ignorance."

"They wouldn't believe us, anyway. They're looking for an excuse."

"They hardly need one," Marten took a deep breath. "Tonight, have a service in the chapel, then move the monks into the passage. Lock it tight, don't open it unless I, or another monk knocks three times, then twice.

That means that it is safe to come out. If I knock five times quickly, it means that I've been captured and have broken under torture to reveal your hiding place. Five times, you and your men flee out the other end of the passage and go into the mountains. Their horses and wagon train can't follow you up there. You'll have to take your chances with the dogs."

"I'll organize it for tonight," the monk said finitely. "God be with you."

"And also with you."

How to accost the commander was the question that lingered in Marten's mind. He could get into his chamber while the commander slept; if he woke, then there would be a melee, which would not favour the young brigand. If he brought him a poisoned snack, it would immediately arouse suspicion if a monk showed up bearing a surprise gift, besides, he knew nothing about poisons.

He sat in his small dimly lit chamber and thought. He looked at the icon on the wall. Saint George, slaying the dragon.

"How do I slay my dragon? Can you answer me that, beloved saint?"

Then it dawned on him. Every room in the monastery has an icon of some sort. Not a gold one, or even a pretty one necessarily, but there was one there nonetheless. He would simply knock on the door to collect it. He would say that the monks didn't want to offend the religious sensibilities of their guests. The commander wouldn't believe him of course. He'd think that the monks were afraid the soldiers would steal them in hopes of selling them in Sofia or elsewhere. Trade them in for a night of a woman's pleasure or the like. But he would allow it. That's the way in the door.

'Now, once I'm in there, how can I do the deed? Hard weapons, like blades or bludgeons, would be detected. I need a soft weapon. Rope can be brought in to strangle him, tied as a belt. Maybe the commander would have weapons in the room? Take his and use it. There is no reason to smuggle in anything. No, that's too much of a 'maybe'.'

Marten exhaled loudly. *'What if I go there and he's on alert. He hands me the icon and sends me out the door. What if the opportunity simply doesn't present itself? There is no need to hurry. If the opportunity is there, I'll take it. If not, I'll simply look about and learn what I can about his chamber, and start planning again.'*

'No, then I'll have to spend the next four hours collecting all the other icons from all the other in order to avoid suspicion. Then knock on the

panel in the kitchen to summon the monks out of hiding, and hope no one noticed that they all disappeared into the kitchen for a few hours. Think!'

'Let's just hope that the opportunity is there. I'll take someone with me, and I'll have him get the monks out of hiding while I get the icons from all the other rooms if it doesn't work out.'

That night, Marten knocked on Mesut's door.

Mesut answered the door dressed in his night shirt.

"Yes?"

"I beg your pardon, Beyefendi," Marten said deferentially. "The abbot has asked me to collect the icons from the walls in the rooms. He does not want to offend any of our guests."

"What?" Mesut looked at the man in monk's clothing. He was dressed in a plain brown cassock, with a rope belt, an empty sack over one shoulder and a wooden crucifix around his neck. "Of course. Come in."

"I'm first?" the commander asked as he opened the door.

"If you refuse, then my errand is cancelled, Sir. If you agree, then the rest of your men will accept it."

"I suppose so. Come on in, I'll get it for you."

Mesut led him into the room and walked to the far wall. His back was turned to the unarmed monk. Mesut reached up and unfastened the icon of Saint George, the monastery's patron, from the wall. As he did so, Martin threw his rope belt over the commander's neck and pulled back with all his might.

Marten had never used a rope before for such a purpose. Rather than crossing his arms as he applied the weapon, in order to bring more torque to force, he gained more speed by keeping his arms open as the rope hooked tightly round his victim's neck. He pulled back and twisted his body, rolling Mesut's larger body over him and brought him down to the floor, belly side first.

Once the roll began, Mesut's hands instinctively went for the rope around his neck. It was wrapped too tightly at his throat, which was contracting under the force of Marten's intent. Mesut pushed his hands further back along the rope to the sides of his neck, and stuck his thumbs into the cavity of the rope behind his head. At that point, he hit the floor, landing elbows first and belly second on the wood planks. Thankfully, nothing broke.

Marten, perched atop the prone soldier's back, placed his knee between Mesut's shoulder blades and pulled back with all his might.

There was a vicious force against Mesut's throat, and his neck wrenched backwards, but the strength of the Janissary's arms around the rope lessened the killing power and held the assault at neutral. Marten was still in command of the conflict, but he could not kill in the current position, he would have to shift in order to kill, or remain in this position until his strength weakened.

Realizing this, Marten lunged his whole body forward and collided his right elbow against the back of Mesut's head. The Janissary's jaw was levered between the wooden floor and the thrust of Marten's elbow. Marten gave only an instant of respite to the commander as he lifted himself again and repeated the violent attack, elbowing the back of Mesut's head again, and then again a third time.

Mesut needed to act, or his attacker could simply continue this until his foul murder was accomplished, and he was already feeling consciousness escape him. He pushed his right arm further back along the rope, and held it fast. This hooked his right arm around his head to block Marten's attacking elbow.   Another attack came, but the blow was cushioned by the blocking arm.

Marten retaliated, realising that he could quickly lose his control of the situation. He whipped his grip from side to side, viciously reapplying force, and jerking the rope like a saw to burn the commander's hands and neck.

With his relatively free left arm, Mesut released the rope and pulled his left arm over his face, grabbing the rope at the same place as his right, and forced the two to roll to the right. Mesut freed himself from the pegging knee on his back, and rolled atop off his attacker, albeit with his back still to Martin, his position was now safer.

It was at this point that panic set into Marten. The rope was still around Mesut's neck, but Mesut was managing to squirm around, and now the former killing torque was moving against the back of Mesut's neck, accomplishing very little. The Janissary was kept at distance from his face only because his torso was trapped between Martin's legs. Martin could hear grasping air moving beginning to move freely through his victim's mouth now.   The soldier was on top of him, his face against Marten's lower chest, and he had lost his early advantage.

Mesut tried to call an alarm, but his throat couldn't spare the breath. Instead, he forced his attacker to do it for him. Ignoring the rope for the time being, Mesut posted the top of his head against Marten's breastbone, and pushed with his hurting neck. This gave him the distance that he needed between their two bodies, and he quickly thrust his hand between

Marten's legs. He grabbed his attacker's testicles, squeezed as hard as he could, twisted and pulled.

Marten screamed and screamed. The guards came running.

Four men dressed in uniforms ran into the room. They freed Mesut and arrested Martin. They rough handled him, but they knew enough not to kill him just yet.

Marten was held back, raging against the three men restraining him as Mesut stood with the assistance of the fourth. When Mesut could speak again, he hissed at his failed assassin.

"You are going to tell us where the rest of the rebels are."

"I'll never talk!"

Mesut laughed coarsely as he caught his breath. "I've heard that before. Take him to an empty room, I'll be there in ten minutes."

Five days later the orta returned to the city square. This time, they had with them a harvest of eighty prisoners of war, walking in chains. The men and women of the city looked at the sullen faces of the rebels. Their wounds scarcely treated and their spirits broken. The procession marched from the southern gate of the city's stockade to the northern quarter, where Veli-Jem had kept his house, and Yusuf-bey (now Veli-Yusuf) had moved to. Many of the townspeople followed the spectacle as it wandered through the city streets.

"Peace be upon you, Yusuf-bey," Mesut said in a grasping voice as he greeted the sipahi. "It has taken us a week, but we've rounded up your rebels for you."

Yusuf and Jenkat looked at the assembly stoically. "Unto you be peace, Mesut-bey. What do you intend to do now?"

"Our job here is finished. We intend to return to the capital. This province is your administration now."

"We thank you for your service, Janissary," Jenkat replied. "We will execute the prisoners tomorrow. Will you stay for that?"

"That sort of thing is your prerogative, and not the affair of my men or I. I want to leave this city as quickly as possible. We will return should the need arise, but we pray it doesn't." Mesut's throat was bandaged, but he nonetheless kept a threatening tone made only grislier.

"God will find that in our prayers as well," Yusuf answered. He stared defiantly at Mesut as he spoke, though he failed to impress the warlord.

"I also bring news from the court," Mesut continued. "The Sultan is planning a spring campaign for this coming March. You two will be called up to serve. Your men will be called away. You must neutralize this province over the winter. When the army of the faithful is away, we shouldn't need to concern ourselves with rebels on our rear front. You need not only neutralize, but also to recruit from here. A couple hundred tribesmen from Eskishehir won't do."

"If this area is to be considered arrears to the campaign, may I ask where we'll be heading? Another venture into Wallachia?"

"Not this time," Mesut answered. "Be ready when you are called."

They turned the prisoners over to the local beys and marched out of the city, heading back home.

Chapter Nineteen – New Arrivals

A flotilla of seven Italian war-galleys and four transports slid quickly over the cold water of the Marmara. The sun was still low in the sky, only now pulling itself up from slumber. The sleepy water of the inland sea was almost glass-like in its calm, a calm that was broken only by the rhythmic oars and chanting from the eleven newcomers. Their triangular sail rigging rested low on their booms, awaiting the command to unfurl in the event of wind. Their long oars rose, rolled, fell and pulled in perfect unison.

Slowly, as the ships sailed past the walled town of Gallipoli, a wind began to pick up. The town, whose name means *"the beautiful city,"* maintained its subdued character, but was now home to a comically disproportionate harbour. On the coast of the small city was a harbour and shipyard that dwarfed the town itself. From their boats, Greek-speaking fishermen cast their nets from the Turkish occupied town. Knowing looks past between old fishermen captains and their young crews as they saw the ships past. Italian trading ships were a common appearance in the trade lanes of the Hellespont, but these ships were ships of war. Their disciplined crews rowed their oars in a seemingly superfluous discipline. Those transport ships were weighted down heavily, they could hardly be shipping grain or regular trade goods. The fact that war was coming was probably the worst kept secret in the east, and now a handful of nameless fishermen were watching the first pieces as they were set up.

Veli-Fayik, the governor of the village, was woken from his slumber some very heavy knocking on his door, followed by a violent stirring. Despite his youth, the Veli's hearing had in large part departed him to the point where he was almost completely deaf.

"How many ships did you count?" he asked his manservant.

"Eleven, Veli," the servant replied loudly and demonstrated with his fingers.

"Warships?"

"I believe so," he nodded.

"Send word to my great-uncle, the Grand Vizier Halil," Fayik liked to constantly remind everyone that his extended family, the mighty Chandarli Clan, was significant, even though the Veli personally lacked any significant gravitas himself. "Tell him that Constantinople is receiving reinforcements on this day. Remind him that we need warships here until we manage to produce a large enough fleet on our own."

"Yes, Veli," the servant bowed respectfully, though he knew full well that the request would go unheeded. If Fayik's family decided that the time was right to fortify the city, the first thing that they would do would be to remove Fayik to a place where he would be less of a burden. The divan's neglect of naval matters was what ensured Fayik's security. "I'll send a messenger right away."

By mid-morning, the wind and waves had picked up and the Italian flotilla soared past the village of Studion and swept past the Marble Tower (which was a misnomer as the tower was made of granite and concrete, it was only encased in a thin marble shell), marking the edge of the city. The rolling hills encased in the city walls peeked over their edges and watched as the war-ships sailed past. The south side of the walls basked in the day's sun, whereas the leeside of the wall was shaded and kept in the autumn chill. Adam Karian, the generalissimo of the Roman Legions, thought that this was a perfect metaphor for the state of the city, keep the cold and hide from the light of the sun, the sun being the light of reason that had since left the east, and was now embarrassingly settled in far-off Italy.

Discounting his normal Armenian pessimism, he looked out hopefully from his guardianship along the walls. He counted the eleven ships sailing along the walls. Seven rigged for war, and four supply ships, weighed down heavily to the point that they were barely afloat. These were hardly old sea hags roped together for one last sail. These ships were taut and new, in their rigging and sails, their hulls and masting. Everything about them seemed shining and new.

'I can't believe that they're actually coming through with anything,' the general thought to himself. *'Warships! And who knows what's in those transports! Crossbows? Harquebusses? Cannons? Those marvellous Italians manufactured such wonderful toys of war! God has truly answered our prayers! In our hour of need, the Virgin sends an apparition of the avenging Archangel Michael, in the form of aid ships from the West.'*

Hope swelled in his capricious heart as watched the lifeline from far away sail across the sea.

"Shit," Vincent announced almost inaudibly. Only the guards standing with him atop the watchtower near the forum could hear him curse.

The watchtower provided probably the best view in the city to observe the comings and goings of the inhabitants on either side of the Venetian stockade. Over the city, and over the walls, they could see naval traffic in the sea, and they could see the activities of the city's main harbour of the Golden Horne.

"What's wrong, Sir?" one of the guards ventured to ask.

"They're flying the standard of Genoa. These aren't ours," the commander looked like a statue gazing out at the ships. Wheels ground in his mind as to what the overall implications of an enlarged Genoese presence meant.

"They'll help us keep the Turks at bay, won't they, Commander?" the second guard asked.

"Dominic Trebianno has no interest in crusade, I'm afraid," Vincent DiCastillo answered, his angry eyes following the ships as they passed. "He's going to offer the Emperor Constantine more protection in exchange for some of the Venetian concessions. This arrival is going to weaken the city before the Turkish horde comes."

"Still, they might help," the guard offered half-heartedly.

"The Genoese are motivated by profit and power, and they're hardly above looting a burning house. They don't understand long-term," their commander answered back. "The idea that you can milk a cow for years, or you can slaughter it once, hasn't crept into their philosophy of governance just yet."

Vincent sighed as the ships sailed past the Venetian concession.

"Go tell the Governor what we've seen," he ordered the young soldier.

"Yes, Sir."

Mario walked up and down the seemingly random streets that connected his home to the great Cathedral of Holy Wisdom. Every morning, he would hurry as fast as he could to observe the morning mass, and he would walk leisurely back home afterwards, like the hundred or so other faithful. What was curious about Mario among those in attendance, is that he was not what anyone would consider religious. To him, clergy was a political ladder for unscrupulous men of low birth, as opposed to the Venetian Senate or Imperial Courts, which were reserved for unscrupulous men of high birth.

His eureka moment came five years ago, when an infant died; one of a hundred infants that would normally die every day, the world over. His faith had been tested by wondering how an all-loving God could take an innocent thusly, but that wasn't what forced his faith into regression. What shook his faith irrevocably was that the local priest refused to allow the infant to be buried in a consecrated cemetery. Because the infant had yet to be baptised, the two-month old still bore the taint of original sin, and was hence unworthy to be buried in a pauper's graveyard alongside baptised thieves, murderers and whores. The priest who decreed the child unfit for burial stayed strong against the wailing and screaming of the distraught mother, and he had the infant disposed of in a public trough-grave. Mario remained a Christian, and observed his vows of the clergy, but he never trusted the worldly institution of the church again. He respected them as he would an earthquake or a fire; they could unleash horrible earthly destruction, but cosmic justice was simply not a qualification to their existence.

Mario had found something fascinating and divine in Holy Wisdom, a shred of bliss and joy. That shred was the pious Ella DiCastillo. Every morn, she would veil herself up and attend the early service. She would go and pray, reverently and piously, and he would wait by the narthex. Every morning as she would pass by him, she would smile. Sometimes he could only see her smile through her eyes, and sometimes, she would 'accidentally' allow her veil to slip to show her full lips and round face to smile at him. Today had been one of those rare occasions when she actually spoke to him.

"God bless you, Doctor Mario," she had said in passing.

"And blessings to you, also, Ella," he returned with a smile. "May I walk you home?"

Her eyes smiled and held back a laugh, and she pointed to the Hippodrome Forum across the square and down the road. "I'm going shopping first, for a new wrap."

"Please, grant me the dual honours of walking you home, and addressing me as Mario. I'm not your physician, as you well know."

Ella acquiesced and the two of them walked across the street. Mario cursed that she lived so close to the church. He wished that she lived across town; he would walk her back to Venice for the company if need be.

"Are you busy these days, Ella?" he asked slyly.

"No, I stay home and help my sister-in-law and prepare for the birth. I fear the stress of impending motherhood is weighing heavily upon her, and in turn upon my brother," she added. "It makes wonder as to the wisdom of marriage and child-bearing."

"I imagine you must spend a great deal of time wondering upon such things, what with all of your suitors."

"All of my suitors?" she retorted in mock shock. "What makes you think that I am smothered in suitors, Mario?"

"A beautiful and bright girl like you must be suffocating under the constant harassment of broken-hearted men, hoping for your love to repair them."

Ella blushed under her veil.

"You shouldn't speak like that. My brother isn't presenting me to suitors this season. Not while Daria needs my help."

"That's a pity," Mario said in a voice that was unnaturally deep and confident. "I'd hope someday to present myself with the lofty title of suitor."

"For that, you would need to speak to my brother. He's not home, but I am, thank you for walking me safely to the forum, Doctor," she refocused her face as stern as possible. "Good morning and God bless you. I must attend to my own needs here."

"Good morning and God bless you, Ella."

And with that they parted ways.

For the first time in Mario's life, there was someone in his life who mattered to him more than his work and his more solitary intellectual pursuits. This was demonstrated by the fact that he was at a church, of all places, every day, silently trying to commune with his own dormant spark of divine light.

He was full of his own version of the Holy Spirit as he walked along the urban hillside of one of the seven hills of Constantinople. From the hillside road, he looked over the abandoned ruins of Bucholeon Palace, and saw a flotilla of ships in the closed Sea of Marmara.

'Genoese war galleys,' he thought to himself. *'The drums are beating harder and faster these days.'*

Mario grimly cursed under his breath. War would mean a tumult in his new life here in Constantinople; especially when he thought about how involved Ella's older brother would be. The timing couldn't have been less convenient.

Bucholeon Palace stood at the foot of Acropolis Point and was built into the Sea Walls of the city. It crept down the hill up to the seashore and had its own private closed harbour on the Sea of Marmora. It had housed some of the most elaborate gardens in Christendom, and every major room was floored by mosaics so intricate that they had taken years to finish.

Like most of the former glories of the city, it lay in ruin. The only remains of the fabled gardens were the creeping vines that encased the red brick ruins like a green shell during the summer, and were now turning red and yellow in autumn's glory.

Sheltered in those ruins was a fully functioning clandestine religious community. Consisting mostly of Bulgarian refugees from the Turkish onslaught in the Balkans, these refugees kept their Manichean-inspired version of Christianity in the centre of the Orthodox world. Because of their thrice low status within the city, as heretics, ethnic minorities and refugees from an unsuccessful defence of Christian lands from the Turkish advance, the Bogomil monks hid in abandoned shelters where they could quietly practice their own dualist heresies away from the prying eyes of the judgemental Constantinopolitans.

And heretical, they certainly were. Rather than Trinitarian Christians, they had a tradition of theistic dualism going back to third century Babylon. They believed in a kind and benevolent spirit force, roughly corresponding to the Holy Spirit, and an evil creator God who had wrested human souls away from communion with that spirit and forced them into our horrible physical exile here on earth. They believed that Jesus was the first, and thus far only human, to transcend the crystal shell of the vulgar world and return to the divide. It many ways, they were the spiritual cousins of the Bektashi cult that ministered the Turkish Janissaries, a fact that hardly endeared them to their fellow Christians.

A spirited monk from the Bogomil cult climbed atop the ruined lighthouse outside the ruined palace and watched the ships sail by. Isodore counted the ships and considered what they meant. While most monks disdained the earthly realm as a spiritual prison, Isodore felt the opposite. He paid far too much attention to the vile creation of the physical world, as he felt that the best way to transcend it was first to understand his prison. It was that revelation that came to him during his travels across Italy which so endeared the renascent peninsula to him.

'Some new strength for Genoa. They're good for Constantine, but I wouldn't want to be in Count Dominic's place today. That strong a rearmament probably won't be here to reinforce him. Since I haven't heard anything about this before, that means that they'll probably be a surprise to the Governor of Galata as well,' he thought absently.

The flotilla of ships arrived into the Pera side of the Golden Horne by mid-day and were met a series of hastily assembled dignitaries, as well as half the colony in tow. Special space was made in the busy harbour to moor the ships and their crews began to disembark.

The first man off the first ship seemed to play the part of conquering Mars coming from Neptune's sea. Dressed in shining steel show-armour from head to toe, this self-describing God of War leapt onto the dock and looked at the stunned silence of the gathered crowd. At the other end of the dock were the gathered notables of the colony, the tallest of whom was Dominic Trebianno, clothed in fine trappings of court and an ornamental breastplate.

"Hello, Cousin!" the iron giant called out as he slowly clanked down the wooden quay.

Dominic lowered his gaze gracefully to welcome the knight.

"Guistiniano Longo. Welcome to Galata," he smiled and extended his hand, palm down.

The newly identified knight knelt before the governor of the colony and kissed his cousin's hand.

"I bring a gift from His Eminence, Umgati, Bishop of Genoa, and from the emperor of the west. He presents to you, Dominic Trebianno, the gift of my sword. A powerful and precious gift it truly is. To the people of Galata, he gives the strength of arms of three hundred men, veterans of the victorious war against Sienna. To our Christian brothers in Constantinople, in honour of our re-union of faiths, I bring a gift for the emperor of the east, Constantine Palaeolagas, Constantine the eleventh, from the Emperor of the West, Frederick the Third. A gift of fine crossbows, cannon, horse and a hundred harquebuses; as well as a promise of more to come! Let it be known that you have rekindled the friendship of the Christians who will now stand beside all in resistance to the advance of the godless hordes of Mohammed."

Whispers abounded among everyone witnessing the ceremony. News would travel quickly across the harbour, and by nightfall, this Guistiniano would be known across the city, and toasted as the heir to his namesake, Flavius Petrus Justinianus.

"Rise, cousin," Dominic commanded. "Welcome to Galata, we accept your gracious gifts."

"Thank you, cousin!" Longo announced loudly, obviously more for the benefit of the crowd than for his cousin. The dignitaries in attendance could detect a frost between the two kinsmen that was only barely under the surface during their public display of familial affection.

"In honour of this joyous occasion, there will be an extra ration of bread for all families in the colony!" Dominic announced.

At that point, even the crowd could tell that there was some kind of competition between the two cousins. In an instant collective conspiracy, they all began chanting "More! More!" It wasn't difficult to hear chuckles by some of the observers.

"Thrice normal rations, then!" the count called out with a forced laugh.

In barely audible tones, Longo greeted his cousin less formally. "Hello, Dominic. Are you surprised to see me?"

The Count smiled one of history's least sincere smiles back at his cousin. "Surprised and overjoyed, I assure you, Guistiniano."

"We could turn around, if you'd like," the knight offered.

"We'll find you some barracks, and you can join us for dinner. I'm sure your sister will be pleased to see you."

"So am I."

The governor barely hid his disgust at his cousin's and brother-in-law's presence but smiled for the crowd. He needed a drink, and he needed to speak to Giovanni Cardillo. He needed to speak to Noah, and if necessary, he would have to speak to the Emperor himself, as the alliances in the city were about to be stretched. Most important, he'd need a moment with his new guest before his cousin found access to some of the city's other notables.

Across the Golden Horne, another meeting was taking place. This one was between Orhan, cousin to Mehmet the Second, and Hectore Pazzi, captain of the Galata garrison and distant cousin to Count Dominic and Guistiniano. Don Hectore was tall and strong. His very presence urged everyone to constantly be on their best behaviour but he found himself on an atypical mission today. Diplomacy and politics were not among the gifts that God bestowed upon his temperament.

They met in the Grand Mosque of Constantinople, a small stuccoed building in the notorious Venetian pan-handle district near the harbour. The room was simple, with windows allowing in light and carpets covering the wooden floor. In attendance were a dozen Turkish men, of varying status and two interpreters. Hectore had wanted to meet the Prince alone, but Orhan would have none of it. The Prince was still a prince, and by virtue of that, needed to be seen publicly subordinating a visiting infidel. To greet him as an equal, behind closed doors would cause a serious loss of face.

"Your highness, I've been asked to speak to you about a grave concern," Hectore began. "War clouds are looming on the horizon between your cousin, Mehmet, and the armies of God here."

The translation that reached Orhan's ears were far more diplomatic than the words that flew out of Hectore's mouth, but such was the nature of diplomatic translations. The profession of dragoman, or imperial translator, was one of honest lies in order to keep the balance. In his limited Turkish, Orhan heard *'armies of Rome'* rather than the more grandiose *'armies of God'* but allowed the mistranslation.

"I pray the armies of the true faith crush your degenerate heresy under the hooves of righteous," Orhan answered without much expression. "For it is only by conversion to Islam, that you may save yourselves. The faith is a fire that burns in my brethren when they capture your so-called *'Queen of Cities,'* and then that holy fire will burn the degenerate Mehmet from the throne and bring me to my rightful place."

"He believes that the Turkish tribes will be successful in their assault, Captain," the Greek interpreter said. "And that discord between heretical movements within the horde will place him on the throne."

"These are both true possibilities," Hectore acknowledged, doing his best to hide his doubt as to the second. "But Galata shall be neutral in the upcoming war. We have always enjoyed a good relationship with your co-religionists, and see no reason to break it on behalf of the Greek heretics."

"I see!" Orhan exclaimed. "You fear the fiery wrath of the true faith, and hence flee from the very prospect of battle. A wise decision, as an army that marches for God is truly unstoppable."

"The Prince believes this to be wise," his interpreter explained.

"The Prince's life will be in danger if he stays here. When the Turkish barbarians come into the city, there will certainly be a bounty on your head," the captain continued. "I bring news from Count Dominic Trebianno and from Black Halil, the Prime Minister of the infidels. I offer you shelter in the Genoese colony during the conflagration."

"I care nothing for your infidel nobleman, but tell me what the great Halil-Pasha has to say! I command it."

"The Prince is most curious to learn your news."

"Neither of these men believe that your cousin will survive the coming war, Prince Orhan." He said in a hushed voice. "We will secure your safety in Galata, and once the war is finished, and your cousin dead, you can return to Adrianople as the new Sultan."

"Hmmmm," Orhan thought to himself. He looked across his busy entourage

"When does he believe the army will attack?"

"At the end of winter, Prince," Hecotore replied. "For your own safety, you should come as soon as possible."

"He invites Your Majesty to begin teaching the faithless on the Galata side as soon as possible," offered one of the translators

"Tell him that I, along with my servants will stay here. This city is to be the future capital of our own great Islamic principality."

"Prince, the count will offer his own personal home for your comfort!"

"The Prince thanks you for your hospitality but rejects your gracious offer," there was a polite finality to those words.

The prince and the captain were both frustrated at the impetuousness of the other, but the two interpreters looked across at each other, their eye-contact giving a silent '*congratulations*' to each other for a job well done.

Hectore's situation was less demonstrably successful than that of the two translators who'd avoided an undiplomatic brawl. The Genoese soldier had failed to secure the interests of his lord and now had to ponder how to go about keeping his own position secure. The arrival of Guistiniano Longo wouldn't bode well for him.

Near the Grace of God Hospital was a cubic building made of red brick. From the outside, there was no decoration, nor adornment, nor anything to identify the building for any purpose under heaven. The only feature on the four walls was a single iron grate door that led into what in the summer time was an oven, and in the winter months was a snowed in void. The high walls prevented the snow from melting on sunny days like today, and turned the housing block into a bit of an ice box during the winter, and prevented the heat of summer's days from escaping during the blazing season. Along the walls, facing this weather trap, were the apartments of twelve doctors, mostly either monks or priests, who worked at the hospital.

There was a knock on Mario Orsini's dormitory in the physician's apartments of the Grace of God Hospital. A nervous looking doctor peeked his nose through the wooden door.

"Who is it?" He asked nervously. "I'm very busy."

"It's me, Mario. Isodore. Vincent's friend." The monk spent his nights sleeping on a stone bed that was partially exposed to the elements, but it was Mario who looked terrible. "Are you alright, Doctor?"

"Yes… yes," Mario opened the door to see his guest. The sun gifted little patches of greenery to the courtyard, assaulting his eyes as the fresh air slithered into his quarters. "I'm sorry, I've been working all afternoon."

Isodore leaned back as the door opened. The smell of brimstone wafted out of the room to burrow into them monks nostrils. "What are you doing in there?"

"Just working on some things. What brings you here?"

"I wanted to speak to you, and see how you're doing. You've been here three months now, and I never see hide nor hair of you. What are you burning in there?"

"Nothing, it's just…" Mario started to protest as Isodore pushed past him to investigate the doctor's apartment.

It was a lower floor cordon which extended from the courtyard. The far end of the apartment dug into the ground, and there was some manner of furnace set up, and walls lined with jars, freshly labelled in various scripts: Cyrillic, Greek, Latin and Hebrew.

"This is a nice place the hospital's given you," Isodore noted and looked about. "Are you a Jew?"

"What?"

"The book on your table over there has a Star of David, and there's Hebrew written in that notebook, open on your desk, and on those jars."

"Quick eyes," Mario grumbled as he resigned himself to the uninvited presence of the unwashed monk. "I'm a Christian, that's not a Star of David, and that's not all Hebrew." He said pointing to all of the locations listed.

"It's a Seal of Solomon then. That explains the smell of brimstone," Isodore replied. "I should have guessed that. One triangle up, and one down. The symbols of fire and water for alchemists."

"You seem to know your science, Monk."

"The star was also the symbol on the signet ring of King Solomon of Jerusalem. He used the symbol, one triangle of copper and the other of lead to bind demons, and other such tales, if you follow these," he added. "But I doubt that that would be your interest. I take it that the Hebrew in your notebook is for alchemical work."

"Yes it's alchemical, and some of the shorthand is Hebrew, but some is Greek and some is Persian, other still in Arabic. All of this to record Latin names. What brings you here today?"

"I wanted to visit you, and make certain that you're doing well in your new home."

"As you see," Mario answered suspiciously. He remembered Isaac's words of interest.

"Did you know that a rather large naval convoy arrived from Italy this morning?"

"I saw that."

"They're from Genoa, the Italian princes are hoping to intimidate the Turk away from attacking. I doubt that they'll meet with much success, the apocalypse is in my prayers, and the Turk is forcing the hand of creation and destruction," Isodore could tell that Mario had little knowledge or care for such esoteric matters. "There's an army of infidels preparing to pound us into road-clay, but you don't seem terribly concerned."

"Well, honestly, I'm not," Mario answered truthfully. "My grandparents were refugees from Milan, everyone said that it was the end of the world when Florence overran the town. My mentor, do you know of Antonio of Padua, Antonio the Wise?"

"No."

"He's a great man, and his city of Padua also fell to other so-called Gog and Magog types in the form of my dear Republic of Venice. No apocalypse. When Rome was over-run by Visigoths, people claimed it to be the end of Christian civilization, yet here we are a millennium later."

"Unlike the Florentines, Venetians and the Visigoths, the Turks are actually sworn to destroy Christendom," Isodore countered.

"Most Pagan and Christian texts on alchemy, philosophy and medicine come to us through Arabic, Isodore. The Muslims aren't the harbingers of the apocalypse. Once this war's blown over and a peace is made, in whatever form that peace takes, as long as the powers that be leave me alone to my own works, which I have full faith will eventually happen, then what do I care if they worship in the direction of Rome, Constantinople, Athens, Jerusalem or Mecca? Knowledge and wisdom transcend the earthly domain of conquerors and base politics."

"That's true, but a visiting horde can still make life quite unpleasant."

"I'll give you that," Mario conceded. "But my work is fairly independent of rulership. All I really hope for is to be left alone to study. There is to be a Caesar in all times, and it matters little to me who that Caesar is. My concerns are elsewhere. Constantinople is not my fight."

"I'll agree with that, but it can be a lonely walk from this earth to the divine," Isodore chuckled to himself. "But I'll caution you about saying that in public. Politics and religion are best avoided around certain men; speaking of which, I'm going to visit Vincent at his home in an hour. He's asked that you join me. Are you available?"

"By all means." Mario replied. Too enthusiastically, as by the quick reaction, Isodore understood his enthusiasm to visit, and could easily guess at the reasoning for the display of enthusiasm. "That would be delightful."

"Won't it be?" Isodore answered quixotically.

Chapter Twenty - The Future Generation

"What wonders God has wrought! You're a big one!" Mesut's gravelly voice hollered in surprise. "What's your name? How old are you, Boy?"

"My name is Hussein, son of Mesut! I'm seventeen," the youth answered with nervous trepidation, poorly hidden by false bravado.

"My god, my god!" Mesut unconsciously touched his still-bandaged throat as he spoke. "Your teacher, Bilgee-Hoja, tells me you're strong as a tiger and quick as wolf. Is that so?"

"I haven't disgraced myself or my teachers in my lessons, my sheikh."

Sheikh is an Arab title for chieftain, and when used by non-Arab Muslims, it usually conveys the idea of *pater familias*, rather than a military or political rank.

"Let's pray you don't."

Hussein, the young Janissary, had finally come of age, and was part of a group of twelve sixteen and seventeen-year-olds that had just completed their ten years of study in the Lion's Den and were standing for their first inspection by their new commander. Their inspector arrived with reputation as being a cruel task-master and vicious warrior. News of how his neck simply wouldn't cut to the blade of an assassin, while not an entirely accurate rumour, had found its way all over the Lion's Den.

Mesut, commander of the Eighth Orta, inspected these newcomers in the mustering ground of the capital's Janissary fortress. Summer's flowers had long left the rocks and stones as Mesut paced around the new Janissaries. Around them, were hundreds of their corpsmen, getting ready to accept the children as brothers, as soon as their commander properly reminded him of the authority structure.

"And your name?" Mesut asked the as yet unmoustached youth beside him.

"Erkin, son of Mesut, my sheikh."

"And where are you from, Erkin?"

"I am from Skopje, my sheikh."

"No you're not, Boy," Mesut corrected him. "You're from God. Your soul is a shard of divinity, trapped upon this earth. Until such time as God beckons you back to Him, you will serve God with the rest of us."

"Yes, Sir."

"Third one, what's your name?"

"Abdul, son of Mesut, my sheikh."

"Where are you from?"

"From God! My soul is…"

Where is your family from?"

"Montenegro, my sheikh."

"No, boy. Your family is here. We are from all over this toiled earth, and together we unite and try to better it."

"Number four, what's your name?"

"Iskender, son of Mesut!"

"How enthusiastic," Mesut chuckled sarcastically. "And Bilgee-Hoja, tells me that you've been a very diligent student, you may even be recruited to the Devshirme. Is that what you want, Iskender? To be spared a soldier's life, so that you can serve in the Sultan's court? Do you think that's a better use of someone like you?"

"I would like to serve God to the best of my abilities, my sheikh."

"A very diplomatic answer, and I'm sure that you'll do a fine job serving the orta from the palace. Just remember, you have to hit twenty-two, first. You've got five years of war to look forward to, before you can think of such a soft life."

"As God wills it."

Mesut walked among the youths and gave them each a personal word or encouragement and a personal rebuke. He inspected their red tunics and white felt caps. Their swords, spears, bows, daggers were displayed. Their knowledge of the Qur'an was tested. Their ability to march in step was demonstrated. Throughout all this, the other members of the orta watched on in silence.

The mastiff trainers, the soldiers of the Kopckci, watched on, unimpressed. None of them had gone through such an experience, they weren't real Janissaries in the eyes of their comrades. They were interlopers forced into the insular soldier-cult of the Janissaries, and they could only watch on with their noses up as new recruits were embraced into the bosom of their brethren.

"Boys," he began after their displays. "Today you've honoured your instructors. You've shown what you've learnt, and my congratulations go to them. Bilgee-Hoja, Eren-Hoja, Emre-Hoja, These boys do you proud. I thank you for your gift, of these twelve *men* here today."

Mesut kissed the hand of each of the old, bearded teachers, and brought the kissed hand to his own brow as a gesture of gratitude and respect. The instructors were also wearing their Janissary uniforms, though they hadn't been on display for many years. Teaching children in the Lion's Den was the closest thing the corps offered to retirement.

"From today on, your honours are your own only among your peers. Outside these walls, all of your honours belong to the corps. Men of all lands will address you, not by name, or rank, they will not address you as Macedonian or Greek, nor will they address you as free-man or slave. They will see only a Janissary before them. Some will love you. Some will hate you. All will respect you, for if they don't, they will witness the wrath that breaks kings, and the fury that builds Empires!

"Let no man doubt that before me, there are no boys, only soldiers in the elite of God's army! You are slaves on this earth, but slaves to God's mission! You are of many nations, but you are one! You are better educated than any heretic Prince! You are better trained than any self-aggrandized knight! You are better equipped than any army in Asia or Europe! You are the sword and spear of God, and those weapons will be drawn from this day forth until the day of your burial. You are now Janissaries. Owned men. Never forget this."

For the rest of the day, the new members trained, ate and prayed with their new orta. They were no longer relegated to the children's wing of the Lion's Den, nor the children's table in the dining hall. The other children, of varying ages looked on in jealousy at their comrade's new-found status. These new members were trying awkwardly to participate in a conversation with their new peers, who were warmly welcoming the new additions into their midst, when their commander came to their table.

"I'm going into the city, and I need two body guards. Which of our new brethren are up to the task?"

Twelve hands shot up in lightning unison.

"Very well, Hussein and Iskender, come with me. Everyone else, enjoy your meal."

The three of them left the mess hall, the two students following their commander to the stable. "We're going to be visiting an old friend of ours," Mesut announced. "We have little to fear from him, or from the citizens in the capital, but there are men who wish us harm, so keep your wits about you."

"Even within the capital, My Sheikh?" an incredulous giant Hussein asked.

"Even among the Divan, Janissary," Mesut laughed. "Dangers are everywhere, when you're always ready to face them, you need not fear. It's those poor bastards who walk around secure in their own safety that find swift death, not us."

"Yes, my Sheikh," they both replied.

The three armed horsemen trotted down the cobbled grid streets of Adrianople. Mesut rode, his violently curled but slightly greying moustache was a familiar sight in the capital. After him came his two body-guards. Iskender tried to stare down every fruit-seller and washing maid that they passed on the boulevard. As for Hussein, at seventeen years of age, the barrel-chested youth towered above anyone else in the Lion's Den, and the same applied to the city dwellers who gaped as they saw the big man. He carried the horse-tail standard of the regiment, so that everyone knew who this traVeling party represented, as though there was any doubt.

When the party arrived at their destination, Mesut dismounted and with a curt hand motion, instructed the young ones to do likewise. They stopped outside of a giant villa, neighbouring the Imperial Palace – though the villa could almost be considered a palace itself. Thirty servants were gathered in the courtyard to greet Mesut. In front of them was the Second Minister to the court of the Sultan Mehmet the Second, the short, bald and vicious Zaganos-Pasha.

"Peace be upon you, my brother," the vizier proclaimed as he greeted Mesut with kisses on both cheeks.

"Unto you be peace, my older brother," Mesut replied. "It's been a long time."

"What happened to your throat?" Zaganos asked seeing the bandage on his friend's neck.

"A misguided attempt at delivering me unto God, Vizier," Mesut grumbled graciously.

"Come in, I have dates from Jerusalem, honey and Bithynia, and Boza from my new lands near Iconium. The servants will stable your horses," the vizier invited.

"You!" he said, indicating Hussein, "Plant your standard in the ground outside my front gate so that I may boast of my honoured guests, and we will sit inside and relax."

Hussein looked to Mesut for confirmation. Mesut closed his eyes lightly, indicating for him to obey, which he did. The three Janissaries were brought into the sitting room of the villa, and given honeyed dates and boza. Boza is a millet based semi-fermented beverage, that if you aren't given a taste for as a child, you can never develop one later in life. It was the un-official drink of the Janissary corps, as they were the only ones who'd dare to slug down the viscous beverage in large quantities.

The claims have been made that it increases a man's virility, a fact which Zaganos insisted was proven by his eight daughters and five sons, from three wives.

"So who are these two young Janissaries you bring with you, Mesut-Pasha?"

"This first one is Hussein," Mesut introduced the larger of the two. "Bilgee-Hoja says that he's one of the most gifted fencers he's seen in years. A future lion of Islam! I have no doubt that children of the orta will be marVeling at his exploits soon enough."

"No doubt!" Zaganos concurred and Hussein blushed.

"And this other one here is named Iskender," Mesut indicated the smaller. "He's been singled out for the devshirme."

Zaganos raised an eyebrow. "Really?" He asked, showing interest. "Maybe you can join me at the Throat of the World?"

"If God wills it, vizier," Iskender answered dutifully, wondering what could possibly be meant by the term '*throat of the world.*'

"These two boys finished their education and joined the orta this morning." Mesut said as he prodded one of his Jerusalem dates. "We expect greatness from them."

"This morning?" Zaganos asked incredulously. "Well, then. Congratulations are in order to you both. Guard your friendships well. Did you know that Mesut and I joined on the same day as well?"

The two boys seemed quite surprised at this.

"No, Vizier." Hussein answered.

"My family was from Morea, while Mesut here was called out of Bulgaria, but we were friends for many years in a Lion's Den, much like that one you call home, only ours was in Macedonia. I was called into the devshirme a few years later, as a scribe and a man of letters. I've been a man of the palace for many years now, but I've never had any truer friend than Mesut. Even when the other ortas rebelled against the sultan, Mesut stayed true rather than appease the other greedy commanders."

His was a fairly typical story, in that most of the senior administrators of the Sultanate were Devshirme, former slaves. Zaganos had been freed of his bonds of slavery by the former Sultan Murat, and allowed to have children, which explained the multiple sons, of varying ages who joined them for fruit, but would not dare speak unless they were spoken to. The greatest regret of Zaganos-pasha was that his sons, born free Muslims, were by custom ineligible to enter the ranks of their father's beloved corps. Their destinies would either be by a secured appointment at court, or as Sipahis, rural landlords and cavalrymen.

“Do you know anything of engineering, Iskender?”

“Some basics were in our training, Vizier,” he answered quickly. “But little by any way of practicum.”

“Your orta is going to be assigned to the Bosporus, young one,” Zaganos continued. “We’re building a fortress on the European side of the strait, directly across from the fortress on the Asian side – It’ll be ready for battle soon. We intend to cut the throat of the strait and hold it there by springtime.”

Iskender and Hussein watched on in rapt attention, as it wasn’t everyday that the third most powerful man in the capital, who turns out to be a former orta-brother, starts explaining affairs of state and the beginning of a war.

“Cutting the strait is going to force the hand of the infidel Romans, and bring about a war. We can’t tolerate a sea-accessible port in the middle of the lands of the faithful, you see, that would be foolishness. So instead, we’ll force them into their walled cocoon and then crush them out like a hazelnut. This will protect our territory and bring glory to the faith.”

“Praise be to God!” Iskender proclaimed.

“The fortresses are finished, and we’ll arm them fully by mid-winter,” Zaganos added.

“The orta isn’t there to haul stone,” Mesut interjected. “We’re there to keep the armies of Constantinople away. The Christian capital is only a few hours march from where we’re building, and if they believe that they can knock off this endeavour and force it into stillbirth, they will.”

“We’ve got an experienced building crew assembled in Gallipoli, and a new expert gunsmith who we’ll discuss later. The supplies are all stored in ships in Varna harbour,” Zaganos concluded with satisfaction. “Mesut-Pasha, would you spare Iskender to assist me in some of the planning and administering of the construction?”

“He could use the experience, so of course,” Mesut replied. “Thank you for the offer.”

“Anything to help my old friend, and my old family.”

Iskender could only do his best to hide his delight as to the direction things were going.

“Now, I’ll have my sons show your two young guards around my home,” Zaganos said. “You and I have some things that need be discussed without these others around.”

The sons of Zaganos and the two newest members of the Janissary corps went quickly and without words. Zaganos and Mesut leaned towards each other and began speaking in hushed tones.

Orban was in absolute shock. His forge had been under construction for over a month, and was now in ruin. Someone had broken into the wood and earth structure by the banks of Adrianople's Merich River and broken nigh everything. Ores were scattered, ash of coal, coke and wood were everywhere. Books were torn apart and their velum parchment burnt in the hearth. It was enough to make the smithy weep… or at least totter there for a few minutes before collecting himself properly.

The Hungarian gunsmith wasted shockingly little time in inventorying the crudely built mill and in appraising the damage. The building was within the realm of repair, but the hearth would have to be replaced, and several tools would have to be reworked or repurchased. The books were irreplaceable, as they were his own notes and his own plans, but he'd gone over them enough times to put them to memory, and he knew what he was doing. This disaster had hoppled the project, but not crippled it.

Into the workshop ran a runner dressed in fine draperies.

"The second minister comes," the courtier blurted out in Greek once he caught his breath.

"Here? Now?" Orban asked.

"The second minister comes," the courtier looked blankly back at him.

Orban nodded, understanding that the messenger spoke no Greek other than what he'd been told to repeat.

"Teshekur," he replied, using some of the only Turkish at his disposal. '*Thank you.*'

At this the courier sprung to life, thinking now that Orban both spoke and understood Turkish. He started talking at a lightning pace, completely incomprehensibly to the bewildered smith.

"I don't speak Turkish!" he tried to cut off the other man, who continued, undaunted. "I said that I don't speak your language, you pig-blooded savage."

It was just as well that he didn't understand the messenger, as he had in his exhausted state decided to explain the virtues of Islam to the guest, in hopes of bringing him into the fold. Much to his puzzlement, he found the would-be convert unreceptive to his homily. Despite his puzzlement, the incomprehensible words he uttered in Greek came true and the entourage of Zaganos, the second minister of state arrived shortly after him to the now defunct forge.

Orban ran out of the building to receive the vice-regal envoy. Orban, now over sixty years in age, knelt down onto the cold ground to show respect. The previous night's rain had already dried, but the ground still held a chill onto the man's knees. Zaganos dismounted from his horse and embraced the Hungarian.

"Peace be upon you, brother," he said in his native Greek.

"Unto you be peace, Vizier," Orban responded in his well-studied, but unnatural pronunciation. "You honour my house."

"Your hand honours God, Master Smith," the second vizier was short, bald, and despite his refined mannerisms, there was always a thuggish attribute which he was never fully able to dissipate. "I came as soon as I heard."

"You heard quickly, Pasha."

"Can you show me what happened?"

"Of course, Pasha," Orban answered. He brought him into the impermanent building that had been set up to the river, safely within the city walls.

"Was anything stolen?"

"I don't think so, only destroyed. Everything will need to be rebuilt, but I should still be able to finish by the spring, if nothing like this happens again," Orban tried to sound optimistic. "But I'll probably need some more money in order to hire on some men to guard the building at night."

"You've been paid enough. More than enough, our exchequer would say," the bald Greek said as he looked around to inspect the damage. "I'll have some of my own guards posted here. You represent a significant investment of state, with a significant project underway."

"I'm grateful for the security and trust that you and the Sultan have placed in me, Minister," Orban tried not to sound overly sycophantic. "I don't know who would do such a thing as this."

"I do," Zaganos said under his breath. "It needn't concern you, but there are many men here in the capital who'd wish this entire enterprise cancelled, and your salary be spent decorating palaces and paying for more servants. They seem to have forgotten the importance of spreading and defending the faith to the ignorant corners of the earth. There are men within shouting distance who'd destroy your endeavour and wish illness upon His Majesty. These people will find their fates soon enough."

"I assure you minister, I wish nothing but the best for his majesty."

"Your well-wishes are well paid-for, master smith."

"Does that make them any less honest?"

"No, of course not. I'll pass them along when next I see the sultan," Zaganos said absently as he inspected the damage in the terrorized forge. "He still has the utmost faith in you. As do I, for that matter. Don't worry about payment, as long as you deliver."

Orban smiled.

"Please accept my full protection while you're in the capital," Zaganos said loudly enough that his guards could hear him. "Any attack or harassment of you will be seen as an attack upon my own person. My guards are your guards, Master Smith."

"Thank you, Minister," Orban replied, pleased to be fortunate enough to enjoy the financial patronage of the Sultan and the personal patronage now of the Second Minister.

"You're most welcome. If it is practical to do so, we can move your forge physically to a more secure area in the city."

"Sir?"

"We can move the forge to the barracks to the north of here. The Sultan's own guard use it as a base for training newly recruited children from the provinces. You'll be safe there, and the soldiers can assist you in any heavy work. They'll also be more available for training with the new equipment. They'll also house you there. It's the best case scenario for everyone."

"That would be fantastic, Vizier!" Orban replied gratefully.

"I'll speak to the commander this afternoon. It's no problem, your work is important, Orban."

"Thank you, Vizier. You've re-supplied my heart with hope in this endeavour. I was afraid when I arrived here this morning that everything had been rent asunder. I'm sorry that I thought thusly."

"Don't worry, we all weaken from time to time. Let's see if we can gather your things today or tomorrow. I'll speak the local commander, and you prepare yourself for a move."

Zaganos was himself quite pleased to have secured the personally loyalty of the man who would be forging the largest cannons the world had ever seen. This was doubly welcome as the entire Sultanate was now getting ready for war. Zaganos was especially pleased with the newly cemented patronage, because all he had to do to secure this vassal was to have the Janissaries ransack the poor bugger's workshop in the middle of the night.

Tables. Tables without chairs. Round tables littered about the great hall in order to house all the dignitaries of the capital. At the head of the chamber was the elevated dais where the Sultan himself sat. At the beginning of the evening, his table was shared with Prime Minister and the Second Minister, the exchequer, Musa Chandarli and Tolga, the father of

Mehmet's wife, Nulifer. After the meal was served, the table was cleared so that individual subjects could approach the Sultan to ask for blessings and to pay homage. The Divan were afterward dismissed to their patriarchal family tables.

After the Sultan's table, the most prestigious table to sit at would the Grand Vizier Halil's table. Normally all the men of the House of Halil would be in attendant, but in the case of the current grand vizier, that meant his three brothers, all of whom were also members of the divan. Halil had no sons. Curiously to many, he had never taken on an additional wife when Ayshe became barren. That rumour could only be whispered, and even then would only fuel the curiosity as to why Halil hadn't taken an auxiliary bride.

At Halil's side was his bodyguard and informally adopted son, Ahmet of Amaseia. Ahmet was widely believed to be a murderer, and many of the notables of the empire were uncomfortable to have a man of such low station and reputation, sharing court with the Grand Vizier, but many were generally afraid to mention this out of fear for the well-deserved reputation of the minister himself. Also around the table were a handful of tribal chieftains. Tribes loyal to the old Sultans Mehmet the First and then Murat, who had now sworn to fight by the side of the next son in order to assist in the holy war against the infidel.

Zaganos watched on in disgust as another tribal cheiftain sat beside the grand vizier and they shared a laugh.

"That's another one for Halil," he said miserably.

Zaganos' own table, was the third most honoured place to sit in the hall. The podgy Hungarian gunsmith was invited there, he wore a silk robe purchased especially for the occasion. *'Purchased far too cheaply to be properly dignifying my office,'* Zaganos thought to himself. The smith had prior to this week given the Second Vizier the loyalty due to a man of his station and his employer. Orban might not fit in among the society of Adrianople, but his presence was important, and his newly affirmed personal loyalty to the Minister was a palpable asset. His presence at the table reminded everyone in the Divan to whom the hero of the day gave his allegiance.

Also at the table was a rakish courtier named Baltaolu. Though was barely forty, he was well respected as an intermediary during the recent interregnum. It was in no small thanks to his lobbying that Mehmet was allowed back as Sultan, and that Zaganos himself was not killed when Mehmet was forced to abdicate his throne. Baltaolu looked at the sheikhs sitting across the hall next to Halil.

Next to the affable and friendly Baltaolu sat the stern Janissary commander, Mesut. Rather than decorate himself in a futile attempt to fit in, such as that courageous, but doomed, effort made by the gunsmith Orban, Mesut wore his Janissary uniform, and uncouthly sported his scimitar in its scabbard by his side. Between him and Orban, the table was critically underdressed and would be publicly ridiculed if not for the fact that the lead table sat so many half-savage chieftains and wide-eyed mountain mystics from the Anatolian highlands. It was socially offsetting to the attendants of Zaganos' house.

"Don't worry, Minister," Baltaolu tried to sound reassuring. "We're all in this together now."

"We're not. I don't trust him," Zaganos answered. "I don't trust the old jackal, I've been betrayed by him once before, and he's plotting it again now."

"No one's been a more eloquent supporter of the Sultan in recent months, My Lord. I think that the Grand Vizier and the Sultan have truly opted to let the past be buried with the dead."

"Men like him don't change, Baltaolu. They just seem less dangerous with age. He's plotting, I can tell. This time, I'll be ready for him."

"The Sultan trusts him."

"The Sultan trusted him before."

Baltaolu's thin face looked across at the squat hairless minister. "You should let forgotten fights stay forgotten, my friend. Now is not the time to revisit these things."

Zaganos was about to launch into a diatribe as to why Halil represented everything that was wrong with the state of affairs in the empire, when a black hand rested on his shoulder.

Kabira, the palace's chief eunuch and warden to the Sultan's personal harem, leant down to whisper into his superior's ear.

"You have a guest who wishes to sit at your table, Minister."

"Who is it?"

"Tolga, the Emir of Kastamonu and of Sinope," Kabira whispered and motioned over to an empty place at Halil's table.

Zaganos looked at Kabira questioningly and raised an eyebrow.

Kabira nodded gently and narrowed his eyes as he did so.

"Please invite him here."

"Right away sir."

Kabira slinked off and returned with the aristocratic figure of Tolga, his head hidden by an enormous green silk turban.

"Hello, Emir," Zaganos stood to greet the prince who was dressed in fine silks, contrasting sharply against Mesut's dusty dress uniform and Orban's humble, though flashy fineries. "I must say that I'm surprised to see you here. I thought that you were invited to sit at the your son-in-law's table."

"I was," Tolga bowed his head, but his back remained strong. "I find the company displeasing to me. The tribal sheikhs who share his table are a crass and rather primal lot. I was pleased to see space available at your table."

"It pleases me to fill it with someone as respectable as yourself."

Baltaolu looked on, calculating the ramifications of this new friendship would mean. Orban ate his food, as he was completely oblivious to the meaning of the Turkish language conversation, but even he could tell that there was something significant to the two men meeting.

"Please sit down, you know the Sanjak-Pasha, Baltaolu, I presume."

"We've met many times over the years, yes."

"And Mesut-Pasha, the commander of our local Janissary detachment."

"Yes," Tolga barely acknowledged the presence of the Janissary, as it was not customary for an Emir to share a table with a slave, even one as important as Mesut. "An interesting diversity with which you accompany yourself."

The Emir then took a seat and acknowledged the rest of the table. His upper body made no change as he gracefully descended to his knees at the table. His meticulously fashioned turban and truly exquisite dress distinguished him from the other guests.

Kastamonu was an Emirate on the Black Sea, with a long standing alliance to the House of Osman. A country of mountains and forests, Kastamonu was one of the most powerful Turkish states in Anatolia, constantly competing with Karaman for position and status. The Ottomans maintained hegemony over much of Asia Minor, but their primary holdings were in Europe. The Emir was a sworn vassal to the Ottomans, Tolga himself swearing oaths to the fourteen-year-old Mehmet when he first became Sultan, granting him his daughter's hand in marriage, and had stayed a loyal ally during the return of Murat. Tolga had been a very loyal ally to Murat, and was very respected by Mehmet. Unlike everyone else at the table, the loyalty was that of an ally rather than an underling. That afforded the Emir a special status of a respected outsider.

"I understand that congratulations are in order to you, Emir," Baltaolu suggested. "Twin sons!"

"God's blessings are indeed wonderful in my eyes," Tolga replied automatically. "I hear that congratulations are also due to you, Sanjak Pasha."

Baltaolu smiled and leant back.

"I wasn't aware how public that knowledge was!"

"I assure you, Sanjak-Pasha, the rumours and affairs of *court* never reach my ears out in the periphery. Affairs of *state*, however, and the appointments for the upcoming campaign, have a tendency to become public knowledge pretty quickly."

"Then allow me to congratulate you publicly then, My Friend," Zaganos spoke up. "You're to be *Kapudan-pasha*, the first Admiral to the House of Osman. A position invented just for you."

"I'm excited about the opportunity to do what I can for the sultan and the faith. I'll be going to Thessalonica to gather the existing fleet, and then we'll be sailing to Gallipoli where new shipyards are building up for a new fleet."

"Do you have much experience with the seas, Sanjak-Pasha?" Mesut asked directly.

"I've sailed from the Balkans to Anatolia many times, and I'm an excellent swimmer. I like to race my young sons across the River Merich," he answered with a smile.

Mesut did not smile in return but mentally added new items to his itinerary of preparations. Emir Tolga did the same.

"Vizier, by my count this is the fifth such welcoming party the palace has hosted since the season began. Do you know if we'll be hosting many more?" Tolga asked.

"That's not certain at this time. We've certainly been successful in bringing allies to the cause."

"These aren't allies," the emir corrected him. "They are mercenaries, they're here for spoil and conquest. I'm beginning to suspect that when this campaign is over, there won't be much left of Constantinople to pay off these *friends*."

"That had dawned on me as well," Mesut added reluctantly. "These tribes want land on which to graze their flocks, and gold to give to pay for their lechery. I think that Sultan will find himself with a large and angry horde on his hands once he secures the single city for which he plans."

"These tribes are the allies of the Grad Vizier," Tolga stated. "Not of the Empire."

"You should be careful with that tone, Emir," Baltoglu warned him.

Mesut looked angrily at the courtier. "Unless you believe the grand vizier to be a fool, you have to believe that the end result of what he does was planned by him. The end result of his support for the campaign is an unwieldy and undisciplined army greedily out for plunder and not personally loyal to the Sultan, but instead here to follow their own agenda. The migration of tribe after tribe into the area of the capital is going to unwind the state, Sanjak-pasha."

"All summer and autumn, the grand vizier has personally mobilized legions of mystic orders to go about recruiting all over Anatolia. He's bought off rogue noblemen so that there can be stability during the upcoming war. He's sent emissaries to the conquered lands of the Christian infidels to muster auxiliary troops. I don't know what more you could possibly expect him to do for this jihad," Baltaolu answered.

"I suppose you're right," Mesut said without any crack in his voice before he turned to the second minister. "I'm only a soldier and I'm not aware of the exact nature of the deals with the Anatolian nobles or the Balkan subjects. I'm sure that there are secrets attached to the deals of which I'm unaware."

"I'm sure that there are many secrets in those deals," Zaganos concurred.

"As am I," Tolga answered conspiratorially.

"Minister," Baltaolu started. "Right now we're enjoying the most unification that the House of Islam has seen in Europe in a generation. You remember the first interregnum, when factions loyal to different sons fought openly in the empire. Then the false start to our Sultan's reign and the chaos in the provinces. Please, Sire. Don't allow suspicion to break what we now have."

"Of course, you're right," Zaganos answered quickly. He was far too suspicious by nature to throw the accusations aground, but he couldn't risk being perceived as a paranoid king-maker. "I'll mention these issues with regards to the tribes to the Grand Vizier when we next meet."

"I'm glad to hear it," Baltaolu said with relief.

Baltaolu was an observant man, but he missed a knowing look of agreement that passed between Zaganos, Tolga and Mesut. A knowing look that started a new party within the capital.

Chapter Twenty-One - Hospitality

Chronography is a strange science. In the ancient world of the Babylonians and Egyptians, twelve was a number of great cosmological import. There are twelve houses of the zodiac, twelve phalanges on each hand, and there are twelve months in both the lunar and solar calendars. Keeping with the significance of twelve, the ancients introduced the idea of the "hour," a unit to measure time as one twelfth of the day, between dawn and dusk, and also for the night.

The process was far from scientific, and completely inappropriate as the system spread northwards. The Abassid Caliph, Harun Al-Rashid gave Charlemagne a gift of a water-clock in the early Ninth Century, which Charlemagne believed to be broken, because of the irregularity of the measurements over the short winter days and long summer days of the year. The tilting spin of the earth wasn't something entirely understood in his day.

People learnt more of the nature of the earth's spin and sun's position as time went on, and by the 1450s' there were numerous marvellous mechanical devices to tell the hours and eventually minutes of a day, from elaborate water clocks, to bell towers, whose *cloche* – the French word for bell – gives the English the word clock.

Generally speaking, the day for a Christian was divided by eight liturgical hours, each with a collection of appropriate prayers. The day for a Muslim was divided by five liturgical hours, each with their appropriate prayers. Finally, the merchant's day was divided by sales of the day, and how things carried on with whichever fate destiny brought them. The idea of accurately setting the time as eight twenty-eight in the morning, would seem ludicrous and obsessive to anyone, but there Longo was at that time.

In one of his pouches, Guistiniano Longo had a marvellous device. It was a spring-driven clock made of iron, and was about twice the size of a normal chicken's egg. Longo could watch the hours slide along during the day, and more importantly for a man of his interests during the night. This allowed him to follow stars and planets more accurately.

Today, Longo used his clock to measure exactly how late his guest was.

Hectore Pazzi arrived at two hours past dawn.

"Hello, Guistiniano!" he greeted the guest and the use of Longo's proper name hung in the air along with Pazzi's breath.

"I don't know who you are, and you're being fairly presumptuous to address me by my Christian name, sir," he said, closing the lid of his technological marvel. "Who are you?"

"My name is Hectore Pazzi, and I'm the captain-general of the colony of Galata," he announced proudly. "We've met before."

"Have we?"

"At Varna, Sir."

"I don't remember you."

"No, sir, I don't suppose you would. You're the great man, and I was then only a junior clerk."

"Oh, you were a clerk. Were you at the castle or Shumen?"

"The castle, Sir. I..."

"Then you were in Varna city, not the battle of Varna, as you tired to imply, right?"

"Well..."

"You were a clerk, not a soldier, correct?"

"Sir..."

"Do you tell your constables and others that you were a soldier, fighting valiantly to defend Christendom, or do you tell them the truth; that you hid away in a castle, and fled with the payroll when the battle was lost?"

"It was the Illyrian mercenaries who fled with the treasury, Sir."

"My appologies, I'm sure you'd never contemplate such a thing. You're here to take me to your master, then?"

"Yes..."

"It's hardly needed, I know the way, but I suppose that brother-in-law of mine wants to keep up appearances. That's a nice cloak you have, it must have been expensive. They pay you well here, Captain?"

"Well enough, Sir," Pazzi didn't appreciate the slight and felt compelled to counter with an accusation of his own. "Your accoutrements are rather nice as well. The wages of your trade must suit you well."

"I afford these niceties by carrying the fight to the enemy, not hiding in a castle, or a city, or a colony, Don Hectore," Longo said bluntly. "Do you think that Dominic will hide or pick up the cross and fight?"

"I'm sure that he'll do what's prudent at the time, Sir."

"Ah, prudence – soft-boiled courage."

"Sir, this way," Pazzi announced and silently led his guest through the winding streets of the hillside colony.

The captain-general was pleased to finish his acrimonious conversation with the guest. He knocked on the door and stepped back, grateful that his role in the conversation was finished. He was thrilled when the door was opened by one of Count Trebbianno's servants who welcomed them both in. Pazzi politely, and joyously, excused himself from the duty, and left them.

Longo, on the other hand, waited. He waited and waited. He was asked to stand in the standing room, and then the servant invited him to sit in the sitting room. All of which he did with a honed patience.

"Ah, Longo, sorry about the wait," Trebianno said when he stepped into the sitting room. He greeted his cousin with a hug and kissed the air on either side of his kinsman's face. "You've eaten, right?"

"Of course," Longo answered. "We agreed to meet for breakfast two hours ago, so I ate before leaving the barracks. Where's my sister?"

"Oh, yes, sorry about that, she's at a reception right now, the women of the imperial court, you know. She'll be back tonight, I'm sure we can arrange a meeting for another time."

"I'm sure," Longo answered patiently, and without surprise. "Perhaps you can take advantage of this opportunity to tell me about your failure to secure union?"

"No," Trebianno tisked him. "It hasn't failed, the project is far from dead, but things take time out here, they can't always work with Germanic precision. Surely the cardinal will understand that."

"The cardinal is Italian, not German."

"I know he's from Italy, but you're hard-pressed to find anyone who more enthusiastically supports the northern princes."

"The House of Hapsburg now carry the mantle of the Holy Roman Empire, Cousin. We have unity through their crown, and through the universal faith. The nuances that are tolerated out here frustrate him."

"They say unity, they mean hegemony, Longo," Trebianno corrected him.

"In this context, they are the same," Guistinianno said quickly. "We're here to extend that unity eastward. To have one large community of nations, under the cross. It gives security and safety to all nations and races!"

"A hundred nations and a hundred races can't be under the same flag, and you know it," the count retorted. "German, Bohemian, Flemish, Italian and Pole can hardly call each other brother, when they don't have the same word for the concept! The universal communion of Christ is nothing but the rule of the Germans, or of those filthy popes."

"You'd prefer the rule of the Italians, I understand. I'd prefer this also, but I prefer the universal rule of anyone, to the anarchy in which we now find ourselves."

"I don't favour anarchy, but local administration of laws has to take precedence over anything as grandiose as what these two foul emperors claim! Why should Syria and Spain operate under the same laws, for example? Their languages are different! Their cultures are different! Their races, their geography, their history, their food, their temperament! They're all different! The very idea of universality of law is impossible!"

Longo exhaled loudly, this was an argument they'd had before, but he it seemed to be an unwinnable position for either of them.

"Because we're not regional! We're all made as one flesh, from the north of Europe, to the south of Africa, we're all in God's image. There is no regional distinctions in the eyes of God. Do you think that because murder is immoral in Ireland, it should be acceptable in Arabia? Rape is in contravention of divine law in the mountains of Bavaria, but not the mountains of Persia? There is one God, one law, and we need only one governance!"

"Cousin, were that the case, then the one God could make his one government and we'd be done with it! As it stands, the reality of life among the Greeks is different than among the Celts, or any other race for that matter. They hate us westerners, and won't adopt our ways. They hate us for very rational reasons – we burnt their city, gobbled their trade, and treat them as second-class in all aspects, and they reject us accordingly."

"They don't need to agree with the law in order to be governed by it! The bible is not a debate, it's divine judgement! Those who act out against it are committing crimes against God!"

"Then God can punish them!"

"Why is Gennadios not dead?" Longo changed the subject, but not the theme of their confrontation.

"We can't just kill the locals who disagree with us! They'll riot and oust us from the city! We're not conquerors here!"

"Why exactly, do you think I'm here?" Longo asked accusingly. "Do you think I'm a pilgrim or a hermit?"

"I know why you're here."

"Then say it."

"You're here, because Cardinal Umgati wants to rebuild the Roman Empire."

"I'm here because there are many in the west who want communion with the east, and don't want the cradle of Christendom to continue to be subject to the heresy of the Muslims. We want one state, under the cross, for the whole world."

"It can't work like that, the eastern brethren are too different!"

"They should be grateful. We're here to drag them, kicking and screaming out of savagery. We're agents of the rebirth of humanism! Would they prefer to live under the infidels?"

"Some would! Gennadios and Stavros have both proclaimed that the sultan's turban is preferable to the pope's tiara."

"Then send them to the sultan," Longo said dismissively. "You still have to take orders, as do we all. The cardinals, the emperor and the pope all want union, which means that you do too. If you don't, then I'm to replace you and send you home to our dear uncle. Now, which other champions of union can I find here in the capital?"

Trebbianno exhaled angrily through his nose.

"The Venetians also favour union. As does the Strateogos of the Legions, a general by the name of Adam Karian."

"What about the emperor?"

"Who knows what he really wants?" Count Dominic threw up his hands when he mentioned the emperor. "He's a mystic, not a rationalist. The wisdom that comes from an analyzed thought isn't the wind that fills his sails. He believes that God will grant him knowledge. Nobody knows what he really wants on any given day, and what he wants can change drastically from week to week."

"The current patriarch, Gennadios, he's against the union, correct?"

"Very much so."

"Noah is the priest that supports it. I've been told to ensure his placement."

"Yes, we've been trying to put him on the pulpit out here, but without much success. He's not assertive enough to do it on his own, so the rest of us have to do all of his self-promotion for him."

"I've already arranged a meeting with Karian for later today, I'll leave shortly. We'll discuss Noah and the state of union."

"I'll wish you good luck, but it'll never work. We'll never have a proper union with the eastern churches ever again. They're too different and too bull-headed to function under western rules. We'll have to treat them as allies, not underlings."

"The gold of their crowns no longer shines, Dominic. Why should we respect the weak? They should be prepared to do as they're told."

"I'm sorry to be the bearer of bad news, but you'll find them very uncooperative."

"There's no room for allies in this war, cousin," Longo answered sternly. "They'll obey us willingly, or we'll leave them to the dogs of war, and let them stand or fall on their own strength."

"Good luck then."

"Thank you. I'll make arrangements to meet my sister in the palace this afternoon. I don't foresee the duty of returning here arising again anytime shortly."

"What a coincidence, neither do I," Trebianno answered.

Longo began retracing his steps to the harbour. He wasn't the sort to let it go unnoticed when he was being followed. Someone was following him through the city as predictably and as visibly as a shadow. Longo couldn't get a good view of whoever it was, but he was aware of their presence, as sure as he was aware of sellers, beggars and vice.

Even in a foreign city like Galata, he could tell that there was someone matching his paces as he weaved his way through the streets and busy markets of the colony. There are some, who when confronted with such a situation, would retreat to the protection of the crowd. They would seek to get lost in the hustle and bustle of the busy streets. Longo was a much more practical man, and retreated to the deserted residential roads of the hillside settlement.

Only a few blocks away from a busy market road, Longo found himself walking down an empty road that was much to his liking. Once he was a hundred paces or so from any intersection, he turned around and waited for his pursuer.

Pazzi was in in an awkward situation, and one upon which he hadn't planned. He was walking behind Longo, on an empty road, and it would be very difficult to falsify any pretence other than the obvious. He was hardly out for the fresh air.

"Hello again, Don Hectore," Longo greeted him as he came closer. "Is there something that I can help you with?"

"No, nothing at all. I'm just making sure that you find your way home safely. The barracks is over to the east," Pazzi said smiling and pointing.

"I know where it is, thank you very much."

"Where are you going?"

"Is that of any importance to you?"

"Everything that happens here is important to me."

"I'm going to the harbour. From there, I'm planning to visit the other side."

"You're meeting with Adam Karian?"

"That's right."

"You should be careful around him. He's not quite as dutiful as he seems."

"I thought that the two of you were friends."

"He doesn't keep friends, just people he can use."

"Well, thank you for your concern, but I'm sure that I can judge another man's character for myself."

"I'd hope so," the captain-general said cautiously, "but these easterners are a little more duplicitous than the men of the west. You should be very cautious."

"I'm always cautious, Don Hectore," Longo stated sternly. "I've heard that you and the Strateogos have a rather elaborate history together."

"What kind of rumours?"

Longo looked dead-pan at his host.

"There's no need for this kind of rudeness," Pazzi answered quickly. "There are few illegal or shady dealings that happen in the capital without the general's notice, and I've had to lecture him about western norms before, but that's the extent of our relationship."

"I'll remember that."

"See that you do."

"Well, thank you for the warning, the advice and the escort. Now if you don't mind, I'm sure that I can find my own way to the docks."

"Of course. Good day to you."

"Good day to you."

"General Karian," Longo announced when he entered the office of the Strateogos. "I would first like to say that I have no cares or concerns about your emperor. I have no opinions about any illegal enterprises that take place in the empire. I don't want to meet anyone in the court, and I couldn't care less about Genoa, Venice, Germany or Greece."

"A pleasure to meet you, too," the curly haired Armenian said walking over to his guest, not entirely certain what brought on such a proclamation. "If you care so little for these things, why don't you tell me about the things that do tickle your interests."

"I care about the welfare of my men and little else. I've been ordered to do what I can for the defence of the city. It has been brought to the attention of the west, that the Turks intend to crush the eastern empire when spring comes."

"You're here to help us?"

"I'm here to lead you."

"Do you speak Greek?"

"No."

"You can't lead us, but I'd love your counsel."

"I'm here to win a battle, Strateogos. I want you to know that I have absolutely no interest in the politics of the city."

"I find that hard to believe. I'm under the impression that you're here to secure union."

"I was told that you favoured union."

"I do, and I'm very active in the politics of bringing it about. I thought that you'd be new ally in that fight."

"The Genoese and Venetian ambassadors should be wholly dedicated to that, as are you. That fight is being fought, so I intend to now dedicate myself to the defence of Christendom."

"No politics?"

"It will be very political when Constantinople stands because of the bravery, dedication and piety of their fellow Christians. I doubt that the patriarch will convert while the Turk's sword is still drawn. I'm very apolitically political. And my mastery of the art comes from neglect."

"I've read about you for many years, and you seem much as I imagined you to be," Karian looked at his desk while he spoke, as though looking for the right papers. "I've read about siege of Milan."

"I'm flattered."

"Do you think that you'd be able to recreate what you did there?"

"In what regards sir?"

"The digging. We're expecting that the Turks are going to try and undermine the walls in order to knock them down. What do you think we should do about that?"

"Start digging now, before winter hardens the ground too much. You should build a large tunnel, running parallel to the walls, about fifty paces outside of them, and about ten yards down. Such a counter tunnel would thwart any attempts by the Turks to dig under the wall and plant explosives. You'd need to man the lateral tunnel with a few dozen men, but that would stop the Turkish miners in their tracks."

"That's great. When can you start?"

"Tomorrow morning, if you can afford to hire us."

"I won't be able to secure your army right now," Karian said realistically. "I can ensure you a salary and give you men to do your bidding, but we won't be able to hire on so many mercenaries until the final hour."

"Then we'll start with what we've got."

"Sounds fine to me."

The two men shook hands, and Longo returned to the harbour to ferry back home. Karian was pleased that the defence was finally beginning. For half a year, the Turks had been planning and readying themselves, and the Romans had done nothing but wait, and try to carry on life as normal. The general was pleased that the neglected tasks were finally being undertaken, and that they wouldn't be caught by surprise when the time came.

Chapter Twenty-Two – Houses

"Achooo!" The sound echoed throughout the ambassadorial manse.

Giovanni Cardillo found the winters in Constantinople quite disagreeable. The cloudy skies, the humid chill, and the inevitable battle with his own failing health were a constant distraction to him. While most men would simply dismiss a runny nose as a normal deficiency of changing seasons in foreign climates, the Venetian ambassador saw it as a personal affront by fate.

Cardillo was the most senior representative of the Venetian Republic within the city of Constantinople. He simultaneously held a seat in both the court of the Eastern Empire and in the Senate of Venice. He was a member of council to the Emperor of the East, and was cousin to Eugene IV, the former Holy Father in Rome. An important man of respect shouldn't show any weakness, and that's exactly what he was now showing. Sniffling, sneezing, coughing and possessing a nasal cavity that was as open as the famous sluice-gates that drained the swamps of his dear Venice, all were signs of weakness that he could never allow for public spectacle. So he did the only thing that a man of his temperament could in the current situation. He hid in his home, speaking only to his wife and three children, and did business through couriers, allowing only his most trusted servants to see him in his depressingly and increasingly human state.

The one non-familial exception to his self-imposed quarantine was Vincent DiCastillo. The two men had been together in Constantinople for over a decade and shared a professional closeness of which most administrations could only dream. Even with this closeness, Giovanni insisted on a wicker wall, similar to a confessional screen, separating the chairs in which the two men would sit when the soldier came to visit the ambassador.

"I pray that you're feeling better today, Ambassador," Vincent greeted him through the screen.

"My health was better when I woke up this morning. I've heard news that the Genoese are making new alliances," Giovanni replied in a rasping voice. "Eleven ships, led by a knight from Genoa have arrived on Galata's docks. What can you tell me of this, Vincent?"

"The knight's name is Guistiniano Longo. He's been sent by the Western Emperor to help in the defence of the city."

"How many men does he bring?"

"Two hundred horse, five hundred foot, include perhaps a hundred firearms."

"Where does he stay?"

"In the Plaza San Luca," St. Luke's Place was the notorious vice-ridden and degenerate district in Galata that housed the colony's barracks. Vincent could hear Giovanni slurp something out of a cup from behind the wicker screen.

"Do you know about him?"

"I know of him," Vincent answered slowly. "He's a mercenary and a brute, but he comes with a good reputation. He earned accolades as a digger during the siege of Milan. He organized a system of tunnels to counter Florentine miners who were attempting to undermine Milan's walls. Those skills could help us in the upcoming days. Apparently Karian's asked him to recreate that work. He's also a veteran of Varna. I don't know much about the man though."

"He comes from a noble family, but they've since fallen on hardship. He's related to Bishop Umgati of Genoa, and is brother to the wife of Count Dominic across the harbour, they're also cousins. I suspect that he was sent by the Bishop more to secure the failed union than anything so altruistic as defending Christendom. Bishop Umgati and Count Dominic have a long history of bad blood, we may want to have a meeting with this *Guistiniano Longo*. Talk to the monk, have him learn the strength of company that made its way here, and then we'll arrange for a conversation between the two of us and our new guest."

At the end of the last breath, the ambassador burst into fits of coughing. Vincent was quite impressed that the failings of the body would never slow his patron's sharp mind. When the coughing subsided, he pressed his master.

"Are you certain that he'd want to speak with us?"

"I assure you that he's not here to help Dominic Trebianno," Giovanni answered between coughs. "He has a different agenda, one that's been dictated from the Bishop of Genoa, not the count over the water. We'll meet with him, and we'll use Karian, as an intermediary."

"Yes, Sire,"

"A second issue: I hear that the Turks have finished arming their fortifications on the northern Bosporus. Is this so?"

"That's what our runners say – finished or nearly so."

"Send Ezera north," he decided. "I want him to sail past the castles and let you know what he thinks. His experience on these matters has served us well in the past.”

“He’s no longer in our service, Don Giovanni,” Vincent pointed out. “He serves his own business. Also, I don’t know when he’s expected back.”

“Give him a pilot’s licence, a roster placing when he returns. Ask him to go there to pick up some copper goods, or something of the like, and pay him handsomely. Tell him that we will also pay handsomely for his analysis of the fortresses. Phrase it as a request in order to satisfy his delicate sensibilities if need be, but have it done. If you need gold to cement the deal, then you have authority to use the vault.”

“I’ll see it done, sir.”

“A third task, either for Ezera or Isodore, or perhaps another party,” the sickly thinker started “Adrianople is building a fleet in Thessalonica. We need to know what’s there as well.”

“I’ll hand that task to Isodore as well, but we’ll need to pay him more.”

“That’s easily done,” Giovanni continued. “Another thing, your doctor friend, I need to see him. Send him to me, he was of great help during the summer.”

“I’ll see it done today.”

“Thank you.”

The walled ziggurat that Vincent called home was lightly covered in white paint. Much like Mario’s apartment block, DiCastillo’s villa walls acted as a cage to keep the sun out. When he entered his home through the sliding wooden door and greeted Ella and Daria the two women were huddled around the baby crib, keeping each other and the baby warm by the roaring fire. A gurgle and wail came from the crib, and Daria snapped her fingers to call the wet nurse, who obeyed with frightening speed.

“Hello, girls!” he called as he entered.

“Hello, yourself!” Daria shouted back. “What brings you home at this time of the afternoon? Wine in the afternoon left you undesiring of staying at your post?”

“As always, wife, it is wonderful to see you, too,” Vincent said, ignoring her and kissing the infant in the cradle, his eyes warming to the nurse before his wife. “Have the servants bring some food upstairs for the three of you. I’m having guests over.”

The two women looked at each other. The child, Alexandra, was oblivious to the notion that conversations were anything other than a random collection of interplaying sounds but seemed to possess enough intuition to immediately fall silent.

"Are we to hide ourselves in our own home because you choose to have your drinking companions from the regiment over before the sun sets?" Daria asked accusingly. "Into your home, with your wife, sister and daughter, you're going to be inviting your baudy friends?"

Vincent exhaled loudly.

"Wife, you and my sister are to cloister yourselves upstairs, while I meet with some people. They are not drunken brawlers here for free wine, they are here for important business, of which you needn't concern yourselves. I can't meet with them at the tower or the castle, because everyone I meet with there gets their presence reported. I'm having some guests here. We'll be done in an hour."

"I suppose that you've been talking to Don Giovanni, then!" Daria said. Whenever Vincent was forced to show deference to the ambassador, he came home in a bad mood.

"Nikos!" Vincent called out to the head servant of the house, who quickly emerged from the kitchen.

"Yes, sir?"

"Set up a meze table in the sitting room upstairs for the girls! I'm having two guests over. Prepare some fish soup and mulberry wine."

"Yes, sir."

Daria stormed upstairs with Alexandra, Ella meekly followed her sister-in-law. Vincent sat down alone on one of the wooden recliners set around the room and took his heavy cape off. His guests weren't due to arrive for another hour, but he preferred to sit in solitude. The wailing of the child ground his nerves like salt against ice, and the wonderful fiery girl whom he'd married had transformed into a frigid, complaining matron since the child arrived, and it wasn't as though she'd exactly been soft-spoken woman beforehand. Ella, he didn't even know how she was doing; all she ever did now was go to church! Vincent had a newfound appreciation for silent solitude in his own home.

Isodore and Mario were greeted at the door by Nikos the servant, who was quickly brushed aside by the commander of the quarter.

"Welcome!" he exclaimed as he ushered them in the door. "Come in, come in. Sit by the fire. Nikos, three flagons of wine!"

"Thank you, Don Vincent," Mario doted. "It's always a pleasure to visit you."

The marble greeting room had a chilly air to it and it echoed all of their words off the lifeless walls. Vincent and Mario both wore the long black coats that were expected of gentlemen to wear and Isodore kept his grey, shapeless robes. The three of them quickly relaxed around the lounge and sipped their hot wine.

"How is your first Constantinople autumn, Doctor Mario?" Vincent joked.

"Much colder than I thought it would be," Mario answered truthfully. "For some reason, I've always thought of the east as being hotter than the west."

"Well, with so many people here, and you accustomed to the temperate summers of Italy, the chill must be hard."

"Actually," Mario replied tepidly, "I rarely ever go into the hospital anymore. I'm only there for two days out of the week. Most of my time is spent at home brewing potions and elixirs, to supply the hospital. I prefer it that way, I don't actually have to interact with the natives, and they don't have to deal with me."

"Why don't you want to deal with the natives?" Vincent asked with a curious note of caution. His eyes seemed to threaten an answer.

"Whatever I say to the patients, they won't believe me. They'll question me, ask about my education, my fees and if I'm married or not, and then the start trying to engage me in some obscure discussion as to the nature of Christ, while all I'm trying to do is determine their phlegm and bile levels! It's infuriating. I'll give them a prescription, and then they'll go and check with the senior Greek to make certain I've given them the correct medication, and not a vial of baby pee or some equally obscure folk medication, to suit my own enjoyment. It's enough to drive a man to melancholia, so I stay away from all this and brew the medicines that the doctors require, and ignore the patients. It works out a lot better that way."

Vincent looked at him silently for an instant.

"That's a terrible decision, Mario," he chastised him. "The locals are a proud race, and they believe in the supremacy of their culture and their religion over all other races, religions and nations. This is despite the fact that their trade is dominated by Italians, their armies are almost entirely composed of foreign mercenaries and all of the significant doctors, architects and engineers in the city today come from our peninsula. They still look down upon us as upstarts in the realm of civilization, and heretics in the eyes of God. They'll never stop to question why God has so blessed us with wealth, technology, military and cultural strength, and yet allowed their once proud empire to fade into the shadows!"

Mario and Isodore exchanged quick glances, as they could see that Vincent was getting himself worked up, and showed no signs of relenting.

"The Turks surround the city on all sides, and it's us that prepare for it! Do you know what the Emperor is doing today? He's observing the women of the court who are trying to march in step, like soldiers. Ha ha! Isn't that amusing?" he asked sarcastically and slapped his recliner. "Hell's horsemen quietly build a castle within a half a day's march of the palace, and he's watching fat court-wives try to turn left in tandem! These people have to be told every day that they're not our equals, let alone our cultural overlords. *We* are the example for *them* to emulate! They don't understand that our religion, our veneration of science and reason has given us dominion over their defeated empire, and that their effete superstitions and asinine mysticism have made it so that they survive only by our assistance! If I'd had my way, the entire city would be abandoned of all Latins and Franks, and let the Turks do their worst to these miserable Greeks!"

Mario gulped his wine.

"I'll try to remember that: *be an example*," he repeated politely. "I didn't mean to upset you, Don Vincent. Please accept my apologies."

"No, I'm sorry," Vincent answered sharply. "I shouldn't have been so angry. I've been having a rather arduous day."

Seeing that his quick flare up had run its course, Isodore blurted into the conversation, "So, what seems to be rubbing your brain the wrong way?"

Vincent blinked, returning his mind to the events before him and away from the long developed antipathy he felt towards his adoptive home. "I have tasks for both of you. Isodore, I want you to cross over to Galata. The Genoese just received reinforcements from back home, they are under the command of a knight by the name of Guistiniano Longo. I want you to tell me what you can about him, how his men are armed, how well trained they are and anything else that you can learn. I'd like you to tell me about this over breakfast tomorrow. Can you do that?"

"Of course, Vincent."

"Good," Vincent nodded before turning to the doctor. "And as for you, I need you visit an old patient of yours. Giovanni Cardillo has taken ill again and needs your help. He doesn't want to go to the hospital, he doesn't like for people to see him ill. He thinks it's undignified. Also, he doesn't trust the native mystics. He wants a scientific doctor."

"Illness happens to everyone, there's nothing dignified or undignified about miasmatic shifts…"

"I know that, you know that," DiCastillo acknowledged, "but he believes that it's undignified, so you're going to go and visit him. Don't worry, you'll be well paid for the effort. Can either of you tell me when my old friend Ezera is coming back to the city?"

"I have no idea," Mario answered truthfully.

"That's too bad. I need to speak with him when he returns," Vincent snapped.

The Venetian commander had a rabid decorum to him that day, and Mario wanted to avoid any serious conflict with him, so he decided that it would be best to excuse himself and return later to speak to him.

"I guess I'll go and see the ambassador now, then," he suggested.

"Good idea, that's appreciated." Vincent said with an uneasy smile.

"Yes, sir," Mario answered. "There is something else that I would like to discuss with you."

Vincent could tell by his awkward countenance exactly what the subject would be. His face was cold.

"Now is not the proper time for this, we can talk later."

"Yes, I suppose," he deferred. "Another time then, but soon."

"Good," Vincent thanked Mario coldly, sent him out the door, and sat back down with Isodore.

"You wanted to speak to me about something else?" Isodore asked.

"Yes. Is he still going to mass?"

"Every day."

"Hmm," Vincent thought. "He's a good man, but I don't like him as a bridegroom."

"You're right to look after your sister, Vincent." Isodore agreed. "Mario has money, but is far from rich, he's of good birth, not considerably so. You've refused suitors of much higher quality than him."

"I have," Vincent recalled. "I need to find someone for her who'll give her a better life back in Italy. Most of those other *better* suitors are Greeks who'd keep her as a foreign trophy and then treat her like a servant. There aren't many good prospects for her here."

"She's almost twenty, Sir," Isodore reminded him. "Those suitors are going to become more and more sparse. Mario's Italian, he's a man of learning, and he's obviously quite infatuated."

"He'll probably never be allowed to go back to Italy, and he's only recently given up his monastic vows. He's a thirty year old virgin who's completely unprepared to save his own state in the world, let alone anyone else's."

"That's true. He'll need a strong brother-in-law," Isodore suggested rather playfully. "What about Longo?"

At that, Vincent was forced to chuckle.

"I need you to get back to me by breakfast tomorrow, Isodore. And don't ever joke about that again!"

"Why the hurry?"

"Because the Turks are assembling a fleet in Thessalonica, and are going to send them to the Marmara, we believe at Gallipoli. I want you to go there and determine how many they are, who's in command, how many ships, of what quality... these things."

"Gallipoli's in Turkish hands," Isodore began to protest.

"You speak Turkish."

"Market Turkish! And even then, everything I say is in the present continuous tense."

"Well, it's better than anyone else!" the Italian joked. "I want you to go there, play it safe, don't do anything to get noticed, and then come back and tell me what's there. I'll give you a horse and some gold, and you can leave after breakfast tomorrow. How does that sound?"

"Great," Isodore replied glumly. He wasn't terribly excited about traVeling the roads at night, let alone going through Turkish lands. "I haven't had a chance to get away from the capital for a while."

"That's the spirit," Vincent assured him. "When you get back, they're always be more work for you. Unless you'd prefer to sit around the old palace with the other monks and pray all day."

"From time to time, I've suspected that my true calling wasn't monastic life," Isodore bemoaned his state with a lame whimper.

"Good luck, Isodore," Vincent wished him.

Trebizond the unconquerable was at one time a radiant light in the east. The city was a vibrant Roman city sitting below the high hills and mountains of the eastern Black Sea. It seemed to lean over the dark and choppy waters of the sea, hanging steadfastly off of the snow-capped forest, they hid mountain raiders of Kurdish tribesmen, Armenian brigands and Georgian slavers. Absent now were the marble glories of Rome, and the red-brick churches of Constantinople; Trebizond was an empire of wood. The city was oaken mansions, pine slums, birch public works and mahogany public houses. All of these buildings, like the forest in which they hid, were covered in a layer of white that reflected the green of the trees and the grey of the sky. The city itself seemed to be an extension of the forest more than a city of ten thousand, but there it stood, the capital of the so-called empire of Trebizond.

When Constantinople fell to the Franks of the western empire in 1204 and a Latin kingdom was proclaimed, it was in Trebizond where Greek polity survived. Loyalists to the old order assembled here and proclaimed a third Rome to have emerged out of the wild forests and treacherous mountains. While the city never truly ascended to honestly hoist the mantle of the true inheritor of the despoiled empire, the locals took great pride in being the unvanquished. They even refused to swear loyalty to the Palaiologi dynasty when the old capital was recaptured in the name of Orthodoxy. The city and people of Trebizond carried a much deserved reputation for being exasperatingly independent.

A local dockhand named Jeorgi jogged down one of the port's three docks, his head covered in a blanket from the rain. He examined a curious looking ship. It seemed to be war-ship that had been grafted for hauling, or perhaps a hauler that had been rigged for war, either way, it was a curiosity to see a ship of its size in Trebizond's small harbour.

"Alo!" the boy cried out to the ship in horrifically pronounced Greek. "I say, is there being a captain of this is your ship?"

Ezera ran to the portside of the Nineveh to see who was calling across to him. He was always happy to find someone who spoke worse Greek than him.

"Alo!" he called back through the sound muffle of light snow. "I am Captain Ezera of the Nineveh! Can I help you?"

The boy below him was a tall, thin lad, with curly blond hair, blue eyes and a giant nose that seemed to take up half his face. He was a stereotypical looking *Laz*, one of the minor races that inhabited the Caucasus Mountains.

"Alo! I am the Jeorgi! I am saying something to you!"

"Well then, Jeorgi, please say," Ezera answered. The name Jeorgi was a common version his own father's name Jeorge, or Saint George. The dragon-slayer was the patron saint of England, Bulgaria and Georgia (named after him), and the name certainly had its fair share of usage out east.

"In the past, you are going to Constantinopoli. In the future, you are not going to Constantinopoli." he called over with a big smile on his face.

Ezera frowned a little bit. "What's the problem?"

"Constantinopoli is closed!" he called up. "Turkish castles are closing Constantinopoli!"

The crew wouldn't like the sound of that one bit. Ezera's eyes narrowed as he thought about the castles under construction he had passed when he came up into the Black Sea six weeks ago.

"Big guns, friend. Big big guns!" the Laz harbour-man said, extended his arms to demonstrate.

"Thank you," he replied and tossed the man a copper akche to thank him for the information. "Who told you this?"

"Other boat." He said pointing to one of the four other boats in the harbour.

Ezera looked at the ship to which he was being directed.

'*Crap,*' he thought to himself as he saw the longship with its square cut sail hiding from the drizzle. '*Bloody Vikings.*'

He'd need to get more information about the '*big gun*' and what was meant by 'Constantinople is closed,' but there was never any guarantee when talking with Vikings. The river men are a mercurial sort, great fun when in a good mood, murderously temperamental when in a bad one. Ezera would have to hope that they're in a good mood.

Mario put his ear against Giovanni's back, just below his shoulder-blade.

"Can you breathe in, please?"

Giovanni inhaled as deeply as he could, and Mario heard a gurgling sound echoing in the ambassador's chest cavity.

'*Definitely a phlegm imbalance,*' he thought to himself.

He pulled his head away as his patient erupted into a fit of coughing.

"Are you ok?" he asked once the fit subsided.

"No," Cardillo answered through a half strangled voice. "I can barely sleep at night, and I can't be seen by anyone in my current state."

"Do you cough blood, sometimes?"

"I can taste it, but I never see any," he coughed again and pulled his coat tightly around him.

"I'm going to have to perform some blood-letting on you, could you please show me your forearm?"

Giovanni obeyed. Truth be told, he wasn't particularly confident in his physician's ability, but he trusted him more than he trusted the only other Italian doctor in the city (a raging alcoholic who spent most of his times in various stages of incarceration), who he in turn trusted more than the mystic healing orders of the Greek priesthood who would advise him to pray for delivery from illness. He grimaced as the doctor pulled a razor over his flesh.

Mario pushed and squeezed the incision and inspected the blood coming out.

"Your blood flows at a fine pace, neither too fast nor too slow," he said. He then dabbed a piece of cloth onto the wound to collect some blood. He smelled the cloth, he examined it, he even dabbed it on his tongue to taste it before he bandaged his patient.

"The problem is definitely an excess of phlegm. You're blood and bile both seem to be fine," he proclaimed. "I'll go back to my laboratory and distil some medicine for you, and bring it over before sunset!"

"Thank you, Doctor," Giovanni gripped his newly bandaged arm. "My factor will pay you by the door."

"There is another thing, Don Giovanni," Mario said timidly.

"Yes?" Giovanni asked politely. *'Here it comes, everyone needs favours.'*

"I've fallen in love with a woman and seek her hand in marriage," Mario began, but was cut off quickly by the ambassador.

"Congratulations, but I was under the impression that doctors were under oaths similar to those of the priesthood. Can you take a wife?"

"Yes, sir. I'm no longer a college physician, so I am permitted to marry, but after this point I may never work in a university again, and I will probably be unable to find work in a proper hospital without some degree of patronage."

"Here in Constantinople, you are my personal physician, and you needn't worry about finding a new hospital."

"Oh that's not a problem, the Greeks don't fret the same oaths as we Latins," Mario said with a smile. "The problem is securing permission to marry from her master."

"You're comfortably wealthy. You have influential friends. You're a man of books, and education. I'm certain that any father would be proud to take you on as a son-in-law, and any wife as a husband. Can you not afford a dowry?"

"It's not that. The woman who is the object of my heart's affection is Ella DiCastillo; the younger sister of Vincent DiCastillo."

"Ah. He can be an intimidating man," Giovanni said through a hacking cough. "I understand your dilemma, Doctor. I won't help you directly, but I can help give you an opportunity."

"Anything would be appreciated," Mario said with a bit of disappointment.

"If I help you directly, and order Vincent to accept you, which I would be out of place to do so, then you've made an enemy of your future brother, and Vincent is hardly the sort of man to tolerate enemies for long.

His rage would be there long after I've gone to the hereafter," Giovanni inhaled deeply and closed his eyes. With all his might he resisted his body's will to wrack itself with a coughing fit, and once the repressed fit had passed, he continued. "I'll take you out of that hospital of yours shortly. As you know, Adrianople is preparing to attack the city. They'll probably come once the winter's snows melt, and they can safely use the road from their capital. They'll march a hundred and fifty miles southeast, and attack the city."

"So I've heard," Mario replied, though truthfully all he really knew about the upcoming war were snippets overheard from the conversations of doctors in the hospital, most of whom were convinced that should the armies of Muhammad cross the threshold into the city, the Archangel Michael himself would arrive to strike them down.

"Vincent and I have been discussing the construction of a field hospital, in the Petrion section of the city – probably in the Chora Monastery. Do you know it?"

"Near the Church of Holy Apostles?"

"It's not important right now," Giovanni continued, ignoring the doctor's glaring ignorance of local city geography. "Do you have experience in such matters?"

"Sir, I'm a physician, not an administrator."

"The support that we're receiving from back home would indicate that you should be whatever you're capable of being, Doctor. No seniority here, only ability," Giovanni answered. "Do you know who Adam Karian is?"

"I believe he's a general…"

"Of sorts, yes," Giovanni's quick mind was outpacing his sickly body, and his arm began to spasm at the shoulder. "I'll arrange a meeting between you two, and he'll show you where the building will be, I'm going to charge you with setting it up as a hospital, hiring surgeons and staff. There are several monasteries and convents nearby, you can find assistance from them to act as nurses. Make yourself known in the Petrion district. Take up this charge with competence and strength, and by the time this Turkish tide wanes, you'll be one of the heroes of the day. Then you can press your claim on the DiCastillo girl. You'll be in a position to demand respect and gratitude from our friend Vincent. How does that sound?"

"Wonderful, Don Giovanni!" Mario thanked him profusely. You are a great man!"

Mario kissed his hand, and the sickly nobleman continued into hacking fits.

"I'm an ill man! Save your gratitude for later, and make your medicine, Doctor."

"Yes, Don Giovanni! Right away!"

"Sir!" a guard called out after coming to attention. "The chevalier Hectore Pazzi has arrived and requests an audience!"

The miniature fortress that made itself home for Adam Karian stood still in the night. It had no sense of its inhabitants, no character to speak of, save for the utilitarian martial attributes of a rather plush barracks.

"Escort him in," Karian replied. Vain by nature, Karian looked into a mirror in a hunter's search for any remaining lint or other imperfections that may have found home on his long black coat or purple sash. Finding none, he readied himself to receive his guest.

"Don Hectore! Benvenuto!" the Megadux, or Grand Duke, called out in outlandishly pronounced Italian.

"Thank you, Adam," Pazzi answered back, happy to remain in his familiar Italian. "May God bless you this evening."

"And also you," Karian smiled politely, but his eyes bore no warmth. He was never as adept at making others feel welcome as he should have been, given his political responsibilities. Truth be told, he cared very deeply for his blood-family and his adopted family in the army, but for those who were neither of those groups, he cared very little; they were just strangers.

"I need to speak to you in private, my general. Are we alone?"

"Of course, come sit with me by the fire. Enjoy the warmth," Karian sat down in a recliner and motioned Pazzi to a similarly set up one.

Pazzi sat and leant back against the cushioned wood.

"I have little taste for these eastern climes, Adam," he began.

Karian smiled politely, mildly irked at the use of his first name by the Genoese captain.

"All complaints on that subject may be delivered through prayer to the almighty, Hectore. There is little that I can do to help you on that matter."

"I suspect that this may well be my last winter out here. We are witnessing the winter of Constantinople, General. Spring will come, and with it I see a horrible decay."

"Many seasons have come to the city, Captain. A thousand winters have descended here since our city became the capital of Christendom, and spring has always thrown off that frozen yoke. Weeds come, so do flowers."

"I'm sorry, if I upset you, general," Hectore answered quickly "but I don't share your optimism. We both know what's coming. You and I know, more than most others here what fate has in store for the Queen of Cities."

"We can't fight God's will, Don Hectore. If God damns this city to be torn asunder by the legions of Gog and Magog, then it is God's will and wonderful in my eyes. If God wills that we return to his teachings, and then saves us, then that too is wonderful. We have little say in the matter."

"You're very fatalistic for a soldier."

"I'm Armenian."

"General," Hectore began slyly. "God truly helps those who help themselves, and I have to help myself for the future. When the winds take away the smoke from the Turkish cannons, I plan to go on living my life, and doing so in a style to which I've become accustomed and if you'll forgive my saying so, I don't think that at your age you're ready to reacclimatise yourself to poverty. This is still a city of immense wealth, and I don't intend to let it fall into the hands of the Mohammedan horde! Their palaces deserve no aggrandisement. Their women need no baubles and their mercenaries need no more coins."

Karian glared at his guest. He didn't like foreigners in general, Italians in particular, or Hectore Pazzi in any way, shape or form. Adam was more than capable of looking past his own hate, were the price right.

"What did you have in mind?"

Light snow was gently accumulating on the Trebizond dock when Ezera walked up to the moored longship. Much to his contentment, it wasn't a very large one, only about seven metres, less room would mean fewer people. Hidden at the land's end of the dock was most of the crew of the Nineveh, hands on swords and crossbows cocked.

"What you want?" a voice called over the ship's side. A burly youth, probably about fifteen years of age, greeted him in a garbled version of Greek. The youth had short cropped hair, and while he wasn't old enough to grow a beard, was obviously brawny enough to intimidate most dock-dwellers.

"I was told that your ship has some knowledge about the gates of Constantinople."

Next to the youth emerged a large blond man with a yellow beard and ferocious green eyes. He shouted at Ezera incomprehensibly in one of the northern tongues.

"My father doesn't trust southerners," the boy translated. "We were to visit Constantinople a week ago, but the Turks have closed the Bosporus. No ships can pass south, so we were forced to come east to trade here."

More people were emerging out of the ship's hold, a child and a beautiful older woman, probably the matron of the family. This longship was undoubtedly a family trading endeavour, probably based among the Rus of Kiev.

"What happened at Constantinople? Do the Muslims have ships there?"

"Some," the boy answered after conferring with his father in their sing-song language. "There are two castles, on either side of the strait, and they are both armed with many cannons. They have small ships at the shore, which stopped us from continuing south."

"All ships? Did they forbid you, or did they merely want money?"

He spoke to his father, who made a rude gesture with his hands. "Gelt! Gelt!" the elder man said.

"They wanted money."

Mario took that in and gave himself a moment to consider what this meant.

"Thank you all," he said at last. He waved goodbye to the Vikings and assembled his crew back aboard the Nineveh. He informed the crew as to what was happening.

"This leaves us with two options: we can run the blockade or we can pay the bribes," he stated matter-of-factly. "We're running Empire goods, and flying under a Venetian flag, if we go back to Constantinople, the bribe will have to be huge. If we go back with lighter trade goods, we can sprint past the Turks without much problems."

"You said that they had cannons," Lorzenzo the oarsman pointed out. "We can't outrun cannons. Especially when we're so laden down."

"They're new cannons, with green crews and we're a moving target."

"What about their boats?" asked Gaspar, the coxswain.

"In closed waters, we'll sail past them, or through them if need be. The Nineveh's forced her way past worse, and we don't have much to fear from a land garrison. We'll approach them at a relaxed pace, and then pick up to ramming speed to race past them and get on to Constantinople."

"Captian," Pere, the crew's eldest member, suggested. "Maybe it would be wiser for us to work the Black Sea routes for a while."

"That's probably wise advice," he conceded. "But if we postpone fleeing, then we'll be stuck here in the Black Sea. We're going to push it as fast as we can, and get out of here before the strait is completely shut. Then we'll stick around Crete and Cyprus for a few months, until things become more stable."

There was a sullen approval from the crew, who returned to their duties, and the Nineveh crept onto the dark waves of the angry Black Sea.

Chapter Twenty-Three - The Cutting of the Throat

One of the curiosities of the freshly built Bosporus fortifications on the European side of the strait, was that it was so easily stumbled upon by land. The arrogance of the three architects - Sultan Mehmet the Second, Grand Vizier Halil and Second Minister Zaganos - was such, that they believed that the Christians would never be able to muster a defence ten kilometres northwards. They believed that the Empire of the Romans was so corrupt and debunked that the only course left open to them was to quietly await the inevitable. With this thinking, it seemed perfectly natural to build a castle meant to house guns aimed at the waterway, and completely ignore the hills against which the castle was built. The whole facility was guarded by only a single orta.

The granite, quarried in Thrace was shipped overland and the buildings were erected quietly, and with minimal security. The castle was built right up against the water's edge; it's walls strong enough to repel any misguided amphibious assault, but the hills of the surrounding countryside would give any spy a bird's eye view into the inner-working of the fort.

For six months, ships passed by this busy site, watching the foundations assemble over the summer, the three towers rise and walls pile up as autumn made its presence known. For six months, reports went all about the capital. Everyone in Constantinople knew of the construction project. Every trading centre on the Black Sea followed the news, and all ships entering the strait would first check in the village of Terabia, near the mouth of the Bosporus, to ensure that the strait was still open. Every Christian community heard the thundering silence of the Empire against this obvious act of aggression.

As 1452 turned into 1453, such was the lack of threat posed by Christendom against the castle, provocatively named "*Roman Castle*," that the hill behind the fortress was guarded by two guards, whose combined seniority within the Janissary ranks was less than a year. Hussein and Iskender huddled together under a canvas canopy that passed as a tent in order to stay safe from their only attacker: the cold. They were talking about history, politics and religion. They knew that their charge was an empty one, and treated it as such. The two of them were involved in empty conversation, as they tried to whittle away the long hours until sundown, when they'd be replaced by two new, equally inexperienced guards.

"You see," Iskender tried to give the impression of authority when he spoke, "Orhan the First was the second Sultan of the line of Osman, he was in fact the first heir to the sword of Osman, but he was the first Muslim leader to permanently arrive in Europe. There's no turning back after that! It's through him that Ottoman state is more than just some local Anatolian Beylik or Arab Sheikhdom. We serve as the standard bearers of civilization in the New World."

"Yeah, yeah," Hussein agreed absently with his little friend. He had never been a student of the same quality as Iskender, but his size and his aggression, both natural and trained, had made him well known and respected in their class, and he was the first of the 'new recruits' to get noticed by the rest of their regiment. "I'm more interested in the near future right now. When do you think we'll take the city?"

"In the spring. Marching season will start in four months, and the city will surrender right away. I can't imagine the Christians putting up much fight. I've heard that there's already a mosque in the capital of the non-believers, and that they're collecting converts faster than they can teach them," Iskender said with his familiar self-confidence. "My only fear is that there will be nothing left for us to conquer once the war starts."

"The whole city won't convert," Hussein insisted. "I've heard that the Christians would kill anyone who learned about Islam."

"They'll probably resist at first, when we conquer them," Iskender agreed, "but in a year's time, the whole city will uniformly Muslim."

"I'll believe that when I see it," the giant answered. "Look over there. Someone's coming."

Iskender squinted at the next hill but couldn't make anything out. It was all a snowy white blur. Hussein, on the other hand, could make out a rider trotting along the white mass of one of Thrace's many unnamed, colourless hills.

"I don't see anything," Iskender replied.

Hussein gave an unnoticed look of annoyance to his friend and then grabbed his head to point him in the direction of the unidentified rider.

"Right there!" he pointed.

"Oh yes," Iskender lied. "I see him."

It was a known and hidden fact among all of the new additions to the orta, that Iskender was functionally blind at a distance. His silver tongue, and willingness to help the other younglings with their studies was the base for the conspiracy to cover this fact from their teachers and officers, but Hussein was now re-considering the wisdom of that conspiracy.

The two young soldiers threw off their canopy and Iskender raised his horse-tailed spear to get the attention of the rider. The rider turned his course to come over to them. The rider was covered beneath a formless cloak that hid his characteristics, but he bore a spear that carried a messy collection of long hair under a horned helmet. The tails of seven horses had been cut off to adorn that standard, in order to identify whoever hoisted it as an agent of a senior administrator. Whoever this rider was, he was an important man. As he rode closer, Hussein inspected the rider more closely. He was armed with a spear in one hand, a short bow over his back, and a shield overtop of it. He had two swords on the left side of the saddle and one on the right. In various pouches attached to the saddle and to his own figure, he had a mosaic collection of javelins, darts and arrows. Hardly dressed as an emissary.

Hussein reached to the ground and picked up his own bow. A Turkish bow was a composite technology; the main shaft of the bow was made of supple wood, such as maple, and was bent over, against itself into a circle. Then to the bent outside rim of that circle was placed the long horn of an animal, like a deer or antelope. The long horn was glued using rendered animal fat, and tightened with stiff leather bindings. Thus when the circular bow was bent back against itself again, the flexible strength of the wood would whip the arrow forward and the harsh force of the animal horn would push the wood for added torque. It excelled as a cavalryman's bow and was capable of propelling short, light arrows for a distance of three hundred metres with accuracy, even further than that as a more random havok. The arrows were gripped with the thumb on one side of the shaft and the index finger on the other side, this was different than the way the Christian armies held their arrows, which usually involved three fingers on the string in the "Mediterranean-style," rather than the two fingers on the arrow of the so-called "Mongolian-style."

With his bow curled into a full circle, Hussein wrapped the opening of it around his right leg and pulled back on the other end, pressuring the circle into a convex arch. The leather-waxen wire of the draw line quickly found its way to connect the two points of the crescent. He quickly placed an arrow across the short bow (directed down to the earth, of course) and called out to the rider.

"Stand and speak! Who are you?"

The cloaked figure rode up to the two cautiously, with his hand raised as a gesture of peace.

"Peace be upon you, Janissaries," the figure said. His face was covered behind a chain veil hanging from his pointed helmet.

"Unto you be peace!" Iskender called back. "Who are you and what are you doing here?”

“I’m here to meet with your commander, Mesut-bey,” he called back down. “My name is Ahmet of Amaseia, on an errand of the divan.”

Iskender knew the name, Hussein did not.

“Come with us,” Iskender called out. “We’ll take you to the castle.”

Ahmet nodded his head politely. He didn’t have many experiences with Janissaries, but those that he had had were hardly positive. He found them to be haughty and overly self-assured, so he was pleased to see the little one afraid of him.

“Please dismount your horse and come with us,” Hussein ordered. “Then, we’ll take you to our commander.”

The youthful giant had no knowledge of players outside his regiment, and unlike his friend, knew nothing of Ahmet’s rather murderous reputation.

Ahmet threw a leg over the horse and slid off onto the snow. He’d spent more time on horse-back than the two Janissaries had been walking. His flawless and silent dismount was punctuated by the clinking thud of the chains and plates of the armour underneath his robe as he landed.

“Lead on, then,” Ahmet commanded the giant Hussein. “I assume you know the way.”

Hussein had distinguished himself in archery, swordsmanship and wrestling during his training in the Lion’s Den, but in those competitions with his fellow Janissaries, as hard-fought as they were, there was always a friendliness to the competition. True, there were odd cuts, sprains and even the occasional broken bone, but if anyone seriously injured anyone else, there was a great shame attached to their actions. Hussein stood a full head taller than Ahmet, who was a tall man in his own right, and was almost half again as wide at the chest, but in the eyes of the smaller man, he saw a goading into competition. It was the first time that he found himself looking into the eyes of a competitor who wouldn’t find shame in injury, nor would he be as eager to indulge in competition for the sake of mere competition. This tribesman wasn’t what the big man was used to facing. This unfamiliarity made Hussein a little nervous.

“I can’t do this, master!” Ahmet had insisted to Halil a few days prior. “I’m not good at that. I don’t speak like a courtier. I get angry. I don’t know anything about politics!”

“Well you have to learn, Son,” Halil answered him. They sat beside each other in the frozen garden of Halil’s Villa.

Unlike the small enclosures of Constantinople that held in the cold like an icebox, Halil-pasha's garden was open to the sun, and was much warmer than most of the houses of the greatest Muslim city in Europe (the Muslim presence in Spain being reduced to Gibraltar and some of the surrounding townships by this point). The two men sat in wooden chairs, enjoying the warm sun, despite the cold air. The garden's summer glory was gone, but the winter sun was warm and nice.

"If you can't do this, you will spend the rest of your days as my most trusted bodyguard, Ahmet," Halil stated in a fatherly form, "but upon my death, you'll be forced to either find a new patron, or return to Amaseia Sanjak with empty hands. You need to learn how to deal with enemies and with friends. You need to learn how to make friends of enemies and enemies of friends, and when it's a good idea to do either."

"I'm not a politician."

"You will be," Halil insisted. "Look at the empire now, my strong boy. During the reign of the great Sultan Murat, it was among the Janissaries, the Devshirme and the Sipahis that power rested. That tripod was how the great man kept order. Now, the tribes are pouring out of Anatolia to enlist in the Jihad. Outlandish religious orders recruit entire lodges from Anatolia and Thrace to come and carry the banner of The Prophet. They come to the standard of the pretender, Mehmet, who would insist to the world that he is a gazi, a fringe warrior who spreads the faith with his own sword. The tribes now outnumber the triumvirate of the old order by seven to one. After this war, the only peace there can be for the empire is by making a balance between the tribes, whose force of arms keep the peace, the old administration, which administers the house of peace, and the Ulema, the religious authorities who keep the laws and traditions that unite us all. The empire that you were born into is not the empire that we'll see in a few years time, and we need to be ready for this. A new triumvirate for a new age!"

"I don't see how this can help," Ahmet repeated. "It seems like a task beyond my ability."

"I want you to inspect the cannons of the castle at the Bosporus," Halil continued. "Remind the Janissaries there that they are subject to the inspection and approval of the capital."

"Anyone can do that!"

"You have to," Halil insisted. "You need to stamp your own presence on the political map, and subordinating that rebellious Janissary is a good first step."

"If I go alone, they might just decide to kill me and be done with it!"

A harsh realization crept into Ahmet's mind at that point. *'Does Halil know about me and Ayshe?'*

"They won't kill you." Halil answered. "But they will fear you. You are known for your past exploits, which necessitates added security. In addition to that, they'll be afraid of your opinion. This is one of the first steps in subordinating them."

Ahmet bowed his head in submission. "Yes, My Lord."

"Don't be confrontational with Mesut. He's a strong enemy or a strong ally. If you're too much of a problem, he'll have you in a watery grave, but we'll hope that it won't come to that," Halil said with a smile. "You need to be very friendly to him."

"What?" Ahmet asked incredulously. "I thought you said that he was our enemy. And that I was to dominate him!"

"He is," Halil agreed. "And you will. But for now, he doesn't think much of you, and we have to use that. If you're being friendly, he'll think that he can manipulate you. He already thinks you're weak, he's a Janissary, they think everyone else is weak, and at this point we're better off not correcting him. You're there to observe the closing of the strait, the cutting of the throat that leads to the Christian capital. He'll be aware that a bad word from you can be problem for him politically, and a good word will be a boon. If you act good natured, he'll believe you to be malleable, and seek to befriend you. It won't be real friendship that he's seeking of course, just trying to ease the tension between his patron, Zaganos, and myself."

"So what should I do?"

"Be nice. Act impressed with the fortress. Commend the performance of the guards, tell him what he wants to hear," Halil answered wryly. "But don't come over so far at first. Then he'll believe it to be a trap. Your presence there will keep him nervous for a few days, convince him that the two of you have potential, and leave him feeling happy that he's made an ally at court. He'll see you as a long-term investment."

"I don't understand how this will subordinate him. The Janissaries are prideful peacocks. He'll never respect anyone outside his own ranks."

"He'll believe that by going along with your ideas, he can secure his own access to the court. He'll believe it to be a temporary submission, but we'll keep extending it until he accepts its permanency."

"This is dangerous and risky."

"If you aren't up to this kind of task, you don't need to accept it, Ahmet," Halil answered him, "You have to think about what you want for your future. I'm trying to help you."

"And I thank you, Pasha," Ahmet answered with resolve. "I'll do my best not to shame you for this opportunity."

Ahmet was escorted into the centre of Roman Castle. Of all the castles he'd seen in his life, Roman seemed to be the most unnatural. The rookery in the Pontic mountains was overgrown with the forest that surrounded it. The keep in Amaseia was weighed down with moss and the memories of centuries by the Black Sea. This castle was new. The stones had neither moss nor memory. Grass and weeds hadn't found their way into the courtyard, only utilitarian mud and gravel adorned the floor. This castle had yet to become a part of the landscape. It was merely an artificial construction grafted onto God's creation. Only time could tattoo this ink of a fortress into the corpulent hills that surrounded it.

The Janissaries all mustered into the courtyard to see who'd arrived. The castellan, the cooks, the tradesmen all peered out from behind the soldierly cordons of the fighting class, their bright white hats flung back and their crimson tunics unnaturally clean in the muddy afternoon.

The cleanest and the brightest of them all was their commander, Mesut. The flawless clothes hid the scarred body of a rather intimidating soldier. Ahmet remembered the scarred hands and cauliflowered ear from when he first saw the Janissary commander, two years ago when Mehmet was first summoned to the capital, and again when Halil was arrested and brought before the Sultan. Since then, the old soldier had gained a rather vicious looking rope-burn along his throat. Despite his grisly appearance, his voice was polite and courteous, if a little gravelly.

"Peace be upon you, Brother," he greeted his guest. "Welcome to Roman Castle. I'm Mesut, the commander of the Eighth Orta, currently manning the twin fortresses of Roman and Anatolian Castles."

"Unto you be peace, Brother," Ahmet returned the salute. "I am pleased to visit. My name is Ahmet of Amaseia, the son of Ali of Amaseia. I am here at the behest of the divan to inspect the fortifications."

"I know who you are, we've met twice, but never in a very formal capacity," Mesut said with a smile. "You must be weary from your travels. I will have your horse stabled and a bed made for you in the quarters. This is a military outpost, and I'm afraid that your quarters may not be as lavish as those to which you've become accustomed in the house of Halil-Pasha."

"I'm sure that the quarters will be fine," he replied politely.

"Hussein, see to his horse and then go and help Iskender," Mesut ordered. "Iskender, see to his person. Go clear out the fourth room of the third building. Make certain that it is clean and presentable, and when finished, come and tell me personally."

"Yes, Sir," the two seventeen-year-olds said in unison. They bowed briskly and went about their assigned tasks.

"Welcome, Ahmet," Mesut said with a stone face, "I received word that you would be arriving, and I'm to show you about the castle and show you the armed strength of the new guns. I would normally invite you in for pleasantries, boza and lokoum, but the hour is late and the shadows are long. If you feel strong enough after your ride across the hills, I'd like to show you Roman Castle today, before nightfall, and we could guide you through Anatolian Castle in the morning. Are you feeling up to that, or would you prefer some rest."

"I'd like to unload some of my personal effects into the quarters, and then see the castle before the sun goes down, if that's possible, Mesut-bey."

"By all means," Mesut said with a smile.

"Good God," Hussein exclaimed as he entered the guest quarters in the as-yet-unnamed third building. "I've never seen a warhorse so heavily laden. That beast was carrying a fully armoured fighter, as well as provisions, two cases of javelins, three of darts, and seven bushels of twenty arrows apiece. On top of that, there was some light barding on the damned horse!"

Iskender stood up from under the bed where he was cleaning.

"He came in here to drop of some of his things before Mesut-Pasha took him to inspect the castle," he pointed over to the corner. "Over there, is a short sword, a broad sword, a scimitar, two daggers, a knife, two composite bows – a footman's and a horseman's – a shield, various pieces of plate armour and helmet with a chain veil. This man was more heavily armed than the Albanian Rebellion."

"He's a diplomatic envoy?" Hussein asked mock disbelief.

"He's something else," Iskender answered. "Bilgi-hoja told me that he worked for the Sultan himself, and killed his enemies for him. Now he works for the grand vizier Halil, and some people think that he killed the divan's secretary and his son."

"He said that he was on a mission from the Sultan's council," Hussein tried not to seem too ignorant of outside politics.

Iskender pointed his head in the direction of the piled armaments. He then looked back at his big friend and raised an eyebrow of disbelief.

Hussein grimaced and nodded in return.

Ahmet paid meticulous attention to everything that Mesut said about firing arches and range limiters about the twelve cannons that were set up about the towers and walls of Roman Castle. Two canons were positioned on the top of the two wind-battered towers, and rocks were set out as range markers by the water. Because of their proximity to the hills, darkness descended upon them far too quickly for finish the tour, and they agreed to continue on tomorrow.

"Tomorrow is the Festival of Sacrifice," Ahmet pointed out as the two men stood on the battlements of the fortress. The sun had set behind them, and while the Bosporus straight itself was being overtaken by the shadows of the European hills, the Asian hills still collected the dying sun's last light. The snowy slopes of the Anatolian hills shone as the umbra crept closer to its shore.

"It is," repeated the Janissary commander. "Will you be honouring us with your presence for the celebration?"

"If it's not a problem, the honour would be mine, Chorbachi," Ahmet addressed him by his formal rank of Chorbachi, or '*Soup-Maker*.'

"Speaking of which," he replied, "I have to attend to that. But I would like to continue our conversation after dinner."

"Of course."

Mesut was not a cook; he hadn't made soup on a regular basis since he was seventeen and at the bottom rung of the Janissary ladder, and only once afterwards as punishment for an incident involving a drunken brawl and some stolen sheep. The title of "soup maker" was indicative that every meal for the entire corps was served to them by their commander. There was a long mess line to get their bowl of gruel, but it could only come from the man himself. The soup ladle was seen as a sceptre of authority. Even on the rare occasions when the Janissary soldiers were given a night's leave, they would never eat in a pub or bawdy house. To do so would dishonour their commander and bringing a personal snack into a camp would be tantamount to treason. It was by virtue of this role that Mesut could never be late for dinner.

Ahmet decided to force down a rancid bowl of fatty stew that would prevent the soldiers from dying by way of malnutrition, but was hardly fit for the kitchens of capital. It was a wise decision, for if he had snacked on his own provisions back in his room, he'd probably have fallen victim to a munitions accident while touring Anatolian Castle the next morning.

"What do you think they're talking about?" Hussein asked Iskender once they finally finished their mutton stew. He indicated their commander and their guest who were sitting at the next long table over in the mess hall.

There was no elevated dais for the commander or his officers, nor were they used to receiving important guests. Six months prior, the entire castle had been little more than hillside, and the soup hall was little more than a wooden cavern designed to keep the rain off of the heads of its inhabitants.

"Shh," Iskender replied. "I'm trying to listen."

"Tomorrow is the big day," Mesut informed his guest. "Tomorrow we'll sever the waterway officially to all traffic by non-aligned ships."

"I look forward to seeing this, Mesut-Pasha," Ahmet replied. "When do you think the Christians will react?"

"If they were capable of reacting, they'd have done so by now," was Mesut's brutally honest answer. "For a half a year we've been constructing this fortress. Everyone knows about it. We aren't hiding. The Christians are a defeated force, waiting to be finally taken off the board by the armies of God."

"I've seen those walls, Pasha. Do you really think that the spring campaign will be so easy?"

"You don't attack from walls, Ahmet-bey," Mesut answered grimly. "The significance of this fortress is that we are now cutting the throat of the Romans. Their economy and political clout in the Eastern Mediterranean is based on their control of this water way. From the city, they've controlled the trade from Central Europe, through the Black Sea, and then to the rest of the world: Egypt, Syria, Greece, Anatolia, Italy, etcetera. We've taken their greatest asset without so much as a sword being drawn. The Romans are quietly awaiting defeat."

The Turkish word for a strait or waterway is *boghaz*, which literally means throat. In Turkish, the Bosporus Strait is called the Rumeli Boghazi – *Roman Strait*, but could just as easily be translated as *Roman Throat*. The ambiguity and implications of the term '*cutting the Roman throat*' was not lost on either man.

"Not everyone shares your confidence, Janissary," Ahmet said cautiously.

"Ah, you're referring to your master, then. Perhaps you could explain to me his strange opposition to the campaign?"

Ahmet puffed himself in mock indignation.

"The grand vizier is hugely supportive of the campaign! No one has done a finer job recruiting and organizing than he!"

"That's true, I'll give him that," Mesut interrupted Ahmet before he could finish his thought. "But he's also known to favour a less muscular approach towards our Christian neighbours. Everyone knows that had he his own way, we'd be trading with them as friends, rather fighting them as God commands us."

"That was his initial intention, and of course peace is always a noble hope, but once the Sultan had decided upon war, the grand vizier steeled himself to that mission."

"So he's a reluctant Jihadi?"

"He's pragmatic. War's can be unpredictable."

"No, they're bloody well not," Mesut answered sharply. "Our forces outnumber the Christians by almost twenty to one, yet our Sultan's plan is now, and always has been the subjugation of a city-state masquerading as an empire. Only a fool would give any credence to the thought of the Nazarene army surviving the fray. Some are starting to wonder what will be done with this giant war-band that your master has assembled once Greek mortar crumbles and Roman steel shatters."

'Where's he going with this?' Ahmet wondered.

"The fact is that the tribal hordes care nothing about spreading civilization. Only the Ottoman State cares about bringing institution of governance and the universal rule of Islam to the world. We're the true Jihadis. That horde is just rabble," Mesut had a darkness to his tone and there was a resentment in his eyes when he looked at Ahmet the urbanizing tribesman. "If the Janissaries, the Yayas and the Sipahis take the city, then it will be a beacon to the nations, a new Cairo, Damascus or Baghdad. It will forever guard our rear flank against warlords and marauding tribes like the Huns and the Mongols, who've charged through Anatolia before. From there, we will forever have a base to continue the constant and permanent war to spread the faith to the faithless and to eventually restore God's rule on God's creation. And that's what all this is about, young pup, God's kingdom on earth! That's why we fight! To bring about a new society, one that the earth has never seen, without borders, without wars, without brigandry or local tyrannies. One world, one law, one great egalitarian peace. Is there any loftier goal for any man?"

Ahmet tried to interject an opinion but was quickly cut off. Mesut was never one to allow dialectic discussion when he sensed weakness in an opponent's position.

"If, however, these tribal wolves descend upon the capital, they'll loot and burn the city into ruins, all to line their own purses with enough gold to pay for a few nightly nightly pleasures and to bring a handful of baubles for some peasant wench back in their home village. Your master could not have his way, and is now seeking to turn the fortunes of our empire to dust! He is betraying Islam, in order to satisfy his own ego. If he dooms the expedition, then he was right all along! That's what he believes! You are giving your loyalty to a dangerous man whom you would be wise to avoid, Ahmet-Bey."

"I'm sorry you feel that way, Janissary..."

"And I know why you are loyal to him, don't misunderstand me," Mesut insisted.

"You don't know..."

"But I do," Mesut said with a hard and angry face. "I also know who killed your brother, and upon whose orders."

Ahmet was silent.

"I'm sure that Halil has promised you some form of redemptive vengeance for the cold murder of your own blood. Surely you understand that catharsis is something that he can never deliver. It's not in his nature. He'll string you along, with a promise of what's barely just out of reach for now, but if you stay the course, you're almost there. How long have you waited, Ahmet? It must be a year by now."

"Nine months," Ahmet answered labouredly. He looked around the crowded hall. No one appeared to be eavesdropping on their conversation, though many were.

"Don't worry about anyone here, Ahmet. Their loyalty is beyond reproach. Just like yours is to your own blood. You've unfortunately allowed the silver tongue of the grand vizier to misguide your loyalty. How many have fallen to your hand since you arrived in the capital?"

"Three," Ahmet answered tentatively.

"And why were none of them the murderer of your own family? Everyone knows where to find him. Did the men you killed ever wrong you in any way?"

"Why do you mock me?" Ahmet was an emotional person by nature, and his rage was bubbling to the point where he was tempted to unleash it. Given that he was surrounded by several hundred professional soldiers, it was a blessing to Ahmet that he didn't try to cut down their beloved commander.

"I don't," Mesut said. "I'm offering you Zaganos. He killed your brother."

"You'd betray your master?" Ahmet laughed dubiously.

"He is not my master!" Mesut shot back angrily. "He was an honoured member of the regiment for many years, but has betrayed us for a career of his own self-advancement. The feud between he and your patron has weakened the empire which I serve with dignity and honour."

"And what do you propose."

"I'm going to be the agha of the Janissaries eventually. I'll place you falsely as one of the guards for his home. You can remove his treachery from the empire, avenge your brother, and escape into the night, hours before anyone knows what's happened."

"And what would I owe you for this favour, Mesut?"

"I have only two conditions. The first is that you keep me informed of the grand vizier's plans. He is too dangerous to be left unobserved, and for his own reasons, he's taken you into his confidence."

"And the second?" he laughed, for the first condition was beyond consideration.

"You will have to wait until after Constantinople falls to have Zaganos," Mesut could see the exasperation on Ahmet's face, so he continued his case. "Nothing is more important than the campaign right now. Vengeance and honour have to wait. That's the price for what I offer you. Sultan Mehmet the Second will visit his most trusted minister, you might be able to find both!"

Ahmet weighed his options before answering.

"It seems that I have few other options left," he said at length. "I accept your offer."

"Praise be to God," Mesut answered. We've done a great service to God's will tonight.

"I pray you're right."

"He'll invite you to betray me," Halil said at length. "This Janissary who you're going to meet with."

"I would never…" Ahmet started to protest.

"You'll agree." Halil answered quickly. "If he believes you to be a secure spy, you'll fall into his trust. This way, we can control what information he receives. If you don't agree, he'll find someone else to do the task, and then we'll have to wonder who they are and discover them. This way, we know where they get their information, and we know what the information is."

"Yes, Halil Pasha," Ahmet was beginning to understand his master's plotting, but he found it to be frustrating. "I'm afraid that I don't have much of a mind for intrigues."

"Don't worry, my boy. You'll learn."

Iskender nervously knocked on the door to his commander's office and was allowed in.

"You wanted to see me, Commander?"

"Yes, Iskender," Mesut answered. "I need you to go on a special mission for me after the feast. I need you to take one of the horses from the stable, and ride as hard and as fast as you can to the capital."

"Yes, Sir."

"Do you remember the home of the Second Minister, Zaganos-Pasha? I took you and your friend Hussein there once when you first joined."

"Yes, Sir."

"I want you to go there and give a message to Zaganos-Pasha for me."

"I'll leave right away, Sir."

"After the sacrifice festival. The message is simple *'Everything went as you said it would.'* Can you remember that?"

"Everything went as you said it would."

"Good. You're excused."

It was with great pride that Iskender prepared for his first great mission.

The next day was the Festival of Sacrifice, where twenty rams and a half dozen oxen were sacrificed in the castle to celebrate God's covenant with the humanity, as well as the establishment of the new fortifications. The festival was a commemorative event that dated back quite some time.

A long time ago, in a land far, far away, there lived a man and his angry god. This supreme being to which he was loyal, was a vicious and jealous god of wrath, who insisted on fairly regular blood sacrifices. Avram (later to be known as Abraham) continued sacrificing live animals to his bloodthirsty overlord; when he first heard the call, and then periodically throughout his Near Eastern travels. He surrendered his wife into the harem of an Egyptian king while pretending to be her brother, cast out his serving girl along with their illegitimate son, and cut his second wife and their six sons out of any inheritance in favour of his preferred son, Isaac. This is the short version of the life of the patriarchal founder of the three great ethical monotheisms.

Oddly enough, his piety is most heavily attested to by his attempted murder of his son. One day, the angry god to whom he was covenant-bound to serve, demanded blood once again. And this time, no ass or she-goat would sate the blood-lust of the all-merciful, nay, this time he demanded Abraham's son be served *in viscera*. Abraham was ready to comply and send wee Isaac off into that good night, when an Angel appeared said "That's okay, we can see that you are loyal indeed, so the boss will let you keep the boy, and you can kill this here magically concocted sheep in his stead." Abraham was thrilled, though possibly not as thrilled as his son, for the turn of events and he joyfully and piously went about slaughtering the sheep. The Muslim narrative differs from the Hebrew story only in that they contend that it was Ishmael, the progenitor of the Arabs, that was on the block, rather than Isaac, the Jewish patriarch.

Christians recreate this good example by insisting that God repeated the fine example set by Abraham in sacrificing his son. This is the Easter ceremony where Jesus is made the Lamb of God, sacrificed by his Father in order to provide an example for which everyone was to aspire. For this reason, many Christians morbidly eat spring lamb at Easter.

That's the antiquity of *Eid al-Kabir*, the holiest of days in the Islamic calendar, and it was in a pious orgy of blood that the non-clerical imams of the Janissary corps went about slicing the necks of animals, bathing the newly quarried granite in blood. On that day, the stones started to collect history, and the nutrients of the blood fed emerging mosses and lichens. The castle would no longer be an artificial fixture on the hillside, but a natural part of the historical landscape of the Bosporus. Next to a waterway that was forever flowing with the blood of empires, the throat was indeed forever cut.

Chapter Twenty-Four- The Long Way Home

Behind him, Iskender could sense the approach of the other horseman across the wind-saturated hills. Armed to the teeth, the tribal zephyr would catch up to him by nightfall, of that there was little doubt. That would mean that the two men would have to break bread with each other and play nice. Iskender hardly relished the thought, as Ahmet of Amaseia carried a vicious reputation with him alongside his more conventional tools of ill-omen. By the time night descended and the young Janissary was forced to make camp, the shadowy figure was upon him.

"Peace be upon you, Brother," he politely greeted the interloper.

The tribesman trotted up to make his presence known and was silent for an instant before return the salute. "And unto you be peace, brother Muslim."

"I'm building a fire, you're welcome to join me, though I haven't brought much water or food enough to share."

"Thank you," Ahmet replied and dismounted his horse. "I've already eaten a large breakfast this morning, and I've got my own provisions. I'll help you with your fire. You seem to be having some trouble."

"Thank you," Iskender smiled. It was a recurring joke among his peers that in a desert, he would be able to create water by simply touching wood; such was his incompetence at fire-building. "We weren't properly introduced the other day. My name is Iskender. I'm a soldier in the Eighth, now based at Roman Castle."

"I'm Ahmet," the guest replied. "I'm in the service of Halil, the grand vizier to the Sultan in Adrianople, heir to the sword of Osman."

"It's an honour to meet you again, Ahmet-bey."

"A pleasure to meet you again, young Janissary."

"Are you sure you're not hungry?" Ahmet asked Iskender once he got the campfire burning. "You've been riding all day."

"I'll be fine, thank you," Iskender replied.

In truth, Iskender was indeed famished, but he wouldn't eat until he arrived at the house of Zaganos-pasha tomorrow. There was no disgrace in breaking his fast with a former Janissary, but to do so with a man like Ahmet would be beneath him. Tribesmen, regardless of their imperial patronage, were respected for their savagery and gazi-spirit, but the men of the Janissary ranks were soldiers of learning and culture, who had no need to descend to the level of the rabble. Iskender doubted that Ahmet was literate, and found himself repressing a sneer when he heard the hillbilly intonations and accent when the tribesman spoke. Despite his prejudice, Iskender was the model of politeness.

Ahmet didn't care for the Janissary's company either. He was young, arrogant, aloof and obviously not at the same level as Ahmet. He would admire the soldier's discipline, as the corp's reputation on the battlefield was legendary, but the effete and insular cult of the slaves bored him. Ahmet had born a Muslim, and was untainted by the Christian legacy that had for so long gripped the famed converted soldiers. That, alongside a widespread reputation for homosexuality and heresy did little to endear the young soldier to the grand vizier's bodyguard. Despite all this, Ahmet was also the model of politeness.

"Have you seen any battle yet, Son?" Ahmet asked.

"Not yet," conceded Iskender. He wasn't pleased with the *'son'* comment, as there was neither kinship nor significant enough age difference between the two to merit it. "I think that fairly soon, that will change for all of us. Have you been in a battle?"

"I've been in many fights, with far too much bloodshed, but only one proper battle," Ahmet answered. "When I was fourteen, my brother and I were levied to go and fight with the Sipahi, Kazim Bey. We rode south and east to Caesarea to fight off raiders from Karaman. We weren't in the main battle, unfortunately. We pounced on a team of Cappadocian horsemen, only a couple of dozen, but Kazim-Bey was a fearless fighter and we crushed them. Some of them were killed, but most of them ran back into the hills and valleys of the highlands."

"Did you kill anyone?" Iskender asked inquisitively.

"Then?"

Iskender nodded.

"I think so," Ahmet answered truthfully.

"What do you mean *'you think so'*?"

"I was an archer, standing among a score of my cousins and clansmen. There was no way to know which arrows were mine, which were my brothers or my cousins; even if we could identify the arrows, the bodies were so riddled that it would be a guessing game to find out which one actually killed the men. I suspect that I killed one of them, but to be honest, I'm not sure."

"I'm almost eighteen, and I'm still waiting for my first kill," the younger of the two mumbled, almost to himself. "I hope to make up for that soon."

"Don't worry, it'll come in time," Ahmet tried to sound like an older brother and stoked to campfire. "Have you ever tired poppy smoke?"

Iskender blushed reflexively. "That's a sin."

"So is killing, but we've both found ourselves outside those regular rules, soldier."

"God's rules don't change by profession, and killing in order to defend and expand the House of Peace is hardly a sin."

"Forcing a conquered people into slavery is also permissible by the Qur'an, it's even a pious act to bring them into service of the faithful. Have you ever seen a freeborn man be broken to the point that he accepts his position as an owned man?" Ahmet made idle his conversation while he fetched a black ball of opium from a pouch hidden at the bottom of one of his many saddle bags. "Or do you remember it?"

"What are you saying, Ahmet?" Iskender asked accusingly.

"It's a heartless thing to see. It takes time and cruel commitment I'm saying that there are many pious and religious acts that lack any form of human justice, and that some acts, while not religiously permissible, are fundamentally good."

"Like your poppy smoke?" Iskender asked sarcastically.

"Among other things, yes," Ahmet answered softly as he collected his long iron pipe and a pouch from his saddlebag. "You don't have to join if you don't want to, friend."

Ahmet tried to control his anticipated tension as he took a stick from the fire. He blew against the red heater end of a stick to remove the whitened ash. When the ember was clean and red, Ahmet pinched a portion of black oblivion from a brick in his pouch and rolled it between his thumb and forefinger. He then placed the red ember into the bowl of his long iron pipe, and broke off the smoldering wood to act as a bed for the opium gum. He gently bedded the black bead onto the burning ash and blew on it again, to gently start the melting process.

"I guess I'll be on watch tonight," Iskender mused.

"Don't worry about that here," Ahmet assured him. "There are no travelers near here, nor are there any bandits. Most people are too worried about the impending war to come anywhere near here. It's just us and the hills tonight!"

There was a certain lupine grin on Ahmet's face that made Iskender quite uncomfortable, but at the same time, this tribesman had a certain charisma. He seemed almost naïve as he inhaled his pipe. He seemed more of a likeable bumpkin than the Janissary had imagined him to be.

"I'll give that a try, I suppose," Iskender relented

When the sun finally began warming the earth in the morning, it brought no relief to Iskender. He felt as though there was a thin wire stretching through his head, going in one ear and out the other. His body simply hung off this painful wire when he stood up and attempted to mumble his way through his morning prayers.

"Good morning to you, Buyuk Iskender," Ahmet chipped cheerfully as he had already packed up the camp from the night prior. Buyuk Iskender is a reference to Alexander the Great, of world conqueror fame. "I thought you were ready to sleep the morning away!"

"My head's spinning," Iskender murmured.

"Don't worry, that should be done by noon-time. Just in time for our arrival into the capital. Are you going into the city, or will you be going straight to the Lion's Den?"

"I have to go the palace, I have to meet someone…"

"Zaganos Pasha?" Ahmet asked.

Iskender frowned.

"Oh, if you'd like, I could pretend to know nothing about your master's master, and you don't know who I serve."

Iskender found it interesting how such a patently false offer could sound legitimate from Ahmet.

"I have some business in the capital," he insisted.

"Of course," Ahmet said. "But you might want to consider a visit to the bathhouse first, you look like you've been up all night smoking poppy in the hills."

"Ha, ha," Iskender snarled sarcastically and massaged the back of his aching neck. "When will we get back to Adrianople?"

"By noon time, in plenty of time to go about other tasks."

Ahmet slapped himself into a corner of the domed bath-house and felt the wet marble bristle triumphantly under him. The furnace bellow heated the water, which heated the stone, and the effluent hot water poured out of taps with which the patrons washed themselves. Unlike his master, Halil, Ahmet would go when the place was busiest, on a Friday afternoon. Among the tradesmen and bureaucrats who came there to wash for their Friday prayers, he stood out with his long hair, large frame, scars and tattoos. He could listen to the bathers grumble about the normal ails of urban life. While everyone wore wooden sandals and cloth towels for the sake of modesty, there was a certain intellectual nudity that followed the conversations going on. For Arto the bathhouse attendant, his exposure to these naked machinations earned him a valuable retainer from the palace's chief eunuch. Kabira paid him a monthly stipend in order to have access to certain gossip.

Lying in the middle of the huge octagonal belly-stone was a humorous looking pot-bellied foreigner. He'd been pointed out to Ahmet before, but he'd never been formally introduced, so he figured that now was as good a time as any. The large tribesman hopped onto the slippery marble centre-piece and slid over to the awkward looking bald man.

"Orban, Orban," He greeted the famed Hungarian gunsmith. "Peace be upon you."

"And unto you be peace," Orban replied and by doing so came dangerously close to exhausting all of his limited Turkish.

"I am Orban," he began by pointing an open palm at himself. He then looked questioningly at the other. "You are?"

"Ahmet," he replied carnivorously, understanding that the foreigner understood very little of his language. Ahmet decided that he'd best speak very slowly and loudly so that the fellow could best understand him. "I'm Ahmet. Are you in order?"

"BytheblessingsofGodIaminorder," Orban had apparently memorised the question and the appropriate response, but obviously understood none of the words, judging by the confused visage behind the calm mask on his face.

Ahmet smiled coldly at this.

"Are you a Muslim, Stranger," he asked without intonation. "You use God's chosen words, and speak of him quite comfortably."

Orban had a foolish looking grin on his face and obviously understood nothing.

"Muslim. Muslim? You?" Ahmet aped loudly, garnering the attention of a room that had gone silent. "Are you a Muslim?"

"Ah." A look of cognition hit the foreigner. "I… Muslim… No. I am being Jesusji."

Not knowing the word for *Christian*, Orban simply added the profession suffic 'ji' to the name Jesus. *Jesusji* would more accurately be translated as someone who sells Jesus, although the word for Jesus in Turkish is *Isa (Jézūs with a Latin "J" in Orban's native Hungarian)*. The word for Christian in Ottoman Turkish is Hristyaniyya. Orban's inability to speak the same language made Ahmet's harassment seem all the more insolent. Everyone in the bath house had fallen silent and was watching the dramatic harassment unfold on the belly-stone. Everyone knew Ahmet's reputation and the disposition of his patron, everyone was equally knowledgeable as to the foreigner's affiliation with the absent Zaganos Pasha.

"Leave him alone, Young One," came a familiar voice from the south wall. Ahmet glanced over quickly to see Musa-Pasha, Halil's youngest brother, his long beard drooped down with sweat. "He's making no oppression to you, let him be."

Ahmet was of course forced to bow to the authority of Musa. Musa was a minister of the divan, the Sultan's councillor, and younger brother to his own patron. Ahmet was also aware of the fact that Musa's entire position in the society of the capital was dependent on the welfare of his elder brother. Ahmet was wise enough to know that having the same patronage hardly made them social equals.

"Of course, Pasha," Ahmet feigned doting cheer. "I'm only welcoming our new guest."

He smiled a toothy grin at the bewildered gunsmith, who smiled back sheepishly.

Musa glared at the two of them and returned to his own conversation. Ahmet in his turn threw his smile all around the room and then slumped away into a corner.

Back at the Palace of Adrianopolis, the young Janissary awaited an audience with the Second Minister. He waited at attention for almost an hour before he was ushered into the great man's office.

"Welcome! Welcome!" Zaganos greeted the young soldier with a smile. "I'm sorry for the wait, but the business of the Empire waits for no one. Have a seat. Are you well?"

"I'm fine, Pasha," Iskender answered dutifully with a bow. "Peace be upon you."

"And unto you be peace," the minister replied mechanically. "Are you ok?"

"Yes…"

"Your eyes seem strange," he said without loosing his polite composure.

"I'm fine, I assure you, Pasha. Though you honour me with your concern…"

"One moment, if you please," Zaganos poked his head outside of his audience chamber and called over two young boys, one in his early teens and the other barely a child. "These are my two oldest sons, Murat and Beyazid. I wanted them to see our visiting guest. Introduce yourselves to the man.”

“Peace be upon you, Janissary,” they both uttered in tandem.

“And unto you be peace, children,” Iskender replied. “Sir, I have news from Lord Mesut.”

“And what would that be?”

“He said to inform you that throat is now cut and everything is going as per your plan,” he replied dutifully.

“Good then,” the minister replied. “Can you wait outside, I wish to speak to my two boys, and I will write a letter to your master for you to bring to him.”

“Yes, Pasha,” Iskender bowed and left the room.

The polite joy left the minister’s eyes once the janissary had left the room.

“My sons, today I have an important lesson to teach you about the weakness of men.”

Ahmet stretched out languidly in his bed and let out a long breath of satisfaction. Ayshe smiled at his dramatics and kissed him on the cheek. She hooked her hand around his neck and held the younger man’s gaze intently. Ahmet hated when she did that. She gazed into his eyes with a warm facial expression that was belied by her eyes. She was thinking, calculating, and Ahmet couldn’t fathom the depths of her machinations. He could only smile back like a fool.

In response to the curt smile from her husband’s bodyguard, Ayshe broke the gaze and diverted her eyes. She didn’t want him to become overly familiar with her own private thoughts. Once she looked away, so did Ahmet with a mild grunt of disapproval. The pillowing mood that had so recently filled their bed made a graceless exit.

“I ran into your brother-in-law this morning in the bathhouse,” Ahmet said, relegating the conversation to what he believed to be small talk.

“Which one?” Ayshe asked absently, her attention and her gaze going out the window.

“Musa. I was giving that foreigner friend of Zaganos a bit of a hard time, he told me to stop it.”

Ayshe’s attention returned to him immediately, and her face seemed to age ten years as shadows overtook the craggy lines of her hawk-like visage.

“Did you quarrel with the gunsmith, Orban?” she asked. Her voice was swift staccato and far more aggressive than Ahmet believed a woman should speak.

"We didn't quarrel, I gave him a bit of a rough time. He's not a Muslim. He's supposed to be unclean to us, but we let him bathe with us. Normally the minorities have their own times for bathing. Let him go with the Jews and Christians!" Ahmet answered indignantly.

"He's an important man, and he's supported by an important man, Ahmet," Ayshe spoke in the business-like tone that Ahmet so disliked. "Did you confront him publicly? Did many people witness it?"

"Most of the folks there," Ahmet answered off-handedly.

Ayshe stared at the ignorant young man whose bed she shared. Ahmet resented her aloofness, all the more so because it came from her own keen mind over his inexperience; that was more painful to bear than the on-principle animosity that he got from the Janissary.

"Sometimes, you can be really foolish, Ahmosh," she told him after a moment of silent glaring. *Ahmosh* is a diminutive form of Ahmet.

"You shouldn't talk to me like that," Ahmet mumbled.

For all her plottings and subtleties, she had little understanding of the cultures of men outside the palaces and harems of the capital. In his eye, she could have seen something new. She could have caught a glimpse of the murderous temper of the tribesman. Unfortunately for her, she didn't see this.

"You need to get wise quickly," she chastised him. "The palace suffers no fools."

Without a thought or a warning, Ahmet's open hand swung forward from his side and slapped across her face. She was flung out of the bed by the force of the strike. Out of the bed she tried to regain her footing before the momentum had subsided, but instead she veered into the wall a couple of metres from the bed and collided with that before collapsing into a pile in the corner of the bedchamber.

'What the hell did I just do?' Ahmet asked himself, looking at the slumped body of his mistress.

Ayshe, in shock, looked up and saw the boy staring down at her. In his eyes was a smouldering fury that she'd not seen before. How could she not have understood what was there, what had always been there. This man had killed men, children and infants, and who knows how many others. In his face was no remorse for striking her, just rage. The two held eye contact for only an instant, but it seemed like so much longer.

"Look at me, Ayshe. Look at me," he said, grabbing her face and forcing her to look upon him. "You have to hide this. If you don't, he'll kill you. I can run away and find a future, you can't."

Ayshe felt like throwing up. She could feel blood rushing into her cheeks and her face beginning to swell from the violent impact. She was silent.

"Understand that!" Ahmet chastised her, and then slapped her curtly with an open hand again. The second slap was intended to focus her attention rather than do any serious harm. "You have to sequester yourself away until the bruise is gone, or I'll kill you myself and ride off. Don't even think of crying."

Ayshe looked absolutely terrified at this point.

"You brought this upon yourself, you foul woman! When you first seduced me in your husband's bed! Have you no decency? No morals for your own marriage?. Now go clean yourself up."

"You bastard," she whispered.

Ahmet held up his right hand, five fingers spread like daggers.

"Don't make me finish the job."

Ayshe steadied her gaze and lifted her chin proudly against him.

"God will punish you for this."

"God's punished me enough. Now go, and for your own sake hide yourself."

Ayshe threw her clothes on and drew a chador over her face; while uncommon in her own home, it was certainly not unexpected of a pious Muslim woman to veil. She left Ahmet's room without another word being spoken.

Once she had vacated, Ahmet sat down on the bed and punched the mattress as hard as he could.

'Damn it!' he held back tears. *'What am I going to do now?'*

There was a knock on the cedar door to the private chamber of the second minister and Iskender was summoned back into the greeting chamber of Zaganos Pasha, alongside two of his sons. The boys were doing a poor job of trying to seem impassive, which only made Iskender nervous. They were stiff as boards, staring forebodingly at the Janissary's eyes but trying not to make eye-contact. Zaganos on the other hand was cheerful and upbeat.

"Sit down, I was just discussing some affairs with my sons. I'm sorry to have put you out like that."

"It's no problem, Pasha," Iskender enunciated and tried not to be distracted by the younglings, seeing, hearing and speaking no evil, but glaring at him as if in judgement.

"We're not going to force you to tarry, brother Janissary, so I'll give you a letter to take to your master. Do you have a horse to return you to the throat cutters?"

"I will bring my horse back to the Lion's Den and exchange him with a fresh steed."

"You'll do no such thing, my boy!" Zaganos clapped his hands twice and a house servant standing in the doorway. "Equip this man with the fastest mare in the stable, a gift to my good friend Mesut to celebrate his success."

The house-eunuch bowed his head deferentially to the second minister and motioned for Iskender to follow.

"Thank you very much, Pasha," Iskender said with a bow. "I'll make sure he gets your letter by morning."

"The pleasure was mine," Zaganos said with a smile.

The sons looked on in judgement.

Dearest Mesut, Son of Abdullah,
Commander of the Eighth Orta,
Slave of the Gate and Defender of the Faith,

In the name of God, the compassionate and the merciful, I greet you and pray that this letter finds you in grace and content with your achievement and humble before the one God who has granted it to you and for whom all credit is given. If God wills it, may a hundred more victories be granted to the faithful through your pious service.

I felt truly elevated when I heard the joyous news that the throat of the heretics is being cut. These are great times for all humanity, as the light of God will soon shine through the darkness that inveils so much of the world. I salute you and thank you on behalf of all Muslims. I will have a dozen heifers sacrificed to celebrate the blocking of the strait and distribute the meat among the poor of the capital.

I must warn you that there are some who are moving against us as I write these words. The threat from the tribes, of which we'd discussed prior to your move to Roman Castle, has become real. On the night of the next full moon, they'll be going through with the inspection. To guard us all, you have to act. I know your wisdom and bravery can bury this threat, like so many others.

Against all this news, I must relate to you another frustration. The boy that you sent to the palace to bear this glorious news also bore the signs of corruption. When you first introduced him to me, you had intimated that he had a future among the courtly classes, but I must reject that recommendation. His eyes and breath bore the earthen decay of burnt poppy. You may discipline him as you see fit, but this boy is never to enter the palace again. He may redeem his sins through martial service, I leave that in your discretionary hands. We've both learnt from past experience what happens to a comrade afflicted by this menace.

Peace be upon you, my brother,
Zaganos, son of Abdullah, Second Minister to the Sublime Porte and the Gate of Felicity

Chapter Twenty-Five - The Inspection

It was never appropriate for a commander to show any fear or panic in front of his troops, and Mesut prided himself on his adherence to the rules of professionalism. Before he marched his men from the now fully operational Roman Castle down to meet the sultan, he'd put the fear of God into each and every one of his soldiers. It was his hope that they would be as afraid as he was, without realising that he too was so afraid. He mustered the eighth orta in the courtyard of the castle and addressed them.

There was a sharp division between the men of the regiment. On the one side, there were many soldiers who were properly trained Janissaries, and on the other were the mastiff trainers, the kopekjis. Their numbers were forced onto the regiment, and the rest of the unit had to carry their burden. They were paid more than the regular soldiers, their dogs ate fresher meat than many of the regiment's men, and they were slated for promotion above men with experience, expertise and seniority. They had numbers, but not respect.

"We have an embarrassment to the corps, men. We have a humiliation that we have to avenge!" he told them. Mesut feared no enemy on the field, death was the inevitable end of service that came for all soldiers. What he feared was the destiny he saw on the horizon, the marginalization on his beloved Janissaries, or worse yet, their supplication. He looked at the mastiff trainers, Janissaries in name only.

"The Sultan himself, your master and mine, is marching to the city of the dead," he called out, referring to Constantinople. "And we will meet him there. We'll be there to stand by his defence, when he fearlessly stands so close to the enemy! Just as his courage won't waver, neither will ours!"

There were quiet nods of approval from his men.

"He should be afraid, though. The Christians aren't without strength and soldiers, and the Imperial party is going to inspect the walls from the nearby countryside! We can't allow this to happen without defending our master. Our job has always been to defend the Sultan and the state, even if our lord Mehmet doesn't understand how badly we're needed. We can't allow the Sultan to fall prey to the enemy, so without any pause or stop, we'll leave the gunners here, and a company for defence of the castle. The rest of us are going to run for two miles to where the Sultan's camp has been made, and accompany him to the walls."

"He's alone?" Erhan, a new recruit called out in worry.

"No," Mesut answered. "He's brought his hunting party with him to act as bodyguards. The falconers are rangers from his exile in Amaseia, and he's taken bad advice from them. He thinks that those undisciplined, unsoldierly men from the forests and hills can do our job as well as us. We have to go there and remind the Sultan of our strength, and our loyalty."

Mesut gave a dramatic pause before continuing.

"Make no mistake, these tribesmen want to take our position as the elites of the empire. They are our enemy, as much as the infidels are. Out of pride and loyalty to the regiment and corps, make sure that you run too fast for them to keep up. Make sure that your drill is too sharp for them to match. In the event of any hurly-burly, obey your sergeants and act quickly and decisively. Remind our Sultan why we are the terror of Christian princes and the hunters are only his fair weather friends. I hope that you all understand the importance of the task that's just come to us."

Silence implies consent. The Janissaries nodded their acceptance of the important display-task before them, and they filed out diligently into their columns and prepared for a brisk morning jog. Their commander led them on foot, and would not weaken his pace.

Over the snowy hills and through the frozen dales of Thrace, the Eighth Orta took flight over the earth. With each unison step, they claimed new dominion and pounded their might into the memory of the earth beneath them.

An hour later, they'd arrived at the camp of the Sultan, full of energy and ready for battle if need be. The camp was a clearing in an unnamed part of the forest; finding them was the easy part. The four hundred men of the orta's vanguard arrived only moments after word of their arrival penetrated the camp by posted guards. Their surprise boded well for the Janissaries.

"Who approaches?" demanded the captain of the camp.

Mesut was shocked by the man's appearance. The captain was a bearded tribesman, a large man who could obviously carry himself in a fight, but was not what the Janissaries would describe as a proper soldier. He did, however, wear the uniform of a proper soldier. He wore a Janissary uniform, complete with red jacket and white felt cap.

"Janissaries! Draw scimitars!" Mesut called to the men behind him before refocusing on the captain before him. "I don't care who you think you are, you and your camp will stand down now, you will take those uniforms off and walk back home naked to whatever village you filthy savages call home and you will never... ever... hold your head high in the

326

presence of a real Janissary ever again!"

"We're the new Janissaries," the captain nonchalantly informed Mesut. "We guard the person of the Sultan. You can turn around and go back to whatever garrison duty you've been shuffled to and stay out of trouble there."

"Mesut!" Came the call from the back of the camp. The young and as yet unbearded face of Sultan Mehmet emerged from the crowd and joined the two feuding captains. "I'm sorry for not greeting you myself. It was Captain Birol's suggestion. We didn't know who you were."

"I understand, Sire. We could have been a mongrel pack of honourless brigands who'd disguised ourselves in the uniforms of the illustrious Janissary corps. In the future, you need not worry, for any such brigands will be hunted the ends of the earth for dishonouring your service so."

"Ah, yes. I have good news, your ranks are going to be bolstered again. As you know, we're preparing for a campaign, and for this we need as many men as we can assemble. I'm expanding the Janissaries, and raising your numbers."

"It normally takes ten years to turn a Christian child into a Janissary, sire."

"To go from heathen to heretic?" Captain Birol suggested.

"Silence, Dog!" Mesut spoke louder and harsher than was appropriate in front of the sultan. "We're already doing our best to train the additions to which you've already bolstered to us. If anymore come, the regiment will cease to be Janissaries, and will simply be an irregular militia, of which there are already plenty."

When Mesut yelled, the rope-burn scar on his neck glistened an angry red. It made Birol feel a residual psychic heat and pain emanating from the old soldier. The sultan felt this as well.

"It's a pity that we're going to work with you *old guard*," the captain spoke as though he couldn't decide on whether words or a yawn were to emerge from his mouth. "I hope that none of my men pick up any bad habits from these disloyal cultists."

Mesut drew his own scimitar with a swiftness that few men could match. The sultan's own swiftness intervened between the two uniformed belligerents, lest blood flow.

"Now, Birol," Mehmet began. "Mesut here is a loyal and true officer – an exemplary of his corps. It was because of him and his regiment that I'm here today, so this man holds a special place in my heart and you shan't offer him such disrespect. It's a pity that the other Janissaries don't model themselves to him."

Mesut's face was like stone. When Mehmet first became Sultan, upon his father's retirement, the Janissaries had heeded to the influence of the grand vizier, Halil-Pasha, and rebelled. They'd demanded a 'gift' from the new administration, and had openly rebelled against their sultan. They'd even set fires in the capital and refused their duty as fire wardens until they'd been paid. Mesut had refused to participate in the uprising in favour of the return of Murat, and his Janissaries had acted as the only defenders of the palace during those nights five years ago.

Mesut had felt that would enjoy a privileged status among the Janissaries, with the return of Mehmet. He hadn't behaved the way he was out of political motivations, but he felt that there would be a recompensed patronage for loyalty proven.

Mesut saw in Mehmet's eyes, memories that hadn't lost their edge with time. The city of Constantinople wasn't the only drive that consumed the young king's thoughts. Serpents coiled and constricted around the monarch's heart, and those serpents' names were vengeance and vendetta. Those serpents were waiting to strike out against those that wronged him, those years ago. The remnants of the Roman Empire were not his only targets in this great campaign.

"Sire, we're here to assist you in any way we can," Mesut said cautiously. He tried a different tact "And when you are this close to the capital of the infidels, you'll need the protection that only the Janissaries provide. These men, whose loyalty you find abundant, can wear a uniform to fool the enemy, just as easily as a woman or child could, but they lack the iron that forged the reputation that goes with uniform. The Romans will see the red and white and be careful, but if well-counselled caution doesn't win the day, I fear for your safety, My Lord."

"We are more than capable…" Captain Birol began.

"Shut up," Mesut spoke with abundant authority but without much effort. His words were simply passing the information to his rival that now was the time for him to be silent.

"You're right, Mesut," Mehmet said. "And I think that it would benefit some of these new guards to watch you and yours in action."

"I'm sure that they'd benefit greatly from seeing how real soldiers act. Then perhaps they can at least play the part with vigour, like children with wooden swords and stern faces."

"Then let's go, everyone," the sultan announced. We're going to the walls of Constantinople! We're going to inspect our targets. Mesut, you'll join the rest of my field divan tonight, I'll look forward to hearing your assessment of the walls as well as theirs. Perhaps from a more… practical… standpoint.”

“As your majesty wishes,” Mesut gave a dutiful bow and began the dispassionate task of calculating possibilities.

The icy wind swept the night’s frost from the mighty walls of the capital, and from those walls, *She* looked out at her dominion. Mary, Queen of Heaven, Mary, Queen of the World, was the mistress of the city, not some paltry dirt assembled into flesh and crowned by metal. Only she, blessed by God as carrier of the sacred seed and deliverer of salvation could be called ruler in the city of Constantine.

When Constantine the Great’s shadow, the eleventh pretender to carry his name, had been a young man, studying diligently in the monastery of Mistra, he’d worshipped her on footing with the father and the son. She alone actually had delivered salvation to an accursed earth, mired down in sin and desolation. From her, all was possible and all was given. Her radiance replaced the sun as Constantine’s great light. She was his mother, his god, his wife and mistress, and all he could do was weep when he was confronted with her glory, face-to-face.

She’d saved the city before. She’d stood on the mighty land walls and called the glorious defenders to arms. That was almost twenty years ago, and only a few who walked the palace grounds had been around to remember it. The patriarch called it a miracle, and the emperor praised the defenders as the heroes of a generation, and for all time. John Palaeologos, the current Constantine’s elder brother, wore the purple at that time, was the man lucky enough to witness this miracle. The younger Paliologos was informed of the witness by letter from the patriarch.

It had always consumed Constantine with jealousy that his brother had been chosen to bear witness to such an apocalypse and not he. He was more pious than his worldly brother, and certainly more well-read. To make the matter even worse, John never discussed the affair with his younger brother. No matter how much he asked, no matter how much he begged, no anecdote outside of the official record was forthcoming.

It wasn’t until 1448, when John was called up to the heavenly kingdom, that an emissary from the heavenly kingdom began to travel down to see Constantine. What he first believed to be an angel, but only later realised was the Virgin Mother herself, came to visit him. She told him about mysteries and secrets of the hereafter. She told him about his strength and his enemies weaknesses. Her beautiful apparition had been appearing to him more and more in recent months.

She appeared to him, she spoke to him, she absorbed his heart, mind and soul while she did so. Her visits were so all consuming that his official apartment in the palace was closed off, and he couldn't hear the banging on his door.

"Appologies, General Karian," Olaf the captain of the emperor's bodyguards told the general. "He's… communing."

The huge Viking blocked half the doorway with his unarmoured girth. The Varangian guard were mercenaries recruited among the river-men of the far north, among the Angles and the Saxons, among the Rus and Danes. They guarded the emperor's person and property.

"Shit!" the Armenian Strateogos yelled and strangled air in stressed frustration. "Of all the worst times possible for this… shit!"

"Appologies," Olaf repeated stubbornly and made no effort to accommodate his superior's needs. "You'll have to wait 'til he comes out."

Adam leaned close to the Norseman and addressed him in his most hushed of voices.

"These are becoming more and more frequent."

"Yes, sir. They are."

"Something has to be done, if his state becomes public knowledge…"

"That's why no one's allowed in, sir."

"Move aside, I'll wake him from his trance."

"It's not a trance, Sir," Olaf's face became serious and fearful. "He's possessed by a demon that rides him. The demon takes over his body for a few hours, and will leave on its own accord. Unless you want to bring a priest here, all we can do is wait."

"Bring a priest here, that's all we need, for someone in the priesthood to know about his affliction. They'd cast him down and put that bastard Stavros on the throne."

"Fine, you can try to rouse him, Sir," the guard relented, "but it won't do much good when he's in this state."

"Thank you, I'll see what can be done," Adam whispered and slipped into the private chambers of the emperor.

The chambers were the model of outward order. Everything was cleaned and arranged daily by the chamberlain and his men. The chamberlain, the guards and the general were the only men who knew of the Emperor's growing madness, and they worked seamlessly together, without need of meetings or spoken orders, to keep the secret from the rest of the world. They all worked together to keep order and stability all around their emperor, in the hopes that the order outside of him would eventually seep into his mind and keep the chaos at bay.

"Sire?" Karian asked as he entered. "It's me, Adam."

The emperor was seated in a plush chair, his knobby legs pulled tightly to his chest. He wore a night-shirt, but was naked below the waist. His head was darting from left to right with exhausting energy and he seemed to be mumbling to himself. He sat at the eastern window that overlooked the harbour and seemed to be pointing to a gate of the sea walls.

"She says she'll come for me there... when I leave the Petrion."

"Sire?" Adam said with stronger resolve. "You need to come out of this. Are you going to be alright?"

Adam looked at the half-naked sovereign shivering in the cold room and gradually approached him. Constantine's eyes didn't even blink as his old friend came up to him and grabbed him. Adam held his master's head tightly in his hands, and Constantine's eyes eventually stopped their erratic diffusion of focus and came to behold their servant.

"Adam?" he whispered. "She was here?"

"Are you going to be alright?"

"She was here, Adam. The Queen."

"The queen, Sire?" Adam questioned. He dreaded the hallucinations worsening and he could only hope that this was a passing daze. "Sire, you've never married, the last queen was your sister-in-law, and she's been dead almost five years now."

"No, no, no, no, no," the emperor insisted angrily. "The Queen of Heaven. Mary, mother of Jesus."

"Yes... her," Adam said gravely. "Is she gone now?"

"She's left me, but she still protects me."

"That's great, now you have to focus. Look at me, Sire," Adam said patiently. "Are you going to be alright now?"

Adam tried his best to ignore the Emperor when he was like this. Constantine's eyes were blurry, red and unfocussed, his skin blushed and covered in white splotches. He shivered and sweat at the same time. Loyalty was a virtue of supreme place in the general's mind, but oh how he wished that his loyalty was to someone more capable than it was. Or at least someone who would be more pliable. Adam knew that someday the time would come where he would have to put his own interests above those of his master, and he felt guilty for thinking so. Nevertheless, reality was his master, and his liege seemed independent of that fealty.

"Yes, yes. Of course I'm fine."

"I'm glad, sire." Now please put some clothes on, we have a situation that absolutely requires your attention."

"What is it?"

"They're here, sire."

"Who's here?"

"The Turks, sire. They've arrived to the walls."

"And... Stop!" Mesut ordered the men of the orta once they'd arrived at the agreed location on the lawn of the Christian capital. He turned around to make sure that his regiment had complied with the order and was doing so with the ferocious rigor that he demanded of them. To his joy, they behaved admirably.

Also to his joy, the falconers were all over the frozen field. They moved like a herd of cats, with independent-minded 'scouts' on all flanks, and sloppy footmen trying to march at the fast pace of the "Old Guard" Janissaries, and then drifting down to a more leisurely trot as their momentum died. They had started their morning march clustered together like the Eighth, but because they were untrained at marching in step, they ended up tripping over each other and colliding in a tangled clot of misappropriated uniforms and bad cadence. They eventually spread out like dollops of batter on a skillet. The wonderful lack of organization was so gleefully obvious that Mesut's heart warmed. He wouldn't have to point this out the divan or the sultan, as it was obvious to all. The sultan's face was frozen in an angry grimace as he watched his loyal hunters fail in their attempt to act the part of soldiers.

Mesut would come before the Sultan later and he would have to do his best to seem magnanimous, rather than snide. That would be harder than some battles. He smiled inside and played out the impending confrontation with Birol in his head. This was turning into a beautiful, sunny winter day.

The Janissaries set up the command tent for the divan to sit and look at the mighty walls. With two kilometers of air between them, Constantine and Mehmet both felt each other's presence and began the process of trying to analyze each other's spirit. This was the first time the two had been this close.

"He's over there, you know," Mehmet said, pointing to the balcony of Blachernae Palace. He's there with his advisors, and I'm here with mine. The old man feels safe in his tower, protected by stone and mortar, and I feel safe out here, under God's sky and with the earth under my feet."

The less-assertive divan members nodded their agreement with their Sultan's assessment of the world as he saw it, and tried to fake comfort as they sat within cannon distance of the giant walls.

"So tell me, Orban. What do you make of these walls?" Mehmet drifted flawlessly into Greek, a language that he spoke with much more formality and grace than the Hungarian cannon-maker did. "Where do you think that they're most vulnerable?"

"Over there, Sire," Orban pointed with pudgy workman's fingers to a section of the wall, about halfway between the harbour of the Golden Horne and the Sea of Marmara. "That's where the cannons should concentrate their fire. It's the longest stretch the walls without the reinforcement of towers, and it's on a mild crest, so the tension will be taking weight away from the centre and towards the slopes. When the wall breaks, it will be there."

Mehmet's eyes floated around the mile and a half of triple walls that encased the capital. When Attila the Hun came to this spot and looked on the walls, he turned his horde westward to harass Rome, believing the walls to be unbreakable. There were no Huns left anymore. Their seed had diffused into a thousand different ethnic, cultural and religious groups throughout Eurasia. The Hunnic storm raged over the Fifth Century, and then gradually abated when their hot blood boiled into steam and was carried off in the winds. Mehmet was no Attila. His accomplishments would not disappear into the mists of time, a legacy to be conquered by the conquered. His footprint on the earth was to be a permanent mark in the memory of God. That city would be his.

For the next two hours, Orban pointed out to the divan where the cannons should be set up, when the time came, and where the siege would be headquartered. Throughout the presentation, only Mesut, the uninvited observer, had a scribe to take notes. He was also the only one who continued to ask questions of the Magyar.

Giant Hussein was shocked when he'd been commanded to follow his commander about to take notes. That was the type of duty that should have fallen to the more scholarly minded Iskender, but Hussein was literate and educated, which was more than he could say for the '*New Janissaries.*' He'd been taught to have a disrespect for those outside of the orta, but this was his first contact with irregular soldiers. They were unshaven, illiterate, uncultured brutes. They seemed to have ferocity in their blood, but the big man wondered where they'd be when that flame burnt itself out. While he was a new recruit to the regiment, he knew that he could run for two days on an empty stomach, and he could stand and box with a broken nose and loosened teeth. These soldiers assembled would be terror when they had an advantage, but how long would they stand when the wind wasn't to their backs? Could they stand, undaunted in the fire? He doubted it. Hussein's broad face wasn't rough enough to merit daily shaving, but he had enough experience to tell the difference between soldiers and fighters. He was the former and these interlopers were certainly the later.

Mehmet looked on in disapproval at the captain of the falconers. His plan to infiltrate the Janissaries with loyalist soldiers was looking to be doomed to failure. The Janissaries' loyalty was no longer the rock upon which his grandfather and namesake had forged an empire in the Balkans, but their professional competence was still enough to shame all other fighting men on the planet. They couldn't be disposed of through skullduggery and political will. They'd have to be kept around for now. Mehmet decided to summon Mesut to a private audience, before they left the city walls.

"That's a lot," Constantine ruminated as he looked at the Turkish soldiers gathering on the Lycus Plain, the flat stretch of land before the famed land-walls of the capital. "How many do you think there are?"

"About a thousand or so, Sire," Adam answered pensively. He tongued a hole in his mouth where he'd lost a tooth to a dentist twenty years ago. It was a nervous habit that helped him to think. "Perhaps a little less."

"Surely, they're not going to attack," the emperor suggested. "Not now, and with so few men."

"They've almost as many men as us, but I suspect it's a scouting party. They have no cavalry, catapults or cannon. They're inspecting the walls. They're sizing them up and planning an attack. They're not afraid of us, and they want us to know that."

"His highness, the Proconsul Stavros of Brussa!" the chamberlain called into indicate a visitor.

"Come, Anthypatos," Constantine called to the new arrival.

Stavros was a man of delicate stature and had the hungry eyes of someone whose ambition was far too unchecked. His voice was one of the loudest in the court and he was feared and respected by most of his peers. Adam Karian and he did not consider each other to be peers, only as rivals who needed to be politely tolerated in the presence of the emperor.

"I came as soon as I heard, Emperor," the falsely aghast voice of the aristocrat was as welcoming as a fungal infection in summertime. The proconsul hurried through the Emperor's shadowy apartment and joined the two men on the balcony to observe the gathering outside the walls. "What's to be done, Your Majesty?"

"Nothing yet," Adam answered on his master's behalf.

"What?" Stavros asked in mock-surprise. "A thousand enemies gather on flat land outside our very gates, and you think that it doesn't merit a response."

"Any response by soldiers would be immediately blunted. Those are Janissaries on the fore, or most of them are at any rate. If your majesty would be willing to make a diplomatic maneuver that might bear fruit, but our military options are limited. I'll remind the Anthypatos that we are not at war with the Turks right now. His Majesty signed a treaty of perpetual peace with the sultan when he first took the throne."

"Sire, they can't have a picnic in our garden and do so with impunity. The Turks have obviously no intention of honoring your gracious peace. To tolerate such an affront is to encourage more!" Stavros made his case with more assertion than Adam was comfortable with. "We have to send someone out to meet them and demand they leave."

"Or invite the commander and his staff for dinner," Adam suggested sarcastically, knowing full well the failure that any military conflict would bring.

"Their excellencies, Vincent DiCastillo and Guistiniano Longo!" the herald announced.

"Send them in!" Constantine called back, eager to end the rancor among his two advisors. The emperor was an affable man, and disliked such bickering. He called out their location to the entering guests. "We're on the on the western balcony!"

"Vincent, welcome," Constantine said once they arrived on the balcony. "This must be the Genoese captain of whom I've heard so much."

"It's an honour to come before you, Sire."

"I'm sure," Constantine added absently. Everyone else nodded and gave their hellos.

"Stavros," Vincent added without enthusiasm. He shared Karian's lack of affection for the Proconsul. "I can assume that you know there appears to be a regiment of Turks at the gates."

"Yes, we'd noticed that, thank you very much," Stavros answered curtly.

Guistiniano looked at Adam and raised an eyebrow. It was his way of asking *'Who is this man and what is he doing here?'* Adam nodded his head imperceptively to the left, as his way of answering the question. *'He's a friend of the Emperor and we have to tolerate his idiocy.'*

"There seem to be two troops in the party," Vincent observed, ignoring the court's interloper. "What do you make of that, Adam?"

"I'd seen that as well," he gazed from the imperial balcony and observed the hodgepodge soldiers gathering outside the walls. "About a third of the Janissaries are running as a vanguard. They're running in step and as a block, the back two thirds is a sort of clustered horde. They're bumping into each other and trying to run ahead of each other. I'm not sure. Maybe they've bought uniforms for the cooks and support staff."

"No, all Janissaries are infantry soldiers, even the support trains. Maybe they've been poisoned?" Vincent regretted the suggestion of poisoning. It was a random thought and one that shouldn't have been voiced. "Perhaps they've costumed some irregulars to hide their real numbers... to keep us at bay through intimidation, or something along those lines. Maybe the Janissaries are losing numbers."

"You give them too much credit, Italian," Stavros said in a courtly manner. "The Muslims are hell-bent on rapine and plunder. There's no possible discipline when those are the only motivators. These are hardly soldiers of Christ."

"Proconsul," Longo spoke with a baiting voice. "I've seen Janissaries fight. I fought in the Crusade at Varna, and these enemies are hardly a disorganized horde."

"Perhaps you can make a litany of failed battles and impress other men," Stavros answered back, referring to the mentioned crusade's lack of success in Bulgaria seven years ago. "But these walls have repelled all comers and given no inch for a thousand years. You'll find that the spirit of our race is not as willing to accept a *'tactical retreat'* as that of our western cousins."

"I'm sorry, I'm a little confused," Longo said patiently, but with a slow boil working its way up in his voice. "My colleague Adam here is the commander of the Roman City auxiliaries and Navy, Vincent DiCastillo represents Venice, her colonies, interests and relations with Rome. I've been invited as overall liaison with the mercenaries, irregulars and recruits. Who are you and why are you here?"

"You should have your superiors explain things to you before you find yourself in my presence, young one," Stavros said with an arrogant smile. "I'm the governor of Brussa and Prime Minister of the Roman Empire. I am the vice-regent and I'm usually not in the habit of explaining myself to foreign subordinates.”

“I’m sorry, but I was under the impression that your ward of Brussa was occupied by the Turks and turned into a tribute paying province of the turbaned sultan, if you want to turn the subject to defeats and retreats…”

“Gentlemen,” Constantine shushed them. “Our mutual enemy is over there, not in here.”

Vincent and Adam were trying to ignore the posturing among the other two advisors to the emperor, but neither could feel that the inexplicably disorganized Janissaries were as big a threat as allowing a minister like Stavros to the table.

The corridors of the great palace of Blachernae were almost abandoned. Everyone had either been sent away or was at one of the western windows to try to catch a glimpse of what was going on at the edge of the empire. Adam Karian hoped to find a moment of calm to think while he walked down the echoing hall, but an old friend would have none of it.

“What were you gentlemen talking about in there?” A voice broke Adam’s meditative silence.

Adam looked over his shoulder, and found a thuggish looking man who’d somehow managed to squeeze himself into the ill-fitting togs of Constantine’s court.

“What do you think we were talking about?” Adam answered back angrily.

“A regiment and a half of Janissaries comes up to Lycus field, has lunch and now looks like it’s packing up to go home, that raises some questions. What does the emperor think about that?”

“Is there something that I can help you with here, Pazzi?”

“I heard that he had another episode this morning,” Hectore Pazzi was the assistant to Count Dominic Trebiano, and periodically represented him at the court of the emperor. When his master was away, he would more typically represent his own interests above those of the Genoese colony of Galata. “I pray the emperor is alright?”

“He’s fine,” Adam looked around as he spoke. He didn’t want to be seen talking to this Italian. There’s an old expression about judging a man by the company he keeps, and no one would want to have the reputation of Hectore Pazzi smear its residual film on them. Adam walked quickly as they spoke.

“These sorts of rumours seem to be growing,” Pazzi said as he followed the general down the hall, his crisp soldier's walk clipping and clopping through the echoing hallway. "It makes you wonder how much longer he can hold on,".

"I don't like to hear talk like that," Adam said with embarrassment. He was quite fond of the emperor, and didn't like to hear his reputation besmirched by the likes of this Genoese. "You should ask your friend Longo about him."

"Longo's not my friend," Pazzi joked. "He's brother to Dominic's wife, and the two of them aren't friends, either. I imagine that you and he probably get along quite well, neither of you have any friends."

"Is there something that I can help you with?" Adam turned around angrily and faced down the other man. "Is there a question you want to ask me, that you think I might answer honestly, and not merely give you some rehearsed platitude?"

"Now, now, Adam," Hectore held up his hands in mock surrender. "I just wanted to know that you and I were still on the same page. We have a big day coming up, and I don't want you to give up on me. I don't want you turning into some tragic martyr, and look out for your emperor, instead of yourself."

"Don't worry about me, Pazzi. I know what's got to be done. As long as you hold up your end, everything will be fine."

"Hey, don't you go worrying about me, either. I never get confused as to what's important and what's not."

"Of course not, and I never start something without having a few different possibilities of how to get out of it," Adam said as a warning. Had there been anyone in the hallway to overhear them, he'd be in a precarious position now. As it happened, there weren't any thirsty ears nearby, searching for rumours to drink. "Don't bring this up here again. I'll talk to you again before the day."

"That's all I wanted to hear."

"Good day to you then, Sir."

"And a good day to you, General," Pazzi bowed in a slow and deliberate manner.

His presence made Adam's skin crawl. In a perfect world, he wouldn't have to deal with the likes of that self-interested Italian. As time went on, Adam had begun to feel worse and worse about what he was planning, but he nonetheless knew it had to be done, for his own sake. It's just that he was uncomfortable thinking of himself as the type of man who'd do it.

When the Turkish contingent had experienced enough of the city wall, when they'd drawn enough sketches and maps of the fortifications, they then began the simple task of returning to their camp to the north-west of the city. For the Eighth Orta, this was a simple task. Mesut called the men to attention, told them to form up in the direction of the camp, and then stood, waiting for the falconers of the Sultan's camp to form up and organise themselves.

The falconers clustered into several main groups. Those who were ready and keen tried to run ahead of everyone else, and began to disappear into the hills, rather than wait for their fellow comrades, officers, commander or Sultan. Some tried to assemble into ranks, a poor man's pantomime of the Janissary's discipline. The majority of them grouped together among friends, and waited for their leaders to tell them to start hiking back.

Mesut couldn't help but smile as he looked back at his soldiers, assembled in groups around their sergeants, who assembled in order behind their officers. They waited in formation for twenty minutes, while the others ran around trying to remember their place. Under normal circumstances, their commander Birol would have been happy with their performance, twenty minutes to assemble and ready was good by their standards. It was obviously not good enough for the standards of the waiting Janissaries, who smugly stood and looked down their noses at the swirling chaos.

Sultan Mehmet was one of the few men on horseback, and he trotted around the camp, inspecting the disorderly assembly.

"Commander Mesut," he called to the Janissary, loud enough for all around to hear. "Would the eighth do the honour of marching with me and my council back to camp now?"

"With pleasure, Sire!"

"Good. Captain Birol!" Mesut then addressed the commander of the hunters. "When you've organised your men, you are free to join us back at the camp, I should want a word with you when you arrive. I trust you can accomplish this before nightfall."

"We'll be right behind you, Sire!" Birol promised.

Mehmet offered no response. He and three other equestrians, the grand vizier Halil, the gunsmith Orban, and Musa the new imperial exchequer joined the ranks of the Eighth for the march back to camp.

"Tell me, Mesut," the sultan asked once they found themselves en route. "Do you suppose these new Janissaries will catch up with us before we make the camp?"

"I can't be sure," Mesut's confidence was reserved for himself and his own, "but we'll stay with you until they return."

Orban was oblivious to the Turkish language conversation, but the Chandarli brothers listened intently. Neither of them ventured their ideas just yet.

"Sire," Mesut had to approach this topic delicately, but he also had to maintain bravado. It was a delicate balance, and political speech had never been his forte. "May I ask a question about my new colleagues?"

"Yes," Mehmet's voice was not as strong as it should have sounded. He was not prepared to be lectured by a subordinate with regards to a failed idea.

"Are they to take the field of battle as the mastiff trainers will, or will they number more with our allies from the gazis of the tribes?"

"They're going to be Janissaries, like you and yours. You'll call them comrades and brothers," Mehmet answered without looking at him. "You should be pleased that your ranks are growing."

"I am, we've got several new recruits who're looking forward to proving themselves," Mesut then inserted an afterthought. "They've spent ten years training for this. Their entire lives so far have been getting ready to prove themselves. None of them have any ambitions outside of the corps, and none of them have any friends that don't wear the same uniform as them. Their sense of self, their pride and their joy, comes from each other. If they ever dropped down the standard shown by these new Janissaries, I'd have them whipped in front of their unit."

Mehmet almost snarled. He didn't like that the slave would be so bold as to make such disparages at his bodyguards, but he nonetheless knew the assessment to be accurate.

"The Janissaries are not the only weapons in the prophet's arsenal, Janissary."

"No, Sire. But we're the sharpest. What happened those years ago shamed me very much, sire. It's your strong arm that wields our mighty sword, and I pray daily that you use that strength to sever the infidel's head from his body, but those rangers will dull the sword to a glorified club, Sire."

"I know," Mehmet said sullenly.

"I thank God for your wisdom."

"I'll be appointing them as sergeants and officers in the existing regiments. They may lack experience, but they're a much needed injection of loyalty into a group that has long been allowed too much independence. Don't you agree?"

"Yes, Sire," Mesut closed his eyes in frustration. His protection of the Sultan those years ago was hardly motivated by altruistic loyalty. He knew then what he was witnessing now: that the seeds of betrayal grew into strangling vines. "A wise precaution, and the eighth can always use more manpower."

"Then they'll be your responsibility. Along with the mastiff trainers, you'll train them to be every bit as hard as your own steel."

"Yes, Sire."

Halil silently watched this little scene unravel and said nothing. For most of the past few days, he'd said little to anyone, save for the polite pleasantries of court. Empty words hid deep thoughts and he watched the only senior Janissary in the empire who'd rebuffed him those years ago, emerge into a potential ally. As an asset, he would be all the more valuable because of his perceived loyalty. Halil knew the youthful indulgence of the Sultan too well. Mehmet would flush the ortas with the hunters, and make new officers loyal to him alone, not to their regiment's dual quests for gold and glory. The grand vizier could speak to his master, and have the eighth spared, because of past loyalties. That could turn Mesut into a very powerful man, commanding the strongest regiment, unfettered by the dissenting conflict. Mesut would be a powerful man in the army, and could be made a powerful man in court, provided he understood what Halil could do for him.

Halil smiled to himself. He was going to steal Zaganos' dagger right from under the second minister's nose. There was a reason why he'd been prime minister for so long.

Chapter Twenty-Six - King's Side Castle

The sight of the full moon sliding over the ripples and waves of the harbour was an hypnotic sight. Olaf watched the silver sphere dance and couldn't help but be taken back. An identical sight could be seen almost anywhere in the world, it was a beauty available to free men and slaves alike. When the young Viking saw the light slip over the water, he felt that he was back home in a land of hills and forests that teemed with life, of the cold rivers that named his race and of dragons and other spirits, some malevolent and others kind.

Olaf had been forced to convert to nominal Christianity in order to wear the title of Varangian Guard, the elite mercenaries of Byzantium. He was as illiterate, ignorant and uneducated as he was large, strong and vicious. That was all that was expected of a man such as he, at least by the soft men of the south who placed their faith in God, but expected the steel and sinew of the Varangians to thanklessly maintain that faith.

Normally, the Varangians were charged above all other charges with the custodianship of the treasury, held and guarded in Blachernae Palace. Tonight, the night of the last full moon of winter, their commander had come to them with a new charge.

"Olaf!" came a call from the darkness. "Is it clear?"

The wild-eyed Viking shook the moon from his head and refocused on the task before him.

"It's clear, step silently," he whispered.

From the shadows of Porphyrogentius Palace, two dozen large shadows crept out into the moonlight.

Porphyrogentius was the palace of the administration, rather than it's more famous neighbour, Blachernae, which was the palace of the emperor's palace of worldly delights. It was in there the once famed treasury was kept, though now it was sorely under-stuffed. For almost a thousand years, river-men from the north had formed the elite guards of both the Emperor's person and his pocket, but alas, these days neither commanded the same respect or loyalty that did it once upon a time.

The Varangians themselves were known for their fierceness in peace and war, but tonight their war-cries were silent, their armour and arms were in barracks, and their feet were padded with soft leather. The river dragons poured down the palace corridors like lighting down a spike but without sound until they broke at the door to the vault itself, which had at one time been the richest treasure trove in Christendom.

The silent crowd of northerners built up at the wall and formed a hole for the smallest man among them, a wiry Armenian aristocrat and soldier named Karian. Without a word, he reached into his cloak and drew out the key to the vault and turned the tumblers to open the ironwood door.

The treasury was in a sad state by imperial standards. There was by no means enough to manage a world empire, consisting of a hundred cities and legions of soldiers numbering in the hundreds of thousands. But for twenty five men, it was more riches than any could well imagine.

"Act quickly, men," Karian instructed them.

Near the palace, aboard a heavy hauler were a few dozen men of Italy, waiting for a special cargo. The ship had no captain in the conventional sense, the man they called "Captain" was their captain on the ground, in the barracks or in the grave if need be. Hector Pazzi, captain-general of the forces of Galata and the Western Roman Empire in Constantinople, looked at the shadows along the harbour walls and waited patiently.

By nature, he wasn't a superstitious man, but the moon was the symbol of Constantinople and the heavenly bodies guided and protected their wards. The bright light of the silvery moon overpowered the tiny red dot of Mars tonight. This city, while weakened, degenerated and despoiled, from years at the hands of corrupt oriental despots and violent heretical sects, was still the city of Constantine, the New Rome.

"Are you alright, Captain?" one of the crew asked. His breath hung in the air, floating crystals catching the frosts of winter.

"No, it's too quiet," he replied at barely above a whisper.

"The sun won't rise for many hours yet, Captain. The city slumbers."

"This city never slumbers," Pazzi chastised the young soldier. "This harbour might be abandoned by tradesmen and cut-throats, but where are the cats? The rats? Those horrible packs of stray dogs? The boats in the harbour don't even have guards posted! It's too quiet. It's unnatural. The Holy Virgin's made them cast their eyes away while our evil is enacted in her holy city."

"Everything sleeps, my captain."

"They're not sleeping. They're hiding."

"Hiding, Sir?"

"They sense us here," Pazzi squinted at the silhouettes of the walls, church spires, palaces and hills of the city. "We're being watched."

The junior soldier looked at the same black masses and saw nothing. He listened for the sounds of gentle waves against the hulls of ships and the dark echo of docks, but heard nothing. The cold winter air absorbed these familiar sounds.

The Genoese captain exhaled loudly and focussed his attention on the crystallizing fog of his breath. This act was to be his final abandonment of his duties as an officer of the city of Genoa, and the Holy Roman Empire to which it was a component. As soon as the men arrived with the treasury, the ship would lay itself in storage on the Pera side of the harbour and get ready to sail away to Avsha, a largely uninhabited island near the Dardanelles. There, they would divide the loot and part ways. Pazzi thought about Cyprus, or possibly Malta as a new home.

Something moved in the shadows. Or did it? If it became known what was transpiring here, there would be a round of executions to make the Massacre of Albi seem gentle.

"You," he indicated a nearby sailor. "I thought I saw someone over there, go investigate."

The sailor did as commanded and searched, but returned empty handed. Pazzi looked out into the night, and his fears and doubts got the best of him.

"We're seen. We have to return to Galata," he said at long last.

"Sir?" the junior asked. "There's no one there."

"Now, everyone! Back home! Quickly and quietly!"

The crew of the transport hauler obeyed without grumbling and the ship slipped quietly back across the harbour to the Genoese side.

The Varangian retinue arrived at the harbour with time enough to hear the paddles of the Genoese boats cut the water, but without enough light of torches to see them go. The soldiers snorted their disapproval, but their officer took it in stride.

Karian greeted the early departure of the Genoese mercenaries with little more than a blink. A fatalist by nature, he always assumed the worst and never proceeded without at least five conditional abstracts.

The Varangians behind him started a murmur. They were carrying heavy chests and sacks filled with the contents of the Palaeologian vault, they were tired and weighed down with gold, and had a traditional way of dealing with traitors.

"Men," Karian started in a loud whisper. "This is a blessing from God, we no longer have to share the treasure with the Italians, we should be grateful."

The Viking's nature was one of barely restrained aggression, and this nature shown through their pale eyes as they stared against the dark at their ring-leader.

"The only setback is that we have to walk a bit uphill. You're all strong and up to the challenge, quickly quickly! The night is ours!"

The human oxen grudgingly lumbered behind the general and they began an ascent up Charisus Hill.

The Petrion District of Constantinople was a cordoned off section in the north-west corner of the city. Bordered by the Land walls to the west, the sea-walls of the Golden Horne to the north, and Charisus Hill to the south, that section of town was cordoned off with a rampart fence, guards and gates. It contained the Blachernae and Porphyrogentius Palaces, the residences of many important officers of state, and even a small private harbour, where Hector Pazzi had been waiting, before being so superstitiously scared off.

When the harbour escape was cut off to Karian, that certainly cut his options considerably, but not enough to abandon all hope. Karian was a fatalistic man, and planned for constant setbacks. He couldn't leave by water, and it would be impossible to leave over land, as all the gates to the Petrion were now closed and guarded by guild militias, outside of his own influence.

Chora, The Forest Monastery, which despite the name was not in fact in a forest, straddled the Petrion compound and the wilderness of the citizenry. It held barracking stables and hostel facilities, and crowned the northern-most hill of the city. Its walls were unmanned, at it was governed by the Armenian exarchate, rather than the Orthodox patriarchate, making it similar to a diplomatically neutral embassy in the capital compound; an embassy with which Adam Karian had very close ties.

That night, while the General Karian was pilfering the treasury, and Captain Pazzi was running from his own shadow, Mario Orsini had made two important trips. The first was to his hospital, where one the surgeons cut his hair and shaved his beard, and the second was to visit Miriam, the local witch.

Mario was by nature a skeptic, and witchery was by law punishable by death. Both these sources of discord were politely silent, however. Everyone went to see the witch sooner or later, it couldn't hurt. Everyone has, since time immemorial, muttered prayers that either went unanswered or were met with an unceremonious "*no*." The witch offered something a tad more pro-active than the salvation offered by the church. Instead of uttering prayers in an archaic Greek that was barely comprehensible, the witch would mysteriously mumble in a tongue that was completely *in*comprehensible. She would burn herbs instead of incense, and instruct the petitioner to imbibe a potion or mumble an incantation; this was in stark contrast to the communion wine and prayers offered by the clergy. As stated earlier, it couldn't hurt, and the visit usually did make people feel better, and when their heart's desire was fulfilled, so was the witches credibility, and if the petitioner's quest proves for naught, it was simply destiny to be thus.

The witch was a friendly enough old woman who lived close to the old Bucholeon Palace. Her house was smaller than Mario's, but unlike Mario, she didn't share a garden with a half-dozen other men; it was just her and her cats, of which there were plenty. She greeted him at the front gate, and brought him through the courtyard into her kitchen. She lived up to the stereotype of a witch in her physical appearance; she was old, her skin was like leather wrapped around a skeleton; her back was bent, and she walked with the aid of a cane that was a ragged and knobby as she. In contrast to this, her face was round and bright. When she smiled, she looked more like a cheerful twelve-year-old than an ageing Methuselah, and she would laugh at her own jokes in a language that Mario didn't quite understand and suspected that she was inventing as she went along. She thought these jokes were quite funny and got a good belly laugh out of at least one of them. Mario smiled and nodded, ever the gentleman.

"I make some tea, and you drink, yes?" she asked through her ancient smile.

"Please, Ma'am," he answered with all his trained politeness.

"Good, good, delicious tea," she sang the words to no particular melody as she put some herbs into a pot. "Ambrose says you are doctor."

Ambrose was one of the men with whom Mario lived, and who'd recommended the witch to him.

"Physic, yes," Mario answered as he looked around. He'd expected to see bats hanging from the ceiling and strange herbal potions, perhaps an altar to Satan. In their stead, he was sitting in what appeared to be a fairly well-stocked kitchen, dominated by a round table in the middle and a large iron-plated hearth where a fire burned brightly. The witch obviously had money. The only prejudice Mario had confirmed in the witches home were the cats, well-known to be familiars of witches; there were eight or so cats of various ancestry. These cats didn't seem like satanic agents ready to do her bidding, they lounged around and looked at the intruder with a contemptuous arrogance, the kind managed by all cats who see yet another uninvited human enter their domain. Mario generally liked animals, but the affection wasn't shared, and these cats were far less hospitable than their mistress.

"Let me see your hand," the old woman reached out and grabbed his left.

"You're a traveller-man," she smiled. "…and you're not finished your travels. You'll see many places in your life, more than old Miriam, I think."

"So far, I have travelled much, but it isn't my past that I'm here to talk about."

"You will have a long future," she began. Mario wondered if she could see anything through her drooping eyelids, but kept silent. "Your heart holds great changes also, the spirit of Hermes floats in your blood. And you are here because you are in love."

"That's true," Mario answered with a boyishly polite smile. While being true, it was also his worst kept secret, as anyone meeting him for the first time would ask if he were a newlywed, or a widower, depending on which way the winds of his heart blew his emotions on that particular day. Alas, keeping the secrets of his heart in his heart, was not one of his great abilities.

"Good luck," she continued absently and poured him a cup of tea, full with ground herbs, whole flowers and bits of spices.

"Thank you," Mario replied, for both the well-wishes and the tea. The tea tasted like dirty grass, but Mario drank it anyway. When he'd finished, the old crone examined the contents of spent reeds, seed shells and spice sparge.

"You will be very happy with your true love, she'll give you children and joy," she said without a smile – her eyes softened as though she has bad news to add on to the banner of good fortune. "But not now. There will be a huge catastrophe, out of which your love will emerge."

"I was expelled from my university and driven from my homeland, Ma'am," Mario quickly deflected her addendum. "I'm pleased that my catastrophe is behind me."

The witch's eyes, which had recently held such playfulness, now held a consoled sorrow. She wanted to comfort him as a grandmother, say that it would be alright, but she could see disaster coming in her milky eyes.

"A war's coming, is that it?" Mario asked. "Everyone knows that."

"That's coming for everyone, Doctor Mario. For you, something different. Something will cheer you and cheapen you. I see a big change in your life."

There was silence for a moment, before Mario broke through with his original purpose.

"I'm going to propose marriage, I came here for a charm," he announced in a rather more business like tone.

"Yes, of course," she said in an equally business-like tone. Gone were the soft grandmother-esque tones of voice, as were both the joy and sorrow of her character. She went to her cabinet and took out a black and white, dried eagle feather.

"Hold this in your pocket and say her name three times, then break it in two while you repeat her name a fourth time. Take your hand out of your pocket, and touch her hand, to shake or to kiss, any deception should do. She'll be unable to resist you. Then, when you get home, grind the feather in a pestle bowl and drink it as a tonic.

"Thank you," Mario reverted to his boyishly friendly tone, but the witch didn't reciprocate. She raised her eyebrows, indicating that a fee was required. Mario put two coins on the table, she gave a non-committal nod, and he began to leave.

"Mercury is in your blood," she said as he made to leave.

"What?" Mario asked, his thoughts quickly turned to his experiments with mercury.

"Mercury, Hermes, the messenger of the Gods," she continued. "He brings knowledge to those who seek it, knowledge and wisdom are things that you'll be doomed to find, Doctor. New experiences will always pull at you."

"Ah," Mario grunted with a smile. "Great knowledge dooms one to unhappiness. I've heard that."

"No, dear boy," she continued in her sad manner. "You'll never be able to stay in one place. You'll either wander the earth, always searching, or you'll stay in one place, unhappy and miserable. Mercury is in the blood that rides your veins."

"You think that I'll be always on the move?"

"Either that or critically unhappy. You'll become morose and cripple the souls of those around you, even of those you love."

"Thank you, Ma'am," Mario said politely.

"Fine, you don't want to hear my warning, that's your decision. But you'll regret it."

"We'll see about that."

And with that he was off.

The following morning, the sun shone warm upon the face of the city. It was spring's first tease to her beloved people, for she was preparing for her long hibernation. A long winter finished his stay as an unwelcome house-guest, and would no more regale the world with his tales of frost and windy survival. Today he would have to deal with his much more popular sister taking her bows. At the back of some peoples' minds was the possibility that this was to be her final arrival.

When Ella Di Castillo stepped out from the shadowy, incense laden mists of Holy Wisdom, she was the picture of elegance. An eternal spring and never ending summer sprung from her face, as though autumn would never crease her eyes or lips and winter was as unreal as fairy stories or Greek legends. She wore a bright yellow veil, open, over the uniformly brown and bland outfit of a Byzantine Lady. Outside the gate of Holy Wisdom, she was met by a rather nervous looking physician in the courtyard. Mario's hands were in his pockets, one hand gripping tightly around an eagle feather which he was rehydrating with his own sweat. He mumbled her name three times quickly.

"God's peace be with you, Doctor Mario," she said from smiling lips.

"And to you."

Mario crushed the feather in his hand and made to kiss her palm. The crushed remains of the feather clung to his sweaty palm and as his hand drew across the space between he and Ella, the feather arched out into the wind between them.

"Uhh," Mario stuttered as a wind exhaled up Acropolis Hill, caught the errant feather, and directed it into the open veil of Mario's targeted love.

The feather swam as smoke through the open gap between where the veil covered her face and where it should have reached down to her blouse. Into her face and into her doe eyes it flew.

"Ah! My eye!" she called out and the throngs of parishioners gawked to see what was happening.

"Ella," he started to approach her, but she withdrew, keeping him at bay with a raised hand.

Mario looked out at the on-looking crowd.

"It's alright," he reassured them in broken Greek, "I'm a physician."

They hardly seemed reassured and continued muttering amongst themselves.

"What is that?" Ella demanded. For the first time since meeting her, he heard some quite unsweet sounds weighed into the metre for her voice.

"I'm sorry, I'm sorry," Mario repeated himself. "I needed to speak with you.”

“Now’s hardly a good time,” came a deep voice from behind him. “We’ve got a busy family evening planned.”

Mario’s vertebrae straightened as he recognized the verbose voice of Ella’s elder brother. The appearance of Vincent DiCastillo made the onlookers quickly find other things with which to occupy their time.

Vincent hopped down the steps four at a time from the cathedral to the courtyard.

“How are you doing, Mario?” Vincent’s face was a curious cross between impish humour and granite resolve. Mario supposed that he’d make a wonderful cathedral gargoyle.

“I’m just fine, sir,” Mario answered, his voice a staccato faster than he had intended.

“That’s good, I always like to see my friends happy,” Vincent put an arm over Mario’s shoulder in a friendly gesture. The difference in size and musculature of the two men intimidated Mario. “It’s a big day at the DiCastillo home.”

“My brother is introducing me to another suitor,” Ella tried her best to appear without opinion.

“You’ll like this one,” Vincent said with a smile. “I like this one.”

“A rich fool no doubt,” Ella replied. “Fleeing prosecution for theft or buggery, I’m sure.”

“Nonsense,” Vincent’s friendly granite smile never wavered, but his eyes met Mario’s for the briefest instant. “No sister of mine will marry a refugee.”

“I’m sure that he’ll be quite suitable,” Mario mumbled.

Ella turned to face him directly, and her eyes bore down.

“I hope so,” she said, peaceably and honestly, not breaking her gaze.

Mario didn’t see the gaze, because he lacked the ability to look up from the ground. Vincent glanced over at his sister and cocked his head towards the doctor, as if to say, ‘*This, dear sister, is beneath you.*’

“I say, Doctor Mario,” Vincent grinned. “You should come over later this week, Daria and Alexandra are now accepting guests. You can inspect Alexandra, tell Daria that everything’s fine, and stay for dinner.”

“I’ll do that,” Mario said quickly before gracelessly excusing himself.

“See you then,” Ella said coldly.

Mario angrily staggered back to his home. While he walked, he punched the air and swore at his own weakness. Passers-by noted the half-mad foreigner and veered away. He stumbled home, seconded himself into his waifish little apartment and did what any sensible soul would do in his hurt condition: he got drunk on the cheapest wine that the market carried.

Over the course of the night, he saw what should have happened. Ella ran into his arms, Vincent shared Giovanni's patronage with him, he became the physician to the emperor! Damn his weak soul! Even in his wildest fantasies, he lived on the avails of the great men of the earth, always under the coat-tails of the powerful! But with each drink, his plans became more grandiose, and more grandiosely squashed. Fate had turned against him! No, it wasn't fate, it was Vincent DiCastillo! And Giovanni Cardillo! It was the fault of Antonio DiPadua! Bishop Isaac DiNapoli! Ezera was probably sharing a chuckle with his friends about Mario's terrible failure. Everyone was to blame but him! Oh, why couldn't he command the respect of these men! Why was he forced to kowtow to them! He was more wise in the ways of logic, philosophy and science; justice was truly blind if she were to allow those men power and keep him a servant! After a few hours of yelling at his invisible accusers, his neighbours finally broke down his door trying to learn what was wrong.

Mario had only vague memories of their visit. The whole evening was a blur that he wished had never happened. He woke up the next morning in crippling pain in his brain and belly.

His head and his stomach rebelled against Mario's custodianship. It was as though they were protesting to the point of leaving their master.

"Wake up, Doctor," came a shrill voice, singing more than speaking. "You have to come with us."

Mario smiled through his hangover and tried to open his eyes.

"We are here for you," the sing-song baritone called again.

Mario finally managed to open his eyes to find that two giants had broken into his home.

"Ahh!" he screamed and launched himself to his feet. "Who are you?"

"My name is Olaf, this is Svend. We are here to bring you to General Karian."

The doctor's eyes focussed randomly from near to far, but managed to identify the two giant northerners as soldiers of the Varangian Guard.

"What have I done?" Mario asked in a brief panic.

The two Norsemen looked at each other.

"Karian wants to show you the hospital grounds. He told us that you were expecting us, so come on then!"

"I can't..." Mario looked as though he were about to lose consciousness.

"You have to," Olaf's musical voice sounded nowhere near as menacing as the glare in his eye as he turned to his friend Svend. "Don't worry, we know how to clear up alcohol in the morning, Doctor."

"We have lots of experience!" The slightly smaller of the two chirped in with a guffaw.

"Oh, thank God," Mario gasped.

Much to Mario's shock, the version of a hangover cure to which the two Vikings subjected the unsuspecting doctor was more terrible than the malady itself. They brought him to the icy fountain in the courtyard, in full view of all his neighbours, and dunked his head. Olaf then grabbed him from behind, around the waist. He pulled his clenched fists tightly into Mario's gut, in a pumping manner (similar to what future generations would refer to as a Heimlich manoeuvre), and used his big, strong arms to lift the smaller man off the ground as he did so. Mario made a terrible racket as he was forced to expel the poisonous alcohol (along with everything else) from his stomach. He was then dunked again into the fountain, forced to drink water, and then forced to vomit again. All of his neighbours watched on at the spectacle. The Greek doctors and physicians gazing on in horror as the foreigners engaged in some kind of semi-consenting assault. No one came down from their balconies, they watched as their quiet, foreign neighbour was assaulted by the Emperor's elite guard and appeared to approve of the process.

During a lull in the 'treatment,' Svend had to call out to the neighbours in the square house apartments.

"There's nothing here for you, unless you want this for you!" His voice was sweet with the lilting notes, but his face and actions did much to dissipate the cuteness of his mispronouncing tongue.

Olaf looked down at the shivering doctor and smiled.

"Do you feel better?"

Shivering wet in the February morning, and still covered with his own vomit, looked up in shock at what the Varangian had just done, and at the foolishness that would present that as a real question.

"No," he answered resolutely.

"Here you go, then," Olaf said, smiling. He handed Mario a red piece of sugar-candy. Sugar's good for your stomach when you've drunk too much. We should go see General Karian now."

Mario looked up at the smiling mountain and nodded.

"Can I change my clothes first?"

"Well, I'm pleased to see you three before noon-time!" Adam Karian greeted the two guards and their ward. "My name is Megadux Adam Karian, Strateogos of the Legions of Rome, and Marshal of Constantinople. You would be Mario Orsini, unless my two men have had some kind of mix-up, which I'll pray is not the case."

"I'm Doctor Mario Orsini," the physician said with a bow. "Doctor at Grace of God Hospital, and of late, Professor of Natural Philosophy at the University of Venice."

'That's a monumental step down, to go from a western university to an eastern hospital,' Karian thought to himself. *'I wonder what he did to deserve such an exile?'*

"The Venetian Ambassador, Giovanni Cardillo, told me that you may have need of my service," prodded the hung-over Italian.

"And I do," Karian said. "You are apparently a doctor of some repute, and you're politically suitable for a task I need done."

"A task, General Karian?"

"We're setting up a field hospital in Chora Church. Do you know it?"

"It's near the palace compound, a few hundred yards back from the walls."

"That's right. We need to set up a hospital there and we've a month to get ready."

"Yes," Mario answered quietly. His head still hurt, though his stomach was surprisingly better.

"Men, leave us!" Karian called to the room, and the twenty-year-old or so blond-haired, blue-eyed behemoths lumbered out of the red stone hall where Karian held court. When the last of them were out, the general walked the doctor over to a bench and sat him down.

"Your eyes are bloodshot and you reek of *retsina*. I don't care whose patronage you enjoy, but I can't tolerate that."

"I'm sorry, general. Last night was a… celebration… of sorts. A much beloved friend is soon to be married," Mario was surprised at how easy it was to lie about his intoxication. This made him a little worried. "It's not a usual event, I promise you."

"If it is, you'll be put in a prison, not a hospital. I'm going to need to tell you things. Some things of high secrecy cannot be revealed to any others, but you'll need to know what's happening. Can I trust you?"

"Of course." Mario insisted.

"I can't tell you anything that I wouldn't want your master, Cardillo to know about, but your tongue is now sworn to silence. On your honour and before God. Do you understand this?"

"Yes, General Karian."

"The Turks, the Muslims, have no friends here, but they do have agents. The Sultan pays well for information, so be aware that there are men, ranked among the poor and from among religious dissident groups, that will try to spy on you, and your affairs. Your new responsibility must be kept a secret for now. For this reason, you'll have to continue working at the hospital. You'll make plans and provide instructions as to how to convert the church into a field hospital. You'll have to go to Chora today to get an understanding of the grounds. By spring, the secrecy of the hospital's location won't matter so much, and we'll move you there permanently, you can leave the hospital then."

"Yes, Sir."

"We expect the Turks to come in March, or possibly early April. By then, the roads will have dried, they can camp *en masse* without serious danger from the elements, and by then they'll have amassed a force large enough to try and force the walls."

"That's why the hospital will be so close to the land walls and the palace?"

"The palace will be properly guarded in the event of a siege, and Chora is near the land walls and the northern part of the harbour walls. It was from the harbour that the Latins breached our walls two and a half centuries ago; we won't be caught without defences there this time."

"Yes," Mario began, but was then caught in a wondering question. "Is it wise to put the hospital in a church? I've heard that the Muslims delight in burning down churches with the clergy and flock in them."

"That's not true," Adam answered quickly. "They'll loot, and they'll kill anyone who tries to stop them, but they won't burn down a church that has gold all over the ceiling. Hopefully, it won't come to that. I have full faith that the walls will hold, they'll try to starve us out, but we'll wait them out. The walls are impregnable, as long as they're adequately defended."

'Everything's impregnable as long as it's adequately defended,' Mario thought to himself, but said nothing. "Is there anything else that I should know?"

"No, but I'll warn you again against the leering eyes of espionage. It's another spear in the side of Christ that here, in the capital of Christendom, there are many who would act as agents of the anti-Christ, but it happens to be so. If you believe that you are being followed, someone asks your neighbours about you, there are strange patients who want to speak to you rather than some other Greek doctor, please be aware of the danger. You'll have to come and tell me about them. Even if it's a mere suspicion, with no evidence. Can you do that?"

"Of course."

"Good. Good luck, Doctor Mario."

"Thank you, General."

Mario left the barracks with a step of greater cheer. He had himself a new patron, and something other than Ella to think about now.

Chapter Twenty-Seven - The First Battles

Erkin was a part of the same class that joined the Orta along with Iskender and Hussein. He was the smallest fighting man in Roman Castle and he was known to be one of the most enthusiastic and tenacious of the younger members. He was charged as an outrider and messenger, and the castle came alive when he charged in with the alarm.

A thin plume of red smoke on the northern horizon had already alerted the castle that trouble was coming.

"Pasha! Pasha!" He cried, tearing into the sunlit courtyard. "My Sheikh!"

"Yes, boy! What is it?"

"There are three ships coming from Terabia!" Erkin said as he rose to his feet. "Three galleys, weighing low with cargo. They arrived about an hour ago."

Mesut listened to the boy and smiled in controlled cheer. Terabia was a Greek village along the northern Bosporus. Any goods from any of the countries on the Black Sea would pass by there on their way to Constantinople. Goods wouldn't be unloaded there and shipped overland, Terabia's tiny docks couldn't handle it and most mule trains couldn't handle the hilly terrain between there and the capital. Ships stopped there to inquire about the state of the capital and the narrow waterway that led up to it.

'*They must be checking to see the status of the castles here. Everyone knows they're here, they must want to see if we have any ships to support,*' Mesut looked at the young man. "What colours were they wearing?"

"The two headed eagle, Sir."

The two headed eagle was used as a standard by Rus, Alans, and what was left of the old Seljuks, but it is most likely that the ships are sailing under the flag of the second Rome, which also flew the two-headed eagle. Any of those banners of course, would make fine targets. Mesut just had to make sure that they weren't the property of any of the Italian cities. He had a sultanic warning that bringing them into this campaign was to be avoided at all costs. "You're sure that they've got the eagle?"

"Yes, Sir!" Erkin answered smiling. "Purple and Gold."

Mesut smiled back. "You've done a good job. Now ferry across to Anatolian Castle and tell them what you've told me. Tell the sub-commander, Abdullah, that we are expecting our first test today."

"Yes, Sir!" Erkin said and he started towards the little ferry boat.

"Alright, Everyone!" Mesut called out, so that everyone in the fort could hear him. "We've got our first opportunity coming down the water shortly. The gunners will be ready in the towers! The archers have to be ready on the walls. The rest of you have to get your bows and javelins and get down to the shore line! Everyone here can fire a bow, a spear or a javelin across the water to the other side! You've got to be ready to hit a boat in the middle now! They are galleys, rowing at top speed maybe as fast as ten noughts, they can't turn around, they can only escape straight through us, or sink! Hit them with everything! Hit them with river stones if you have to! Get the row-boats and ferries ready to pick up any survivors as prisoners, we'll ransom them for a pretty price! Get yourselves ready! You will tell your grandchildren about this! You are to fight in the first battle of a great war that will be remembered by all the faithful from today until the Day of Judgement! God is great! Get ready! God is great!"

Three single-masted galleys began their journey down the winding way of the Bosporus Strait. The water was deep enough to be safe, and the tide-less current helped them along their journey.

By a unique feature of the waterway, there were actually two currents at play. Along the surface, freshwater ran southward from the top of the Black Sea, the effluence of the Don, Volga and Danube rivers, along with a hundred other smaller cousins. A few metres below this aquatic wind, raced the northbound saltwater from the Aegean and Mediterranean Seas. Skimming atop the lighter, freshwater were the three galleys that were to be the first initiates into the newly severed strait.

While the currents were friendly to them, the hills and mountains most certainly were not. They bent and bowed at seemingly random intervals, approaching and retreating from each other, leaving the Bosporus to snake through whatever space the erratic coast allowed it. This made it so that the ships were denied maximum speed. If they rowed themselves too fast, they would be unable to turn in time for the random coasts of the waterway and run themselves aground. The galleys rowed slowly and carefully upon the water. Their sails were tucked carefully down mast to avoid a random gust of wind sneaking over the hills and taking them to the shore.

Mesut observed the four cannons of Roman Castle. They had been stationed in twos, two facing northward and two on the southward wall. The three cannons in Anatolian Castle had been likewise stationed along the castle's sea-wall, with all three pointed across the strait itself. They would be able to fire at ships coming, passing and leaving. All of the Black Sea merchants of Constantinople knew of the old Anatolian Castle and most knew about the construction of its young sister across the water, so the Greek captains would be wary but, if God willed it, they would be completely unprepared for the newly armed strength that the two castles were prepared to wield.

Over the winter, the cannon-men of the two castles spent several hours determining the range on the three installments. How far a target could be, and how near, were both determined. This meticulous testing undoubtedly warned the denizens of the capital, but that was calculated into the Ottoman plan. Six months ago, the Roman forces had been too weak to stop the construction of a fortress less than a day's march from the capital. On that morning they heard the cannons of the completed project, announcing its presence to the world. Both the construction and completion of the project showed the Roman's unwillingness to act. To the mercenary army that found itself responsible for the Empire's defence, the echoing thunder of the upriver cannons was a reminder that they may have accepted employment on the wrong side.

The men on the ground around the two castles learned the range of the cannons, and they marked the range of their bows and javelins. Fourteen middle sized row-boats, big enough to carry a dozen men, were readied for boarding actions or the rescue of prisoners from the freezing autumn waters, depending how the situation presented itself. All of their preparations had, however, been laid in anticipation of but a single vessel.

"Wait until the second ship is in range." Mesut counseled the cannon chief. "Then hit the first one. If we hit them too soon, then the other two will turn around and abandon the project."

"If we hit them too late, they can still speed through." The gunner delicately countered.

"That's the balance, sergeant. This tower position is geared to weaken them. The middle is where we try to capture them, and the far wall will sink any who escape. May God steer your fire."

The ships came trundling over the chilly currents.

"The first ship has passed the boulder, Pasha," the gunner warned as the ships drew nearer. Along the eastern shore of the strait was a boulder of grey sandstone that had been determined to be the furthest reach of their cannons. They were using it as a signpost. The first galley creaked past the innocuous marker.

"Steady, my children…" Mesut watched as the second galley reached the marker. "God is Great! Fire! Fire, my gazis! Fire true! Strike true! Bury them against the anvil of the water and scour their ignominious names from the memory of God! Fire!"

There was a thunderous blast from the castle walls. The echo of the blast rebounded from hill to hill. A cloud of smoke rose from the busied walls and two watery explosions erupted to the port side of the lead galley. The third cannon shot landed squarely into the fore castle of the ship, sending its rear woodworks flying into the split currents.

"Again! Again! Health to your hands and fire again!" the soup-maker-commander shouted. He knew that one for three was shockingly good considering the range, but he had hoped in his heart for a more decisive opening volley. "Make those cannons as waterfalls of iron and crush them! Load faster!"

The drummers on the three galleys had tripled their cadence. Mesut gave thanks to God for the original success, knowing that the fore-castle attack may well have damaged the hydro-dynamism of the lead ship, pushing them towards the hilly banks of the strait. Unfortunately for him, that prayer met with no response and the lead ship began to careen around the bend in the strait and begin to speed towards the capital.

The front battery managed another three volleys at the lead ship before it came too close and they were forced to change their focus of fire to the second. They only managed to send one volley at each of the second and third ships before they escaped the cannons of the first tower and slipped into the range of Anatolian Castle's cannons.

Seeing the short comings of the northern battery, the wall battery of Anatolian Castle raged against probability and tried to rain as much fire as possible.

"Focus on the lead one!" Mesut screamed vainly at the cannon crews. "We need to take at least one as a prize!"

The lead was pounded at flank four times at close range before she managed to limp past the second battery. The second and third ship took inconsequential damage from the arrows, javelins and hand cannons from the men ashore and were catching up to the lead. The row-boats remained in dock for the time being. As the forward galley rowed its way past Anatolia Castle, Mesut cursed their crews and captains and spoke several colourful invectives regarding their dubious parentage.

By the time that the commander had levied himself upon the southward wall, the cannons were already firing. "Hit the damaged one!" He cried. "Sink it! Incapacitate it! Cripple it! Just don't let it escape!"

Hope was beginning to abandon the old warlord. He watched the second and third ships paddle out of range, and the first lead ship, although damaged, was still seaworthy enough to lurch forward. Then, from almost nowhere, fortune blessed their endeavour.

A cannonball struck the port side of the damaged galley and took half the bulwark with it. The commander's face lit up with joy when he saw the port side oars fall into the dark water.

"Send out the archers! Run down the coast and keep at them! Cannons, keep going!" he yelled down at the small flotilla of boats in harbour and gestured frantically to the crippled galley. "Go, men! Go!"

The lead galley had been paralysed. Half of her oars, as well as many of her oarsmen had seen their last day. They were still under fire and had no way of withdrawing. The Turkish land archers were approaching on both sides of the strait, as were a dozen small boats to take them.

Mesut's brief exuberance returned to rage as he saw the other two ships pull into a treacherous reverse. They approached the besieged hulk and cast lines to her. "No!" He yelled, watching his prize get stolen. "Sink her! Fire faster! Faster!" The last shot fired at an arching elevation came just shy of the target as the two healthy ships dragged their battered sister safely out of range.

"God curse them and their inbred families!" Mesut swore, a rarity for him, before he regained his composure.

The first engagement of the battle of Constantinople was doomed to be unsuccessful.

Two days after their original disgrace, the orta was given another chance to prove their worth. First they saw a plume of red smoke rising from their station at the Black Sea egress, and then word came to them by scout that a single ship was approaching the two castles from the North. This time, she was a three master. A much more laudable prize than any of the single masters that had slipped past them earlier. Also, as a single ship, and apparently much larger (ergo, easier to hit). Regrettably, she wasn't an imperial galley, but on the bright side, she wasn't Genoese, either. She was a free trader, sailing a run from the Crimean Peninsula by way of Trebizond, and was by their report, weighted down with cargo.

The men in the two castles waited as the Nineveh began to make its way down the strait.

Earlier that day, when the Nineveh had first arrived to the Bosporus, the first thing that was done was to weigh anchor outside of Terabia, and send her boat ashore. Ezera and a half-dozen crewmen landed the craft in the chilly waters next to the dock, and Ezera ran up to the wooden public house next to the jetties.

The village itself was darkening from the afternoon sun, as spring and the western hills brought dusk unnaturally early to Terabia. There were only a few dozen wooden structures, and none of stone. While never boisterous, the village seemed strangely more abandoned than usual, there were no merchants or open public houses. As the delegation from the Nineveh approached the harbour master lodge, they saw a telling sign next to the village square. Five spears, horsetails hanging, were planted in the ground outside the lodge.

"Captain?" Lorenzo asked.

"I see them," Ezera said in Catalan, lest anyone overhear their plotting. "Let's see how bad this has to be. We might have to fight our way out of town, so keep your hands near your arms, lads."

The other pirates (*read* merchant sailors) looked about each other as their captain bounded onto the veranda of the wooden harbour-castle and to meet a waiting reception.

Outside the lodge were three men, two sitting on a long bench and one standing, waiting to receive the captain. The man standing was dressed in a long black coat with a white frock, dressed in the manner of the Roman administration. He was fair-skinned and fine-featured, and had the look of a beaten dog to him. The other two sitting men were leather-skinned and dark haired. They were dressed in brown woollen coats, with brimless woollen hats to keep the cold at bay. One had short hair, invisible under a felt hat, and a cropped beard and moustache, the other long hair and a clean-shaven face. They shared a look of apathetic violence.

"Good afternoon, Gentlemen," Ezera greeted them in Greek as he came into the office.

The two leather-skinned inhabitants took to their feet immediately started barking orders in their language, for which the man in the black coat tried quickly to translate.

"What Ulash-bey is trying to say is that your guards must wait by the docks. Please, Captain," he said in a pleading and conciliatory tone. "This won't take more than a few moments. Please."

"No problem, of course," Ezera said with a smile on face and he told his crew to wait.

The short haired Turk pursed his lips and snarled a tisking sound at the captain. The Roman official saw this as his cue to enter into the conversation.

"These agents of the Turkish Sultan have come to secure the safe passage of ships through the straits and protect commerce," he began. "What is your cargo?"

"Lumber from Kaffa and furs from Trebizond."

The man in the long coat translated to the man with the short hair who sat back and spat words that sounded both aggressive and apathetic at the same time.

"Ulash has asked that ten percent of your cargo be put into warehousing here."

"Asked?" Ezera was hardly a patriot of the eastern empire, or a champion of Christian solidarity, but he still considered the Turks to be a fairly universal enemy.

The official shrugged.

"Let me ask you something," Ezera asked without ever breaking his polite demeanour and friendly smile. "How long has the empire been doing this sort of work for the Sultan?"

"It is a temporary arrangement, I assure you." He answered dismissively.

"I believe that," Ezera agreed "though I'm not certain that you realize just how temporary it will be."

"Captain," the Roman bureaucrat said tepidly, "we both find ourselves slaves to reality here. We must obey this current Herod, with the knowledge that they will pass like a storm, vicious and horrible, but the will pass. Christ's Kingdom is eternal. This Tartar clay shall crumble to dust in time."

"Good Sir, I believe that I'm a little more experienced in weathering storms than you, and this storm is one best avoided."

"Captain?"

Ezera turned his back to the three of them, and began to walk down off the veranda. As he did so, the long-haired man stood up from the bench to protest and Ezera spun around quickly, his smile nowhere to be seen. At that swift motion, the crewmen from the Nineveh hurried up from the docks.

"You tell that man to sit down or there will be blood on the floor before I raise my voice a second time!"

The official began speaking in Turkish to the long haired man, who would hear none of it. He reached again for Ezera's shoulder, and Ezera in turn raised his right hand to block the grab at the wrist and crossed his left over, thumb extended at his attacker's eye. The thumb hit true and the long-haired man's head bent back to absorb the impact of the thrust, which raised his chin and exposed his throat. Ezera stepped forward and with his right hand that was at the other man's wrist, he thrust with all his might to collide his fist with the extended jaw.

The peak of the jawbone took the full brunt of the punch, which then distributed the shock to the mandible joints, where the jaw connects to the skull below and in front of the ears. The impact was enough to slide the jaw bone against the skull, tearing the cartilage that kept the bone in place. He fell backwards and briefly tried to stand again, before collapsing unconscious with his lifeless jaw hanging off his skull like an unwound yo-yo.

The entire violent episode lasted only seconds, by which time the crew was rushing to the lodge, the other agent was on his feet and the man in the long coat looked like the sky was about to collapse.

The crew came in with swords drawn and incapacitated the bureaucrat and the short-haired man, who was fuming angry.

"Hold! Hold!" Ezera called out to steady everyone. "Pere! Check the man on the floor. Is he alive or dead?"

The old man rushed to the incapacitated body on the floor and checked his eyes and his breathing.

"He'll live, but I don't think he'll be eating any apples for a while," he joked

"Good," Ezera replied, looking at the short-haired man. "If he died, then we'd have to kill everyone here."

The other man's face was contorted in rage, but he didn't act out.

"Now, gentlemen, we're going to keep on our way, wish the nice people here a pleasant day, and we'll hit Constantinople before nightfall."

Swords still in hand, the seven sailors backed away from the harbourmaster's ledge and retreated to their ship.

As soon as the men clamoured back aboard their ship, Ulash rushed inside, to the stove and grabbed a red clay jar. In the jar was a powder with a base of nitroaniline, a dye used for colouring wool. The chemical is incredibly toxic and by handling in such a cavalier manner, Ulash was courting a slow, painful and cancerous death. He scooped the powder with a wooden spoon and shovelled it into the stove. From the chimney of the harbourmaster's lodge belched red smoke. This smoke was seen from the Bosporus castles and the alarm was sounded.

The Nineveh slowly crept along the Bosporus in the afternoon sun, staying off-centre of the waterway, and gently rounding the waxings and wanings of the nature-carved pathway. There was no point in pushing the oarsmen as hard as they could until they came within range of the castles. A slow, leisurely pace would get them to the bottleneck with full strength left in the oarsmen's arms. And they would need their full strength to glide through the gauntlet. The Turks would probably float some boats to try to slow down this veteran of the sea-routes, but a ship this size would simply cast the little river runners aside in her bow wake.

The slow pace also allowed for the lengthening shadows to creep out from the western hills and onto the waterway itself. While this would normally make for dangerous sailing, Ezera had navigated the strait enough times that it would be less dangerous than trying to run past the castles in full light of day. The dark wood of the ship against the dark waters of the Bosporus would make for a more difficult target. This timing was also beneficial in that the archers on the ground on the Asian shore would have the setting sun blaring into their eyes as they tried to shoot at the dark mass. None of these factors alone would ensure that they'd survive the day, but combined, they made for elevated probabilities.

Eventually, the Nineveh rounded the last bend before the castles came into view; First the new Roman Castle, and then its Anatolian counterpart.

"Gentlemen," he called out calmly. "Keep your pacing. When I yell for speed, you give it to me with all your might. Mind the shields on either side of the ship, you won't get hurt, but listen to me and listen to Gaspar. We're the ones who'll tell you to turn, to speed up, to reverse. I'm at up top, he's down in the belly with you! We'll see you through this run, and we'll be drunk in the wine houses of the capital tonight. Don't panic, just keep pace and do what's commanded of you."

The crew hardly needed any address to motivate them. None were new to this sort of thing, and most were veterans from the Comnenei uprising, in which they all saw more dangerous situations than a few passing ballistae. Cannons were inaccurate, slow to reload and completely impractical against a moving target. The crew had no serious reason to fear, but even without serious reasoning, fear had a nasty way of creeping in uninvited.

The signal to triple their rowing speed from sailing to ramming speed came alongside the sound of cannon fire. The two cannons atop the northern turret of Roman Castle blasted their cannon balls simultaneously into the air in the direction of the Nineveh. Kitted as a merchantman, she still kept the memory in her grain that she was once a warship, regardless of her cargo hulls now being filled with heavy lumber from the forests that circled Pontus. The sound of cannons seemed to reawaken something inside her and lunged forward as if of her own volition. Her hull seemed greased for the chase and half of her cargo weight seemed to dissipate into thin air. Ezera smiled as the old girl regained her form.

Two splashes erupted from the water, dangerously close to the ship's prow, then a third, further away.

"Steady!" Ezera called as he inspected the castles.

He could make out the tower cannons pointed north and south on Roman Castle and the forward battery along Anatolian. There were hundreds of men in red tunics with huge white cones of hats manning the shoreline.

"Luis!" he called out to his wheelsman, who was steering the rudder from the aft. "Have us skim the starboard-side shore! The men on the ground won't be able to see our shadow in detail against the sunny side, and the Asian side won't fire against us because they'd hit their own castle! Do you understand?"

"Yes, Sir!" Luis called back and relayed the directions to Gaspar, governing the under-deck bowels of the ship.

"They're coming at us…" the chief gunner said in a confused tone. "Sir? Are they going to try and ram the castle?"

Mesut shared his bombardier's disbelief for an instant.

"Damn," he whispered as understanding crept in.

They would only be able to fire a few more barrages from the cannons before the target ship was too close; you can't very well fire a pack cannon downwards. Once they were close enough to the Roman Castle, they'd be immune to the Asian battery as well, and they'd retreat along the shore until they came back within range of the southerly cannons, and then only for a few instances before this fat laid-down merchantman retreated safely to Constantinople. A second failure against what should have been such an easy prey was not an option.

"Everyone with bow and musket to the shore line!" He called down from the north tower. I want no supplies left! Hit them with everything! Man the boats! Ten silver akches for the first man aboard that ship!"

"Luis! Under the deck!" Ezera instructed his wheelsman as he took the wheel himself. Arrows were raining down among them and the senior crewman needed no double incentive to retreat down among the oarsmen. Ezera sheltered himself with a long shield large enough to cover him from the broadside direction of the arrows. He stabilized the captain's-wheel with a peg and said a silent prayer to God, or Neptune or whoever was listening to guide them through this gauntlet. He looked towards the sun-marked eastern shore and smiled as he mentally noted that they had crossed the halfway point of their run.

Smaller boats slid into the icy water and unsailorly men rowed towards the coming behemoth. Many of them tripped over the wake of the larger ship, as Ezera had predicted they would, but something happened that he'd not predicted. Many of them were armed, not with boarding equipment and fighting utensils, but with nets and chains; Nets and chains that were aimed not at the ship's deck, in order to board her, but at the oars. They couldn't cut through the thick oars with axe and sword, but the weight of chain and strength of net was enough to slow down the oars on one the starboard side, which would run the Nineveh aground unless he ordered the port-side rowers to slow down as well.

"I need ten men from the port-side up here now!" he called down to the rowing galley. "Come armed to repel attackers! Gaspar, make certain that they keep time with each other, otherwise we're going to maroon against a very inhospitable shore.

The coxswain obeyed and sent the men up, while he tried to keep order among a tumultuous crew, made nervous by the turn of events.

The small Turkish ships rowed strait at the stumbling galley. Ropes and grappling devices flew up towards the deck and were cut down the superiorly trained crew of the Nineveh. Screaming curses into the air, the attacks fell into the cold water as they tried to take the prize for being the first to board the enemy vessel. One ship, sailed past the aft-castle where most of the excitement was happening and rowed at great speed ahead of the limping boat.

"Closer, come on," Hussein instructed his rowers towards a tangle of net and chain that clustered four oars together. "Almost there…"

"Are you sure about this?" one of the rowers asked just in time for Hussein to leap from his small boat onto the netted clot of oars just above the water's surface.

His enormous weight pushed the nest of rope and chain down into the water, but not to a dangerous degree. His legs soaked up to the knee, the rest of him was still safe, but he needed out of the water. He lunged his torso atop the planes given to him by the oars that cut a slope towards the ship, and with all his might he gripped one of the oars and pulled himself up completely out of the water. Another arm he threw over another oar, and he began to pull himself up towards the ship deck.

It was at this point that Hussein realized that his plan had a major flaw in it, that flaw being that the oars didn't actually lead up to the top. They led to a deck just below the top deck, and about two meters shy of the battlefield of on deck. He cursed himself and his bad judgement for not realizing this beforehand, but the commitment was made and had to be followed through.

Hussein forced the shrieking sounds of his comrades out of his head. At the main battleground of the aft-castle, lines were being cut, climbing attackers were being cut down before they could gain a foothold on the ship. Friends were falling into the water and their own probable death and the ship was still only mildly inconvenienced by the presence of the attackers.

The heavy giant continued up the oars despite all this around him. His presence, while unnoticed by the aft-castle fighters, was certainly noticed by the men on the rowing deck. His weight lifted the top sections of the oars up to the ceiling of the galley and immobilize them there. It would take two or three men's weight to bring it to an even keel, so that they could try push the oars out of the ship. The men who manned the adjoining oars tried to club him with their oars as he climbed closer and closer.

None of this was very successful, and the wet oars bent too much to lever him away. The clubbing was ineffective, and he shifted oars twice when they were pushed out of their sockets by the crew.

"Let him climb, let him climb!" Gaspar called out and drew his sword and approached the portal in the bulkhead where the oars exited. "When he gets here, I'll cut his face off!"

Get there he did, but not yet close enough for Gaspar to reach him with his sword. There was a half meter of bulkhead between the deck and the outside, and Hussein had no intention of getting that close. When he was close enough to stretch his long arm up to grab one of the ropes attached to the main deck guard rail, he gripped it hard.

Gaspar immediately realized what was happening and ordered the oar opposite of the attacker to be raised and slid sideways across the deck. It jutted out the same portal as Hussein's base oar and rammed him in the hip as he tried to hoist himself up on the rope, which all of a sudden seemed much less stable than he had hoped. The giant had hoisted himself above the portal, hooked his foot over the guardrail and finally managed to pull weight onto the main deck.

Hussein rolled onto the deck of the ship and into a pile by the railing to catch his breath. As he panted, trying vainly to restore oxygen to his strained limbs he heard an alarm cry out in Catalan.

It was a cry to arms by Ezera, gripping the rudder-wheel with all his might to prevent the ship from veering aground. His words needed little translation to the doubled over Janissary interloper who saw Lorenzo, the largest crewman aboard, leap down from the aft castle and charge directly at him.

Hussein quickly grabbed his *yata-an* from the scabbard over his shoulder. A yata-an is a sword that was cruelly curved inward in the manner opposite a scimitar. He swung wildly at the oarsmen. The sheer force behind his swing wielded the sword less with the finesse of a fine blade, and more with the brute force of a lumberjack swinging an axe. It was enough to clobber Lorenzo's blocking sword arm and to throw the attacker's broadsword. This surprised the attacker, who then smashed into the shoulder of his target.

Lorenzo was shocked to realize the size of the man he'd just attacked, but wasn't to be deterred. Having smashed into close range and found himself disarmed, he threw one arm to trap Hussein's sword arm and threw all his weight against him in order to push him backwards onto the guardrail. Hussein rolled with smaller man's weight as he threw all of it against him. The giant's strength, when combined with Lorenzo's momentum, was enough to hurl the sailor half over the rail.

Lorenzo's legs wrapped a scissor form around the rail to save him from falling overboard, but his weight had shifted enough for Hussein's sword arm to regain its mobility. With his newly won freedom of movement, the Janissary clutched his concave sword with one hand and stabilizing his target with the other. He chopped down onto the other man's midsection, prone on the twenty-centimetre-wide rail. The force was enough to upset the bindings of rail underneath him, not to mention the horrific damage done to the victim's ribcage. His feet fell loose around their perch and a second subsequent chop, this time to the upper body, finished any possible resistance. Hussein kicked the body off the ridge, where it bounced off the oars on its way to a watery grave.

Adrenaline rage raced through the young man's veins and he charged the aft castle at the rear of the ship. The captain at the wheel was screaming for reinforcements from bellow and ordering men above to do something to stop the charging juggernaut.

From atop the aft castle's scaling ladder to the main deck, where Hussein stood, another boatswain stabbed down at him with a glaive, a pole-arm with a long, curving blade. Hussein stepped back from the sailor's thrust and reached overtop the lunge to grip the pole with his maw of a fist. In a single motion, he pulled himself halfway up the steps and let his sword swing a full semicircle overhead to crash down on the boatswain's skull, ostensibly halving it like a melon.

This brought the giant as high as we would get on the floating mountain of the aft castle. He stood on the deck for but an instant, when another boatswain, Luis, hit him sidelong at a full short dash. That sent the two of them falling backwards, down two metres onto the wooden planks of the main deck. Luis was barely hurt by the fall, as he landed his full weight onto Hussein, who was now using all his furious energy to try and rip oxygen from the air to feed his aching body. He could barely recognise the glint of a steel dagger in the hand of the man straddling his chest until the dagger came crashing down onto his chest.

The pain was excruciating as the dagger rebounded off his sternum and left its chipped point behind. It hurt almost as much as when the now jagged and broken blade that came down a second time onto his chest, losing its thrust in the muscle tissue of his *pectoralis major* muscle group near his left shoulder. With the man kneeling over his chest, there was little that Hussein could do except kick as hard as he possible could, and hope that his long legs could reach the back of the other man's head.

As fate would have it, his foot couldn't reach that far and the boatswain stabbed him again, this time piercing the pectoral muscle wall and barely missing the big man's heart and lungs.

What seemed like a defence was more of lucky spasm for the downed Janissary. His descending leg from the unsuccessful kick collided at forty-five degrees with the step ladder ascending the aft castle. The dagger thrust into his chest caused his entire musculature to tense in hope of turtling his heart. That spasm was enough to throw the mounted attacker off, and consume Hussein in more spasms. Believing the giant to be either dead, or well enough on his way, the boatswain rushed back up the ladder to find that the aft castle had turned into a melee ground with Turkish soldiers climbing aboard, and Captain Ezera having abandoned the wheel to fight hand to hand against the boarders.

Mesut watched with glee as the boarding took place. From up atop the south tower of Roman Castle, he watched the ship lose its direction and veer perpendicular to the flow of the strait. She had lost any hope of continuing on, and her crew were pushing themselves through the portholes for the oars. They were risking a frozen death in the cold water rather than face the rumoured cruelty of the Turks. He smiled from cheek to cheek as he saw his first victory of the new campaign unfold.

'The first victory of many to come,' he thought. 'Shame about the giant boy. He earned his spot in paradise on this day, he did. The prophet himself will be toasting his gallantry – and so will I!'

Chapter Twenty-Eight - Always on the Run

The cold flow of the Bosporus tightened around Gaspar as he crashed head-first through hard surface. It felt as though some invisible hand inside his belly clenched a fist and pulled all of his hair follicles into the case of flesh in which he dwelt. He resisted the instinct to cry out in freezing anger when he dove through the conflicting currents and resurfaced a few metres southward. His blurry eyes scraped against the shadows and wrath poured out of his nostrils, and he regained his bearings in the water. Without thinking, he took a deep breath and forced himself back underwater, in the direction of the nearby shoreline.

He kicked his legs and pushed his body until his lungs burned like capsicum and he was forced up to take another controlled breath out of the dusk air and then dive back down to continue on to the shore. On his third dive, his hands found stones and mud to block his progress, signaling that he'd met the shore. He raised his head enough out of the water to breathe, and pulled himself the last metre with his hands. Without looking back, he hurled himself out of the water and ran into the forested hills that held the mighty strait and kept running.

His soaking wet clothes slowed him down, in addition to making a horrible slopping noise with every stride of his pace and left an obvious trail that would make tracking him easy for anyone who took up the task, but that was a minor consideration now. Gaspar pushed himself to the point of exhaustion, at which point he finally took refuge under a tree, and began tearing his wet clothes off. He hardly relished the idea of being naked in the cold forest, but the wet clothes would only make things worse. There was no frost left on the forest ground. It had been replaced by a cold, damp mud everywhere, and grey-green foliage that was hardly enough for him to really hide behind. Gaspar bent over to catch his breath, and then heard a rustling behind him. Someone was tracking his rather obvious trail.

Abdul the kopekchi had seen the Roman sailor leap from the boat and swim ashore. The sight he'd seen pleased him, as he knew that it would be a contribution to his own glory to hunt down a survivor and bring him in personally. This would bring him the recognition he needed in order to be considered a full member of the orta. Following the trail left by the Roman (all Christians were Romans in the eyes of the Janissaries) was a simple matter, even in the descending night. Broken branches and sticks cut a swath through the country side and left a watery trail among the trees. This was more of a child's game of hide-and-seek than a morbid hunt to enslave the refugee.

Gaspar controlled his breathing to the best of his abilities and hid behind a birch-wood. Naked and in the dark, he could hear the charging of his novice pursuer coming closer and closer. The ship-less sailor gripped a hold of a wooden log he had picked from the ground and tried to stop his body shivering and his teeth from chattering. Damn the sounds! He couldn't stay still in the cold air, his breath was visible, he'd be seen for sure! All he could do was close his eyes and listen as the man behind him came closer and closer, thundering through the darkness of the forest.

Abdul could sense blood in the water as he leapt through the forest around the unlit trees. Soon, oh soon he would be upon the coward who ran, and then he would have a slave of his very own. He'd drag him back to Roman Castle by his hair, kicking and screaming. He couldn't help but smile, imagining the honours that would be lavished upon him once he stood before Mesut with the last survivor of such a glorious victory. He would be decorated, his name would be among those called with glory. These thoughts added a spring to his step that helped propel him faster through the night.

So fast, as it turned out, that he didn't even see the naked man with wooden log-club.

Gaspar swung the club round-house from behind the tree to cut off his pursuer's stride in mid-bound, smashing his shoulder and knocking him to the ground. Gaspar cursed that he hadn't hit a more vital area, or at least done some damage to the shoulder, but accuracy suffers in adverse conditions, and the shivering naked man in the dark was operating at diminished capacity for a wide variety of reasons.

Abdul was thrown into a thorn bush, and he thanked his stars for the coarse clothing he was wearing. His eyes widened as the other man bounded towards him to strike him again while prone, but Abdul was given a second reason to be thankful. The man's bare feet crumpled against the harsh dry pin-pricks of the surviving thorns and he fell atop his intended prey, dropping his club.

The Janissary found joy again, now that his attacker had sacrificed both surprise and weapon, and for some reason not immediately apparent had also surrendered his clothing. Abdul wrapped his arms around

Gaspar's torso, pinning the Catalan's arms to his sides, and pushed up with his own leg, rolling atop. This pushed Gaspar, naked back, against the pins and needles of the thorn-bush, with his adversary atop him.

Gaspar returned the hold by wrapping his legs around his attacker's waist in a guard lock and tried to scissor his legs to collapse Abdul's chest. The muscles in the youth's chest were too strong for Gaspar's weakened legs, but the diverted energy allowed for Gaspar to free one of his arms. He could hardly punch at the man's face or jaw from his current position, but Gaspar began punching a clenched fist first against Abdul's ear. Abdul tried blocking but by that effort only allowed Gaspar to free his other arm.

With both arms free, and his enemy trapped between his legs, Gaspar lurched forward and slithered one arm under Abdul's jaw. He then grabbed his own wrist with his free hand and managed to leverage Abdul's head against his armpit and pull back with both hands, counter-pushing with his legs. With convulsive strength, Gaspar whipped his full weight back, pulling and twisting on the other man's neck. There was a sound like that of a wet log snapping that came from the Janissary's upper spine, and Gaspar finally had a moment to catch his breath. He was no longer being followed, and now he had a warm red tunic to get him through the night.

Shivering, Gaspar limped across the rocky pathways of the forest. His feet screamed pain as every step re-invigorated the memory of the thistle bush which he'd stomped through barefoot during his melee with the Janissary. The stolen boots and looted tunic were far too small to provide respite from the elements, but they were better than bare-footed nudity.

He thanked God for the small mercy of the rising sun that eventually crept over the horizon. With it, crept the promise of warmth and heat that might dry the mud-caked uniform that patched the elements away from his skin. Unfortunately, while the sun was starting to light the day, it did so through the heavy clouds that globed overhead and hid the blue sky. It was as if he had stumbled into a blind-spot of creation and his maker couldn't quite make out where he was.

Shortly after the sorry excuse of sunrise, the coxswain came upon a pathway. It was neither cobbled nor properly cleared enough to be called a road, but it was there to remind him of his proximity to human civilization. In his newfound religiosity, he gave thanks again and started limping southwards on the path. The excruciating pain on the soles of his feet allowed him to apply pressure only to the sides of his feet, so he walked bow-legged, on the blades of his feet with their bloody soles turned inward. He picked up a felled birch log to act as an awkward walking stick to help him along.

He stumbled along thusly until he could hear voices. Because of his rough state he had actually heard the voices prior to registering them as communication. He only really became aware of them once they abruptly stopped, having become aware of his own presence. The cold, to say nothing of the emotional shock of loosing the Nineveh, and dulled his senses and reflexes to the point that he was barely aware of his surroundings.

The voices that had gone silent called out through the forest in Greek.

"Who is there?" A gravelly voice came from out of the misty morning.

"Help me," Gaspar called back. "I'm the only survivor of the Nineveh, a ship molested and captured by the Turks!"

There was some swift discussion among the other voices.

"If you continue south, you will find Constantinople by midday!" the voice called back at him. "You can go there, Christian!"

"I can't walk! My feet bleed through my boots! The cold air chills my bones and I need water! Please, Christians! God will remember you actions today and return your kindness or your wrath tenfold in the Kingdom!"

The voices started mingling again and three figures emerged on the pathway. Their heads were covered by cloaks and their bodies by furs, they seemed half-animal enough to dwell naturally in the forest.

"We all have our problems, Traveller," the lead one said as the three of them closed in on Gaspar. "Now lie down and take off your boots."

"Thank you, thank you," Gaspar mumbled in relief. "God will return this mercy…"

He was cut off by the lead of the three removing his hood and throwing his cloak as a blanket onto the Janissary-clad sailor. The man's nose was red and bulbous to the point that its swelling had closed the left nostril completely. His right eye was the yellow of a lilting daffodil and his lips had retreated so far from his mouth that the black crapulence of his rotting teeth was exposed to the elements when not hidden behind a scarf.

"I'm sorry, Traveller, but thus far I've found God's mercy to be a tad lacking."

Gaspar looked on in shock as the other two men appeared to be equally deformed. Their gangly frames and deformed visages were terrible and frightening to behold.

"He's afraid of us," the second one, a dark-skinned Semite, said.

"He should be," the yellow-eyed first speaker said.

The club footed third woodsman gesticulated at the other two of them, as he apparently lacked the ability to speak.

"You're right, of course," the gangly Arab answered in accented Greek. "We'll take him back to the camp for now.

To this, the mute responded a gnarled sneer and rolled his head in the direction of Gaspar. Gaspar, for his part, did nothing.

The three ghoulish-looking men from the forest dragged Gaspar's body through the forest by aid of a three-log sled that acted as a stretcher. They emerged into a grey clearing and presented their ward to a man who awaited their return.

"Who is this man, and what is he doing here?"

"We found him stumbling through the woods, Father," answered the stumbling Arab. "He needs help. Look at him for God's sake!"

The three deformed men put down the sailor's body and the priest knelt over him. The priest himself was as ugly and grotesque as his flock. His face was an unwholesome and angry shade of red and it produced sores and warts as though they were being expelled from his core.

"My child, are you awake?"

"Who are you?" Gaspar groaned.

"My name is Leonidas. I'm a priest."

"You've got to help me, Father," the bleeding man moaned. "I'm dying."

"Is he dying?" the priest asked the three men who brought him in.

"Probably a bit faster than the rest of us," answered the man with the bulbous red nose and yellow eyes. "He sure looks like he had a rough night."

"Can you make it to Constantinople?" the priest asked gently. "It's not very far from here, we can take you to Diplokion."

It was at this point that Gaspar became mildly more aware of his surroundings. In an outcropping of the forest, there appeared to be a walled compound, too small to be a village, but large enough to host a handful of buildings. The palisade walls that surrounded the compound were covered in thatch and vine, making the camp difficult to recognize amid the surrounding forest. The only exposed plane of wood was the door, and it was adorned only with a green Maltese cross. Unbeknownst to

Gaspar, the cross of Saint Lazarus identified the camp as a leper colony.

"Please, Padre," he pleaded. "I can't walk. My fingers are numb. I can't stop shaking. I need sanctuary!"

"My child, I can't let you into our village, for your own sake. It's forbidden. We'll take you to the harbour village, it shouldn't take more than an hour or so, and they can bring you to the capital."

Gaspar moaned in agony.

"Padre," interjected one of the deformed rescuers. "Maybe we should take him in for a few days."

"That would be a curse to him. You know that he would never be allowed into their world again. God's commanded us to a life of solitude, and our woe-filled company would only curse him. Take him to Diplokion, but don't let any of the villagers see you. Then return home."

"He might die on the way," answered the man with the yellow eyes.

"Then that's the will of God, and it's not our place to question it," the priest replied without much thought before turning back to Gaspar.

"Listen to me, Christian. Listen. We're going to send you to Constantinople. You'll have to forget that you ever saw us here. Please, swear to God that you will not tell anyone that you saw us."

Gaspar's unfocused eyes darted around wildly.

"Good enough," the priest muttered and he sent Gaspar and his minders away.

Chapter Twenty-Nine - Wounded Lions

side from the Janissaries cohorts stationed there, Roman Castle was also home to many animals. There were a few dozen horses in the stable, alongside a host of pack-mules. A kennel had been built to house the mastiffs; and roaming around the courtyard were a gaggle of geese, a few dozen chickens and an over-aggressive Angora cat with an under-active thyroid named Bonjuk.

Of all the birds that lived freely in the fortress, the alpha was brazen rooster with blue-black feathers and a cruel comportment. He'd been a champion combatant in the flesh-pots and opium-dens that hosted such competitions and was now enjoying his retirement from the rigours of bloodsport. Everyday he would make demands on his harem of hens, favouring any who tickled his fancy, and then moving on so as not to create too much of a dependency upon any of the individual females. He'd been known to rake at the eyes of even the mighty Bojuk in order that the big cat remembers her place. The humans who dwelt in his domain were equally subordinate to his will. When he'd arise in the morn, he'd call out and tear them from their beds. They would come and feed him and his harem; change their water, clean their filth and remove those troublesome eggs from the ladies. The attachment of potential new chicks was a constant threat to the rooster, which is why he allowed the men to devour his unborn children. It kept him secure and it kept the hens in line. It's a demanding job, to be the master of a castle, but it was a duty that this rooster took great pride in, as he soberly understood that no other was capable of such responsibility.

From the slit window of the inland hill-side tower, Ezera watched the drama unfold among the chickens and their rooster overlord. He watched as the larger geese were cowed by the rampant aggression of the more vicious fowl.

'That rooster's a real bastard,' he thought to himself and smiled. *'Mean and aggressive, but he always gets his first bite at the food, and he takes the girls when he wants them. That used to be my life.'*

The former captain of the now vanquished Nineveh looked about his squalid room. It was new enough that it hadn't any of the familiar legacy of filth that contaminated other such prisons, and the yellow sandstone made it seem almost clean. Sun crawled in through the long and narrow window and brought enough light to see plainly. Enough light to see what was left of the only other survivor of the Nineveh.

Pere had survived the boarding, but had sustained a grievous wound in the belly that festered. Last night, he crossed the horizon and found his own way out of their shared prison. Ezera would have to wait until mid-morning when they were brought breakfast gruel, to ask that the body of his deceased crewman be removed for burial.

Ezera watched the Janissaries in the yard go about their morning routines with less affection than he gave the beasts. They fed grain to the birds and then meat to the dogs. The dogs seemed to eat better than the soldiers. At an hour after sunrise, the regiment gathered in the mess hall for their own meal, and then began the daily tasks of a fortress. Most of the soldiers were absorbed in the task of the fortress' ongoing construction. All that activity belied the emotionless cruelty of the outside walls. To the ship sailing down the strait, the fortress on either side was just towers and walls, but from the inside it was a bee's nest of activity.

The sun gradually lit up the entire castle, warming away the cold night. The castle responded in kind, by getting busier and busier as the light grew brighter. Ezera thanked his stars because he knew that feeding time would come shortly afterward. He needed to speak to his jailors and get the body of Pere taken out of the cell. His beloved old friend was starting to exude gasses and stiffen.

The jailors came like clockwork and opened the iron frame door that had been battened into the stone walls. The guards came in pairs. One brought food, water and a new bucket for the necessities of waste, and the other kept his eye on the prisoners, with his curving sword drawn.

"Wait! Wait!" he called as the man with the food and bucket stepped in. Ezera had to hope that these men understood Greek. "My friend is dead! You must take him!"

The guard eyed him suspiciously. The guards were young men of eighteen or so. Two of a dozen who'd joined the orta recently and, as they were bereft of seniority, were tasked with the ignominious duty of feeding prisoners and carrying away their filth. On the positive side, it was better than cleaning the latrine or the kennel.

"Dead?" the young Janissary asked nervously. *"Oldu mu?"*

Ezera made a slicing motion towards his throat to indicate that Pere was no longer among the living.

The young jailor knelt down and confirmed the prisoner's diagnosis. He wasn't entirely sure what to do at that point. He'd assumed that all was expected of him was food delivery and retrieval of waste. This was a most unexpected extra duty. He had to appear as though he knew what he was doing.

"Wait here. I must tell my sergeant," he instructed Ezera. The Janissary's Greek was better than Ezera's.

'*Where the hell am I going to go?*' Ezera thought to himself.

Ezera was left with the sword carrying youth while the first one ran through the tower looking for his sergeant. From the cell, he could hear him rattling on doors, open gates and calling out a name. This was the first good news Ezera had learnt since his incarceration began three days ago. His jailors were inexperienced juniors, who were unsure of how to act without immediate supervision. That will be an import factor to remember when the time came.

The first sign that something was happening came in the form of a plume of white smoke coming from the north. Then from outside in the courtyard, a trumpet call came out. Someone on the water-side wall was raising an alarm, and work stations fell abandoned as their masters threw down the tools of craft in order to replace them with the tools of war.

The two guards hurried themselves out of the room, and left Ezera there with his previous company.

'*That's strange*,' Ezera thought to himself as he inspected the fortress from his window.

The cannons were not being manned. Their crews were mustering in the square as the galley approached the fortress. Once it came into full view from his slot-window, it made more sense. The ship was sailing under the unfurled purple and white banner of Tolga - the Emir of Kastomonu and Sinope, the strongest Muslim principality on the Black Sea. The ship slid up to the fortress and beached herself scrapingly against the rocks.

Ezera cringed as saw the random utilitarian navigation that was doomed to run that ship into a shallow grave some day. Poor seamanship and poor construction, combined with a general disrespect for seafaring tradition kept the Turks out of naval predominance, and allowed for the relatively tiny Republic of Venice to muscle trade away from them.

'*I've got to get out of here*,' he thought.

From the long cut in the stone that allowed him to look out from his tower at the drama that was arriving, Ezera silently watched. He watched the Janissary commander ready himself to welcome his guest.

Mesut straightened himself in preparation for his guest. The Emir's galley beached roughly against the rocky shore and crewmen leapt onto the shore and began securing ropes to haul the ship into place and fasten it to the beach.

Mesut watched on, his felt cap and tunic keeping out the bitter north wind that ripped down from Russia. The wind tugged at his big bushy moustache, it tried to knock down his conical white hat, its ice daggers tried to find unpatched holes in the old soldier's cloak; all to no avail. He stood like a red and white tree before the arriving ship, and with all due hospitality, prepared to give a warm welcome on a cold day.

The ship finally ground to hard jolting stop against the cold rocks of the European side of the Bosporus and rocked against the impact. The ship was a low castled galley with a high bottom, making it more of a barge than a proper seafaring vessel like the Nineveh. That, and the Muslim shunning of anthropomorphism and reluctance to personify and name the vessel would earn the utmost disgust from the imprisoned captain.

All this, Ezera watched from his window. Sharing a cell with the corpse of an old friend, he watched the drama unfold as the great man landed and met the captain of the local guard. Whoever he was, he dressed in fine silks that whipped about the wind when he stood on the ship and stepped down the gangway onto the shore. The dandy guest kissed and hugged the commander when they greeted each other and the Janissary led the finely-accoutred dignitary into the fort.

'*That man,*' he decided. '*... is my way out of this jail.*'

One of the largest rooms in the fort was the medical hall. Tripling purpose as a recovery room, apothecary and surgery, it now housed a dozen soldiers recovering from the throat-cutting adventure that captured the Nineveh and brought the Black Sea under the Sword of Osman. Their guest of honour was a grievously injured giant by the name of Hussein.

The '*Giant of Two Continents,*' as his young comrades were now calling him, lay on a straw-stuffed mattress on the dirty floor of the unfinished hall. Seven of his ribs were broken, and he had suffered from serious internal bleeding. On the first day that he'd been brought here, Mustapha-hoja, the oldest man in the regiment (hence the responsibility of chief surgeon) had told him to make preparations to meet God, for he would surely not see morning. From his wounds aboard the ship, he bled and suffered. A fever enveloped him and his internal organs swelled. Mustapha-hoja didn't give him serious medical attention as his survival was dismissed by triage as being halfway between fighting soldier and honoured martyr, and it was accepted that he'd soon take the second laurel.

The next morning his fever still raged, but he finally received proper attention. His bones were painfully reset and many of the young members of the regiment came to pray with and for him. Even the Chorbachi himself came to check on the departing and evoke his name in his prayers to the almighty.

On the third morning after the battle, Hussein's fever broke and his belly ceased to swell out. The flesh of his back had turned purple from the settling of unspilt blood, his health was to be in question until the inevitable day of his death, but it seemed apparent that God had decided to postpone the harvest of the young man's soul.

As he recovered, all of his classmates from the Lion's Den came to pay their respects to him. His officers were less gushing but let it be known that he had earned the respect of the orta for both himself and his class. These guests did more to elevate his spirit and assist his recovery than any of Mustapha-hoja's prayers or leechings.

When Emir Tolga arrived to visit the fortress, it was mandatory that he inspect the gunner's crews that had brought such a great victory to the House of Peace, and of course to he visited the wounded in the hospital, to thank them for their sacrifice.

Hussein tried to stand when the Emir of Kastamonu arrived, but Tolga motioned with a hand for him to remain reclined.

"Peace be upon you, Lion of God," he greeted the wounded.

"Unto you be peace, sir," Hussein responded in kind.

The only other 'great man' from outside the small world of the regiment that Hussein had ever met was Zaganos-Pasha, the second minister. Unlike the short, stocky minister in Adrianople, Tolga had a grace that came from being born into status. He had not converted to Islam or gained position through his own force, he comfortably walked the path that had always been his. Whereas he may have lacked the intensity of the former Janissary, he had a peaceable soul and a sharp mind that came across by his mere presence.

"Your commander has told me about your heroics against the infidels," Tolga said with a smile. "My congratulations go to you."

"Thank you, Emir."

"He also says that your recovery is equally miraculous. No doubt a favour from our grateful God. I saw your body from afar when I first entered the hall, and I saw a wounded man, lying down as if to prepare for slumber. But here, up close, I can see something quite different. I see a great warrior. I see a man whose greatest accomplishments have yet to be realised. I see an ember behind your eyes that is far from burning itself out, young gazi. You'll heal, and your conflagration will be one long remembered among all nations, I pray."

Hussein blushed at the flowery words.

"If God wills it, My Sheikh."

"If God wills it, My Lion."

In the Grace of God Hospital on the south slope of Acropoline Hill in Constantinople, very little light penetrated, giving a shadowy presence to the stone halls and rooms. The smells of burnt sulphur, blood and human filth dwelt in the darkness, and even the occasional blades of sunlight that entered through the windows couldn't free the hospital from the feeling that it was anything but an earthly purgatory, a waiting room before transfer to the tomb.

"Doctor Mario!" One of the surgeons called to the Italian physician. "We have a man in the sanatorium who says that he knows you. You must come."

Mario frowned at the surgeon. In the politics of any civilized hospital, no surgeon should ever use the word '*must*' to a physician. Mario, being a foreigner whose command of Greek was limited, had a status below that of most physicians, and it pleased the lower classes to no end that they were allowed to exert authority over someone who should be their social better.

Before he could begin to berate the physician, another idea entered Mario's head. He recalled Adam Karian's warning about spies, here was a man who insisted to speak to him. Mario became instantly aware of a possible threat.

"Of what nationality is the man?" Mario asked, hoping for some clue as to the man's identity, also, he couldn't allow himself to respond instantly to commands from someone who should well be his underling.

"Catalan," the surgeon spoke with disgust. "He was brought here in from Diplokion an hour ago. He was brought out of Saint Lazarus, he shouldn't be allowed here."

Catalans still bore the brunt of a staunch racism among the Constantinopolitans. Catalan mercenaries had made up the bulk of the Empire's defences until they rebelled and looted while the Turks gobbled up land in the Balkans. Mario would be lucky if the patient was not mistreated by the nun-nurses that triaged new arrivals.

As for the second note of disgust, that he was brought from Saint Lazarus, Saint Lazarus was the name of a leper colony just north of the city. A man goes into that colony like a flesh-bore beetle goes into a man: it enters and then 'til death do they part.

"Take me to him now." Mario answered immediately, all thoughts of spies having flown from his head.

"I need to tell Doctor Marcion…" The meddlesome physician began.

"I'll find him myself," Mario said with disgust. He was unwilling to wait through the honorific stalling for which the surgeon was preparing, and he barged past him into the triage hall.

"Sister!" he called out to a nurse and then addressed her in his limited Greek. "I'm looking for a man. He's Catalan, he's looking for me."

"He's at the end of this row," the brown-robed nun pointed to a row of a dozen or so beds that stretched to the far wall.

"Thank you, Sister," Mario answered. He liked the nurses, they were the only ones who were nice to him. They were also the only ones who understood how dangerous the illiterate butchers-surgeons were without the guidance of the educated physicians.

The last bed at the end of the row was occupied by a prone man, his feet bound together and bandaged in grey cloth. There wasn't enough light to make out the face of the man who lay there, but his stature prohibited it being Ezera. This man was tall and thin, as opposed to Ezera's stockier build.

"I'm Doctor Mario."

"Doctor," the patient grunted in Italian. "It's me, Gaspar."

Mario remembered the coxswain from Nineveh immediately.

"What's happened?"

"The Turks. They've closed the Bosporus. We were hauling cargo from Trebizond and they fired cannons at us." Gaspar moaned. "They've sunk the Nineveh."

To this, Mario had no comment or expression.

"Ezera's gone. Pere's gone. Everyone's gone," Gaspar's eyes wetted. "My family for almost ten years is all gone. I'm the only one left."

"I see." Mario took a deep breath, and then put all his emotions to the back of his mind. "Let's take a look at you. I'm going to send a nun to fetch Vincent. You'll have to tell him everything. Can you do that?"

Gaspar nodded apprehensively. Mario recalled Ezera's early warnings about Vincent.

"Alright then," Mario said with confidence. "Let's look at these feet of yours."

The keys to the iron gate of Ezera's cell clanked through the tumblers and pulled the bolt back. The door opened and his two red coated guards stepped through.

Ezera was sitting by the slot window, trying to breathe in fresh air rather than the putrefying odour of death that Pere's earthly remains imparted to the cell. The guards were taken aback by harsh smell they'd forgotten. The first guard grunted some words in Turkish to the second, who then accosted the captain.

"Up, Up!" he told him and began searching his person for a hidden blade or other possible weapon. After finding none, he spoke to him again in Greek.

"The Emir will speak to you," He began. "He will address you in Greek. You will avert your eyes at all times, and call him 'my Sheikh.' Do you understand what I am telling you?"

"Yes," Ezera answered gruffly as his pouches and pockets were turned inside-out by the young Janissary.

The door opened again and the soft-faced turbaned man from the boat entered the chamber. The two Janissaries immediately froze at attention. The first look on the Emir's face was one of utter revulsion at the smell.

"Is that man dead?" he asked, pointing to the man on the floor.

"Yes, My Sheikh," the senior Janissary answered.

"Prisoner, what is your name?"

"My name is Ezera. Ezera of Barcelona, my Sheikh."

"Come with me, we will walk along the walls of this castle together. I won't speak to you in this coffin of a cell. You won't try anything foolish, will you? My friends here wouldn't like that."

He motioned to the four guards behind him.

"No, my Sheikh,"

"Good."

The two men walked out of the prison tower and onto the bridge of the curtain walls that connected the three towers. The cold wind contrasted to the warm sun on Ezera's face. On their right they could see the strait, bubbling along as it always did, next to it was the empty shell of the Nineveh, broken beyond the hand of man to repair. To their left was the courtyard of Roman Castle and beyond it, the hills of Thrace. The breeze was cold, but the sun was warm. Behind them walked four guards; armoured tribesmen, not Janissaries.

"My name is Tolga, I am the Emir of Sinope and Kastamonu, and I bid you peace."

"Thank you, my Sheik."

"That is an empty title to you, please don't use it," Tolga chastised him and then pointed out the cannibalised hull of the Nineveh by the shore. "I understand that you were the captain of that ship."

"I was," Ezera said sullenly. He tried not to look at the skeletal wreckage by the seashore directly. "For twelve years, we sailed the Mediterranean, the Adriatic, the Aegean and the Black Seas together."

"It was once a warship, I believe," the Emir insinuated.

"It was that. She fought in two major battles, and dozens of skirmishes over the years."

"Always for Rome?"

"No, Sir. Sometimes under the flag of Venice, though usually for ourselves."

"Venice. That's a republic, isn't it?

"Yes."

"I've often thought of how a Republic could be perfected under Islam, rather than our current trusteeship system."

"I don't know much about these things," Ezera conceded.

"You don't know much about politics?" Tolga asked in mock incredulity. "But it's important. Look at what happened in your city of Constantinople last year. Dreadful riots. Were you there at that time?"

"Yes."

"All over notions of the divinity of Jesus. Was he all Godlike, or half-God and half-man? Or wholly God and wholly man at the same time? We Muslims of course believe that he was a man like any other, but revere him as a vessel for God's message; Similar to Moses or Joseph – certainly important but not divine. What do you think?"

"You ask me about things for which I have no answers." Ezera replied suspiciously.

"How would you ready a navy for a battle, Captain?"

"Ha ha! That I can answer!" the Catalan's face lit up. "It would depend on how many ships, what kind of ships, what kind of waters, what kind of sailors, what kind of opposition. I could speak for hours without resting on that subject!"

"Good, I'm glad," Tolga said slyly. "You care little for politics or religion, and are very knowledgeable on a subject that is of very timely interest. Mesut , the Janissary commander is a friend of mine, is by right to turn you into a slave, you know this?"

Ezera was silent.

"You see, you are a prisoner in a holy war to liberate God's creation of earth from the shadowy grip of the infidels. As a prisoner, you are rightly to be turned into a slave. That means that my friend will have you beaten, tortured, humiliated, until every drop of your own identity is gone, and you will then blindly obey what your master says. Any master. These Janissaries are slaves themselves, and nothing pleases them more that to vicariously avenge their own past humiliations upon someone else. Anyone. That hardly seems like a fitting end for a man such as you. Have you ever transported slaves in your sailing career?"

"Yes."

"Disgusting trade," Tolga shook his head. "An appalling example of human cruelty. You don't want to be subjected to that, a man of your age probably couldn't survive it."

"I'm a young man still," Ezera smiled, despite his condition. "Though, not quite that young. Do you have another idea?"

"That I do!" Tolga smiled. "I'm going south, overland. We're going to Gallipoli, there, under the supervision of a vizier by the name of Baltaolu, the Sultan is assembling a navy. I'd like to bring you along, to help with the supervision of the fleet. I understand that you're pretty wry when it comes to such things, Captain."

"I am, but why would you do this great favour for me?"

"I assure you, the favour is to our mutual benefit. The admiral has no experience of naval life outside of a ferry-boat and playing with his children in a nearby river. I need someone to help familiarise him with his new responsibilities. You'll be a direct agent of my house, not of the Ottoman state. And of course, you'll have to convert."

"You want me to accept servitude and abandon my religion?"

"First, servitude is your destiny for now, either with me or with them," Tolga said matter-of-factly. "Second, you have no religion. You know as well as I do that Christianity is a rusting chain around the leg of the adherents. For the benefit of your own conscience however, I'll give you a chance. If you can name any six of the twelve disciples of Jesus right now, I will personally see to it that you are set free this day. Can you do that?"

The Emir looked at Ezera with a straight face.

"Mathew, Mark, Luke, John," Ezera remembered the names of the four apostles. "Judas…"

Their eyes locked as Ezera's mind searched and searched. Tolga was quite surprised that he'd found five, and would act on his word if Ezera could actually do it.

"Mary?"

Tolga smiled quietly

"No, I'm sorry. Mary was not a disciple. It was a noble effort, however, and I respect the fact that you were willing to guess when you didn't know the answer. Most of my advisors are too afraid of being wrong to say anything that may be questioned. As for accepting servitude, that's not what I'm asking. You'll be a paid retainer. You can accept a life of luxury and respectability with me. Or hardship and an early death with them down there."

He pointed to the off duty Janissaries lounging about the courtyard.

"The choice is entirely yours, but I leave here overland to *The Beautiful City* within the hour. You won't need the hour, however. I believe you to be very reasonable man."

"You seem to know me pretty well."

"Your reputation has preceded you, Captain Ezera," Tolga smiled.

"So what's entailed in this conversion?"

"A few repeated prayers in Arabic, and a small sacrifice on your part. It should be finished in no time."

"What kind of sacrifice?"

"Wake up, Gaspar."

The voice came from out of the darkness that permeated the hospital. Consciousness tapped from underneath set eyelids and tried to break out, to no avail.

The tight frame of Vincent DiCastillo emerged from the darkness and knelt next to the wounded sailor. His face crept closer to Gaspar's and he let out a gentle whisper.

"Wake up, Gaspar."

That voice pulled the sleeping patient up from his slumber.

"Don Vincent," he stammered.

"I'm glad to see you alive, Gaspar. I'm here to listen to you. I want to know exactly what you saw. I want to hear what you remember from the other day."

"Of course," Gaspar replied hesitantly. "I was down in the hull, keeping pace for the oarsmen at time, so I didn't see a lot."

"That's not a problem. Just tell me what you remember. I'm curious as to what it took to sink the Nineveh and my old comrade, Captain Ezera with it."

Gaspar told him everything, from when they first heard about the closure when they were in Trebizond, to the brawl at the mouth of the Black Sea, to his escape. Vincent listened unblinkingly. When Gaspar was finished his tale, Vincent asked him confirmatory questions about cannons, and men. None of which Gaspar could answer with any degree of accuracy. At the end of the interview, Vincent got up and left.

"Good luck, Gaspar," Vincent smiled a soulless expression as he spoke. "I hope that God speeds your recovery. Doctor Mario is doing a fine job, I assume?"

Gaspar nodded.

Vincent tilted his head in acknowledgement and left the ward. Mario was waiting patiently for his exit.

"I'd wanted to speak to you, Don Vincent."

"Of course, what is it?"

"My patient seems quite frightened of you," Mario said. "I hope you didn't distress him too much."

"Yes," Vincent was a little perturbed by the innocuous conversation but kept his well-maintained comportment. "What did you want to speak to me about?"

"Ah, yes," Mario began shyly. "How was the meeting between Lady Ella and the would-be suitor that you spoke of last time we met... at the Cathedral."

"Unfortunately, he met with the same lack of success as all the others. Marrying off my beloved sister is turning into far too much of a challenge." Vincent answered patiently, but his tone let Mario know that he should hurry.

"I wanted to ask for your permission to court Ella," Mario blurted out. "She has me quite enamored and I would like..."

"Stop," Vincent cut him off. He'd been anticipating and dreading this conversation for several months now. "I like you, Mario. I want you to understand that. You're an educated man, and I know that you're a pious fellow and an all around good Christian. You're the kind of person I'd love to have in the family, but unfortunately you don't have the wealth to climb in station and I'm not rich enough to bankroll you as an encumbered brother-in-law. Don't try to exceed your class. You're a refugee and you only have enough money to live in a small apartment with a shared courtyard. Ella deserves more than that. Everything else about you is fine, but on the matter of wealth, you have neither lands nor office. You're here under begged patronage. You understand that, right?"

Mario's face blushed. All of the courage that he'd been building up since the rooftops in Venice, since their conversation on the island eight months ago vanished into the thick air of the hospital.

"Do you understand that?" he repeated.

"Yes," Mario answered in a voice that was half way between a whisper and a sob.

"I like you, Mario. But because of this conversation, I can't have you as a guest in my home any more. Surely you understand *that*?"

Mario nodded.

"Damn it, straighten your back, harden your face. You look like a child," Vincent scolded the doctor. "You'd do the same for your own blood, and if you wouldn't then you're a despicable man and I don't think that you are a despicable man. I have to get to work, but if you're not going to actually *be* strong, at least try to pretend you are."

Mario's face turned crimson, though he tried his best to clench his visage like stone. It failed, coming from someone so obviously unused to it.

"That's better," Vincent lied. "Good day to you, Doctor Mario."

"Good day to you Don Vincent," Mario answered in un-breaking monotone, and Vincent left through the main gate of the hospital, leaving the doctor alone with his thoughts.

After a moment's focus, he returned to his duties and inspected his patient. Gaspar seemed quite upset by his surprise guest.

"Are you alright?" Mario asked him.

"I'll be fine. You're not a friend of Vincent DiCastillo, are you?"

"Not friend," Mario said with muzzled emotions. "Though we're on good terms, he's a good chap, I suppose."

"If you think that, then you obviously don't know him very well," Gaspar mumbled to himself.

Mario took a deep breath and checked his patient's dressings.

The best kept secrets are the ones that everyone knows about. An aunt's drinking problem or a man's predilection for girls younger than his wife, or the annual pilgrimage of Saint Nicholas to all the children of the earth. Once everyone understands the lie, it becomes self-fulfilling and no longer dishonest. In the courtyard of Roman Castle, the Janissary orta assembled to watch an important ceremony. A forced conversion is a false conversion, but since everyone knew was it was false, was treated as true.

In the incomprehensible syllables of Arabic, Ezera bore witness that there was no god but God, and that Muhammad was indeed his prophet. That part of the process was easy enough, the difficulties arose when it was time for Ezera to be marked with the Abrahamic covenant. Circumcision was the symbol of the covenant between God and the first voluntary adherent to his laws, Abraham. It had passed down through the Hebrew prophets in the land of Israel and jumped south to find

Muhammad, and all Jews and Muslims are intended to keep this mark of the flesh as sacred. Christians believe that the supercession of Jesus over the old laws of the Hebrew Bible, the so-called Old Testament (a linguistic concept brimming with the idea that it's been replaced by a new one), cancels this tradition and throws the ritual sexual mutilation of children to the dustbin of history along with kosher dietary laws.

While Jews and most Arab Muslims perform the practice to infants, Turkish men normally undergo the trial by ordeal on or around their seventh birthday; seven being the age of reason in Islam. Converts must undergo it at the time of their conversion. Ezera was around forty, though his exact age was uncertain, even to himself. Unlike Abraham who took the knife to himself, the duty for Ezera fell to the imam.

The task was performed in the open air, to allow the most light, and the ritual hardly went unnoticed. A crowd gathered around for their first bit of entertainment since being posted to the castle. The audience of Janissaries had all undergone the ritual as part of their enslavement as children. Their bondage began at the age of seven, and upon their first week of capacity, they went under the knife. They were all quite vocal in letting Ezera know how painful it would be. They jeered him as he prepared. Tolga had told him to show no fear, and that if he wept, or cried out, it would be a serious dishonour to Tolga, and that Ezera would be put to death for a false testimonial of faith.

Ezera lay down upon a carpet that was placed on the stony earth of the courtyard, and he pulled his breaches to his knees. He looked up at the sky, and said a silent prayer to God, a prayer of apology and to implore forgiveness for what he had been pressured to do. Lastly he asked God, in what would turn out to be the second last prayer of his life, for deliverance from this mutilation. God was characteristically silent.

The imam used a metal thong-clamp to retract the foreskin of Ezera's penis. Once exposed to the elements, a scalpel like instrument, cleaned only minutes ago in the Bosporus, made the original piercing into the foreskin and began its orbit. The slow, downward sawing motion of the blade, combined with the tension pressure from the pull of the clamp swept the tissue away in less than a minute. In those seconds, Ezera was forever marked as a foreigner to his homeland. Even the whores he visited across the seas would be suspicious.

Throughout the operation, he defocused everything around him. The tearing pain of his body, the shouting of the crowd, all became as unnoticeable to him as the earth beneath his body. Upon the completion of the cutting, the real pain began. Ezera was as motionless as the balm was applied and his member was bandaged. The imam gave a final blessing in Arabic, to which Ezera replied an acknowledgement as to the wonders which God has wrought.

"Very stoic, Ezera-Ayoub." Tolga smiled down at his newest servant.

It's traditionally among most major religions for a convert to adopt a new name, to go with his or her new identity, and *Ayoub* is the Arabic name for the prophet Job.

Ezera looked back up at him emotionless.

"I'll have my other servants carry you to bed now," He continued.

"No, thank you," Ezera said. "I can stand and walk for myself."

"You're free to try," Tolga offered dubiously.

Ezera rolled a sit-up and gingerly pulled his legs into a foetal position. He then outstretched his arms to act as balancing anchors and rolled himself up onto his feet, then slowly thrust himself up erect. Standing tall, he looked out at the observant crowd, gathered to see the event, and he refused to waver. The hooting and jeering stopped immediately as they saw him standing, naked, bloody and bandaged from the waist down, but standing nonetheless. Ezera was intending to show them what *invictus* looked like.

He stood and looked at the silent crowd, and then saw upon a wooden table by his feet, the soiled instruments of his surgery, and a piece of bloodied flesh, which had only recently been an important part *of an important part* of him. It was at that point that his consciousness failed where his stoicism had survived. The rest was a complete blur as he fell to the ground.

Chapter Thirty - Rising Squall

Barely two hundred metres from the Grace of God Hospital was the manse of the Venetian governor, Giovanni Cardillo, his health now precariously restored with the ending winter. In his large office, a warm brazier smouldered away, keeping him and his two guests warm in the late afternoon. Giovanni was dressed in his traditional flamboyance, with a crocodile smile on his face. His first guest, Vincent DiCastillo knew that his master's appearance was carefully constructed as to be friendly, the way a coral viper's spots and stripes make it seem like a harmless stick. Adam Karian, the third man in the room had dark skin and curly black hair, wore a long black coat and a colourless emotional mask; he was a dark sight indeed. Around such a man, Cardillo hardly needed to hide his fangs, but appearances had to be maintained.

"Now," the governor began. "As you know, General Karian, the Bosporus is now completely sealed to us. The Turks have cut off access to the Black Sea. Most of the Eastern Seas are essentially now a Muslim lake, with the exception of Constantinople herself. I must ask, what *exactly* are you doing about this?"

Karian looked at the two men. He alone in the court of the emperor believed that Giovanni's nature was wholly opportunistic. Most of the other courtiers believed him to be a bit of a well intentioned simpleton when it came to politics, though an educated man in philosophies and sciences. With regards to Vincent, Adam had no doubt as to the man's vicious mercenary ethic.

"I've come to ask you for assistance," he began. "There are devils at our gates, and without your help, I believe the gates will burst open, and allow in the flames of hell."

"You've invited it, Karian," the governor answered. "For the past four centuries, your empire has used the Turks as mercenaries. They would win battles for one emperor over some rogue family members in exchange for a bit of land here, and a bit of land there. They fought alongside your emperor's cousin and against his brother, with you at his side, if I so recall. They armed themselves and you did nothing. They governed Christians, and you did nothing. They built Muslim fortresses within Christian lands and you did nothing. They've severed your trade with the Aegean and Black Seas, now all business, trade and commerce has to be done through Venice and Genoa. All the while you've done nothing, because the Eastern Empire lacks the strength to stand up to their enemies.

"Against this impotence, I made you an observation. For five years we negotiated union between the churches and between the two halves of the Empire, the Western Empire and other Western states would come to the aid of our Eastern cousins, but you then spurn us. Why do you think we would help you? And honestly, what could we do. You're a general of Rome, but you have no soldiers, save those Varangian bullies. You command some thousand shopkeepers as a town watch. The city is defended by Venetian Mercenaries, contracted by us on your behalf, paid for with Genoese gold. You might want to consider an honourable surrender, good sir."

"We are all Christians, Don Giovanni," Adam replied. "The greatest defence that the West has is us. Constantinople is a city with access to the sea. It can be reinforced easily, and it is in the middle of Turkish yoke. With a strong Roman Empire..."

"The Eastern *Empire* is long gone!" Vincent dismissed his claim. "You represent the city of Constantinople, any other claims you make are preposterous."

"The Holy Seat of the Patriarch of Constantinople still bears influence throughout the East, Brother Christian," he answered back. "From Russia and the Balkans to Egypt and Syria, there are millions of us, and if you can protect the city then the Orthodox world will forever be grateful to..."

"To the nations of Mamon?" Vincent entered. "That is how your patriarch refers to us, is it not?"

"Peace, Vincent." Giovanni re-inserted himself into the conversation. "What the general says is true. If the Muslim hordes no longer have to defend two borders, one of the Balkans and one of Greeks, then they can advance into Europe. The accessibility of the city to the sea is a thorn in their side, for that reason they'll attack, and never cease to do so. If they take the city, then we have to start looking at Hungary and Croatia as buffers, and personally I'd prefer to help empower these Orthodox, rather than a potential Catholic rival closer to home. The only question for discussion is if the city can actually withstand the coming firestorm. That's why you're here, is it not? Your concerns are more practical than those of your emperor and patriarch. Or at least that's my assumption."

"We need more men," Karian said. "The Turks aren't properly trained soldiers, one of your mercenaries is worth a hundred of their armed slaves."

"I've spoken to a witness of the closing of the Bosporus, General. He's in the hospital just down this street," Vincent said. "Professional soldiers and sailors were cut down by these Turks. They're hardly listless slaves."

"Undoubtedly your professionals were sadly outnumbered, and possibly overconfident. The sons of Muhammad must have been lucky."

"Outnumbered they were, and Captain Ezera is traditionally overconfident. But outnumbered you are, and luck and confidence are hardly in abundance here."

"Governor," Karian said returning to Cardillo. "Is it your intention to abandon us to these scavengers?"

"No, of course not," he didn't need any time to consider the option. "But from now on, all sermons, everyday will thank God for the assistance of the Doge of Venice. I want every Constantinopolitan praying for his health like they used to. I'll summon forth as many mercenaries as I can, including ships and cannon, I still have friends here and elsewhere. But you must make it clear to the people here, the court and the Emperor, all understand the sacrifices undertaken by Venice to ensure the survival of the *'Empire'*."

"Of course."

"And you will also surely agree that the current patriarch Gennadios is unacceptable. He preaches hate against your only allies in the world and his influence has lost you the assistance of thousands of soldiers in the upcoming trials. I'll send my request for reinforcements to Venice as soon as I hear that he's permanently out of office, and our mutual friend Noah is re-elevated to his place."

There was a moment's silence to allow Karian to fully understand the meaning of permanence.

"I'll speak to him and tell him to step down."

"That isn't enough," Giovanni answered. "He's been a constant thorn in the politics between the eastern empire and the civilized world to the west. He'll continue to denounce us and the alliance. He's hoping that the Virgin Mary will come and keep the Turks at bay. That kind of fanaticism does you no favours."

"He's needed to keep the peace!"

"Peace in the city was kept at too high a price, General," the governor scolded him politely. "Your Emperor's fear of rocking the boat has almost sunk his empire. I'm afraid that you're in a position where you're going to have terms dictated to you, either from us or from the sultan. Now, Gennadios should be taken out of the equation, permanently. If you can't get rid of one man, I don't know how you plan on dealing with an opposing army. He has to go."

"That should be later today," Vincent added.

"You speak with the subtlety for which your race is famed," Karian said to Vincent.

"Just have it done," he answered back.

"We'll all do what we can," Giovanni said to close the meeting. "If he's not, then Venice will declare its neutrality, like Genoa. We'll take our mercenaries with us, and you can defend your safe and stable religious empire with prayer alone!"

Isodore's donkey clipped and clopped her way into what was a century ago the Turk's first permanent conquest in Europe, Gallipoli. Surrounded by fertile fields, and then ringed with the Thracian hills, the city had been an economic backwoods since antiquity, and had traditionally been vulnerable to attack by land. During a Byzantine war of succession, the city was conquered by soldiers of Orhan, the second Sultan of the Ottoman Dynasty. From Gallipoli, the Turks would move north to conquer Adrianople and eventually move their capital there, to be closer to the front.

Gallipoli, *The Beautiful City*, housed the largest Turkish-controlled harbour and port on the Marmora, only a hundred kilometres south of Adrianople. More than just a harbour, the fishermen of the bustling port provided the recruits for a Turkish navy and the expertise in shipbuilding that were so necessary for the task.

The city was walled by a wooden fortification, hardly strong enough to withstand a proper siege by an army, but inconvenient enough to channel civilian entrants. A Turkish militia man with a hawkish face stopped Isodore and his flatulent donkey at one of those channels.

"Stop! What is your business in this city?" he asked.

"I'm coming from Constantinople. I'm here to pick up supplies, and then continue on to Athos," Isodore lied. "I'm on the pilgrimage road."

Athos was a monastic site in Macedonia to the west of Gallipoli. A century prior to the arrival of Ottoman suzerainty, the mountain monastery was the centre of the Hesychast movement and the last great cultural flowering of Byzantium, called the Palaeologan Renaissance. It's been a pilgrimage sight for mystical-minded Orthodox Christians for centuries since.

"The gate tithe is a dirham."

"Here you are," Isodore cheerfully handed over the smallest unit of currency used in the sultanate. "I've never seen the harbour so full. Is something going on?"

The guard shrugged. "God knows. They've been hiring sailors and shipwrights from all over the Marmora for the past year. There's an important visitor in the city today."

"Most impressive," Isodore said nonchalantly. "Is it safe for me to take a look, or is the harbour under armed guard?"

Many people find bureaucrats and guards to be ornery and dour, and treat them as such. Isodore had made the observation a long time ago that if you are friendly to people, they'll usually be friendly in return. Once the toll was paid, he and the guard started chatting away like old neighbours.

"Be careful when you go there," the guard warned. "That important guest that I told you about is inspecting the harbour, making sure all the boats float, I guess. I really don't like boats, but the whole city's been turned into a shipyard. You Greeks sure love your boats."

"That we do," Isodore smiled. Truth be told, Isodore was Bulgar, not Greek, but the distinction between Christian subjects would probably have been lost on the guard, and Isodore wasn't one to add extra information when it wasn't required. "The sea is beautiful and peaceful. It allows you to forget about the bloody soil back here."

"I don't swim, I don't sail and I don't eat fish. There's something… unwholesome… about the sea. There's no progress or memory to the landscape. Just the constant coming and going of waves."

"You're a philosopher," Isodore joked. "Someone should tell God that Rhazes has leapt from the grave and is now guarding the gates of Gallipoli."

"Don't joke like that," the guard said trying unsuccessfully to conceal a smile. "Move along."

"Peace be upon you, Muslim."

"Unto you be peace, Christian."

"And over here, we have yet another mighty war galley being assembled into service for God," Veli-Fayik announced as he played the part of guide to his assembly.

Admiral Baltaolu looked on with pride, and Emir Tolga smiled politely and pulled his coat tightly to keep out the sea breeze from the cold waters of the Marmora.

"We'll have at least a hundred ships ready by the end of March!" the admiral boasted.

"And they'll all be warships?" Tolga asked redundantly.

"Of course! Single deck galleys, broad ships!" Baltaoglu motioned with his hands to show that the ships would, in fact, be broad. "Each will have a single cannon, and iron ram and enough men to storm any Roman vessel we encounter."

"How many enemy vessels do you suppose they'll meet?"

"At last count, there were almost two hundred ships in Constantinople's harbour, but only ten of them are warships, the rest are fishing vessels and cargo trawlers."

"Very well, worthy cousins," Tolga nodded his head. "You're both doing a great service to the faith here. Tell me, what are you doing to train the fleet?"

"The men of Gallipoli are practically born in boats, Emir," Fayik answered. "Still, we send the fleet to patrol the water between here and the village of Lapseki, on the Asian shore. All ships flying the standard of Rome are stopped. Of course, we let the Italians through."

"Ah yes, Halil's wonderful policy that would halve our prize by allowing the foreigners to retain their privileges. We are ever to remain grateful to the prime minister," Tolga boasted

Fayik wasn't certain of how to respond to any insults at someone who was so senior to everyone assembled. In the end, he chose to simply remain silent and pretend that he hadn't heard.

Behind the conversing principals, walked a collection of servants, slaves, toadies and general hangers-on. Most were trying to hide their boredom and hoping to catch someone else failing to do so. The games of great players were aped poorly by their underlings.

One man among them was paying no attention to his crowd, and only marginal attention to the conversations of the masters. Ezera of Barcelona, re-christened "Ayoub" the Arabic name of the suffering prophet Job, looked about his world and shook his head. He could see a massacre in the brewing. There could be no doubt as to the result of the war at sea. This Turkish fleet, an inaccurate term as the fleet itself was composed almost entirely of Greek sailors, would outnumber that of Constantinople and would eventually bring about victory, but not without suffering terrible casualties.

This presented Ezera with a quandary. Should he help his benefactor, who rescued him from what would most certainly be a gruesome fate, or remain silent and plot his escape? The best option seemed to be to follow the Veli's example and remain quiet.

This, as fate would have it, was not a realistic possibility, as Tolga fully expected to tap his expertise.

"Ayoub," He called to his newest servant.

Ezera leaned on his walking staff and pulled himself towards the conversation. The stitched pain in his lower regions still flared when it would brush against his clothing, and dream-time adventuring tore him away from slumber every night, but other than that he was coping well.

"Yes, my Sheikh?" It was always wise to show deference in public.

"What do you make of these… ships?"

"They look to be finely built for the fishing season, sir."

"I'm glad that the meet your approval," Baltaolu joked.

"I'll see if my cook approves," added Fayik with a chuckle.

Ezera was perfectly willing to tolerate minor humiliations until he could ensure his ultimate extraction from his current situation, but insults to his knowledge of such matters was a slight not to be suffered under any circumstances. That residual pride is why slaves who are not properly broken in spirit usually end up under the ground faster than those whose souls are beaten down to the point that they could be worked to death.

"You're going to have a fleet of a hundred barges, Admiral. Flat-bottomed transport ships that can race across the Marmora at high speed on a clean day, but have to be dragged up onto land as soon as any wind picks up. Look at that so-called warship in the dock," Ezera pointed with his birch staff. "It's deck if three feet above sea-level and it's empty. When it's full of men who are rowing, it'll be closer to two feet. They'll be one strong wave away from disaster."

"All it has to do is get our soldiers to our enemies' ships, and they'll board without much trouble," Fayik corrected him.

"A Venetian galley deck is at least ten feet above the waves. How are your soldiers going to board? Will they jump? From two feet to ten feet, from a moving platform to another moving platform. Are your soldiers used to fighting at sea? Or do you think that the Italians are going to give them a hand up onto to their decks and fight them *mano a mano*? The Italian marines will throw daggers, javelins, arrows, bullets, and darts down at your crews from the safety of the deck. Five Venetian warships will sink your entire navy of a hundred, even if you double it to two hundred, then the massacre will only be greater."

"That will be enough, thank you," Tolga interjected without emotion.

"Who is this… man?" Baltaolu demanded.

"This man serves me, Brother," Tolga answered gracefully.

"I'll not suffer the council of a slave, regardless of what he says. He says that he's a convert and I say that he's still a Christian, and should rightly be treated as a labouring slave! We need no assistance from him or his failed civilization!"

"Some of the greatest warriors of the faith are converts, brother. I don't suppose you would reject our mutual friends Zaganos and Mesut for their infidel pasts."

"That's different!"

"It's always different. God brings us all together by different paths to find the straight road. Many streams flow into the same great river, and he's flowed into ours."

"We have no need to tolerate anyone who speaks so out of place."

"What I find interesting," Ezera began, "is that no one seems to argue my assessment."

"He's like Orban," Tolga said gently to Baltaolu, ignoring Ezera's words. "We'll listen to his expertise, and respect his knowledge. He'll never speak against you in public again."

With that Tolga looked at Ezera with severity.

"Will you?"

"Of course not." Ezera said in a tone that let no one to believe him.

"Work with him, Baltaolu," Tolga adjured. "There's already too much riding on this."

"We'll see," Baltaolu sneered.

Isodore the monk watched all this transpire from the shadows of a nearby warehouse. He couldn't hear what was being said, but it was a simple enough task to see what was happening. Ezera, who'd apparently been injured, had turned Turk and was now counselling the Muslims. He'd only met Ezera the one time, last summer at Vincent's home, but the captain had made quite the impression.

The spying monk didn't know about the loss of the Nineveh, nor was he currently knowledgeable to the closure of the northern strait. All that he could see of which he was certain was that the Catalan pirate, a friend to Doctor Mario and Don Vincent, was speaking, and apparently arguing with agents of the sultan. It was the arguing that was more damning, because it proved to Isodore that he was not a prisoner. Were a prisoner to speak so aggressively, he'd be strangled.

This sent Isodore's mind racing. He would of course report this to Vincent directly. Vincent would be furious... or not. The commander had been a mercenary himself after all, but siding with the enemies of Christ is a little too cold-blooded to seriously consider. He could have been pressed into service, but that would have had him rowing oars, rather than inspecting shipyards. He must have hired out his expertise. What if Vincent knew about that? Giovanni Cardillo certainly wasn't above sending him as a mercenary expert to spy on the Sultan's navy. The Venetians played that game alongside the Genoese in a very sinister capacity. That must be what was transpiring here. Ezera would not only relate intelligence, but issue bad advice to the infidels.

That then raised the question of what it meant for him to be there. Obviously, they hadn't heard anything from their agent, so they sent Isodore to investigate. They didn't tell him this, because they didn't want the secret identity of their informer to be known – in case he'd been killed or moved. Isodore would have to find a way into the Veli's mansion to speak to Ezera. Fortunately for them both, finding a way into places uninvited was something at which Isodore had some experience.

The sun began to creep down towards the horizon over the hills of the Gallipoli Peninsula, and the call to prayer echoed towards the setting sun. In the mansion of Veli-Fayik, an extravagant supper was being served to the great men, and a modest and humble meal was being served to the servants downstairs.

Ezera ate with the other servants, all of whom cast disparaging glances his way. He, who'd forgotten his place and spoken so harshly was not a welcome addition to the family. They believed that someone without respect for the rules invariably had no respect for those who did. Ezera, for his part, did little to dismiss this perception, as he in fact had no respect for those who accept their lot as being so miserable. He was committing the heinous sin of being uppity.

The true sin of slavery and servitude is not the violence done to human beings by whips and rods. The evil of the practice was that after the flashes of violence had come to their natural end, they lingered in the minds of the victims. The slaves accepted servitude to end the violence, and then accepted servility as a way to minimize the further affliction of that horror. This was constantly reinforced with fear, and the truly horrible de-humanization occurs when the violence is no longer needed. When healthy men and women accept that their die is cast and that this is where it rests. This self-defacement is evil. The violence that brings it about is evil. One of the most damning aspect is reflected when that horrible sin is internalized to the point that the slaves jealously rage against those who don't internalize. Those who reject their own enslavement are hateful in the eyes of those who've accepted theirs.

Ezera's colleagues stared daggers at him over the dinner table, as he sat with his back straight and refused to allow his head to bow any more than was necessary to eat.

"Old man!" one of the guards shouted into the busy kitchen. "Where's the old man who thinks he's special enough to speak to great men like they're minions?"

The captive captain looked up, non-committed.

"I'll answer to that charge, but I'm not so old to be identified as such." Ezera said with a commanding presence that made everyone in the servant's quarters more than a tad unnerved. "What do you want?"

"You have a summons from the constable," the guard answered.

All eyes in the busy kitchen looked over at Ezera to see if he'd flinch. Tolga's chief eunuch had a triumphant look on his face when he heard the news. A justification was on the horizon, that this interloper would properly learn some respect for the way of things.

"Where is the culprit?" demanded a rather young looking constable with a hawkish face, standing at the servant's entrance.

The constable's glance seemed to stake him a position beyond his physical stature, and the entire roomful of servants felt immediately under his observation.

"I'm he," Ezera answered with a baritone voice that allowed no hidden fear to show itself.

"Alright then," the guard escorted Ezera, who resisted the urge to of struggle when so surrounded. "Come along! I'll have him back in an hour or so."

'*One guard?*' he thought to himself. '*I'll have better luck against one child-guard while I'm shackled than against a room full of this lot without the chains. It's just time to steal a horse and ride 'til morning.*'

Once outside, the still limping Ezera saw a second militia man waiting for him.

'*Two. This might be a little harder than I thought.*'

"Good evening, captain," the second guard greeted him in Italian.

Ezera looked puzzled and tried to make out the other man's shadowed face.

"Do I know you, friend?"

"We met last year at the home of Vincent DiCastillo. My name is Isodore of Phillipopolis."

"The priest?"

"Monk," Isodore corrected him. "Our mutual friend sent me here."

"Let's get the hell out of here, I'm a prisoner…" Ezera whispered.

“You mean you’re not spying for Giovanni Cardillo?”

“Of course not! I hate that bastard!” Ezera answered with joyous enthusiasm.

Isodore’s eyes were black like coal rather than glass. No light reflected, nothing was there to show the machinations of the brain behind them, only dull black nothingness.

“Do you have a horse ready?”

“No,” Isodore answered slowly. “I’ve enlisted this boy to help me speak to you, using the pretence of issuing a warning. His help’s been bought for that service, but helping a prisoner escape from here isn’t what was paid for and would only land us both in a prison.”

“You can come back tomorrow, with better preparations.”

“No,” Isodore said again, this time more quickly. “Your eyes are seeing the fleet and your ears are hearing the plans, are they not?”

“What? Of course, this Tolga-Pasha wants my help…”

“I want you to find a way to record everything important about the fleet and get it to me. I’ll work on finding one of the house staff who can help us, it may take a few days to secure a way for you to transmit the intelligence to me, but I’ll then bring it back to the capital.”

“Are you insane?”

“No, but you’re in a position to help more than anyone else, Ezera.”

Rage came so close to boiling over, but was tempered by the realisation that he was being offered an opportunity.

“When you get back to the capital, speak to Giovanni. Tell him that I’ll do all of this, but only in exchange for a renewal of my pilot’s license, and an availability on the roster in the Republic,” Ezera insisted. “And money! Lots of damn money!”

Ezera’s desired concession referred to fleeting practice in Venice, whereby anyone with a pilot’s license could captain a ship for a trading house. They would be hired directly by a merchant, for a merchant ship, and they would be allowed to recruit crew, and post passages from the customs houses. With roster availability and pilot’s licence, Ezera would be a wealthy man, and without it he would be a pirate and brigand.

“I’ll pass on your conditions to him when I return.”

Ezera nodded, and was escorted back to the dining hall.

Later that month, as winter made its final withdrawal into memory, and the warm breezes of spring entered the days, the nights were still cold. Behind a stall in the fish-market of Gallipoli, two young, springtime lovers quickly met to exchange the sorts of pretty words that only the young do.

"I have something for you, Serap," Niyazi said and reached held out his hand.

Serap looked over her shoulder, making certain that no one was witnessing their moment.

"Yes?" she said excitedly.

Niyazi then opened his hand slowly, to reveal a gold ring. Serap's hands flung to her face to cover her mouth and eyes. Niyazi smiled and Serap's eyes watered.

"My father..." she started.

"He can't say no," he protested.

"But he doesn't approve of you. You know this," Serap was on the verge of weeping openly, so she looked about again to make sure that no one could see her come so close to loosing control. "He wants me to marry his elder brother's son as soon as I turn sixteen."

"He's more than twice your age, and your cousin!" Niyazi raised his whisper by dropping an octave.

"He's got a farm, he's got wealth. What do you have, my love? Oh, my sweet love, my father just wants the best for me."

"In five years, the Veli will give me a *timar*, my own farm. I'll be on my way to becoming a Sipahi."

"In five years I'll be twenty, who'll want me then?" Tears streaked down her face more openly now.

"I'll love you when you're a hundred."

"Oh no," she sobbed. "Look at me now, see what you've done. I'm crying openly. Look at this."

Niyazi raised his hand to try to wipe he face clean, but she pulled back.

"Just go, I'm sorry. I'll always love you, but I can't meet you again. It's too hard for me."

"Wait..."

"No," she insisted tearfully and closed her lover's hand. "I can't marry you, and I can't ever see you again."

With that she hurried off, darting between stalls of fish and vegetables, leaving Niyazi alone with a ring.

It was a long walk home for the crestfallen lover, he was so caught up in his own unrequited love that he failed to notice the bearded man walk up to him on the road.

"Peace be upon you, brother," the unidentified man greeted him.

"Yeah, peace," Niyazi replied informally, without looking up.

"I'm sorry for your troubles, Friend, but take consolation that your situation need not be permanent."

Before he looked up to assess who was speaking to him, Niyazi turned on the interloper and made as if to throw him to the ground.

"Mind your own affairs, whoever you are!"

He then saw that the man wore the clothes and beard of an Orthodox monk, a fact that only served to reinvigorate his anger.

"What do you think gives you the right to speak to me that way, *Christian*?" he said, hissing the address out of his mouth rather than speaking it.

Isodore raised an open hand to calm the angry young man.

"I'm here to help you, Friend," he said.

"I'm not a friend to you!"

"Not yet, but you will be soon, for I'm here to help you, if you're willing to help me."

Isodore slowly opened his coat and reached into one of his innumerable pockets and pulled out a pouch of that jingled of coin.

"I have a fee for a service here," he began. "A regular fee for a regular service. How much are you paid for a month's service to the Veli?"

"Three silver akches," Niyazi lied. He was paid six dirhams, or one silver akche. "What's it to you?"

"Well here's five," Isodore motioned towards his little black pouch. "And another five when you complete a service for me. Are you intereseted?"

Niyazi grabbed the pouch and counted out twenty copper dinars.

"What do you need?"

"You are a cook at Fayik Veli's mansion, are you not?"

Chapter Thirty-One - *Pietas, Veritas and Patientia*

The city of Adrianople was gradually blooming into spring, and the city was abuzz with excitement. The wooden palisade walls that surrounded the capital were overflowing with people. Clan after clan of Anatolians camped and barracked outside the walls, the spidery emblem of the Uygur Clan flying above this camp, the eagle feathers of the Samot Clan reverently elevated above that one. Even the cross embossed the shields of Serbian and Bulgar levies who prepared to do their duties for their overlords were present. Among all these various symbolic showings, the most feared was the soup pot of the Janissary corps. All these symbols of tribal affiliation, even the revered horse-tails of the house of Osman, were subordinate to the grandest banner among them, that of Holy War.

The banner of the Prophet, proclaiming the unity of God and Mohammed's prophetic stature was to be flown about the horde. The army was *sine qua non* one of Islamic expansion. While the Christian levies were kept in line by the force of those horsetails, the clans were recruited, pressured and commanded by faith to move under the leadership of the Great Khan, Mehmet the Second. In his capacity of the sultan, he was limited to commanding a handful of battalions, infantry and cavalry, Janissaries, mercenaries and press-ganged Europeans. But when the banner of the prophet was unfurled, and he took the mantle of Ayoub the Great, the companion of Mohammed who led the assault on Constantinople in the Seventh Century, he received blessings to make holy war, and that made him the true carrier of the sword, not only of Osman, but of Islam itself.

This mantle brought legitimacy to his call to arms. Once the Mevlani religious lodges had accepted his role as gazi, they brought pressure throughout all the tribes of Asia Minor, and recruits started to trickle to the cause. Those clans who were unmotivated by religious devotion were motivated by a lust for gold. Some were bought off with the gold from conquered Bulgaria, and others by promises of land in Macedonia and Serbia. The bashi-bozuks (literally broken heads – meaning clan-less rabble) enlisted as freelances for the promise of mere booty. All told, one hundred and sixty-five thousand fighting men rallied to the cause, and that number again as support.

The only standing army that was to take the field was that of the Janissaries. Unlike anywhere else in Europe, they were soldiers in practice instead of theory, even during times of peace. Mesut, a rising star among the regiments and commander of the prestigious Eighth Orta was given overall seniority of the twelve slave regiments. The men in his command would be responsible for the northern half of the wall up to the Golden Horne. The European levies, conscripts and mercenaries would be placed under the command of the Prime Minister Halil and be given responsibilities for the south. It was among them that the cannons were stowed, the sultan would camp, and the overall command be centred.

The hodgepodge of clans and mystics that made up the Anatolian Army was placed under the command of Zaganos Pasha. He was very good at managing the conflicting temperaments of his wards and he would march them first to Roman Castle, and then south to Constantinople. He would surround the Genoese colony of Galata, and neutralise the north shore of the harbour.

Hundreds of kilometres away, Baltaolu prepared the fleet to sail away from Gallipoli and head in the direction of Constantinople. They had instructions to overrun the village of Diplokion and then to anchor there, keeping the mouth of the Bosporus closed and prevent any reinforcements from arriving and securing the harbour. Baltaolu was also charged with harassing the four kilometre long southern wall of the city, forcing the egregiously outnumbered Romans to defend that wall as well, diverting soldiers from the defensible land wall.

One of the most important men to take the field was an unassuming Hungarian intellectual mercenary named Orban. Orban had a rotund, doughy figure and a disposition that failed to instil any awe whatsoever, but he could do what no one else could do. He forged cannons. Enough cannons to send the furies of hell into a fierce retreat. The centrepiece of the artillery corps was a monstrous masterpiece of a cannon that had been dubbed "The Basilisk." The Basilisk was twenty-seven feet long. Its barrel was eight inches of bronze and was thirty inches in diameter. The cannons had to be pulled by a team of a hundred oxen.

Many of his courtiers believed that at the age of eighteen, Mehmet was not yet mature enough to truly appreciate the magnitude of what was happening. This was a popular misconception. As far as he was concerned, he was about to vindicate his ancestors' struggles in Europe. The greatest city in the world, a prize like no other, was about to be plucked from the tree and placed gently into his basket, forever leaving his name in the annals of human history. He understood the magnitude and planned accordingly.

Halil ate his dinner alone. In an hour, he was scheduled to meet the Sultan and the divan for their daily breaking of bread, but by habit, the prime minister would eat a full meal before the banquet. He thought that he would seem undignified if he gorged himself at the sultan's table. It was in his best interest to always seem sated. Also, it would be easier for him to carry on the constant interplays of conversations that would go on over the meal. After he ate the last of his lamb dish, he nodded to his cook in appreciation and washed his hands by the prepared basin.

"Where is the lady of the house?" he asked the cook. "I've not seen her all day. She's being quite mysterious."

"I believe that she's upstairs, Pasha."

"Well, go and summon her. I'd like to see her before I go," he said gruffly.

His wife had always been independently minded, and Halil had a long tradition of humouring this, but this was the eve of battle. Tomorrow morning, one of the largest armies ever seen my human eyes was to begin a march to capture one of the greatest prizes ever won. Halil would not be ignored by his wife on such an auspicious evening.

After a few moments, the cook came down.

"She says that he's ill, My Lord," he reported.

"Ill?" Halil asked incredulously. "At the crack of dawn, I leave for what could be a very long time, and she denies me?"

The cook looked nervous.

"What's wrong? You don't believe her? Of course she's lying! I know that! She's angry at me for being unable to divert this folly. I've invested enough wealth in her and her ignoble family over the years to make any woman weep in joy, and now she's disapproving of me? I tell you, these last few months have made her approval or lack there of a source of treason to my own conscience!"

The cook remained silent and swallowed nervously.

"What?" Halil demanded, seeing that something else was bothering his servant.

"Ahhh…" he stammered. "My Lord, I think that you should go to her."

"What are you talking about?"

The cook looked around and gave his master an imploring look.

"I don't have time for this!" Halil pronounced and prepared to storm out of his mansion. "Ahmet! Ahmet, where are you?"

"Here, Pasha," the tribesman answered quickly, stepping out of an adjoining salon. "Are you ready to leave?"

"I am," the vizier answered. "Wait here, I'm going to check on the Lady Ayshe, I won't be a moment."

Halil hurried out of the room, leaving Ahmet and the cook in the kitchen. Ahmet's stare bored holes through the frightened cook as they heard the master of the house's footsteps climb the wooden steps above them. The cook felt as though the devil's own rage was stirring up from an infernal slumber.

Constantinople's Chora Monastery compound was a typically Byzantine structure. Its red brick walls, capped with round domes would place it as an iconic establishment in the Fifteenth Century metropolis. When it was first built, it was constructed a mile outside of the city proper, but before the city walls. Now, while still outside the urban sprawl of the capital, it was at the intersection of roads that connected the sea walls of the Golden Horne to the land walls of Theodosius. It was only twenty metres north of the Lycus Aqueduct, that fed water to the city from a series of lakes, rivers and springs in Belgrade forest. There was even a fresh-water cistern for the monastery to use. Because of its location, General Karian had designated it to be transformed from a semi-abandoned, quasi-heretical monastery into the major field hospital for the ensuing siege.

Mario Orsini arrived and inventoried the facility. The monk's barracks were to be evacuated and converted into two tiers. The upper level would be the quarters for the physicians, surgeons and nurses of the hospital. And the ground floor would be used as a sluice gate for the incoming wounded. Tents would be put up in the walled compound to house the wagons to bring injured men from the walls, and would also act as a triaging area. Mario had intended the courtyard to also function as an overflow for the hospital, but the land was too slanted downward towards the barracks for it to be a stable work area. Also, the late March air was still to cold to allow weakened men to sleep outdoors. The day's sun was warming and sweet, and April would eventually be upon them, but the days were deceptive to the sting of night.

Mario was happy to be out of the Grace of God Hospital. The monastery was a more open building than the hospital, by far. The wind could blow the corrupt air away, and the sun shone everywhere. General Karian had come to inspect the renovations underway and had conveyed the thanks of the Emperor Constantine the Eleventh, in front of the entire staff. After an endorsement like that, the prideful attitude of the local surgeons and physicians hid itself rather than risk offence to the court.

Everything was sunny and wonderful for Mario, once the ensuing war was taken out of the picture. Once the Turks were turned back, Mario would be a household name in the capital, and he would probably be the physician to the court of the emperor and be entrusted with an appropriately heavy purse. What would Vincent DiCastillo have to say then?

On the morning of March 24, 1453, a final grace entered the Chora compound.

Ella DiCastillo entered the compound and found Mario yelling at labourers, who were trying to set up a tent in the cold muddy ground.

"Bury the pole!" he yelled in his constantly improving Greek, and demonstrated his intentions with his hands. "I don't want it to rain on my patients if there is an accident."

The workers clearly understood what he was trying to say, but they knew nothing of tent building. Mario suspected that he should have hired a handful of soldiers off the wall to do this job properly.

"Doctor Mario?" Ella asked diminutively to get his attention.

"Yes…" Mario answered tersely before he saw who was speaking. "Ella?"

"I've come to help you," she said proudly. "I've taken temporary vows and I would be a nurse here, if you need me."

Mario was speechless. Truly he didn't need any more nurses, but he was hardly above forcing one of the bossier existing nuns out onto the street.

"We always need more nurses," he said quickly. "Does your brother know that you're here?"

"We discussed it last night, and he was opposed to it. What I've done I've done without his permission, but with God's Grace. I'm a bride to Christ until the end of this trial." Ella couldn't keep eye contact while she spoke those words.

'*The vows are temporary*,' Mario thought. "That's wonderful!"

"What should I do now?"

She looked so adorable, tightly wrapped in freshly tailored and washed clothes that were intended to seem plain. Even the plain habit of a nun was a luxurious gown when it hung on her ample frame. Her honest smile and warm eyes brought an even grander smile to Mario's face and heart.

"Let's get you a room and have the nuns teach you what you need to know about healing," he said simply.

Cloistering vows were not permanent commitments, as Mario well knew, having himself spent ten years as a priest in order to teach natural philosophy and medicine at the university in Venice.

She smiled at him and averted her eyes. Mario let his gaze linger just long enough so that she wouldn't mistake his intentions as anything less than those of an undeterred suitor. This coming battle had the potential to be the greatest thing that had ever happened to him.

There was a cold fire burning under Halil when he entered the harem of his home to find his wife hiding behind a changing blind.

"Come out from there!" he called out. "I am to leave on a mission that will either destroy our family or leave us as the greatest Muslim dynasty in Europe, and you refuse to come downstairs to bid me farewell! What villainy have I done to deserve this?"

"I'm sorry husband," she called from behind the veil. "But I cannot have your eyes see me. I am unclean to you."

"Unclean," Halil dismissed her claim offhand. "I'm not here to fuck you, but I bloody well demand a goodbye when I go on such a task!"

Behind the screen, where she'd hidden once from Ahmet and his brother, Ayshe held back her tears and held her face in her hand. Her eye was no longer swollen shut, but her cheek had remained a corrupt shade of purple where Ahmet had struck her during a recent rage.

"I'm sorry," she repeated, barely audibly. "I'm so sorry."

Halil became uncharacteristically aggressive and stormed over to the wooden blind, to force her presence in front of his eyes.

He saw Ayshe packaged into black robes, tightly pulling a woollen shawl over her shoulders to keep warm. She sat on the floor and her legs were tucked under her body, her knees giving cradle to her down-cast head. Her hands shook from rage and depression, and she'd obviously been crying.

"What happened?" Halil's temper immediately subsided. He loved his wife very much, and his first instinct upon seeing her in this state was to lower himself to a crouch to see what he could do to help.

He put a hand gently on the back of her head, but she refused to raise her gaze to meet his. If she did, he would see the welt on her face. Ahmet's rage had been visited upon her more than once.

"Janim," he said, using the Turkish word for *my soul* or *darling*. "Look at me."

"I can't," she wept. "I'm so sorry husband. I've wronged you so grievously."

"Look at me," he repeated, this time with more force.

For the first time in their thirty years of marriage, Ayshe obeyed her husband against her own will, and raised her face to look upon her husband's. She expected him to break down in weakness at the sight of her. At the realization that another man had touched her, both sexually and violently. He would call himself a cuckold and a fool and blame her, but she saw none of this.

Halil's face was like wood, though his eyes pooled slightly. He gently moved his head towards hers and quietly kissed her purple eye.

"Ahmet?" he asked with only the faintest trace of disappointment.

Ayshe couldn't keep her eyes up. Her downward glance answered for her.

"Ayshe," he said slowly. "I've always loved you."

The iron-matron of the harem managed to hold back a sob, but she knew full well that once she began, she would be completely unable to stop.

"I'm going to go now, but always remember that I love you."

Ayshe looked up at him incredulously, and Halil kissed her on both eyelids. After that, he rose and left the room. The two would never see each other again.

A war council met in the private secretariat of the Roman Emperor, Constantine Paleologus. The chamber was lit by the sun's bounty that reflected around the pastel pinks and reds of the chamber, but the day's beauty did nothing to soothe the tempers of those present.

"We need more men for this to work!" General Karian proclaimed to the Emperor and pointed an accusatory finger across the table at the Genoese governor. "On the other side of the harbour, Trebianno has in his charge an additional six hundred mercenaries, well equipped, and ready for battle!"

"Indeed, we have, Old Friend," Trebbianno replied plolitely. "But they are not mine to give away like toys to children. Genoa will never put her servitors under the command of the Venetians or their allies. On top of that, we've sworn official neutrality in this conflict."

"Damn Venice! Damn Genoa! Where are your reinforcements! You promised assistance and forgot about us!" Karian turned his rage to Giovanni Cardillo.

"Most of your soldiers are Venetians," the Cardillo reminded him. "If the Genoese join us, as they well should, we would be pleased to welcome then in a united defence of Christendom. As for our lack of reinforcements, we would have spent the last two years scouring the earth for soldiers enough to defend the walls of Christendom if we could have, but you rejected the west and put that fool Gennadios in the pulpit. Any assistance after that folly is something for which you should be eternally grateful, despite the ramshackle nature of a speedy recruitment.”

“We have to defend our own walls, Giovanni, and we’ve already sacrificed one of our truest friends as councillor to your cause,” Tebiannno added in Greek, resisting the urge to drift into their native Italian. It would be an unforgivable insult to the office of the Emperor to do so in his presence. “You seem to forget that the buoy line that protects the harbour may indeed start in the administration of Venice, but the chain needs to be fastened hard in Genoa to keep ships out of the harbour. If we don’t defend Galata, the Turks will overrun our city, sever the chain, and occupy the harbour. They won’t need to pierce that great wall of yours then, Emperor.”

The emperor didn’t reply to the suggestion, none was needed. In 1204, that’s exactly how the city fell to the French and German soldiers at the behest of the Doge of Venice. Genoese official neutrality would keep the harbour closed, and hence one of the three sides of triangle of Constantinople would be secure.

“And what of the Ottoman fleet?” he asked.

“Ah, yes,” Cardillo perked up with some enthusiasm. “We have an informant among their ranks. They have a hundred and twenty light galleys, rigged for boarding and transportation. They’re going to hold Diplokion, a two hour march from Trebbianno, and use it as a naval base for the siege. From there, they’ll secure the islands as the siege wears down. They’re not strong enough to force the buoy, but we won’t be strong enough to force our way out, either. The harbour will dissolve into a stalemate fairly quickly, I should think.”

“Would they be able to attack the sea-walls along the Marmora?” asked the emperor.

“No, sire,” General Karian answered quickly. They had gone over this before, and the Emperor should have recalled it, but his memory was notoriously short-lived for everything except for affairs of court. “If the Turkish fleet abandons their assault on the buoy to attack the south wall, then our fleet would break free of the harbour and be able to harass them, sink a few, and then retreat to the comfort of the defended harbour. They’d be fools to try such an attack.”

“So it all comes to the great wall,” Constantine surmised. “How many men defend her?”

“Forty-two thousand men.” Karian answered. The two Italian governors looked at each other dubiously.

“Sire,” Trebbianno began in his most diplomatic of tones. “There are seven thousand real soldiers. A handful of locally trained fighting men, but mostly mercenaries from Italy, and a few from the lands of the Rus; the rest are all refugees from the Balkans, local fire-brigades and whatnot.”

“We have an extensive support network,” Karian said, trying to sound positive. “And the wall network has defended us for a thousand years.”

“It’s fallen twice before,” Cardillo countered.

“Once to an earthquake, and that doesn’t count, and the second time to traitors from you country, Don Giovanni.”

Cardillo smiled politely.

“Countrymen who came in smaller numbers and accompanied by less malice than this foe.”

“Enough of that, thank you,” Constantine cut off their little argument. “Trebianno, how much would it cost the imperial treasuries to lease your mercenaries for the next few months?”

“Sir?” Ahmet asked with bated apprehension.

Halil stood like a statue before his bodyguard. Smaller, weaker and older, the old minister still radiated a stony strength of mind that put the tribesman on his guard. He said nothing, but stared into the eyes of Ahmet. The cook left the room quietly without excusing himself.

“Are you alright, Pasha?” Ahmet asked again.

“Pasha?” Halil asked. “That’s a very formal title, young one.”

“You’re an important man.”

“Yes, I am. I’m an important man from an important family. My father and my father’s father before him have been advisors to Sultans since before the sword of Osman stabbed into Europe. Despite that, I’d hoped that you would have considered me to be more than simply a great man. I’ve shown you great kindness, haven’t I?”

“Yes, Pasha.”

“I saved you from certain death at the hands of the sultan’s minister, Zaganos, the man who killed your brother.”

“Yes…”

“And I’ve promised you an eventual opportunity at vengeance. When this adventure in Constantinople falls apart, Zaganos will suffer the humiliation. The task of his elimination would fall to you. You don’t think that he'll prevail, do you?"

"Of course not, Pasha. I…"

"And how do you repay these acts? I brought you into my house and called you son. What kind of a son are you?"

All of the colour drained from Ahmet's face and he swallowed hard.

"Pasha, I am grateful to you," Ahmet began, but his voice was swallowed by a swelling in throat.

"And you've shown that gratitude by lying with your own mother. The Glorious Qur'an proscribes death for that sin. What do you say? Do you agree with God's law?"

"Pasha, I'm sorry," a whirlwind of thoughts stormed through his mind. His crime with Ayshe, his dependence on the poppy, and the murders, especially baby Kareem and Sadullah's son, spun in his brain. "I've wronged you. I've sinned against you."

"Go. Never come back," Halil said quickly and without emotion. "I've brought dishonour to myself and my house, by allowing you in, by trying to help you, I've weakened myself at court, in the eyes of my family and now even my wife. I'll pay for my own sins. But you, Ahmet, son of Ali are to pay for your own. You're banished from the kingdom of Islam. You're forbidden from being a gazi, you must go and live among the infidels, the enemies of God, and await the arrival of destruction. You go and stand in that buring house and wait"

"Pasha,"

"Don't call me that. You're banished from this point on. Take a horse and go. If I hear that you are back in the House of Peace, I'll have you hunted down as a thief and murderer."

Blood and adrenaline raced through Ahmet's veins. He knew that his own disgrace would be more than he could handle. He could flee into the Balkans, but Halil had mentioned his father, Ali. His family would bare disgrace as well.

Unlike all of the other viziers, Halil had no children, extra wives or significant harem, he didn't have the legion of servants that was normally expected of his office, the two of them were completely alone.

"I said go, get out of my sight," Halil repeated, this time with a growing rage.

Ahmet looked him in the eye and took a deep breath.

"I'm so sorry, Halil. God cannot forgive my treachery and sin." And he looked down and closed his eyes. His thoughts went to the daggers in his boot and on his belt. He thought of the shame that would be visited upon his family's house when word reached there, and his father would be cast out of the Sipahi's home. Ruin awaited the humble house of Ali.

Halil looked at him coolly. Ahmet's eyes slowly opened, and he looked at his master. Tears welled in his eyes and his hand gripped the dagger behind his back and contemplated what he saw as his only safe way out.

"I'm so sorry."

"Go!"

Ahmet quickly released his dagger and left the kitchen. His vision was blurry and swallowed sobs that would otherwise have escaped his mouth. He prayed to God that his path would never cross that of Halil Chandarli, ever again, and the Grand Vizier gave a similar prayer. Neither of their wishes were to be favourably received by the almighty.

Three days later, Guistiniano Longo and Hectore Pazzi reported to the office of Count Trebbianno, as they were commanded to do.

"You'd wanted to see me?"

"Yes, events have started."

"Count?"

"The sultan left Adrianopole two days ago, with a hundred and sixty thousand fighting men. They'll be here by the end of the week."

"So it's finally begun," Guistiniano.

"It has indeed, and the emperor has agreed to pay for the services of your boys. You're to take your men and your ships and cross the harbour this morning."

"How are they going to pay for our services? The empire is bankrupt!"

"The city of Galata is guaranteeing the loan."

"The colony treasure or your own?" Guistiniano asked

"That doesn't concern you right now, *cousin*," Trebbianno said with a smile. "The Emperor and I came to an understanding, and you're needed over there. Take down any trappings of Genoa or the Western Empire. You can't compromise our neutrality in any way. If we side with Constantine, then we'll be overrun, the harbour will fall, the wall won't hold and Christianity falls in the east."

"We won't be put under the command of that Venetian dog, Cardillo, will we?"

"No, no! You have to present yourself and your men to General Karian. The Venetians will be fighting under their own banner and under the dubious leadership of the Spanish mercenary, Vincent DiCastillo."

"And our pay?"

Hectore shuffled his feet, trying not to show is anxiety.

"You'll be paid at the end of the campaign. Don't worry the trust is guaranteed in Genoa."

Guistiniano smiled.

"Thank you, brother."

"Thank me when the Turks break, I'd hate to put those coins in your eyes," Trebbianno replied with some understated sarcasm.

"I think I can cross that river myself," Longo answered.

"I'd like to volunteer to go over with Don Guistiniano," Pazzi spoke up. "It would dishonour me as a Christian to stay here while the Holy City is lain siege."

"No," the Count said adamantly. "You'll be needed here."

"Sir, I…"

"Your devotion is admirable, but you're needed here, Hectore."

"Of course, Your Grace," Pazzi held his tongue and decided to bide his time for now. There was still an Emperor's wealth stowed away somewhere in the capital, and one way or another, it was going to finance a new Pazzi dynasty.

The captain-general spoke in his most doting and dutiful tones, but knew that he had to leave from that point on. There isn't much that can convince someone of his rank to desert a post, but Adam Karian was hiding the wealth of nations somewhere across that harbour, and he was determined to find it.

The Ottoman fleet stationed in Gallipoli set sail on March 25, 1453; two days after the army left Adrianople. Admiral Baltaolu stood at the helm of the flagship and looked to the Eastern horizon as he sailed against history. Ezera looked backwards in horror. Among the hundred and nineteen other ships, he saw the spirit of chaos emerge from the black depths of the cold spring sea and bat the ships from side to side. The hirelings were mostly unemployed fishermen and landless peasants, with no idea how to row in cadence. Oars clashed against oars on the same ships, barges were swinging dangerously close to one another and the brisk breeze of the day created waves for which the green crews were unable to properly cope.

Time and again, he had warned Baltaolu as to the need to train his teams, at land and then at sea. The Admiral had dismissed his claims and warned him that if he continued to cast doubt as to his command or the campaign, that he would be tried by what he called "the justice of the seas." This did little to encourage morale among the skippers, many of whom had now begun speaking to Ezera about how to properly train crews and prepare for the inevitable events such as naval combat.

The old pirate surmised that given six months and total command, he could have turned the fishermen and croppers into the first great professional fleet under the crescent since the Arabs sieged the city seven centuries prior. That possibility having evaporated, his survival rose to be the utmost priority. Since victory was a complete impossibility for the untrained navy, his survival would have to depend on his escape, or the removal of his admiral.

'God, thy will is hard, but it shall be done,' Vincent prayed quietly in the chapel in Giovanni Cardillo's manse. His wards, his wife and his sister, had both been taken care of, only he remained. Ella, Daria and their daughter Alexandra had been sent to stay in the colony of Galata (He was as yet unaware of Ella's rather rash decision to stay). *'Give us the strength needed to weather the storm. May our enemies be guided to our shores like waves to a cliff, and may they break as waves. May their terrible strength and vicious fury be feverously resisted. If the darkness of this storm blocks all light from the sky, we will remember that there is a light that can never be extinguished, and that the beacon of your grace will guide us through the storm. And once it has passed, as all things come to pass, may we once again bask in the warmth of your sunshine and never take that simple joy for granted again. Amen.'*

Giovanni waited politely for Vincent to finish.

"You still do that," the governor stated. "Even when there isn't anyone to watch."

"Yes, Sir," Vincent answered, equally politely. "You can see, and maybe you'll stop courting disaster and realign yourself to the church that you advocate and defend so valiantly."

Giovanni looked as though he were about to stab his lieutenant with words on the subject, but he quickly decided against it. They'd had the argument enough times that it didn't need to be rehashed in the lengthening shadow of an impending war. He chose instead to the change the topic.

"Do you think you'll have a problem with Guistiniano?"

"Yes," Vincent answered truthfully. "He's a sharp mind, but an insufferable soul. We need his men, and his expertise, but I'm not looking forward to breaking bread with him.”

“You don’t have to be his friend, Vincent. Just listen to him when you need to.”

Vincent nodded, he understood that well enough from past experiences with similarly infuriating individuals. He recalled younger days, with Ezera.

“Do you think that they’ll arrive tomorrow?”

“No,” Vincent answered. “They’ve already arrived. We can see their camp fires at night. They’ll be on our doorsteps *en masse* shortly, but they won’t set up during the day. For the sake of dramatics they’ll set up at night. They’ll wait for the rising sun to show off their numbers and their might, and hope for that surprise will help cow us into surrender. That’s what they did last time.”

“I don’t know, Vincent. All of my sources tell me that this new sultan, Mehmet, is a different kind of man.”

“No, sir,” Vincent replied without room for debate. “They’re all the same. Every Bulgar Tsar, every Turkish Khan, every Arabic Sultan and every Persian Shah. They’ll attack. And once they’ve thrown themselves against the city to their own exhaustion, like all the others, they’ll crawl back to their dark caves, like all the others. This city is a monument to Eternity and the Queen of Cities is dedicated to the Queen of Heaven. Our victory’s been assured since before the first arrows flown or swords unsheathed.”

“Are you becoming even more religious on me, Commander? You’ve spent enough of your life killing your fellow Christians.”

“This is different, Sir,” Vincent insisted. “This is the defence of Christendom. Don’t you feel that in your bones? That’s the Holy Spirit there to guide us to victory.”

“I feel the cold of winter stored tightly in my bones. I’ll feel the Holy Spirit only when I see the backsides of their retreating army, and I’ll thank you to keep that in mind.”

“Don’t worry, Sir,” Vincent said in a reassuring voice. “I’ve enough faith for both of us on this one.”

Mario stumbled down the stone steps of the barracks attachment to Chora Monastery. Through a sleepy haze he hurried to the narthex door, where his unexpected guest was waiting for him.

“Lord Karian,” he greeted the megadux by bowing and kissing the grand duke’s ring.

"Good evening, doctor," Karian replied.

In the moonless darkness of the night, the only light to illuminate their encounter came from the torches held by three Varangian body guards.

"The campfires of the enemy are in sight of the wall," he began slowly. "The battle will start when the sun rises. There are a lot of them. More than we'd anticipated."

Mario said nothing, but listened.

"This monastery is special, Doctor," Adam looked the Italian in the eye. "You need to understand that. In the event that the Turks storm the gates, and break through at Charisius (the gate nearest the monastery), I need you to do exactly what I say. Can you do that?"

"Of course," Mario answered immediately, if suspiciously. "What is it?"

"You need to surrender the hospital. You have to offer to treat their wounded."

"What?"

"This church is built on a hill, Doctor. There are secret doors and cupboards and hollows that you don't need to know about. We've hidden bibles, religious tracts, manuscripts, illuminations and trinkets in there; nothing of value to a marauding soldier who wants something shiny to spend on a wild night. If the Turks find these, they'll just burn them. In the event that the city falls, we'll come back here in peacetime, and fetch the legacy of Cominius. Civilization and Christendom have to weather this storm."

"I understand," Mario said. His eyes focussed on a place far away. Mario was a far cry from being the most political man in a city famed for its intrigue, but he could usually tell when someone was lying to him. Adam Karian spoke to him the way Antonio did, that night in Venice. Defeat was in the air on both evenings, and Adam Karian intended to save what he could for himself, and didn't care about what would happen to others. The parallel was strong enough for Mario to taste.

"Heroes are made of greater things than I, your grace," Mario addressed him the way he was forced to address that despicable Bishop Isaac.

"Don't sell yourself so cheaply," Karian laughed. "I suspect that you're a man with surprises, rather than secrets. But remember that your charges are the wounded, and the church. What goes on beyond these is none of your concern."

"You can count on me, My Lord."

And with those words, Mario was through being a true and loyal subordinate to Antonio of Padua who sold him to save his own position; of Vincent DiCastillo who thought he'd never be good enough for Ella; of the sickly Giovanni Cardillo or the scheming Adam Karian. There was blood in the water, and Mario wanted his piece of flesh.

"Good," answered Karian with a strong nod. "I've been told that about you and I sensed it right away: You're dutiful, honest, and patient, three grand virtues that are in high demand!"

The tree virtues of the servile and the weak were listed off to the unwelcoming ears of Mario Orsini, and they were not received warmly onto his breast.

"Thank you, Megadux. Now, I suppose we should both get ready for tomorrow. The war begins."

Chapter Thirty-Two - The Island

It was the last day of March, and a harsh and brutal storm struck the Aegean, forcing the ships to find refuge. Atypical of the normally hospitable sea, the uppity winds shoved and dragged the three ships for two days before they found the relative shelter in the sound between the Island of Chios and the Anatolian mainland, north of Smyrna.

In the clouded dark of midday, the ships threw themselves against the pebble beach and slid over the round wet stones. Their crews leapt from the creaking hulls and collected ropes as they hit the rain drenched shore. Painfully out of unison, the three ships and their three crews, heaved themselves further up onto land, until their flat-bottomed transports were out of reach from the grasping hands of Poseidon's might.

Still, the rain continued to pelt the men, and returning to shore didn't give them the immediate respite for which they'd hoped. The rain coming down from the sky to their faces was a nuisance, but nothing more. The rain that fell onto the mountain that sloped all the way down to the sea was the greater enemy.

During hot Aegean summer, the sun burnt any significant vegetation that tried to establish itself on the mountain side, which left this part of Chios with little topsoil enough to hold the rainwater. Instead, the runoff tumbled down the hill and turned the ship's respite-bay into a wadi-river for about four days of the year. The sailors aboard were unfortunate enough to find the bay on the fifth of those yearly four.

Next to the mountain, safely away from the wadi's path was a tiny monastic outcropping. A square building, alone between sea and mountain, it's windows sporadically lit by candles and lanterns beaconed the marooned sailors.

"Over there!" A shrill voiced yelled. "We're saved!"

"Anchor the ships to shore first!" a deeper voice retorted, overpowering the first one. The voice belonged to an ancient mariner that demanded compliance, and even in the storm his will was meticulously obeyed. "Anchor down first!"

The three ships were beached whales on the rocks and the anchors seemed redundant, but men scurried like crabs over their precious ships, throwing tarps over decks and dropping anchors against the pebbled ground. There was no telling where the ground would be in comparison to the water when the weather or tide change.

Once the ships were secure, a mob of almost five hundred men began the treacherous rise up to the unknown building.

The doors to the building were opened to let in the refugees from the storm.

"Come in. Bless you," a monk mumbled to each man who entered the building. "Come in and God bless you."

Most of the men smiled politely as they rushed into the dryness. No one had any idea what the old bearded man was saying; it was truly all Greek to them.

"I speak Greek," came the shrill voice from the unscheduled guests. He spoke ecclesiastic Greek with the staccato of the Italian peninsula.

"Welcome, Brother," the bearded priest greeted and kissed him on the cheek. "My name is Iohannes, I am the abbot of this community."

"My name is Bishop Isaac DiNapoli, representing the expeditionary force of the Doge of Venice. I'm here with my brother, Balias," he gestured to another man. We're here on crusade, to help defend Christendom from the wrath of the Turks."

"May God be with you on this quest."

"And also with you."

"I regret that we are but a small abbey and possibly inadequate to the task of lodging so many men."

"Any comfort will be appreciated, Brother Abbot."

"All comforts that can be extended will, Your Grace." Iohannes said with a bow. "I'll have as many blankets as possible brought, though it shan't be enough, I'm sorry to say."

"It'll do, Brother Abbot."

"Though we should be able to give enough porridge to everyone."

"We have millet aboard the ships, we'll replace your stockpile when the rain settles, thank you."

"I'll return when there is food ready to feed you men, Your Grace."

"I look forward to it."

Iohannes bowed, and Isaac returned the courtesy.

"It'd be better to face the wind, than to take shelter among these heretics," Isaac grumbled, almost to himself.

"Peace, brother," Balias reassured him. "They've given us shelter from the storm and are now preparing food for our bellies. We should all have such charity in our hearts."

"They're still heretics. Why should we break bread with them?"

"They're fellow Christians, and if you recall, the Emperor has pledged himself to communion between the Holy See and the Eastern Metropolitans."

"Those promises have been given before. We can't trust these easterners to fulfil their commitments."

"You're right, but that doesn't mean that we should abandon hope. The prodigal sons of the east are finally coming home to the true faith of Rome. We shouldn't chastise them for their centuries of blasphemy, but welcome them back to the table. For three and a half centuries, our Eastern brothers were lost, but they're now found. We should rejoice in that."

"They need to be reminded the price for heresy. All of their dead relatives are now burning in the sulphurous pits of hell for insulting God," Isaac grumbled. His eyes darted about with a fury that was new to him. He saw his enemies everywhere, and lacked the calmness that used to give him such strength.

Balias exhaled angrily.

"If you're not careful, we'll end up before a court again! Now is not the time and place…"

"We are on a mission to protect God's Kingdom, not to be politically expedient! We swore an oath upon the Holy Bible when we left Venice, that we would conduct ourselves, and command our soldiers to protect Christendom and obey God's Holy Law."

"Stop this!" the third man insisted angrily. Captain Francisco was an aged seafarer, who had no direct authority over their mission, unlike the Cardinal and his less-decorated brother, but nevertheless commanded the respect of the five hundred soldiers and sailors huddled together; certainly more so than the two new interlopers in their insular words. Hungry men milled about the entrance hall to the Abbey and were now beginning to take notice of the altercation between two of their leaders. "We're here to ride out a storm, not start a new one!"

Isaac lifted his chin and tilted his brow back menacingly. "God sent that storm to test us!"

"Will you two knock it off!" replied the new complainant. "You're making the men nervous and your fighting is just plain rude!"

"The constable is right. We're here for a short time; our war is still a week away, in Constantinople. There's nothing to gain by fighting now. Accept their hospitality as it's given. Can you do that, My Lord Bishop?"

Isaac glared at the layman in his haughty way.

"You'd sacrifice God's grace for a roof over your head and meal in your belly! You'd have been asleep when the soldiers came for our Lord, you would! But not I! I remain vigilant this time!"

"Bishop," Francisco began. "I will be vigilant in protecting you from your enemies on the road to Constantinople, even though now that enemy be yourself."

"Isaac," Balias said as soothingly as he could in his squeaky voice. "Our fight is not here. Please hold your tongue, and then their emperor will tell their patriarch what he must do. It's *fait accompli*. All you can do is inconvenience us, please make no more of a scene than you have already."

"Fine," the elder brother said curtly. "You'll get no more trouble from me."

Neither of the other men believed him, and they cast doubting glances at him.

"I'm serious," he insisted. "I care not for these ignorant animals. If they are aware of the truth and embrace falsehood, let them prepare to muster into their places in the brigades of hell."

"That's the spirit," Captain Francisco smiled without enthusiasm.

"Are we really to break bread with these heretics, My Lord Abbot?"

"Yes, Grigori," Iohannes replied with mild annoyance. "We will extend them every hospitality, and then they can continue along their way once the storm breaks.

"They're excommunicates," the younger of the two insisted.

"They are, but they number half a thousand and they're not staying. I've invited their leaders to dine with us tonight, during which time you'll be as diplomatic as you are able."

"If they try to practice their heresy here, then we'll need to speak up."

"If they have a service of their own, it won't matter. There is no reason to disturb our peace here."

"This is a bad idea, Abbot."

"What can happen, Grigori? Only one of them speaks Greek and none of us speak Italian, so I'd wager that everything should jump along peacefully, so long as the intention's there."

Grigori's face showed his disapproval.

"Relax, My Friend. They're only here for a night."

Grigori smiled politely, and mentally returned to his worrying and fretting.

"Of course I'll be well behaved!" Isaac snorted to show offence. "I'm quite familiar with how to behave at dinner. I've shared halls with princes and popes, captain. Have you ever been invited to such banquets, *Captain*?"

"There are no princes or popes here," Balias interjected with patience, pushing himself between the captain and cleric. "Because of our status, you don't need me to remind you of how important it is to be polite to our hosts. Isn't that right?"

"He seems to think I need a lesson in manners from him," DiNapoli said pointing to Captain Francisco, "and I suppose that you also think I need a lesson in politics from some vagabond seafarer. Maybe the eastern schismatics here would be so kind as to teach me theology."

"Your brother's far too eager for a fight," Francisco said to the constable. "We should leave him here, have the men keep an eye on him."

"He's still a bishop, Captain, and he's the only one who speaks proper Greek." Balias answered back quickly, irked at the captain's willingness to side-step the proper ecclesiastic authority of their mission. "He's more than capable of putting on a good enough impression."

"Why are we bringing Francisco to the dinner anyway?" Isaac demanded. "He's a tradesman of low-birth and no education. If we bring him, why not the whole unwashed crew?"

"Because I'm the Captain of the three ships, your grace! I'm the one who makes all of the decisions until we reach the capital."

"If we reach the capital."

"If you have the ear of God nestled so tightly between your lips and shoulder, why don't you ask him to change the weather?"

"Do not tempt me or test the Lord, lest you learn just how ferocious God's wrath can truly be!"

"Gentlemen!" Balias interrupted again, this time at his wits end. "Again I say, be nice, behave. We'll meet the abbot and his assistant in a few hours, share a bowl of gruel and a jug of wine, go to sleep, wake up in the morning and leave. You both understand that, don't you?"

Balias was furious at his brother's intentions, but he'd witnessed his elder's formerly famous social graces diminish him into anathema. Over the past six months, the stresses and rigours of Venice had stripped the flesh from the bone of his beloved brother and left a panicking skeleton in their wake.

The problem was that he couldn't be seen to accommodate orders from Captain Francisco, who was shockingly below him in social status. The captain's barking of orders at the church prince was making the newly religious bishop dig his heels in even further in resistance. This phenomenon was ironically why he didn't think that they should press the Greek Rite Christians in the abbey to convert to Latin Rite here and now. If they tried to force their ideology down their throats, the Greeks would insist on sticking to the old ways out of ornery stubbornness, not out of any loyalty to God. If instructed by their own, they would acquiesce.

"Captain, please go and attend to your men, I'll summon you for dinner in a few hours."

"Of course, Captain," Francisco bowed to both of them before turning to leave.

He severely disliked being dismissed like that. He was the captain of three ships, a respected man, and he was used to having his orders be obeyed. Taking two gentlemen along on the trip was frustrating, and Isaac DiNapoli was a boorish fanatic, who was fleeing Venice under some unknown circumstances. Francisco didn't trust the bishop, he seemed more uprooted than pious. Isaac had the hunted look of a cornered street cat, and his brother was constantly trying to calm him down, it was apparently a role for which he had little experience.

Francisco also distrusted the devotionalism that the cleric instilled the soldiers that they were transporting. By Francisco' experience, holy warriors were men for whom all was justified and conscience was abated. All fine and good for war, but an incorrigible nuisance to deal with and transport.

"Don't worry about him," Balias assured Isaac once the captain had left. "He's angry about being marooned here."

"He needs to recall his place."

"That he does, that he does," the younger brother parroted himself. "I know you can handle yourself among these Greeks, I'm only worried that you and Francisco are going to start fighting in front of them. Doesn't give the right impression of Christian unity, does it?"

Isaac smiled. Despite his intemperate character, he had a truly contagious smile.

"Don't worry about me, Brother. Go talk to Francisco and make sure that he can keep that Illyrian temper of his in line."

"I know you'll be fine," he lied calmly with an honest-looking smile on his face. "I'll go talk to Francisco and make him remember that the onus is on him. Thanks for not losing your temper at him."

"Not at all."

Isaac needed to be lied to like that periodically. His ego had to be petted in such a way that he could still believe himself to be the reasonable one, pious and noble, and that everyone else was twisted in their actions and beliefs.

"Good," Balias answered. There would be a time in the future, he knew, when he'd no longer be willing to stroke the growing spiritual mania of his brother, but that was still some time away from now. "I'll go talk to Francisco and make sure he understands."

The chapel of the monastery was dark and cool, but it was dry. The light from the candles and lanterns danced over the reflective glass mosaics, giving the room the illusion of sneaking dawn.

"That's a beautiful piece of art, is it not?" Isaac asked to no one in particular.

"It certainly is, your grace," one of the soldiers answered. He was huddled up in a blanket, but after an hour in the monastery, everyone was feeling much better than they had a few hours prior. "I can feel God's presence here."

"Can you?"

"Yes, Sir," the soldier answered with an enthusiastic nod of his head.

"Well then, I'll ask you to tell me what you see."

"In the painting?"

"In the fresco…painting, yes."

Isaac stepped back from the fresco, and the soldier looked on. There were almost three dozen other soldiers observing Isaac's lesson, all of whom were quite glad that they had not been chosen as the foil of the lesson.

"I see Jesus… he has a halo… and a book."

"Any book?"

"The Bible?"

Isaac nodded. "In which hand?"

"His left."

"Yes, the sinister side. And what of his right?"

"What of it?"

"What's he doing with his right hand?"

"Uhhh... He's doing this," the soldier positioned his fingers with two up and three clutched together, as though he were making the shadow-puppet of a bunny-rabbit.

Isaac smiled that contagious grin of his and the other soldiers chuckled quietly.

"Do you know what that symbolises, my child?"

"A rabbit?"

Everyone, except the bishop, laughed aloud.

"It's a symbol of eastern heresy. The three fingers together indicate the trinity, God the Father, God the Son and God the Holy Spirit. On that count, they believe as we do," and then the Cardinal's eyes narrowed to slits and he raised his hand for all to see with two fingers pointing up. "But here is where they believe folly. The two indicated that they claim Jesus to have been in possession of two natures, to be both wholly human and wholly divine. They believe that he was a mortal man, who ate, drank, and shat, womanized. No more than a dirty sinner himself. They've been taught this by their Muslim conquerors. It is because of things like this: their breaking faith with God, their mimicry of the infidels; that God has forced them under the heel of the enemy. This is what happens when you quietly accept falsehood on equal grounds to truth. Compromise, meeting halfway, is not a rational virtue. Midway between truth and lie is untruth, my noble soldiers of Christ."

"You mean these monks aren't Christian?" one of the soldiers asked.

"Oh, they believe that they're Christian. They believe this because they've wandered so far from the truth that they no longer know truth from lies. We shouldn't hate them for their confusion, but we shouldn't support their confusion. We're here to bring them back into the embrace of God, and into the communion of the one and only institution of God's grace, the holy church. Remember the importance of what we're doing. We're saving them, not only from the infidel, but from themselves as well."

The soldiers all nodded knowingly.

"So tell me then, Is this a beautiful piece of art?" Isaac re-asked the same question to a new soldier.

"No, your grace," he answered with strength. "I see only filthy heresy."

"Good answer," the Cardinal concluded. "Now I have a question for everyone. What do we do when we are confronted with vile heresy?"

"Don't worry, Francisco. I know how to handle my brother," Balias reassured the Captain. "He just needs to be shown some proper respect, and then we'll be fine until the next crisis."

"People like him make crises," Francisco answered back quickly. "He's the last kind of person you want with you on a mission like yours. He's a fanatic, he can't work with you or me. How's he going to work with Venetians and Genoese, let alone a Greek army!"

"From what I've heard, there isn't much of a Greek army with which we need to contend."

"It doesn't matter how many soldiers they field…"

Francis was cut off by the sound of stone hammering on stone in the next room.

"What's that?"

"I don't know," Balias answered. "Let's go."

Without another word, the two men bound into the hall and barrelled towards the chapel in which the majority of their company was barracked. They almost tumbled over each other as they slammed through the door and into the chapel.

Aghast, they looked at the ground on the far wall. Across the ground were strewn bits of painted plaster and stone. Upon the wall was a stony grey hole where once a masterwork had stood. A lolly-gagging crowd of soldiers looked on, not sure whether or not they had gone too far.

"Brother, what have you done?" Balias asked breathlessly.

"God's work!" Isaac shouted back triumphantly.

Grigori stepped into the chapel to see what the commotion was and stopped dead in his tracks. And that was when things got really out of hand.

Francisco had wanted nothing to do with the monks. He had wanted to sleep on land, and get back to the job of bringing his mob to Constantinople. Once the hammer had fallen upon the wall, that goal was unattainable. There would be no polite dinner, no friendly rapprochement, and no talking his way out of this. The only way out of this situation would be to go forcefully through it.

"Get him!" Francisco called out, pointing at Grigori. "Quickly!"

A small group of sailors leapt onto the unsuspecting monk and tackled him to the ground with ease.

"What are you doing?" hissed the younger DiNapoli.

"My hand is forced," Francis replied. "We can only commit now."

"This is madness!"

"Perhaps," the captain acknowledged before barking instructions at the other men.

"You two, hold him here! The rest of you, tear this monastery apart until you find every lying, thieving monk you can grab with whatever force is needed and bring him here! Do it now! Search every room, and come back here quickly!"

As the men ran out into a frenzied hunt throughout the monastery, Isaac sauntered over to the captain, with a magnanimous look on his face.

"It seems that you can be conscripted into God's duties after all, Captain."

"Not another word from your mouth. Because of you, Christian blood will be spilt by Christian steel tonight, and if you're not careful, God will find yours among it."

"I assure you that they are not true Christians, so my conscience is clear, Captain. As will be those of all our noble soldiers of the cross."

"Why have you done this?!" Balias exclaimed, his naturally shrill voice tightened by the strain of exasperation. "It's so unnecessary!"

"It is necessary!" Isaac hollered back at his own flesh and blood. "We are all soldiers in this holy crusade! We need no allies but God! Any compromise is sacrilege, and can only result in us losing favour with our Lord."

"Just shut up!" Francisco yelled at him.

The two soldiers who'd stayed behind shuffled their feet and pretended not to hear as their captain continued to berate their cleric.

"We'll detain the monks until we leave, then release them," the captain growled commandingly. "In the meantime we'll plunder the building. Fifty percent of the loot will be divided among the crew, as per contract, thirty percent goes to myself, and twenty goes to the commissioner of the endeavour. You, Balias, are the representative of the senate of Venice here, so that means you. That leaves nothing for the good Bishop who started this whole ugly situation. Do you ever wonder why the Greek Christians don't care much for their Latin cousins, Your Grace?" Isaac shook his head in disgust at the Captain. "Your lust for gold is why you'll get none."

"You'll receive nothing of the plunder," Isaac said mater-of-factly. "For we're on a mission to honour God, not men. As such, our papal dispensation means that all gold and other treasures seized will not go to enrich the lives of mortal men, but of our immortal church."

"By immortal church, you mean yourself and the princes of Rome?" Francisco asked.

"I mean the church. Maintenance of God's administration costs money, brothers. And by denying the monies given to you by God for the church, you are committing the sin of stealing from the church. On pain of excommunication, and permanent imprisonment in the bowels of hell, I will justly claim all the plunder from this raid."

"Ha!" Francisco called back and turned to Balias. "Your Brother's an unconscionable mercenary! I wonder what the cost would be of selling you?"

The constable and captain stared icily at each other for an instant before Francisco again interjected himself.

"This is what I like about you clerical types!" he claimed sarcastically. "You are free to murder, rape and steal. There are no laws of God or man that apply to you, because of your favour in the church. That means one of two things to me. Either you are truly Christ-like when you sin in these most vicious and depraved manners, or you truly know that it's all shit, and nobody'll ever punish you for acting in such a deplorable manner. Tell me, *Your Holiness*, which one is it?"

"You risk your soul, Captain," Isaac answered back.

"You'd be an expert on that, would you?"

Isaac's face had an ugly mask upon it, like a lean and starving winter-wolf that just eaten it's fill for the first time in months.

"I'll tell you this, priest," Francisco continued. "If you try to get between these men and their money, they'll kill you. Their religious devotion isn't as strong as you think. Just because you've absolved them of sin, don't think that they have any more conscience than you!"

"I'm not the one confused on the motives of men, Captain."

The night winds swept the clouds from the sky and sent them racing over to Anatolia. The soldiers and sailors of the Venetian expeditionary force emerged from the monastery and met the shining sun of morning. Out of the dark cocoon they emerged, their souls steeled by the knowledge that they were an uncompromising force. They had been tempted by Satan overnight, and they had survived.

When God was proud of his servant Job, Satan tempted God. A lofty plot for a lowly demon, but such was God's pride in his servant. Satan believed that even this pious servant of God would turn his back to the Lord if he experienced enough duress. So Satan attacked him with boils, with rain, with beasts of the earth and monsters of the sea. Job kept the faith and was rewarded by God.

Bishop Isaac DiNapoli told the men how the serpent had become more subtle in the years since then. Truly, it was Satan who sent the storm to instil fear in the hearts of the men. Surely it was the Devil's work that brought them to the Isle of Chios and to the monastery. There, the Devil offered a warm bed, warm soup, shelter from the storm. All the men had to do to receive the benefits, was break bread with heretics; men of false faith.

The men refused and kept the faith of Job. They found no comfort in the fruits of Satan, and for that were all named as Knights of Christ once it was time to re-embark upon their ships. The men were proud at their award from the bishop, so much so that they didn't mind carrying the plunder, content that it would be used for God's purposes, under the watchful stewardship of Isaac.

With deeds done, with piety restored by rage, wrath and blood, the ships returned to bring their gifts of faith to the people and the struggle of Constantinople.

Chapter Thirty-Three - The First Day

April 6, 1453

Dawn stretched itself westward over the land. The silhouettes of men emerged from the darkness. The first to form out of the void were the soldiers of the combined Christian armies. Perched atop the long double-walls of the capital, they turned their faces to the spring sun, and let it warm them from the cold night. Looking then westward, they saw the massive challenge before them emerge. The light of day crept over the thick inner wall, its stout octagonal towers, and storied gates defended the citizens within from the sight of the outside world. After that wall was ten metres of potential killing ground, cordoned off by the outer wall; a small space in which any attacker would have to set up siege equipment. That gap was what turned a hundred armies to flight, because the outer wall which would have to be scaled in order to reach that killing ground was tall, flat, and far too thick to knock down by ballistae, catapult or trebuchet. In front of the outer wall was a moat. It wasn't deep or wide, but any invading army would have to wade or swim through the cold April water, carrying ladders and scaling equipment to get to the wall, set up their ladders from the moat and climb the wall to get into the killing field, in order to set up the scaling equipment yet again for the second set of walls. All things being equal, it would take an entire day for an group, and that's without any defenders firing arrows, quarrels, darts, knives, bullets and shot down on them. The defending army was hardly without their advantages.

On the other side of the moat, the shifting figures were noticeable in the dark of night. As the morning sun bent over the top of the wall, the mass became more detailed. Banners emerged, tents that had been set up hastily in the night had their poles re-vetted. Whinnying horses added their voices to a Babel of humanity on the doorsteps of Jerusalem's heir. They were out of range for the bows and muskets of Constantinople but the sight was still frightening to behold. A new day was upon the Queen of Cities; Lucretia awaits Tarquinius.

The inside of the city was a true shock to Ahmet, who rode his brown horse quickly along the cobble-stone roads. He'd seen it once before, from across the harbour, and then it was only a series of walls and towers to his eyes. Now, it was a mish-mash of settlements. More like a thousand little communities grouped together around churches and connected to each other through guarded highways. It contrasted so sharply with the more compact and functional Adrianopolis. The beauties that he rode by, the palaces and the churches, were more beautiful than anything he'd seen before, contrasting to the muddy spring roads and random squalor were something equally perplexing to him.

He'd entered the city last night, only hours before the gates closed in the face of the army marching from the north-west. Both he and his mount were exhausted, so he cautiously found a tavern in the first built up area of the city. He knew no one, he knew none of the sights nor sounds of the Christian capital, and the only words that knew in Greek were general purpose expletives that would be of limited assistance. He knew that there was a mosque by the harbour. There, he could find people who could help him, and he struck off in that direction once the sun rose.

Ahmet had fled from Adrianople without any kitting. His only real friends, his bows, swords and lances were back in the home of his old master, the Grand Vizier Halil. He had a horse, elaborate clothes (he was dressed for a formal state procession when he found himself banished), and a pouch full of electrum. The electrum coins in his possession were the same alloy of silver and gold that the Byzantines used, but they were stamped with Arabic calligraphy, proclaiming the universal rule of Islam, rather than that of Constantine, as such Ahmet didn't want to go spending or showing them about town.

He noted in disapproval the pain in his back from sleeping in the public house he found the night prior. There was a time when he could easily sleep in the forest, his time in the palace had apparently softened him.

He trundled through the collection of villages and communities that made up the city until he reached the Venetian Quarter, overseeing the harbour. The quarter was cordoned off with armed guards, who yelled at Ahmet as he tried to pass. They tried at least three different languages on the wandering Turk, none of which he understood. The armoured guard eventually out of simple desperation allowed him to pass into the Turkish panhandle of the city.

Once in the panhandle, he set about finding the elusive Osman, a long burrowed thorn in Mehmet's side. There was one minaret in the district, and no great man could be great without the greatness of God. Ahmet trotted briskly to the mosque and found Prince Orhan, son of Beyazit and grandson of Mehmet the First, holding court outside the mosque.

The man looked like a clown, a poor mockery of his young cousin,

Mehmet. He wore a turban, poofed up to a ridiculous degree. Ahmet chuckled at the thought of what a handsome sight it would be to watch him pass through a doorway. His moustache was greased outwards menacingly to look like horns, and he walked with a girth to show his wealth and status. In Ahmet's eyes, he was fat, vulgar and corrupt – the worst of palace glory, but without the culture and grace. Ahmet cursed his own luck that had led his life to the point where he needed to petition a man such as he for patronage.

"Peace be upon you, Prince," Ahmet announced as he rode up to a gathering of twenty men, mostly old men who were there to pay daily respect to their "great leader," who'd lost any real claim to greatness when he'd accepted the status of refugee. There was a religious precedent for his status, the Prophet Muhammad himself had been forced to seek refuge in Medina, when his violent opponents tried to hunt him down in Mecca. The Prophet grew powerful in captivity, and eventually led an army from Medina to crush the soldiers of Mecca at the Battle of Badr. Prince Orhan was received in Constantinople with considerably less warmth than he'd hoped and little opportunity to march on Adrianople.

"Peace be upon you, Gazi," the prince raised a hand return the salute. "You bear the countenance of a messenger, have you brought be news."

"I bring the possibility of great news," Ahmet said once he'd dismounted and given the reigns of his horse to one of Orhan's courtiers. "My name is Ahmet of Amaseia, son of Ali. I am not a messenger, but a warrior. I bring to you a sword, not crusted with jewels but forged in bone and sharpened on flesh. I offer you my services of arms. I have come to seek a place at your court."

Ahmet knelt the way his master Halil had taught him and kissed the hand of the pretender prince. In the instant that the tribesman bent his knee and averted his eyes, Orhan gave a quick look to one of his less elderly advisors. Ahmet didn't actually see the look, but he could tell it had taken place by the way the prince's hand tightened, and the stiffness in the councillor who looked away. In an instant of friendly pleasantries and presumptions of fealty, Ahmet identified immediately that he was surrounded by enemies.

"Word of your valour has reached far and wide, Gazi Ahmet," Orhan said magnanimously. His obtuse moustache seemed like a mockery of a smile. "Even far away here, we have heard of your tales. Your presence comes with a warning, Ahmet, son of Ali."

Ahmet knelt motionless in the early spring mud. He could sense movement around him. He counted in his mind the men-at-arms that were around the uncrownable prince. At no point would he avert his eyes from the ground in front of him, to do so would violate rules of protocol, so he was forced to tally men through his peripheral vision. It was like he was hunting from the Rookery back in Amaseia. He was perfectly still, while he heard words that were designed to buy time for those who surround him, so that he could be captured and ensnared.

"I was under the impression that you served another master: Halil Chandarli - the corrupt servant of my beloved uncle who now serves that imposter, my honourless but blooded kin, Mehmet. I didn't fall for these sweet words last autumn, and I won't be do so today. Are you planning on infiltrating my court, and then delivering me to your master?"

"That's not true," Ahmet said at a whisper. His eyes had glazed over and he was preparing himself. Blood was floating in the air, all that was needed was the storm of Ahmet's rage to cast it down onto the earth.

'Best not to kill today,' Ahmet thought to himself. *'I can't stand to be hunted, and the siege is about to start. Flight is my best option. These are all old men, no young soldiers serve him, only old loyalists from lost campaigns.'*

"If you don't require my service, Lord," Ahmet began slowly, rudely raising his gaze to meet that of the Prince. "Then I will take my leave and let you and your men be in peace."

"I'm sorry, but I can't allow that," Orhan said with an arrogant smirk. Your master's plan has backfired, and he'll have to pay dearly to get his prized assassin back."

Ahmet smiled calmly at Orhan. Unbeknownst to the prince, he had said some golden words to the tribesman's ears. Once he had said that he wanted him taken alive, Ahmet knew that his life wasn't in danger from swords or spears. A brawl against a half-dozen soldiers who were decades past their prime was not something to strike fear in his heart.

"So be it," Ahmet concluded in his calm baritone, as four of the six old, fat bodyguards descended upon him.

Two spearmen stood back, as not to get in the way of their compatriots who jumped onto the opportunity to reaffirm their worth. For many years, they had idly served their master, a task that consisted only of trying to look menacing, as there weren't many threats to the royal person within the panhandle. Their task had never been a difficult one until now.

Ahmet sprung up from his knelt position, just as the four guards were upon him. Away from them meant that he'd lunge straight at the Prince himself. The guard beside him was holding a spear, the dangerous point was too far up the shaft the spear of any use once Ahmet closed the gap, so he wasn't a huge concern to the tribesman. Ahmet raised his foot quickly in the form of a foot-jab, directed squarely towards the Prince's chest. The thrusting power of the strike came mostly from his back leg, with added thrust from his hips. This caused his foot to pivot and he to face the spearman after Orhan fell back.

The force of the kick threw the prince to the ground, separated Ahmet from the four men who were about take him, closed the gap between him and the first spearman, and caused a distraction that threw the city square outside of the mosque into an instant panic. The panic suited Ahmet well.

Orhan hit the ground hard on his back, and his bodyguard gripped his spear to counter attack, but Ahmet was a metre away, too far inside for the spear to be much good. The spearman tried to take a step back to make space, but Ahmet continued with momentum and brought his leg around, kicking with the shin-blade into the upper-leg muscle group of the retreating guard. This caused him to fall over, trip over a drum and into the mud. His spear fell from his hand and the wooden shaft split under its owner's weight.

Ahmet didn't see this to verify. He didn't need to, he heard the snap. He spun around immediately to catch the first of the other guards charging him. A big guard with a grey moustache was sprinting to him, trying to mimic Ahmet's success against the prince and his guard. The man was barrel-chested and twice as big around as Ahmet, though the guard was a half a head shorter than his intended prey.

Ahmet leapt directly at him, forcing the collision between the two a tempo sooner than the guard had anticipated. That brief second was time enough for Ahmet to jab through what limited guard the man possessed, stopping him cold just long enough for the Ahmet to continue with a second punch, this time a right hook that struck the side of the poor bastard's neck, just under his jaw line. The rotund guard staggered for an instant and Ahmet swung another right hook, this time solidly to his jaw bone, knocking the man over, his head spinning further around than his bone structure would normally allow.

Ahmet looked around for the first time and quickly took stock, the first spearman had thrown himself overtop Orhan, effectively removing him from the conflict, one of the four footmen was unconscious on the ground, the other three were closing in on him quickly. The second spearman was trying to wade through the crowd to get to the melee. He could avoid considering him for the meantime. Ahmet judged that he had a split second before two of the three standing guards reached him, so gave a good strong kick to the guard on the ground. There was no sense in running the risk of him re-entering the fray.

The third guard swung a wild arm at Ahmet, trying to ensnare him. Ahmet was the strongest fighter in the fray, but if the guard could hold him at neutral, his friends could finish the job. Fortunately for Ahmet, he could see that coming, and he countered by stepping back, just out of range of the wild arm, letting the momentum carry the other man for an instant, and then stepping in with a stern, harsh knee to the bollocks. The attacker doubled over and collapsed.

As he fell, two more collided into Ahmet. This time, Ahmet had neither tap nor tempo, and the two managed to dictate pace. The first collided with Ahmet and found success where his compatriot had found air. He managed to wrap an arm around his target's waist and grab on tightly. Despite Ahmet's attempts at slipperiness, his attacker wrapped his arms around him and locked his fingers. Given time, Ahmet could pry himself free of the simple hold, but the other attacker threw an open handed strike at his head, boxing his ear. Ahmet barely held on to consciousness. His eardrum rang like a trumpet, he writhed against the grip like a snake thrown into a fire, and his equilibrium dropped to the point that he couldn't offer much resistance to the man wresting him in place. His knees buckled and the world started spinning.

If not for the inexperience of the two older men attacking him, Ahmet would surely have been taken prisoner. The man who threw the ear boxing strike stood to observe his handiwork for just an instant, and what transpired in his mind was the briefest of victories, quickly transformed by Ahmet's quick reaction.

While being held fast around the waist by one guard, Ahmet raised his feet quickly and struck the other man, the one who'd struck him, down to the ground. His kick did very little damage to the person of attacker, but it was enough to push the striker away, and push Ahmet and the man holding him to the ground. The momentum of the collision to the ground gave Ahmet enough grease to push out of the trap-hold and see the whites of his attacker's eyes. He couldn't raise his arms enough to punch, and his legs were equally pinned in the octopus of humanity that held the two of them together on the ground. Ahmet could make luft enough to raise his head and leverage a head butt, which was short and without adequate force. Ahmet could sense the striker converging on them quickly, so craned his neck and bit the cheek jowl of the man who held him. The man screamed and released his hold, Ahmet rolled up in enough time to meet the charging striker.

Before Ahmet was fully on his feet, he lunged forth and used his unusually long reach of arm to swing wide and collide an open hand of his own to the man's head, right at the ear.

'*Serves you right, you fat old bastard*,' Ahmet though to himself. It was his first really conscious thought since the fray had begun. Conscious thought was usually the enemy of vicious fighters. Ahmet would consider this a sign that he was getting old.

Ahmet would have continued his assault on the man, but the second spearman had finally arrived on the scene, and tried to stab at the interloper from Adrianople. Ahmet had to sidestep the spear blade, back away from the striker, worry about the rising man on the ground with the bleeding cheek from Ahmet's bite, and ignore the ringing in his head.

Again, the inexperience of the older guards was helping the younger fighter. The second spearman over-thrust his spear, and Ahmet was fleet enough to side-step. A spear is a great weapon when used properly, when there is a distance of a metre or two between the combatants. It can reach over a rank like in a Greek phalanx or keep an attacker at bay. The problem with a spear in melee is that it becomes a liability when the range is closed. Ahmet jumped the length of the spear from where he narrowly avoided the tip, to the middle, where the man wielding it could barely defend himself, able only to use the spear as a blocking timber of wood.

Ahmet grabbed the stave with one hand and crossed with a straight right fist followed by a second, quickly knocking the spearman to the ground and taking his spear. Ahmet hopped back the distance of three paces and extended the spear to keep the three guards at bay.

'*Where's my horse?*' he thought angrily and looked about frantically.

"You'll not lay a hand upon the prince, boy!" The striking guard yelled loftily.

Ahmet looked for an exit to the square and barely noted the conversation. He saw the road upon which he'd entered. His horse had apparently either been taken away or run away in the confusion of the scrap.

"I'm leaving the quarter!" he roared so that everyone in the square could hear him. "Nobody come after me! Your friends are hurt, not dead, and they'll be fine soon! Anyone who follows me won't be so lucky!"

More footmen and body guards started to try to circle him, but he kept them at bay with his spear until he was out of the square, at which point he threw the spear to the ground and ran.

"Chase him," Prince Orhan screeched at his guards. "I'll give a purse of gold to whomsoever brings me that assassin's head!"

In the light of the afternoon sun, the monks of Chora Monastery sought out the darkness of chapel one last time before temporarily abandoning their home as a hospital. The city held itself in an eerie silence when the bells rang over the hilly terrain. Normally, people would ignore the clanging and the chimes, but today there was a siege. Outside of the walls were an uncountable number of men from all nations, Anatolian Turks, Serbian Cavalry, Bulgarian archers, Vlachs and Macedonians had come to their doorsteps, and prayer was something that would best be heeded in this dark hour.

For Mario, the prayer times brought him solace.

It was during these hour or two-hour sessions, that he had the opportunity to search through the church, the monastery, the dormitory, the tannery, the brewery, the kitchens, and search for whatever it was that Karian was hiding. Mario didn't believe Karian for a second about the sacred texts. Whatever it was, he needed it hidden away, and Mario's intellectual curiosity found it offensive that the oriental generalissimo would try to hide something under his accute nose. There was but one building left for Mario to search, and that was the ossuary.

The cemetery of the compound had been large enough to support the community for its first few centuries of existence, but as time wore on, the number of monks who died of old age, disease, and in one instance of an enraged and jealous husband, the corpses began to add up. Land within the city walls was abundant, but the Eastern Orthodox Empire wasn't prepared to lease out new land to the Oriental Orthodox Armenian churches. A minor difference relating to the consubstantial or dual-nature of Christ, was not enough for warfare, purges or heresy pyres, but it was enough to effect land leases. At any rate, the monastery had more bodies than it could handle, so it took to digging up the skeletons of its revered past, drying the bones in a kiln, and storing them in properly labelled shelves in a purpose-built structure, hospitably placed next to the women's chapel.

With bells chiming behind him, Mario Orsini crept into the ossuary and began looking for something. The recurring problem, into which he ran with every location he searched, was that he really wasn't sure what he was searching for.

As a doctor, he was used to corpses, they were an inevitable part of life and death; some men achieved greatness, others did not, all men achieved finality at some point. Bones were less clinical to him. There were no readings to observe, no balances of fluids, only the empty skeleton that once carried the life of a human being. Looking into the hollow eyes of a skull seemed to Mario like wearing a dead man's shoes. It was built to comfort someone else, not you, but you're alone to perceive it. Blood and guts didn't frighten the good doctor, but eternity did. The thought that these bones were lives, great and small, but that they were all pushed out of their one special spot on this earth, by the needs and demands of others who didn't consult them. They were pushed out of their own graves. Mario looked in the eye sockets of a shelved skull.

"That's a hard hand, Friend," he spoke, more to himself than the ghost who haunted the bones. "It won't happen to me."

Through the shelves, he found bones, boxes and other miscellanea, until finally, behind one shelf, he found something that made his heart jump. A glimmer of gold caught some of the sun's rays and reflected it straight at Mario's eye. Mario thrust his arm into the hollow between the shelf and the wall, and took hold of the box, gripping it with the tips of his fingers and jimmying it out of its tomb.

He started to lose consciousness of what was around him. He pulled the box, as long as his forearm, and covered in gold plating close to his chest. He then sat down on the floor, dirtying his long black coat, shaking his finger's as he opened the case.

In it, he found a skeletal hand.

"Damn it! Nothing again!" Mario cursed himself. Even the sheeting that he thought was gold, was in fact an alloy of such poor brassy quality that he cursed himself for being foolish and greedy enough to believe it.

"Are you alright, Doctor Mario?" came a gentle voice from the door to the ossuary.

Mario blanked for a second, panic hitting him as to what to say, before he placed the voice.

"Good morning, Ella," he stammered.

"Good afternoon," she corrected. "What, may I ask, are you doing with our darling saint?"

"Saint?" Mario looked up at her, and then down at the hand, and realised that he was desecrating a reliquary. "I didn't realize what it was, I should put it back."

"Saint Eutyches' hand is the most prized relic of the monastery, I'm sure that you don't want to have the monks angry at you," Ella replied soberly, but with enough of a lurking smile to make Mario seem at ease.

"I've never cared much for relics, many of them are completely fraudulent, you know. Certified for a price, and sold for a higher price."

"So how long were you a priest?" she asked, not quite changing the subject.

"I was never a priest. I took the vows, you have to in order to teach at the university, but I was never an evangeliser or a presbyter. I had no need for a flock."

"I'm sure that you'd have been a fine shepherd."

"A shepherd has two goals for his flock, first to fleece them, then to kill them. I have no intention of doing that to gullible peasants, or pretending that I can cast magic to save their lives."

"Many say that doctors and healers are magicians, of sorts," Ella was carrying on a conversation, but was uninterested in the topic. She had something else on her mind, but Mario was oblivious to human affairs once his big brain got working.

"*Many secrets of arts and nature are thought by the unlearned to be magical,*" Mario quoted to her and laughed. "Roger Bacon said that. My master, Antonio DiPadua, my old master I should say, he would chastise me for quoting him. He believed that no civilization was possible north of the Alps."

Mario smiled and chuckled.

"My beloved sister-in-law would say the same applies across the Adriatic."

"I'm glad that your spirit's strong," Mario said, smiling gently. "Most of Constantinople's citizens have sough refuge in either the church or the tavern."

"I'm a nun and barred from the tavern, so I suppose my decision's been made, and what of you, ex-priest?" she laughed.

"I was thinking of getting a goblet of wine and attending the second half of the afternoon prayers, would you care to join me?"

They both laughed for a minute, before she composed herself and scolded him for blasphemy.

"You shouldn't joke of these things, now is the time when we're to be most prayerful."

"Do you think that prayer alone would save Constantine's city?"

"Miracles have been known to happen, there are precedents."

"Will you marry me?"

That was so out of place that that, that Ella felt as if her prized horse had turned into a cow. She looked at him confusedly, and then started laughing again.

"I'm serious, speaking as a former man of the cloth, to a current nun, what's wrong with that?"

"My brother would never stand for it!" she chortled.

"I'll make you a promise, if we both outlive this war, then God must intend for us to wed, we'll be rich, powerful, and make a quiet life for ourselves and raise a family, perhaps on an island somewhere in the Adriatic, where there are no others to come and spoil our earthly paradise."

"I never thought of you as such a dreamer, Mario."

"But you do think of me, don't you?" Mario asked with a charming smile, gracefully changing the tempo. "I know that I think about you."

"You're hiding something," she stated, this time changing the subject deliberately. She looked into Mario's eyes and her own narrowed slightly.

Mario's first instinct was to turtle away, but much to his own surprise, he held her gaze, and he held his smile. He felt the blood flow to his ears increase, but he made a solemn vow to himself that he wouldn't blush, which is what he would normally do in such a confrontation.

"From the bottom of my heart, I promise you that I'm not hiding anything. Quite the opposite, in fact," he added mysteriously. "I'm what the monks here would call a seeker... of sorts."

She had no idea how to read his enigmatic smile.

"Yes!" Constantine shouted and strutted into his inner sanctum chamber. In the middle of the room was a table with a map of the city drawn across it. Clay figurines sat atop the map and smeared the afternoon's shadows across their field. The room was littered with mechanical devices, games, banners and mementos of Constantine's first half century on the earth, most of which was spent in religious courts in the Morea. A tired looking Adam Karian waited patiently next to the board, where he'd been for the past two hours.

"An emperor's prerogative, Your Majesty," Karian uttered without wasting a breath. "I've used the time here to properly review *your* plans in my mind."

"Review is always good, Strateogos," the emperor said as he took off his coat and handed it to one of the many aids who followed him around, doting about. He liked to address Karian by his military title of strateogos, which outweighed his court title of megadux. The strateogos of the Empire was the supreme commander of all forces, whereas megadux was a landless Armenian grand duke. "Be glad that you have the simple task of a military man, my friend. The politics of court would drive you batty. Lords and ladies, all seeking out a bigger piece of the pie. Thankfully we have some good allies at court."

Adam made no effort to smile. The lords and ladies of whom the emperor spoke were inbred cousins to the emperors, and unfortunately the shadow cast by God upon the earth seemed to believe that politicking with municipal nobility, gentry without land but in possession of lofty titles, was of greater importance than the swath of humanity on their doorstep. Worse still, the allies he referred to were sycophants of the worst order, incompetent men like Stavros of Brussa, who were trying to worm their way into the rotting core of state.

"My liege, you've commanded me to report to you daily, do you still wish this?"

"Yes, I do," the aging monarch said with a smile that he hoped correctly mimicked a combination of wisdom, and the veteranly camaraderie. "Tell me, Old Soldier, is it as bad as those cowards in court say?"

"It isn't a situation to be envied, Your Majesty."

"Tell me how it looks!" he commanded with faux youthful exuberance.

"Well, My Lord," Karian looked at his beautiful map, with the exacting models that had been placed about it, and he sighed, knowing that his emperor would never really understand what it all meant. He immediately considered one of Constantine's favourite pastimes. "This map is like the board of a chess combat, and two armies have now aligned themselves in opposition to each other."

A glimmer of reason and intelligence sparked off the cold stone that had thusfar been all Karian had witnessed of the emperor's interest in the war.

"The Muslim army may well seem like a random hodgepodge to many who look upon it, but it's as meticulous as a chessboard," the general pointed to clay turban on the map-board. "The Sultan is protected at the back, his retinue keeps him safe, and he wouldn't be moving much during the campaign. The tents set up as his headquarters are large, and well-guarded. No one will see the machinations that happened inside, but from the green tents would flow all of the important decisions of the campaign. Mehmet the Second won't be moving until the endgame, until then he'll stay safe and protected.

"The Queen of the Turkish army would be the Janissaries. Under the soup-ladle sceptre here," he indicated the appropriate figurine. "The loyalist corps can move faster and further than any other force on the field. They're in the rear for now, defending their sultan, but when they take the field in motion, there's very little that would be able to stand in their way, and they've had a long tradition of controlling the field, wherever they've been.

"To the north of the city, an army of a different sort mustered. They were the elephants (*bishops in modern English*). They were mostly on horseback, and they've peacefully gathered along the hilltops north of Pera."

"If they're cavalry, wouldn't they be the knights?" Constantine asked with a tone of correcting wisdom.

"No," Adam answered quickly. "Like bishops, their strength was their mobility and their ability to move anywhere quickly. Like bishops who are restricted to one colour or the other, they were forbidden from rough terrain around the headwaters of the Horne, and city walls could hardly be leapt by their horses. They're the tribes and their movements are blocked. They're commanded by Zaganos-Pasha, second minister to the sultan, they're lightly armed and armoured, and within a matter of hours, they could be anywhere, from the Bosporus, to the walls of Constantinople, to the city of Pera and the shores of the great harbour itself. They're mobile, but limited, that's why they're bishops and not knights.

"The knights of the army are the navy here. The strength of knights lies not in its mobility, they don't move far, but in that they can move through defending pieces, slipping in and out of a fray, they can thusly attack many places at once, and it's always a wise strategy to deploy knights to the centre of the board." Adam pointed to boat-shaped model in the south-west corner and moved it to the strut of land on the European bank of the Bosporus on the map. "With this in mind, Admiral Baltaolu, the Turkish commander, is having his flotilla row along the coast so as to catch up with main army by nightfall. We have a spy among them, so we've some very accurate information about them. Their instructions are to take a hold of Diplokion, and from there, they could command the Bosporus, the Princess Islands, the Golden Horne and the southern Sea Wall. They could also fetch supplies for Chalcedon on the Asian shore, should the need arise. The central perch at Diplokion should serve the knight well.

Constantine nodded and squinted at the other pieces.

Rukh is a Persian and Sanskrit word that means "Chariot" and enters our language as Rook.

"The chariot was the supreme war engine of the ancient world, heavy and powerful, it would run down anything that stood in its way. The modern war machines that takes this mantle, in March of 1452 are the creations of that Hungarian smith named Orban whose service you failed to engage, against my recommendations.   It should take him a few days to set up most of the cannons, and his elite treasure '*The Basilisk*' has been carried in more than a hundred parts, but once they're all set up, those cannons'll barrel down straight at the walls of Constantinople with a force against which only our prayers can offer resistance."

Unbeknownst to Karian, the Basilisk was in fact so big, that it would have to be mostly buried into the earth so as not to fly back half-way to Adrianople after each shot was fired.

"In front of all these important land soldiers is a rogue's gallery of Anatolian humanity: the pawns. Aghas and Sheikhs have gathered their extended families as makeshift battalions and dervish orders chanted a procession along the hilly ground from the upper headwaters of the Golden Horne to the choppy sea of Marmora. The largest contingent of all are the Bash-i-bozuks – the broken headed. These men are mostly criminals, released from prisons with an offer to receive their freedom. The others are beggars, rounded up from their city squares, would-be mercenaries who couldn't find an army to join and miscellaneous adventurers. There was no uniformity to their appearance or kit, and they added to the Turkish army's reputation of *horde*. These are the pawns, set up at the front, potentially dangerous, but not as of yet. For now they are just a multitude."

"This seems like a strong army to stand in opposition, General," Constantine noted.

"Alas, the Christian armies have been set up with less precision," he conceded. "We're in no position to attack the Ottoman horde in any way, as we've built up a Greek defence that's designed to cover our attackers rather than attack them. You're the king, here in the castle, which is unfortunately dangerously close to the wall. I know that you don't want to move, but I think that you'll have to as the siege drags on. The pawns are our city auxiliary, untrained in combat and shouldn't be trusted not to flee and be slaughtered if they were confronted by any serious threat. The rook would be the city walls that can stop any assault.

"The two knights of the Risen Christ would have to be Venice and Genoa. The two mercurial players are both handicapped by being either partially or wholly neutral in the campaign. They could change their positions far too quickly to be counted out, but they wouldn't play an equal role. It's the mercenary professional soldiers of Venice that man the land wall. Their muskets, pikes and swords can guard the wall and prevent anyone from storming over the wall or through the gates. The knights over in Galata would prevent the enemy bishop from sweeping across the unassuming sea wall, or enemy knight from finding too much comfort on its roost in Diplokion.

"The defending bishop is the Roman and Italian fleet. While they'll be trapped in the harbour during the opening phases, the attacking fleet would be trapped at Diplokion to match them. If the attacking fleet abandoned the town to attack the Marmora sea walls, then our fleet would be allowed to strike at Chalcedon, or they could isolate ships from their untrained fleet. This is our strategy: to grind the siege to a halt as quickly as possible. We have enough food stored away that the city could survive for a year, or possible two. We don't know for certain how well provisioned the Turks are, a hundred thousand people need a lot of food, and they don't work for free. Two years would be more supplies than we defenders need, and more time than they can afford."

Unbeknownst to the two participants in this discussion, their strategy was exemplified by the German word *"zugzwang."* Zugzwang means *'forced to move'* and its connotation in chess is that since players are forbidden to pass on a turn, they must move every turn, and a player is in zugzwang when any move they do will result in lost material. Constantine and Karian were conspiring to force Mehmet into such a position.

"Your Majesty's army formed an iron shell, into which the Turks would have to crack. If they try to wait out the great city, they'd be forced to disband and go home. If they try to force the merciless walls, they'll be cut down by our glorious defenders. If they try the harbour, they risk war with Genoa and the Western Empire. If they try to strike at southern walls, they'd open up the sea lanes and allow our navy to pick them off and bleed them in small numbers. Waiting out the storm was a strategy that has served us well in past years.

"Since they have opening initiative, I suppose they're white and we're black," Constantine said with a smile.

"Yes, Sire."

"Do you think that they have a chance at victory?"

"Yes, sire, a very strong one."

"And us?"

"Less strong, but still present. Yes."

"What do you think we would need for victory?"

Karian now made the effort to smile.

"That bad?" Constantine asked.

To punctuate the point, a crack of thunder reeled over the hills and leapt over the city walls to reach their ears. It was followed by an explosion of stone as the first granite cannon ball smashed into the first tower, filling the evening air with dust.

"My God!" Constantine called out. "They're attacking!"

"No, Sire," Karian replied slowly. "They're testing their range. They won't start the attack until tomorrow."

Chapter Thirty-Four - The Second Day

April 7, 1453

For most of the city, the first day of the fateful siege was dominated by a horrendous quiet. Each neighbourhood of the city would function as if it were its own independent municipality, and the municipal auxiliaries called out for a mass muster. Everyone reported for their feudal duties. Many were relegated to fetching water for the soldiers on the walls. Those boys who were neither too young nor too old were readied for street fighting, should it come to that. Most of the auxiliaries were tasked with loitering about the Forum of Saint Romanus and waiting to be put to some use.

The rest of the metropolis became a city of women. They walked freely about the streets, toddling about and seeing only each other. Some women tried their hand at running their husbands' shops and some sparse commerce happened, but not enough to call the day typical. The city had always been fairly free for women to roam about, unlike many other places on earth, but all of a sudden there were no alleys that were barred or neighbourhoods wisely avoided. The unwittingly feminized city took on a new character, and no one was quite certain as to how they should best respond to the change.

What a shocking difference in comparison to the other side of the walls. Inclusively, there were more than two hundred thousand men gathered for the event. The army was mono-sexual in the descriptive sense, as it was only men. No women cooks, the comfort women that usually followed armies were barred, the extended families that would normally accompany the tribal factions were told to stay at home, lest they lead their soldierly men to distraction. The army assembled under the banner of Sultan Mehmet the Second was composed of men, mostly between the ages of fourteen and thirty, with a few younger children in the Bashi-bozuks and a few older veterans in the Janissaries and tribes.

That first day was quite uneventful for the citizens, but the besiegers were full of movement. They had felt tents to set up, twelve great mess tents and a granary; the horde would eat a lot. Latrines had to be established near the upper estuary of the Golden Horne and by the north shore of the Sea of Marmora, all that food had to go somewhere; the last thing the Ottomans wanted was for the inevitable outbreak of disease to arrive sooner rather than later.

The diggers, conscripted out of occupied kingdom of Serbia, began their tasks right away. First, they had to make earthen casings for the cannons. Bronze was used to make cannons, and bronze (an alloy of copper and tin) is heavier and stronger than iron, and cheaper and more pliable than steel. The strength was needed for their destructive purposes. Because of the use of bronze, rather than the lighter steel that could be mounted upon carriages, the cannons had to be entombed in the ground, surrounded by earth to prevent recoil or shifting. Once they were held tightly, they could be tested for range and accuracy. This was a frustrating task for the artillery men, and horrifying to the soldiers on the wall who witnessed volley after volley crash before the outer walls, or over their heads into the city behind them, ready to randomly fall on field or fountain, moor or mountain, breaking the morning quiet. Once the diggers had finished installing all of the cannons, they would start upon building tunnels to undermine the walls.

Rounding the walls to the north of the city, Zaganos-pasha commanded the hill country of Pera. While he himself stayed at the field headquarters just north of Galata, his mostly mounted tribesmen had many advantages that were denied the main army. They had the use of Roman Castle as a barracks, as well as a store house. They could receive supplies quickly from the Black Sea before sending it to the Sultan's army, and because the Anatolian levies that he commanded were a smaller number, the logistical nightmare of feeding and looking after them was much lighter than the heavy weight upon Halil's shoulders who was administering the larger camp.

The third Ottoman command was perhaps the simplest, logistically speaking. Baltaolu commanded a hundred and twenty ships, which sailed along the coast to the mouth of the Bosporus at Diplokion. No resistance was offered, and the flotilla was only using the docks and bay as a base, they weren't there to occupy. The village behind the docks wasn't big enough to house such a multitude, so many of the ships weighed anchor in the bay and their crews settled there. There was no need to worry about setting up facilities, as the ships were all effectively self-sufficient, they would restock at Chalcedon when and if the need should arrive.

The placement of the ships into the limited space of the bay was a source of comedy for the village locals. Ships smashed into each other, one ran aground and was so damaged that her crew had to be diffused into other ships. The only reason that they eventually settled into a docking pattern was because of the diligence of Ezera, the captured pirate, who requisitioned some rowers to ferry him about the bay to shout orders at the individual captains so they could finally find rest. The general incompetence of the fleet was visible from the capital, and the reports of it lightened the hearts of all who witnessed them.

Despite that comedy, the Ottoman forces at the close of the first day were exactly where Mehmet had intended them to be.

On the morning of the second day, the Christian fleet was sheltered in the Golden Horne. Most of the ships were comfortably at anchor and without a care in the world. The reason for their sense of security was that there was a giant chain that separated their harbour from the open sea. Six hundred metres of heavy wrought iron chain, buoyed on wooden pontoons, floated on guard at the harbour's entrance. One end was affixed to the Acropoline shore of the city, and another was fastened in the Genoese colony. This was palpable assistance going from Genoa to Constantinople, but the Genoese end of the chain was unassailable because if Zaganos attacked it would bring Genoa and hence the Holy Roman Empire into the war. Attacking the Constantinopolitan end of the chain was equally foolish, as the Acropoline shore was bare-face rock and the Turkish navy was hardly ready for any precision missions.

Nevertheless, Baltaolu was preparing his fleet.

"Sir," Ezera insisted with untrained patience. "We can't sail over the chain, it will rip holes in bottoms of our boats. They'll sink in the Horne without a shot being fired."

"So we can unfurl the chain then," the admiral said with a dramatic flair. "Cut loose the wooden planks that keep it above water. Then it will sink to the bottom with enough weight to either uproot its anchors on either side of the strait, or lower enough for us to get our ships over the barrier. The decks of our small ships are only a metre or so above sea level, it should be simple enough to have men lean over and do this. If we'd had the giant ships that you insisted we'd need, we'd find ourselves at a huge disadvantage, wouldn't you say?"

Ezera liked it better when Baltaolu wanted nothing to do with him. Now, the Kapudan-pasha wanted him to be the man to relate his foolish orders to the crews and captains of the fleet.

"No, admiral, that's not what I'd say. When our ships accost the line, their ships will meet us there. It's a bottle-neck. Our ships need overwhelming numbers to stand against theirs, and we'd also need to attack them from different sides. Your plan is going to have our ill-equipped, ill-rigged, untrained, poorly constructed ships stand fast against theirs. Their ships and crew are faster, higher in the water, better trained, more motivated and more experienced. We really can't do that and hope for a positive outcome."

"We're here for a battle, not a jolly sail around the sea."

"Then let's attack the islands," Ezera pointed to the seven islands off the coast of the Asian shore.

"There's nothing's on the islands!"

"These men need some training, otherwise you're sending them off to their deaths, Pasha. A landing, a charge up the hill, then rough up some monks and villagers, it'll do wonders for them! Instead of attacking the Roman fleet, we can send a messenger up to Pera, ask their commander to lend us some men to occupy the islands. Our green boys'll gain some invaluable experience."

"It irritates me the fickleness of a convert's faith, Ayoub. An army that fights under the banner of God is unstoppable, and history has proven thus."

"Sir, it is a sin to remind a convert of his roots," Ayoub-Ezera replied, never raising his voice and keeping the sarcasm to a minimum. "I'm sure you wouldn't take that tone with the second minister. And in case you hadn't noticed, upon these hundred or so ships, you and I are the only ones who pray towards Mecca."

"Enough of your constant second guessing! Loyalty and submission to authority are virtues you simply lack! Inform the captains, we'll attack after noon-time prayers," he snapped, showing more of his strained temper than was appropriate for a man in his situation.

"Sir, do you wish me to die with the men, or shall I stay here hiding with you during the battle?" he asked accusingly.

"I'll have you lead them, Ayoub," Baltaolu glared at him.

"Of course, sir," he stated flatly "It's always an honour to serve with those who don't fear death."

And with an undisciplined bow, Ezera began ferrying messengers to the different ships to prepare them for day's travails.

On the other side of the city, the cannons began firing as soon as there was enough sunlight to safely load their incendiary packages. Their missiles were mostly rounded stone, and the army had a team of stonemasons quarrying and rounded the next battery for their engines. To the attacking army, the artillery was like a lumberjack, the tree wasn't ready to fall after the first hack, or the second, but without anything to stop

452

the woodsman's axe, time would eventually knock down the mightiest of oaks.

The loitering auxiliaries of the city were immediately put to work on the second day, they were tasked with picking up the stone debris fallen from the walls, and move it to support the curtain outer walls.

To the defenders, the destructive ability of the cannons was most apparent. Causing no significant risk to the attackers, the defences of the city were being beaten into the earth, and there was nothing that could be done about it. The Cataphracts, the famous heavy cavalry of Byzantium, could not go charging out into the swarm of humanity and cut down the cannons, they were dug into the earth and too well defended by the massive infantry structure.

Smash! The octagonal towers that stood at intervals along the wall violently received the wrath of the attackers.

Smash! The squat outer wall shook as the missiles tested the ancient stones.

Smash! A crack formed in the curtain wall at the mesotechion, equidistant between the Horne and the Sea. By noon on the second day of bombardment, it was obvious to all that the wall would not hold indefinitely.

Shortly after the sun's daily nadir, the call to prayer echoed out from Chalcedon on the Asian shore. The proclamation of Muhammad's prophet-hood signalled the time for the Turkish fleet to depart Diplokion.

Thirty ships made ready to put to battle. Their sails were lowered and their oars were readied for speed. Ayoub-Ezera couldn't help but twist his lips to smile, while he was going to be involved in a catastrophe, at least he would be in command of a catastrophe.

He'd met that morning with thirty captains. The primary qualification to be a skipper in the Ottoman navy was to have at least two years sailing experience. Most were Greek fishermen in their mid-to-late twenties. Their crews were shepherd's and farmer's children. It was hardly a force to intimidate their enemy.

The plan, as he'd explained it to the captains, was to have two lines in the engagement of the pontoon bridge. The first fifteen would row as fast as possible up to the barrier, and the strongest axe-men of each ship would be at the bow, ready to hack away at the wooden attachments, thereby loosening and sinking the chain.

The next battle line would row up arrears the first, each line had a counterpart in the other, and attach themselves by ropes. They'd then get ready to row at maximum speed into the sea to take the first line with them once the first line had taken too much damage and could no longer attack the chain.

This would leave the defending fleet with two options, they could either lower the boom and chase the limping thirty into the open sea, at which point the eighty ships of the main flotilla could meet them, or they could stay in their huddled morass, and undergo the same form of attack again and again. It was Baltaolu's idea that they should meet the Italian and Byzantine fleet out at sea, where there were fewer rocks and shoals to oppress his inferior ships.

Following that reasoning, Ezera turned ship number sixteen, the first ship of the second line, into the flag-ship of his mission – a ship that went unnamed despite Ezera's numerous suggestions. After the post-noon prayer finished its haughty claims, the expeditionary flotilla sailed out from Diplokion harbour and approached the strait that separated Pera and the Acropoline bluffs.

The church bells of both Pera and Constantinople clanged out a warning as the first line sped towards the barrier. Ezera's ship was the furthest outside, and from his vantage point he had the best view of the sea, the harbour and the Bosporus.

"Damn this weather," he mumbled under his breath. He didn't want the captain to hear him, but it was obvious to everyone that they were going to run into difficulties. The spring wind was making the sea rather choppy, and the black water looked very cold.

Ezera motioned towards the trumpeter of his ship, who let out a long protracted blast from his bugle. One long blast meant that it was time for the second line to turn around and place themselves in position to help the first line escape when the time came. Ezera saw that the second line was doing a slow job of that in the rough water. He knew that this would also make the retreat hard, as ships weren't aqua-dynamically built to reverse, and they probably couldn't get the ships out of harms way as fast today as they could have if they had launched this attack at dawn, or on a milder day.

Ezera watched as the first line smashed into the barrier. When they hit, the ships of the harbour were still loading their crews. Ezera smiled, knowing that their tarrying would buy the axe-men more time. Of the fifteen ships that hit the barrier, only thirteen did so successfully. Two smashed their bows into the barrier itself, colliding the hulls of their ships against the metal and wooden obstacle. The crews had paddled too quickly, and hadn't stopped abruptly enough to position themselves well. One ship appeared to lose a crewman over the edge when they collided.

"Steady to those ships quickly!" Ezera called over the prow to alert the next ship over. His shouting could be heard by the next ship over, who in turn called over to the next, and so on.

The first line began their task in earnest, and with a few exceptions, seemed to be coming along just fine. Each ship had three axes attacking the chain and the wooden pontoons. While chopping down from a floating platform to another floating platform was difficult, given time it would eventually be successful.

The second line was having more difficulties. A wind had perked up and many of the ships were stumbling about the sea, trying to turn around, their oars were clanging into each other, moving out of sequence, and the rocking sea wouldn't give them a chance to recover much. On top of this, the commotion caused enough sound pollution as to deny any shouting communication from one ship to another. By the time the second line was backing their rears into the first and securing ropes, the first few defending ships were starting to approach the barrier.

Two ships, Venetian biremes, approached the melee post haste. Biremes were so named because the had two decks of rowers, making for four blades or oars that would slice the sea at once, they also had two main sails, but like their opponents, their sails were stowed away. Each ship had a hundred and twenty men aboard, and their decks would normally be three metres above the surface of the water. These ships were equipped for battle, and since their hulls were empty, save for the personnel, their decks were now four metres above sea level.

The two ships quickly arrived at the front and made their presence felt immediately. Crews of archers, harquebusiers, and javelin throwers appeared atop the prow, a good three metres over the heads of the Turkish ships. Arrows flew, muskets exploded and javelins rained down upon the heads of the Greek conscripts and mercenary fishermen.

Three ships of the first line flew white flags from their aft castles right away. These signalled for their counterpart ship to start pulling forward, while their own crews started reversing as quickly as possible. Their immediate priority was to get out of harm's way as quickly as possible.

One of the ships that collided with the boom too quickly flew its white banner immediately, and her second-line counterpart started to row. What happened next was a disaster for the thirty five men aboard. Their ship's collision with the metal and wooden death-trap that closed the harbour had rammed the spokes and spikes of the barricade into the hull of their little ship. Their hasty withdrawal was unadvisable, as the strong pull at the stern of the ship tore the body of the ship back over the barrier, cutting holes through the ship's keel. This damage caused drag, added to by the flat and non-hydrodynamic rear of the ship trying to cut through the angry waves. The ropes attached to the aft castle had too much resistance, and began to tear the poorly and hastily built ship apart at the seams.

The event had all the makings of a catastrophe foreseen. Two ships were bringing a flotilla of thirty to its knees, and a third and fourth were joining the fray.

"Horn!" Ezera called to the trumpeter. "Two times!"

The trumpet blared twice to signal for all the ships to step back from the boom, but at that point it was more of a formality, as most of the boats had already begun to pull back. There was no way to properly stand against a modern warship, for a handful of untrained sailors it could mean only a watery grave. Ezera looked at the crew of the one ship that tore apart and he cursed himself. Her crew was trying to swim to neighbouring vessels, all of which were starting to pull away.

By that time, a third vessel joined the other two at the line, just as the opponents were falling back. She was lower in the water and smaller than the other two Italian galleys.

"Oh, shit," Ezera said as he saw the dromon join the other two. "Horn! Three! Now! Three!"

The trumpeter signalled with three blasts, the call for an all out retreat. Row if you could, swim if you had to, but get away from the line.

There were only two ships close to the line when the low riding dromon arrived. At the very prow of the deck was what looked to be a cross between a hose and a cannon, and it contained the secret science which had defended Constantinople for centuries.

Greek Fire was a concentration of four major ingredients, the collection and refinement of which paid for Mario Orsini's home. Saltpetre, or salt-stone, was distilled from a collection of caves in the forests surrounding Constantinople; brimstone (sulphur), a burning crystal used since antiquity, was imported from Kaffa, on the Crimean Peninsula; quicklime – calcium oxide – was known for its explosive properties, again by way of a Venetian doctor; and naphtha, a cocktail of gummy flammable chemicals that kept the substance in liquid form until it was ready to be lit during the fury of combat, again, delicately concocted by the expert hand of the Venetian alchemist.

When the crews of the Ezera's ships finally realised what was upon them, the panic spread faster than the fire would. Oarsmen abandoned their rowing, boatswains ran down the length of the ship and tried to jump to their ferrying tugs, their captains did the same. In the chaos, only the inexperienced child crews of the ships didn't understand what was coming, and it was them who had been earmarked by the almighty for suffering.

The liquid sprayed out of the cannon hose at the head of the dromon and onto the rowers of the ship unfortunate enough to be in its way. The burning liquid had the consistency somewhere between pine sap and molasses, stuck wherever it landed. The fire burned upon this base, slowly but with great heat. A cup of the vile mucus would normally take half an afternoon to burn itself out. The screams of the unfortunate rowers could be heard from the Golden Horne to Chalcedon. An eruption of pain and suffering to which no ears should be subject, was unconscionably visited upon fellow human beings.

Men jumped into the freezing water, abandoning their ship to the flames and the rest of the remaining twenty-eight ships of the attack force fled off to the open sea. The defending ships made no attempt to follow the retreating attackers, but in a rare act of battle-time kindness, did try to rescue the survivors from a frozen watery grave. Ezera led his first command in service to the sultan back to Diplokion.

The bombardment of the city brought the first casualties into Chora hospital. They were mostly civilians, victims of cannon shots that flew over the walls and randomly entered the city when the Ottoman army was fine-tuning their artillery.

This was morbidly positive for Mario and his staff, as they had small numbers coming in at first, so they could prepare themselves better for later, when large numbers would come in flooding. The bombardments were so loud, and there was so much visible smoke from the nearby wall, that even though the doctors in the hospital couldn't see the fighting, they had to know right away how bad it was going to be.

"Surgeon," Mario began a conversation with one of his assistants.

"Yes, doctor."

"How many have we had so far?"

"Seventy four patients, sir," the sawbones answered. His apron was covered in dried blood, as were his hands up to the forearm. "Most of them got sent home after some stitches and wine."

"How many beds are taken?"

"Eight, Sir, but I think most of them can get out tomorrow."

"Great, not bad for a first day of this foul business. There's fighting at the harbour, we can expect more this afternoon.”

“I’ll pray to Saint Eutyches that we’ll have fewer still, Doctor.”

“You do that,” Mario said with a smile. “I’m sure you can find his bones round back.”

“Don’t blaspheme, sir,” the surgeon replied gruffly. “We’ll need all the help we can get.”

“Yes, I know,” Mario corrected himself quickly. “I mean his reliquary is in the ossuary, for prayer.”

“No, Sir. The relic is buried in the women’s chapel and we can’t well go visiting it there,” the vulgar butcher informed Mario. “It’s buried under the altar. Women go and pray there for healthy pregnancies. The hand gets brought around the monastery on special holidays, Easter and Christmas like.”

“Yes, I’d forgotten that,” Mario said absently. His brain ran back to yesterday when he’d found the reliquary in the bone yard.

‘If the reliquary’s out there, then what’s under the altar?’

In the mid-afternoon sun there was a huge celebration in the harbour district. The sense of dread that had typified so much of the previous days, so much of the previous years in fact, was temporarily forgotten in a half-hour battle. Three ships had annihilated an attacking flotilla of thirty without a single injury. Glory, Glory! What a celebration! In that celebration, there were songs being sung, different boats challenging each other to sing alternating choruses more loudly than they could, musicians from the taverns and brothels of the mainland came out to their send merriment to the victorious sailors. The Venetians were especially proud of their two warships, and the Greeks were singing songs of the success of their dromon. The Genoese, out of antipathy to Venice, also cheered the success of the dromon and her crew.

In the chaos of the harbour revels (the celebration was limited to the harbour – the wall was still tense and dangerous) many people travelled across the Horne. One such person was Hectore Pazzi.

Count Dominic had forbidden him permission to leave his post in the city, so Hectore disguised himself with a stranger’s clothes and a false beard, and abandoned his post. He hired a boatman to take him from Galata Point, across the harbour to St. John’s Gate.

He hadn’t seen Adam Karian since winter, but he knew that once the gold had been taken out of the vaults, it wouldn’t stay in the open. It had to be hidden somewhere in the city, and Pazzi was going to find it. God’s mercy would best be prayed for anyone who tried to get in the captain-general's way!

Ezera arrived on the deck of Kapudan Pasha Baltaolu's trireme and was met with suspicious gazes that quickly turned away at his arrival. He was escorted by men at arms to the drawing room of the Admiral. The boatswains admitted him into the office and closed the door behind them so that the two men could speak alone.

Baltaolu didn't look up from his ledger, Ezera stood at attention. Each man was waiting for the other to break the silence.

"You've failed, Ayoub," Baltaolu said at long last.

"The plan failed, as I said it would, Admiral. We gave it as good an effort as was possible under such a foolhardy stratagem. A loss of four ships and few crews depleted is, in retrospect, not so bad."

Baltaolu looked up and gazed with and cold-fire burning at the former pirate.

"I want you to take the twenty-eight ships that you brought back to me and go to the Islands. Leave three ships to control the islands, one on Antigoni Island, and the other two on Prinkipios. Escort the crew from one of the ships to the Monastery of Saint George and bring back whatever treasure you can find."

"Yes, Sir," Ezera answered. "Do you want to send a runner up to the Pera garrison and ask for some men to do the job of occupying?"

"No, Ayoub, I don't. This is a part of financing this war, and I believe that the experience will do our men some good."

"Yes, Sir. I can also understand that you don't want to ask the second Minister for any assistance. After the battle that they just witnessed, I wouldn't want to speak to them either."

"You may go at first light tomorrow," Baltaolu pretended not to hear the accusations

"Yes, Sir."

Ezera bowed in an exaggerated way, with arms swimming through the air and head duly downcast before concluding his dramatic exit.

The sun finally set, enrobing the battered city in the warm blanket of temporary peace. The cannons stopped, the pontoons were safe, and the auxiliary conscript men returned to their homes, to regale their wives and children with tales of their heroism that day.

While they were all going to rest, three men embarked on three radically different, though braided, missions.

Mario Orisini, doctor and administrator of the Imperial Hospital of Constantinople, snuck quietly over the small wooden fence that protected the women's quarters of the Chora compound from that of the public. Over grassy hillocks and cobblestone pathways he went, finally reaching the women's chapel. It was unguarded and sequestered, almost an afterthought to the main chapel, but it was the home to one of the religious commune's most prized artefacts. Mario carried with him two important items on his night's quest: the keys to chapel and a muted lantern.

The keys let him into the building quickly, but he was still too apprehensive to bring the lantern to full glow, so he kept it at half wick. He strode quickly across the sanctuary and arrived at the altar.

Thank the maker for his miracles, the altar was wood, and although heavy, not immovable. Mario lifted one end infinitesimally off of the stone surface of the altar and pivoted it out of the way. Under the altar was a discoloured stone, bits of dust surrounded it. It had obviously been moved and replaced. Mario tried to find enough space to reach his fingers into holes to grip the stone to pull it away, but to no avail. He would need some kind of prying device or lever in order to unearth its contents.

He knocked the floor around the stone and heard nothing but a deadened thud, until he knocked on the altar keystone itself. There was a hollow underneath it. Mario lacked the expertise of a stonemason and was hence incapable of judging how big a hollow, or what was there, but he surmised with absolute certainty that it wasn't Saint Eutyches' hand, and the hollow would be at least large enough to hold the large reliquary. He would have to find a tool tomorrow. He went to bed and allowed his gifted mind to start wondering about what secrets the hollow held.

The second man on a mission that night was Hectore Pazzi. He had secured himself a room at a local tavern, in a run-down district near the old Bucholeon Palace. No one would find him there. Hectore went out that night, looking throughout the city, trying to find where Adam Karian could possibly hide something of such value.

That was a simple matter, he was on the north point of the triangular city. Getting there was simple enough, all the soldiers and guards were busy. They were in a siege, and acted accordingly. Hectore couldn't go to Adam and Karian couldn't go to Pazzi.

This raised a question in Pazzi's mind.

'If he can't go anywhere, it would have to be near him.'

This was sound initial reasoning.

'If it's in the open, it would have to be guarded,' he continued to reason. *'Where can it be near him, under guard, but away from prying eyes?'*

Pazzi explored the Palace district. The largest building was Blachernae Palace.

'The palace is too obvious, he'd get caught.'

There was a royal harbour at the disposal of the Emperor.

'Too open, too accessible. He wouldn't risk it.'

Porphyrogentius Palace was almost abandoned to decay, it now served as stables, administrative centre and prison, but it was still under heavy guard because of its proximity to Blachernae.

'Random soldiers could stumble upon it and either return it or run off with it. Probably the later.'

Chora Monastery was the only complex left, ergo it was there where he'd find that for which he sought.

'Holy Mary, mother of God. That's perfect. He's hidden it there. I've found you out, you wily thief! I've found you out!'

The third man on a mission that night was Isodore, the Bulgarian monk. He'd gone to the inn near his home in the abandoned Bucholeon Palace in hopes of sneaking a few drinks before returning to his austere compound. When he sat down, he instantly saw through the false beard and creatively simple clothing of another diner at the inn. The man's posture was that of someone used to observing and being observed. His hands were big and strong, but not those of a workman; the possibility of a professional soldier became likely. His face and eyes were obviously not those of an easterner, he was definitely from either northern Italy or perhaps even further afield. He had to get a better look at the man's face. Isodore would never forget a face.

So he got up and walked to the kitchen, ostensibly to complain about the stew, but in reality to get a better look at the stranger who was seated nearby. One close passing glance, and he immediately recognized Hectore Pazzi, the Captain-General of the soldiers of Galata, and close friend of Count Dominic Trebiano.

'What the hell is he doing here?' he wondered to himself.

Time would tell.

Chapter Thirty-Five - The Third Day

April 8, 1453

“Come to me! Muster a line!” Mesut called out as he rode through the Janissary ranks in the pre-dawn hours. He hated horses, but they were convenient beasts of war. Obedience to the rules of drill brought every small group of ten out of their tents and into rows.

The sun was pinking the sky with dawn, but torches were still necessary to draw attention. Around the Orta, wake up calls were going all about, and orders were being shouted in a dozen different languages. Ahead of them, Iskender, Hussein, Erkin and their former classmates in the Orta could identify orders being given in Bulgarian, Serbo-Croatian and Macedonian. Iskender looked up at Hussein to see a smile visible through the darkness, something in the way that his eyes caught the torchlight.

“This is it,” the big man said euphorically. “Now we’re charging the walls!”

“If God wills it so,” Iskender said with less enthusiasm.

“Muster up! Muster up!” the gravelly voice of their commander called out.

The Janissaries obeyed instantly and eagerly.

“The day breaks!” Mesut cried out. “A new day dawns on us! Today will be the first day of a great battle! Your signatures will grace a page of history that will live through the ages. My first command to you today is to survive this battle! Glory is now yours and will never be taken away!”

Hussein’s eyes watered with a combination of pride and excitement. Iskender’s were cold and concealed his nervousness. Erkin tried his best to seem unemotional, but the fear and enthusiasm for the day made an impossible combination in his heart, that was reflected in his face.

“The first testing and prodding of the walls will be done by the auxiliaries. The broken headed! The Christians! The levies! You have to hold back! You’ll be doing policing!”

Hussein looked down at Iskender, whose spirits lifted.

“I want you to go to the supply tents, and come back with halberds. We’ll follow the auxiliaries onto the field, and make sure that they don’t retreat! They’ve got the scaling equipment, so you won’t be crossing the moat unless I command it! We’ll start the charge to the walls when the cannons all fire a single shot each! If the cannons fire again, that means return here! This is a raid! It is not an all-out assault just yet! We’re going to let those Christians know that they can't hide forever in their castles, and that we're coming to find them! No one is going to wait this fight out! Now go! Get your halberds!"

The soldiers all ran to the supply tent to equip themselves. As they were retrieving their pole-axes, Hussein and Erkin turned to Iskender.

"That's it? We're just going to be policing?"

"Don't worry about it, it's part of the big strategy," Iskender assured them and tried not to seem too relieved. "This is our duty for today and we should do this as we do everything else, with obedience and diligence."

"You're right," Hussein said in a disappointed grumble.

By the time the sun had risen high enough in the sky to light the landscape, the Lycus Valley was full of ready soldiers, readying to cross the shallow moats and attack the walls. The spectacle was being watched by the defenders, especially from the tower at Charisius Gate, where the defenders made their temporary headquarters. At the top of this defensible tower, Adam Karian, Guistiniano Longo and Vincent DiCastillo watched.

"It's a jab that's coming, not a serious attack," Vincent surmised. "How quickly can you bring the trebuchets up from Kaligaria?"

"Why bother? These fools will break like waves," answered Karian.

"Fire the trebuchets over them, aiming at their camp. We can do some serious damage while their cannons are forbidden. They can't exactly shoot through their own numbers."

"I'll volunteer for that," Longo interjected.

"Run the trebuchets?" Vincent asked.

"No, but I've got a hundred horsemen," he stated flatly. He didn't care much for the cautious strategy of entanglement.

"Are you insane?" Karian asked.

"No, look, let's do this quickly. Their attack is in the middle-north of the wall, their best soldiers are behind them, look, the Janissaries are marshalling the raiders. My horse can come out of Pege Gate at attack the south. Just make sure that the Saint Rhegium Gate can open to let us in."

"You'll come back through their numbers?"

"Through their retreating numbers."

"Through the Janissaries?"

"Who are tasked with policing their own men."

"You'll lose half your men!" Vincent scolded the testy Genoese.

"No! We have to attack, not huddle behind the wall. I'm not afraid of dying, and you may have noticed that staying here indefinitely won't work. Sooner or later, those wall will crumble! If the Christian armies are unwilling to take the fight to the enemy, we're doomed. There's too many of them. We have to force their retreat."

"Do it," Karian commanded. Ride out from Pege, if you can reach their cannon, that would be great, if not, do what damage you can before returning safely. Let everyone see you returning safely, don't engage the Janissaries, we want the men on the walls to see victory. They need to see that victory is possible to those who take it. That sight is more important than fighting our enemies right now."

"Ask and yee shall receive, My General!"

"Go, quickly."

Guistiniano complied with the command and ran off leaving Vincent and Adam alone with a handful of guards and officers.

"He'll probably die, you know," Vincent informed him.

"I know. He's reckless and I don't trust him so the individual is no great loss."

There was silence for an instant and they watched the Ottoman horde slowly approaching their fortifications.

"Adam, do you trust me?" he asked quixotically.

The Strateogos winked in response and they both watched the drama on display before them.

The cannons were all ordered to go off at the same time and they more or less did within a space thirty seconds or so. A single volley flew from the various batteries in the Lycus Valley and smashed into the towers and walls of the great city. That was the signal.

"My Children!" Mesut roused the Orta. "March! March on and keep these lazy bastards honest!"

The orta was equipped as halberdiers and they marched all in tandem, an orderly army standing behind the random mishmash horde. The kopekjis were right behind the Janissary infantry, ostensibly to catch any fleeing soldiers who got through the main line, but the corps perceived them to be there to catch any of their numbers who fled.

The regiments ahead of them were a more chaotic site. Some were carrying ladders, some grappling hooks and rope ladders. Some still had long wooden pikes with which they intended to vault over the outer wall. With a variety of blood curdling roars from commanders and participants, they began the charge of the walls. They sprinted ahead of the Janissaries.

Hussein looked over at them and bobbed his head around the halberd in front of him to see what would happen next.

The outer moat was barely flooded and did little more than slow down the chaos of the charging horde.

Once the first quarter of their numbers had crossed this eastern Rubicon, the defenders let loose their attack. Crossbows, longbows and short-bows were paired with harquebuses and hand cannons. The defenders had seven cannons and a few trebuchets, but none of them were in the same league as the giants that the Turks had brought to the arena. The defending cannons were used for making holes in the enemy's lines. The charging horde had no lines, it was a charging mass of flesh and metal.

They began with sound and fury, charging with varying degrees of enthusiasm into the muddy swamp that was the moat. The water itself was only up to a man's knee, but the mud underneath it sucked that knee down to the waist, and the charging horde quickly got bogged down.

The soldiers on the wall held their fire and watched the morass bump into one another and get pushed from behind as they tired to cross the man-made swamp. Only once large numbers of the horde had freed themselves from the mud on the defending side of the moat did the archers and harquebusiers take aim at the horde.

Those who were in that first quarter of the charge freed themselves from the mud and ran strait to the outer wall. Those in the second were cut down in the mud and water of the Lycus moat. The slower, or less enthusiastic, half of the charging horde stopped tight and made an effort to fall back.

Behind them were the Janissaries, ready to convince them otherwise.

The glorious first quarter found their glory because they were not fired upon as they approached the walls. They escaped that travail, and their ladders and hooks found the walls and they climbed up to the terrace that separated the solid outer wall from the towering inner wall. In that ten metres of peaceable grassland stood two hundred Greek shop keepers and tradesmen, normally volunteers in the city's fire brigade, now consigned to wall duty on this fateful day. They fought tooth and nail against the broken-headed attackers, denying them access to the plain between the walls. They fought and knocked down the scaling equipment and ladders. One attacker, an ingenious pole-vaulter threw all his energy into his assisted leap, only to find that his pole was a few feet too short to pass the wall; he fell to his death after knocking his body unconscious against the upper wall. The first quarter fought valiantly, but the defenders were more so. The city's Fifth Municipal Fire Battalion was to win their first and only combat honour in their eight centuries of existence.

The second quarter of the great charge was shot by arrow, quarrel, bullet and cannon. They retreated and joined the rest of the aborted charge in hasty flight.

"They're coming at us," Iskender said.

"Here come the cowards," Hussein snarled. "Are you ready, Brother?"

"Ready yourselves!" came the bellowing voice of Mesut.

"I'm ready, thanks be to God." Iskender prayed under his breath.

Towards the southern end of the middle of the wall, the Pega Gate opened. With all the commotion at the northern third, near the palace district, the opening of the military gate went unnoticed by the sultan's eyes.

The wedge of armoured knights that stormed through the gate rode without standard or command, they all knew their orders and their targets. By the time they had crossed the moat over the narrow road, they had formed a line and were charging diagonally across the field at the cannons, in particular Orban's monstrous Basilisk.

"Halil!" Mehmet screamed from his tent and grabbed his prime minister by the arm and pointed to the south. "They're attacking! You said they'd never do that!"

Halil's eyes were not as strong as his eighteen-year-old sultan's.

"They wouldn't do that, they'd be doomed!" he said and squinted at the horizon.

Despite Halil's protestations, a line of heavy cavalry, in the spirit of the cataphracts of yore, charged the field and was straightening their line diagonally against the dug in cannon batteries.

"Send the Anatolian levies, quickly!" Mehmet ordered.

"Sire, they're bowmen and skirmishers! They'll be cut down!"

"Cannons! Fire!" Mehmet cried out. "Bring back my Janissaries! Defend the camp!"

Chaos erupted as the sultan's will was done.

An instant before the wall of the retreating horde hit the Janissary police, the alarm was raised by cannon fire.

"Pull back!" Mesut called out, riding about and shouting orders at his men. "Don't kill any of them! Let them retreat back to the camp!"

From his horse, he then saw what had caused the early retreat.

"Children! My children! The camp is under attack! Charge to the south! Right turn! Right turn!"

The Orta, as always, did as commanded and began their charge to the southern hill, where the Italians were congregating.

"Kill them!" Shouted Guistiniano. "Kill them all!"

His men were only too happy to obey. The only soldiers standing between them and the prized cannons were a handful of Anatolian tribesmen and a few unchecked Falconer-Janissaries. The falconers flung arrows at Longo and his men, their dervish sheikh danced and spun among the fighters, all for naught once the heavy cavalry hit. A dozen of the unready soldiers were run through, more were run down and others simply fled in the panic. Guistiniano had a clear line of sight to the cannons.

"Charge! Don't let anyone distract you! Get the crews!"

And charge they did.

The commander of the gunners, the master gunsmith Orban screamed as the knights arrived at the top of the hill. He, like all the other unarmed artillery men, turned and ran. They hoped for escape, but few are the men who can outrun horses.

"Run, everybody!" Over the course of the past year, this was the only thoughtful command he would ever give. He was placed in command of the gunners for his technical expertise, not his combat prowess.

The last thoughts of the Hungarian mercenary, before the spear of an unnamed Genoese mercenary ran him threw, were pious thoughts, prayers that he would be forgiven of his sins, and a final hope that God would grant victory to those for whose defeat he had worked so hard. Like many men, he hoped that a final drop of regret, shortly before the end, would outweigh a lifetime of less than ethical behaviours. The only mercy he found was that of a swift death, although one that was surrounded by men of different countries of languages, rather than by his loved ones far away in distant Hungary.

Longo looked around once the crews had been dispatched; their expertise, like their blood, fell away into the earth. To the north of them, the Janissary infantry was charging, but they were still a long way off.

"Sir!" One of his men yelled at him. "We've done it without casualties! We should return!"

"No!" His commander yelled back. "Everyone! Charge the great tent! Kill the boy-sultan before his men come back! Land and gold for whomsoever kills him! Quickly! Before the rest of the soldiers return!"

As though there was a random gust of wind, throwing dried leaves aside, the horsemen changed their direction in unison and pushed inwards to the centre of the camp.

The camp beyond the open lines was guarded by Christian forced conscripts, ill-disposed or prepared to stand against heavy cavalry,. They guarded a vast series of tented pavilions. Long, makeshift halls and atria were formed from hollows between pegs and canvas. Tarps sheltered the insides of the two-day-old impromptu palace. Into this maze of temporary splendour and fleeing officials stormed a hundred horses, their riders directing them towards blood.

"Your Majesty! Come this way!" Implored Emir Tolga, courtier and friend to the Sultan. "Our soldiers are this way, and theirs come."

"No, Your Majesty!" decried Halil. "They're coming this way, we need to retreat!"

"They're coming from *this* way," Tolga pointed to the left, "and you'd have us run *that* way?"

The Emir of Kastamonu pointed increduously to the right.

"That's where they're going, and faster than us!"

"We're going that way!" Mehmet, unused to chaos and command, shouted. "To the Army!"

The three great men and their entourages ran northwards towards their army, as fast as their legs could carry them.

A mere instant after they left their tented chamber, the horsemen ripped through the walls to find it abandoned.

"Knock over those braziers! Start a fire and let's get out of here!" Guistiniano Longo commanded at the crown chamber turned muster ground. "Now, and let's get home while we still can!"

The braziers were brass containers, holding coal, charcoal and coke. They smouldered and brought warmth to the room on a cold April morning. Seven of them were knocked over and their contents were thrown against the dry canvas walls of the tent before the horsemen began their triumphal retreat.

The horsemen sprang out of the tents quickly. Although it was only fifteen minutes ago that they were in the Pege Forum getting ready to charge, it had been a very busy quarter hour. Longo led the charge out from the tents, his bugle in hand summoning the other horsemen to him.

At their emergence from the enemy complex, cheers were raised all along the mighty wall. The new heroes, new Myrmidones, new Knights of Jerusalem, new Draconistrarum, were galloping across an open field towards St. Rhegium Gate. To the north of them, even the charging Janissaries were too slow to catch pace. To their rear, the smoke of the main camp was floating skyward, carrying with it the victory prayers of Byzantium up to God for closer inspection.

From behind them, archers emerged. Their sinewy bows cast their wooden death at the retreating horsemen, but to no avail. Saint Rhegium opened his grace and brought the warriors to his breast.

The attacking army abandoned the day's assault and set about the task of extinguishing the fire.

Far away from the scene of the battle, Ezera was having a wonderful morning. Antigoni Island was sparsely populated, and had more or less given over everything of value in their monastery without the need for stern words. Saint George on the other hand, was at the top of the mountain of Prinkipos, and involved some invigorating hiking.

Ezera was by nature a physical man and enjoyed the long trek to the top of Saint George's. The last time that he'd seen the village at the base of the hill, he'd been here with the Venetian physician and the DiCastillo brood.

He had worried about this task. His men were all Christian. They had no pre-existing loyalty to him, and only antipathy to the cause of the Ottoman war. They lacked the loyalty, ferocity, skill and metal of the Nineveh's crew. Oh, the Nineveh! The greatest crew and greatest ship on the seas! They could be trusted to do whatever was required of them.

The Greeks in the fleet surprised him. They were more than capable of brutality to their own co-religionists, though they were a little too enthusiastic in its application. The monks seemed to sense this right away and turned over anything that looked like it could be exchanged for wealth.

On their way down from the mountain-top monastery, they couldn't see the smoke from the battle at the wall; their angles were poor for seeing over the hilly peninsula. The clouds of the day disguised the plume of smoke rising up from Mehmet's headquarters. They did, however, have a clear and distant view of the sea lanes.

"Captain!" called out one of the sailors who was lucky enough not to be lugging booty back to the ship. "There are more ships coming!"

"I see that," Ezera quickly answered. He jumped up to the nearest elevation of rocks and stood perfectly still. His eyes squinted at the horizon and started counting. "Three vessels. They look like transport galleys from here, but they're too far away."

"Are they with the Turks, or the Romans?"

"They're Italians," Ezera answered quickly. "We don't have any big ships in the fleet. Those are reinforcements for Constantinople."

"Will the rest of the fleet fight them?"

"I suppose they will. Are you upset that you're missing some action?"

"I wouldn't say '*upset*,' Captain," he laconically answered.

"Look, the fleet's starting to move," another sailor said.

"Let's hurry down to the ships, maybe we can get there in time," Ezera perked up. "Don't lose the gold."

"There's so many of them," Balias mumbled when he saw thirty five galleys rowing across the sea to meet them. Unlike yesterday's choppy waves, the sea was as flat as poured glass this afternoon.

"That doesn't matter, the strength of the test only increases the honour of victory. You'd have bettered yourself by learning that lesson, Brother," answered a rather confident sounding Cardinal Isaac.

They watched as their ship, and the two other ships in their group, turned slightly to the starboard side.

"Captain Francisco! I demand to know why we're coasting out to sea! We shouldn't flee from the Saracens!"

The captain of the vessel had tolerated the constant second-guessing and ill-informed advice that had come from the cleric for the greater part of two months now, and had decided to suffer no more.

"Enough from you! Lock yourself in the state-room, or I will personally throw you to the sharks! Now get out of my way!"

In reality, there were no sharks in the Sea of Marmara, it's far too cold. Isaac didn't know this and chose to take a temporary vow to silence.

Once away from the shore, the three ships joined together and drew in their oars. Ropes lashed the three together, so as they would form a wooden castle, floating in the sea. The fleet of Kapudan-pasha Baltaolu reached the floating fortress a half a kilometre south-west of the Ivory Tower, the cornerstone of Constantinople's walls. The drama that was about to play out was going to do so in full view of the embarrassed land army.

Mehmet ordered harquebusiers and archers to deploy at the shore, with orders to fire only if the winds of fate would bring the ships closer to land. The burial of the cannons, the only thing that saved them from destruction in the morning raid, unfortunately kept them out of the afternoon battle. Sultan Mehmet the Second, and his entourage of bodyguards, ministers of state, friends and allies, all set up a tent from which they could watch the battle from the safety of the shore. At Newgate, Vincent DiCastillo, Adam Karian, and the champion of the hour, Guistiniano Longo were joined by an honoured guest for the same purpose.

Emperor Constantine the Eleventh made one of his few exits from the palace at Blachernae. He was surrounded by at least four dozen toadies and doting courtiers, including his most presumptuous advisor, Stavros of Brussa. They proved to be little more than a nuisance to the commanders, but their presence represented the approval of God for the battle and could hardly be ignored. The Emperor, ignorant and conceited though he was, was still the Emperor and commanded respect.

"I say, what are they doing?" Constantine asked, examining the crowded horizon.

"They're joining up, Your Majesty," Karian answered factually.

"I can see *that*! Why the devil would they do such a thing? Now they can't go anywhere!"

"Sire, if I may?" Longo volunteered, and the Emperor nodded. "When they're together like that, they have three fronts where they can be attacked: the left, the right and the rear. The fronts of the ship are too pointed, no one can scale them…"

"And when they're separated, they would have nine such openings – I understand. It's very defensible," Constantine proclaimed with authority. "But they still can't escape, and look at the size of the fleet that's attacking them! You could walk from the Sea Walls half way across to Bithynia without wetting your feet!"

"They're getting their sails ready, Your Majesty," Vincent added his contribution. "If a wind finally picks up, it will take them right through the attackers and once they're free of them, they can sail and row their way into the harbour."

"Won't the Turkish ships block them?"

"Look at how big the Venetians are," Karian pointed out. "They outweigh the little Turkish galleys by at least three to one. They'll be batted to the side without much ado."

"My, this is all very scientific of you three," Stavros attempted humour.

"We've put a lot of thought into this, *Proconsul*," Guistiniano said with an unspoken accusation that wouldn't pass the muster of being even microscopically veiled.

Karian glared over at him and he shrugged.

Constantine let the slight pass as though Longo hadn't registered it, but Vincent scowled at Longo. Longo scowled back. He wasn't prepared to suffer any subordination to the Venetian.

The white-turbaned young sultan watched with dire frustration as his navy outnumbered the Venetians by more than twenty-to-one, and was unable to force them. Attack after attack he watched, and he cursed. The elderly advisors were around him, Halil and his damnable brothers, semi-literate tribal sheikhs, mystic dervishes, aghas who did not propose any suggestions, but answered for everything that *'It was God's will.'*

'This is not God's will, but mine,' he thought with rising fury.

He had to keep his youthful blood down, because screaming out his frustration at the day's horrible events would cause him to lose face with the Divan, but he was quickly losing his patience. Already, the frustration of the day's spectacle was forcing his skin to rebel in cross-looking acne. Normally, one of the women of court would be assigned to hide the affliction, lest it remind everyone of just how young their sovereign really was. His face had acne and his beard wasn't full, these flaws were on broad display for all around to see.

All he could do was watch the battle and try to act sombre.

He remained quietly composed for the first hour. For the second hour of inertia he was beginning to show signs of testiness. During the third hour, his breathing and his body language was making the rest of the Divan uncomfortable. When the fourth hour clocked in and the sun started to set, he had had enough of patiently waiting, and announced it.

"I am the sword of Osman! I have no business waiting here! I must lead my army!"

And in an unwinding spring of frustration, he got up and moved. He wasn't entirely certain where he'd be moving to, but he was going there quickly.

"You!" he accosted a nearby equestrian guard. "Off that horse now!"

"Sire?" the confused Sipahi asked.

Mehmet grabbed the man by the thigh and pulled him off the horse. Even the charger seemed to accept the outlandish demands of the Sultan and allowed him up.

The divan looked on at the strange behaviour of their sovereign, as he rode the beast down to the water's edge and wetted her hooves in the shallows.

"Kill! Fight! Attack! Win!" he screamed over the waves, to little avail.

He paced on horseback, watching every attempted board and every repelled attack. He even rode his horse into the water to be closer to the battle. The archers manning the shore-line weren't quite certain what to make of their sultan's screeching wrath.

And then, fate answered his calls. Fate, as fate would have it, was not without a sense of schadenfreude.

The sea rippled, and then rolled, as an eastward wind started to pick up.

The cannon fire stopped, and the sails of the floating fortress unfurled, and they began to move eastward, freeing themselves from the tangled knot of the Ottoman fleet.

"No! God's rage, and spit, and hate fall upon you all, you filthy motherless whores!" Mehmet screamed as he watched his ships capsize in the wake of the enemies' flight.

Those words definitely deducted from the Sultan's aura of gravitas.

Wind tore the three ships free of the clot, and pulled them eastward to the harbour, whilst the Ottoman fleet mired themselves with clacking oars, bumbling over each other like a basket full of blind moles.

"Double the pace again!" commanded Ezera. "We'll hit them soon!"

Ezera's fleet had crossed the opening of the Bosporus an hour prior and kept going. He ignored the two or three dozen ships there, quickly noting that they were sitting still and showed no sign of readying themselves for anything. They were at anchor and weren't planning on doing any fighting anytime soon. Distantly ahead of them, he saw the cluster of ships that was undoubtedly under the command of his ignorantly fearless leader, Baltaolu. The fact that there seemed to be another spectacular failure unfolding was of no surprise to him.

He sailed his twenty-eight along the southern sea wall towards the fight they saw brewing from Prinkipos. They kept a safe distance from the walls, knowing that a single archer within range could do terrible damage to an open-deck galley, the type of ship that the fleet was unfortunately using. Because of that distance, once the three retreating Venetian war galleys broke away from the main conflict and started to close the gap between Ezera's flotilla and their own, they were set to pass Ezera on the inside. This was fine for the Catalan.

Ezera was in the lead boat and he ran up to the back of the aft castle so that the skippers behind could see him as he tried to gesticulate his plans.

He motioned with both arms pointed in the direction of the horizon, and then pumped his fist three times, and made a "come here" wave, indicating that three ships were coming towards them. He then made a circling motion with his arm to say that everyone in the fleet would do the next command. He then made rowing motions with his arms, then chopping motions to say "very fast," and punched his open fist, demonstrating that it was his plan to ram the ships rather than grapple and fire upon them. The skippers near him then tried to relate it to those behind them, and like a game of Chinese Whispers, a variation on the plan eventually disseminated to all twenty-eight other ships.

The wedging rows of ships turned inward and picked up speed as they readied to meet the three heavy warships speeding along the wall.

The first ship sped the crashing gauntlet of the ramming galleys, the experience of Captain Francisco' crew outweighed the numbers of the Ottoman fleet, and the crew cheered as they passed the final ramming ship.

One ramming ship managed to collide sideways with the second ship of the fleeing Venetians. They tried casting up grappling hooks, but the warship's crew had temporarily abandoned their oars in favour of sail power, and they cut down all of the aspiring hooks and cables. The wind kept pulling them through the threat and into the relative safety of open water.

By the time the third ship entered the killing field of sea, it was a crowded mess of smaller galleys, through which she couldn't possibly navigate. She was hit side-on by two vessels, one right after the other. She in turn rammed a ship that was in front of her, though not intentionally. That smaller ship capsized, throwing her crew into the Marmora.

The two ships that hit her side were too light to damage her sturdy hull, but the impact was enough to push her. And push her they did, right into the rocky shoals at the bottom of the sea walls. Unlike the attackers, those rocks were hard enough to damage her hull. She started taking water instantly.

"Reverse, Reverse!" Ezera shouted and ran about so that the other skippers could see what he was doing. "Get the hell away from the wall! Get back!"

All of the small Ottoman ships were doing just that, and Ezera nervously watched the parapets of the city walls. The wind over his ears, and the clatter of oars slashing against one another brought to much noise to his ears, if anyone cried out in pain from a well-timed arrow, he wouldn't be able to hear the screams until they were safely at sea.

"One archer behind the crenels will shoot us all!" he despaired.

He ran to the prow of the ship and looked at the murderous walls above them before bellowing a cadence to his men, working his hardest to get them out of the killing field of walls as quickly as possible. He had to deny panic a home in his voice, but the position of the ships here was more precarious than it had been at the boom, when the dromons poured their liquid fire onto them.

His ship finally liberated itself from the shoals and reversed into the open sea.

"There aren't any archers," he said slowly, the realization of relief slipping into him. "The wall's undefended. All their soldiers are on the land wall."

His face smiled, and then the smile turned into an outright laugh. He leapt for joy and let out a "Whoo!" of celebration.

"Captain, what's happening?" one of the crewmen asked.

"Let's get back to Diplokion, things have just picked up, and today is a glorious day for all of us."

"There's more of them," Balias said frightfully to Captain Francisco. "Look, another fleet."

"I can see that, but I don't think that they'll be much danger to us," the captain answered back.

"How can you tell?"

"They're still at anchor, they never thought that we'd make it past the first fleet, so they're completely unprepared for us. They'll also be pretty frightened if we made it past their original numbers."

True to Francisco's prediction, the Diplokion fleet stayed at anchor and patiently observed from their harbour as the two surviving ships of the Venetian reinforcements settled close to the boom, which was lowered to allow them to pass. An honour guard of Venetian galleys and Byzantine Dromons waved flags and lit torches to welcome them into the harbour after such a long journey. The sun was descending into the west, and shadows from the seven hills, the walls and palaces of the capital stretched across the waters of the harbour. The bright flames of the torches were a warm welcome after their long stretch at sea.

"You don't suppose that your brother is going to try any of his tricks here, do you?" Francisco asked Balias.

"I pray that he won't."

"You should remind him, diplomatically of course, that this isn't a city of monks, and during a war, people like him end up killed by their own.”

“In a better world, he wouldn’t need the reminder, but I’ll pass it along nonetheless.”

“In a better world, men like him would be in prisons, rather than pulpits, sir.”

It would have been inappropriate for Balias to agree outright with the captain, but his silence implied what his worlds would have been, in a better world.

Chapter Thirty-Six – The Third Night

April 8th, 1453 – Continued

Sunset, for the Ottoman army, mercifully brought a close to the horrors of the third day. It also brought a manner of carnival into the encased yolk of Constantinople. The forums became gathering spots for revellers, celebrating the day's victories. Guistiniano Longo and his cavalrymen were famed and toasted in every taverna in the city, their raid on the Sultan's camp became more grandiose with each telling, and by morning some believed that the Genoese knight had stood *fisticuffs* with the Sultan and forced him flee with his tail between his legs.

Songs were sung of the Jannisaries fleeing before the charging horsemen of the west. The nuances of falconer, mastiff-trainer, or old-guard Janissaries were unknown to the locals, but everyone heard that the red jackets and white caps of the feared Turkish slave-soldiers were turned in flight, and those who stayed to fight were killed by the city's champions.

A very special toast was raised by the locals for their own. The Fifth Municipal Fire Battalion, long thought to be drinking club for men who sought to avoid direct military service, had seen their members display some heroics significantly beyond any realistic expectation. Many of them took the opportunity to turn those tales of heroics into carnal celebrations in the brothels about town.

The harbour was also in carnival. When the three Venetian transports rowed into the harbour, they were greeted by cheering droves with banners, icons, torches and wooden swords. Wooden swords had long been a gift given to children to remind them that they would someday be soldiers, showing a wooden sword to adults was a way to say that the time to fight was upon them, it was the local way for the townspeople to show support for their defenders. Room was made for them in the imperial harbour at the base of the palace.

Against the backdrop of all this tumultuous celebrations, one man sought out the quiet of the shadows.

Mario Orsini retraced his steps from the previous evening and quietly entered the women's chapel of the Chora compound. Without wasting time or uttering a sound, he pushed the wooden altar table aside and brought the pry-blade of a lever against the altar stone. The stone was heavy, but once it cleared the floor's surface, it easily slid out of its hole, exposing the hollow cavern.

Mario swallowed hard and looked about, making certain that there was no one to witness either his sacrilege or his uncovering another's sacrilege. He brought the light of his lantern over to the hole, and peered down. There was what looked like a small chamber underneath the altar.

Grabbing either side of the egress with each hand, he lowered himself into the cramped room. It was a few feet in depth, and difficult to tell how far back it went. The width and length of the chamber were both obscured by burlap sacks, leather satchels, cloth bundles and other bags. It was too cramped for Mario to enter all the way. He had to content himself with standing in there and gazing over the piles with what little assistance his lantern gave him.

He grabbed hold of the first bag available and brought it out from the hole and set it on the sanctuary floor. He opened the bag and pulled the edges down to see what was there. In the bag he found: several dozen electrum coins, a brass armlet with red coral-stone, a turquoise hippopotamus the length of his index finger, a gold ring with a large pearl, and an ivory miniature, cracked down the middle, probably from the rough move to the chapel.

Mario said nothing but looked around quietly and lowered the light on his lantern. There were at least a hundred other bags just like it. He absently stowed the hippopotamus in his pocket and put the bag back before leaving the hole. Silently he replaced the altar stone, and then the altar table. He blew away any dust that had emerged from his work and would betray his presence here tonight. He left the chapel and locked the door behind him. He finally went back to the hospital barracks to lie in bed and think. He had a great many things for his mind to consider.

Two years ago, Mario was an emotional wreck of a man, whenever he was confronted with any ethical dilemma. The thought of mistreating another man would weigh heavily on him and rob him of sleep, over even the most insignificant moral trepidations. He'd once been wracked by four days of anxiety for accidentally wandering off with his master's Zeno-folio.

His thoughts were not the fussing and fretting of morality and a conscience in crisis. They were the mathematical queries of logistics and inventory. Mario's mind had more determination when confronted with these practical matters, the calculations of which made no demands on his ethical capacity.

It was several hours after the sun had set when the last arrivals to the fire damaged tent of the Sultan finally arrived. The last time everyone in the chamber had met was three weeks ago in Adrianople, but recent events had necessitated their congress.

Sitting on pillows and carpets in a tent lit with burning braziers, different men, different factions, and different opinions sat about. They were served coffee and baklava, all rules of politeness were observed before words could be said, but there was a palpable stress in the air.

Halil sat surrounded by his brothers. They represented the divan, the exchequers of state and harpies of the court. Like everyone else, they tried to hide their impressions of the day's events, but everyone knew what they were going to say. Scrap the enterprise, pay off the levies and go home. Accept whatever tribute Constantine was willing to pay as a down-payment on future tributes from the lowly City-Empire.

Baltaolu sat with Emir Tolga. The admiral knew that he was going to need the political warmth of Mehmet's father-in-law after the double failures at the chain and again with the Venetian reinforcements.

After them were Zaganos and Mesut. While their contributions were limited to the campaign thusfar, they had no major disasters to carry. Politically they knew that they'd best quietly allow reality to blame Halil and Baltaolu for the disaster of the day.

After everyone finished their sweet dessert and bitter beverage, Kabira, the black agha of the eunuchs ushered all of the guards, servants, slaves and retainers out of the main room, so that the war council could speak more freely. He then positioned himself by the curtain to overhear everything that was said without himself being seen.

"Peace be upon you, everyone," Mehmet started the meeting.

"Unto you be peace," everyone grumbled in unison.

Mehmet then stood up from his comfortable cushion and walked to the back of the hall, picked up a rolled carpet and walked into the middle of their large circle of cushions. He rolled the carpet out, and it measured four metres by three, a large one o f Cappadocian origin.

"A work of beauty, this one. Is it not so, Father?" he called out to Tolga.

"Yes, Your Majesty," he answered. At such a meeting, no one wanted to be singled out for anything.

"That it is," agreed Baltaolu beside him.

"I didn't ask you," Mehmet said dispassionately without looking at the admiral.

He went back to his own cushion and produced an apple, red, sour-looking and out of season. He then walked back to the middle of the circle, placed the apple in the middle of the carpet and returned to his cushion.

"Grand Vizier Halil," he returned to the conversation. "I would like you to get that apple for me. Can you do so without stepping on the beautiful carpet?"

"Sire?" he asked.

"I asked you if you could fetch me that apple, without stepping on the carpet?"

"Sire, I don't think that I could do that."

"I see. Is the problem that you don't understand my request, or that you're unwilling to try? Kapudan-Pasha Baltaolu!"

Mehmet had the ruthlessness of youth without consequences. He was the youngest man at the council, and his eyes betrayed an unfettered aggression that made elder men uncomfortable. He stared a challenge at his admiral.

"Yes, Sire?"

"I put the same request to you. Is it within your abilitities?"

Baltaolu wisely decided that it was in his best interests to at least give it a try, so he stood up and walked to the edge of the carpet. A metre and a half from the short side is still a long reach. He tried stretching his arm, without reaching it. He tried stretching out his leg, but met with no more success.

"Alas, Sire. I cannot."

"Sit down then. That apple is Constantinople. I've asked you to get it for me, but you only say '*No sire, I can't.*' I should be happy with you I suppose, at least you tried. You failed abysmally and sacrificed what dignity you had left, but you put in a good effort. A pity that you wasted our time with your unproductive acrobatics. Do you find horrific dishonour in your failure, or are you comfortable with it?"

"It dishonours me greatly, Your Majesty."

"As well it should," Mehmet capped that line of conversation testily. "Your failure costs both strength and money."

Mehmet reached down and picked a pistachio nut from the tray before him.

"Any of you, more experienced advisors, planning on showing me a useless effort? Another honourable failure? Wholehearted effort that's just going to fall a little short?"

"Sire?" asked Mesut.

Mehmet stared blankly.

“Would you like to try, Janissary?”

“If I may.”

“You may.”

Mesut arose and walked to the carpet. He reached down and started to roll the brim inwards, stepping on the burlap flooring under the carpet as he rolled it up. At the halfway point he grabbed the apple and brought it to the youngster.

“Thank you, Janissary,” he said patiently, and with a touch of stolen thunder. “That was very clever of you. Now, does anyone have anything good to say about what happened today?”

“I do,” Baltaolu ventured tepidly.

“Do you now? I hope that you haven’t chosen today to develop a sense of sarcasm, Admiral.”

“No, sire,” The Kapudan-Pasha knew that his position was the least tenable of everyone at the table, and he would have to make try very hard to keep his place there. “The three Italian ships were not completely successful.”

“That’s right, there were three ships that sailed against your hundred, and I understand that you did manage to put one to wreckage against the sea walls. Their crews, I’m sure, were rescued by the Romans.”

“No, sire… at least not right away.”

“So they had to shiver in the cold sea for some time. My heart goes out to them. I’m glad that you’ve found some victory in today’s events.”

“Not victory, sire, but intelligence. It took three hours for Roman soldiers to come to the aid of the men who washed ashore. Three hours!”

Mehmet’s face was blank, this registered as nothing.

“Sire, the sea walls are completely undefended. All of their soldiers are guarding the land wall. When we attacked the buoy yesterday…”

“Another spectacular failure,” Halil added before a shushing gaze came to him via the young sultan.

“Admittedly not successful,” Baltaolu wasn’t about to cede complete defeat. “When we attacked them, our attack was fended off by four ships that broke out of their docks. Only four! The ships aren’t manned. Those men are also at the wall.”

“So, they have all the men they can spare at the wall, what of it? We knew that!” Halil chided the admiral.

“We didn’t know to what extent,” Baltaolu answered back. If we could land men at New Gate or elsewhere, they could enter the city easily. If we could send some cannon over to Zaganos-pasha, He could enter the Valley of Springs and sink the Christian fleet. As far as the naval conflict has gone, it hasn't been an unremitting disaster. We've only lost a handful of ships. We still have many possibilities open to us, your majesty."

"Hmmm," Mehmet wondered. "What do you think of that, Second Minister?"

"Send us some cannons, and we'll come down from Pera and occupy the Valley of the Springs. If the ships are really as defenceless as our friend insinuates, we would sink their entire fleet. If they're not, they'll destroy our artillery. Do we have something other than your observations, Kapudan-Pasha?" Zaganos did not like being addressed as by title alone, especially when the sultan was angry and erratic.

"It doesn't matter, sire," Halil piped in. "Our cannons can't move. We can't make more of them, and our crews are dead. There are only a few dozen men who know how to properly use those beasts now. We need to retrain crews for the equipment."

"How long does it take to train an artillery-man?"

"Properly can take a long time, and we need more cannons, Sire."

"Don't continue along that line, Grand Vizier," Mehmet instructed him.

"Sire?"

"If you want to say that we should abandon the siege after only three days, then that means that we have to pay all of these filthy mercenaries and levies that you've hired, the state will go bankrupt, as I'm sure your brother Musa will concur."

"We could extort a handsome sum from the Romans, Sire. Surely enough to cushion the blow from this adventure. That option must be considered."

"Considered and rejected," Mehmet answered without looking at him. "Mesut-bey, since I know what my vizier thinks is appropriate, what do you think that we should do?"

"Oh, that's simple, sire. Your original plan was working fine. We should continue along those lines."

"Were today a success, Janissary, we wouldn't be having this meeting," Halil interrupted.

"We could never take this apple without paying costs, sire. The cannons are still pointed in the right direction, and training a crew can take place during the war, we don't need them to attend the university in Cairo, just give them simple instructions. Given time, they'll knock the walls down. Our diggers have started their task, the soft earth is doing us a great service. We know that their numbers are so low that they can't defend their city. Time will win this war."

"Musa-bey," Mehmet addressed the younger Chandarli brother, the secretary of the treasury. "Under the current conditions, how long can we keep the siege going? If there are no more dramatic failures."

"Without a serious problem, until the first of May should be no problem, sire. Longer if we keep losing men," that didn't sound as positive as he'd intended it to. "After that, we have three options, Sire. You can borrow money; you can grant the men rights of plunder, to compensate unpaid wages; or you can abandon the siege."

Mehmet didn't want to borrow money from the nobles, especially the wealthy Chandarli Clan. Any loans meant new wives, and new claims on his dynasty. Granting rites of plunder, with an army this size, would pulverize the city into sauce rather than take the prize whole. Under no circumstances could he abandon the siege. That would take him off the throne, and half the Divan would try to put Orhan in his place.

"Mesut, you're right, the situation isn't as bad as it could be. The most important thing is that they receive no more assistance from the west. Thank you for your reminder of our strength," Mehmet looked around the room. "The siege continues, and its triumph is once again assured. I thank all of you for coming. I would ask the Divan to leave with our blessings. Baltaolu and my beloved father-in-law, Tolga must remain, as must the prime and second ministers."

Musa and the other Chandarli brothers bowed and backed out, as did Mesut.

"Tolga," Mehmet began. "I have a great favour to ask of you."

"Anything, Sire."

"I must ask you to ride with Zaganos-pasha to Pera, and from there to Diplokion. I have to ask you to take command of the fleet under the rank of Kapudan-pasha. Would you do me this service?"

"Of course, Sire."

"Thank you. You and Zaganos may go."

They did so without another word.

"Halil-bey," he began when it was only himself, the grand vizier and the now former Kapudan-pasha. "What do you think should be done with Baltaolu?"

"Sire, I…" Baltaolu tried to speak in his defence.

"Silence," hissed the Sultan. His face contorted in beast-like proportions. Everyone in the room froze. "Don't ever speak to me, especially out of turn! Understand that you incompetent ox!"

Halil waited for the fury to pass. He knew better than to tell the angry young boy to calm down. That would only invite more rage.

"I recommend exile, Sire," he said once calm had restored. "If you kill him, the men will say, apparently correctly, that you placed a fool in command. This would bring questions as to your judgement. Quiet exile is better."

Mehmet ground his teeth, a disgusting habit that he'd inherited from his father. It was when he did that that Halil saw shades of thoughtful old Murat in his undisciplined boy.

"Your words are wise," he acknowledged. "You may go into exile now, Baltaolu. I understand that you have family in Karaman. Go there."

Baltaolu swallowed, then bowed, then glumly walked out of the room, leaving the sultan and his minister forever.

"What do you think, Halil?"

"I..."

"Before you answer, I want you to know something," Mehmet's eyes were resolute, they seemed somehow older that they were at this time last year. "If you tell me anything that plans for peace rather than victory again, I'll have to dismiss you. It won't bring me any pleasure, but I'll do it nonetheless. Once thrust, this dagger can't retreat."

Halil considered his former pupils erratic mood swings over the past hour, and thought it wise to agree.

"I think that it would be wise to slow down the pace of the campaign, as the Janissary said," he replied. "Your patience and the cannons are better warriors than their navies and soldiers, my lord."

"I'm glad to hear that. You may go," he said.

"Good night, Sire."

"Goodnight."

Isodore was relieved that Hectore Pazzi was not a man of exceptional intelligence. He left the inn at a predictable time, and rarely looked over his shoulder to see if he was being followed. He had the utmost faith in his own anonymity, and that miscalculation bolstered Isodore's faith in his own.

In his third night in the capital, Pazzi left the tavern as soon as the sun set, like he did the previous night. Isodore patiently kept his distance, but always observed which turns the man made, and to whom he was speaking.

Isodore's greatest help to his urban camouflage was the simple ordinariness of his appearance. He was slightly overweight but not fat, had a priest's beard, but not a big bushy hermit's beard, he was tall-ish but not giant, and he had light brown hair and hazel eyes. Describing him in great detail isn't necessary because he's the type of person anyone would walk past on the street and make no register of. His outside was so typically typical that even the shopkeepers whom he'd been visiting for the past three years in town didn't know that he was a regular.

The monk's atypical nature was entirely mental. Considered by Paulines to be a Burgomil, by Burgomils to be a Manichean, by Manicheans to be a Monatist and by the Orthodox to be a heretic, his religious bend would place him sternly and irrevocably into the category of "miscellaneous."

His inability to sit still, both religiously and socially, probably stemmed from his affable nature. While he enjoyed arguing with anyone who didn't have the crazy eyes of a fanatic, he would fundamentally accept solipsism as normal. Having different ideas, many of them being contradictory, meant that he had no problem thinking of everyone as being basically correct. God was of three attributes, and Christ of two natures, or a single nature, and we mayhap we needn't actually divide God into three, and maybe Christ was wholly human, wholly divine and half-and-half. Isodore's appreciation and tolerance of nuance made him an affable man, very easy to get along with, but a terrible monk. The others in his order were fine to let him wander as far as his feet would take him.

Because of his many wanderings, both physically and religiously throughout the city, he knew the back alleys and differing religious institutions better than most. It was because of this that he realized right away what Pazzi was doing. This night, he first visited an abbey barracks of the Armenian exarchate, then another boarding house for the Oriental Orthodox Patriarchy, then a lodge that was frequented by the retiring Armenian Rite Katholikos of the city. Pazzi was hunting an Armenian.

Last night, he'd been scouting the Palace compound of Blachernae, which contained one of the largest Armenian religious centres in the capital at Chora. Putting one and one together was not a problem for Isodore. Chora had been converted into a field hospital for the siege, the monks had been uprooted, they would have been sent to one of the other Armenian temples. Pazzi was looking for someone displaced from Chora by the temporary hospital.

Pazzi's stays at all of those buildings was brief. He entered the buildings only long enough to ask a few questions at the door, and was then on his way again. He finally was received at the Hospice of Saint Nishan and brought in.

'He must have found who he was looking for,' summed up Isodore's

thinking, where he disappeared for a half an hour.

The monk walked in the main gate to the hospice and presented himself to guard at the door. He wanted to learn what he could about the object of Pazzi's interest.

"*Bari Yereko. Anun's Isodore'e*," He greeted him and introduced himself in Armenian, and then said that he was looking for someone from Chora. "Unek Choratsi."

"Are you with the Italian gentleman?" the guard asked in Greek.

"How much did he pay?" The monk asked slyly, thankfully shifting to the more familiar tongue.

"Two bits,"

"Here's three, where might I find them?"

"They're on the second floor, third door on the right, Brother Isodore. The man's name is Father Abaven."

"Thank you, Brother."

The building was a normally a convalescent home for elderly clerics. It was dark, quiet and sombre, as would be expected of such a place. Such a description suited the lively monk well tonight, as he stuck to the shadows when he walked through the vestibule and up the stairs, and then began slinking down the hall. It mildly distressed him that he was a little out of breath once he reached the top of the wooden staircase, more for reasons of stealth than health. He none the less forced his breathing to regulate and crept towards the aforementioned third door on the right. He put his ear to the door and listened.

He heard nothing for an instant, and then heard footsteps coming to the door.

In a quick panic, Isodore jumped quickly to the left and walked in the neighbouring door without knocking. There was an elderly man getting ready for bed, by candle-light, who looked up, startled at the intruder.

"*Barev! Vonts ek?*" he greeted the stranger, stepping into the room and closing the door just as Pazzi exited the next room. "Hello! How are you?"

The old man started speaking back to Isodore faster than he could translate the words in his head; Isodore's Armenian was far from fluent, but he could certainly tell that the man was very angry. Isodore nodded his head at the man's angry words, smiled imploringly and then backed out of the room into the darkness of the hall.

"*K'nerek, k'nerek,*" he apologised and returned to the safety of the outer hall, closing the door behind him.

He listened to the darkness and heard no signs of Pazzi. There wasn't even the distant patter of footsteps; it was as though his presence had been erased from the night. Isodore pushed open the door to Father Abaven's chamber and stepped in silently.

"Hello?" he asked the darkness of the chamber, which gave him no reply.

The moonlight coming through the window was enough to illuminate a lantern on a night table, and Isodore sparked it from his flint to see around. The lantern was quickly receptive and cast its light about the bedchamber.

Lying on the bed was the earthly remains of Father Abaven. His nose was a bloody mess, blood that was also all over the pillow on the wooden floor before his bed. Isodore quickly checked the man for breathing, sensing nothing, he then looked about in a panic.

This wasn't the sort of thing that he normally ran into. Watching, thinking, observing, that was his trade. A corpse was something unfamiliar to him. He looked at the still warm body and his eyes blurred for an instant. He'd never seen a corpse before, the shell without the ghost was something new to him and he didn't like it at all. He stumbled out of the room, gasping for breath. He closed the door behind him and ran out of the Hospice. Only to regain himself after hours of wandering the street in a psychological mess.

"A word?" Halil posited as he waddled over the grass, his beard and belly presaging his arrival.

"Yes, Prime Minister?" Mesut turned to face to face the aristocrat with the same level of dispassionate respect as he held all members of the divan. His formal graces and controlled emotions made it difficult for others to read him.

"Peace be upon you."

"And unto you be peace. What is it?" Mesut began the reply before Halil had finished the greeting.

"I suppose that you've heard of the Janissaries defending the cannons?"

"The falconers, yes," Mesut wouldn't refer to them as anything but. "I understand that they were cut down."

"Many of them have gone to God, yes," Halil replied. "It's a pity that they lack the fortitude of your soldiers."

"It's a pity that our reputation has suffered so greatly, Halil-Pasha," he corrected the vizier. "It's a pity that our enemies saw men in Janissary uniforms turn and flee. It's a pity that untrained children were convinced that they could stand and fight like the mighty."

"I assure you, I share your embarrassment."

Mesut ventured no words or expressions to confirm or deny such a brash assessment.

"I agree with what you said to the sultan during the inspection of the walls, that these new Janissaries are blunting your blade. We need to take soldiers from your ranks to stay here to defend the sultan's person. Would you be able to spare the mastiff trainers?"

Mesut's eyes betrayed a hint of suspicion.

"With pleasure. Why would you be so willing to lift this burden from us?"

"We need the steel of the Janissaries to be sharp, Brother. We don't need you to be weighted down with men whose competence is untested. That and we need more people to protect our beloved Mehmet."

"Of course," Mesut nodded his head to agree with the elder statesman. It was obvious that he was trying desperately to curry favour with Mesut, the only Janissary commander who hadn't revolted to depose the sultan last time. Halil's transparent plan was to strengthen the Janissary, weaken Mehmet's personal defence, and accrue a boon from Mesut in the process. Halil was fooling no one. "I'll send them over, first thing in the morning."

"Thank you, Chorbachi," Halil said magnanimously. "I pray that this favour will strengthen both of us."

Mesut wanted to slap the back-biting minister. There would be no transference of loyalty over such an obvious ploy. If Halil believed the Janissary officer to be so easily manipulated, he was sorely mistaken.

"I'm sure that it will, Pasha. Good night."

"Goodnight, Janissary."

The most chronic sound of winter in the Venetian palace had been the intermittent hacking cough of the ambassador, Giovanni Cardillo. Spring had not brought an end to it, and now Cardillo's body was tired and weary from the convulsions and shivers that accompanied the constant hacking.

His meeting chamber was alight with candles, torches and braziers, keeping him constantly warm. He'd been to the Venetian doctor, the Greek doctors, he'd invited herbalists to his home and even had that old witch brought in through the servants' entrance. Nothing that anyone suggested seemed to be able to do any good for him.

He'd tried everything but honest prayer. He would go through the motions every Sunday, as it was expected of his office, but he would never consider the option of honestly humbling himself before the almighty.

He wasn't an atheist. He believed in God, his Son, the Saints and Sacraments of the one true church, Catholic and Apostolic. He just didn't like God the father. He reminded him too much of his own father, aloof and uncaring. He loathed God the son, who was given the kingdom, for which all he had to do was die. Everyone dies, that carpenter lived a life without responsibility. The Church had a special spot reserved in his heart, a spot it shared with nothing else, as it was the root of so much evil. Left to their own devices, the secular rulers of the earth would simply enrich themselves by administering to the needs of the population. Simple functional necessity would allow civilization to flourish. The Church was a ruthless secular power that would contest the secular powers of all others, because they had the near magical ability to turn men against reason and to take up bloody violence against their own interests. Religion was evil because it was its nature to create and spread evil. It was unfortunately an evil with which Giovanni had to work.

For this reason, Giovanni was less than enthusiastic about meeting his two guests. He'd heard rumours of Isaac, of a fast rise and equally speedy fall, but knew very little of the younger brother. He'd worked with their cousin, many years ago, and found him to be an irrepressible scoundrel.

"Señor Balias, from the Senate of Venice, and Bishop Isaac of Naples!" announced the doorman of the embassy.

He knew better than to announce Isaac prior his brother. Anyone who placed a church nobleman over a landed gentleman to the ambassador was taking his life in his own hands. Here, a penniless squire whose dominion was an island that sunk at high tide would get consideration above the Pope himself.

"Gentlemen, welcome to my home," Cardillo greeted them.

Balias, the younger of the two, was the first through the door and hopped to embrace the ambassador.

"Hello, Don Giovanni!" he smiled widely, but his eyes failed to hide some shock. His voice betrayed nothing. "It's good to see you again, old friend. It's been many years."

"It has, young Balias. Many years since I knew your cousin, Leonardo DiNapoli," Cardillo added.

"You look very robust. The eastern climes must be invigorating for your health."

"That they are," Giovanni smiled. The lie that he saw in his guest's eyes felt like a slap in the face, and it let him know how seriously his health really had decayed. "And this is your brother, Bishop Isaac, of whom I've heard so much."

"I have that privileged title," Isaac said and tried to resist the urge to blush with embarrassment and fury. He held out his hand to await a kiss.

Giovanni observed the rules of decorum and kissed the ruby ring, but did so with an almost criminal lack of enthusiasm.

"Welcome to the Venetian Quarter of Constantinople," he said formally. "You'll both have apartments here in the embassy, my servants are already moving your belongings. Later in the week, I will present you both to the emperor. Have you met with my lieutenant, Vincent DiCastillo?"

"The Spaniard, yes," Isaac seemed less than impressed. "I'm sure that the Doge could send you a more qualified Venetian gentleman to be your assistant. Surely there exist such men in the Republic."

"There are many qualified gentlemen back in the Republic, but Vincent is a known commodity here in the Empire, and I wouldn't trade him for Neptune's Trident," he answered jokingly before a fit of coughing overtook him. "Pardon me, a residual winter cold."

"Yes, of course," Balias had a stern face, but one that had been dedicated to the unfamiliar territory of honest suffering for the past year. "I'm sure that modern science and God's grace will be able to fix your spirits."

"Someday, yes," he answered, thinking of Mario's inability to cure his ailments.

"God cures illness, not science," the stern bishop informed them.

"Yes, and God sends illness to test the faithful. 'All things, both good and evil, are possible through him, as I recall."

"Indeed," the cleric nodded. "I should like to meet the new Bishop of Constantinople."

"Yes, of course. You'll meet him when you meet the Emperor."

"That should be quickly, Mister Ambassador. I have some very important letters for him, regarding the rules for the mass in Holy Wisdom, to celebrate the return of the Greek churches to the Christian fold."

"Yes," Giovanni smiled politely. "That should happen in a few days, in the meantime, you've brought men with you, correct?"

"Yes, your lieutenant, the Spaniard that we met earlier, has taken them to barrack."

"Good, good. How many of them are there?"

"Three hundred and seventeen. We lost our third ship against the walls of the city. That ship was carrying our equipment. The men are all safe, but our armour and weapons may well be at the bottom of the Marmara."

"No, I've dispatched some of my own house guards to the sea walls. The ship wrecked against the shore there, and while she's no longer sea worthy, most of her cargo was safely brought over the wall. It's difficult to bring the crates up the wall, but with time, the task should be accomplished."

"Oh, that's wonderful," Balias answered. "We've crossbows, harquebuses and armour in that cargo. That along with more than three hundred men to wield them should aid well in the defence of Christendom."

"On the subject of which," Isaac interrupted. "I have specific instructions from the Pope, which need to be attended to before we put those men at the service of the Emperor."

There was an awkward silence. Cardillo suffered another coughing fit, breaking that silence, before he went on to ask the bishop:

"What kind of instructions?"

"I am to witness his baptism."

"I'm sorry, Your Grace," Giovanni spoke like any man who was born with an ability to lie and make up a story with little or no preparation. "But that's been done. At the holy altar of the blessed cathedral of Holy Wisdom. There was a three day festival. We can't very well do it again to satisfy a letter. I'm prepared to swear on God's holy law that I witnessed the event personally, if that would assuage your worries."

"I'm sorry, but it will not do," the Cardinal answered quickly. "We'll have to re-enact the ritual. The emperor should have waited for my arrival."

"I believe that he let his newly found faith carry him away when he sensed the Holy Spirit in the letter he received from the Holy Father."

"Be that as it may, we'll have to have an event to which I will act as witness. It shouldn't bother anyone, a rebaptism is hardly a sin. If anything, it will serve to reaffirm his commitment to Christ."

"Yes, of course," Giovanni replied before he was again lain aside by his coughing.

'*This man's going to be a problem, but not for too long,*' the ambassador surmised.

Chapter Thirty-Seven - The Fourth Day

April 9, 1453

“Come on, easy does it!” Vincent called down the ladder once he'd arrived at the top of the Marble Tower. “You can see the whole battlefield from up here!”

“Yes, just a moment,” insisted Balias who finally emerged from the narrow vertical passageway that led to the top of the structure. “I say, it is quite the sight.”

From the top of the tower, the observers could look north along the walls that stretched up to the top of Mesotechion, and then crested down to the Golden Horne, which was out of direct sight. Eastwards along the sea walls, they could see the southward defences, and to the south was the Sea of Marmora.

The big sight to see was to the west. Over a few dozen acres of land was stretched one of the largest armies ever put to field. Not only was it the shear size of the horde that impressed, but the variance of it. Armoured knights alongside light archers, professional soldiers and ragamuffin crowds, all running in and out of a complex of tents and shelters made the army seem like a giant traVeling carnival.

“My word, there certainly are a lot of them,” he exclaimed.

“A hand, please,” came the irate voice of the bishop, trying to scamper up the ladder.

“Of course, Your Grace,” Vincent helpfully lowered a strong arm to help the Prince of Christ up the final stages of the ladder to the parapets. “Are you alright?”

“I'm fine. Thank you, My Son,” he answered while trying to catch his breath.

Balias smirked as he listened to his brother. Isaac spoke in a much more formal manner when he was near foreigners. His intonation was quicker and with a more didactic air. He constantly sought to subordinate non-Italians.

“There they are, your grace! The Vikings use a word, ‘*Gruzn*’ which means both terrible and great at the same time. It usually applies to some monster of legend, like a dragon or whatnot. I think the term certainly applies to these enemies.”

“There is nothing great about the enemies of Christ, Spaniard,” Isaac spoke as though he were correcting a pupil who'd mislearnt a lesson.

"Those who live outside the Latin communion are damned and not deserving of any respect."

"Even our Greek friends?" Vincent joked, but with a grain of sobriety.

"Those outside the Church of Rome are not our friends."

"Under normal circumstances, I'd be the first to agree with you," Vincent laughed. "I don't have much patience for their bizarre mysticism and oriental ways. But that argument has to be postponed until the Turks are driven back. I've been asked to explain that to you."

"I'll thank you for your interest in religion, my child," Isaac said condescendingly. "But *I'm* to judge what is and is not appropriate in this field."

"I see," Vincent nodded and looked out at the field of battle.

"*Smash!*" went another explosion from the cannon battery. They'd been less frequent today, as a result of their new crews.

"Is it safe up here? I mean from those cannons?" Balias asked, trying to break the awkwardness.

"Oh yes," Vincent answered. "Very safe. All the cannons are aimed at the middle of the wall. There's nothing to worry about, in terms of cannons. The tower here is too tall for arrows as well."

Vincent looked over the edge and then turned back to his two guests.

"The Emperor has not converted to the Latin rite and has no plans for doing so, Isaac," Vincent began, leaving out honorific titles. "He's accepted the idea in principle, arrested the major opponents of union, and he'll host an ecumenical council to unify the churches after the war. The soldiers hired on for the task of bolstering the defences were hired on as mercenaries, not as crusaders. You're going to have to stop your religious posturing."

"It's not posturing!" he shouted.

"Oh yes it is," Vincent opened his cloak wide enough to show his sword, alongside a small arsenal of knives, daggers and some form of truncheon. "And we'll not tolerate that here and now. The alliance is in everyone's interests, and if you betray that faith, then I'll cut your belly like I'd drain a sheep, say that a Turkish assassin got you and you need to be avenged. At least then you'd be of some service to our war. Once the Turks pack up and go home, you're free to fight whatever battle or debate you want, but until that point, you have to choose to be an ally or an enemy. My impression of you leads me to believe that you're more likely to choose enemy of the endeavour. I look at you and I see someone who would let the Muslims capture all of Eastern Europe, rather than ally with someone whose knee doesn't bend to Rome."

"You seem to have warped ideas as to what the 'sides' are in the battle between truth and lies, my child," he said with all calmness.

"Don Balias, you're in charge of your men, not this holy fool. Can you control *him*?"

"He won't be a problem," Balias insisted. "Is the ambassador behind this little conversation?"

Vincent looked at him coolly, answering the question and then turned his attention to the cleric.

"Bishop, if you step out of line, and I need you to understand this without reservation, you'll never see Italy again. You'll be buried in an unmarked grave under Muslim soil, to rest there until the day of judgement. Do you understand that, or should I just go through with the inevitable outcome now?"

"I understand," Isaac said, but with too much defiance present in his eyes. Vincent didn't see it, but his brother did. Balias knew that this would be the end of nothing, though he hoped for the best.

The gradual bombardment didn't stop all day long. It was slower than it had been yesterday, but it hadn't stopped. The stones kept flying, and the walls kept crumbling. The injured kept mounting and Mario kept busy with them.

Most of Mario's day consisted of running from the front gate to the barracks and the hospital priory. Mostly what he was doing would be considered triage or diagnostic evaluations.

"Doctor Mario!" came a familiar shout.

"Hello, Isodore," Mario said smiling. "How wonderful it is to see someone healthy walk in here. How are you?"

"Terrible, I need to speak to you urgently. I think that you're in great danger."

"Why?"

"Can we speak somewhere," he lowered his voice, "Alone?"

"Yes, of course," Mario pointed to the barrack building near the entrance. "I have an office in here."

"Good, good. That's good," Isodore replied with uncharacteristic jitters.

It unnerved Mario to see the monk so shaken up, so he was most curious to see what was wrong. It was the early hours of the morning, after dawn, but not significantly into the day, so the influx of injured was slow.

"It's a good thing you're here this morning, things are pretty slow. The past few days, the cannon fire was intense, and we had many, many people coming in, and yesterday, oh, the first real fighting started. Today, the cannons are slower. They must be out of sorts, given how much slower my business is here."

"Yes, I'm sure," the monk answered and looked around Mario's office.

The room was covered in charts, labelling different shades of yellow, and the room smelled like a latrine. There were several dozen half-full vials of urine on the shelves, and a book open on a counter.

"Do you know Hectore Pazzi?" He began.

Mario shook his head.

"He's the captain of the guard on the other side."

"An Italian working for the Turks?"

"No, no! The Genoese! The other side of the harbour! Not the other side of the wall - listen!" Isodore hated it when he became emotional. He felt that it rattled his otherwise good judgement. "He's here in town."

Mario looked blank.

"What of it?"

"He was here, scouting about the palace compound two nights ago," he began to relate his tale. "And last night, I followed him around half the Armenian religious establishments in Constantinople."

"I though the Armenians were all Orthodox,"

"He's not looking to convert! He was looking for someone. And not all Armenians are Orthodox - do you know Father Abaven?"

"Yes, I do. I met him briefly a month ago. He's the Abbot here. Or at least he was before the war. He should be again once this place reverts to ecclesiastic control after the Turks run. Why? Is he Western Rite?"

"He's dead."

"Sorry to hear that."

"Pazzi killed him."

"What?" Mario asked. "Why would he do something like that? Did they have a disagreement?"

"I don't know for certain, but I was there when it happened."

"You were there? Have you told Vincent?"

"No, forget Vincent! He wasn't looking for him because of something personal. He's hunting something else. I heard him at the door, he was interrogating the man before he killed him. It has something to do with this monastery."

"Why would anyone..." Mario's eyes glazed over and he looked as though he was focussing on something just outside his optical perception. His face blanched.

"You know something," Isodore said right away. "What's going on?"

"I don't know, let me think for a second."

"Tell me, and I'll help you."

Mario traced his fingertips over his eyebrows and stared into Isodore's eyes.

"I can't tell you the truth and I don't want to lie to you."

Mario was a fairly solitary creature, and Isodore was one of the closest things he had to a friend in the city. Except of course for Vincent, though their friendship was strained and would undoubtedly take a downturn when he learned that Ella was here. Ezera, he presumed to have died when the Nineveh was sunk.

"I can tell you later," he said after a moment's thought.

"What is it?"

"I can tell you later," the doctor repeated. "But I need you to let me know about Pazzi. Keep an eye on him. I'll speak to the guards here and ask them to increase the force here, but I don't know what good it'll do. Everyone's guarding the wall."

"I know," concurred the monk. "There are no police or guards on the streets or in the towers. On this side of that fence, there's nothing."

"Do you know where to find him?"

"He's staying at an inn near Bucholeon."

"Well, keep an eye on him, but be careful."

"You don't need to remind me," Isodore leant in so that his whispering could be heard. "I really need to know what he's after, though. I swear that I won't tell anyone."

"Don't be so persistent," Mario answered. "The less you know, the better at this point."

North of the city, along the fabled Bosporus, halfway to the Black Sea, stood Roman Castle. Since it sat right on the waterway, it was an idea meeting spot for Zaganos-Pasha, the second minister of the Ottoman State, and Emir Tolga of Kastamonu, the acting admiral. Their meeting began, as all such meetings did, with an exchange of well wishes of peace.

"Peace be upon you,"

"And unto you be peace."

"Congratulations are due to you, Emir," Zaganos said with a bow.

"Yes, thank you. Though it's a shame that our friend Baltaolu can't join us for the rest of the campaign."

"He was a good man,"

"He's not dead, and his goodness wasn't my experience," Tolga replied. "He started last year, knowing nothing of what he was doing. That's not a sin, but accepting ignorance as unchangeable, most certainly is. He refused to learn, he refused to listen, he thought that this appointment was licence to mint his own coins, and is now riding east on a borrowed donkey, like a pilgrim without a kurush to his name, to Karaman to live with his uncles."

"It's God's will."

"Let's not worry about God's will these days so much as our own," Tolga said before switching over to Greek, Zaganos' native tongue. "May I present my castellan, Ayoub. He's of your race."

Zaganos took one look at the Catalan and knew that not to be the case. He behaved politely nonetheless.

"Hello, Ayoub. Where are you from?"

"Barcellona, Vizier." He answered. They shared a glance where they both understood that '*your race*' means convert.

"Welcome to Roman Castle, Spaniard."

"I'm Catalan, and I've been here before, though in remarkably different circumstances."

"Welcome back, then," the short, bald minister of state corrected himself. "It was you that called this meeting, my Sheikh, so I presume that you've got some news?"

"Yes, not so much news, as a private announcement of which only you need be aware," Tolga steadied himself and prepared to speak. "I know nothing of sailing, naval warfare or training men for either. I know nothing of ships, aqua-dynamism, trade winds or currents. I thought that you should know that."

"I already knew that," Zaganos jovially answered. "The question is, how much can you learn and how quickly?"

"Nowhere near enough, I'm afraid," he answered without shame. "That's why my assistant here is so important. Ayoub is an experienced sailor and captain. And it was he who ran the Venetian cargo ship aground. He also led a raid against the Marmora Islands, and against the buoy line. He's the most experienced soldier we have for these things."

"Well then, I repeat myself when I say '*welcome again*,'" The minister seemed a tad impatient. "What do you think of the naval situation?"

"Terrible. Irreconcilably so," Ezera answered with candour. "The only thing that is preventing the Romans from sailing their fleet out of the harbour and sinking every ship we have, is that they don't have the time or manpower. They're defending the wall, they've only a few ships in fighting condition. If the pressure on the wall ever lightens, they would probably do away with our entire fleet."

"It can't be that bad. Baltaolu…"

"Baltaolu was unforgivably foolish," Ezera cut off the minister before he could finish the sentence. "Baltaolu was given a city to turn into a shipyard and a forest to turn into a fleet, and he had them produce fishing trawlers and then convert them into fighting ships. There was no thought and no plan at the beginning, and no good fruit grows from a poisoned root."

"And your plan would reverse that, I presume?"

"Oh, goodness, no. If Baltaolu was a paid agent of Byzantium (an ironic comparison, as that was exactly what Ezera happened to be), he wouldn't have been able to do more damage to the naval campaign. My recommendation is that we abandon the buoy. It can't be taken."

"Well, I wouldn't suggest that to His Majesty if I were you."

"No, but you'll have to do it anyway," Ezera conceded. "So I'll have to ask you to listen carefully when I explain the new plan."

Zaganos looked over at Tolga with what would be a raised eyebrow, if the second Minister had any hair on his face. The Emir of Kastamonu nodded to let him know that the reformed pirate was indeed serious.

"Alright then, Ayoub-bey," he began. "What's your plan?"

"The ships that Baltaolu had built are all the same, flat bottomed hulls, they're made for fair weather sailing on this Roman lake, not the high seas."

"You have many complaints but few suggestions."

"Flat bottomed boats are meant to be hauled onto land at the end of a day's fishing. Their hulls are strong enough to bear the weight of the ship as it gets dragged over pebbles and rocks. They can even be transported over land for small distances."

"What are you suggesting?"

"I want your men to work quietly and inconspicuously. I need them to carve a pathway through the trees, leading from the Bosporus to the Valley of the Springs. We'll haul the entire fleet over Pera Hill, and drop them into the upper stretch of the harbour. We'll surprise them and sink their entire fleet there."

"I'm sorry," Zaganos said, returning to Turkish in order that his objections not be heard by Ezera. "This man is mad, that can't be done."

"He demonstrated to me this morning," Tolga answered nonchalantly and in Greek in order to re-include the Catalan. "The ships can be hauled by their crews over land and set back in the water relatively quickly. With the help of your soldiers, we should be able to move the whole fleet in one night."

"We need you and your men to clear a pathway up the hill and down the other side. And do so without being seen by the Romans, or the Italians, also to guide us through the channels at night," Ezera added.

Zaganos did not like receiving orders from someone so distantly below him in social strata, but he was willing to listen.

"But if our navy is still not capable of defeating their ships, as you've said, then what of all this? I presume that you were there when three ships outfought our hundred."

"Three ships escaped sixty on the open seas, and then one was sunk," Ezera corrected him, out of mildly wounded pride. "What we're talking about here is a surprise attack at dawn, with ninety ships, against a half dozen ships that have sleeping crews. Most of their ships can be boarded and captured before the alarm is raised. Do you know what that means?"

"We'll take the harbour, then so what? They'll close those gates and we'll still have to bash down the land wall. I realize how important the sea is to you, but it's a side spectacle to the land wall, which is what's important to the sultan's plan."

"No," Ezera spoke with irritation. "Then the Romans have to divide their men. Half for the land wall and half for the harbour. This plan will halve their strength on the land wall, and eliminate any chance of help from abroad. If we can succeed, the war is effectively won. That's what you have to explain to the sultan."

Zaganos smiled from ear to ear. He didn't like being talked down to, but on this occasion he'd tolerate it. If it worked, he'd usurp the grand viziership from that conservative old curmudgeon Halil, and if it failed, he'd blame this foreign mercenary.

"That sounds like a brilliant plan, Capitan Ayoub. I'll have my men start cutting a swath tonight."

Ahmet awoke earlier than normal, and rolled out of the hostel bunk where he'd been staying for the past two nights. Not only had he slept through his morning prayers, but the second liturgical hour of the day was quickly coming to fore. He stepped out into the daylight of the hall and sensed something very slight.

He looked down the hall and saw the inhospitable innkeeper speaking to two men obviously Turks, who were asking him questions in the infidel's language.

Ahmet didn't swear, or even breathe loudly. He stepped quietly and quickly across the wooden hallway and opened the door across from his own. The door was another hostel bunkhouse, abandoned by all except for a handful of religious pilgrims caught in the siege. They were busy praying and took no noticeable interest in another man coming into a public room.

Ahmet crossed the room and looked for a window from which to escape. The innkeeper had apparently had problems with guests retreating to avoid paying rents before and had the windows sealed tight.

He still resisted the urge to swear aloud, but instead scratched his scalp hard with his fingernails and pulled a lock of his hair, a habit from his childhood. He positioned himself by the door and listened for what was happening. He heard the two men ready themselves outside the door to his now unoccupied sleeping dormitory, and briefly affirm that God was great. The two men then hurried into the room with daggers drawn.

Without making a sound or wasting a movement, Ahmet stepped out from behind the door and turned down the hallway to the exit. As the two unnamed assassins stepped into the room, he stepped behind them and walked his exit. He took a hard look at the innkeeper as he left, allowing his eyes to cast a threat that no words would translate. Were it not for the necessity of silence, the innkeeper knew that his blood would be freed from bodily constraints and Ahmet would have nothing but a vague sense of satisfaction in exchange for it.

Outside, in the midday sun, Ahmet hurried down the muddy road towards one of the city's many fora. He knew he'd be able to disappear into the crowds once he found enough people, but he was also acutely aware that the two men he'd just avoided would be back again. It was best to avoid a blood-feud with anyone right now, but if they found him again, Ahmet would have to stand and fight. He could only hope that they were hired thugs and not somebody's nephews or cousins out for revenge. The last thing he wanted was someone else wanting to tax vengeance out of his flesh.

"Ella," Mario tapped the nun on the shoulder. "Could I have a word?"

"Yes, of course, Doctor."

The two walked onto the campus of the complex, the tented area that was still expecting larger numbers of wounded. Larger numbers that through God's mercy had yet to arrive.

"How are your duties coming along?"

"Harder than I thought. The nurses aren't very helpful here, they don't like me very much."

"Of course not, they don't like new people," Mario said cheerfully. "They don't like non-Greeks, either, so don't take it too personally."

"I don't," she laughed lightly. "I don't know anything about medicine or healing, all I do is bring our patients bread and watered-down wine. The old nuns don't think that this is a great time to teach a new girl what's to be done. How do you deal with this?"

"With what?"

"Well," she searched for the words, "My brother's racism towards the Greeks embitters him, and I don't think that it's healthy, but they don't like us, either. They don't care for the Italians coming into the hospital for treatment. I just want to scream at them, sometimes. Italy's blood is defending their home, would they prefer we stayed away?"

"They'd prefer that, yes," Mario said smiling. "They'd prefer the Turks went back to the steppe-land from which they came, the Armenians to go back to the mountains, the Bulgars to return to their hills, the Vikings to their rivers and us to our western peninsula. They think we're all a part of the same problem. We're not them."

"I can't understand it,"

"How's your sister-in-law doing?"

"I'm worried about her and little Alexandra," she began before she realized the implication behind the question. "Ah, yes. She can be a little headstrong, but not to the same degree."

"She loves you and your brother, so she's put much of her prejudice behind her," Mario stated. "That's the only way people can get over the xenophobia which has been taught to them from birth."

"Are you saying that you should find a nice Greek girl to wed, Doctor Mario?"

"Oh, heaven protect us all, no!" he laughed. "You know, my eyes have been taken by a young and beautiful Italian girl."

She blushed. Mario didn't. It felt wonderful for him not to be the one blushing. He felt somehow empowered by not being the one whose emotions were squeezing out of the tight grasp. The rehearsal helped.

"I have something for you," he said.

"I should get back to work."

"I don't hear any cannon. No one will come for a while. Don't worry," he said gently, and then reached into one of the pouches in his black doctor's coat.   He produced the finger-length turquoise hippopotamus. "Here you go."

"Oh," she said curiously and examined the stone carving. "Is it an elephant?"

"It's a hippopotamus."

"A river horse! I've never seen one before," she said, examining the figurine closely. "Are they really blue?"

"I've never seen one myself," he admitted, "but I think that they're grey or white."

"It's beautiful. Thank you."

"You're beautiful. And you're welcome."

She blushed again.

"Where did you get this?"

"Well," Mario considered his answer carefully. "I have a cache of wealth that I've managed to accumulate recently. Money isn't a problem for me any more."

"Congratulations, but I think that money's always a problem for men."

"That's true, I've got a host of problems today that I didn't have when I first arrived here, but I'm a humble man and I can avoid the big problems of big wealth. Now my only problem is finding someone to share my life with."

At the thunder of nearby cannons, they made eye-contact for the three seconds that elapsed before the nearer crash of stone on stone when the cannon ball hit the wall.

"More wounded," she whispered.

"Maybe not."

"Maybe not," she exhaled. "Mario, you are a very good man, and any woman would be happy to call you husband."

"I don't want just any woman to call wife."

"My brother has refused you as a suitor."

"He'll change his mind."

"What if he doesn't?"

"He will," Mario said confidently. "I've faith in that."

"I can't accept your gift," she said and held out her hand.

"Keep it, Ella," he kept eye-contact, drawing strength from her faltering. "Keep it as payment."

"Payment? What kind of services are you expecting?" She joked to try and break the tension.

"You don't understand it now, but you've given me a great deal. The potential of what may be has given me more strength than I could have imagined."

"Pfft," she spat, jokingly. "That kind of drivel doesn't come naturally from your lips, Doctor."

"Accept it, or my words will become even more degenerately honey-laced. To the point that their very sound will rot your teeth and make you fat," he proclaimed with comedy.

"Fine, fine," she looked at him and smiled. She looked at the gate to the compound to see if anyone was coming onto the tented campus, and saw none. "Thank you, Mario."

When she said this, she reached over to him and kissed him quickly on the cheek. She speedily turned about and hurried back to the hospital barracks to check on the patients there.

Mario didn't see her face, but he didn't need to, to know that she was smiling and blushing. She had just done something so colossally out of character that it seemed like someone else was riding her feet. She was impressed at her own self-transformation, as was he.

Late in the afternoon, Hectore Pazzi went down to the common room of the inn in which he was staying and ordered a bowl of stew, some bread and some wine. He wasn't the type of person to normally savour a meal, especially one as simple and utilitarian as the one in front of him, but something slowed him down.

He could sense the eyes of a stranger on him.

There was a monk, a bearded hermit, the kind that crop up everywhere in the east. The eastern monks all generally look the same, bearded, unwashed, unclean, and with the glassy eyes of someone who thinks that God's on their side. Pazzi normally had no time for any of them, but he had no time for any threats to his anonymity right now either. Something would have to be done about this.

Pazzi was hardly without experience in such matters. He finished his meal and went out into the street, walking slowly, changing directions occasionally and altering his pace. Everywhere he went, this monk followed him like a shadow, creeping in the setting sun, sometimes hidden but always there.

He followed him along the main Via Christo to the Forum of Theodosius. The square forum was normally a clothing bazaar, that was today a total free-for-all, what with the men of the city all occupying the walls. The women were frightened by tales of the debauchery of godless savages at the gates, but the lure of inexpensive textiles in a city of women was too tempting for them to stay home and fret.

Pazzi had originally thought it would be a fine place to avoid his pursuer, though it proved not to be so. The soldier was a full head taller than everyone else, and being the only man in the crow did lend him to standing out a fair bit. Pazzi ducked in and out of shops and around vendors and hawkers, selling various meats on sticks and candied fruits. The carnivorous shoppers did little to help him hide, and he doubled back around to return to the Basilica District.

When he entered the round Forum of Constantine, he entered an open air Agora that would have been a hub for all activity in the Venetian Quarter, but was now a ghostly barren plain. No one was there, they were all at the neighbouring clothing market. Hectore didn't want to get caught out in the open like this, so he quickly and sharply turned right and hurried along the *corso* northwards towards Holy Wisdom.

By the time he arrived at the piazza that separated the Cathedral of Holy Wisdom from the Hippodrome, he was certain that he'd lost his follower, but he had to check. He turned a corner and ducked into a shop that sold salted pork. There he grabbed a few strips of the desiccated ham and paid a bronze *solidus* for the treat. All the while in the shop, he kept his eyes on the entrance. If the monk was following him, he'd have to walk past here because of the sharp double turn he'd taken.

This stratagem paid off, and once the price of pork was paid, Pazzi saw a monk hurry past the front of the shop his eyes scanning forward and looking around. Their eyes met for a brief instant, and at that point Isodore knew that Pazzi was on to him.

Pazzi struck out onto the streets chasing his shadow. The warm April sun was losing ground to a wind that still remembered March and Isosore quickened his own pace.

Isodore had no intention of remaining prey for long. He wasn't blessed with a clear head when it came to stressful situations, and he was still rattled from the murder last night. The sight had frightened him and the perpetrator was now in his pursuit.

Along the side of the road was a wooden stockade, separating the Venetian Quarter from the rest of Constantinople. It was too high to jump over, and the gates were left open and unmanned during the day. The neighbourhood was shifting from the shops of the fora and piazzas into the dull islands of residential compounds. This was not good for the monk, because the barrens that separated the residential complexes were homes to gangs of ruffians and packs of dogs, neither of which he wanted to run into. He had two quick options available to him, either go to the harbour, or go to the Turkish panhandle. It was at the instant of mulling over those two undesirable options, that a third one entered his head, and he began to hurry down towards the Perama Gate.

He looked over his shoulder and could see the big Italian had started to break into a jog. The empty land between the piazza and the gate was a simple random spattering of cobbled road and occasional housing squares. If he was caught out here, no one would see them, Isodore supposed that he could be murdered on the street in broad daylight an no one would know what had happened. He broke into a sprint to escape from his pursuer. He ran with the full belief that his life depended upon it.

Pazzi chased him over a hillock and stopped dead. Into the side of the hill was a masonry tunnel, and an open iron gate.

"Jesus!" he swore aloud, not caring if anyone was near enough to hear his curse. "What kind of maniac goes into the sewers?"

He looked into the darkness beyond the entrance. No light penetrated the deep, so his hare had no candle or lantern to chase. Pazzi knew nothing of the sewers, except that the underbelly of Constantinople was said to be as large as the city above, and he would be out far out of his element.

"Damn!" he swore again and kicked the iron grate. "You're a coward! I'll find you another time and make you pray for a nice swift death! I've seen your face, Monk! I'll see it again!"

And that being said, he sulked off, leaving Isodore, never the fighter, to shiver in the dark and worry about the future.

Book Three:

The Fall of Constantinople

Sailing To Byzantium

Stanzas Three and Four

O sages standing in God's holy fire
As in the gold mosaic of a wall,
Come from the holy fire, perne in a gyre,
And be the singing-masters of my soul.
Consume my heart away; sick with desire
And fastened to a dying animal
It knows not what it is; and gather me
Into the artifice of eternity.

Once out of nature I shall never take
My bodily form from any natural thing,
But such a form as Grecian goldsmiths make
Of hammered gold and gold enamelling
To keep a drowsy Emperor awake;
Or set upon a golden bough to sing
To lords and ladies of Byzantium
Of what is past, or passing, or to come.

William Butler Yeats

Chapter Thirty-Eight - The Breach

April 21, 1453

The days began to blur into one. For the army on the doorstep of Constantinople, their days were shockingly dull. Sit and wait while the gunners gunned. The Janissaries broke up the periodic fights that would break out between unoccupied soldiers. Musa the exchequer would oversee the kitchens to make certain that no one was ever overfed. Only the artillerymen and the diggers had anything important with which to occupy their time. The new cannon teams weren't as fast as their predecessors, but they were learning, and the diggers were gradually getting closer to the walls.

Zaganos' hilltop group had spent the first week of the siege trying to find things to occupy their time, but were now always busy. They slept in shifts during the days, and spent their nights cutting down the forested hills of Pera Hill, in preparation for the slide paths.

Ezera, or Ayoub to his colleagues, dedicated his days to the task of screaming at the fishermen who were slowly transforming into sea dogs. He had them rowing races to the islands and back and then portaging over the hills. Picking up superfluous supplies from Chalcedon and running them to the army's main camp, where they'd potentially come under fire once they beached and unloaded at the land wall. He was doing the training tasks that should have been done during the winter at port.

In the city, a different stress entered people's lives. The mentality of being surrounded brought everyone's tension to a slow boil. The economy ground to a halt and city became dirty and dust filled. Spring rains brought a reprieve from cannon fire but stirred the mud on the city streets into a dirty clay. The city was a red and brown dust bowl once the sun started to dry the streets.

Ahmet found himself living in an "inn" in the grubby industrial district, near the road to the Golden Gate. It had taken him little time to find a hell to descend into. The basement of the bawdy house was a basilica-like chamber where the damned came to burn away their final hours.

The black tar blew its wind onto all, regardless of race, religion or nation. Ahmet lay down on pillows next to Armenians, Slavs, Greeks and races of which he had no knowledge.

Ahmet spent hours, perhaps days, laying about in the dark and dank hall, hiding from the biting light of day, that would sneak in and attack his eyes whenever some inconsiderate soul opened the door. He let what little money he had leak out of his purse in exchange for pipes, bowls and coals, and someone to periodically check to verify that he was still alive. When he was like this, he didn't worry about food.

A woman who worked in the inn above came down to check on the passive inebriates, make certain no one had lain back and swallowed their tongue. Ahmet watched her through his mental daze. He watched her body. Her skin was completely covered by her clothes, but the tar of opium gave him the imagined ability to see through those rags. Her face, pock-marked and bruised from a hard life, became beautiful in the tribesman's eyes. Her eyes, while cast down in disgust at this part of her job, Ahmet believed to be enticing him towards her.

The big man rolled off of his pillow, and tried to entice her with his sweet words.

"*Benim ismi Ahmet*," he slurred. The words had no recognition in the barmaid's eyes, who took a frightened step backwards.

Forgetting for a moment, that almost no one in the city understood his Uygur-accented branch of the Turkish language tree, he went about professing his love to the poor wench, who spoke some angry and mutually incompressible words of warning to him. Ahmet didn't understand a word of it, though there was some recognition of panic when she screamed.

A foggy kaleidoscope of colours flowed down the stairs to the subterranean opium hall, and three men from the bar above charged in to see what was transpiring.

"It's all okay," Ahmet said in Turkish, to no one's understanding, though with what he believed to be soulful sounding words. "I just wanted to talk to this beautiful girl. Maybe we can get married."

The innkeeper and two of his most trustworthy regulars accosted the foreigner with their fists, knocked him to the ground and kicked him. The phrase 'knocked senseless' would be inappropriate, as he was well past that point when the assault began. Ahmet mounted no defence, and was only marginally aware of what was happening to him. As happened every time he smoked poppy, he found himself wallowing in self-pity and unable to cope with the outside world.

He regained consciousness somewhere outside the walled-in Psarmathia district. It was hilly and empty land, with cobbled roads and unkept greenery in the shadow of the land wall. He was lying face down in what could have been an herb patch, were there someone to manage it.

He sat up and heard the sound of a dog growling. A mutt had arrived at the patch in which Ahmet had been recovering and it seemed to be ready to take back his prime sleeping spot. Ahmet thought to growl back, when he felt the earth tremble under his feet. The dog ran away.

Ahmet looked beyond his herb patch to see a troop of cavalry trotting along the wall road. It was the Italian mercenary, Guistiniano Longo and his horde of knights, out for another raid. They turned into one of the gates, cheered themselves and disappeared. The guards atop the wall cheered them as they went.

'The war,' Ahmet thought to himself. *'That damnable war. I should be fighting that. Like a gazi, a jihadi. But here I am, lying with the dogs and living among the infidels. What's happened to me?'*

Alas, he knew the answer to that question. He knew that his own vices, his unchecked lust and debauchery had cost him his status, his brother, his ability to ever return home. This curse was all of his own making. He'd known that for a long time, and he'd done nothing about it. This was not a new revelation, but a repetition of an old regret. He'd stared down that unfortunate reality before.

He had a eureka moment, an epiphany. He knew, then and there, what he needed to do in order to redeem himself before God. He would prove to the almighty that he was a great warrior and a sword to wield against those who'd done wrong on this earth. Mehmet, the son of Murat, had visited such terrible evil upon him, that he couldn't let it pass. Ahmet swore before God to avenge his honour by assassinating Mehmet at his moment of triumph, when he entered the city. As to whether or not God took notice of this oath, he couldn't say.

Guistiniano Longo charged again out of the Pege Gate. His fame had grown to the point that boys and men of the city, anyone capable of procuring themselves a horse or pony in any condition had run to his side. His numbers had swollen past the point where he knew everyone in the group, and there were many who couldn't communicate with him because of a language barrier.

Unlike the third day of the siege, now a distant memory of two weeks prior, the Ottoman army was now prepared defensively at the crest of the hill where the cannons lay. As Longo's cavalry made a line and began to charge, Ottoman soldiers from a dozen nations ran out with pikes and shields to form a line of their own. Behind then, archers lined up and began firing at the charging horses. Longo's men were undaunted, until they came up against the most brutal defence of the cannons that the

Muslim army had devised: a furrow trench.

Only a few feet deep and a few wide, the trench was hidden by a minor rise in the land. Over the ditch were scattered some branches and straw to hide the pit. Such a simple construct of engineering was poised to do vicious damage to the charging horses. The first row of the cavalry charge was the first to encounter the obstacle, and that began the blizzard. Many horses crumbled onto each other, and the horses behind them couldn't help but get dragged into the mess of horse, hoof and rider that began to coagulate along the line.

"Turn Right!" Longo commanded, and a little more than half of the charging horsemen managed to save themselves from the painful fall into the ditch.

For those who didn't, the Kopekchi Janissaries with their angry dogs of war ran into the horse clot as a phalanx of tooth and claw. Many men caught under the weight of their horses met a terrible demise, while surrounded by blood, fangs, steel and confusion.

This swift minor victory over the Roman raiding party was to be a feather in the cap of Halil for his command of the main force. The grand vizier watched the retreating horses racing towards the Romanus Gate and the safety of their walls. He couldn't help but smile. The Romans had just been dealt their first bloody nose. The first of many, if God wills it so.

His feeling of proud superiority was put on suspension when he looked to the north of the retreating Italians.

The red jackets and white hats of the Janissary corps were easily identifiable on the battlefield, and they were running south-eastward on foot, trying to catch the fleeing horse.

"What in the ninety-nine names of God are those fools doing?" Halil wondered aloud.

The Gate of Saint Romanus was one of the largest of the twelve major gates, second only to the southernmost Golden Gate. It consisted of two rectangular pile towers, and two large wooden doors, tall enough to accommodate a man on horseback twice over. The fortifications straddled both the outer and inner walls of the city, and it bridged the gap from the outside world to the inside world of the city.

The men of the Eighth Orta hit the gate just as the last of the horsemen charged through. The first Janissaries bounced off the doors and through the gates like a marble going down a funnel. In the killing ground between the inner and outer egresses of the gate were two dozen unarmed auxiliaries manning the doors. They were prepared for the pushing and pulling required to open the giant doors, not for fighting. The swift scimitars of the charging red-clad plague of locusts tore them to shreds before all of them knew what was happening. The doors were pulled wide open by the new occupiers.

"Into the towers!" Mesut yelled. "Quickly, occupy the towers, keep the gates open! They can't reclaim the towers once we've taken them!"

The Janissaries all moved in a tandem blur. Doubling back onto the towers, climbing their steps them from their gates that faced the insides of the city, they began the first occupation of the wall.

The towers were not keeps, their hollow interiors doubled as grain silos. Along the sides were stairs that led up to the top of the inner wall, and from there they led again to the tops of the towers.

The first man to reach the top of the stone stairs was the man with the biggest stride in the army, the recruited slave Giant Hussein. He bound onto the unoccupied top of the tower gate and charged the raised banner, picking up the red and yellow shield of Constantine and tossing it over the edge like a javelin. In his free hand he carried the standard of the two-pointed sword, the white serpent's tongue on a field of red. He hoisted it as high as he could and waved it so that all could see. In the city to one side, and the army camp to the other, his figure was beheld by all, waving his banner with conquering ecstasy.

More of his comrades began to arrive at the top of the towers and see a sight that had previously been allowed only to the defenders. The huge army camped on the doorstep to the extensive walled fortress of Constantinople. And for the first time in his life, Hussein saw the city of Constantine, and was less than impressed. Patches of urban sprawl, neighbourhoods within a wilderness of patchy agriculture were what he saw when he looked at the apple of the Sultan's eye. It seemed less desirable than Adrianople.

"Glory, My Son!" Hussein heard yelled at him from across the gate, on the other tower. There was Mesut, cheering him with his gravelly voice. "Glory!"

Hussein could never have felt prouder in all his days. He stood there as the champion who first raised the flag of the faith over the capital of the enemy. The look on his face at that moment was of such pride and joy, that his friends would remember him thusly forever, long after his subsequent death.

The Roman camp broke into immediate shock. Positions on the wall were ordered abandoned as the entire Greek-Italian army began to merge on the Romanus Gate.

"I told you his glory-seeking wasn't to be trusted!" Vincent DiCastillo yelled at Adam Karian. "Now we've been breached. If they can hold this long enough for the rest of the army to arrive, the city's fallen!"

"I'll kill that Genovese bastard myself once we reach there," Karian was on the verge of tears. The Empire that had lasted for over a thousand years was about to crumble, and do so under his protection. He feared that he would be remembered forever as the villain who slept while his lord was taken into chains.

The two commanders rode hard southward to where the fighting was taking place, and it wasn't long before the sight of the red and white sword was visible at the top of the tower.

"A curse on all of them!" Karian shouted out.

Vincent was past the point of cursing, and when they were nearing the battle site, he quickly dismounted his horse and took his musket from off his armoured shoulders.

A musket is a heavier and more precise version of the harquebusses and hand-cannons that most of the Italian soldiers were using. Vincent's gun was heavier, longer, more accurate and had a longer range than the armaments of his men. It was his most prized possession, after his home and his family.

Vincent took aim at the top of the Romanus Gate and found the biggest target up there. He focused his attention on the flag-waving giant and carefully shot a single bullet. The gunpowder exploded in fire and gas, and propelled a small ball of cheap lead out the barrel and through the air. It soared through almost two hundred metres of air before finally hitting the giant straight side-long at his right temple.

At that range, the momentum of the bullet wasn't enough to pierce the big man's skull, but it was enough to knock him back.

Erkin watched blood explode from his friend's head as the bullet cut deeply through flesh if not bone. He staggered back with faltering consciousness and the back of his thigh collided with the crenels of the tower wall. The unproven Janissary youngling lunged at his friend to try and grab him, but the big man's weight was too much, and he fell over the edge of the tower, down twelve metres to the dirty ground between the two gates. He died of his injuries shortly thereafter.

Iskender and Erkin ran to the edge to see where their best friend of the past decade (more than half their lives) had landed. The obtuse angles of limbs and back from the collision forced the young Janissaries to pause for but an instinct, but their training kept him in touch with the world around him.

Iskender grabbed the fallen standard from the ground and ran defiantly to the edge from where the shot had felled his friend.

"Here's our flag!" he cried defiantly at the charging Christian soldiers. "Here it stands! Here I stand! Never to fall! Never!"

The commotion was not lost on Mesut, but his head stayed clearer than the fiery youngsters. He stood at the edge of the tower, facing his army and waved his arms at them, beckoning them on.

"Come! Come, brothers! Victory is here for us for the taking!"

He then ran back to the other side of the tower top, facing the town. He drew his bow and fired an arrow randomly into the crowd of soldiers gathered there. He didn't check whether he hit anyone or not before returning to the army side of the tower.

There he saw the uncountable numbers of the Ottoman Horde in confusion. Some wanted to charge, but others were unwilling to. There was no decision in the horde, and inertia is stronger than momentum when numbers are great. God be praised, at least the bashi-bozuk skirmishers were charging all about. Disorganized they may be, at least they were willing to follow through once the barrel had tipped.

"Damn it, we have the gate! We've got it!" he yelled at the distant soldiers. He could not see the Sultan's tent from his vantage point, but he called out to Mehmet, knowing that the young Sultan would never hear him. "I hold the apple, My Sultan! It is ready to be plucked!"

The walls were turning into corridors of troops as the defenders ran down towards Saint Romanus, the horses of defeated raiders were even turning around to return on the Janissaries. Their position could not be held without help.

From the Ottoman camp, horses fled to the regiments, the white turbaned officers of the Sultan had their orders and were finally bringing them to the companies.

"Hold your ground, fire true!" Mesut announced with glee. "They're coming! Fight fierce and don't let them settle. The city is ripe!"

To the horror of Mesut, he saw the officers and the units staying put. The bashi-bozuks were now arriving, but the rest of the army was holding. The heavy infantries from Adrianople were absolutely needed to fend off the charging Christian soldiery. No cavalry! No shelter in the gate! They would get picked off and Halil would have the army sit back and watch, as though this were some kind of Thracian wrestling match.

“We can’t hold it,” he shouted in disgust. “Fall back! Take your comrades and fall back!”

Iskender’s heart sank. It was for naught. He ran down the stone steps of the tower to see Hussein’s body, damaged by musket fire and broken by the fall. The biggest man he’d ever known, in terms of heart as well as size. Iskender needed Erkin’s help to carry him with the retreating corps.

The long retreat back from the Gate of Saint Romanus, over the greenery and moat bridge, and across the field back to their lines, was an ignominious flight from glory. Mesut ran away from the gate, knowing full well that defeat had been captured from the mouth of victory, and someone needed to pay for this dishonour.

Two hours after the failed horse raid and the Janissary thrust through the defences, the court of Constantine gathered in the great hall of assembly. There, overlooking the Golden Horne, General Adam Karian was brought to explain the events of the day. Because of the breach, Karian was being forced to wait while the emperor saw to other responsibilities.

The big room had walls of red brick, a ceiling with modern frescos depicting the Assumption of the Virgin, and the floor was decorated with some of the eastern Mediterranean’s most detailed mosaics. The crown of Constantine was on an elevated dais, under which the bearded emperor sat in all his splendour, crown-capped and meticulously groomed. Surrounding him were men in black coats and women in long white dresses. Among the assembled were the two Italian emissaries.

“Sire,” Balias announced with a bow. “It brings me great pleasure to stand before you today. I come with several hundred of the finest soldiers of the Venetian Republic, ready to serve in defence of Christendom.”

“The soldiers please me as much as your greeting, Venetian,” Constantine said gratefully. “I watched your ships arrive from New Gate. I’ve seen with my own eyes that God watches over you and yours.”

“I pray that His good graces continue as the men take position among your own, in honour of your wisdom.”

“I’ll pray for this also,” Constantine knew that Karian wanted to speak, but thought to make him wait a bit more. “Tell me of Italy. Does your republic still find itself at odds with the Holy Father? I assure you that I won’t hold such a political uneasiness against you, as I’ve been known to find myself at odds with the bishop of Rome from time to time.”

There was a polite fluster of laugher in the hall.

"Minor disputes exist between the Doge and the Senate and the current inheritor of Saint Peter's diadem, but we are like brothers with a compromised past," Balias' eyes seemed to lose focus for the briefest of seconds. "Some problems exist, but our mutual love carries the day. We are all overjoyed to re-commune with our eastern cousins."

"As are we with our western brethren. Who is your elaborately dressed friend?"

There was another round of giggles.

"Your Imperial Majesty, may I present to you my brother, Bishop Isaac DiNapoli, of Venice. My confessor and spiritual appointment for the mission."

"Let him stand forward," Constantine leant back into his throne to assess the priest. He'd been warned that the man was unbalanced. "Welcome to Constantinople, Bishop."

"Thank you, Sire," DiNapoli said, only slightly lowering his head in bow. "I bring a message from his holiness the Pope, who wishes to welcome the eastern churches back into the Holy Communion of Rome."

"Thank you, it feels liberating to know that we are together under the Holy Communion of Christ," The emperor knew better than to allow someone like Isaac to indulge in a public conversation, so he ended their verbal transaction there. "I'm honoured to have you both in my court. You may now take your places among the peers. One of our other cousins, from even further afield east than the rest of us, has something to report."

"Thank you, Your Majesty," Balias bowed and Isaac lowered his gaze minimally. They both stepped aside and allowed Adam Karian to take the floor in front of the lord of the eastern horizon.

"My Lord Emperor," he bowed upon his arrival into the cold, open air chamber. "I've come to report on the day's events."

"And you have much to answer for," Constantine uttered. He had a stronger voice that he used in the assembly hall. Adam had got used to his softer, less commanding persona in the office.

"Sire, this morning, we launched a horse-back raid against the infidel army. The raid was unsuccessful," he began, but was cut off by the voice of one of the assembled noblemen.

"I'll say it was unsuccessful," an unseen stranger joked.

Karian turned about purposely and focussed on the voice.

"I believe that is Stavros, Anthypatos of Brussa, is it not?" he asked.

The overheard nobleman straightened his back and smirked arrogantly, as the rank of Anthypatos meant that he was the proconsul governor of a province; much higher than Megadux Adam Karian, who had a rural title.

"Good sir, your province was conquered by the Turks a century before your birth. You've contributed no soldiers, no ships and no grain to the cause of the defence of Christendom. I'll ask you to remain silent until the Emperor petitions your opinion, for reasons of his own choosing, I can see no reason to deal with you," and he returned his focus to the imperial throne.

"My Lord Emperor," he began again. "The morning raid was unsuccessful, and a company of Janissaries followed the retreating cavalrymen into the city through the Gate of Saint Romanus. They were then reinforced by some militias. Sixty-five of our soldiers were killed and a hundred were injured and are now in the Hospital of Chora. The Turks held the gate for no more than a half an hour, and were then forced back to their lines."

"How many of them were killed, General?" the emperor asked.

"We're not entirely certain, Emperor," he hesitated to speak on this subject because it was hard to give an accurate answer. "The Janissaries took their dead and wounded with them. Their militia have lost a hundred men to death, injury or surrender. Those who surrendered have been taken to the prison at Aemilianus Gate in Psarmathia."

"What do you make of what happened today, Megadux?"

"It was luck for them, luck that the Janissaries were in the right place at the right time to charge, and luck for us that the main army couldn't act swift enough to take advantage. Because of the organization of our defenders, especially the Venetians, we were able to act faster than them."

"What do you think should be the course of action for our glorious defenders now?" the Emperor asked.

"They should be congratulated for their quick reactions, Sire." Karian didn't like where this was going. Constantine was leading him somewhere, which meant that he'd been pressured by the useless men at court to take some foolhardy decision. "Not all eventualities can be predicted, and the unpredicted can only be reacted to. The reaction of the thema and the tagmata both distinguished themselves and brought honour and life to the city."

"Do you believe that there was a breakdown in their leadership?"

"No, Sire."

"Hah!" came a chuckle from Anthypatos Stavros.

"Peace, nobleman," Constantine ruled. "We're here to help the cause. This great cause of all ages. We're not here to pick flesh from each other's bones.”

“Sire, may I ask what decision has been made in my absence?”

“Adam, my old friend,” Constantine spoke in his most gentle and friendly of voices. “This command weighs heavily on your shoulders, and I’d like to lighten your burden.”

“Am I to be removed from the command, sire?” Adam felt panic for the first time since the siege began. He was a man of plans and alternate plans, but it was always stressful when one of his backup plans should be needed.

“No, no. Of course not.” Constantine’s voice echoed with false sympathy. “You’ll act as second in command.”

“And the overall command?”

“I will assume that responsibility, personally.”

Stavros smirked at the public demotion of the Armenian general.

“As you wish it, Your Majesty.”

“I knew that I could rely on you, Adam,” the emperor said and tightened a fist to show his faith.

In contrast to the polite change of offices at the palace, there was hell to be paid in the atrium tent of Sultan Mehmet the Second.

“Halil!” screamed a furious Janissary raging through the tents. “Where is that that decrepit traitor who calls himself counsellor?”

The slaves and servants of the Divan and the Sultan scattered about the tent as Mesut stormed about, red faced and sweating.

“Do you know where he is?” he accosted one of the slaves before turning to Kabira, the chief eunuch. “What about you, you filthy mule? Tell me where he is!”

“I don’t know, Master Janissary,” Kabira answered quickly. He didn’t want to anger the vengeful soldier any more than he already was.

“He’s here with me,” announced a sombre, if not quite authoritative voice. Mehmet emerged from behind a curtained wall with the grand vizier in tow. “Now control yourself! Peace, Brother! Peace!”

“We had it, My Sultan! My Sheikh! We had it!”

“Stop yelling, you had what?”

“The city, the gate! The brave men of the Eighth Orta took the fifth gate. We held it! I personally stood atop it and looked down to see the city, the palace and the harbour. To the south I could see the Sea of Marmora! We had taken it!”

“But you couldn’t hold it,” Halil chided.

"We *did* hold it, damn you!" Mesut insisted. "For half an hour, we stood alone, while you watched! You, you sent out riders to tell the army to stop! You left us there to die rather than push the assault! We could have taken the wall this afternoon!"

"You charged the gate without telling a soul!" Halil made a disgusting grimace when he spoke to the uppity slave. Gone was the rapprochement between the two. "You thought that you would capture glory on your own and that the rest of the army would simply follow your lead. What did you think? Did you think that we would telepathically know?"

"The broken-headed knew, and they had no instructions. The Anatolians knew, but they were called off, by you! You consciously decided not to push the advantage!"

"There are over a hundred thousand soldiers here!" Halil argued his case to the Sultan. "When he went out of line, he could have sacrificed the whole battle plan, my sultan. We can't move an army this big without preparation, and we couldn't stop them if things went wrong. I didn't think he could hold the gate. This proved to be true, as he and his men are back here at the camp and not there now. If we charged headlong, and they had lost the gate, we'd loose uncountable numbers against the wall. You ordered us to wait. Not to cross the green, Sire, and we haven't."

"Janissary," Mehmet asked impatiently. "How long did you hold the gate?"

"Twenty minutes, perhaps half an hour."

"Probably half that," Halil tutted.

"How long does it take to reach the gate, Commander?"

"Five minutes at full charge for the heavies, less for the skirmishers or the cavalry, My Sultan."

"I see," Mehmet exhaled. "Halil, you followed my instructions. Thank you."

Mesut glared at the minister.

"Wait here for a moment, Commander," the sultan commanded. "I wish to speak with you in a moment. For now, I need to discuss things with my vizier."

Mesut's face was ashen with rage, the only colour was the rope scar around his neck that burned crimson. He bowed and stood at attention while Mehmet walked into the other room with Halil.

"Is what he says true?"

"Sire, I followed your instructions. An assault would be doomed, and would cost us dearly. These are your wishes, your decision."

"True, and I'll commend your honouring of my commands," Mehmet nodded his head, though his voice was burning with frustration. "You say that the cavalry raid was stopped?"

"Yes, your majesty. The trench stopped them in their tracks," Halil said with precise diction, secure in the knowledge that what he did was the correct course of action.

"Good. Now go assemble the Divan. I want to meet with them right after sun-down prayers and before dinner is served."

"Of course, Your Majesty."

Mehmet then turned about and marched quickly back to where he had left the fuming Mesut.

"Peace be upon you, Commander," he said quickly and without thinking.

"And unto you be peace, sultan," the angry soldier answered.

"How many men did you lose?"

"I've lost five and twenty valiant sons today, Sultan. I don't know how many of the bashi-bozuks fell," he answered grimly. "I knew each one by name. One was less than a year out of the Lion's Den."

"I'm sorry for your loss," Mehmet managed to sound both heartfelt and businesslike at the same time. "I would attend the funeral, but I believe your order grieves privately."

"We are all honoured in life and death to be slaves to you and God, Your Majesty. We would be honoured again to have you at the funerals."

"It will be so, then," Mehmet looked troubled. "I wish I'd seen the battle, Mesut. I listened to the council of my vizier and waited in safety at the rear of the camp, rather than at the front, watching the army. I would have ordered everyone into that breach you carved. This costly war would be cut short and victory would crown me with conquest."

"Yes, Sire."

"I've decided to make you an officer of the Divan. The exact title and responsibilities will be determined after the war, but in the meantime, I want your level head. I'm going to introduce you at a meeting of the Divan after sundown. Until we can formalize an office for you, you'll be the acting agha of the Janissaries. You'll co-ordinate the other Ortas. I don't want another opportunity to be lost because of someone's unwillingness to take what's presented."

"Thank you, your majesty," Mesut spoke sternly.

"Don't thank me just yet," Mehmet joked. "You haven't dealt with the rest of the Divan yet. They aren't quite as friendly as your comrade Zaganos, who I'm sure will be thrilled to have you at the table."

"It's funny, sire. I've known your second minister since we were both seven years old, and I'd lay my life down to save his, knowing full well that he'd do the same for me. However, in all my years, I've never heard anyone describe Zaganos as friendly."

"Friendly's relative, Agha."

Night fell and the Ottoman fleet sailed gently from Diplokion's docks. Only a few hundred metres northward along the Bosporus, the ships were one by one flagged into a tiny embank by a posted guard. The ships rowed themselves slowly aground, and the crews leapt out. There were a dozen men at their disposal to help each crew to carry the vessels over the rocky inlet and onto the grassy slope of Pera Hill. Once on the slick and soft greenery, there was a path that led them to take their heavy ship up for five hundred metres towards the crest of the hill and towards the Valley of Springs.

The Valley of the Springs is a wadi that captures the spill-over from Pera Hill and Hellas Hill. Once the boats were hauled all the way up to the crest of Pera, they were then carried over the shallow run of the hill to the gully separating the two hills. Then the ships were rested into the gully, it was a straight walk from to the upper reaches of the Golden Horne.

The only threat came in the form of Galata. While the city had declared its public neutrality in the war, everyone knew that the Christians living inside the walls were much more sympathetic to the Christians across the harbour than they were to the Muslims besieging the city. Individuals, if not outright Genovese agents, would deliver the intelligence to the capital. The ships would have to hide in the forest, unseen until shortly before dawn, when the ships would be put into the water to fight the Christian fleet. Any sooner and the Christians would be ready for them.

Quietly, and two hours faster than anticipated, the portage found completion. When the sun next rose, the new day would bring a new phase in the life of the Queen of Cities.

Chapter Thirty-Nine - The Harbour

Even under the worst of circumstances, a clear sunrise can be a thing of beauty. During the parting days of April, 1453, the heavens opened the day with a certain lifeless beauty. The sky turned from black, to grey, and then pink and finally blue. It wasn't quite as natural as it could have been, for there was something wrong with the world. The deer in the hills were more invisible than normal, the dolphins that played in the harbour irrespective of the buoy-line didn't surface. Even the spring larks had flown away. The sound of that infernal cannon, the fighting and dying of men had replaced the beauties of nature. The hills seemed barren and the wealth giving sea was bereft of her former glory. Stripped down to its soulless functionalism, the sunrise still held some of her residual, if diminished, beauty.

The first rays of light that tipped over the hills of Bithynia and leaked into the harbour, arrived to be seen by only one pair of eyes from the southern shore. Captain Francisco was an early riser, and was unhappy with his accommodations in the capital. He'd been hired on to sail soldiers and supplies from Venice to Constantinople, and was now a prisoner in the harbour because the war had broken out before his patron had anticipated.

His boredom and frustration were amplified by the very real possibility that he and his crew would never escape. One of his three ships had been sunk; he'd not contracted for warfare. The ships were hardly prepared to defend themselves; they were transport galleys, not warships! When he finally got back to Venice, perhaps the senate would compensate him for his losses, but they could just as easily reject his claims outright. Such were the vicissitudes of life for someone who made their life by the sea. He dealt with in the only honourable way a man could: with functional alcoholism.

The hung-over captain staggered out of his cabin on ship and walked towards the harbour-side prow of the ship in order to allow for his first relief of the morning, and he saw something stir down harbour. It was well past the harbour of those filthy Genoese, it was up the estuary, almost in the hills and forest. Why would anyone sail all the way up there? There's nothing that way except for Turkish scouts.

Light gradually filled the harbour valley, and realization sunk into Francisco's dehydrated mind like reluctant sobriety when he identified what it was that he saw.

"Ships," he whispered. "Christ protect us all, they're here."

Seven… eight… more and more were pouring down river and into the Horne.

"Alarm!" Francisco called. "Alarm!"

Luckily for him, the word was understandable to men of all languages.

The Ottoman skiffs soared over the flat glass-like surface of the morning water. Though the drums of cadence were silent, the crews kept time with the metronome trained into their motions. The small ships of the Turkish fleet were like compact little falcons, attacking bigger, but less ferocious albatrosses.

Of the seventy Christian vessels in the harbour, only about twenty were capable of making war upon the enemy. The rest were fishing, hauling or trading ships. Of those twenty, only two of them had crews aboard. The rest of the ships had crews that slept on land, or were stationed along the land wall.

The cry to arms broke the silence of the morning and was soon echoing from walls and gates throughout the harbour. Inns and makeshift barracks were emptying their residents in the general direction of the harbour, and volunteers for pitched defence flew out of the Phanar and Theodora Gates like field mice from a looted granary.

The bells and horns of the harbour were loud enough to reach Blachernae, where Constantine slumbered. He rolled out of the four-posted bed and staggered from his bed chamber to the western balcony of the imperial apartment.

The rising sun lit the inside of the city's fabled wall with yellows, oranges and reds. He could see over the barrier and there was the Turkish army; still encamped, still resting in the morning's semi-darkness. The cannon crews didn't work at night and had yet to fire their first shots of the morning.

Puzzled, he put on his red robe and listened carefully. He could definitely hear the church bells sounding out alarms, and the commotion of what sounded like it must be battle. He followed the sound through his private study and into the lounge where he would normally dine on breakfast before facing the rigours of the court. On the other side was of the hall was the eastward balcony.

'*East?*' he wondered. '*Please God, don't let it be rioting. The last thing we need is more obstinacy from the clergy.*'

By a stroke of good luck, his prayers were answered positively and he strode onto the larger eastern balcony. The citizens of Constantinople were indeed not engaged in a self-destructive riot.

Conversely, by a stroke of bad luck, the once bustling harbour was busy again. It was almost impossible to see the glimmering waters of the Horne. Flowing down from the upper estuary were dozens upon dozens of small ships, all sporting the white crescent on a forest green banner.

"Oh, no," he muttered.

He hurried into his chamber and threw his clothes on and rushed to the egress to the imperial apartment. Outside were twenty Varangians, the chamberlain, and many other functionaries ready to attend to the Emperor's person.

"My Lord," began the chamberlain. "I have terrible news…"

"Yes, I know," Constantine cut him off. "Have my horse prepared. I will ride down to the harbour in a matter of moments. Where is Megadux Adam?"

"I don't know," the chamberlain's words didn't sound honest to Constantine's ear.

"I hope that you're not trying to hide from me the fact that he's at the harbour," the Emperor said flatly. "Because then I'd have you punished for dishonesty and he for disloyalty."

The chamberlain's head dropped.

"I'm sorry my lord. He left your house as soon as the alarm sounded."

"He should have waited for me," Constantine said without emotion. "A pity for him that he can't adapt to his new role, I suppose that I'll have to remind him of it. Make certain that my horse is ready. Assemble the nobles as a war council. I'll meet with them upon my return."

"Yes, My Lord," said the chamberlain with a bow.

The torrent of the Ottoman ships was too much for the few Roman ships to withstand. Only two ships of war were able to emerge from the docks in time to meet the wave. Greek fire was stored in its composite parts and would only be mixed in preparation for a battle, it was far too dangerous to keep in a ready form for storage. The two ships that went out to meet the attacking navy were rammed in the centre of the harbour, in full view of city's inhabitants. The attacking navy was not as skilled or experienced as the defenders, but not embarrassingly so any more. The Turkish ships were weighed down only by troops, as each skiff carried with them as many soldiers as they could safely manage without capsizing.

The attackers were not waging an assault on the harbour's sea walls, nor were they paying much attention to the defenders on the shore or atop those walls. They were attacking the sleeping fleet. The ships that had swum like harbour dolphins around them twice before were now being grappled, boarded and captured without any resistance. Several ships were being outright stolen by the attacking soldiers.

For half an hour, the battle raged in all parts of the harbour. Men fought atop ships and on the docks that led to the city itself. There was even fighting on the shore near the gate of Saint Theodora, where the fishmonger's guild was responsible for turning a skirmish into a bloody victory of attrition against the seventy tribesmen of the Turgut Clan from Manissa, who had tried to press their luck by storming a gate in the manner of the now famous eighth orta.

Notwithstanding the rarity of the fishmonger's victory, the harbour seemed lost before the sun had finished its daily task of rising.

Constantine's retinue of Varangians came to a halt at Phanar Gate. The Emperor gasped and looked at the top of the wall. His horse neighed angrily at his coarse stop.

"Do you see her?" he asked the guards, wild-eyed but not panicking.

"Her?" Olaf the Varangian asked.

Atop the gate stood the Holy Virgin. She was coming to him as she had shown herself to his elder brother ago, the last time the Turks had besieged Constantinople. She was clad in red and yellow robes, the emblematic banner of the surviving inheritor of Rome. She looked at the Emperor and spoke with a soft velvet voice that had echoed in his dreams since he was a pubescent boy.

An eerie calm overcame Constantine. He'd lived most of his life in monasteries in the Morea, perpetually prostrating himself before this image. He'd always allowed her grace to overcome his own sinful nature. She'd help him overcome onanism during the years of his youth, and had always represented that pure idea. If God could bring purity to something as perverse as a woman, surely he could visit grace upon him.

'Worry not, my champion,' she spoke in her wordless voice. *'You will be victorious, as I am with you.'*

Constantine jumped down from his horse and staggered towards the gate before falling on his knees.

"Holy Mother!" he cried. "I will defend you! I will defend your glorious son!"

The worried Varangians looked at each other, as did the peasants and townsmen who were rushing to the harbour to offer what assistance they could. Was the emperor mad? He certainly seemed so. The Constantinopolitans immediately recognized an ecstatic vision when they saw one, though the less mystically inclined Vikings were less enthused to do so.

The Holy Virgin held out her two hands and light formed on each. In her right hand was the moon. For centuries prior to the advent of Islam, the crescent moon had been a symbol of the Queen of Cities. In her left was the golden throne of heaven.

'*When you drive the infidel back, my son shall return to you,*' she said in her immutable voice. '*And govern the earth, with you at his right hand. He will call you brother, Constantine.*'

"Yes, yes!" the emperor threw himself onto the mud of the cold spring ground. "Your will shall be done, Holy Mother. Your will shall be done!"

'*Defend the church, my son,*' she said as her image lost its solidity. '*Only the true faith can turn back the heathen.*'

"I will, My Queen. Queen of Heaven and Earth," Constantine poured salty tears onto the grey mud. "A new kingdom of Christ will emerge by my hand. I swear it!"

The Varangians had now dismounted from their steeds and surrounded their prostrate emperor. They lifted his psychically battered shell and brought him into the guard tower of Phanar Gate to recover. The citizenry from the city of Constantine circled the tower with almost the same enthusiasm as they charged to the harbour.

An explosion of fire and screams came from the eastern edge of the log-jammed harbour.

"Neptune's whores fellate me!" Ezera shouted, and then wished he hadn't sworn in his present company. "They've managed to ready the Greek Fire! I'd hoped it would have taken them longer."

From their hill-side shelf built onto the slope of Pera, Ezera, Tolga and Zaganos watched the carnage unfold. This was Ezera's first time watching a sea battle from the safety of the shore, and the experience was not entirely to his liking. The frustration of seeing so much, and not being able to yell directions, having to rely on the good judgement of men who lacked it, was vexing the pirate.

"Emir," he addressed Tolga. "You must fire the retreat."

"What?" Zaganos interrupted testily. "Retreat at the first sign of a fight? We can knock them over now and take glory for ourselves!"

"No we can't," Tolga corrected the Vizier. "We don't have the men to take the city, only to neutralize harbour. We should fall back with what we've won."

"No, give them more time!" Zaganos demanded. "They're massacring the Christians! Now is the time to do the most damage we can, if we don't continue now, we'll never surprise them like this again!"

"The surprise is over, Vizier," Ezera answered. "We've destroyed several of their ships. Even better than that, we've captured some to strengthen our fleet. Their archers on the shore will take lives from the army and the fire will take the rest. We have to retreat back here to the estuary. Take the captured ships with us."

"I agree," Tolga replied. He didn't like holding the position of Admiral, and he generally allowed Ezera-Ayoub to make any decision related to the office. The politics of his position was that he had to keep Zaganos happy. The second minister of state wouldn't tolerate being overruled by a pirate who underwent a dubious conversion for very long. "Fire the rockets."

Several rockets were lit. They were powered by chained blasts of gunpowder, each infused with ground seashells, exploding in an indigo blast of smoke. The series of blue explosions garnered the attention of everyone in the valley of the harbour.

The Ottoman fleet knew the signal and began rowing their ships back to the mouth of the estuary and the Valley of the Springs. Their victory was incomplete, but the damage was severe. The three wise men watching the battle from the slope observed their fleet reassemble below them, but they also saw what was left of the Roman navy. They counted four ships of war and seven fishers, traders and haulers. While it wasn't a total victory, it was a decisive victory for the Sword of Osman, and a crippling defeat for Byzantium.

"Doctor Mario, there's a man to see you," one of the guards of the Chora compound announced.

"Send him in quickly," Mario answered.

The sounds and smells of the battlefield could waft their way into the hospital, as would the wounded, the inevitable result of all battle. With the exception of men in various stages of gore, it was rare for the hospital to have word from anyone outside its walls. The monastery had become an island in time, knowing only suffering.

A bearded man was brought to the doctor. Mario observed him appraisingly.

He had broad shoulders, but was intentionally lurching them down to appear less intimidating. He wore a beard that didn't quite match the colour of the hair on his head. Alone that's not suspicious, but there were many inconsistencies to the man who came into Mario's dank office. His eyes had a definite intelligence, but his hands were those of a workman. He dressed like a mendicant, but he had the deportment of someone used to the pleasures of luxury.

Mario smiled and wore his most naïve looking face.

"What is it, Brother?" Mario addressed the stranger in Greek.

"I've come to volunteer my services, Brother," the stranger replied in perfect Piedmontese Italian.

'*You're Hectore Pazzi*,' Mario thought without a wasted second. "You speak Italian?"

"Of course, Brother," the provisionally identified stranger answered with a bow suited for court and a voice suitable for violence. "My name is Filipé, I'm from Padua."

"My name is Mario Orsini, I'm from Venice," he greeted him with false warmth. "My master was from Padua. Do you know Antonio of Padua? He's a physician of great renown, though he's been gone from Padua for many years. He's now rector at the University in Venice now."

"Of course I know of him, though I've not had the pleasure of meeting him personally," the stranger claimed. Mario could tell there was no recognition of the name in the man's eyes. Padua had been under the rule of the Venetian Republic for a half century, and all Padovani of any education would know of their greatest champion in academia. "I studied at the Universidà Padova until my father's untimely death, not in Venice. I've been wandering the east since then."

"Well then, welcome countryman," Mario smiled. "What can I help you with, for I fear that I shall be very busy, very soon."

"I was trained as a physician, though I must confess that I didn't finish my education. I've acted as a ship's doctor for many years, and a field surgeon for many wars. I'd like to help as you as a surgeon, if you are in need."

"We're always in need," Mario said politely. "Do you speak Greek?"

"And a touch of Turkish, yes."

"Let's hope we won't need that," Mario joked. "Do you have a letter of introduction from the Venetian fleet, or the University?"

"Unfortunately, no," Filipé-Hectore said gently. "Many of my personal effects were lost at sea during a great battle against the Turks."

'*A handy answer, I can't let on that I know,*' he thought and played his part. "Alright then, I'll put you under the supervision of one of our senior surgeons here, and when he vouches for you, we'll write you into our books. Welcome to the enterprise."

"Thank you, Doctor Mario. I'm sure you won't regret this."

"I hope not," Mario smiled back.

After he introduced the new doctor to the chief surgeon, he hurried back to his office and wrote a letter, which he immediately had couriered by one of the guards to the monastic community that had occupied the Bucholeon palace.

> *My good friend, I.*
>
> *I pray that you'll forgive the brevity of this letter, but I have precious little time. A man has come to me at the monastery and offered to work as a surgeon. I believe him to be none other than the man of whom we spoke. I ask you to come and confirm this for me. Please do this as quickly as possible.*
>
> *If it is the man you spoke of so seriously, then it is best that he is kept here, where he can be observed. If he is here for some skulduggery, as you suspect, then we can alert our mutual friend Vincent to his presence. I know what he's looking for, come quickly and we can discuss this in further detail.*
>
> *Your good friend, M.*

Constantine arrived, covered from head to toe in the mud of the city streets from where he received his vision of the Holy Mother blessing the battle. He transformed the gate-house of Phanar into a temporary war office, and had his two Italian counsellors of war summoned to him there.

To his surprise, it was his uninvited counsellor who arrived first. It was just as well, for he needed to meet with him.

"My Lord," Karian bowed when he entered the small room where the emperor was hiding himself. "I bring terrible news. The Turks…"

"Stop for a moment," Constantine interrupted him. "It seems that it was only yesterday, when I told you that I was to be taking over the responsibility for the defence of the city. It was yesterday, was it not?"

"Yes, Sire…"

"I had full intentions of keeping you involved in the administration of this war. When I awoke this morning, when I needed your council as to how to proceed, you were nowhere to be found."

"I was here, My Lord," Adam replied incredulously. "I was commanding the men from the wall, and it was through those efforts that the Turks were turned back. We bought time for the use of Greek Fire that's ended the fight."

"A rather horrible battle result, it would seem."

"It could have been much worse, Sire."

"I don't think that's correct, Adam," the Emperor said sullenly. "I had a vision today. The Holy Mother came to me and sent prophesy through me. She said that I will be victorious. That I must lead the faithful to victory. I'll trust in her wise words above those of someone who leaves my side at the first sign of combat."

"Sire," Adam spoke slowly so as not to be misunderstood. "You are on the verge of making an unwise decision."

"I shall do as the Holy Mother has commanded me," he said resolutely. "I shall lead the armies of Christ personally."

"You've always been the leader of the armies, Sire," Adam could only hope to assuage the randomness of the Emperor's mercury now. "Always in your name, and always with your instruction."

"And now with my more direct hand," Constantine announced. "I will keep you as an advisor, but you're to be addressed by your court rank of Megadux, no more will you be addressed as Strateogos. You are an Arch-Duke still, and a general no more."

"If your will be so," Karian answered with a bowed head. His eyes focussed on the earth, not out of formal deference, but out of a need to hide the violent rage and resentment that his eyes would betray.

"I'll expect your advice, Adam. I trust and respect it. But the men, they need their Emperor. They need to know that God sanctions us."

"Yes, Your Maj…" Karian was unable to finish his response when the doors to the gatehouse were opened to allow entry to Guistiniano Longo and Vincent DiCastillo.

"Ah! Welcome, gentlemen!" the emperor stepped around the stunned Karian and greeted the two Italian knights. "I understand that I have the two of you to thank for our survival of the Turk's treacherous surprise attack this morning."

"Our survival is something to be celebrated," Vincent said with a hint of apprehension. "But the battle of the harbour was a crippling loss, Sire. You have to appreciate that."

"I don't see losses any more. Only temporary setbacks," Constantine reassured them both, unsuccessfully. "Adam, these two men and I must discuss things that no longer concern you. Would you please wait for me back at Blachernae?"

It's interesting how the most insulting public displays of dismissal can adopt the form of a question.

"Yes, Sire," He answered and left the room with what could pass for dignity. He declined to make eye-contact with either Italian.

"Now, then. Let me continue," Constantine restarted his strategic pedagogy. "Our previous plan, of sheltering ourselves like a turtle will simply not do. Even were it successful, which I now doubt would be the case, the Turks would simply slink back to their holes and prepare to do the same again. Here, we are going to stand firm against the tyrants, and drive them back, not only from the city walls, but we'll follow them across Thrace. We'll pursue them back to the city of Adrianople, where we'll avenge my noble ancestor Valens. It is from this dark time and place that a new kingdom will arise. I was told this by no less authority than that of the Holy Mother, Mary, Mother of the Risen Christ!"

Guistiniano and Vincent exchanged glances very subtly. Neither of them was quite certain what they were hearing.

"I will address the court this afternoon, and tell them of my vision. Chroniclers will post it on every street and forum in the city!"

"That's wonderful to hear, Sire," Vincent said diplomatically. "But we still have to deal with the enemy's success in the harbour."

"It's not their success. It's their weakness," Constantine cut him off angrily. "You don't see opportunity, only adversity. That's why we're losing this battle."

"Sire," Longo intervened for the first time in the conversation. "They have over a hundred ships, geared for war, and we are now depleted to only six. We've lost almost all of our strength in the water, and we'll now have to permanently move valuable soldiers from the defence of the land wall to the harbour. We've been dealt a horrific blow."

"I suppose that you'd want to discuss surrender with the Turk then?" Constantine asked the two of them accusingly.

"No one said that," Vincent spoke. "But after this morning, it might be wise for you to consider tribute to the sultan. We can't hold on forever."

"You're both pessimists, like that dour Armenian," the Emperor scolded them. "We need to attack them now. Strongly, like Señor Guistiniano did in the first few days of the siege. They expected us to hide and it was you who drew blood from their proud faces! We need more of this! From now on, I would like to hear the word '*attack*' come from your mouths at every instant. If not, then there are other strateogoi who can advise me in what's needed to find victory!"

Vincent looked at the emperor and assessed. It was best to keep him happy until his religious euphoria wore off, and after that point they could marginalize him. The Italian mercenaries wouldn't listen to his Greek instructions anyway, it was only the domestic regiments, unready fishmongers and merchants conscripted into civic duty, that would follow the mirages of Palaiologos. He was frustrated by this turn of events, but he would have to keep that frustration in check.

"Of course, Basileus," Vincent said, using the Greek title for the Emperor of the East. The term was archaic, but appropriate. "We'll begin making such plans for you this hour."

"Yes, of course," Longo added, he obviously had the same impression as his Venetian counterpart.

"There's no need for it. I've done all the planning required, here in this room. It took only an *instant of clear though*."

Both advisors to the emperor were aware of the fact that nothing of value could be prepared in an 'instant of clear thought.'

"Would you care to enlighten us, *Basileus*?" Guistiniano asked, stealing Vincent's word.

"Yes, of course," Constantine straightened himself. "You'll ready the fleet to counter attack this afternoon."

"Your Majesty, that's ludicrous," Vincent let slip. His plan to hibernate through the emperor's winter of wisdom was thrown to the ground.

"If you no longer have faith in Christ's victory, Captain, you'll be dismissed as my minister."

"Sire, if you dismiss me, you dismiss Venice. Damn near all of the real soldiers on that wall and most of the battle ships left in the harbour are here because they were commanded to be here by the Republic, not your empire!"

"Vincent," Longo tried to warn him to reign in this anger before he said something that couldn't be taken back.

"No! Wait a moment!" Vincent was shouting now. Twenty years of capped rage at eastern ways boiled to the top, and the Venetian had just lifted his finger from the floodgate. "You are the emperor of Rome in name only! You are the mayor of Constantinople! A local baron! The empire of the east has fallen! You speak of avenging Valens? Adrianople fell to the Goths almost thousand years ago! Half the members of your court are nobles of lands that were conquered before your grandfather was born! Half of your fabled city is occupied by Venice, and that little Genoese colony across the river's managed to steal almost all your trade! Your churches are emptied of their relics to pay for gifts to your noblemen! And now, now you intend to run this war. You're a priest, a fourth son of a cousin to a former emperor! What do you know about war? You've just dismissed the only man in your court who knows anything of the subject! Tell me, who were you thinking of replacing him? Who? That prancing peacock, Stavros?"

Constantine stared blank-faced at his accuser.

"Excuse me," Longo spoke up. "I don't mean to spoil a conversation that should best be postponed, but the Emperor here, might have a good point."

Vincent was growing to hate the Genoese and his expression left no wonder as to his feelings when he moved his gaze from the emperor to the knight.

"They have a large navy on the other side of the harbour. They have no docks at which to rest, and no room to manoeuvre. They're cluttered together for now, but by tonight they'll have some order. They'll also move cannons from the land wall to the hills north of the water. They'll hit the ships on this side of the harbour from the safety of the hills, and only then will they move their troops over. The harbour is lost. Tonight they'll fortify and tomorrow they'll attack again. We've six ships, let's load them up with Greek fire and run them into the other fleet to do what damage they may. Then, we should dismiss the ships to safety. Send them to Trebizond or Kaffa, or some other such place."

"That's what I like to hear," Constantine said accusingly at Vincent. "Not the empty complaints of someone who doesn't realize how lucky he is to have a voice at the table of Christ's regent."

"We need Adam Karian's voice in the war council, Constantine," Vincent said, using the Emperor's personal name: a faux-pas that would warrant severe consequences from anyone else at any other time.

"His counsel is for my ears," the Emperor replied. "As is yours. I would suggest you speak to your master, Don Giovanni, and ask whether or not he's prepared to recall all of Venice's commitment with as little thought as you were prepared to do, Don Vincent. You will both come to my audience chamber after Hesperinos Prayers at sundown. I expect to hear of your successes this afternoon. Good day, Gentlemen."

Constantine left the gatehouse and returned to the palace, leaving the two commanders there to discuss what had just happened.

"We need to find Karian," Vincent said.

"Why? We all agreed on his plan, it was sound. If we continue along those lines, I'm sure that the city can outlast the morale and purchase price of the Turkish army. He's thought of enough tactics and counter plans for the siege, so I don't think that he'd abandon that habit outside of his office. I'm sure he's done enough for himself to deal with this eventuality as well. Besides, the old man's spoken and if we go around his back, he'll just get more irritable and more erratic. It's best if we just tell him that we're obeying him, and continue to do what we'd already planned for."

"The Emperor's gone mad as Caligula!"

"Quite possibly, but it doesn't matter," insisted Longo. "He'll make pronouncement, but the soldiers look to you and I for leadership. He'll command the mob with his mystic talk, making political issues, but that'll be a problem for Cardillo and Trebbiano to deal with at a later date."

Vincent hated to concede a point to the Genoese, but he knew that Guistiniano was right, and the two quickly went about readying the fleet with Greek fire for a final counter-attack before the harbour was conceded as a defeat.

The life of Ella DiCastillo had been a simple one since her parents were taken by plague so many years ago. She'd been forced to leave Barcelona and take residence with a brother whom she'd never met. Vincent, much to her surprise, had welcomed her with open arms and an open heart. Daria welcomed her as a sister as she'd been given everything a young girl could want.

Now, she was an unwed girl, past her twentieth birthday, and had all but officially made her nun's habit permanent. She had now but a single suitor, the rest having been driven off by her protective brother. Her options in life seemed very limited.

Her first taste of life outside the DiCastillo mansion since the long sail from Iberia to the East, was a bitter dish for which she was shockingly unprepared. She eventually had to step back from barracks, which had turned into a dungeon of pain and suffering.

She had seen men shot with arrows, shot with bullets, and crushed by falling rock. On the day that the Gate of Saint Romanus had temporarily fallen, she'd learnt how to tell the difference between the slashing wounds of swords and the thrusting damage caused by a spear. Today, after the battle of the Golden Horne, she'd seen the horrific consequences of fire.

Faces that held the mixed emotions of all humanity, were turned forever into hideous masks. Street children would forever point and mock at these unfortunate survivors, in order to share a laugh amongst themselves. Ella wondered if saving them really was wholly a mercy.

She sat in a darkened corner of the cloister and tried to hold back her tears. The reality was that she wasn't very good at hiding her suffering. Every time she exhaled, it seemed as though tears would come from her eyes along with the breath from her lungs. She regulated her breathing and tried to let the severe emotions pass. It didn't really work.

"Sister Ella, is it?" a stranger's voice asked. "Are you alright?"

Ella looked up, her eyes were wet and red. She didn't recognize the bearded man.

"My name is Felipé, I'm new here," he said. "I'm sorry to disturb you."

He had dark and intelligent eyes, so it wasn't out of place for Ella to conclude that he was a doctor, or possibly an important person of court coming to inspect the hospital.

"It can be truly horrible what those savages do to their enemies," the stranger said. "I suppose we should take heart in knowing that the Christian army names itself among the servants of God by looking after our fallen. The Turks will leave their wounded where they lie, let them perish as they may."

This was of course not true, the Ottoman hospital was a series of tents that was much better staffed than the small one that Ella and Filipé were now sharing, but they had no way of knowing that.

"Yes, God be praised," she replied mechanically and wiped the budding tears from her eyes. "We should be thankful."

"I've been in situations like this for many years, with the horrors and gore, and it can be difficult to endure. I hope you don't mind my noting, but this seems as though it's your first foray into this nightmare. If you need to find strength, it is sometimes good to tell someone what's troubling you. If you'd like, I've been here before, and I'm a good listener."

"Thank you," she said sniffling, and she tried to fake a smile. "You're very kind."

"I do what I can," he cautiously passed her a handkerchief.

Hectore Pazzi knew full well that the worst thing you could do in a situation of such extreme stress was to open up. That would only lead to more anxiety and eventually a psychic collapse. The seeds of such a collapse, he was now planting in poor Ella. He wanted to be there when all of her defences fell, and she needed someone to lift her. Trying to seduce a nun was hardly the worst crime that he would be charged with on Judgement Day.

He wasn't about to get distracted from what was important, however. He had to wait until the fall of night, and then he'd start searching. The looted treasury stores had to be here somewhere.

The Second Battle of the harbour lit the afternoon sky into evening. The fishing fleet of Byzantium were loaded to the brim with the mixed components of Greek Fire. Their rowers crossed the harbour at ramming speed, and then lit their cargo, before swimming back to shore.

The floating fires collided into the Ottoman fleet, harboured tightly together in what little space the Upper Horne provided them. The fires of the ships lacked the grandiose explosive nature of black powder, which came with a loud gas explosion, but the Greek Fire burned hotter and its flames were more destructive.

Eventually, enough of Zaganos' archers arrived to kept the demolition ships from getting too close, and enough of the ships were hauled back on land and away from the flames – but the damage was done. By the time the flames were out, a little before dawn on the morning of the twenty-third, the Turks were down to forty-five combat-ready ships, and the Eastern Roman Empire had two seaworthy warships to her name.

The harbour now needed to be guarded, and the walls manned. At a huge cost of life and material, the Turks had won the day.

Chapter Forty - The Empty Tomb

April 30, 1453

It was a pale shadow of a day that came, stained as it was by bloody victories and losses of the past week. The sun rose from slumber and prepared to watch the earth spin before her, one more time on her axis. The dawn was barely noted by the long suffering inhabitants of Saint Lazarus.

"What are you doing, father?" asked a man with a deformed nose.

"You know what I'm doing," the priest answered back.

"He's surrendering. That's what he's doing. Same as every other morning," the jaundiced Semite completed his pardoner's reply. "He surrenders every day, and there's no one to surrender to! That's what I find embarrassing. That nobody ever bothers or demands or ensures how broken we are. It's a given."

"That's not it, and you know it, Kabil," the priest replied as he affixed the white flag to the gates of their camp, as he had every morning.

"Well you can forgive me, because it looks like you're trying to surrender, and I don't see an army anywhere demanding it so I know that can't be right."

"They're out there, you hear them every day," Leonidas the priest turned to his two accusers once he'd finished with the flags of surrender. "You know that they could come here at any time."

"We're not even a village! We're eight men and one woman! We're afflicted, for Christ's sake! No one's going to come and occupy us."

"That's true, My Child. But if they come, they'll kill us and burn down Saint Lazarus. That's why they have to understand that we're not worth the effort. The humility of the Christian soul will help us to survive."

"What humility? Those damnable Christians wouldn't let us into their city! They left us to die out here in the country!" yellow-eyed Kabil demanded. "The city, to keep its beauty, cast us out and even these marauders won't receive us!"

"God's testing us."

"God's testing them!" psoriasis-faced Mordecai protested. "We're helpless, and they had the opportunity to help us! They did nothing! They washed their hands of their fellow Christians, and went back to fighting with the Latin buggers!"

"We mustn't descend into bitterness, Mordecai," was a constant warning that the shepherd gave this member of his flock. It was a constant warning because it was a comfortable bed in which to lie for those who carried the cross of leprosy. "If the Mohammedans are turned back, then we'll carry on as we always have. If they triumph, we'll do the same. We have to keep the outside world at bay, and go about our duties."

"We won't stand up for Christ and fight, because we're afflicted." Kabil asked. "During the Crusades to liberate the Holy Land from the infidel, the Knights of Lazarus were a fighting order of lepers. They were one of the most feared orders of knights by the Saracens."

"They weren't feared because of their strength, they were feared because they had the appearance of an army of the damned!" Mordecai obviously found the idea quite ludicrous.

"They were feared nonetheless."

"Those Christians wouldn't stand up for us," Mordecai answered flatly. "Why should we die for them?"

"We won't involve ourselves in the wars of this place," Leonidas answered back with a sense of finality. "We'll gird our souls for the hereafter, and don't fret the mortal coil."

Their recurring discussion was cut short by an eleven-year-old boy named Adelphos came running into the camp. While leprosy had robbed him of his fingers, his eyes could still see and his feet could still propel him as quickly as was needed.

"They're coming! They're coming!" he shouted as he ran in.

"Who's coming?" Leonidas asked.

"Turks! The Turks are coming!"

"How many?"

"I don't know, Father. Many! Maybe it's not a hunting group! There's more than ten, possibly twenty!"

"Kabil, are you ready to translate for us?"

The Arab nodded, but couldn't shake the worry from his face. They closed the wood-thatch gate behind their young scout, and Kabil stood up on the rampart to address the Turks when they arrived.

Leprosy is a generic term for a variety of different afflictions. Though scientists would eventually define the bacteria and symptoms, there have been millions of people over the millennia of human history that have suffered from a plethora of illnesses, all of which were considered under the umbrella term "leprosy." Only five of St. Lazarus' nine inhabitants suffered from what later scientists would properly identify as "Leprosy," the rest suffered from other, unrelated debilitating skin infections.

Kabil had been a translator of Persian and Greek into and out of, his native Arabic. He'd lived a healthy life until his thirtieth year, when an itchy infection arrive and spread. His ankles, knees and elbows swelled, and the pigment started to leave his skin. He'd spent the past ten years of his life in Saint Lazarus, trying to pray enough that God would forgive whatever sin he'd unknowingly committed to deserve such baleful punishment. For ten years, he'd kept self-loathing and bitterness at bay, and tried to find acceptance and peace, insomuch as it was possible in his condition.

He waited for the pathway to the camp to turn into a muster ground for whatever army the Turks would field. None appeared.

He continued to wait, and he could sense the arrival of scouts in the forest, but none were visible under the green canopy of nature that hid them from Kabil's failing eyes.

"What's going on?" Leonidas asked him in a loud whisper.

"I don't know," he answered, looking around. "They're here, they're in the forest, but I can't see any of them."

"Where are they?"

"Everywhere, I think we're surrounded."

"Greet them, tell them that we're not their enemies," the priest instructed him.

"Peace be upon you!" Kabil called out into the forest.

The sound of his words seemed to be absorbed into the emerging greenery of April's end. There were no birds or animals to return his greeting, and no human voices were uttering the proscribed response.

A rustle in the trees here, it was just the wind. A rustle in the trees there, and it was unnoticed. Through the canopy of spring, the first arrows flew. The first arrows landed ineffectually into the courtyard of the camp, sticking up from the mud. These arrows weren't simple wooden shafts with bone, stone and steel, though. They were long arrows, measuring a full metre, and their ends were covered in a sticky mucus alight with flame.

"They're going to burn us down!" Mordecai was the first to realize what fate the Turks had planned.

The other inhabitants of the camp took their lead from him and began to panic. The wooden palisade around Saint Lazarus was not a martial wall, it was designed to keep bears and wolves from breaking into their store. It had kept the sombre denizens more like a Zorastrian Tower of Silence, than the defensive walls of Constantinople. The wooden stockade now functioned as the walls of a crematorium.

There was only one exit to the camp, and it was to that door that the nine inhabitants ran, and it was outside that door where the attackers lay in wait.

The raiders were clansmen, not Janissaries, Sipahis or Yayas. There were nineteen men and boys of the Ak-kuyu Clan from Safranbolu.

The first few out the door were cut down by arrows after they left the wall, the next few tripped over their wounded and dying friends outside the door, and then the shock-troops of the clan stormed the forced open door. The scimitars of bored soldiers carried enough speed to make short work of the inhabitants of Saint Lazarus, and five minutes after the lepers were first warned that the enemy was approaching, they were all dead. The morning had been barely disturbed.

Ezera ran into his master's tent and disturbed Tolga's book-keeping.

"Tolga-Pasha, something's going on up on Pera!"

Tolga wasn't one to trust scribes when it came to measuring balances of monies, and he liked to administer the books of his own enterprise. His elevation to admiral had also been an economic hardship, as he now had to pay for the crews and provisions of the fleet – an honour that he wasn't entirely financially prepared for. He was realising how much faster the siege needed to progress in order to be profitable.

"What? Where?"

"On Pera Hill! They're fighting, I don't know why."

"The Genoese?"

"I don't know."

Tolga rubbed his face and groaned as he stood up. He then tried to force his eyes to adjust to the day, once he stepped out of his tent and into the noontime sun. A few hundred yards above them, at the top of the hill, there was some kind of melee going on for all to see. It was undoubtedly visible from Galata, and probably from Constantinople as well.

"Ayoub, get horses for yourself and ten guards."

"Already done, for twelve."

"Wonderful, go find out," Tolgo answered lightly. In the darkness of his study, Ezera could see a man haggard by the stresses of situation and office, but as soon as he was out in the light of day, it was a new man. He seemed serious and light-hearted at the same time, which was exactly what the men in his command needed to see.

Showing the purple and white of Kastamonu, the party rode quickly and were met by guards who quickly brought them to see their commander. The camp was in overall disorder. Men were praying, screaming and crying. Some were scrapping with one another, and it looked as though some of the tribes were trying to leave, only to be prevented by other tribesmen. The whole camp seemed about to run off in every direction.

Zaganos was in a frenzy.

"Peace be upon you, how many men did you bring?" he demanded of his guest.

"And unto you be peace," Ezera answered politely. "A dozen. What's happening?"

"One of the tribes went off in search of plunder, and found a leper colony," Zaganos mourned. "Are your men Christian?"

"Yes, why?"

"Good, we need them as burial detail."

"Of course, they're big strong lads. I don't understand what's going on."

"Of no concern right now. Your men all speak Greek, correct?"

"Yes."

"My son will take you to where the burial site is, and they'll have to bury the corpses. The tribes are afraid of contagion. They think that anyone who touches the lepers will carry the disease."

"So they're happy to let Christians bury the dead."

"Exactly."

"Great, and me?"

"You supervise, hurry, otherwise we'll have a military riot starting here and spreading everywhere. I'll go and tell the tribes that the dead are going to be buried by the Christians. The clan that stirred up this bee's nest is going to be expelled."

"What about my men?"

"They'll be safe. I need you to get the bodies of the lepers. They're all dead now. Go to the colony, bury everyone and set the land to pyre."

"The clan that attacked, are they?"

"About to get murdered if you don't move."

"Why? Are they lepers, too."

"No, of course not. They've just come into contact with them."

"And your men would kill them for contact?"

"You have to understand, the tribes and clans, they're rabidly afraid of infectious diseases. They have no fear charging any enemy, but panic at the slightest sniffle."

"How do I know that your men won't try to kill us and force us into the pyre?" Ezera asked. "On their own initiative, of course."

"You think quickly, Ayoub," Zaganos conceded with voracious humour. "Fortunately for yourself, you think quicker than the men. If you boys hurry, I'm sure that you can finish this before they realise that option. I'd thought of it, too."

"We'll hurry, then," Ezera agreed and left the tent.

The eleven-year-old son of Zaganos-Pasha presented himself to Ayoub, and wished peace upon him. Ezera returned the well-wishes and followed the child to where he and his men could procure burial equipment. Once they started on their journey to the future barrow, he called the attention of one of his sailors.

"What's your name?" Ezera asked one of the crew.

"Miccah, sir,"

"Alright, Miccah," Ezera whispered as they prepared to bring the ox-carts down the hill to the soon-to-be pyre of Saint Lazarus. "As soon as we're out of sight of this camp, I want you to hide in the woods, and if you see any soldiers following us, you have to run and tell me."

"Yes, sir," Miccah whispered back.

"What's your name?" he asked another.

"Olysseus."

"You're going to do the same, a little bit later."

"Yes, sir."

"Great, now smile. We're all friends here."

No one smiled, they glumly collected their carts and followed a guide over the hills.

Mario packed up his kit prepared to go back to Chora. Even during the hardship of the siege, he still had to visit his patron and patient at least once a week. Unfortunately, Giovanni Cardillo knew as well as Mario that the visits were doing less good than was needed, and that the inevitable comes for all.

After such a routine visit, Mario was about to have the servants gather his horse, when he saw a dangerously familiar man sitting in the atrium.

The high cheekbones and pale green eyes of Bishop Isaac DiNapoli were instantly recognisable, and Mario's blood rushed to his face. A mixture of fear, anger and resentment fermented in his body and puffed his reddening flesh, his body started to release adrenaline and Mario's stomach felt instantly less stable. The fight or flight instinct began to assail his rational mind, and he clenched his fists until the knuckles were white from the pressure.

What was this hateful man doing in Constantinople during a siege? Why was he not made aware of it? What's going on in Venice? These questions and many more found their way into Mario's logical consciousness, which fought a vicious battle against his emotional instinct, and was eventually victorious.

Mario noted that this horrible man, who'd lied to and intimidated him so badly only a year and a half ago, seemed to be a shadow of his former self. His cheeks were more sallow. His eyes, which had before held a predatory calm, now darted about like a hunted rabbit. He still wore a bishop's crown, he'd apparently found no small amount of success, but he had obviously lost very much, as well. The priest was obviously aware of Mario's presence in the shadows, watching him, but he didn't make eye-contact. He was pretending not to notice him.

'He doesn't want to talk to me,' Mario surmised. *'He could be afraid, but I don't see why. He knows I'm here, and I suspect he recognises me. He's trying to seem aloof, but failing. He knows me as a former pawn. I'm rising and he's falling, that's why he doesn't want to see me. He's still above my station, but the gap is narrowing. That's why he's afraid.'*

Mario had no great desire to speak to the man, but a nascent streak of aggression had been developing in the womb of his mind over recent months. That streak crept out of his instinct and pushed his logic into an action that he wouldn't normally have pursued.

"Good afternoon, Bishop," he politely announced and walked into the spring sun of the atrium. "Welcome to Constantinople."

"Thank you," Isaac said. He squinted, pretending not to recognise Mario. "How are you, Doctor…"

"Mario Orsini. We met last year in Venice. I taught natural philosophy at the university, and was a loyal disciple of Antonio Di Padua."

A face of disgust contorted onto the cardinal's face.

"Yes."

"What brings you here, Your Grace? So far away from your post in Venice?"

"You know very well, what brings us here, you miscreant dog."

Mario was taken aback, he wasn't surprised to hear such brutal language from a priest, but to hear someone known for an imposing will and sharp intellect, name calling was so unseemly.

"Your Grace, I'm sorry to cause offence…" Mario wanted to kick himself for sounding so toadying, rather than assertive.

"You're sorry! Well let me explain things to you, you… you…

insignificant nothing! I am a prince of the church! Favoured by God! You're a Satanist and a servant of Demon-worshipper! I'll speak to Don Giovanni right now and have you expelled from his service! You deserve no better! You have the gall to come to me and try to gloat? You'll find yourself on the streets begging again, then when you see me again, it won't be to gloat, it'll be to beg! Beg!"

"Brother, stop!" Balias yelled and hurried into the atrium.

"This man! He's a servant of Antonio, he's been sent to spy on me!"

Balias turned around. Mario recognised his egg-shaped head, but his rim of hair had gone from jet-black to more of a charcoal grey over the past months. Balias looked at him for an instant and seemed to recognize him, but paid him no mind.

"Peace, brother. No one's here to spy. He's Cardillo's doctor."

"He's a spy! An assassin! A heretic!"

"Why don't you go and tell Cardillo all about it then, Brother. I'll get rid of him. I'll kick him out of the embassy. Don't worry."

"I don't need to worry about the likes of him! Or his master!"

"Of course not, I'll take care of him. You go and see Don Giovanni."

Isaac crumpled up his robes and stormed out of the atrium, and into the shadowy darkness of the rest of the embassy. His face had contorted in a bestial way. It was as though all reason and logic had been picked from his bones, leaving only a skeleton of anger and frustration. Balias and Mario were left standing where they were.

"I can find my own way out, thank you," Mario said, doing his best not to seem dumbstruck by the former titan. "I know the way."

"I'll come with you," Balias answered. "I'd like to explain a bit of that."

"Then this way, please."

The two of them walked silently to the stables, where Mario's borrowed horse was waiting patiently, having been freshly brushed by the embassy serving staff.

"Are you still in the employ of Antonio Di Padua?"

"No, I was never really in his employ. I worked carefully with him for many years, and he has my respect and sympathy, but I haven't received any correspondence from him in the year that I've been here."

"A year, that sounds about right," Balias confirmed. "About nine months ago, Florence and Venice went to war, and Florence seized Padua. Pope Nicholas owes his papacy to the Florentines, and he gave holy sanction to their aggression and elevated my brother to cardinal, in order that he could assuage the senate with more authority."

"But he's dressed as a bishop. Why is he banished? Why is he so afraid of his own shadow?"

"That goes to your friend Antonio. Don Antonio had so many friends and family in Padua, in the university, and the chaplaincy, that he developed a rather effective intelligence community. He became a senator and spy-master to the Republic. He's had a good year. As soon as perpetual and permanent peace was temporarily restored, he devoted all of his resources to upending my brother. He had spies in our house, he turned one of our own cousins into an informer. This trip with the soldiers to Constantinople isn't a holy task, we've been run out of the republic. The senate forced him to return the cardinal's cap."

"I see," Mario was neither magnanimous nor condescending. He seemed to have no opinion at all.

"You didn't know about this?"

"No."

"Well, he's still a bishop, and I'm captain-general of the expeditionary force."

"Do you answer to Adam Karian, or Vincent DiCastillo?"

"The Spaniard."

"I oversee the hospital at Chora, and I answer to the Armenian. I'm sure that I'll see you again. And as for your brother, I can't say that I'm sorry to see him suffer, but I hope that God comforts you for your… burden."

"Thank you, but I'm sure that my brother will be back to his old self any time now."

Mario doubted that, as diseases of the brain and spirit were usually much slower than ailments of the body when it came to making an exit. The alchemist thought of Isaac handling the cinnabar ore with his bare hands and wondered about the possibility of madness brought about by mercury poisoning. He wouldn't regret or gloat such a possibility.

"Thank you for the information about back home, Don Balias."

"I'll thank you to keep the bishop's condition to yourself. It could become a problem for us if it became known. I know you have cause to hate him personally, but you have greater cause to support the catholic union of Christendom."

"That's true and you needn't have said so," Mario said in a bit of a daze. "But I don't hate your brother."

"Thank you," Balias answered. "Have a safe trip back to the hospital then, doctor."

"Thank you, and good luck."

Mario began the hour-long trot back to the Chora, giving him lots of time to think.

He thought of the glorious success that his old friend and patron had found. His second father, the man to whom he owed everything. His master had sacrificed him for his own salvation, and Mario had reluctantly accepted that as the way of things. Still, the promise of his redemption, that as soon as things were stable again, had been a goal. Mario had long ago stopped waiting for the promise that a resurrected Antonio would emerge from the ashes of Venetian politics and lead him to triumph, but he hadn't realised that Antonio had given up on him as well.

Antonio was doing as he always did, self-defence, self-aggrandisement, and then when the time came, the vicious destruction of his enemies. Isaac seemed to be a broken man, exactly as Antonio had promised he would be. That did marvels for the Padovan's ego, but little for the abandoned doctor.

"No one'll look out for you in this world, Flora," he told his horse, who seemed to listen intently as she walked. "There's no point in relying on others, only yourself."

He then felt guilty.

"Don't worry, I'll look after you," he reassured his horse as an afterthought and patted her back.

Antonio was dead to him now. He'd leave the spirit of his hateful mentor in a cave, and he'd go out to do build his own future, without any added patronage from him, or from the dying Giovanni Cardillo, or the soldierly Vincent DiCastillo. Honour was the prize he intended to take by his own hand. He was going to be looked after by no one, and he wouldn't look after anyone.

A speck of guilt pained his thought.

Vincent was right, he couldn't look after Ella, if he couldn't look out for himself. He'd have to be as hard as possible until this storm passed, and he had to cast aside any doubts or feelings of sympathy. His priority now was to get the treasure out of the chapel and count on no one else's strength to do it.

"Captain, they're coming!" Miccah announced whilst the other sailors were finishing the task of burial.

"Shit," the erstwhile Ezera announced, as though he were identifying a common type of flower. "Everyone, downhill, run for the camp, do so as quietly as you can. Where's Olysscus?"

"I don't know," Miccah answered.

"Too bad for him, everyone hurry."

The twelve men from the redirected burial detail broke into flight, heading downhill, through the forests and towards the Horne.

"Stop, stop!" Ezera called out after a few minutes of chase-less flight. "They're not up there, they're on the road to the south of us."

To the south of them was the Galata Road, the highway that connected the Genoese colony and Adrianople. South of the road, there was no forest, only open plain.

"Look over there," he pointed down the road. "Horsemen. They'll cut us down when we try to cross the plains. We'll have to wait for nightfall."

"Why would they want to do that?" one of the sailors asked in a panic.

"They think the lepers were contaminated, which in turn contaminated us. They're paranoid about these things."

"I don't see them," Miccah whispered loudly, trying to surreptitiously glance down the pathway. "Where are they?"

"Exactly where you'd expect to find Turks: riding up behind you Greeks."

Ezera had intended that as a light hearted joke, but the men were darkly shamed and silenced by it.

"Oh, come on, it was funny," Ezera-Ayoub insisted.

That was the first time that Ezera noted that his men didn't take this as a simple mercenary job any more. Some of them were starting to see themselves as Judas-goats, betraying their emperor and patriarch in exchange for the pittance being paid them.

"Fine, if the only way you guys'll be quiet is by insulting you, so be it. Just wait until nightfall to make the run."

"Welcome, Ayoub," Tolga said at long last. "I was wondering if you'd finally make it back here, or if you'd run off and rejoin the Christians."

"They tried to kill us!"

"Who?"

"The tribesmen on the hill! They chased us through the woods!"

"They didn't try to kill you," Tolga reassured him. "Zaganos wouldn't have allowed it. He came here a few hours ago and told me about what happened. He also returned the one of your number that he found in the forest."

"We've been hiding in the woods. His men were hunting us down."

"They were going to bring you back here, you fret too much."

"They had us bury the lepers and then…"

"Oh, stop there," Tolga dropped his friendly tone and seemed quite serious. "There were no lepers."

"What?"

"You have to understand this, Ayoub. During a protracted siege like this, any whisper of plague will remove more of our men than any counter-offensive the Romans are capable of mounting. Even a rumour, and the tribes will destroy each other and flee."

"They massacred and looted a leper colony, and then the other tribes expelled the looters, and then we buried everything because the rest of the tribes were afraid to touch the bodies, and none of this happened?"

"Oh, we know that it happened," Tolga agreed. "And you saw how violently afraid they became once they thought they'd exposed the contagion. Because of that, there were no lepers."

"Fine! No lepers! What was the problem up there, in case anyone asks."

"A miracle," Tolga said without intonation. "I'm drafting an announcement and a letter for my son-in-law."

"A miracle?"

"Yes," Tolga looked down at the paper in front of him. "Eight hundred years ago, the early Muslims laid siege to the city of Constantinople. They were led by a soldier sharing your name-sake, Ayoub. Ayoub, the Arab general, was unfortunately killed during the failed battle. Praise God and his miracles, our brother-in-faith, Zaganos-Pasha has discovered his tomb."

"The tomb of Job?"

Tolga shrugged. "It's better than plague bearers and civil strife."

"No one will believe that."

"Oh, you'd be surprised what frightened and stressed people would believe. Our army is as much under siege as theirs. Boredom, money shortages, population pressure, food and sanitation – all these are against us. As well planned out as the siege was, every passing day brings us closer and closer to defeat. Those heroics at the harbour did a fine job at bringing victory closer, but tomorrow is the first day of a new month. This siege was supposed to be over by now. Granaries are emptying, morale is tense. Our foes in the city are still protected by those walls, and unless the cannons break them down soon, we'll have to abandon all this. We need miracles."

"The sultan's army is so huge…"

"It's so unwieldy. Think of your old ship, how many men did you have?"

"Fifty."

"What would you do with five hundred on that same boat?"

"Sink," Ezera laughed.

"Exactly," Tolga grunted and returned to his correspondence.

Chapter Forty-One - In the Forest of the Night

Chora Monastery was built two miles outside the city walls of the capital, and there it stood for several centuries. The name "*Chora*" means '*in the forest.*' Centuries passed after its original construction, and while this house of God didn't move, the city around it gradually did. In the seventh century, the walls of Constantine fell to a powerful earthquake, one of the perpetual banes of civilized people. By that time, the city had outgrown the walls to the point that there were over a thousand people living in permanent dwellings that were outside of those protective walls. Living inside the walls connoted security, and everyone wanted that status. What was the point of denying them? The Emperor Theodosius rebuilt the walls further afield, and now the isolated monastic house of Chora found itself within the Metropolitan region of the capital.

As though it weren't enough to bring the city to the forest, the isolated commune found itself with neighbours for the first time. Next to Chora, Porphyrogentius Palace was built. It found glory as the suburban home of the imperial family until the fortunes of the emperor raised to the point that the empire's treasury could justify the building of a new palace. From that wealth, Blachernae emerged, and Porphyrion sank into disrepair. Because of the importance of the palaces, the district was cordoned off from the masses by wooden stockades and stone gates. Over the centuries, the Petrion district had seen many strange residents; families competing for the imperial crown and an alphabet of visiting Arabs, Bulgars, Catalans, Dalmatians, Ephesians, Fatimads, all the way to Zengid ambassadors, as well as the men of nations that had since been forgotten by even the long memory of history.

A new collection of players had assembled in the district for a new drama to unfold, and the scene was set in Chora.

"Are you sure that's him?" Mario asked Isodore. It was a silly question, as Isodore wasn't the type of man to say close enough when it wasn't.

"As sure as the day I was born," he reassured the doctor. "That's the one who's been hunting you down all over the city. He killed the priest and chased me through the old city. If he's a doctor, then I'm Prestor John."

"He must have been in league with General Karian," Mario surmised. "They must have had some kind of dispute over the money, I don't know the details."

"Karian? What does he have to do with any of this?"

"There's a horde here, Isodore," Mairo whispered.

"I know that! Everyone knows that!"

"Not the army out there," Mario motioned over the walls with a bit of frustration. "I mean in here, in the monastery. A horde of treasure's been stowed away for a rainy day. Adam Karian organized it, Hectore Pazzi learnt about it and he's now hunting for it."

"Karian and Pazzi have a long history together. Between the two of them, there's not much that goes on here that they're unaware of."

"That makes sense. Karian stole some money, probably from the treasury, but I can't be certain. He hid it here in the monastery so that no one would find it, and then he turned it into a busy hub for the war so that no one could sulk around here in secret."

"That's a good idea," the monk admitted, "but how would he get the horde out? Someone like him wouldn't risk exposure as a thief for a handful of baubles, how much are we talking about?"

"A lot," Mario said with a lop-sided grin. "More than you and I could carry."

"If the Christian army successfully defends, then he could get it out at his leisure. A note of warrant from the Strateogos is as good as from the Emperor. If the Muslims take the city, may God forgive me for considering it, what could he do?"

"Wait them out, the cache is hidden and secret. This place is an area of high importance now, but things will change soon, one way or another, and will eventually go back to some version of normalcy. People will stop worrying about a monastic community at the edge of the walls. He could come back then."

"He's a general in the Emperor's service, he can't disappear! He'll be killed for certain, or at least ransomed off to... well, no one I guess."

"That's right, he's got no nation that would pay the sultan's bail money. He'd rot in jail until his dying day," Mario concluded.

"So?"

"So he'll have to leave the emperor's service before the city falls, or stay at his side until after the attackers are repelled. It isn't actually that hard for a man to hide in a city once the veil of civilization is lifted from the old hag's face."

"I like your mind, Doctor," Isodore joked. "What do you plan to do with the general's loot?"

"Take it," he said without any pretence. "I want to get married and settle down, raise a family, own a house and lands. This can do that for me."

"Not if Pazzi takes it away, or Karian appears rather suddenly."

"That's why I've got to move it."

"Who else knows where it is?"

"Me, Karian, and whoever moved it, one man alone couldn't have done it."

"Varangians."

"Probably. They'll come back to loot if the battle goes poorly."

"Are you sure Pazzi doesn't know?"

"I'm sure. He's still looking around at night, when he thinks everyone else is sleeping or praying. If he knew where it was, he'd be recruiting workers, not searching. I'd like to move the gold elsewhere so no one could find it, and then come back myself for it, regardless of the outcome of the battle, but that's impossible with our Genoese friend lurking in the shadows."

"So what can we do about that?"

"Distract Pazzi."

"And how, pray tell, Doctor?"

"That, I haven't planned out quite yet. But this siege can't go on much longer. The walls are buckling, the injured are adding up. I'm sure that they've got similar stresses on the Turkish side. One way or another, the opportunity is going to come sooner rather than later, and I'll have to seize it when it does."

Ahmet, son of Ali of Amaseia, was thrice cursed. He was haunted by the ghost of an unavenged brother. He hated and was hated by the rulers of his own country. More baneful than these two curses was the third curse, he had degraded himself from a casual eater and smoker of poppy, to an outright opium fiend.

Since his expulsion from Adrianople a month ago, he had been sleeping in alleyways, urban fields and gutters, eating where he could and scurrying like rat from the light of day. He'd lost weight, grown a dirty excuse of a beard, and worn through his once fine clothes. He looked like a beggar, where he had once looked like a prince. Only a month ago, he had once been one of the most feared men in the capital of European Islam, and was now devolving into a rakish skeleton. His current state was a direct result of his choice to pursue the poppy rather than other, more productive, glories.

Ahmet was cursed in his life in the capital of the infidels, for he had spent his last diram, and squandered his last resources on opium. He no longer paid for food, he stole. He no longer paid for lodging, he slept in fields, in places where the dogs found resting unsuitable. But after a week without the black tar smoke to ease the pain of the horrors to which his life had fallen, he couldn't sleep anymore. He couldn't sleep, so he stayed awake, and waited for the rest of the city to slumber.

By about an hour before sundown every night, the cannons stopped their bombardment of the city, and the townspeople were able to do their daily routines. It was then that the men of the auxiliaries went to their homes and ate what their wives had made during the day. It was then that they would go out to the fora of the city and meet with their friends in a more social environment. They would tell stories of adventure to the children, who would be eager to learn how their fathers had all single-handedly turned back the infidel advance that day.

Like all merry-making, it eventually came to an end. Darkness overtook the second city of seven hills, and the inhabitants went to rest. When that finally happened, Ahmet came to life and act out on his curse. He hurried among the expanded shadows of night towards the Petrion district, and Chora Monastery. Everyone knew that the hospital was there, and Ahmet knew that where there was a hospital, there would be opium. So he went in search of his vice, hating himself for doing so.

When the city was first besieged, Karian turned the inner workings of the civic authority into a military camp. There were guards who would serve at night, keeping every street safe, reassuring the locals that there was nothing to fear. The Emperor would protect them. This strategy worked, and people, for the most part, felt as safe as possible, all things considered.

When Constantine dismissed the General, his strong hand was no longer there to reassure the people. People's morale faltered a bit, not seeing soldiers on the streets, but it was warmed, knowing that the Virgin Mary had appeared to the emperor and promised victory. The reality that there were no guards to the Petrion district bore little weight on people's sense of safety.

Ahmet walked peaceably into the District and walked past the main entrance to the hospital compound. It was guarded by two men, Greeks, who were shivering in the cold spring night and talking about charioteering; the permanent discussion of the Reds vs. the Blues. Ahmet, of course, had no idea what they talking about, he just walked past them and circled the compound, counting out his steps and keeping away from the torchlight. They eyed him suspiciously but did nothing.

The compound was bigger than he had anticipated, and there was gas lighting all throughout the district, much to the amazement of most new residents and visitors. Ahmet finally found a corner where the shadows overhung the light enough for him to try the walls of the monastery. The wall was too high to jump, but the red bricks were irregular and stuck out enough for him to grab handfuls here and there.

Ahmet was still strong, he'd lost weight and some of his strength, but he still had enough to hurl himself up an uneven wall and his fingers were still sensitive enough to find secure ledges. His body was long and lanky, and he'd always been a good climber of walls, trees, houses, anything that would drive his mother to worry as a child.

He rolled himself up to the top of the monastery wall, and lay there in the shadows. He could count four buildings, and a large tent between them. There was a big church, a little church, and two buildings that looked like barracks. There were people sleeping outside in the tent, so Ahmet presumed that the barracks buildings would be filled to the brim by now.

He examined the inside of the wall before he jumped down, and noted that it would be hard for him to escape. He certainly couldn't talk his way past the guards at the gate. He would have to go into one of the barracks, find the opiates and appropriate something to act as a ladder. He could then escape the same way he came in.

He landed noiselessly on the grass at the foot of the wall. The compound was one of the few places left in the city that still had grass, rather than stone or mud. He walked as quickly and as quietly as he could towards the first building.

"Bismillah," he said when he opened the front door and found it to be unlocked. *'Thank God.'*

He stepped into darkness, which was better than stepping into light. He could feel his way around until he could identify an apothecary, and then worry about finding light to identify the right compounds, although he could probably identify by smell.

He found the dispensary in the third room he searched, and began to wonder where he could acquire a candle or torch, when he heard a rumbling down the hall. Someone was coming with a lantern, so Ahmet hid behind the door.

"I'm certain that there are some bandages in here," Ella said stubbornly as she stormed into the room, lantern in hand. She opened a cabinet and pulled out a pile of white linen bandages and handed them to a man impersonating a Doctor named Felipé.

"You're very patient with me, Sister," Hectore said in a low voice that made Ella uncomfortable.

"Well, here you go, now go look after your patient."

Pazzi made no indication that he was going to move.

Ella stepped away to circumvent him, but he sidestepped to block her path.

"You're a very beautiful woman, Ella," he said slowly, glaring into her eyes.

"I am a nun, Doctor." She said more as a warning than a statement of fact.

"You're a woman, and I know what burns in the hearts of all women. I know what burns in your loins, and I know that you haven't always been a nun, and that you won't always be one."

"If you don't stand out of my way, I will scream, sir," she girded herself.

"You won't," Pazzi said, barely louder than a whisper. "You want this as much as me."

He moved closer to her and tilted his head to one side, making to kiss her.

Slap!

Ella stared him square in the eye, defying him and breathing nervously.

"Let me pass, Doctor," she said, summoning as much strength of will as she could.

Pazzi took a step back, raised his leg backwards to hook the door, and swung it closed. Had he been looking behind him, he would have seen the exposed and surprised Ahmet, crouching pitifully in the dark.

Pazzi then flung himself onto Ella and covered her mouth quickly. He pushed her body, front first, against the wall of the apothecary and held her tightly, reaching around to grab a breast through her habit.

All of what was in front of him was bad, Ahmet knew. He quietly swore at his bad luck. Unlike Pazzi who considered himself to be forcefully suave, knowing that this woman would eventually surrender to the act, Ahmet could tell rape when he saw it.

As damning as the curse in his brain had turned him, Ahmet was still not quite so remorseless and without conscience that he would remain silent.

If he was caught at such a crime scene, he knew that as a foreigner during wartime, he'd be executed as a rapist. If he escaped, then he'd deserve no better than such an execution. Ahmet swallowed hard and looked at the gait of the attacking man. He was obviously strong and knew how to carry himself in a brawl. The last thing that Ahmet needed would be a fight or an alarm to be raised, so he took a deep breath and acted as his conscience and reason dictated.

He ran to the violent coupling on the far wall and grabbed the aggressor by a tuft of hair on the back of his head. He kicked a pointed toe to the hollow behind Pazzi's knee, stealing his balance, and pulled back on the hair with all of his considerable might. Pazzi folded backwards and his skull bounced off the flagstone floor from the whiplash of the assault. It was over in less than a second. Pazzi's was on the floor bleeding from the back of his skull, and Ahmet jumped back from the carnage.

Ella found the hand removed from her mouth and started to scream before she even turned around. When she did she saw Felipé/Hectore lying on the ground, black liquid chortling out of his convulsing body, and a lanky stranger standing in his place. Her scream changed pitch from one of alarm to one of fear.

"*Hayir, hayir!*" Ahmet whispered and motioned for her to be silent. "*Soos, soos! Lutfen, Soos!*"

Seing that the alarm had indeed been raised, and that the woman he'd just saved had no intention of quieting herself in the immediate future, Ahmet turned and ran out the door, seeking shadows elsewhere.

The two guards outside the hospital compound shook themselves from their sporting conversation and came running into the housing when they heard Ella's cry. By that time, Ahmet had disappeared into the black mass of the night. They looked about and couldn't seem to make up their minds as to what to do.

Isodore emerged alongside Mario when they arrived to see what had transpired, he stayed out of the room, intending to stay unseen by the murderous Hectore Pazzi, regardless of his condition. He instead focused his attention on the two confused auxiliaries. He told one to remain at the gate, as that was the only way out of the compound, and the other one to look through the first barrack building, and he would investigate the tent triage area and take it from there.

The monk hurried along the maze of cots that covered the green clearing in front of the chapels. Finding nothing, he was about to investigate the second barracks, when he caught something out of the corner of his eye: the narthex door to the main chapel was ajar to a very slight degree. There wasn't enough light to see this, per se, but the shadows in the darkness allowed for a purple black of the first door to overlap a grey black of the second just enough to raise the attention of this most observant of monks.

He approached the door and poked it open with the tip of his toe.

"Ya-su," he called out a polite greeting in Greek, before trying his native Bulgarian and then a few other languages he'd picked up over the years. "Zdravei? Saluto? Abkhaz? Parev? Merhaba?"

The darkness of the chapel answered him with silence.

"I'm coming in slowly," he announced in the deepest voice he could muster, trying to sound peaceful and fatherly. "I'm unarmed and I just want to talk."

He peaceably extended his hands and fingers to show that he was indeed not carrying a weapon, and walked very slowly through the ajar door.

The chamber room of the main chapel was in total darkness. Not the regular darkness that one finds in a normal night, but an inky fog brought by no stars, no windows and now lantern. There was only a whisper of the open door that exposed a regular night's blackness to contrast.

Isodore closed his eyes, and let his senses wander about the large room. The hair on his arms and face stood out like the sensors of a cave crab, trying to get a feel of perception in the permanent night. His curiously round ears tweaked as high as his ability to hear allowed. He could barely make out the sound of breathing from somewhere in the stone chamber.

"Hello?" he whispered musically. "You've just attacked a very bad man, I'd rather thank you than arrest you."

Isodore heard a loud inhale come from his left side, much closer than he had originally thought. He ducked and stepped back, facing the direction of the sound.

"Greek… No." a very deep voice whispered. "Turkcheh, biliyormusunuz?"

'*Oh God*' Isodore thought '*It's a Turk.*'

"Az az, yavash yavash," he said carefully over-pronouncing every syllable. '*Little little, slowly slowly.*'

Ahmet breathed for a moment, the sound of his panting identifying his place, while he thought of what he should say and how he should say it.

"The man attacked the woman. I was only there to steal, I didn't want to hurt anyone. But I couldn't watch that, so I hit him, and then ran. I hope he's not dead," Ahmet said, far too quickly for Isodore to properly understand.

Isodore looked into the blackness, and started to repeat the gist of what he thought he'd heard.

"Man, the man, Pazzi, the bearded man?" he asked, miming a beard off his chin.

"Evet!" Ahmet said positively.

"Attacking the nurse, Ella, the woman?"

"Evet."

"You are running."

"Evet."

Isodore exhaled loudly. That seemed to help him think.

"I'm going. Talking to woman. You…" he realized he didn't know the word for stay here, so he improvised. ".. sitting here. Is this alright?"

There was a moment of silent consideration.

"Evet."

"Alright then, not much of conversationalist," Isodore reverted to his native Bulgarian for an instant before telling the darkness that he would be back in an instant. "Bi daka."

Isodore left the room to find Ella.

Ahmet's knew that he was incapable of leaping the wall, and he didn't know how many other guards would be out there on the compound, so he had no rational choice at this point but to stay. He paced in the chapel, he was much to agitated to sit as instructed.

"Can you see me?" Mario's voice crossed an ocean of consciousness to reach his patient's ears. "Can you hear me?"

"I... I can't move," Pazzi answered, he was incapacitated and on his side.

"Good, don't try," the doctor answered. "Your skull's broken in two places."

Hectore looked around the small operating room. It was lit by candles, it was still night. "What happened?"

"You were attacked, we presume. Ella, one of the nuns here, found you and called out for help," Mario answered. He knew no more than that. "It's still night, we won't try to take out the bone fragments from your head until we have daylight, which is still many hours away. Can you hear me?"

"Si, si," Pazzi said, reverting to Italian. "Who?"

"We don't know, Doctor Filipé. But some men are looking for him, he couldn't have got far."

"Buono," he muttered before passing out.

"Thank God for small miracles," Mario mumbled past sentiments to himself and began clearing the head wound of bone fragments and dirt as best he could before the sun brought enough light to do the job properly.

There was a harsh knocking at the door to the nurses housing dormitory. The door was answered by a fat elderly nun carrying a candle.

"What is it?" she demanded.

"I need to speak to Sister Ella immediately," Isodore counter-demanded.

"I'm sorry, but that is impossible," the round little woman answered. "The poor girl is beside herself with shock."

"Nevertheless, I am an old friend and I must see her."

Isodore put his sandaled food against the door to keep it open. The nun braced herself at the door and made it perfectly clear that she would not allow the man to pass.

"No! You must leave us!"

"I must see her," he insisted.

"Fine!" came an angry shout from the room, and Isodore could hear the charging footsteps of a very angry soul. The door was pulled open, and there stood a weepy-eyed Ella DiCastillo, face and eyes red and wet with tears and sweat. "I'm here. I'm fine. Now I'll thank you to leave me in peace, Isodore. Are you happy now?!"

Isodore looked into her face and could see the shock brought on by witnessing a man almost killed before her, but he looked carefully into her eyes, those gateways to the soul, and could see something other than surprise and shock hiding back there, in the depths of her humour. Shame was back there. Shame because of the actions of another. Shame because in her mind she would have brought something upon herself. It must have happened as the Turk said.

"I'm sorry about what's happened, Ella," he said gently when he registered her emotions. "I'll pray for you."

"Fine, you do that," she said, turning her back to the door and walking off in angry tears, into the privacy of the dormitory.

"There! You've seen her!" the fat nun surmised. "Now go!"

She was obviously aware of what had happened and was trying to protect one of her wards.

"Yes, Sister," Isodore said and left the women to their peace and returned to the chapel.

"I'm back," Isodore announced as he re-entered the chapel, this time with a lantern in one hand and a bundle of clothes in another. "Are you here?"

Ahmet emerged from a side apse and waved a hand to his brow as a greeting.

"Peace be upon you."

"And unto you be peace," Isodore replied with more formality than was really appropriate for such a standard greeting. "Come come."

Ahmet approached the lantern and Isodore could see him for the first time. He was a big, gangly looking man. Tall and thin, obviously very strong, the light of the candle made Isodore feel less safe, now that he could see the anonymous Turkish Samaritan.

The same way that Isodore could tell what was wrong with Ella, told him what was wrong with Ahmet: the eyes. The frantic desperation and brown discoloration, when combined with the gauntness of the rest of his face, started to make sense to the monk. If this man was a regular thief, he'd have been looking for the church's strongbox. He was looking in the dispensary because what he needed was kept there. He must have been after Mario's supply of opiates. So be it, he had still saved Ella, and by Isodore's reasoning was owed a favour.

"Clothes," Isodore said, trying to hide his apprehension. He was frustrated that his control of the Turkish language was limited to the present continuous tense. "You're wearing these. You're sleeping in a hospital bed. You're not speaking. Tomorrow morning, I and you are going. You're not speaking, are you understanding?"

Ahmet took a minute to make heads and tails of Isodore's garbled Turkish, and he thought he understood.

"Yes, I understand. Thank you, Stranger."

"Come, Arkadashiyim" Isodore had meant to say '*my friend,*' though it came out as '*I am a friend.*' Turkish stative and possessive cases are distinguished by context, fortunately the mistake was still appropriate.

Ahmet smiled and approached the unknown stranger who insisted he was his friend.

"Good.   In the morning, we're going together," everything the monk said he motioned with his hands. "Tonight, no..."

He didn't know the word for opium, so he carried out the body language of smoke and a dizzy head, and then made a slicing motion with his hands, to summarize his opinion on the subject.

"No. Are you understanding?"

Ahmet exhaled loudly, and he could actually feel himself blush in shame.

"Yes," Isodore concluded. "You're understanding."

That night was a hard night for Ahmet. He slept in a bed for the first time in weeks, and he slept in a stranger's clothes; and a Christian's clothes at that. Around him were the wounded of many nations, they kept their own slumber, oblivious to the drama of the night.

Alone as he was, guilt visited him, by this point an all-too familiar guest in his psyche.

He was a gazi, in his heart, or so he had always felt. One of God's chosen warrior, selected among all the men of all the nations of creation, to spread and glorify the faith. This was a title and ambition to which he was failing, and doing so in a most miserable of fashions.

The look in the eyes of that man, the monk who spoke such bad Turkish, held such pity. Not fear, such as what a heretic should have from a warrior of God, but pity, like you would have on an animal that had fallen into a forgotten trap.

What right did he, an ignorant savage from the lands of falsehood, have to pity a fearsome warrior such as he? None!

Not for the first time, Ahmet promised himself never again to let his curse get the best of him. Not for the first time, he swore a renewal of faith. Not for the first time, these lies gave little comfort as he tried to find sleep.

Mario put his head in his hand when he heard the news.

"If it's a consolation, she seems fine," Isodore reassured him.

"A minor one," he said as his head spun. It was he, who'd allowed this murderous slime into the hospital. Mario shouldered the guilt, but he was a man of the same emotions as any other. His reason, however, would always step in, to keep those passions in check. This had resulted in a very stable, albeit boring life, for years. "Where is this *Turk* now?"

"I've put him in the cots outside."

"I'll go secure all of the opiates," Mario said without thinking. His brain would always focus on the routine machinations of normalcy, rather than try to understand any of the human politics with which he was presented. "I should see Ella."

"She's not receiving guests, there's a fat little nun who's keeping watch on the door. It's probably best to let her sleep."

"I suppose."

"I'd like to talk to you about the treasure," Isodore proclaimed. "I know that it's late, but I have an idea."

"What is it?"

"Pazzi's stopped searching now."

Although the situation with Ella seemed more important, the situation with the treasure was something that he could do something about now, so it seemed a better target of his attention.

"That's true. I'll keep him drugged so he stays in bed."

"I know how we can move the treasure easily and safely," the monk smiled.

"Wonderful. How's that?"

"I'll need two horses in the morning, and I'm going to conscript our Turkish friend as a labourer."

"He's an opium fiend!"

"We can fix that."

"No, No. Look at me, Isodore," Mario said seriously. "I'm your friend, and I'm grateful to you, and to this man who took care of Pazzi for us, but once a man partakes of opium recreationally, his soul is dead. He'll destroy everyone near him. He's lost, cut him loose."

"I'll take responsibility for him."

"You don't know him!"

"That notwithstanding, he's strong enough to carry his own weight, and he's incorruptible. No one in the city can try to bribe him, because he only speaks Turkish. No one can talk to him and he'll tell his secrets to no one."

"You and I both know that soon there will be many of his countrymen everywhere."

"If he were in good standing with the Turks, he'd be with them. If he was in good standing with the refugees in the panhandle, he'd be with them. He's alone, we don't have to worry about that."

"He's alone because of the opiates," Mario reminded him.

"You should be kind to the stranger who dwells among you, for you, too, have been strangers in the lands of Egypt. That's the advice of Exodus on this subject. I think we can fix him."

"We? I can't believe this idiocy."

"*Credo que absurdum, Mario.* In case you hadn't noticed, I haven't agreed to help you abscond with the palace jewels. Tithing is ten percent to the church, in case you'd been away from the church for too long."

"This is the first time we've spoken about this, I thought that you didn't believe in monetary wealth."

"Oh, I don't. Although I too would like a soft retirement. Ten percent of a treasury such as you've described should pay for my stay in one of the greatest monasteries of our beloved Italy until my dying day."

"I suppose I could settle for ninety percent."

"Seventy-nine percent. It'll be ten for me, one for the Turk, and ten for the captain of the ship that takes us out of here."

"Do you know of a ship?"

"Ezera's alive."

"What?"

"That's a secret of state now. I'd been feeding information to Cardillo through Vincent, from Ezera for months. He's an assistant to the Turkish admiral. I can find him, he can get us out."

Mario was dumbstruck.

"Fine," he conceded. "But I'm going to need to know your plan."

"Of course, we've got a few hours until sunrise. I'll need some horses and pocket money as well."

"Done, now start talking."

And Isodore did just that, until sunrise.

Chapter Forty-Two - A Meeting

Away from Chora, though still in the Petrion was Phanar Gate. It led from the Petrion District into the harbour district, sparsely populated by the city's miniscule Jewish community. The Jews were wards of the Emperor, and their concession was an annex to the imperial compound. Without the defence of the Emperor, the tidal whims of the religious inhabitants of the city would have undoubtedly devoured the religious minority.

Because of its isolation from the rest of the city, it was to chosen to serve as the host for the first meeting of two of the city's prime Christians. It was in a reserved public house that a table was set, food was prepared by the local staff and the guests were welcomed with anonymity.

The publican welcomed his first guest, Noah, the Patriarch of the City, with the warmth that would extend to an old friend, and his second guest with consummate formality. Isaac was not as enthusiastic about meeting in the Levite district as his counterpart.

The two clerics were left alone by their hosts, as they'd been instructed to do. He was a host and not a participant in the meeting.

"It's a pleasure to finally meet you, Patriarch," Isaac said once the two of them were alone. "Though I must say that I'm a little confused by your insistence to meet in this home."

"Unfortunately brother, there are politics at play in the city even now," the old man huffed his words as though they could be his last at any moment. Despite the obvious decay of his earthly coils, his mind was still a sharp blade. "While I've prayed daily for the union of our two churches..."

"There is but one church, Patriarch, not two," Isaac interrupted.

"...yes," the elder continued without missing an instant. "The Greek-speaking people are unfortunately held back by a terrible curse of the soul, when it comes to our Latin brothers. The years have not brought their hearts together as much as they should have."

"That is indeed unfortunate, Brother," Isaac had no qualms about using the fire behind his soul to intimidate the elderly, and while it might not though put fright into such an eminent man as Noah, it would still cause him to choose his words carefully. "But with a return of the sectarians to the fold, there will be one less barrier between our races. I pray that this will expedite the process."

"Yes, I'll pray for this also, but you have to be aware that the resentment in the city to the foreign influences, particularly to the Italians of Venice, Genoa and Rome, is very strong and not to be underestimated."

"Nor should the power of God's grace be underestimated... or his wrath, as you well know."

"Of course," Noah was becoming a little testy. "We, the Greek-speaking priests who are loyal to the idea of the one church, have had to walk a very narrow line to keep the peace. It was not to long ago that the city rioted at the prospect of union with your church..."

"*Our* church."

"...yes. The road that we've chosen to travel, in order to bring the excommunicates into the fold of Saint Peter, is one of gradual movement. We now carry the favour of the Emperor, and we appoint our own, gradually building our numbers until the matter of Universal Catholicism is *fait accompli*. It might not be as fast as some would prefer, but it is the only way that this endeavour can succeed."

"By which you mean, that you, the podium of Holy Wisdom, don't publically embrace the union of our churches."

"Well, not exactly, no," he stammered.

"Excuse me," Isaac got up from the table and made way to the exit.

"Wait, Your Grace, you have to be reasonable."

"No, Noah, you do. You're choosing to compromise here on earth, and burn in hell for eternity. That is a terribly unreasonable decision in my mind. I'm choosing to do as God commands, and be rewarded with paradise. Don't tell me who you think is reasonable and who you believe to be a fool. I will not negotiate away God to please some chauvinistic native elements."

Isaac left the lounge, and made no effort to thank his host for the trouble. He stormed out and angrily marched to his carriage.

There was silence in the main hall of the Palace of Blachernae. No one would speak to disrupt the most sacred of late-night ceremonies that was underway.

Candelabras stood at regular intervals along a walkway of marble and under a ceiling of gold-leaf mosaics. On either side of the implied road were the lords of Eastern Christianity. Duxes, megaduxes, magistroses and hypathoses wore their best clothes for such an inauguration. Constantine stood before his assembled court, with a sceptre in hand.

"My friends," he began solemnly. "We would normally meet during the light of day, when we could see each other more clearly, but today it seems appropriate to do this in the dark of the night. The capital of God's nation is under siege by those who would twice murder our Lord. It is a dark night for many.

"But fret not, champions of unconquered Rome. For the God of the Israelites, of Moses, of Christ and of Constantine shall warm our cold bodies in this dark night. As the psalms promise, His rod and His staff shall comfort us. We have a table prepared before us, very much in the presence of our enemies, but we fear not their evil, knowing that our Lord is with us.

"As our Lord has not abandoned us, we shall not abandon Him. Our swords and spears, shall march to Calvary, and defend His crucified son as he prepares to rise up amongst us. This is not an easy task, but one that we will complete nonetheless, because He command it of us, His new tribe of Israel.

"I accept the mantle of Moses, as a proxy to lead this tribe, but the vestments of Joshua are currently barren. There is but one among the men of the empire who is fit to rise as such a man. I introduce the court to the new Strategeos: Stavros of Brussa!"

There was polite applause by those assembled.

Giovanni Cardillo was always the very image of politeness, though the two men who stood with him, Vincent and his Genovese counterpart were not able to maintain his standard. To be generous, they tried their best.

"Stavros, my friend, this is a sceptre of wood. One just like it was wielded by Valens, by Valentius and by Belasarius. Do you accept this heritage? Do you accept command of the legions of the Empire of Rome, both in Roman lands and in the lands of our conquest?"

"I do."

"Do you accept the responsibility that goes with this? Do you accept to liberate the lands of the Roman Empire, of Edessa and Iconium in the east, from the Tatars?"

"I do."

"Do you accept the responsibility to liberate Egypt and Syria in the south from the Saracens?"

"I do."

"Do you accept the responsibility to liberate Adrianopolis and Sofia, in the north from the Turks?"

"I do."

"Do you accept the responsibility to liberate Athens and Thessalonica in the west, from the terror of the Mohammedan hordes?"

"I do."

"Then stand proud, my friend, that I may kiss you and call you brother."

Stavros stood up with a look of such glowing pride on his face, knowing that he'd just become so much more than a general. A Strategeos was a mere office, he was effectively assuming the title of Caesar; Second only to the Emperor himself. Since Constantine was a mule and had no children, Stavros could one day be the father to the future emperors, perhaps even the progenitor of a new dynasty. This was truly the happiest day of his life.

"How long do we have to stay and watch this farce?" Vincent asked Cardillo.

"You can leave after you pay your respects to the new Strategeos," the Venetian ambassador answered in a disinterested voice and through a fake smile. "Not until then. Try to smile."

Vincent smirked. That was as close as he could get, under the circumstances.

"What do you think this'll mean for us?" Guistiniano asked the smirk-wearing Vincent. When he spoke to him, he devolved his speaking to a patois that would be considered completely incomprehensible to the Greeks. Vincent and Giovanni would be able to understand him, but no one else in the assembly hall would be able to pierce their linguistic veil. Vincent's Italian was what he'd learnt in court and commerce, so he had some difficulty making the linguistic descent to obfuscation, but he managed to do it respectably.

"Let's hope he's not serious," Vincent said. "If this idiot thinks he's Caesar now, we'll have to remind him quickly that he's the junior member of the war council. I can't believe this farce."

"Does he have any experience with leading men in battle?" Guistiniano asked almost rhetorically.

"None whatsoever. He calls himself landed gentry, but his lands have been occupied by the Turks for over a century, I suppose you'd say that they were his great-grandfather's lands."

"How does he support himself at court?"

"Same way his father and his father's father did, imperial pensions. Orthodox churches charge their tithes, which support the glory of Christendom. That's this pageant."

"Do you ever think..." Guistiniano felt guilty at the suggestion, "...that perhaps God would want to bring this all to an end?"

"Nothing can or does happen against the will of the Almighty, so I suppose we'll find out soon enough, one way or another."

"But all this," the Genovese motioned at the court, all taking turns kissing the hand and congratulating the new general on his appointment. "It's not right. These people are an inbred nest of rats, not the hand of God. This can't be the Christian empire that God commands."

"It's not," Giovanni interjected before turning his head politely to allow for a minor coughing attack. "This is a flaccid remnant of a once virile Empire. Certainly, I'll grant you it's nothing but shadows on the cave wall now, but the Roman Empire of the East was once what it has always purported to be. It was from this city that new languages were first translated, and new alphabets composed. Missionaries from these seven hills went out and converted whole nations to Christianity. The wisdom of the ancient Greeks, Romans and Oriental races was preached in the schools and remembered by the learned. This place was consecrated to be the first city of Christian world, where there was no history of paganism to drown out the glories of the new order. Don't dismiss Constantinople because of the sad state of her current affairs. These men are dwarves and jesters, unfit to claim descent from Theodosius, Justinian, Constantine, or even Julian – a personal favourite of mine. But from humble beginnings, greatness can grow. This root may have rot and cancer all about it, but it's not dead yet. Victory here means a continuation of Christendom in the east; Defeat means that the east will be lost to us for perhaps many generations. It's been nine hundred years since the Muslims stormed into Egypt, and they show no signs of leaving any time soon, my boys. Keeping this city alive keeps the spark of civilization smoldering out here, and a tiny spark can turn into a mighty conflagration if allowed not to burn itself out. Please do not continue disparaging the nobility of the Eastern Empire. We're here to champion not what is, but what was and what may be again."

"I'm sorry, Lord Ambassador," Guistiniano said and lowered his head. He didn't like the idea of showing humility before a Venetian, but the ambassador was indeed right, and he wrong. "I forgot my place."

"See that it doesn't happen again, Longo," Cardillo squeezed the words out before coughing again.

"Do you want me to take you home?" Vincent asked with concern.

"Not until after I congratulate the new general, and speak to the emperor. I also have concerns about Karian's replacement, and you'll both forgive me for pointing this out, but such concerns are better to come from me than from you two."

"Yes, Sir," both men agreed simultaneously.

Despite having what even his most generous critics would call an old soul, Isaac was still blessed with youthful health. He left the public house and entered the carriage waiting for him. Isaac didn't care much for the ambassador's carriage; it was too much like the man. Colourful and garish on the outside, for all the world to see, but dark, frugal and unadorned on the inside.

"Bring us back to the embassy, Driver," he instructed the liveryman, who seemed most unwilling to obey.

"Pardon me, Sire," he began to say in whispered tones. "But we're being watched."

"By whom?"

"I don't know, your grace, but there've been several people waiting at intervals along the promenade. Their faces change, but their positions don't."

"What of it? Everyone here's watched by everyone else! It seems as though the natives have nothing better to do than constantly spy on everyone. Their morbid curiosity excels that of even the most ignorant northern villagers!"

"That's true, that is!" he joked before returning to his serious tones. "But if you look at the street that goes out of the quarter, it's empty."

"So?"

"Look, Sire. No lights. Every window is closed, no one's looking. Nobody's going to accidentally see us, they've all turned away. We might as well be invisible."

Isaac looked down the road and saw shadows of shadows cast about. There were four gas lanterns burning before the final dark mass of Phanar Gate. There were no open windows. No people. No dogs, cats, rats, pigeons or bats to be seen.

"Get us out of here, and do so with haste, Boy. This is a night of foul conspiracies."

The carriage started rolling down the eastern periphery road of the Petrion towards the darkened gate. From behind them, Isaac could hear the clip-clopping of new horses, entering the night. Isaac was in a closed little box and could hardly make out where the horse clips were coming from, but he could certainly tell that they were out there somewhere. He looked frantically from one side of the carriage to another, hoping to catch a glimpse of whoever else was out tonight, but he couldn't; the night was too dark for him.

The liveryman kicked up some speed on the horses, and the ambassadorial coach gained velocity on the smooth roads of the district. By the time they passed the first gas lantern, Isaac could count seven shadowy men following them on horseback. Their faces obscured and their clothes as dark as the night.

"Heaven save us," he prayed, as much to his driver as to God.

The carriage rolled through Phanar Gate and onto the open road. On the highways between the districts, there was nothing for the carriage to worry about, it would be a bumpy ride, but single horses wouldn't be able to catch up with a four horse engine on open road.

Heaven seemed indeed to smile down upon them and the seven shadows behind them didn't follow them out of the gate, though Isaac kept an eye on all directions for the hour-long ride back to the Venetian Quarter.

"Your boys didn't hurt him, did they?" Stavros asked Olaf.

"No, Sir. Just as you said, we followed him good and close, but we didn't lay a hand on him. We wore masks, so he wouldn't see any our faces."

"He wouldn't recognize any of your faces anyway, Varangian," the nobleman said with vain indifference. "I'd be more worried about him seeing you and a half-dozen other blond men, and the piecing the puzzle together from there."

"We'll you needn't worry, Sire," Olaf had no love for their new master. This new man of court had no interest in getting to know anyone in the elite guard, and he thought that they, like all foreigners, should simply be happy to be in his city. No matter, once their new master did away with their old master, there'd be no one to catch them looting the treasury that was buried in the quarter for themselves and fleeing back to Scandanavia..

"Did you see him show any signs of panic?"

"I suppose so, Sir. The wagon fled like a doe in a field, we couldn't exactly see his face, but we can imagine."

"Leave the imagining to me, Olf," Stavros mispronounced his name for the tenth time of the night. "I want him to be afraid for his life and his church. I want him making decisions as only a panicking man can, when he thinks he's facing an assassin's dagger. We'll get rid of these unionists and Italians soon enough."

"Yes, Sir."

"**D**o you like horses?" Isodore asked his travelling companion. "Yes, I love horses," Ahmet replied, smiling for the first time in what seemed more like an eternity. "What's her name?"

Isodore looked at him in confusion. Ahmet patted the horse's flank and asked again.

"Ism-mi?"

"Name?" Isodore questioned, and then supposed that the Turk was trying to learn Greek. He helpfully told him the Greek word for horse. "Ism hippos."

"Hippos mi?" Ahmet asked. Hippos seemed like a very strange name for a horse, better to be named something more glorious and aggressive, but who knew, maybe Hippos meant *Conqueror* in Greek. Ahmet scratched the horse's neck, not understanding that this particular beast's proper name was the even less masculine Flora – Flower. "Hippos. Good."

The two men led their horses from one end of the city to another. Corso Charisius led from Charisius Gate, right next to the hospital, all the way to the hippodrome (Greek for horse race). From there, it was a quick trot down the hills towards the Sea of Marmora until they reached the abandoned Bucholeon Palace.

They trotted their horses to a green clearing, overlooking the sea. The sun shone warm upon their faces and the sea breeze felt sweet."

"Chok guzel," Ahmet said as he looked out at the blue waves, and the green mountains on the distant Asian shore. It was the first beautiful sight he'd seen in a very long time.

"Very.... beautiful," Isodore said slowly as he made the same observation. "Chok guzel, very beautiful."

"Veh-reh b'you tifa," Ahmet tried.

"Close enough for now," Isodore conceded as he dismounted and handed his reigns to Ahmet. "On Daka – ten minutes. You are sitting here. Ok?"

Ahmet nodded to his new friend, and prepared to content himself by enjoying a spring day in a forested glade by the sea. There were far worse things that he could be doing.

The palace was a ruin of forgotten glory. Red bricks built into waves of arches and spires, were left to crumble into disuse when the palace was abandoned. Now it was encased in a spring glory of flowering vines and mint and basil bushes, all of which perfumed the air with the glories of nature that no human hand could replicate.

Isodore went into the wreckage of Bucholeon and began searching. To no surprise, there were many mendicant friars all about. Isodore waived at them politely and went to the store-room to search for his personal effects. Not finding anything, he called out to one of the friars to assist him.

"Yes, Brother Isodore. It's been a while since you've returned to us," the sombre man said, his face partially hidden by a grey-brown cowl. "I thought that you'd abandoned us for more worldly desires."

"No, of course not. I was trying to help a friend who'd been befallen with difficulties."

"If God visits difficulties upon someone, it's not our place to remove what God has wrought."

"No, of course not," Isodore repeated. He had been losing patience with his religious brethren for some time, and was not in the mood to constantly reaffirm the nothingness that separated God and man. "I had a collection of books here, notebooks, where are they?"

"We are a family of but one book, Brother."

"Fine, yes, be that as it may, where were those other pesky books that were here last week?"

"Into the fire, Brother."

"What?" Isodore asked incredulously. "Those were very important books. I had very important things written in them."

"They are worldly things, that have gone as all worldly things, into the void."

Rage almost wrested control away from reason in the monk's mind, but not quite. With an instant sprint of his legs, he ran through the palatial debris to the fire pit, in what had once been the palace kitchen. Blessings upon blessings, the fire was never kept at a high burn, and it burned fuel slowly enough to remind the monks there of the ever presence of winter's unforgotten chill, lest they become too comfortable in their earthly prison.

Isodore ran into the room and knocked over a large wicker basket that contained logs, twigs and paper. He turned it upside down and the papers fell heavily onto the floor. He fell to his knees and started leafing through all the documents at his feet. All handwritten by him, his journal, his meditations, his drawings, and finally (and most importantly) his maps.

"Thank you, oh God, master of my soul!" he breathed as though it were but a single word.

"You shouldn't thank God for anything here, Brother," echoed the bothersome monk who'd apparently followed him across the wreckage. "If you care too much for the trappings provided by the Demiurge, you will fall away from the light, as so many before you have done."

"You know, I've been thinking about that," Isodore said, paying more attention to his notebook than his questioner. "And would you like to know the wisdom that I've found?"

"What would that be?"

"The world in which live, Brother, is truly damnable. There is suffering and woe that is more than anyone can really stand. That's one of the founding principles of our order. But where you and the others here go wrong, by my understanding, is when you start to think that life is something to be out-waited. You wait long enough, and you eventually die, as all living things die, and you believe that then you'll join the divine reality and break bread with God in heaven. I've started to think differently. I've started to think that we've been presented with so many terrible horrors in this life, and that these horrors aren't something to be endured, they're something to rage against and when we die, God will judge us not by how steadfastly we refused the temptation of corruption, but how we tried to alleviate the suffering of those too weak to help themselves. Remember, brother, that sloth and apathy are both sins. Sins that our order's been slipping into for too many years."

"Brother Isodore!" the other monk said in a sort of shouting whisper. "You must stop this at once, I fear for your soul! We must reject temptation! Babylon has no fruits, Brother!"

"I'll worry about my own soul from this point on. I'll remember to pray for you. Now, you must excuse me."

Isodore walked past his former religious brother and made his way through the rubble of a forgotten palace. Out from the darkness of his impromptu monastery, he cathartically emerged into the bright sun of day. There, he found Ahmet still looking out at the peaceful spring day.

"Veh-reh b'you tifa," he announced at the glorious sights of nature before them.

"Yes, very beautiful," the now former monk agreed, speaking very slowly so that his friend could understand each word. "Now, we've got to get to the harbour. Do you know anything about boats? Uhh... Tekne tecruben var mı?"

Ahmet tisked his lips and tilted his head back, raising his eyebrows. Isodore correctly interpreted that as a negative response.

"Me neither. Let's try and learn, then. Come on! I feel like getting some fruit on the way."

They rode their horses up the south slope of Acropolis Hill and rounded the Sphendoneh of the Hippodrome and crested the hill past the great cathedral. Once they were in a position to look down at the harbour, Ahmet seemed agitated. He couldn't make out exactly what was going on, but there seemed to be some movement in the Turkish camp across the harbour, and reciprocal commotion on the south shore. Whatever it was, it couldn't be good.

Ezera watched with a heavy heart as the tribesmen of the northern army began digging their peg holes. Zaganos paced the seaside like a Janissary mastiff, overfed and waiting for more.

"You can't do this, Zaganos-Pasha. It's a mistake. It's a terrible, terrible folly."

"Let me explain this to you, again, Ayoub," the bald minister spoke to Ezera in his native Greek. "Your opinion isn't needed as to what can and can't be done. I ask for your master's opinion, because he's an important man. You're his slave, so your opinion is as he tells you. If you insist on speaking out of turn, I'll have you whipped and nailed up there with those poor bastards."

"What my servant is saying, is that this is perhaps unwise," Tolga explained in more diplomatic terms. "You must remember that all of the men in our navy are Greek Christians, and this obvious display of sacrilege will not sit well with them. Also, it will embolden the defenders."

"It will remind them that there is no way but surrender to the sword of Osman," Zaganos chastised them both. "You two should concern yourselves with the navy, and not worry about the events that happen on land. It's my decision to make clear to the inhabitants of the city what will await those who fight against us."

"They'll see what happens to prisoners! They'll know that they have to fight to the death!" Ezera used what he referred to as his *'captain's voice'* which was deep and animalistic, it often cowed men to obedience.

"That would be fine as well!" Zaganos said. "Then the empty city could be populated with victorious faithful! An unrepentant glory to the faithful that you're both shying away from! I've given the order, and it's to be carried out by my men! All that's demanded of you, Tolga, is to turn over the prisoners on the ships. All that's demanded from your slave is obedience. And you should be careful around those slaves who forget their roles, my friend."

"I'll remember that, *Janissary*," Ezera sneered.

"I am a slave to God and the sultan! I don't forget where my obedience and loyalty go."

"Peace, Minister," Tolga motioned Ayoub-Ezera to be silent with a slight wave of his hand. "We'll turn them over now. Come, Ayoub."

Ezera was furious at such a command, but he knew that he would have to comply. The admiral and his assistant went down to the water to collect the prisoners that had fallen into their hands during the opening of the battle for the harbour, a battle not yet fully over.

"Emir," he said with laboured patience. "He's going to crucify those men publically. That will shock our men, and probably drag Galata into this debacle. It's an unnecessary cruelty!"

"This is a war, there are always unnecessary cruelties."

"This is inhuman, and it's being done for no good reason!"

"It's being done because the vizier commands it. It'll be no surprise to the Sultan, either. What goes on outside of the water's edge, is really not anything for us to worry about."

"Our men will rebel or flee."

"First, they are not *our* men, they belong to the Christian nation of Thrace, which is a nation owned by the Khan of Khans. Second, the decision's been made, you may as well complain about the weather, because there's no way to change it."

"You didn't even try! How can that bastard give such a command, they're his own people!"

Tolga stopped walking and turned to face Ezera.

"Listen to me, because this is important. Men like Zaganos have no country and no people. Those who are born into an alliance can be practical and think clearly about it. Those who are plucked from their mother's arms, who are taken away from everything they know and replaced in a new world are denied pragmatism. Zaganos was a Janissary and Devshirme boy, as you pointed out. He believes in loyalty to his comrades and his master, but all others are human filth to him. Don't expect to find mercy in his shallow heart or his big brain. You're not a Janissary, a man of the Devshirme, or the Emperor. He doesn't care about you and never will. He doesn't care about those who you call his countrymen, because he only knows the countrymen of his service. He only cares about them. The only loyalty outside of that community that he understands is loyalty to and of God. He knows that you're not a real

Muslim, regardless of any protestations, so he thinks that you're a spy among us."

"He's a fool and a traitor to his own race."

"Don't say that. He's much more than that. He's a gazi, spreading God's governance, so that all men may live in accord with God's law. He's liberating humanity, by his understanding. He's also usually right in terms of questions of philosophy, and he's quite a mathematician. Don't discount him as a fool or traitor."

"I don't want any part of this."

"Don't worry, his men, the tribal levies of the Pera Army, will do all of the dirty work. You concern yourself with men in the harbour."

"I'm recalling a portion of the bible which reminds us that farmers will reap what they sow."

"That would be from the Gospel of Mark, Ayoub," Tolga said with a smile. "But you're neither a Christian nor are you a sower of seeds."

"How is it that you've come to know so much of Christianity, Tolga-Pasha?" Ezera asked, unintentionally redirecting the conversation.

"My mother is a Christian – was a Christian, she died many years ago – and she taught me accordingly in my father's harem."

"So you don't hate Christians as much as your friend Zaganos?"

"How could I hate my own mother?" he asked rhetorically. "I could no more hate her, than my paternal aunts who taught me of Islam, or my father who taught me of politics. One of the most important lessons he imparted to me was to remember that God will do as God will, and men who believe that God's will needs their personal defence are all mad and best kept happy and at arm's length, lest they cause serious damage to those around them."

"We're going to execute prisoners in full view of the other army, how is that preventing damage?"

"We'll turn over the unruly and unmanageable among the prisoners, save us some difficulty. The rest we'll keep for ransom later. The tribesmen would prefer a cut of the ransom anyways. They don't share the minister's lust for blood and glorification of the faith."

"If that's the best that can be done for now..."

"What I do is always the best that can be done, under current circumstances, Ayoub. Have faith in me and obey my commands. I'm sure that's something that you've had to demand from your men in the past."

"Yes, Tolga-Pasha."

"Good, then," the emir straightened himself. "Let's assemble the unfortunate then, shall we?"

"I had hoped to speak with you alone, Emperor," the Venetian ambassador said when he sat down in Constantine's private office. "I have to speak with you of affairs of state and the war, not of palace intrigues."

"Giovanni, we're all friends here! Don't be so dour!" Constantine tried to elevate the mood with his jovial nature. "Stavros here has been a loyal friend for many years, you can trust him as you trust me, as he must be aware of all aspects of the current state of affairs."

"Yes, ambassador!" Stavros spoke up with false humour. He had never cared for the Venetian ambassador, he thought it was unbecoming to show too much deference to a foreigner and a heretic. Not that it mattered much, soon there would be no need to tolerate any of them. Until such time it was best to feign politeness. "You look excellent, Cardillo! You've lost weight."

The ambassador looked at the general as if he had just complimented him for losing an unwanted limb. His illness was ripping the life from his body and was an inappropriate topic for small talk.

"I'm sorry to bring bad news to your doorstep, Emperor, but there is grave concern about your new Strategeos. I'm afraid that my captain has little faith in his abilities, and I must concur with him. I've known this man for many years, and he's a creature of the palace, not of the battlefield."

"If Vincent doesn't want to call me 'brother,' that's fine," Stavros said as though it were some kind of a joke. "He can take his little battalions of foreigners and leave the fighting to us."

"If that is the wish of the emperor, then we shall accept it. I'll send a messenger to the Turkish sultan and ask for permission to sail back to Venice unmolested."

"That's not what Stavros meant," Constantine said, mildly annoyed at his general's impertinence. "We want to unite Christendom, and we value the contributions of our Italian allies, of men, of wealth and of expertise. I respect Vincent DiCastillo and give him a grandfather's love. Please tell him not to worry, as I have full faith in Stavros."

"Yes, Your Majesty," Giovanni said before sipping his tea in an effort to keep his throat from clenching again. "He knows that you have full faith in this man, but my man doesn't, and neither do I. I've also discussed the issue with Guistiniano Longo, the Genoese mercenary in your service, he is in agreement."

"The Italians all agree to keep the Greeks out of the council. I'm shocked," Stavros said in mock-indignation.

"I understand that you've left Adam Karian in command of the harbour districts. May I ask what he's done to merit such a demotion?"

"He's still Megadux, a man of hardly modest wealth and position, there was no significant demotion," Stavros said. "He can still serve the empire with honour from where he is."

"My boy," Giovanni said in a raspy voice, and patted the new general's shoulder. "If there comes a time when I lose control of my senses to the point where I would take your advice seriously, I pray that God would mercifully take my life then and there."

"I am an officer of state and you, Sir, are but a guest who has overstepped the boundaries of politeness by leaps and bounds on this day!"

"Peace, Stavros," Constantine said calmly. "Giovanni, I understand that your countrymen are nervous, the war has not been as successful as we had at first hoped. There are, however, great signs that things will be turning around soon and that victory is possible. Not just possible, I should say assured."

"You refer to… your vision, Emperor?"

"I do. I understand that there are some who doubt me."

"Not your sincerity, Basileus," the ambassador caught himself before he finished the sentence by casting a dispersion on the man's sanity. "But if you don't return Adam Karian to the council, then I must apologize, and break faith with you on this day. The siege has thus far been successful for us Christians. They've not held a breach of the wall. Their navy is, though in a better position now, still in shambled chaos. Our stores are still holding strong, and we can still access the sea if need be, by re-opening harbours at Langa or Contoscalion on the Marmora. Karian's plan and command have been very successful, for which he should be thanked and rewarded, not demoted and marginalized."

"Sire," Stavros started but was halted by Constantine raising a finger to him for silence.

"How does this sound to you, Giovanni," Constantine tried as always to seem wiser than he really was. "I will offer him the title of Domestikos. He will command the soldiers of the city of Constantinople. It is still a rank that is subordinate to Strategeos, the commander of all forces, as he'll be limited to the city, but for now, most of the imperial forces are here, anyways."

A sad face hung from Giovanni's skull when he looked into the eyes of the Emperor. He hadn't realized just how far into delusion the Emperor had fallen.

"I believe that he can be persuaded to carry such a burden, Sire," he said lowly.

"Good then!" the emperor was happy at the news that his old friend Adam would be back at council. He had never been comfortable with the idea that Adam be way from him for so long anyways.

"Sire, I believe I hear a commotion outside," Stavros said changing the subject.

The three men hurried to the harbour-side window to see what was happening.

Thirteen men, a number of biblical significance, were marched to the shores for their execution. Holes were dug in the ground and thirteen crucifixes were brought before them. Thirteen of the most unlucky men of Constantinople, many of whom had been asleep when their ships were originally commandeered by the Ottoman raiders, were brought out to the crosses, kicking and screaming. Many of them had to be battered and beaten to the point where they acquiesced to the ordeal, though some were already in mournful acceptance of the inevitable. Their arms were tied to the crossbar, their feet to the main pole. Nails were driven through them to keep them in place and bleed out their once infinite seeming lives.

The screams that came out of men so ruthlessly oppressed were filled with an ugly concoction of rage, pain, desperation and sorrow. The sound of which found everyone's ears in a similar fashion.

The Constantinopolitans heard and watched the events with horror in their hearts. They saw their brothers, fathers and sons hoisted like a flag onto a pole, there to die slowly and in horrible pain. They saw the potential of their own futures there. True to Ezera's prediction, that reminded them what would happen to them if they surrendered. There was only the promise of a painful death to those who threw themselves on the mercy of their enemies. The seeds of resistance were being watered with the blood of martyrs. The futility of brutality paints it's epitaph in red.

To the men of the Ottoman navy, the screams brought the shame of Judas to all of their hearts. They were responsible for the capture of these men, whose only crime was to defend their homes. They had accepted their surrender and by doing so, agreed to treat them in an honourable fashion, as Christians. Instead they were treating them the way the

Romans treated Christ. Every man of the navy felt their hearts sink when they saw the evil that they had helped commit. The seeds of rebellion and of an impending mass desertion were there sown.

Contrary to the perception of the Turkish army in the eyes of the defenders, they weren't beasts. This was not a cause for them to celebrate. Every one of the soldiers in the Pera Army had been promised many things. They'd been promised money, of which they had seen precious little. They'd been promised victory against the infidel, and they'd been waiting about for over a month. They'd been promised battle, and they'd become the murderers and executioners of unarmed men. They had come hoping to find excitement or at least gold. Instead, they watched on at the suffering they'd inflicted by commands of others. Many young men the world over; regardless of race, religion or culture; aspire to prove themselves as great warriors. Very few aspire to be torturers. This was not what they wanted. The seeds of abandonment flower in the spring sun.

Stavros of Brussa saw things differently. He was excited by the opportunity he saw emerging. Such public anger was something that only a fool would throw away! He excused himself from the presence of the emperor and the ambassador, and flew through the palace to the stables, there he procured his horse, ironically named *Conqueror*, and rode hard southward to the Marmora shore, and the prison of Psarmathia, with two dozen of the feared Varangian Guard riding behind him.

"Prisoners!" He called out upon his arrival at the gates of the jail. "I want fifty prisoners here now, in chains and ready to be marched northwards!"

"Who are you to make such demands!" The warden accused as he came to the door.

He didn't know of Stavros personally, but he recognised the wooden staff of the Strategeos and the Varangian guards of his entourage, and he immediately went about procuring the requested number.

"I don't care what their state is, just bring them to me! Bring them in chains! They'd best be ready to meet their kinsmen in hell, for that's where they're all headed anyways! We'll burn them alive while their heretic brothers watch on!"

The march through the city was the closest thing Stavros could experience to a triumph. He led his Varangians two kilometres northwards, from Psarmathia to the harbour, collecting well-wishers along the way. Angry and tearful women, old men who'd drunk fermented courage all afternoon, as well as enthusiastic children gathered along the road and cheered the soldiers and threw stones at the surrendered prisoners. The procession travelled over the cresting hill of the peninsula and entered the harbour district with spontaneous fanfare from the inhabitants, and hostility from the newly appointed harbour-master.

"What are you doing?" Adam shouted when the wild-eyed new general arrived with prisoners in tow. "You're going to start something foolish!"

"Peace, Megadux," Stavros spat back at him. "You're a man now whose obedience is more valued than his opinion."

"You can't massacre prisoners!"

"We most certainly can!" he announced proudly.

"Listen to me!" the former general implored him. "No good can come of this!"

"You don't understand, Adam. You've never understood. You've hoped that we could've waited out this storm without getting our hands dirty. You'd though that the glory of the empire should cower behind the walls and survive. Greatness isn't achieved by timidity, old friend. Our strategy's changed now. When they march against us, we'll march against them and give no quarter. When they attack our walls, we'll attack their camp. We'll make them pay so dearly for every inch of land that they try to abscond from Christendom, that they'll be the ones who turn back and hide behind their walls! Now isn't the time for patience. Now is the time for courage and glory!"

"And when they declare themselves the enemies of civilization, by murdering prisoners, you'll turn your back on Christian mercy and God's laws of war?"

"In a heartbeat!"

Adam really should have known better. Stavros now had two good reasons to continue on with his massacre. The first was that he couldn't possible be seen to publically waver, all the inhabitants of the harbour were there watching. And secondly, he had to show Adam Karian his new place in the order of things, his role was no longer to be played in a decision-making capacity.

"Your ward is the harbour, Megadux," Stavros reminded him. "I command you to ready scaffolding and gallows, to hold fifty men. I'd suggest that you hurry, as the masses are frightened and angry."

"Murderers!" came the cry from the crowds, half directed at the barbarity across the water, but now focussing on the group of frightened looking prisoners that Stavros had force-marched from Psarmathia Prison. A rock flew from an unnamed hand and struck down one of the broken-headed prisoners who'd been captured by the now famed Fifth Municipal Fire Batallion.

"We'll have an uncontrolled massacre on our hands if your men don't stack wood together fast enough, Karian. Now come on and get to work," he ordered the former commander of the legions, and then turned to address the crowds.

"Friends! Citizens of the Empire!" Stavros addressed the crown in his aristocratic tenor. "You've witnessed sin! You've witnessed the murder of your countrymen and the relish with which our foe indulged in such depravity. They think that they'll intimidate us! They think that we lack the fortitude to meet them!"

There were grumbles about the masses of crowds gathered.

"They thought that they would take the buoy, and our sailors stopped them dead, and forced them to flee! They thought that they'd come around the mountain and surprise us! Instead they found that we fought them on the water, on the docks and even in the fish markets! Then, they thought that they'd go back across where no one would bother them! There we were again! I was with our sailors! I led the charge across the harbour, where half their fleet was sunk in a blaze of glory! Now they, think that they'll show how merciless they can be by mocking the suffering of God! Well, my brothers and sisters, well indeed! They'll kill Christians? I've got a half century of Mohamedans here, what do you think we should do with them?"

There were rousing cries from the ever changeable citizenry. True to form, they were getting angrier and angrier, and they were blessed by having a Greek commander now, and foreign enemies. In their minds, everything was as it should be.

Justice was finally meted out that evening. The scaffolds that the harbour guard built were not for gallows, but for a pyre. The screaming mercenaries were painted in a brown wax paint, and lit up to burn through the night. By morning, there were only ashes.

And so evil begot evil. The opposing armies looked smugly at the barbarity to which their enemies were capable and the words of Virgil were reformed in the eyes of all witnesses. "Yield not to evils, but attack all the more boldly." Hearts were hardened for the upcoming conflagration.

Chapter Forty-Four - The Plagues

Iskender the Janissary woke up feeling fine. It was the middle of May, and after four weeks of siege, he was starting to consider himself a veteran. While he was only nineteen years old, he'd already hobnobbed with ministers of state and savage tribesmen. He'd fought a battle at sea when the Bosphorus was severed. He'd been among the first Muslim soldiers to stand on the walls of Constantinople and fly the colours of the sultan and the eighth, and there he'd watched his best friend die. At nineteen, he'd seen more than many older men could dream of in a lifetime.

On that auspicious day, Iskender and his section went through the daily ablutions of an encamped army. He woke up, prayed and then had breakfast. He performed guard duty alongside the cannons for two hours and then helped haul earth from the trenches away from the camp. Aside from a troubled belly, it was a perfectly normal day when he returned to the Janissary mess hall for his noon-time bowl of soup.

After lunch, Iskender put his brow to the earth with the rest of his regiment and recited his prayers. After a few minutes of bowing and standing, and standing and kneeling, kneeling and bowing, he felt dizzy, as though all the blood in his body was trapped in his head. He moved to the side wall of the tent-mosque, hoping in vain for a moment's peace. A crowd of his concerned brethren quickly encircled him

"Are you alright, Little One?" Bilgi-Hoja asked him gently. "You look… spotty."

Iskender looked around at the crowd of red jackets and white caps that had surrounded him. He blinked wildly and stuttered when he tried to reassure everyone that he'd be alright.

"It's nothing. I just stood up to fast."

Bilgi-Hoja put his hand on the young man's forehead and confirmed that he indeed had a fever.

"I'm sure it's just a minor illness," the old teacher assured him. "I'll take you to see Imam Abdul. He'll give you a tonic and you'll feel better, if God wills it so."

"If God wills it so, My Teacher," Iskender replied automatically but in a confused voice.

"Can you walk?"

"I'll help him," volunteered Erkin, before his former classmate could answer.

"Alright, come along," Bilgi-Hoja motioned for the two of them to follow him into the tent city that existed a few hundred metres from the enemy's wall.

The three of them walked through the muddy pathways that connected the various tents of the camp. A little over a month ago, this land had been a budding meadow. Now, its green spring had been trampled by soldiers, horses, donkeys, oxen and wagon wheels into a muddy pit of filth.

"Ohh!" Iskender moaned after a few hundred paces through the corruption and staggered on the road.

"What's wrong, My Boy?" the elder asked.

Erkin's face contorted in disgust and then went through a cycle of fear and confusion.

"He just shit himself," he exclaimed. "It's everywhere!"

Bilgi-Hoja's nose confirmed the diagnosis.

"Calm yourself," the old teachers told him quickly. "You're a Janissary and people everywhere can see you. Don't ever act upset again, hurry up and help your friend."

Erkin obeyed and forced his march faster than before. His comrade, despite being perfectly normal only an hour ago, was now mumbling to himself, and his face was red and burning. He smelled as though death had just flown out of his bowels, and poured out onto the earth.

After a few more minutes of horrid discomfort, they arrived at the hospital tent.

"Peace be upon you," two men at the entrance greeted him and quickly took Iskender off of their hands.

"And unto you be peace," the two Janissaries said in tandem.

The soldiers followed the orderlies into the giant tent hospital and were aghast at what was before them. Beds were overflowing, cots were set on the ground, and there were some men lying on canvas cloth set out on the muddy earth. How could there be so many? Coughing, screaming, mumbling and dying. And the smell! God and His miracles could be all that would turn aside such horrors! Both Bilgi and Erkin covered their mouths to stop the stench of faecal mortality from assaulting their senses.

A bearded man in his forties hurried towards them, running over an obstacle course of patients, orderlies and cots.

"Janissary!" he called out to Bilgi-Hoja. "Stop there, please!"

"Yes, Imam Abdul?"

"I need your help," the doctor said quickly. "I need your men to construct an expansion to the hospital, you're the only ones who can requisition the tents and build it quickly."

"I'll pass on your request to the Agha," he said. "I didn't know that the situation was so dire. How much will you need?"

"We need to double the size of this place and quicky! We need room for another half-thousand, at least. Possibly more."

"What?" Erkin blurted out. Bilgi-Hoja scowled at him again for showing his emotions.

"What my young friend meant to say is that he's also surprised that the situation is so severe."

"It's getting worse," Abdul answered. "Tell me, is your master Mesut-Agha?"

"He is," Ekrin replied proudly.

"He sits on the Divan," Abdul said emphatically. "You must tell him to come. Someone from the Divan needs to see things here. They won't accept my audience."

"We'll tell our master."

"Thanks be to God," the doctor breathed. "We have an unholy cloud among us."

"We can see that, and we'll say what we've seen."

"Thanks be to God," he repeated. "I'll pray that he'll come quickly."

The two guests exchanged their selams with their host and started the filthy trek back to their tents.

"I'll speak to Mesut, but don't tell anyone what you saw," Bilgi-Hoja instructed the young soldier. "If the men learn that a plague has descended on us, they'll panic."

"They wouldn't," Erkin said. "We don't fear death, only God."

"That's noble, and true for our ranks. For the rest of the soldiers here, it's not the case. Look around us."

Erkin looked the mud-patch of a camp and he saw a strange mixture of humanity. There were Christian levies who would run away the first time they were presented with an opportunity. He could identify disgruntled tribesmen who were growing bored and uncomfortable with a siege that had already far outlasted their expectations. Then of course there were the unpredictable broken-headed skirmishers, they didn't even have proper tents for when the rain fell upon them. The grand army was indeed much more fragile than it had seemed.

"God protect us," Erkin conceded to his teacher.

"God protect us, my boy."

"Peace be upon you, Sire."

"And unto you be peace, Janissary," Mehmet greeted the most junior appointed agha. "Did you visit the hospital?"

Mesut never liked being the bearer of bad news, and he bore serious ill favours today when he stood before the Sultan in his master's tent.

"I did, my lord, and I have grave news to report."

"Is it plague?"

"I'm sorry, Sire. The rumours are true."

Mehmet didn't bat an eye. No one in the Divan did. No one would speak until Mehmet had finished ruminating on the possibilities.

Mesut had experienced an awful day. For all his readings of science and medicine, of which there had been many, he had no knowledge of words like '*Salmonella Enterica*,' he only knew the broad umbrella term '*plague*.' He was centuries behind germ-theory, still a bizarre notion to anyone unfamiliar with it. The idea that there are little organisms, so small that they defy detection to even the sharpest eye, and that these organisms can invade a human and bring them to an early grave, would just seem silly, almost blasphemous. Man had dominion over all other life forms and was certainly not subjected to invisible colonies of murderers.

Nonetheless, Salmonella Enterica had crept its way into the camp; a particularly vicious and menacing branch, of the Salmonella family, named Serovar Typhi, to be more precise. Typhoid, as it would eventually come to be known, struck quickly with a terrible fever and attacked the intestines. The bacteria spread through unsanitary conditions and were almost impossible to extract from a population once it settled in. The best cure for a city attacked by this plague was depopulation and wild fires.

The danger of typhoid wasn't the disease itself, it only killed about a quarter of those afflicted. The rest died from the dehydration that went along with the diarrhoea, or various other intestinal or lung infections that attacked the body that had been crippled by the invisible attackers.

Mehmet closed his eyes in hope that some bolt of lightning would come from God and tell him exactly what to do. No such bolt came.

"Prime Minister," he began slowly. "What do you think that we should do?"

Halil knew that he had to be careful about how he answered this question. If he suggested abandoning the venture, as prudence would dictate, he wouldn't survive the week.

"We should split the army, sire," he answered after consideration.

"You would suggest that!" Zaganos decried him across the chamber.

"I would suggest it because it's prudent, Second Minister," he answered. He knew he had to quickly follow up with his rationale, so he didn't stop to allow a full retort.

"Your majesty, this illness comes in a bad wind. We have to take people away from it. Zaganos-pasha's army atop Galata is safe from the miasma, as is Tolga's navy in the harbour. We should separate the main army into a series of camps, each with their own hospitals, open to the elements, that God may wash away the ailments with rain and wind and sun. We should move soldiers away from the main camp, to Studion, Diplokion and the two castles at the throat. We could move some of those whose loyalty is more in question over to Chalcedon, on Asia's shores."

"What would that leave here?" Zaganos grumbled.

"The artillery, the Janissaries and the skirmishers," he answered instantly. "The tribesmen, your cavalry and the Christian levies will all be less than a day's march away, and they can be reassembled again when the time to attack is upon us."

"The attack on the wall will be vulnerable," the bald second minister countered. "They could charge out again and strike. Without all of the army to defend the cannons, they could be attacked and destroyed, or worse, captured! The battle would end then and there with the cross of the non-believers soaring high above their city still."

"Enough, stop," the sultan commanded. "Mesut, how many men are now afflicted by plague?"

"More than four hundred are in quarantine now and the number's been doubling every three days for the past week."

"Damnation!" Mehmet roared and threw his brass teacup at a canvas barrier that flapped to accept the sultan's gift. He was aware of how bad it was to show this level of personal emotional distress, especially in front of the Chandarli brood, but he couldn't help it. A plague was worse than an unsuccessful skirmish, because it couldn't be outrun or waited out.

"Does the army know about it?"

"They'll start to suspect soon, your majesty, and then we'll have a rout on our hands."

"Do you think that the Janissaries can defend the artillery long enough to break through the walls?"

"Yes! Of course! We'll defend it until Judgement Day if need be."

"Your Majesty," Musa the exchequer ventured into the foray, diverting the topic away form the plague. "We had expected that the walls would have fallen by the end of April. We were set back by losses that Zaganos-Pasha and his warlords hadn't forseen, may I ask them now, honestly and without posturing: How much longer do they suspect it will be until the walls fall? We have provisions and pay to think of, since the subject of rout was raised by the honourable Janissary."

"By the end of the month, the tunnels will be at the walls, they'll be undermined and fall like petals from a flower," Mesut tried to sound certain.

"Like petals from a flower," Musa repeated. "Sire, this cactus has no petals. We'd lost more than we planned for, and we've stayed for longer than we've planned for."

"I believe that your brother has been lectured about defeatism," Mehmet cautioned him.

"I'm not suggesting a retreat, My Lord," Musa answered quickly. "But we have to consider the economy of this venture. If we prolong the siege anymore, we can't pay for it! You will have to promise the men their rights. Without that, they won't stay out of *good will*. The only other option is to attack now and let God determine the victor."

"Sire, I would caution you against that," Mesut spoke up. "Their army is still largely intact. The Christians have taken a heavy losses of material by way of the fleet, and position in the harbour and their cavalry, but if we attack now, we will be repelled. We need to either weaken their army somehow or break down the wall. As it stands right now, we would crash against the land walls the way the waves crash against a cliff."

"What do you think that we should do then, Agha?" the Sultan asked his new counsellor.

"Separate the army, Sire. Do as the grand vizier suggests."

"If we do that, then we might as well pack up this entire adventure and go back to Adrianople!" Zaganos cried, but was quickly hushed by the sultan.

"Wouldn't the artillery prove to be a target worth an all-out assault for the intact Christian army?" Mehmet questioned the agha.

"Cut it down then, Sire. Move more of the guns to the Valley of Springs and batter the Palace, and the harbour walls from there. The land battery will be less tempting when the Christians weigh the potential gain against the potential loss of an attack, and hence they'll be more easily defended."

"That means more time, and therefore more money," Musa answered back.

"Do what Mesut says," Mehmet said after a time. "And give the men the promise of three days of plunder. They can have their damn rights."

Mehmet was becoming embittered towards the venture. His apple was collecting too many bruises and worms.

There was an emphatic knocking at the door to the private office of the Emperor. A Greek palace functionary, without significant name or status, entered the room and bowed lowly before the five assembled men.

"Yes, what is it?" Stavros demanded. He had taken to speaking on behalf of the Emperor, who no longer wished to speak to anyone outside his immediate council.

"Sire!" he stuttered, out of breath. "Outside! The infidels are on the move."

Everyone perked up at those words. Guistiniano, Vincent and Adam hurried to the East balcony and looked out to see an army breaking camp. Stavros and Constantine followed leisurely behind them.

The question of what this meant lurked in everyone's imagination, but no one would question the sight for fear of sounding ignorant.

"They are fleeing, my friends," Constantine said at last. "As the Virgin promised me, the enemies of Christ are fleeing before me."

"Yes, my lord," the strateogos concluded. "They are fleeing before an empire that is resurrecting as our Lord."

"What do you think," whispered Longo to the two other compatriots.

"It's too early to tell," Vincent replied. "It could mean a number of different things."

"They're not retreating," Adam added. "If they were preparing to leave, they would have given one last attack, to try to force the walls. Or at least they would have tried to cross the Horne again. Their ships are trapped-in instead of out; they're not about to abandon their fleet."

"I'm curious, Megadux," Stavros invaded their conversation. "In all your years of reading events before you, have you ever taken the time to read the Acts of the Apostles? Specifically the story of Doubting Thomas?"

"I believe you'll find that tale in the Gospel of John, not the Acts of the Apostles," Adam never addressed Stavros by his blood title, anthypatos, as he had no lands to qualify it, nor by his military title of strateogos, for he didn't recognize his qualifications there, either. "You'll also find that the story is called Thomas the Believer, for he is still blessed with sainthood even though he demanded proof of a resurrected Christ. I see an army on the move, but not one in retreat. I don't see the nail holes in Our Lord's palms, nor the spear wounds in his side when I look out from this balcony. To answer your original question: Yes, I have read *both*. Have you?"

"Ha!" Constantine smirked. He liked the Armenian, despite the bitterness in him now. He truly wished that Adam would be more accepting of God's work, and would place less hope in the dull acts of men.

Stavros blushed.

"I'm sorry, but I can't answer for certain as to what's going on with the enemy," Longo said with a straight-faced grin. "My Lord Strateogos, could you please interpret these events for us? We, not having the benefit of your rank and experience are confused by the complicated machinations before us. Enlighten us, please."

Adam rolled his eyes side-wise and held back a grin of his own.

"Yes," added Vincent in an instant of uncharacteristic sarcasm. "We men of the West obviously lack your foresight. Please be a rising sun to us and impart some of your worldly knowledge."

"The army is on the march," Starvros said in his most solemn voice, "Because they have been commanded to."

The silence was deafening for the three junior members of the war council. His striking grasp of the obvious was noticed by even the mystically inclined emperor.

"Because…" Longo coaxed.

"Because they are realizing that we won't be shaken from God's country," Stavros answered quickly, and with renewed confidence. "The steadfastness of the Emperor's soldiers has put fear into the hearts of the heathens, and now they run! This is a time for rejoicing. We should have the bells of Holy Wisdom ring aloud!"

"Anthypatos," Vincent began in a shockingly condescending tone. "Look over here. Do you see the cannons?"

Stavros glared silently at him, rather than the cannons at which the Italian was pointing.

"They are the most difficult thing to move for the army. They're big, they're heavy. That's why they should be the first thing to be packed up when they were going to leave. The big ones aren't being loaded into oxcarts. They're obviously not going anywhere, though a few of the little ones, as you can see, are. Ergo…"

Again, silence.

"Ergo they're moving part of the army, but not all of it," Vincent finished after a suitable period of silence had elapsed. "Why would they do such a thing? Their army is already spread out over Pera, Thrace and Chalcedon. We haven't forced them to move, so they must think that there's something to gain by it. What could it be, *Strateogos*?"

"Sire," Stravros turned away from the Italians and their Armenian cohort. "The enemy has pressed Christians into the service of the infidel, they must have a rebellion on their hands. It is indeed as the Virgin implied."

"That's certainly a possibility," Vincent agreed and looked away at the horizon. "One of many. Perhaps the Christians are rebelling, perhaps there is an outbreak of plague, as always happens in protracted sieges. Perhaps the enemy commanders don't get along quite as well as the five of us and needed to be separated. We should continue to watch, and see what happens. I can't answer for certain as to what's going on until I see more."

"Would you care to hazard a guess then, Captain?" Stavros asked with a poor imitation of the Venetian's own sarcasm.

"Not at this time. Ask me again in an hour or so, when we have more information available."

"If you won't even try to guess, then what good are you?" Stavros accused. His head was superiorly in the air, to the notice of none of the assembled.

"It's happening, Don Giovanni," Bishop Isaac said with glee, echoing in the halls of the Venetian Embassy. "Their army is in full retreat!"

"What?" Cardillo's first reaction was one of shock, but it lasted for only a few moments before his more typical cynicism took root. "Who's said this?"

"Everyone at court! I've seen it with my own eyes! Ha ha!"

The only thing the Venetian ambassador disliked more than the princes of the church, were triumphal princes of the church.

"Where's Vincent?"

"Oh, no doubt your Spanish mercenary is trying to curry favours with the new general, trying to insist that it was he who'd planned the turn of events. He and that Genovese discredit themselves, the way they prance about for the Emperor. They're kept poodles trying to impress their master!"

Giovanni drank some of the herbal mixture Mario had prepared him from an earthenware cup. It was helping his coughing, but he'd lacked the energy to attend court for some time now, since the investiture of the new strateogos.

"I'll wait for him to return and report."

"You put too much trust in him, and not enough in divine providence, Mister Ambassador."

"I've found more wisdom in his judgement than in the whims of the almighty, Bishop. Now what's going on at court?"

"Everyone is most pleased with the new general, they're all happy to have one of their own in office, and many of those at court have their hooks in the new man. He owes favours to everyone, unlike his predecessor who seemed to have had knowledge of everyone else's secrets."

"That's to be expected, Stavros is a rising star, everyone will want to be his friend now. Adam, bless him, had many enemies at court, he was a foreigner, and he favoured union. There's no way he would be missed. Is there anyone left at court who still favours union?"

"You, me and my brother."

"Wonderful." He answered glumly. "It won't be too long till they force Patriarch Noah into retirement."

"Our cause would flourish if we had a more vigorous champion in the pulpit, Ambassador."

"For now, we need someone who won't start a riot, you can worry about those things once the current crisis is over."

"The eastern empire's had a history of one crisis after another for over a millennium. After this crisis passes, they'll be another one, and then another. There will never be a time when there is no crisis, when there is no rational reason to postpone these issues. Now is the time to press harder on the new Caesar."

"Don't start any new infighting now, Your Grace. Now is not the time."

"I answer to a higher call, Mister Ambassador," Isaac replied calmly, but enjoying every word. "I have with me a petition from the Holy Father in Rome, saying that if Noah is unable to secure a union of the churches in more than name only, that I'm to take his mantle as Katholikos."

"Oh, don't be stupid. The office of Patriarch is by the appointment of the Emperor, and at the recommendation of the Metropolitan of Constantinople. No pope has held any sway over the office since they split with Rome in 1069."

"If the Emperor is serious about union, then he'll acknowledge that this is a decision to be made by our Holy Father, and not by petty earthly princes."

The cancer that had made a home in Giovanni Cardillo's body, peered out of his eyes and into those of the Bishop. For the first time in a long time, Isaac realised that he'd overstepped himself.

"You'll remain silent on this and on all other issues. In order to assure that, you may consider yourself to be under house arrest, from this moment on.”

“I beg your pardon? I’m a prince of the church!”

“You’re excused,” he growled and kept his voice from breaking. He rang a bell that he kept on his desk and several of his house servants came as summoned. “Please take Don Isaac to his apartment above us and fasten the locks. He’ll be staying there indefinitely.”

“If any of you raise a hand against me, you imperil your very souls!” he defied the servants to obey their order.

“Don Isaac, if you don’t submit to arrest, you’ll have to flee, and if you flee then you’ll no longer enjoy the protection of Venice. I’ll send men to fetch you. Serious men, Don Isaac. Now, why don’t you follow these men up to your chambers?”

“I’ll do no such thing!”

“In that case, no one here can force you, so you know where the door is. Please remember that I’ll see you again, Sir.”

“I’ll see you burn for this, Giovanni! On this earth and in the very pit of hell!”

“Sticks and stones, Your Grace. Now run away or run upstairs.”

“No need!” he answered. “I’ll stay here for now, but you’ll find that your prison holds us both, Mister Ambassador.”

“Perhaps, but I’m closer to escape than you,” Giovanni answered before turning round and surrendering to his hacking lung convulsions.

“Oh, God!” Iskender cried out. “Why are you doing this to me?”

Abdul patted him on the head. The pain and suffering of a body racked by this plague was palpable to any observer.

“Peace, peace, by the merciful blessings of God,” he whispered into the Janissary’s ear.

Around them, the sick were multiplying. No one was moving those in bed, but the tell tale signs of the outside world let anyone with the wherewithal necessary to perceive that the army was on the move. The ground was shaking, the sounds of pipes, drums and trumpets were all outside, letting soldiers know which banner to follow and where to go.

“It hurts, it hurts,” his patient muttered, oblivious to the tumult.

“I know,” Abdul replied. He looked down at his patient.

Abdul had learnt from his observations of the other patients that dementia came along with the fever. Five times a day, the doctor prayed that the dementia was temporary, for he knew that there were many illnesses that would permanently reduce a man to a jabbering lunatic until the end of his days.

Iskender pointed wild eyes at the doctor, who closed his own rather than stare into his patient's madness.

"I'll be back in a moment, My Son," he whispered slowly.

Abdul went into a cordoned off room within the tent-city that served as hospital. He came back with a small stick of cedar wood, cleaned of its bark, in one hand and a medicine pouch in the other.

"Sit up. Come now, boy! You're a Janissary, champion of the faith! Be strong and sit up for me!" he said with false bravado to convince his patient to straighten.

Iskender pulled himself up on his elbows, more reclined than sitting.

Abdul reached into the little pouch he kept for special cases. While all schools of Islamic jurisprudence strictly forbade the use of intoxicants for the enticement of pleasure, they generally agreed that they were to be considered acceptable for the treatment of severe pain. From the pouch, he took out a syrupy black-green mass and he ran the cedar stick over it, collecting the sap on the wood.

"Chew this," he said as he carefully put it into the boy's mouth. "Between your back teeth. There's a chemical there that will stop the pain."

Iskender obeyed and chewed the wood, sucking the sap from the pores of wood, and his lunacy abated into torpor.

"That's it, my boy," Abdul whispered and stroked Iskender's curls. "You'll sleep well for a few hours."

He then looked around at all the other ailing victims of the plague.

"I wish we could do this for everyone."

The less-famous Palace of Porphyrogentius stood south of where the current and more-famous Palace of Blachernae stands; they were unequal neighbours in the Petrion district. The older and poorer sister had been sacked by the soldiers of Venice, Champagne and Basel during the fourth crusade, and was now but a shell of a building. Everything of value had been moved to Blachernae.

The only functioning parts of Porphyrogentius were the old courts, which now functioned as stables, and the granaries that could act as a prison for the palace. Wedged in the Petrion, between its own triangle of city and palace constabularies, between land walls, harbour walls and city stockades, it was rarely home to more that a few dozen people at any given time. Over the past two and a half centuries, it had hosted family members of rebellious nobles, whose wayward spirits caused them to lead armies against the capital. There weren't too many of those men left.

What was left was but a single prisoner. He had no relatives of any significance, no noble office, current or past. He was a bearded old man who lived his life in the dark of ruined greatness; and while he did so, he occupied a half dozen Varangian soldiers of exceptional brutality to keep him in place.

Those brutish northerners would step aside for only two men, the Strateogos and the Emperor. When the Anthypatos of Brussa arrived into the dilapidated prison, they reluctantly stood aside; they preferred their former master.

"Open the door," Stavros commanded Olaf, who obeyed. The Vikings were hardly enamoured to the new strateogos, but he didn't seem to care. They obeyed and that was all he wanted, he didn't need their love or their approval.

The resident of the little cell was busy praying in a garbled voice and paid no attention to the intruder on his meditation.

"Hello there, Your Holiness," he announced himself with a heel click. "I hope that you've been treated well here. A man of your eminence deserves to be treated like a prince. While this room isn't to my personal liking, you can take heart in knowing that many princes have waited out many years in this very room."

"You may leave me then," the old resident stated simply. "I am waiting here for deliverance by our Lord and not by you, Stavros of Brussa."

"I'm flattered that you remember my name, Your Grace," Stavros was mildly perturbed that the old man didn't look up from his desk. His eyes stayed on scripture, rather than the opportunity for earthly salvation that was about to present itself.

"I know who you are, Anthypatos. I've known you for many years, and your father before you. The court is not a stranger to me, though I am to it, now. Or at least so it seems from here."

"Many things have come to pass since your incarceration."

"I've been here for over a year now, I'd imagine that things would have to."

"We are besieged by Turks."

"I know. I can hear their cannons"

"We are out-numbered by their soldiers, and their cannons are flattening our walls. Already, the Golden Horne has fallen to their might. Genoa stands neutral, and Venice refuses to hear the Emperor's orders."

"The enemies of Christ outnumbered him in his lifetime and after, so that is no surprise. Nor am I shocked to hear about the Italians' betrayals. Pity for the harbour, but this land abandoned God long ago. It seems only fitting that God abandons us."

"That seems to be a popular opinion these days. Shared by many men, but not so by one woman in particular: the Virgin Mary herself."

At that comment the old man finally raised himself from his desk and he tottered over, strongly favouring his right leg, to meet the intruder on his solitude. He stepped into the light revealing the haggard face of Gennadios, the former Patriarch of Constantinople, until rudely imprisoned by Constantine at the behest of the rapine Italian interests.

"You should not presume to speak on Our Lady's behalf, Child. Unless you are going to claim that she appeared to you, which I find doubtful, considering your detestable past record of compliance."

"I make no claim for myself, but for the emperor! Constantine the Eleventh was visited by the Virgin at Phanar Gate. She came to him in front of witnesses and told him that by the next full moon, he would be victorious."

"Constantine is a fool!"

"The Holy Family has shown themselves to fools before and may do so again at their leisure, not your approval, Patriarch," Stavros chided him with a snigger. "But she gave him one criterion for victory, a restoration of the rules of Christ. He now believes that if he allows the Venetians to continue to command the defence, God will allow the city to fall. He's taken command of the army personally, and plans to lead the charge against the enemy when the time comes."

"He what?" Gennadios seemed shocked. "He's a glorified monk! He's afraid of horses, for the love of Christ!"

"He's been given a new steel in his soul, Patriarch."

"That's wonderful," the old priest said, sitting back down like a disappointed child. "I'll pray for his victory."

"You'll lead the prayers for his victory," the nobleman said slyly. "From the Cathedral of Holy Wisdom. I'm here to restore you to grandeur."

"This is the Emperor's wish?"

"It is."

Gennadios's grey eyes unfocussed as his mind wandered through alleyways that had almost gone forgotten in his own mind. The past months faded instantly into the fog of memory.

"When do I leave?"

"Soon. We'll take you to a bath house and clean you up, and prepare you for this. We'll surprise that Italian collaborator who thinks that he's giving the mass," he said with a smile before continuing along.

"Last year, your sermon made men see the light. Men heard you and then took up arms against the enemy. We need that again, today more than any other day in our history. I only wish that Constantine had sided with you then, and driven the Latins from our home. You have to preach to the men, extol them to victory against all infidels. Both the Turks and the Latins. Prudence would tell us to drive the Mohammedans back first, but they have to be reminded that the only friends of Christ are those who've stayed true. Not those who glory in their inheritance of Peter's betrayals instead of his redemption. They've taken their own side."

"Is that a condition?" Gennadios asked with a disbelieving laugh. "Why not insist that I must breathe air, drink water and eat food?"

"Let's go get you cleaned up, Your Holiness."

"How many men?" Mehmet asked Halil.

"Five and twenty," the grand vizier confirmed.

The news that the plague had spread from the main camp to one of the subsidiary camp at Studion was ominous.

"Sire," Halil began slowly. "You have made it perfectly clear to me that you want advice for victory, rather than peace. I don't think I can give that right now, for that's not the choice that we're looking at now. Our army will wither and die here on the field, and more Christian reinforcements can arrive for the city at any time, our fleet in penned into the harbour now, because of the ill-thought-out stratagem of your second minister. Sire, if we stay, this could quickly cease to be a siege and turn into the greatest rout the faithful have ever faced. We cannot stay here and die. We have ten doctors for a hundred thousand men, all of whom are breathing the same air and eating the same food as the plague-bearers. My words are dulled by my past opposition to this endeavour, but I beg you hear their wisdom nonetheless. I implore you to defend the faith, Sire. Waste not your strength, or the strength of your ancestor's legacy."

And with that, Halil sat quietly. Mehmet pushed his finger against a lump in the carpet in front of him, undoubtedly caused by some disobedient pebble. Nature had put an imperfection onto such a beautiful carpet.

"And what do you think, Zaganos?"

The former Janissary scratched his bald scalp. His skin wasn't as taut as it once was. The stress from the past month and a half was ageing him faster than he'd thought. He knew that his future was tied to the success of the battle, but that success seemed so far away.

"I think that there's wisdom in Halil's words, Sire. We may have to return to Adrianople to avoid a catastrophe. If they get reinforcements, we could lose more than the battle here."

Mehmet grunted an acknowledgement.

"And you, Agha?"

"Sire," Mesut tried not to get dragged down by the pessimism from the rest of the council. "We're not dead yet. We still have the possibility of victory. We can't stay here forever, obviously. Our friends here have made the case for retreating to safety, but I'll put forth the case for staying:

"Our sappers have almost reached the wall. We believe that they are within twenty paces of it! Working day and night, they can undermine the barrier at the mesotechion, and it will crumble to rubble before you. Your soldiers have captured a gate before, we know that it can be done again.

"While our men fight plague, we don't know about theirs; they perhaps suffer as well. In one week, the walls will fall, and the banner of the prophet may fly over the shadow of Rome. The owl can pluck the spider from its web. Victory is immediately before us. Please, Sire, I beg of you. One week of courage can bring glory for eternity, and an instant's hesitation will have the faith retreating from the infidels for centuries. This decision is more than a simple one of tactics. It will determine the balance between truth and heresy for centuries. Please, sire. The Janissaries are ready to fight alone if need be! It would be better to die as gazis, spreading the faith, than as defeated old men, secretly whispering prayers to God under the cross of the enemy."

Mehmet grunted and poked the stone under the carpet again. The stone imparted no wisdom. He knew very well that if he withdrew, he was finished, and all other considerations had to take a back seat. Damn the sword of Osman, damn the banner of the Prophet, damn the plagues and the invisible hand of God. He wasn't going to retire like his father to a lodge in the Anatolian highlands, and he most certainly wasn't going to go back to hunting parties in Amaseia and Zonguldak-Sanjak.

"What is the date today?"

"The twenty-second, Sire," Kabira answered dutifully.

"We attack on the morning of the twenty-ninth, then. You all have seven days to prepare for this. God will determine the victors of this enterprise. God is great."

"God is great," the rest of the council echoed with varying degrees of enthusiasm.

Chapter Forty-Five- The Last Day

May 28, 1453

Alone in the dark, they continued to dig. They started as three teams, press-ganged in Belgrade and brought all the way across the Balkan Peninsula to serve in the army of their hated conquerors. They dug five metres straight down, and then started their laborious journey eastwards. The soft earth of Thrace had largely thawed by the tenth of April, when they'd started their subterranean drive to the walls.

The dig was run by a series of crews and sub-crews. Some men dug. Some men hauled earth. Some men built reinforcing structures to keep the tunnel from collapsing. They built a system of tunnels underneath the battlefield so that only the ants and moles would understand the ground better. Every day, they would have to report to Halil Chandarli, who would note with disapproval their lack of progress.

Those three original teams didn't last. After Guistiniano Longo's charge of the cannons on the tumultuous third day, one team was re-assigned to become trainee gunners. The grand vizier had decided to keep two tunnels going at normal pace, rather than to slowdown the pace by under-manning three teams. The second team was less fortunate than the first. One day, two of their twenty fell ill, the next day, seven more. Working together in such cramped quarters proved to be a playground for the invisible typhoid virus. The second team was disbanded and its healthy members were sent to bolster the remaining tunnel team.

Maps and compasses were of vital importance to them, less they wander astray. Crude liquid levels were used to make sure that they didn't go too far down. Had they done so, they'd hit bedrock. Had they slanted too high up, they'd get too close to the surface, where armies were fighting and certainly they'd suffer from a cave in. Most of all, they had to keep the tunnels wide and strait. The time would come when many men would have to run down these tunnels very quickly. That day came on May 28, 1453. One day ahead of Mehmet's final schedule.

It was on that day, that the counter-mining tunnels were uncovered.

Longo had abundant experience with mines and tunnels during his previous campaigns in Italy. He commanded a team of Greek auxiliaries to dig under the wall, at six metres, and make the passages under the wall, narrow enough for a single man to pass. He didn't want to undermine the wall while trying to defend it. On the other side of the wall, a larger tunnel was built. Three metres broad and once and half as high, this massive tunnel went all along the wall, on the outside border, from the harbour to the sea. It was originally defended by ten Genoese guards; not enough to fight off an underground assault, but certainly enough to raise the alarm when the time came.

The first connection between the two digs came when the unseen sun was just about ready to reach its peak for noon time. One of the diggers stabbed his shovel into the earth, and glided through to hollow.

"Tsht! Tsht!" the whole team started whispering, and everyone went silent.

The eldest among them moved to where the shovel had pierced and he got down on his belly. He carefully brushed dirt away from the hole, and he could see light. Light from one of the guards' lantern was a distance down the lateral tunnel. The Serb edged himself closer to the opening and managed to look out into the tunnel. They'd finally hit the city. He smiled at his accomplishment. After almost two months of labour, it felt good to reach some kind of resolution, even if it was for your enemy and against your own.

He pulled his head back, and threw a sack-cloth over the hole.

"Back we go," he whispered.

The miners withdrew from their tunnel and returned to camp to summon up reinforcements.

Guarding the trench was one of the most boring jobs in Christendom. Four men, stationed by the new strateogos rather than the ten of the old order, would be constantly walking up and down the three kilometres, supposedly always looking for signs of enemy incursion. Were the task done by Longo's men, it would have been a strong defence against the mining of the enemy. A lack of men and need for them elsewhere meant that the four men who walked the black mile, did so as punishment for some camp infractions. Thus, the guards were usually the most lackadaisical and unruly sort.

Four unmotivated guards were hardly enough to hold watchful vigils over every inch of the tunnel, and no one was within sight when the dirt flew from a hole in the upper wall of the tunnel. Ten Janissaries, armed with bows and scimitars silently climbed out of their hole and into the tunnel. Running in the dark, they hurried towards of the lanterns; hardly enough to light much past a few metres around the bearer, but bright enough to be seen by the raiders. They became targets rather than tools for their bearers. The silent bows and blades that cut down the defenders and quickly secured the tunnel. Once their silent deeds were done, the sappers emerged from the Ottoman tunnel, carrying barrels of gunpowder.

Potassium Nitrate is a curious chemical. It's interesting because it's so easy to produce and harvest, it can be leached out of almost any organic material, though the process can be time-consuming. For the Turks, straw was used, it was then contaminated with horse manure. The mass of straw was kept away from the elements for a year, kept moist with urine, and then finally the straw was leached with water. The water was boiled away, and at the bottom of the boiling pot was the nitrate. This chemical was then mixed with ordinary charcoal and yellow brimstone to make a black powder, descriptively referred to as "Black Powder."

Seventeen barrels of black powder were placed with care under the walls, and packed in tightly with earth. Fuses were set and the Janissaries, alongside the Serbian sappers, retreated to a safe distance down the tunnel, before lighting the fuses and running as fast as their legs could carry them back to the exit to the surface.

When the black powder exploded, an explosion of gas flew from the fragments of the solid chemical. The gas explosions were strong enough to make large holes in the earth, globe-making from their epicentres. The series of explosions seemed like a single earthquake, which could be felt from Chalcedon on the other side of the water. Smoke clouds bellowed from the five tunnel entrances along the city-side of the wall, as well as from the remaining Ottoman tunnel, which turned into a long range horizontal chimney-pipe.

Black powder made a big noise, and a big flash, but it was hardly strong enough to break through the stone rock of the walls. That's why it was used for cannons and other firearms. It can propel a bullet, but it won't melt the barrel. It's not too weak, it's not too strong. The explosion, in all its destructive glory, wasn't strong enough to damage the wall directly in any significant capacity.

Of course... it wasn't supposed to. They made cavities under the secure teeth of the walls and towers of the city walls. They rotted the root to weaken support. Gravity would now start it's assault on the engineer-wrought wonder that protected the city.

The miners and Janissaries were still fleeing out of the tunnel when the explosion rocked the camp. Halil was happy to see the men emerging safely, a few steps ahead of the smoke, before the tunnel collapsed, making a ditch that pointed from the Ottoman camp directly to the city walls.

Mehmet paced about the camp, showing obvious signs of emotional stress.

"Look," he said to the Janissary agha, almost at a whisper. "Mesut-bey, look at that magnificence."

A sink hole began underneath one of the squat octagonal towers that dotted the wall. Right in the middle of the glorious impenetrable fortress of Constantinople, a tower began to lose its footing.

"*Hamdu Lilah*," Mesut breathed as he watched the sight unfold. '*Thanks be to God.*'

The tower of the Mesoteteichon, the midpoint of the wall, loosened its grip on the earth and fell down in one solid polyhedral mass. Soldiers who'd been standing in there, dwindling away the hours on what had been looking to be just another slow day of waiting, jumped from the falling building, and whose who didn't manage to escape before the tower was unceremoniously received by the shaken earth.

"By all the wonders of God, did you see that?!" Mehmet screamed joyously at the agha of the Janissaries, who was also grinning from cheek to cheek.

"Thanks be to God for all things!" Mesut cried back before grabbing the young sultan's hand and kissing it in congratulations. "The battle is almost over, and victory belongs to you and God!"

A ruckus cheer arose throughout the Ottoman camp. Every man, from the erratic broken-headed, to the disciplined Janissaries, and then all broke into cheer. Their two-month wait was coming to an end.

Then something unthinkable, undreamable even, happened. The curtain wall that connected the now fallen tower to the next tower southward, began to join its former root in rubble. Too many cannon balls, too much stone and too much metal had taken its toll on the wall, and it gave up its ghost, then and there. The wall cascaded down like a child's set of coloured blocks, creating a huge cloud of rock and mortar dust where the permanence of the defences had once stood.

Everyone stood in shock at the degree of destruction to which they now bore witness. As the wind cleared the dust away, the green hills and meadows of the urban no man's land of the capital region was visible. The wall was down for a hundred-and-twenty-seven metre long stretch of land.

The reaction was cacophonous. Even the normally grim and severe Janissaries cried in laughter, sending their white tower hats into the air. The trumpets and drums of the imperial band broke into spontaneous music, and everyone cheered and danced.

“Call back the army!” Mehmet ordered through an unconquerably broad smile. “Call them all back! We attack tomorrow! Tomorrow it ends! Bring everyone back now! Cannons, smash that other wall, smash it down, too. Hit it all day, spare no time! Spare no powder or ammunition! Use it all up today, for tomorrow we conquer!”

Messengers rode out to the other camps, to fetch the Chandarli family and their wards at Studion, to gather Zaganos at Pera, boats were dispatched to fetch a few irregulars form Chalcedon. The army began to reforge itself.

Mehmet went to the stabling barrack and found the biggest strongest horse that was there, a big white courser with a grey mane. He had her quickly saddled and he rode out into his army, hoisting his seven-tailed spear overhead. He galloped throughout the encampment, to the cheers of every regiment that he visited. He rode in full view of the impotent Romans on the other side of the broken wall, cheering, and being cheered by his men.

The men on the other side of the wall were less inclined to rejoicing over the day’s events.

“Doctor Mario!” Isodore called across the commotion of a suddenly busy hospital, rocked by nearby underground explosions.

“Now is not a good time, Isodore,” Mario yelled back. “We have wounded and dead coming in by the horse cart. At least the dead won’t take too much of our time or supplies.”

“Now’s a perfect time, this chaos is great!”

Mario looked around at the hundreds of people, running, walking, limping and bleeding about in all directions.

“I’m needed here, give me a minute. Go check on Pazzi, and then meet me with your Turk friend in the women’s chapel. I’ll be ten minutes.”

“Ten minutes,” Isodore repeated and went off to the stone barrack house with Ahmet.

The two ducked into the small ward and quickly found the short, angry nun who’d given him so much trouble on the night when ‘*Doctor Felipé*’ found his way into the hospital bed.

“How is the doctor doing?” he asked her.

“He’ll be fine, but his head’s all bandaged and broken. In time, I’m sure he’ll recover,” she had a thinly hidden vein of hatred in her words, but she saw no reason to explain the details of it to Doctor Mario's foreign friends.

"He's conscious?"

The nun looked over her shoulder at the wounded man, four beds over and confirmed this not to be the case.

"No."

"That's what I wanted to hear. God bless you, Sister."

Isodore and Ahmet left the ward and hurried off to the women's chapel.

Hectore Pazzi watched the familiar man question the nun about him through the grid of his eyelashes. He was wide awake, but he kept that fact hidden from the interlopers. He had no idea who the big foreigner was, but the bearded one, he recognized immediately from his chase throughout the Venetian Quarter.

Pazzi's mind was still in full order, and he was capable of moving should the need arrive. The reason he was standing still was because Doctor Mario had told him to, and it'd sounded like sooth advice. Now learning that this monk was obviously a spy, probably working for Adam Karian, it meant that Mario Orsini was in on the conspiracy to deny him treasure by keeping him in bed.

Once the two men left the ward, Hectore got up and watched the two of them cross the crowded green to the women's chapel, a building he'd searched and found nothing when he'd first arrived at Chora. A short time later, he saw the doctor joining them there. He found it incredibly doubtful that the three of them were overcome by a sudden need to pray in the women's chapel, so he needed to see exactly what was going on there. It hurt to walk, but he was a man used to enduring pain.

"Please, Doctor," Iskender implored the Imam Abdul. "I'm better! God's cured me, thanks to your ministrations."

"You still have a fever, young pup," Abdul said peaceably. "Now sleep."

The young Janissary's eye lids drooped in trained obedience.

The doctor returned to his regular rounds, and the still wakeful Iskender prepared to make his escape.

True to the young soldier's self-diagnosis, his immune system had indeed purged itself of the Typhoid Fever, and he could count himself in the lucky few for whom there were no significant gastro-intestinal side effects. He still had a fever, though, and was to be a likely subject for re-infection, were he forced to stay. For reasons that he couldn't possibly understand, escape really was in his best interest; unlike Hectore Pazzi, for whom escape was demonstrably foolish.

Finding invisibility among the throngs of a plague camp was easy, no one was paying attention to anyone else; they were all too engrossed in their own suffering. The patients were all too ill or too mad to pay attention, and the handful of overworked doctors could be absorbed by only one patient at a time.

Iskender walked out of the hospital tent, and into the muddy festival that was the celebratory camp. Music was echoing over his head, and people were singing obscure village songs, many with fairly impious lyrics.

His head still burned with fever, and he staggered along a muddy path. He wasn't sure which way was which, but he knew that the Eighth Orta was in front of the army quartermaster's tent, which was where they kept the drums and trumpets. With that in mind, he followed the sounds of the imperial band.

A chill filled him as he walked through the wet mud and he shivered along his way under the deceptively warm sun until he found the banner of the two bladed sword, the home of the Eight Orta. For many days he'd been dreaming and hoping to see his family again, and he was pleased to find the camp in the condition he'd left it, but in front of the camp, was a sight that he hadn't imagined.

The city walls had fallen.

Not completely, but over the crest of the hill, he could see inside the city. He could fire an arrow into the city, admittedly without any accuracy, but in a straight line. The shell was broken forever.

He stood there shivering with purple lips, looking at the victory that he'd missed witnessing.

"Iskender?" a voice asked upon seeing him.

"Erkin?" he replied. "It's good to see you."

"Iskender!" Erkin ran over to hug his friend. "I thought you were called back to God!"

"Not yet!" Iskender answered half-honestly. "What happened?"

"The miners! They detonated the tunnels under the wall, and it collapsed like a card castle! The middle of the wall gave way, and first a tower fell, then the wall. The whole thing took ten minutes! Iskender, it was great! And I was with the sappers! I'm a real gazi now! I fought in the tunnels, I killed my first infidel! I get to carry the standard tomorrow!"

Erkin showed the horse-tailled spear that served the orta as a rallying point to his sick friend.

"That's great," Iskender said, with a touch of sadness. He'd spent ten days in the hospital, and missed so much. Even Erkin had shed and drawn blood, while he was still uninitiated.

"Are you sure you're ok, you look really pale."

"I'll be fine," Iskender insisted, puffing out his chest and trying to seem as war-ready as anyone.

"Bilgi-Hoja said that everyone in the hospital tent is under quarantine. Are you sure that they said you could go?"

"I don't need a doctor's permission to fight for God!" he answered with irritation.

Erkin looked at him in a concerned way.

"You should go and tell Bilgi-Hoja that you're back."

"There'll be time for that later,"

"Iskender, if you're sick, the rest of us could get sick, too."

"God damn it!" he swore. "Listen, I don't want to die in there with all those sick people. I want to storm the gates again tomorrow, if you turn me away, or tell Bilgi-Hoja, then I won't go back. I'll throw off these clothes and join the Bashi-bozuks. I need to fight tomorrow."

"But you're sick."

"What would I tell the class of kids after us in the Lion's Den? Until the day we die, we're going to be asked by new recruits about the Fall of Constantinople. What would I say, that I heard about it from my bed? Would I lie to them and say otherwise? I can't go back, If God decides to take me to paradise, better to do it tomorrow. Better to visit hell than abandon this cause. Please, help me get a tent, get a clean uniform on, and we'll let God decide what to do with me after that, okay?"

Erkin hooked an arm around Ahmet's neck and gave him a big kiss on the cheek.

"I'd be proud to die with you at this place, Iskender."

"If God wills it, then it's glorious in my eyes, Erkin."

The two friends excitedly made arrangements to sneak Iskender into the battle lines.

"Sire, the walls have fallen!" an exasperated Vincent tried explaining to the Emperor.

"They aren't marching into the city, are they?" Stavros countered. "The Virgin protects us still."

"That's because they're trying to knock down the northern wall with their cannons now, as we speak!" Guistiniano Longo decried the wisdom of the new Strategeos. "They've already cast down the southward bend!"

"By a stratagem that you were supposed to negate, Italian!" he answered back.

"I had counter-mining tunnels built, if you'd kept them properly manned and defended, none of this would have happened! We'd have captured their crews and collapsed their tunnels! Perhaps even get a shot at their sultan in his own camp. In case you've forgotten, I've done that before!"

"Yes, I know. In Italy. Strange, isn't it, how much better results you yield when you're defending your fellow heretics, as opposed to now when you're tasked to defend the the True Faith! Perhaps if we bent over further for your blasphemous pope, we could have avoided this catastrophe!"

"Silence!" Constantine yelled at the two of them. "I have had enough of your bickering! I've had enough of this siege! I've had enough of all this!"

"Well then, Sire," Vincent tried to sound amicable. "If you'd like, we could ask the sultan to pull his soldiers back home to Adrianople, because his ambitions bore you. Perhaps he'll agree."

"Enough, Vincent," Adam scolded him. "Sire, we're breeched. We have to offer a peaceful surrender, lest the city be ransacked. All we can hope for now is for our allies in the west to liberate an intact city. If we offer to surrender, then the city will suffer as it did before, but if we continue this lost war, we'll lose everything. The Turks will ravage the city, they'll kill or ransom the men, women and children, they'll have their way with us, and they'll steal everything that isn't too heavy to carry off."

"They'd do that if we surrender or not," Stavros growled with contempt.

"Surrender, and a hope for liberation and redemption is our best option at this point," Adam repeated.

"Sire, I agree," added Guistiniano. "Once they start the assault, which will happen as soon as the second half of the mesoteichon falls, probably tonight or tomorrow, there'll be nothing that can be done to save the city."

Constantine exhaled through his nose and frowned as if pestered by a fly.

"How much is left in the treasury?"

"Almost nothing, Sire," Stavros answered. Adam blushed imperceptibly at the news. "We cannot offer any significant tribute."

"Then, it must truly be God's will that we ride out tomorrow and defeat our enemies," Constantine said with a confident smile. "Are you ready to blow your horn, Joshua? The walls are already down."

"I believe that the Israelites were attacking the city of Jericho, in that tale, Sire."

"And we'll be the ones doing the attacking tomorrow, Gentlemen," the emperor stated with ignorant courage. "I will personally lead the charge out from destruction where the wall once stood."

There was silence around the table.

"This is ludicrous," Vincent said at last. "Sire, if you do not want to pursue a rational peace, then I will take all of the soldiers of Venice back to the Venetian Quarter and negotiate a separate peace on behalf of the Republic."

"Do so, by all means," Stavros said. "An army that marches in the name of God doesn't need heretics as allies."

"My men are here for the money," Longo stated. "But the money's no good without a capacity to spend it. If Venice withdraws, so do we."

"And you, Karian?" Stavros said accusingly. "Will you abandon us with your friends here? All you foreign races stick together!"

"Emperor, if it be God's will that I die at your side, then so be it, there I shall die," Adam had a voice that sounded like he truly meant it. "When all others have fled, I'll take the spear from your side, and bury you at Golgotha."

Constantine looked hard at his old strategeos and smiled warmly at him before looking as his replacement.

"And you, Stavros," he asked leadingly.

"Sire, I was planning on staying here to direct the defence, if the enemies entered the city."

"If we try to make a stand. This is where we'll have to do it," Longo steered the topic away from Stavros' dubious courage and pointed to the model that Karian made of the city. "That's at least a rational plan. We can move the cannons there, and keep the crossbowmen and harquebusiers positioned there as a bottle neck for when the Turks try to funnel in. For the rest of tonight, we'll have to keep the walls from opening anymore."

"And archers on the walls and towers nearby," Vincent added. "It's as good a place as any to make a stand."

"I'll muster my horsemen south of there at Saint Romanus. We can charge out and flank the army if they get too far in," Longo continued the thought. "Who knows, since the Sultan always stays so far to the rear, we might even get a shot at him if his army outperforms."

"A silver lining," Vincent said half-heartedly.

"Then we have a plan for first light," Constantine surmised.

Everyone agreed for once.

It was a busy afternoon in the hospital of Chora. The wounded from the collapsing tower and wall were minimal, but the constant barrage of cannons kept rock debris flying from the walls and into random parts of the surrounding city. Chora was close enough to the breach to shudder with every impact. Civilian injuries were also walking in, as the city was now open to direct fire, through the collapsing wall. When night fell, for the first time the battery didn't break for darkness. They continued on. It had become obvious to all that the time would be soon at hand.

"Ella," Mario said as he passed her among the wounded. "I'd like a word if I might."

He motioned her into a corner, where they could speak more privately.

"Darling Ella, the city's falling," he began.

"I know," she noted with impatience. Everyone knew. The earth shook when the walls crumbled. "Everyone is saying that tomorrow will be very hard, and that we'll have to pray all night to ensure that Constantinople survives and that the Huns are turned back. I was going to do this, but it seems that your friend Isodore has closed the women's chapel."

"Yes, that's an important matter, but not one to discuss now," he smiled grimly. "I'm worried about you."

"Me?"

"I'm worried about if the Turks take the city."

"Surely, Doctor, you don't think that's possible."

"Oh, don't be so innocent!" he said louder than he'd planned to. "The Muslim horde is at the gates and they'll charge them tomorrow. We have to make plans to get out of here."

"Mario, you're the doctor in charge of this hospital! You shouldn't be planning to run away!"

"I'm not a Constantinopolitan, and neither are you, Ella. This is their city, and they'll defend it, or they'll lose it. They've been offered so much help from us, we've given more than we could rationally be expected to, now I don't want to die here, or be sold into slavery!"

"So you'll run."

"Yes! Now listen, I have money. We can flee, get married, and we can pay the ransom for any of your friends that are captured when the city falls, as it's doomed to do. Look outside there, there's rock dust everywhere. Listen to the blasts of their cannons! Feel the pulse of the explosions! This city will be rubble before the next Sabbath, and we'd be fools to stay here and have our blood mortar the stones."

"Every day we try to heal men who've given so much, and you want to flee rather than mirror their commitment," Ella looked at him with disappointment, a sentiment that Mario had seen her show to him before, at the Cathedral when he'd tried to propose marriage. He tolerated it then because he'd been disgusted with himself, but he wasn't about to tolerate it anymore, not after all that he'd done.

"The poor are born, they suffer, and they die! These peasants here are on the road from the second to the third stage of that cycle and we try to postpone their destination as long as possible, but that's about it! They suffer because they want to suffer! They sacrifice because they are commanded to sacrifice!"

"We're all commanded to sacrifice, Mario."

"By whom?" Mario was shouting now. "By whom, Ella? Really! By God? If God wants us to die here, than he can come and kill us both! We'll say that it's God's will! If we live, then we'll say that's God's will! I suppose you think that it's God's will that you stay so stubborn and bite the hand that feeds you here!"

"Doctor, that is enough!" she spoke back angrily. "Enough! Flee like a thief in the night if you want to! I'll stay here and help in the only way I can! You can help yourself!"

"Excuse me," interjected the squat head nurse. "Would you mind keeping it down, you two are disturbing the peace."

"Fine, Sister!" Mario reverted to Greek. "I have to go elsewhere."

It was to their good fortune that almost no one could understand them arguing in Italian, a language as indecipherable as Chinese to the uneducated masses that found themselves in harm's way during a battle.

One man understood every word.

Hectore Pazzi understood that Mario had the treasure and was ready to flee now. He'd done all the legwork, and had a plan to escape. What luck! The monies were in the women's chapel.

Pazzi ran a finger over his forehead and felt his bandages. He pushed lightly against his head to see if there really was the degree of damage to which the Doctor had intimated. He felt some cushioning against the bandages. It hurt his head, but didn't feel as though his brains were about to pour out of his bone-helmet.

He looked over at his strong box. Unlike the other patients in the ward, who came here in a rather impromptu capacity, he'd planned to stay in the hospital, though the injured head hadn't been factored into his planning. He had papers, passes and notes of permission from the Emperor's office in there, but most importantly, he had two pistols and a rather stern dagger. Two shots for the two workers, the Turk and the spy, after the heavy lifting was done, and a knife with which to menace young Doctor Mario until the plan was obvious to him. Then he could do away with the young man and return home. No more of these eastern intrigues for him. He was obviously enamoured with that tease of a nurse, so the way to keep a hold of him would be through her.

He smiled and prepared himself for what he knew would be a long night.

That long night brought no respite from cannon fire or from the volley of arrows that continued to keep the spreading gap of the mesoteichion free from defending soldiers. The fearful sounds of galloping horses could be heard by men on the crumbling walls, and the silhouetted shadows of gathering soldiers were still discernable, despite the moonless night.

Oh, the moon! Symbol of Constantine and his city. It's lunar cycle was associated by most responsible physicians and astrologers with the Virgin Mary, the spiritual defender of the city. Tonight, the night of darkness and of menace, was a night when moon failed to grace the city of its astrological patronage. The defenders seemed truly abandoned.

Constantine rode out to the hole in the wall and inspected it uncomfortably from horseback. He looked like Moses standing before the parted sea. The metaphor failed in the eyes of the witnesses, who knew that this Moses planned on bringing them from the promised land of Constantinople, through this great chasm to meet the armies of Pharaoh on the field, rather than to safety.

Around his equestrian figure stood the imposing footmen of the Varangians. Each of their number were carrying torches, and they followed their leader as though he were an oracle of yore. Constantine wore a suit of armour that was polished to almost mirror-like proportions. When he joined the defenders of the city before the falling wall, he wore the spiritual crown of Leonidas, the beard of Moses and carried the glory of Alexander. Everyone stopped and took notice of his arrival.

"Christians," he spoke without shouting. Had he chosen to whisper, the distant cannons of the enemy would have stopped to allow his voice to carry. "We've arrived at Calvary."

All eyes of all soldiers, Italians, Scandinavian and Greek, leaned in towards him, glistening black in the torchlight.

"The wolves are gathering, and they plan to pounce on us before the sun rises. They are no more than a few hundred yards from where we stand. They think that they may walk into the city of Christ, and warp the city to their own ways. They think wrong. We won't fight them on our streets, or at our gate. When someone comes into your home, you don't allow them to bring the filth from the street in with them. These men bring their heresies and their barbarities with them, and they won't be invited in. We'll charge out and meet them on the plain. It's there that we'll drive them back into the night.

"I'm here to march into battle. Before the sun rises to end our long night, I want to see first-hand, the rapacious savagery of our foes. I'll stand with my sword in hand, and celebrate their defeat. Here's to our victory," he shouted, sword arm raised high. "If this sword falls, there will be a hundred other hands to hold it high! There will always be more! Every time that night falls, those enemies will be there, ready to attack. Every time that dawn readies to break, new hope arises in the hearts of the faithful. Victory is in our grasp, and there it shall always be!"

The men of Byzantium, the last men of the Empire, girded themselves to charge out of the mesoteichion, to meet whatever fate was written for them in God's agenda.

"God protect me," Iskender breathed as he trotted back from the latrine, again.

"Are you ok?" Erkin asked and hurried to his friend.

"Yeah, yeah," Iskender didn't feel bad about lying to his friend, because he knew that Erkin saw right through him. "I'll be ready for tomorrow."

"If God wills it."

"That's all you can say for anything, Erkin," Iskender smiled. He was pale and still shivering from the cold of the night and his remaining fever. He looked as if he'd lost half his weight from the beginning of the siege.

"The Soup-man's summoning people, can you make it?"

"Of course I can, but don't draw attention to me."

"No one's going to turn you back to the tents for this, Iskender," Erkin said with a laugh.

"Our commander's an imperial agha now, he has to observe the rules."

"God's law blesses the gazis."

"God's law blesses the gazis," the sickly waif repeated. "I hope I die tomorrow."

"I hope so, too," Erkin said enthusiastically. "This would be a great place to die."

Iskender put an arm around his friend and laughed.

"Let's go see what the great man has to say!"

"Let's!"

"Everyone, gather around," Mesut announced quickly, and the Eighth Orta did as commanded. "It's a nice night, everyone. I hope you're all good?"

There was cheering and applauding among the men. They were indeed feeling very good.

"Ok, I'm just returning from a meeting with the sultan, and the rest of the divan, and here's what's going to happen: in ten minutes, the skirmishers are going to start on the gap. We're going to be behind them and to the south. We aren't going to attack until dawn. At first light the bashi-bozuks are supposed to retreat to let us storm in and finish what's left of the defenders there. The skirmishers and the archers will probably make short work of the city auxiliaries that are there, but the Italian mercenaries won't be so easily moved. They've got armour, guns, crossbows and they don't rattle. Expect that. That's why you're going in with scimitars in your hands and short bows on your backs. Their light armour won't be too effective against a good heavy blade. Men from the Ozgur and Uygur tribes are going to have our flanks, in case any of their horses try to surprise us from the sides.

"My Children," he started again, this time less commanding and more fatherly, "I've never been prouder in my life than I am tonight. Tomorrow morning, we all march side by side. Some of us will march into the city, and some of us will march into paradise, but it will certainly be to a better place that we go, for we're all going there together. Whatever each of us finds at the end of this march, I want you to know, just how proud I am to call you all my children. Many of you, I've seen since you first came into the Lion's Den. I'll be proud to see any of you die with dignity. As God wills it for us all."

"As God wills it," they all repeated.

They then watched the poor skirmishers ready themselves for their great charge into history.

Chapter Forty-Six - Predawn

4:00 am – 6:30 am

Water and religion have always been the two predominant realities for Byzantium. The city was founded by the Greek adventurer Byzas of Megara, a town on the Isthmus of Corinth, in days of old. Byzas was told by the famed Oracle of Delphi that he was to build a city on the water, opposite the '*land of the blind.*' According to the legend, he sailed all over the Aegean, and then moved on to the Sea of Marmora, preparing to visit Pontos Axeinos – literally *The Inhospitable Sea,* what would eventually be called the Black Sea. On his way to the Inhospitable Sea, so named because of the savage tribes on its coasts and the rough weather that tore over its surface, he came upon the urban centre of Chalcedon.

The people of this town had settled upon a peaceful little plain near the mouth of the Bosporus. The town was at the foot of Asia's rolling hills, and possessed only modest defences. What blindness afflicted these poor villagers to have settled here? They settled on the indefensible seaside, rather than the glorious peninsula that pointed at them, only a half a mile away! This must have been what the Oracle had meant! Byzas settled his kinfolk on the curving scimitar of land, and set down the roots of what would someday be the greatest city in the world. The tip of the land was high enough to observe far and wide. That hill would eventually become an acropolis and dominate all trade in and out of the Black Sea, regardless of how inhospitable the land there was. The Acropoline Hill would defend the settlement from sea raiders, as it lowered sharply and dangerously, southward and westward into the sea. It also had a northern lee. It sloped unassumingly into the waters of the Golden Horne, and protected the harbour from the wind. The defences from human attacks, and from natural catastrophes that the land gave Byzas, meant that the explorer had found his home. He claimed the spot for his new city and dedicated it to the goddess Artemis, the mistress of the hunt, and sacrificed a ram in her honour. The banner of the white crescent on a field of red unfurled and the first streaks of ink began to write a new tome of history.

Byzas named the settlement Byzantium, after himself. It was a glorious spot for a village, and the Greek colony swore its allegiance to Athens, beginning what should have been a rocketing future to the stars. The city had everything needed for success, after all. It had natural defences. It had a natural deepwater harbour. It was well situated for trade. It had alliances with a mighty patron. It was surrounded by water.

617

Salt water.

Unlike Chalcedon, which was blessed with underwater rivers and easily accessible wells, Byzantium had only the Lycus River, which ran dry in the summer, and deep ground wells had to be dug, most of which would hardly yield enough water for more than a few hundred settlers. The perfect place for a city, opposite the blind, seemed to have an Achilles Heel. It would never be able to mature into a proper Polis without water. It was only because of the patronage of Athens that the less imposing soldiers of Chalcedon didn't sail across the strait and subjugate Byzantium before the village got out of hand.

Empires rose and fell, as they always do, and Byzantium stayed a quiet little provincial town on the Bosporus, largely forgotten by the affairs of the outside world. But forgotten things can be found again, and the town of Byzas' hill was to be found by the legions of expanding Rome. The small city had sided with Pescennius Niger in the war for the imperial diadem against the eventually victorious Septimius Severus, and the city was besieged and conquered by a vindictive Roman army. While getting conquered is generally a bad thing for those who have the misfortune to live through it, the Legions of Emperor Septimius Severus brought with them more than their vengeance and fury; they brought Roman engineering. They brought the aqueduct.

North of the city, the hills of Pera housed numerous lakes, rivers and springs. Enough water to quench the thirst of an almost limitless multitude was there, just waiting to be drunk, and the Romans had about as much interest in maintaining a dry village as they had in letting natural resources go to waste. The springs that emptied at the high altitudes of the hilly forest would be the sources for the city's growth. All that needed to be done was to bring it to the city. Water flows downwards, in accordance with the laws of gravity, so the trick was to make a slope that would go constantly downwards, bringing the water from the springs in the Thracian hills, down to sea-level Byzantium, five miles away. The slope had to be constantly and invariably sloping in one direction, or the water would back up and spill over the countryside. Roman engineers were nothing if not meticulous and the slope was constant. The water could come. The people could drink. The crops could be irrigated, and the animals raised. The city grew.

The water flooded into cisterns that held the never stopping waves of water that came. Those cisterns emptied into canals which brought water to reservoirs and fountains for the citizens to collect. The earliest permanent buildings in the city were these waterworks. They cluttered the landscape, making room for themselves at the expense of the growing city's markets and other such civic functions.

In AD 330, the Emperor Constantine first decommissioned the city of Byzantium and then established the city of Nova Roma, or New Rome. The streets and buildings were the same, but they now had new names. He dedicated the city to the Virgin Mary, the celestial matriarch of the newly legalised Christian religious community. The red flag with the white crescent of Artemis was kept, though a white star was added to symbolize Mary, the queen of heaven. In one of those strange coincidences of history, the flag is almost indistinguishable from that of the battle standard of the Janissary Corps, or the flag of the modern Turkish Republic. Constantine's city was established upon the old polis, to be the new capital of a new empire, theoretically undiluted by paganism. The empire was to be Christian through and through, and the wealth of the Roman Empire poured onto the peninsula in order to bring enough glory as to properly demonstrate the city's role.

The problem with building a new city on the limited land space of the peninsula was that almost everything was covered in canals, aqueducts, viaducts, cisterns and reservoirs, and without them the city would die of thirst. The sewage crowding wasn't the only problem facing these ancient urban planners. The monuments that Constantine and his successors wanted to build needed flat, open space, and the hilly peninsula had precious little of that to go around. The city engineers were at an impasse, and the situation seemed impossible without some kind of divine intervention.

When an impossible situation meets a virtually bottomless purse, magic happens. Cisterns were rebuilt as high as possible on the seven hills of the New Rome, as high as the aqueducts downward flow would allow them. The canals snaked along the hillsides, and reservoirs were built low in the valleys. Then pillars were built. In a shocking display of what can be accomplished when genius maries money, a new ground surface was built, connecting the hills overtop the water system. Some of the mighty hills seemed to disappear as flat land emerged overtop valley-based reservoirs and connected one hill-top to the next. The city flattened enough ground to build its monuments and hide its water infrastructure. The Cathedral of Holy Apostles was built atop the Cathedral Cistern, and Holy Wisdom atop the Basilica Cistern. Christ's city, a world capital was built overtop a network of more than two hundred and fifty kilometres of canals, tunnels, and passages.

In the darkness of Constantinople's underground, there are very few people who could navigate themselves through the labyrinth without a map. While the Bulgarian monk, Isodore, was not capable of finding his way in the dark, he had the help of a map, and the help of some friends. It was there, far away from the arms of the attacking army, from the rays of the sun, or the discomfort of his former lodge, that the self-indulgent mystic was to meet his fate.

Mario's pride was such that he hated the idea of asking again once he'd been refused, but the sad reality was that the situation demanded it be done. He walked up to the convent's barracks in the dark hours between Matins and Lauds, and knocked on the door. The door opened swiftly and that damnable elderly nurse showed herself again.

"Is there an emergency, Doctor?" she asked before he could speak. "It's the middle of the night."

"Yes, I'm sorry about the hour, Nurse. I need to speak to Sister Ella."

"She's sleeping."

"You can wake her."

The squat matron of the nurses stood firm and looked the doctor up and down before giving her snarling acquiescence.

"A moment," she grumbled and closed the door.

After what Mario assessed to be significantly more than a moment, Ella emerged from the behind the only door to the women's barracks. Her eyes were beautiful in the candle-light, and her sleep-puffy cheeks were red from slumber. She tried to take an air of superiority over Mario, as she'd done outside Holy Wisdom what seemed like an eternity ago, but now she couldn't seem to manage it with the same grace as before; Mario had become resistant to the intimidation of an idealised woman.

"Good morning," he greeted her.

"Morning is it?" she said sternly. "I suppose dawn is closer than dusk but that hardly makes it morning. Why have you come here?"

"Listen to me," he started before being interrupted.

"No, Doctor. I have listened to you, and I think that I should do so no more. You're preparing to run now, aren't you?"

"Fine, if you won't listen to me, then listen to the night," and he motioned with his eyes to the darkness away from her doorstep. The clash of steel and explosions of gunpowder could be heard, the Turks were trying to force the wall again. "They've numbers that can't be counted, Ella. They'll take the wall before dawn, and the rest of the city before sunset. Listen to them! They'll take everyone! Come with me now, and you can spend the rest of your life wondering about martyrdom. Stay here, and my love, you'll find out about it soon enough. Please, Ella, I can't bear the thought of living my life without you."

Ella was not the type to surrender an already ruled-upon opinion, but reason walked arm-in-arm with self-preservation, and given time, those two bed-mates would lead her down the garden path to survival. Ella looked out into the night and her eyes began to water. She could hear the horrible sounds of death and war on her doorstep. Over the Chora wall, and just outside the Petrion, an eternal struggle was taking place. She listened, as women have always listened to the horrors of war, and she felt the same fear that millions have felt before and since: that the victorious would come and demand a tithe of flesh from the conquered. She wanted to stay strong, but she weakened. Mario saw that weakening and made no effort to respect or give credence to her doubts.

"Today is going to be a terrible day, regardless of what we all do. Many are going to die, and not by disease or old age. I choose not to do that here today. I'm going. You spoke to me of their courage and their sacrifice, those who are going to busy the angel of death today. I'm going to Venice, and I will remember their sacrifice. I'll honour their courage, by telling everyone about what happened here. You should come with me, and help me to chronicle what transpires here. Honour Constantinople by not allowing it to be forgotten, but we can't stop the city from falling. Come with me."

Ella didn't speak, nor did she move.

Mario slowly took her hand and raised it to his lips. He kissed her fingers gently, and she refocused her eyes on him. He smiled at her.

"Come with me, be my wife, and let's live. Don't choose to die here alone, among strangers. You deserve so much more."

Ella's eyes darted about for an instant, and then in a moment of clarity, she agreed.

"Yes," she said with a reluctant smile. "Your offer sounds like the better of the available options."

"How romantic. Thank you"

Ella laughed for the first time in recent memory, then her eyes watered and she looked as though she were about to cry. This wave of emotions passed over again, as many others had in recent weeks.

"So where do we go now?" she asked once she'd recomposed herself.

"Isodore and Ahmet are waiting for us. You'll have to change into some warm clothes, and quickly collect anything that you can't leave behind. Don't let anyone see you."

"Who's Ahmet and where are they waiting for us?"

"Oh. Yes. Those are two very good questions, both of which have answers that you probably won't like."

Ella raised an eyebrow and agreed with Mario's earlier statement that this day would be remembered as terrible.

"Get changed."

"You can't be serious," Ella proclaimed as the two of them approached an inconspicuous stone and concrete gateway into the side of the hill behind Chora.

"I assure you that I am very serious in this and in all other things, or at least for today," he smiled warmly at his future bride. "Come quickly, the sun will rise in a few hours, and the fighting's getting louder."

They approached the grated metal door and found it as Mario had left it, unlocked.

"Follow me," Mario instructed and held out his hand for Ella to take. She took his hand with a nervous determination to see the day through, and the two began their descent into the bowels of the city.

"I hope you know the way," she said in the dark.

"I do, just stay close. I'm at the first step now, there are fifteen more, going down, come with me and count quietly. Here we go. That's it."

The two navigated down the steps in the dark, and then Mario put his hand on the wall, remembering his way like a garden shrew.

"I think I see a see a light up ahead," Ella said hopefully.

"That's where we're going."

The stone hallway turned to catch the indirect light from down another hall, and then turned again to arrive into a large room, lit by three hefty lanterns. The room was large and centred around a wide canal, perhaps two metres across, with a stout little bridge crossing over it. Two small boats, small in the harbour but giant in this small room, were floating in the canal, moored to the bridge. There were also two men sitting on the bridge apparently waiting for them.

"Lady Ella," Isodore stood up and bowed. "I'm glad to see that you've decided to join us!"

"Brother Isodore, I take it that this adventure is of your design?"

"In part, I deserve some credit, though in all fairness our good doctor friend deserves more than a quiet mention of credit."

"And that is a servant?" she motioned to the big man behind him.

"Ahh, not exactly a servant *per se*, but he'll be helping us today.

Ahmet, this… is… Ella.”

Ahmet stood tall above everyone else in the chamber. He bowed his head politely and managed to utter the words “Hello. Ve-reh b’you tifa,” by which point he’d effectively exhausted his command of useful Greek.

“Thank you,” Ella replied, understanding that the big man spoke none of her language. She looked at his face and tried to place it. It didn’t take very long. “I believe that I owe your servant a great debt of thanks.”

“I don’t think that that’s necessary, My Lady,” Isodore answered.

“I think that it is. Please tell him that I am very grateful for what he did the other night. He saved my honour. And tell him that when all of this is over, there will be a place of honour for him in my brother’s house, or my husband’s, if he needs it.”

Mario bit his tongue, reminded of the fact that he as yet didn’t have a house.

“My Lady…”

“Please translate that.”

Isodore’s command of Turkish was limited at best, and Ella was trying to communicate using courtly words. The former monk, on a point of pride, decided to give it at least a modest try, lest people understand his limitations.

“Teshekur ederim,” he began by saying *thank you*, and realized that he didn’t have the ability to continue on with the rest of Ella’s message. If he stopped there, Ella would realize that her message wasn’t properly conveyed, so he continued. He used his established oratory skill of saying very little with as many words as possible. “Ve, chok teshekur ederim ve selam-u alaikum. – *and thank you very much and peace be upon you.*”

He decided that was long enough to put that piece of polity aside for now.

“Wa alaikum as-selam. Bi-shey dehil, Abla.” Ahmet answered. “*And unto you be peace. It was nothing, Sister.*”

“Well,” Isodore proclaimed by clapping his hands, eager to move on from his lacklustre job as a translator. “He says it was his duty as a stranger in a strange land. I guess we can get started then!”

“I take it that we’re near Valen’s Aqueduct?” Ella asked.

“We’re in the aqueduct,” Mario answered. “The aqueduct is underground, the viaduct is above.”

Ella didn’t look to be impressed with her fiancé’s knowledge of trivia.

“We’ve got a map of the aqueduct,” he continued undaunted. “We’ve got a king’s ransom to carry to the harbour, and the best way to do that undetected is by boat along the canal, so here we are. We’ll tow the boats up to Cathedral Cistern, and then down to Basilica Cistern, and then down again to a reservoir on the other side of the harbour. Then we'll hide there until it's safe to cross the harbour to neutral Galata. From there, we'll hire a boat to take us back to Italy, with the gold. We can also ransom and rescue as many prisoners as possible."

"Where did all this treasure come from?" Ella asked incredulously. She looked into the two boats, both of which were packed to the brim with small chests and burlap sacks.

"That's a long story, and we've got to be on our way," Mario answered, hoping to dismiss her claims right away.

While it didn't dissolve her fears, it shelved them enough to take them off the docket for now. The four of them began to lug their little boats up the canal, against the stepped current, and towards the Cathedral Cistern.

Hectore Pazzi's coal black eyes stared across the chamber from the shadows. He couldn't believe his luck. The three men and their whore had been so kind to him. First, they'd found the treasure, something that he'd been unable to do. Then, they'd found a way to transport the loot, something that he could hardly have done on his own. They'd even supplied a map of the endless tunnels of the under-city for him. In addition to all of this, they were now even supplying the labour for the hard task of hauling the treasure against the current and up Saint Irene's Hill.

Pazzi was man for whom logistics would always take precedence over matters of pride and principle. That's not to say that the latter category should be ignored. He also relished the opportunity to do away with that bearded spy, who'd confounded him before. More important than him though, the big Turk was apparently the man who'd confined him to a hospital for the past couple of weeks. He was looking forward to taking his due from him.

Following the four of them would be an easy task. The only light in the caverns was from their lanterns, and they weren't making any effort to be silent, as they thought that there was no one to follow them. Hectore could watch them, and creep silently behind, ever the shadow.

He stood up to follow them into the long corridor of the canal, but tried to do so too quickly. His head swelled and protested against the sudden movement, and Pazzi surrendered to the pain by seating himself and allowing it to pass.

He had to be careful. When he moved quickly, the pain from the Turk's vicious and (in his mind at least) undeserved assault still afflicted him. If it struck him in these tunnels, he might lose track of the lanterns, and then he'd be trapped here until he could find his own way out.

He'd let the four of them work in peace until they climbed to the first reservoir, which would be the highest point of the underground aqueduct, everything was down-water from there. Then, he'd do away with the three men, and take his prize.

Keeping track of time while underground is a futile task. Try as they might, none of them could do so. It was only through Isodore's map and his understanding of the locks and levels of the great aqueduct that the four of them managed to walk along the stony canals, towing the laden boats along with them, to find the Cathedral Cistern.

The great cistern was a giant chamber, hundreds of yards in both length and width. It had over seven hundred columns, reaching up to support its vaulted roof, high above the travellers, but far below the feet of the city's denizens.

"My God, it's huge," Mario said when they finally reached the last leg of the canal. They tied the boats down to another stone bridge over the canal and took a brief rest from their labours. "How high is it?"

"Eight metres," Isodore answered while catching his breath.

"It doesn't look like eight metres," Ella said suspiciously.

"I mean from the bottom, My Lady," he corrected. "There are probably about five metres of air here now, so that means the water is three down, nice and deep."

"It's beautiful," Mario said looking at the corridors of columns that emerged from the city's water supply, tapering off into the darkness. There was the sound of flowing and dripping water echoing through the chamber.

"That's what we thought when we first came through here with the boats," the monk acknowledged. They weren't weighted down, so then we could sail across the hall. We raced, Ahmet here won the day."

"Why does this Turk serve you, Brother Isodore?" Ella asked.

"You'd have to ask him that, and I'm sorry, but he doesn't speak Greek," he said with a wily look in his eyes.

Ahmet, for his part, was aware that they were speaking of him, but didn't seem to care much. He hadn't been impressed with the city when he first set foot inside the walls, but he could now see how glorious it was. So much meticulous effort, a glorious convenience that no one would ever see, but from which everyone would benefit. What other secrets did the city hold? How many more invisible wonders lurked within the walls? What lurked in the shadows, ready to mystify all with unseen wonders?

Click, Fwwt, Tok.

"What was that?" Ella asked with surprise. She looked around and then turned back to Mario and Isodore.

Mario and Ella both saw the arrow's shaft sticking out of Isodore's lower chest at the same time. The monk looked down at his chest and opened his mouth as if to say something, but only voiceless air escaped his mouth. He fell back onto the stone steps beside the water. He was still conscious of what was going on, but he lacked the wherewithal to do anything about his circumstances and he started to slide into the water.

Mario jumped to his side to inspect the damage and prevent him from falling into the water. Ella began screaming, and Ahmet jumped to attention. He took one look at his only friend, and wasted no time dallying. Whoever did that was still out there, and with murder on his mind.

Mario thought he saw an arrow in the monk's chest, but Ahmet knew better, it was a bolt, a short arrow, or long dart, that came from a crossbow; an ugly, graceless invention that could shoot through steel armour. He quickly threw himself to the side of the wall, next to the egress of the chamber from which they'd just emerged.

He filtered out Ella's screams and could hear enough clicking to understand that the crossbow had been loaded once again, and that the assassin was in the canal corridor, ready to strike as soon as the weapon was again loaded. He looked down at Isodore and swore when he saw the bloody damage. A belly wound. He'd bleed for hours before he died. Damn.

Ahmet pushed Mario aside roughly and rolled the suffering Isodore on of the skiffs. He had a plan, but he had to explain it to this man without a functional common language.

"Siz," he began, pointing at Mario and Ella with his fingers, indicating that he was addressing the two of them.

"Gime'le," he pointed at the boat and took hold of the vessels' lead.

"Git," he motioned in the direction that they'd been heading.

"Ben," he placed his open hand on his chest, indicating that he was now speaking of himself.

"Sonra gelecem," he rolled his hand in the direction he'd instructed them to go, and hoped that they understood that he intended to join them after dispatching their attacker.

Just as he finished explaining a plan that he hoped the two non-turcophones would understand, another crossbow bolt flew through the darkness, barely missing Ahmet's head.

'*Wonderful,*' he thought exuberantly. The attacker now had to reload, that would take a moment. Ahmet needed no more than an instant to turn around and sprint down the tunnel from which the bolt had come. He ran on the right hand side of the canal, on a walkway no wider than an average man's stride, and certainly narrower than his own. The light from the lanterns behind him illuminated him as a giant silhouette, an easy target, and his growing shadow gave room for his attacker to hide in. It was far from a perfect situation for Ahmet, but better than getting shot while fleeing.

He saw a minor flash of light from across the canal; a glint of steel in the light reflecting from the distant lanterns. Another bolt took to air and crossed the canal into Ahmet's person.

The quarrel ripped into the tribesman's thigh about a palm's width above the knee. The velocity of his legs while running prevented the wood from sticking in there, and instead deflected it away into the water, but the impact still cut muscle and damaged tendon. Ahmet fell down fast onto the narrow stone walkway. He bounced off the stone wall and then splashed into the frigid water.

Hectore couldn't believe his fortune thus far. In the dying of the light, he could see the big Turk flailing around in the water. He restrung his crossbow and followed the light to catch the last two and nab his fortune.

No sooner had he taken his first step in pursuit, when there was a splash from the water at his feet. Ahmet reached out from the icy depths of the canal to grab at Pazzi's legs and bring him down to the ground. Hectore sidestepped to first wild, clutching hand, but the second grabbed him by the ankle. The grip stole his balance and he landed belly first on the stone walkway. His foot was still held by Ahmet, who then lunged up from the water and threw himself on the immobilized limb. He grabbed on tightly with the ferociousness of a leg-hold bear trap.

Ahmet held the ankle and lunged himself up onto the stone to secure Pazzi's leg up to the knee. He wrapped his arms around the appendage, throwing his weight at the back of Hectore's knee, and then tried to roll back towards the water.

Pazzi scrambled his hands looking for a knife at his belt. He knew that he was still wounded from his concussion and was hardly in any shape to brawl with anyone. He finally found the knife just as his leg was pulled into the frigid water. Pazzi gripped the knife underhanded and stabbed it backwards at the man wrapped around his leg.

The first stab hit a true mark in Ahmet's shoulder, but it didn't cut deep enough and the grip remained. Pazzi stabbed him four more times in the same spot of the shoulder, never allowed enough leverage to properly apply killing force from the angle he had. Ahmet put his legs against the side of the ledge and pushed with all his might, bringing Pazzi into the water on top of him.

Pazzi's first thought when he hit the water wasn't of his attacker. It was of the flint-box in his pouch. With that being wet, he would be trapped in the darkness unless he could catch up with the remaining two members of the boating party. His mind went into a panic before he reconciled himself to the fact that he was being wrestled in the water by a much larger man.

The slow moving canal began pulling the two down-current, away from the fleeing Mario and Ella. The light grew dimmer and more distant.

Ahmet pushed aside the shocking cold of the water and took a deep breath. He squirmed his arms under Pazzi's and began to squeeze with all his might, forcing the air from the bewildered Italian's chest. Surrender wasn't something that came naturally to Pazzi, and he slipped and slid in the freezing water, trying to escape the vice like grip of the heavier man. The panic of the drowning sensation gave him added speed and an adrenalin fuelled strength, but it also clouded his mind in panic. He darted his head left and his body right. His arms went to and his legs went fro. The panicked momentum couldn't extricate him from Ahmet's grip, and eventually the temporary might of adrenalin began the inevitable surrender to the other man's strength, and the icy water of the aqueduct began to occupy his lungs. The water eventually filled him, and the cold wet blackness of the underbelly of Constantinople finally pulled life away from Hectore's grasp. The veins that brought life to Byzas' potential took Pazzi as a blood sacrifice, and allowed Ahmet to lift his own body, shaken, exhausted and bleeding, onto the walkway to breathe.

Looking around, Ahmet saw nothing, only a foggy darkness. He couldn't even see his nose in front of his eyes. With great effort, he managed to stand up and ready himself to continue after Mario and Ella. He stood perfectly still and listened, but all he could hear was the drip, drip, drip of water. He could see no refractive light coming from any directions, and his body shivered with intense cold. His teeth began to chatter and his lips numbed.

"Mario!" He yelled, hoping to hear anything more than an echo. "Ella!"

Nothing.

In the darkness, Ahmet stretched out his fingers and put them on the wall to the right of him, and he started to limp along it. He had no idea which direction it was, but as long as he kept a hand on that wall, he hoped that he would eventually manage to make his way out of the labyrinth of the aqueduct. He was cold, but he had an abundance of water, if not food, and plenty of time. It was either follow the wall or prepare to starve to death. Ahmet hated himself for the life he'd chosen, but he wasn't ready to give it up just yet. He'd already made a promise to God that he'd redeem himself. As he walked he prayed that God had made a reciprocal promise to him.

Far above Ahmet's head, the sun rose and a new day began.

Chapter Forty-Seven – Dawn

The black of night gave way to the purple and then pink of a cloudless sunrise.

The skirmishers lived up to their pseudonym of "broken-headed" with a tenacious effort. For almost two hours, they kept the defenders running, fighting and blocking. They attacked without a uniform front, forcing the soldiers to run and frantically react to a dizzying danse macabre. The rubble of the mesotechion became a hunting ground for men more than a battlefield.

"There're more coming through in the third quarter!" Vincent yelled out to alert his men. They occupied the edge of land where the rubble broke onto the plain of the city, and their border was alit with hundreds of torches.

In front of them, the rubble afforded the skirmishers cover, and the night blanketed them in safety from the archers stationed above them. Only the crazy few, who were mad or greedy enough to try and force the lines outside of the detritus, would charge out of their protection, only to die with merciful swiftness at the steel of the defenders.

At the rear of the defenders were four men on horseback, surrounded by some of the most vicious guards the north could produce.

"Why don't they charge?" Constantine asked his generals. "Why don't they fight us?"

"Sire, they're afraid to stand against us. Mehmet must imagine that your soldiers have the fury of old, and the bottleneck will break his forces as happened to Xerxes at Thermopylae," Stavros assured him.

"Oh be quiet," Adam snapped at him. "Sire, they're tiring us. They're using their weakest and least valuable soldiers to wear us down, and deny us rest. Once the sun's risen, their real soldiers will climb through the fallen wall and find us sleepless, hungry and wounded."

"If you know how they think so well, why have you allowed them this far?" Stavros accused his theoretical subordinate.

"Sire," frustration was evident in Karian's voice. "I recommend that we take this opportunity to angle our cannons as mortars. Keep a barrage at the entrance to the bottleneck, prevent the attackers from resupplying or retreating."

"Do it," the Emperor replied instantly. He was a little worried about his Armenian friend, who had been turning more desperate and irritable.

"Sire, we should advance now, they don't have the numbers to hold us back!" insisted Stavros, committed to reasserting himself.

"Stavros, how about you go and check on the supplies, make sure that we have enough powder and shot to continue until noon-time," Adam suggested coolly.

"You forget yourself!" he fired back in anger.

"Stavros, go," Constantine said flatly. He had apparently lost any willingness to mediate between the two commanders, and it had become obvious to him rather quickly that the anthypatos' reputation for quick thinking was limited to the court and failed to transfer to this arena.

As the sun moved from a state of swelling in the east to the point that its yellow starburst could now reach the distant earth, trumpets sounded. The Ottoman military band played a seventeen note refrain, which was the sign for the broken headed skirmishers to begin their withdrawal.

It was hard for the defenders to see if anyone was withdrawing or not, as their pell-mell attackers had been hidden in the rubble. From the tops of the two remaining towers of the Mesotechion, flags waved.

"Emperor," Vincent pointed to the waving flag, and read their meanings for the bewildered monarch. "The skirmishers are pulling back, and another force is coming."

The sniping perches raised a yellow flag and lowered a green one to half mast.

"The Janissaries are coming," He concluded.

"Good!" The Emperor proclaimed with exuberance and he rode up to the defending Greek irregulars. "They're coming! Keep up that mortar fire! They're coming, my glorious soldiers! They're coming not to harass you, but to kill! They don't want to play a game and go home, they are here to kill you, and everyone you love! They are here for your homes! They are here for your goods! They are here to whore your women and enslave your sons into their ranks, Men! When they climb over that fallen wall, you have to fight with everything in you, fight until your body is exhausted and emptied, so you can be filled with nothing but the fighting spirit of the archangels! There can be no honourable surrender! They come now! Raise your swords! They come!"

The trumpets lifted Iskender's spirit and fortified his beleaguered innards. He saw the distant sun peak over the distant horizon and he knew that God's eye was on the affairs of men today. The giant kettle drums of the military band echoed through the air as they trudged through the mud and muck of the dry moat outside the city walls.

Ahead of them, he could see the random mass of the bashi-bozuks jumping away from the fray, as they'd been ordered to do. They ran like lemmings off of the rocks and rubble and wall fragments that had freshly found earth. Dressed unlike their comrades, the random force looked less like an army and more like a crowd of active spectators. They cheered the Janissaries as the horde ran helter-skelter, screaming with exuberance at the night's events and the morning's promise.

All of Iskender's fears went flying out the window. He entertained no thoughts of death, or worse, dying slowly and forgotten on the field of battle. He actually wanted to laugh. He wanted to run out ahead of the corps and take on Rome all by himself in fisticuffs. His mild insanity was perhaps an after-dinner belch from the typhoid.

"Are you ready for this?" Erkin asked, with a sly smile. "We'll be the first and second regiments to take the wall."

"Hassan's watching all this," Iskender said confidently.

"Oh, lighten up," Erkin answered and laughed.

"No talking in the ranks!" their sergeant admonished them as he patrolled the groups. "Get those knees up and sling those bows, men! We'll skirmish before we fight!"

The entire regiment slung their bows and readied their morale to go into the rubble between them and their enemies.

A scream cut through their quick preparations. Atop the two towers on either side of the Mesotechion were archers, who began to rain their arrows down on the two flanks of the Orta. At this range the defenders' bows were hardly accurate, but with the Orta so tightly together, they didn't need to be.

"Into the breach!" Mesut called. For one last time, the commander of the regiment wore the uniform he'd always worn. He'd yet to forsake it for the less functional outfit of his court station. "Into the breach! Into the breach and on to the other side! It's near us now! Glory awaits! Cross through the rubble and emerge in paradise! Chase the sun and cut down all who stand in your way! God is great! God is great! God is Great!"

On the other side of the rubble, gunpowder mixed with steel and wood to conspire against the Janissaries. Venetian and Genoese mercenaries alongside the less experienced soldiers of the empire sought to hold their piece of land against the advancing horde. Their cannons and trebuchets acted as mortars, throwing rubble against the advancing Ottoman soldiers in a parabolic arch. Firing irregularly weighted and shaped objects blind was hardly the exact science of ballistics, but it was accurate enough to force the Janissaries to hurry through the wreckage towards the waiting defenders.

To the left, right and fore of Iskender, explosions shook the sky and filled his nose with the smell of burnt sulphur. He managed to fire his bow several times up at the crow's nests of Italian snipers in the southernmost tower. A bow was faster and more accurate at this range than the vulgar but lethal hand cannons used by his enemies but to his disappointment, none of his arrows found flesh for certain. He did think that one of the snipers was injured by his arrows, however. It wasn't enough for him to boast of his first kill just yet.

"Iskender!" Erkin slapped him lightly to get his attention away from the distant snipers. "Look, there they are!"

No more than five metres away, soldiers in blackened steel mail emerged from the smoky dawn. They carried crossbows, arbalests, hand cannons and swords, and they marched in a unison similar to that upon which the Janissaries prided their monopoly of discipline.

"Scimitars!" their sergeant shouted as they prepared to enter the melee.

With a liquid flow of movement, the boys' bows were unstrung and their curved steel blades out of their scabbards and into their hands.

"To battle!" came the sergeant's call. "To battle! Charge! Victory! God is great!"

Southward from the mesotechion bottle-neck, the gates of Saint Romanus opened quickly with controlled enthusiasm. From those gates, a tornado of defenders stormed through the opening, and four hundred men on horseback roared out without need of battle cries or instructions. The horsemen of Guistiniano Longo didn't need anymore last minute instructions, because this would be the third time they'd done such a charge.

They knew to ride as fast as possible northwards along the inside of the moat, to stay away from enemy pike-men. They would speed along the wall from Saint Romanus to Lycus and the gap, and from there they'd turn back into the city, charging through the surprised Janissaries, cutting through the Sultan's elite and immediately returning to the camp of the Emperor, there to dismount and return to the battle as footmen. The analogy that their commander used was that they were 'threading a stitch.'

The horses galloped as fast as a three-bit gait could take them. They charged down the no-man's-land between the outer wall and the muddy moat, riding at eight men across, and fifty ranks deep. The ground shook. The riders at the front were the most experienced horsemen, they were men who'd fought with their commander for years, in some cases a decade, all over the northern root of the Italian Peninsula. The experience lessened as one moved focus towards the other end of the formation, ending with the inexperienced new-recruits at the rear, some of whom could barely ride a horse.

On the other side of the mud channel, the extended Gokhan Clan awoke from an early morning trance when they saw and heard the charge of the heavy knights. Their family patriarch shouted at the horsemen as though he thought they would stand down out of his simple force of will alone. He wished that he still had his own horsemen, but the beasts had been requisitioned by the Ottoman bureaucracy and hadn't been seen since the first week of this hateful siege. They'd probably been served as stew some weeks ago.

As if the seizure of livestock wasn't bad enough, their arrows had been rationed down to barely enough to be used. Everything they'd arrived to campaign with had been taken by order of the Sultan! Their job this morning had been to use the pikes that the imperial quartermaster had given them (flimsy long spears, with a cut point rather than steel heads) to deter any such cavalry charge. With the cavalry charging on the other side of the moat, their influence had just become negligible.

"Throw the God-damned sticks!" the Gokhan khan commanded his clan. "Take out as many as you can, and imagine that sultan's agent's face on their bodies! Kill them all!"

A random barrage of long spears, short javelins, darts, sling-stones and occasional contraband arrows flew from the Gokhan Clan to Longo's famous cavalry. One projectile, a heavy hand dart, took a strange trajectory. Measuring only about the length of a man's forearm, it flew up and over the moat towards the horsemen, before the heavy iron of the head overpowered the velocity that the twelve-year-old arm of its young thrower had given it. It then began tilting towards the earth at a hard angle from above. It found a random victim and gravity brought the lethal point right through the gap between the collar of the fortuneless man's steel breast-plate, and the flesh of his neck. It pierced the flesh, broke the clavicle and entered the rib-cage by five centimetres through flesh and rough muscle. Its victim's name was Guistiniano Longo.

Pain spiked through his entire body as the dart pegged his torso from above. He contorted in surprise and bent low, using his horse's neck for support. It wasn't enough and he felt himself about to fall from the saddle, but some unseen force seemed to hold him temporarily in the saddle.

'*They can't see this,*' he thought to himself as the pain continued unabated. He couldn't let the horsemen in his charge see him weaken, let alone the enemy.

He garnered all his strength and reached up to his neck, where he found the offending metal barb. He wrapped his gloved hand around it, prayed, summoned what mettle he could and plucked it from out his flesh. I geyser of blood spurt from his shoulder.

That was too much for the ageing soldier.

His brain surrendered his consciousness to pain, and the Genoese champion fell from the horse, in front of the charging four hundred. Trampled over by his own men, the much lauded champion of the third day, the man called the '*Sword of Christ*' by the emperor himself, lay bleeding to death.

The horsemen crashed into the southern flank of the eighth orta and their spears reigned down terror on the unprepared soldiers fighting amongst the rubble. Iskender ran for higher ground and stood on a collapsed tympanum archway to lift himself above their spears and swords. He quickly returned to his bow and fired wildly into the advance. This time he saw his first blood, as one of the horsemen caught his arrow in the shoulder and buckled in his saddle. He postponed his rejoice long enough to hit a second and then a third. The second was also wounded, but the third was shot in the stomach; he'd be a corpse by nightfall. Iskender was giddy at the prospect. He was now a new recruit in the eyes of no one.

Further up ahead, he could witness Erkin trying to make a stand against a charging mass. What was the fool thinking? Why not head for the higher ground the rubble offered? Erkin swung his scimitar wildly and was impaled by one of the charging courser's spears.

"Erkin!" he yelled out, surrendering his euphoria briefly.

His concern for his friend wasn't so all-consuming as to make him forget his training, or do anything so foolish as run to his side to hear any last minute pearls of wisdom. Iskender kept his perch, out of spear range and he continued to harass the chargers until they'd passed. He shot his fourth man and a few occasional horses, but could see that his aim was weakened after the shock of watching Erkin fall.

Once the charge had passed over them and into their own camp, only then did Iskender run to his friend to see if he were wounded or lost. He was gone.

"You haven't died in vain, Erkin," Iskender said, rising quickly. "You died in glory and will be welcomed into paradise with eagle's wings. May my death be so glorious."

"He's fallen!" the first of the riders called out once he'd arrived into the Roman camp. "Captain Longo's fallen!"

"Damn!" Adam swore calmly. "Such things happen. May God grant him permanent grace."

"God bless him," Vincent quickly added but was not distracted by the loss. "Ready the troops to push back against the Turks. We'll hit them again. Rider! You're captain now, ready the men to advance on foot!"

"Rider, wait!" The emperor's voice bellowed over that of even the cannons and the engines of destruction. "Where is your captain?"

"He's dead, Sire," the Italian veteran seemed about to lose tenor. "He's fallen!"

"Where, man?" Constantine repeated. "Where is his body?"

"Outside the walls, he didn't make it into the breach!"

"Then we'll go and get him!" the emperor yelled back. "Men, let's go and fetch the captain! Guistiniano Longo's spirit longs for Christian soil! Let's give it to him!"

Vincent and Adam looked at each other and instantly shared the same idea, that such a venture was doomed folly.

"Sire!" Adam was the first to voice his concern. "The breach is full of Janissaries! We can barely get in there, let alone through and back!"

Constantine gave him a passing look to indicate his displeasure.

"Men! Christians!" the emperor got everyone's attention by shouting and raising his sword over his head. Once those assembled brought all eyes to him, he issued what would be some of the last words of his reign as Basileus. "Let's go! Collect our fallen friend! Charge!"

And with that, Constantine led almost a thousand Greek peasants and city-dwelling irregulars, professional soldiers none, undaunted and fearless against a professional, trained military cult that was the terror of the world. The veteran mercenaries could only look on in disbelief before they were shamed to follow suit and retrieve their own.

The defenders struck out against the attackers. The days of hiding behind walls and weathering storms were now past them.

"Commander!" one of the scouts accosted Mesut. "They're charging! Along the southern periphery!"

"Where the cavalry just hit?" the commander asked incredulously.

"Yes, Sir!" the young scout answered quickly.

"Everyone to the south!" Mesut yelled to all those around them.

The military band changed their cadence to a tune called '*The Drowned Rose*,' a deceptively upbeat tune that told those who could hear it to turn right. The Eight Orta employed their infamous speed and turned right in the middle of their advance, and moved their focus from the main defender's line, to the outstretched thrust to the south. Mesut hoped to grab the battlefield jab as a wrestler immobilizes an attacker by trapping a wayward arm or leg. Force would be met with superior force and no ground could be given at this point.

"To the south!" the commander's grisly voice called over the ruins of the great wall. "Show them why whole nations fear us!"

When the Christian advance came into the breach, Iskender ran to the rubble for coverage. A huge advance of armoured knights passed him; some holding spears and on horseback, others on foot with swords or crossbows. There were few other Janissaries near him, in the wake of the cavalry advance.

"There he is!" Constantine proclaimed once the advance party reached the edge of the breach. "Pick him up, and let's get back to camp!"

The Venetians, bolts ready and swords drawn, were most eager to do so, and they hoisted the Genoese's body onto a horse, and started a hurried retreat back to their camp.

"He's still alive!" Adam called out when he brought Guistiniano up to the horse. "Barely, though."

"That's providence, God's protecting us!" The emperor announced triumphantly. "Bring him to Chora, the rest of you, regroup at the camp!"

With less collective grace than the Janissary horde, the unwieldy mix of Italians and Greeks turned on itself and eventually faced back into the city. With much shouting and stumbling, they prepared to hurry home. By the time they were ready to start, the Ottoman elites had sturdied themselves amongst the rubble and waited for the Romans to come to them.

The Janissaries caught the retreating Genoese cavalry side-on and at a full charge. The red and white uniforms of the corps crashed into the horse and foot of the grey steel armour-clad knights, and scimitars met broadswords while foot surprised horse. The charging, killing strength of the horsemen had lost both surprise and momentum when they unthreaded the needle and re-tramped the same way they had charged. Carrying their honoured commander over the laden ground, their enemies were ready for them and thirsted for their blood.

The horses couldn't gallop over the rubble and through the crowds. A crossbow couldn't parry a scimitar's slash. The two armies bogged down into rubble and began the crime against peace that would take so many more lives. The defending armies had now lost their bottleneck.

What an opportunity this presented for Iskender. He was hardly an archer *par excellence*, owing to his nearsightedness, but clustered groups of enemy soldiers took away the need for accuracy, so he could rely less on luck and aim, and more on speed and probability now. He quickly, and admittedly randomly, let arrow after arrow fly into armoured clusters of knights, and into the ranks of the cavalry that were trying to retreat past his newfound sniping roost.

The randomness of his grand effort came to a halt when a noble spirit emerged from the hazy blur of anonymous figures. Draped in red and purple, with a golden crown upon his head and a sword held aloft, charged the noblest prince in Christendom, and the most valuable target for any of his comrades: Emperor Constantine the Eleventh.

"Bismillah," Iskender whispered as he quickly drew the string of his short bow.

The sinew-string, made of hemp and tempered with bee's wax and animal fat, flung the arrow over the composite bow at a velocity of slightly over two hundred feet per second, slowing down to half that before it came to an abrupt halt after piercing the emperor's throat and lodging between the vertebrae of his neck.

Constantine's neck fell back and the arrow bent skyward from its neck-lodged pivot. There was a thunderous reaction from the Janissaries before the Christians knew what was happening.

Iskender felt as though his heart were about to take wings, but he didn't take the opportunity to celebrate. He kept loading and reloading his bow until all of the arrows in his quiver were gone, and then he drew his sword as the last of the retreating knights passed by. Even after the field was taken and the enemies had moved on, his mind was still in the battle. He didn't notice when his commander arrived to inspect the victory.

"Where is he? Where is that archer?" Mesut demanded once the defenders had retreated from the breach. "Who was it that shot down the prince of the unbelievers? Which one of you?"

The men of the orta all enthusiastically brought him to Iskender, who was bent over, trying to catch his breath after following the enemies out of the rubble jungle.

"Iskender!" Mesut exclaimed joyously and embraced the young recruit. "Your first year in the orta and you've made history, My Soy! Bless you!"

"Thank you, Father," the plague-rattled waif began, before his commander cut him off again.

"Now everyone form a line again!" he commanded with enthusiasm. "They're in a panic, we have to hit them now and hit them hard! Make a line and move together! When we make it to the plain of the city we'll surprise the hell out of them and make them run. The city is ours! We're the first! The city is yours! The honour is yours! The glory is yours! Form a line!"

With trained discipline, the six hundred men of the eighth orta quickly formed a line and began the charge to the city side of the mesotechion. The panic ridden defenders were in no condition to resist them.

"I'm taking Longo to Grace of God Hospital in the Venetian quarter," Vincent said to Adam once they'd escaped the breach. "He'll get medical attention there, and the Turks won't advance on Venice, we've still got treaty rights."

"Are you insane?" Karian screamed as a response. "If you leave here, your troops will go with you!"

"That's the idea, Adam!" Vincent retorted. "The wall's fallen! They're coming! Escape while you can and look out for your men! These Turks aren't here to take prisoners."

"You filthy coward! You're abandoning us! Just like that whelp Stavros said!"

"Your emperor is dead, your wall's down and your city in ruins! What do you want? Your citizens have barely stood up to defend it! You've left it all to us, and now you want to blame us? Well fuck you, Karian! You Armenians, and Greeks, and Slavs can all go to hell for all I care!"

And with that, the command was given.

Pull back. Abandon the mortars and trebuchets where they were. Load the wounded in stretchers, and pull back to the quarter. Through the hasty retreat, Karian was cursing the Italian peninsula and all its inhabitants, but he knew that it was the right move to make.

"Men," he was forced to announce, "back to the Petrion. We can't hold ground here. We've got to fall back to the palace and send emissaries to the Turks."

"The Emperor," a soldier asked.

"No time," Stavros stepped in. "Give me his crown. Put his body on the horse and get him away from here. Hide him among the dead. Don't let the Turks identify his body."

While Karian didn't like the idea of someone as vulgar as Stavros of Brusa handling the imperial diadem, hiding the body would be a priority for the rest of the morning. A general retreat was sounded.

When the Janissaries emerged from the rubble, to the city side of the breach, they were primed, fresh and ready for a fight. They found an empty plain with two retreating companies of soldiers; one heavily armed heading to the east, and one not so well armed and armoured heading to the north at a much faster pace.

"Which way, Commander?" Iskender asked Mesut.

"Stay here, hold ground," he said instantly. "Send standard bearers up to the tops of the two towers on either side of the breach, I want every soldier who enters the city in conquest to pass under the banner of the eighth. The day's ours. Send the messengers to the other end to call the army forth. The city's fallen."

Julian the Apostate had been the last Emperor of the Eastern Roman Empire to ride into battle while in the purple. He fought the Persians and died from wounds received at the battle of Maranga in AD 363. Things were different now, the Eastern Emperors wore red shoes, not purple robes to signify their position, and they certainly did not leave the palace for anything that hadn't been planned years prior.

Julius Claudius Julianus had also been the last non-Christian to wear the imperial diadem, and did so with paganic pride. His rejection of the tradition of his predecessors in the Constantinian Dynasty was complete when he forsook the drab carpenter's faith for antiquated loyalty to Jupiter and Mars. In some ways he was a terrible cap on a great Christian dynasty, in other ways tried to return antiquity's soul to the East.

What Julian was to the house of Constantine the Great, Constantine the Eleventh, Constantine the Last, would be to the Palaeologi. Leaving the palace as a memory, the former monk from Mystra donned armour for the first time in his life at age forty eight and rode out to defend the empire with his own hand. A hero's death is a right for anyone, from a lowly foot soldier like Hassan to an emperor like Constantine. Blood follows blood, and glory never dies. It never passes with the cycles of seasons or the passages of days.

Julian's last words were the vile spitting of "*Vicisti, Galilee! – You've won, Galilean.*" He knew that with his death, the empire would fall into the vulgar arms of Christianity and the glory, culture and honour of her past would be 'ere forgotten. His death signaled a new era and inevitable era. Constantine gave Muhammad's band no such epitaph.

This day was still far from over.

Chapter Forty-Eight - Morning

9:00 am – 12:00 am

"**G**ood God," Ezera whispered a silent prayer as he watched the destruction from across the harbour. "Protect us all."

"Indeed," Tolga answered him, substituting himself into the conversation in place of the almighty. "We should all pray a prayer for Constantinople. The noblest of cities, it seems, is about to be ravished by the marching slum which Zaganos will let loose."

"You know," Ezera/Ayoub began, "You're an ally of Zaganos, but you don't seem to share the angry man's enthusiasm for all this."

"I'm dedicated to ideals, Ayoub. He's dedicated to earthly alliances. I have more patience for a virtuous enemy than an unscrupulous ally. He thinks that those calling themselves Muslims should have dominion over the earth, regardless of anything else." the emir had a faraway look in his eye. He focussed himself on the boats in the harbour, and the tribesmen about them watching the drama across the water. "I respect God's dominion over humanity. If God wanted everyone to be Muslim, everyone would be. If God wanted everyone to be right-handed, again everyone would be. If God wanted everyone to be honest, everyone would be so. You get the idea. God allows for differences, ergo God loves the infinite variety of his own creation. If someone chooses to be honest, instead of dishonest, that's wonderful and they should be honoured; likewise if someone chooses to be Muslim rather than, oh say, Christian, Jewish or Zoroastrian, they should likewise be honoured. I want to see the city become Muslim, not rubble."

"You put thieves in prison, and chop the heads of murderers, why punish them rather than accepting their difference as being directed by God."

"That's a silly argument, Ayoub," Tolga dismissed the old pirate's attempt at philosophy without so much as a second thought. "Thieves are jailed and murderers killed to protect the rest of society from them, not punish the criminal. But back to the city. God surely guided the first Christian emperors of Rome to build this monument to civilization. Inside those walls are buildings devoted to God's grandeur, that have never been equalled anywhere between Al-Andalus and Cathay."

"So you believe that God can guide Christians? I thought that you – sorry, we Muslims were supposed to hate the infidels."

"When you were a Christian, were you taught by your priest to hate

642

the Jewish prophets? Moses, Adam, Noah, Abraham and the rest of them?"

"No, of course not."

"Of course not, the religion of Israel was an early form of God's purer faith of Christianity. It was inspired, it just needed to be refined into Christianity, and completed as Islam. It's my hope that when my liege Mehmet becomes prince of this city, he'll refine the city to God's purpose, and correct the faith of the faulty."

"Do you think he will?"

"No, I think that he'll listen to Zaganos and the divan will tell him what they think he wants to hear. Destroy the infidel where you find him and build a monument to God anew. Such a waste."

"What do you think about forcing me into Islam?"

"You chose."

"Not very nice choices."

"True, but it was your choice, nonetheless. When all of this is over, you'll have the choice again, you can flee to Christian lands or stay here in the House of Peace. There's an offer for you that we'll discuss later this evening, once things calm down. You can believe anything you want, or deny anything you want. I'd council you against denying anything too publically, that can be dangerous, but choice isn't something that anyone can give or take away. I hope that you'll choose to stay, to learn about Islam, and to someday believe. I hope that you'll have dozens of sons, and they can be brought up in the faith. I forced nothing upon you, Ayoub. I offered you a choice out of a jail cell where you would be until the guards grew bored of feeding you, and a new life. I hope that you don't begrudge me for the offer."

"No, I don't. I'm grateful." Ezera replied before lightening the mood. "And I also hope that my dozen sons await me in the future, and not the past, spread out over a hundred countries."

They both shared a brief chuckle. Tolga got some vicarious enjoyment out of his servant's tales of drunken debauchery around the known world.

"You once told me that no rational man is wholly religious," Ayoub said, referencing his liberation from Roman Castle.

"Earthly religions are corrupt human institutions, I believe in God and the innate sense of morality that he gave each one of us. We all know, deep down that murder is wrong, and that helping the poor is right. It's just rational nature to believe that. Believing that there are three aspects of God, two natures, seven cardinal virtues and more saints than any of us

643

can count, is a purely human theological construct that I want no part of. I consider myself to be obedient to God, not partisan to any human faction. By my experience, rational faith is consistent with the cultural norms of Islam, and I identify myself that way. It's about cosmogony and truth, more than culture."

"I suppose."

"There goes our commander," Tolga segued out of their conversation and brought them back to the battle at hand.

All the horses of the Pera Hill Army were laden down with two riders apiece and were commanded to run up to the headwaters of the Horne, cross, and charge on straight towards the city walls at the Palace District. The high-walled Petrion quarter had been immune to bombardment during the siege because of the heavier fortifications there, and also because Mehmet had intended to preserve the wealth of the Empire, as much as possible. No fighting had taken place there because the high walls were too intimidating to attack without bombardment.

Once the mesotechion fell, once the Janissaries had taken their first steps into the city, that all changed. The Petrion walls didn't go anywhere, but their defenders did. From across the river, everyone could see an army fleeing inside the city's walls. Over hills and along the crest of the peninsula, the flags of Genoa and Venice fled from the wall, the two-pointed sword of the Janissaries, and the three crescent moons of the Ottomans took their place. The attackers now had little to worry about.

"Do you think they'll get in?" Ayoub asked Tolga.

"Eventually. Without any defenders, time is all that will mater."

They watched the horseback Army of Pera disembark peaceably at the first gate of the palace district and accost the Gate. It was locked, but a sturdy door doesn't stand long against thousands of intending guests. The soldiers battered the door down with a ram and hurried into the Petrion on foot.

"It's almost over," Tolga said while watching. "Thank God for that. Let's get the fleet ready, we'll be expected to cross over soon."

"Court!" Stavros commanded to the assembled noblemen and women of the Imperial Court. He stamped his feet as he walked into the room and wasn't prepared to surrender any momentum to debate just yet. "Assemble quickly. I need a word."

The dour-looking men and even dourer-looking women trotted into an assembly in front of the strateogos.

"The Emperor is dead! God bless him. The flames are no longer smouldering at the gate but burning inside our house. Unless you want to stand in the fire and burn, we need to act quickly so here's my plan:

"First, you all must unanimously and spontaneously proclaim me to be the new emperor. Then I fly the flag of parlay and meet with the sultan. I'll agree to pay whatever tribute must be paid to keep the city and then we dedicate the empire to union with the West. We will have to, at least temporarily, accede to their religion to get proper military assistance and lead a crusade to remove the Muslims from Europe. There's no room for anything else now. Does anyone else have a better suggestion?"

There was silence from the normally talkative assembly of harpies.

"Alright then. Who would like to nominate me?"

A hand raised and one of Stavros' many cousins nominated him to the position. Another nameless courtier glumly seconded the nomination and the white flags of parley and surrender flew from the palace balconies.

"Where is Doctor Mario?" Karian demanded when he burst into the Chora compound with forty men from the Varangian Guard in tow. "I need to speak to him now!"

"He's gone! No one knows where!" the stout nurse cursed his very name to anyone who'd listen. "He ran off with that Italian nurse and the other Italian physician's gone from his bed as well!"

"What?" Karian couldn't believe her words at first. "They've all betrayed us?"

Karian was never a man to let fury superimpose itself over logic.

"What Italian nurse? What Italian doctor?"

"The nurse was the sister of some Italian soldier in the Venetian Quarter, I gather that her and Doctor Mario were betrothed. The other doctor's name was Felipé. He was a stranger who came here a few weeks ago."

"What did he look like?"

The nurse went on to describe the likeness of Hectore Pazzi in a fake beard. Adam made no motions to betray his thoughts, but returned to business quickly.

"I have here the body of the Emperor. He's dead, shot in the throat by a Turkish bow. I need you to place him amongst the dead. If we survive the day, we'll need to bury him properly, if the city falls, the Turks mustn't be allowed to identify him. If they do, they'll put his body on display in the forum, and turn him into a spectacle. I need him to disappear in a manner that he can be retrieved only if need be. Can you do that for me?"

The squat, angry nurse nodded fiercely at the grave task that was being given her.

"Good, now I need to check something. Varangians! Come with me!"

The party of Vikings followed their Armenian commandant into the women's chapel, a building that was now being used to hold injured men who had developed gangrene, a creeping necrosis that was incorrectly believed to be contagious.

The party pushed themselves through the sanctuary and passed by the nun-nurses who were watching over their wards. They made their way quickly to the altar and quickly moved the table aside. Before investigating the cache, Karian could tell right away that the hollow under the altar had been tampered with.

"Damn. Open it up," he quickly ordered the guards to do, and they readily obeyed.

The large marble block was pushed aside to reveal a hollow hollow, empty of its horde of gold, silver and treasure.

Around them, the frightened nurses looked on and then tried to busy themselves to their tasks. They weren't sure why these foreigners were despoiling their church, but certainly no good could come of it.

It was at this point that Adam lost any willingness to obey the rules of decorum and decency. He marched over to the first nurse he could find.

"Doctor Mario Orsini! Where is he?"

"I... I don't know," she answered quickly.

"Then what of his woman? Where can I find the Lady Ella DiCastillo? Can you answer me that, Love?"

The frightened nurse shook here head in panic, and another nurse stepped in to answer the question for her.

"No one knows where they went!" she answered boldly. "Now let us get back to our duty! You must do the same! There are Turks everywhere and you're trying to brawl with brides of Christ!"

"Someone has to know!" Adam yelled. "I'm going to tear this hospital apart until I either find them, or at least someone who knows!"

A scuffle broke out at the door to the assembly hall of Blachernae Palace. The castellans had been told quite deliberately not to quarrel with the Turkish delegation, and the commotion perturbed Stavros as he stood on the dais, waiting for the emissary to come.

The senior castellan ran quickly towards the dais and prostrated himself.

"Your imperial majesty, a representative from the Turks. *Zaganos-pasha* wishes an audience."

"I wish for no such thing!" came an angry shout from the second minster of the Ottoman state. "I make demands of those who call themselves 'Emperors by Christ!' I make no requests, and ask for no permission and I seek no favours! Where is Constantine? Where is the emperor? I have seen his face before and it is not you!"

Short, hairless and full of destructive energy, Zaganos-Pasha was like a clothed barrel of black-powder with arms, legs and a sword. His command of the language of the court left little doubt as to his origins and his comportment left little doubt as to his intent.

"Alas, Constantine has been called to God. I am Stavros, general of the legions and basileus of the eastern empire…"

"Congratulations!" Zaganos replied sarcastically. "If you're lucky, your new master, Mehmet the Second, khan of khans, king of kings and now master of Constantinople, will allow you to stay on as a titular head, but I doubt it. He'll probably simply have you killed and be done with it."

"You've been invited here to discuss the terms of surrender."

"Invited? I've had no such honour, your majesty. I'm here because the soldiers of the faithful now run free over the city. You are the general of no armies and the emperor of no empire!"

"We would like to discuss tribute with your master. We invite him to this chamber to…"

"There is to be no agreement on tribute, Christian," Zaganos spoke in a perfect, formal Greek, mixed with a concoction of rage and resentment that made everyone in the assembly hall quite uncomfortable. "You are all under arrest in the name of God. You've denied the true faith of the compassionate and merciful God, as explained by the last prophet, Muhammad, and you've made war against those who've promoted and protected the faith. We're here to take you as a prisoner, and we'll present you to the sultan when he arrives. Everyone else in the hall, you're now slaves! You'll address me, and any other Ottoman officer, as master and you'll do as you're told or you'll be killed. Don't worry, your condition won't last long, I fully intend to sell you to Rome, or Venice, or Genoa; whoever will pay your ransom can have you back. Until then, this gilded hall is your prison, and if anyone tries to run, they'll be killed. Does everyone understand?"

Silence held court for the first time in Blachernae's history.

Zaganos turned his back to Stavros and walked over to the first of the black-coated courtiers and grabbed him roughly by the collar.

"I didn't hear you."

He then thrust a dagger into the man's belly with too much speed for anyone to see the act done and then ripped the blade up the length of his victim's chest. People realised the murder only when their tormentor withdrew the blooded knife from the man's belly held it high for all to see. He then walked over to the next one and grabbed him by the scruff of his neck.

"Do you understand?"

"Yes," he answered quickly.

"Does everyone understand?" Zaganos repeated with frantic volume.

This time everyone did.

"Now, who will be so kind as to show me to the treasury?"

"Come with me, Sir," Olaf instructed Adam.

The general was not accustomed to taking orders from a subordinate, but the situation was far from normal.

"What is it?"

"Come with me, Sir," Olaf repeated and motioned towards the ossuary.

Adam reluctantly accompanied the senior Varangian to the monastery's bone house.

"What is it, Olaf?" Karian demanded, reclaiming his gravitas.

"Money. Treasure. And an empty hole," Olaf answered with disquieting calmness.

"We're looking."

"Your friends disappeared into the night?"

"They weren't my friends, they've stolen from all of us."

"You'd originally planned to share the treasure with the Italian."

"That was a long time ago," Karian answered dismissively. "He's stolen it."

"Maybe we should be looking across the harbour."

"We can't exactly cross the harbour right now, can we?" Adam was getting indignant at the Varangian's insistence, perhaps dangerously so. He was embarrassed that his plan hadn't worked out properly. He was embarrassed that he'd been robbed by at least one of his former associates. It's a rough feeling, being in command and having others suffer for your mistakes. It's enough to drive anyone of conscience in a managerial role straight to sociopathy.

"I think we can, there's a war going on, nobody's looking for a few dozen guards and a disgraced former general."

Adam didn't much care for such a description.

"It would be much harder to find one soldier, a doctor and a nun!"

"Then perhaps it's best if we just cut our losses and collect as much as we can."

"You mean run?"

"Not exactly. There'll be a bounty on your head soon enough, general."

"How dare you even suggest..."

"We've been talking, general," Olaf continued his thought. "and we've decided that the ransom of a general to the Grand Turk should be more than enough to finance our safe trip back home."

"You traitors," Adam seethed. "Just like that filthy mercenary..." his voice trailed off into thought and found a line of reasoning. "Two of the three who've run off with the treasure have homes in the Venetian Quarter. Mario Orsini has a home there. Remember, I sent you and Svend to fetch him a few months ago. He's the physician to the Venetian ambassador and the chief pharmacologist at the Grace of God Hospital. The woman, his woman, is the sister of Vincent DiCastillo, a Spanish mercenary in the employ of the Republic of Venice. The Turks are in the city, so the only safe place to be once the looting starts will be in the Venetian or Genoese Concessions - which is exactly where DiCastillo ran off to. They'll go to the Quarter now and try to sail over to Galata once things calm down."

Olaf was taken aback by the momentum of Adams thoughts.

"Send five guards to the harbour to try and find them if they try to escape. The rest of you'll come with me. We're going to the Quarter."

"To do what? We're only twenty men! fifteen when I send some to the harbour!"

"We'll burn down the embassy if we have to and crucify DiCasillo if need be, but we're going to get what's ours!" Hatred was burning its embers through Adam Karian's mind.

Zaganos tapped his foot impatiently while he waited for the chamberlain to find the right keys to the vault. The imperial treasury was a series of chambers of mythic proportions. When visiting emissaries from barbarian tribes would come, be they Goths, Huns or Bulgars, they would always receive a tour of the palace's bank, as that was known to impress everybody.

The chamberlain finally managed to roll the two adjoining tumblers over to open the great bronze door and open the entrance to the gate. The metal plate pushed back with much coaxing from those assembled and the treasury chambers were opened for all to see.

The second minister walked brazenly into the inner sanctum of once-proud empire.

"Where is it all?" he had to ask.

The chamberlain wasn't completely surprised at the contents of the first chamber. The wealth of the empire had been steadily dwindling for as long as he could remember. The legends of wall-to-wall treasure had always seemed a tad comical to the ears of those who knew the truth. There were still works of art on the walls, gold-laid furniture and shelves with hundreds of scrolls, containing the financial documents of a thousand year tradition, but that seemed somewhat empty. The series of labelled chests that contained gold ingots and bullion seemed to be absent from the main room.

Zaganos, who'd read about the room from the journals and notes of a long pedigree of travellers, resisted his first instinct of flying into a fit and decided to investigate the two neighbouring rooms. All three rooms were high ceilinged chambers with no windows and very thick walls. They had to be lit by torches and lanterns. The dark inside them did little to hide their emptiness.

The second chamber contained mechanical devises. Metal lions, tigers and cheetahs would roar when their tortional springs were wound. There was more large art and furniture, and no gold. The third chamber proved to be equally anti-climactic. It seemed as though every piece of portable wealth had been carried away some time ago.

Rather than speak, Zaganos snapped his finger and pointed at the chamberlain without looking. Three of his men were upon him in an instant. They threw him against a wall and held him there for Zaganos to speak to.

"Where is the rest of it, Chamberlain?"

"Please, sir, I don't know," he said with frightened tones. "This is the first time I've been here in years."

"Don't lie to me, those bastards upstairs are alive because someone will pay for their release, no one cares about you, so we'll either kill you or let you go. Which one we do depends entirely on how you answer my questions here. Now, where is the rest of it?"

"I told you, I don't know! Please, Sir! I'll do anything! I'll convert!

I'll tell you anything else I know, but I don't know what's happened here."

"Break his arm."

One of the men who was holding him against the wall hooked his arm in a joint lock and began to hyper-rotate the chamberlain's shoulder socket. The tendon's in his rotator pulled and stretched between the bones like the spring of a mechanical lion, but didn't tear. They were only supposed to feel as though they were about to tear.

"There are three keys!" he finally answered.

"That's good," Zaganos replied with biting simplicity. "So where are the other two?"

"The emperor has one," the chamberlain was crying by this point, "and the general has the other!"

"Go bring me that little man who wears the crown," Zaganos instructed one of the soldiers nearby before returning to the interrogation. "And who is the general of whom you speak?"

"Adam Karian!"

"I see, and where can I find this '*Adam Karian*?'"

There was light at the end of the darkness. Measuring time without any visual record of events is almost impossible, so Ahmet had no idea how many hours had passed in the shivering cold of the sewers. Always walking with a wall to his right hand side, he'd run the fear of walking in a circle, if he'd found a track that was closed. He had no way of telling direction. All he could do was hope that he was on the correct side, judging by the rising and falling of the pathway, in accordance with the vicissitudes of the hills of the peninsula.

When he finally saw something, he rejoiced in his own mind at the discovery that his eyes still worked. The path upon which he was walking eventually led to a sluice gate that emptied into a public reservoir near Eis Pegas Gate.

The simple joy that entered Ahmet when he saw the distant light, the first thing that he'd seen in hours, was hard to imagine. He hurried down the invisible walkway, limping faster than he probably should have, such was the excitement of the prospect of escape.

He eventually reached a metal grate door; a sewage service entrance next to the public fountain. When he could put his long arms through the grate to feel warmth of the day, he smiled. He lost the smile once he realised that there was no way to open to door without a key, but being trapped here was better than being trapped in the dark.

He thought to call out for help, but he didn't know the Greek word for '*help*.'

He'd have to wait here and shiver in the cold for a bit longer, until someone came along. He'd then have to either pretend to be a mute or a fool, until someone could let him out, and then he'd be on his way to do his duty and kill the sultan when he entered the city. He hoped that he hadn't missed the auspicious event.

He also hoped that no children came along and found him. He thought that he would give them nightmares of a dangerous monster that lived in the sewers, and they'd never be able to sleep again. He laughed at the dark humour of accidentally scaring children.

At least he could laugh now, he was out of the deep cold umbra, and the sun was high in the sky.

Noon was approaching.

Chapter Forty-Nine – Noon

12:00 am – 2:00 pm

Oghlen prayers rang from the mosque in the Turkish pan-handle of Constantinople, calling the faithful to their second prayer of the day. On most days, the conclusion of the noon-time prayer would insinuate not only community's observance, but it would call to court all of the elders of Orhan's court. They would prostrate themselves towards Mecca; the Ka'aba in Mecca was the focal point of Muslim piety, and would then feel pure enough to go about the onerous duties of homage, fealty and obedience to the man who could be king.

That had always been a real option with Orhan. Since the days of his childhood, he had always been favoured by his grandfather, Mehmet the First, also known as Mehmet the Gentleman, Mehmet the 'Support Pillar' and the unofficial second founder of the Ottoman state. It was Old Mehmet who wrestled control of the empire away from warring factions, and united it under his rule. It was he who'd moved the capital from Brussa to Adrianople, away from the internecine warfare of the Turkish tribes and into the hinterland of Europe, where the action was and where the gazis collected. It was he who'd sired enough children to repopulate an entire city with his own kin.

It was his fear that the empire could one day find itself without a legitimate heir, so he claimed a privilege to father as many children as God would allow. A duty that he undertook with all appropriate severity. Because of his enthusiasm for the task, the empire would never be without pretenders to the throne, and Orhan's role would be to step into the palace of Adrianople in the event of something unfortunate happening to his Uncle Murad's children. Sure enough, all of Sultan Murad's fit children died but one, and all under less than transparent circumstances. The only survivor other than Mehmet was mentally deficient and not allowed out of the harem. A child himself and a childless sultan, Mehmet the Second had already been deposed once, and Orhan's potential was always a factor to consider.

As the prayers ended, Orhan walked out of the mosque into the stark midday sun and looked around. The world seemed different.

Courtiers slowly filed out of the mosque behind their prince, and then approached him to show their respect as they normally did daily, but today they did so with less bounce in their steps. Today, they were slow in their saunter and graceless in their words and kisses. When the full coterie of

653

the court had assembled in the forum outside the mosque, Orhan addressed them. Everyone knew that today was an auspicious day. They could see raiders in the neighbouring districts and everyone was thinking about their own lives, rather than those of a faction that now seemed all but lost.

"Friends, Muslims, Brothers, listen to me," he began. "The soldiers of our unworthy cousin Mehmet come after us. They are here to kill me, and I have no doubt that whomsoever accomplishes that foul murder will be richly rewarded by Mehmet, the false son of Murad, the false son of my beloved grandfather, Mehmet. If it were any of you who betrayed me and turned me over, I would bear you no ill will, and I would pray that God forgave you the wretched disloyalty, as it would seem the rational thing to do in this chaotic time."

Orhan had anticipated an outcry of denials and protestations of loyalty at that point. None came and the crowd was silent. That silence worried the prince, who decided to get to the point quickly and not give those assembled too much time to think things over.

"We pray five times every day towards the Ka'aba, in the Holy City of Mecca. It was there that God's final prophet began his teaching, and it was there where the soldiers of the ignorant first came hunting for him. They came for him in the middle of the night, and his son-in-law Ali warned him, ushered him out of the house, and took his place in bed, so that when the soldiers came and found him, they found Ali instead. The Prophet Muhammad, peace be upon him, had fled to safety in Medina."

The story of the Hijra, the migration of the original group of Muslims loyal to Muhammad, was so integral to Islam that the date of it marks year one of the Muslim Calendar, 622 years after year one of the Christian Calendar and 4382 years after the Jewish Calendar.

"I plan to flee," Orhan announced after proclaiming precedent. "I've been offered sanctuary in Galata, across the water, and invite you to come with me. But we need someone to stay, to wear my clothes, and pretend to be me. Someone to take the role first performed by the future Caliph, Ali, Peace be Upon Him. Who would volunteer themselves for this honour? Who would risk their life without a sword in hand, to stand against an army so strong, and know that because they were protected by God, they would be invulnerable? Who among you is ready for such a responsibility?"

Silence again.

"Ishaq?" he quickly pointed out a less-than-enthused looking youth. "Will you take this duty, before God?"

The young man blushed and nodded.

"Alright then, those who would come with me, be here in half an hour, we'll pay a ferryman's tithe in gold and flee to Genoa. You're all dismissed."

Orhan hurried quickly to his home with the conscripted youth in tow. He needed out of the Venetian Panhandle quickly.

"Your Excellency, the commander of the army is here to see you," the announcement came quietly, as the servant knew, as did everyone else in the embassy, of his master's grave malady.

Giovanni Cardillo coughed an answer, nodded his head and motioned with his hand that he wished an audience be granted post haste. Balias was at his side but habitually chose silence in the presence of decision makers, be they Isaac, Giovanni, or anyone else with a vision for leadership.

"Vincent," the ambassador mumbled in a gravelly whisper. "Pardon me, for I cannot stand. You'll have to come closer to me, because I can't speak loudly or hear too well. What's happening at the wall?"

"The wall's fallen, Don Giovanni," he answered in a businesslike tone.

Perhaps because he'd been watching the ambassador's health deteriorate for the past two years, he was only aware of its more immediate effects when he was away from his patron for long periods of time. Cardillo's skin was now a pallid and unnatural shade of grey-pink, and his eyes seemed lost in shadows. This was truly a man close to death.

"The gaps were exposed yesterday afternoon, I sent a messenger to tell you of this. We fought through the night against them, and then at daybreak they charged through with their heavy infantry. The Emperor Constantine is now dead, the Greek army fled to the Petrion, we don't know how they're doing in the Imperial Quarter, but they're probably not doing well, if they're still resisting at all. I've collected the Venetian garrison and the remaining Genoese mercenaries and withdrawn to here. The wounded have been brought to the Grace of God Hospital, Guistiniano is among them. I imagine that he'll live, but he was shot with a dart and then trampled by horses."

"He's strong," Giovanni's voice was barely above a whisper.

"Yes, sir," Vincent conceded quickly. "The Turks are now in the city. They've broken through the mesotechion and the Pera forces are going to the Petrion. As I said, we don't know how long that will last, but we think that they'll finish securing the wall before they invade the rest of the city.

They'll have to occupy Psarmathia before they push their way to our walls."

"The walls will hold,"

Vincent was silent for a moment, and considered his answer delicately.

"No, sir. The great wall's fallen, our little wooden stockades won't keep them at bay for more than a few hours. We need to negotiate a surrender."

"I don't think that he understands you, commander," Balias said at last. "He's been slipping in and out of lucidity for a few days now."

"A fine time to lose his grip," Vincent swore. "You have your papers from the Senate, don't you?"

"Me? I'm here as an envoy from the senate to the Eastern Empire. I don't have…"

"The emperor's dead, there's no court left, and there are no ships that can take you back home just now. You'll have to speak to the Turks."

"Surely you know the situation better than I."

"Yes, I do. I'll be with you at the table, but I'm not an officer of the Republic, all of my decisions and commitments are subject to the approval of the ambassador, who, as you see, is not up to the task."

"I've never negotiated anything in my life! My brothers handles these things."

"Well you're going to have to start now because your brother won't be speaking to anybody if I can help it! Refugees are going to be coming into the quarter as fast as their legs can carry them. We've got to organize some housing in the quarter, transportation to get them out of here, food and water which now all comes out of territory controlled by the Turks. We're probably going to have to pay an extortionate tribute to the Sultan in order to keep the trade concession here, but there's no way they'll honour our political and military rights here the way the emperor did. The empire had spent the last thousand years dying. These Turks are just being born."

"What do I do?"

"First, summon a scribe or secretary," Giovanni spoke up from his death-like silence. "Then record the terms of surrender that you're willing to offer. I'll dictate them. You probably won't be remembered fondly for this back home."

"I can live down a forced surrender, but I don't want to give away the concession, it's one of the most important trading centres in the eastern seas."

"It's slipped from Constantine's grip," Giovanni was interrupted by a fit of coughing before he could continue. "You'll have to take what we can get and be happy with that. I'll have my men run up the colours for truce, and try to arrange a meeting with their commanders."

"Wait!" Balias was confused and angry. He didn't want to be known for signing away one of the brightest jewels on Venice's fingers. Regrettably, he knew that it was his destiny to be such. "No, you're right, set up the meeting. You'll have to be with me. Do we have a Turkish translator?"

"All negotiations in the east are done in Greek, Captain." DiCastillo assured him. "Do you speak Greek?"

"No. I studied at the university, but I don't think I could speak the language as a conversational tongue. Can you speak it?"

"Yes."

"Good. Good, then," Balias tried to reclaim the dignity that his temporary confusion denied him. "DiCastillo, make the arrangements."

Vincent nodded and prepared to leave the room. He looked sadly at the still living shell of the ambassador and felt bad. He'd seen so much death today, but it had all been lively and hot-blooded. It seemed so much more comfortable to go quickly and with honour and glory, than quietly like Giovanni.

"God bless you, Sir."

Cardillo looked at him with what would almost be interpreted as a sly or disapproving glance. Even towards the end, the old man was unrepentant on that topic.

Vincent bowed to him and then left the room.

While Vincent and Balias were conspiring to surrender, Orhan stood alone at the pier. No one had come with him. It could have been far worse, no one had come to arrest him and claim bounty, but of the almost two hundred courtiers who'd been waiting on him for the past ten years, not one would join him as a refugee.

They'd already spent ten years as refugees. Well financed refugees, Orhan's court received a yearly allowance from Adrianople of a hundred and fifty thousand akches of silver; certainly more than enough for the most loyal to be comfortable in their exile. It became apparently to the prince very quickly how fickle those purchased loyalties really were.

Alone was best, he supposed. It gave him anonymity. There was no one to call him by his proper titles and prostrate themselves before his presence, so there was no way for anyone to know who he was. He would be able to purchase passage on a ferryboat to Galata, and he'd be dining with Count Dominic tonight. There, the Genoese would certainly be able to understand his worth. Certainly more than these Romans, who cast him into a dockside slum and forgot about him. Certainly better than those fair-weather friends who smiled in the mosque, kissed his hand in public and then scattered like cockroaches when the light of day came. No, alone was definitely best.

The docks were in absolute chaos.

There was a chaos around him that circled in a vortex of languages and panic. There were Turkish ships landing along the docks of the upper and middle Horne, ever coming nearer to the panhandle. The ships docked and Turkish foot soldiers disembarked and hurriedly ran in through the many harbour gates. The Turkish soldiers were running past the fleeing refugees and paying them no heed.

'*The battle must be over now,*' he thought to himself. '*The fighting is done, and now the tribes are trying to loot as much as they can before the Janissaries can restore order.*'

"In the boat, hurry, go," the boatswain of the ferryboat was hurrying people along into the vessel collecting an extortionate dirham of silver from each refugee who wanted aboard.

"Not so fast, Mustafa," he said when Orhan tried to pay and follow suit. "They won't let you into Galata, Turk. Back to the panhandle. Next!"

"I have an invitation from Count Dominic Trebianno himself," Orhan proclaimed, but was accosted by the angry refugees who only now realised that they had a Turk amongst them. Multicultural sensitivity was waning during the violence of the siege and tempers were short.

"Sure you do! And I've got an invitation for drinks from the sultan after a hard day's work! Now get your ass out of here!"

The angry and frightened people on the docks became angrier, pulling their hair and gnashing their teeth. Orhan was forced to fear for his life and he fled the pier for the safety of the harbour side chaos.

In front of the Gate of Saint John, he saw the flagship of the Ottoman navy were taking berth. Aboard it were three flags: the three crescent moons of the Ottoman state, the green banner with white Arabic proclaiming that there was no god but God and that Muhammad was his prophet, and a third flag, the purple and white of the Emirate of Sinope.

"Tolga!" Orhan exclaimed out loud. He recognised the colours of his benevolent uncle, a man who would never cast him aside. His luck was finally changing.

Orhan ran as quickly as he could to the ship, shouting at it to get the attention of his uncle.

"Tolga-Amja! Uncle Tolga!" he cried.

Tolga heard the shouting of his name over the chaos and looked about, trying to determine from where it was coming. No one on the ship would call his name, Ayoub bore the sole responsibility for the affairs on the water. The shouting was coming from somewhere on the docks. His eyes eventually focussed on a running fat man in his mid-thirties, with a comically gigantic moustache and unfitting clothes.

"God be praised, Orhan! Orhan? Is it truly you?" he was one of the first off the boat, soldiers piled out after him and raced into the city, hoping to find that the legends of gold and silver were true. "What are you doing on the pier?"

"Uncle Tolga, you've got to help me. When Mehmet comes, I'll be killed for sure! My council's abandoned me. Please! I'm the last contender from the line of Mehmet the Great. If I'm lost, then my cousin will cast the empire to fiery embers, with me on top. You have to help me!"

"Calm down, Nephew. You shouldn't be here. You should be in hiding. Is there nowhere for you to take refuge?"

"No. They've all forsaken me!"

"I can't help you, Orhan," Tolga said in frustration. "There's a bounty on your head of two hundred thousand akches to whoever brings you to Mehmet. Once they find you, you're done."

"You can hide me in your ship."

"When the soldiers come back, they'll figure out who you are. Your bounty is higher than that offered for the Emperor Constantine!"

"Then I can't go back, they'll turn me over without a splinter of thought."

"You have to get on one of the ferries to Galata."

"I can't! They won't let me on! I'm Muslim! They think that I'm either a spy or an enemy! I'm as much a refugee from Mehmet as anyone else! More so!"

"Then first get rid of turban and moustache, you stand out like a cow in chicken coop!" Tolga said. He tore the head-wrap from his nephew and threw it into the Horne, then counted out a handful of coins. "Now here's enough silver to make the damn ferryman stop asking questions. Go and don't look back."

"Bless you, Uncle. I'll pray for you."

"Pray that no one saw me speaking to you and no one tells your cousin! Pray that prayer once you're safely in Galata. Now go."

"God bless you!"

"Go!"

With the chaos of day's events, and the erratic movements of soldiers from one end of the city to another, no one took any notice of the Emperor's bodyguards crossing the stockade gates into the Venetian Quarter. They quickly traversed the forums and avenues to the centre of neighbourhood governance, the Venetian embassy.

Half mansion and half fortress, the embassy was built on a small plain near the cliffs of Acropolis Point. The façade was grey granite and red brick. It was normally staffed with a hundred bankers, accountants and officers of different trading houses and such. It also normally had a garrison of fifty guards, all of whom were now manning the stockades. The office functionaries were also absent, as the war had more than mildly hampered the city's international trade.

Arriving only minutes after Vincent's departure, Adam and the Varangians had no problems forcing an audience with the ambassador. They found that the ambassador had moved to the atrium, shivering under a blanket in the sun.

"Giovanni Cardillo, I am here to call you a liar and a thief!" Adam announced himself, more for the benefit of the potentially rebellious Vikings than to intimidate the ambassador, though that was motivation as well.

"What is the meaning of this?" Balias stood up to meet the accuser and his assembled coterie of violent-looking Norsemen. "The ambassador is ill, and shouldn't your soldiers be busy defending your Emperor?"

"Peace, Balias," Giovanni Cardillo spoke with icy calmness that seemed always to teeter at its tipping point. "What do you want, General Karian?"

"The emperor is dead," Adam couldn't help but loose emotional momentum when he announced those words. "The city is being looted by the children of Gog and Magog, and the treasury looted by Venetian deception!"

"We're busy here, we have no time for your complaints, General," Balias had met Adam a few times at court, but they'd said nothing to each other, other than the usual pleasantries of '*bless you*' and '*nice weather we're having.*'

"What do you mean, Adam?" Giovanni asked.

"Where is Vincent DiCastillo?" Adam demanded of Giovanni, not caring to address himself to the ambassador's protesting underling.

Giovanni stared glass-eyed at his accuser. He made an effort to seem strong and unmoving, but it was obvious to Karian that the old man was now beyond knowing too many details of what was going on. DiCastillo must have acted alone.

"Your name is Balias DiNapoli, isn't it?" he said turning to the underling.

"You know that it is!"

"I don't remember every pontificating Westerner who thinks that we Easterners should be impressed with your titles, your money and your greed. I don't care if you want to call yourself the Grand Duke of Christ's left testicle, but if you don't tell me exactly what I need to hear, then I'm going to turn you over to these Viking brutes behind me, who're going to rip the calf muscle off of your leg, cook it in basil sauce and feed it to you. I want to know where I can find Vincent. He has conspired to rob the treasury, and has made common cause with Hectore Pazzi, Doctor Mario Orsini, some unheard of monk and his Turkish bodyguard, in order to enrich himself. Now I've asked you as politely as I can, so now I'll ask as directly as I can: Where... is... he?"

"Commander DiCastillo is at the keep near the Theodosian Forum, he's trying to arrange a parlay with the Turks rather than fight them in the quarter. He's very busy. There are more important things happening today than some treasury problem," Balias answered.

"There will be no peaceful surrender of the quarter, Sir. Venice fought alongside the Empire, the Turks won't care that your senate didn't vote to go to war or not, they'll treat you and your precious 'republic' with all of the delicacy that I'll treat a burglar who creeps into my home intending to steal my gold and my family. Which is, by shocking coincidence, what you've tried to do to your own allies. I hope you all burn in hell for your sins. You're a republic of Judas, and may God be more merciful than I would be, given half a chance."

"You're excused, Strateogos," Balias said icily.

Karian turned his back on the Captain; an act of verboten rudeness. He looked at Olaf's cold blue eyes and thought to give the command for the execution of two members of court, and then decided against it. Come what may, he was still an officer of the Empire, and not some cheap-alley cut-throat. He might as well act like it, regardless of how he felt.

But he really wouldn't have felt bad if the Varangians took matters into their own hands at that point.

"Vincent wouldn't steal from anyone. He's too stubbornly righteous for that! You've been misled, General." Cardillo said from behind him, waves of sanity lapped up into his conversation before receding back into mists.

They stormed off angrily nonetheless, leaving the ambassador and the Count to prepare themselves to meet the Ottoman emissaries to negotiate a peaceful end to the war. This was turning into a terrible day for everyone who was not marching under the Ottoman banner.

"Hey! Hey!" Ahmet yelled. To his shock, the first person to pass by his line of sight since he found his way out of the sewers was a Turkish soldier, not a Greek pedestrian. "Help me!"

The soldier stopped at looked in disbelief to see one of his own trapped in some kind of prison.

"Peace be with you," he mumbled and approached Ahmet.

"And unto you be peace," Ahmet answered back cheerfully. It had been almost two months since he'd last been able to speak to someone properly in his mother tongue. "You have to help me out of here. I followed some rich man into here, and he double backed on me and locked me in the sewer!"

"Ha! You got fooled by an old man!" the looter laughed.

"Yeah, yeah," Ahmet answered in mock shame. "You've got to help me out of here. What's going on out there?"

"The Christian army's disappeared, the city's completely open, everyone's looting, and I want to get back to that quickly, so let's do this quickly."

The soldier took out a metal rod that was intended for twisting and breaking locks.

"This lock's thick, it might take a bit."

"Why don't you leave the rod with me, and you can get back to plunder?"

"It's a two man job and I'll need this back. I'll twist the lock, but you'll have to hold it in place. Can you grab this?"

"Of course."

With pressure applied by the soldier and maintained by Ahmet, the lock snapped in no time and Ahmet was free.

"Thanks," he said gratefully. "Has the Sultan's retinue come into the city yet?"

"I don't think so," the soldier answered. "He wanted to come through one of the gates in triumph, like the old Roman Emperors. Let him, I say. We've been given three days to grab what we can, and I'm not going to waste my time sight-seeing!"

"I don't blame you, thanks again. May God be as merciful to you on Judgement Day as you were to me today."

"If God wills it," the anonymous Samaritan suggested.

"If God wills it," Ahmet confirmed

Ahmet then hurried himself into the warm end-of-May sun. He was still soaking wet, his lips were blue, he was covered in caked blood and he was shaking from the cold, and the sun was gift from above. So, too, was the information about Mehmet's plans. The emperor would come in the gate closest to the palace, Charisius Gate, right next to Chora in the Petrion. Ahmet knew where he had to go now.

The only problems for the would-be-assassin now were the lack of weapons, a plan or knowledge of when Mehmet intended to enter the city. In all likelihood, he'd try to do that as quickly as possible. The Sultan was not exactly a patient man.

Ahmet's day was starting to improve.

Orhan walked morosely into the Panhandle. He'd been refused passage on three separate boats trying to cross the harbour, and he eventually decided to return to his mosque, there to await his captors.

Bareheaded, he walked down the dirty streets of the Turkish district and into the square before the Al-Aqsa Jami, the mosque was named after the Grand Mosque of Jerusalem, its name meant *The Furthest Place*.

Orhan could see the crowd assembled as he approached, but he kept his head down and paid them no heed. They were chanting and rejoicing at the '*liberation*' of the city, as they were welcoming the Muslim soldiers, and hoped that their homes would be spared the looting that would come unabated to Christian, Jew and Muslim alike.

"Where is the pretender?" demanded a soldier on horseback; A Sipahi Turk from far off Smyrna who rudely interrupted their politically adroit celebration. "He must be surrendered to us now!"

"He fled!" came the unanimous answer.

"He ran to Galata!" came an adjunct.

"We have no prince but Mehmet!"

"God protect Mehmet the Conqueror!"

"You protected Orhan!" the Sipahi chastised the crowd. "This community was the scabbard that held a dagger intended for the throat of your sultan for years! And now you think your new master will forget your old loyalties? Do you think he'll forgive you if you don't turn him over? He will not! How could he ever do that?"

"We have no prince but Mehmet!" the crowd called out in answer.

"I don't believe you! You're hiding him!" We're going to burn down the whole district! You'll all die alongside him! I hope you like flames, because that's how you'll be tormented for eternity! You've turned your back on the brotherhood of all believers! There is but one permanent punishment that's fit for you all!"

'*It would serve these traitors right, to allow them to die here,*' Ahmet thought with morbid delight. '*They forgot me, by what rights can I be commanded to remember them with anything but wrath?*'

The Sipahis started brandishing their horses and torches, people started panicking, and the panhandle was about to erupt in a flame of chaos before any physical fire spread.

"Wait!" Orhan called everyone to attention. "I'm here. I'm here to surrender myself to Mehmet, son of Murad... or whomever."

There was a static tension that collected in the Panhandle, as they saw that the prince they'd forgotten had not forgotten them.

'*The fools,*' he thought to himself. '*These ignorant peasants think that I've come back intentionally to spare them. Oh well, I might as well have some nobility in my surrender. The story might endear me to people for when Mehmet's reign of terror is overturned.*'

"Do not shed the innocent blood of your fellow Muslims," he commanded the sipahis in his most regal tone. "There has been enough blood of the faithful already spilt. I surrender myself without condition or reservation. I only ask that I be allowed one last instant, to thank these people for their hospitality, and to thank God for giving me the opportunity to do good while on this earth."

"You may," the sipahi answered in a bored manner that hinted he was aware of Orhan's ploy.

Orhan centred himself in the city square and faced the people. The people he never cared for, and now hated because of their disloyalty and cowardice.

"My Friends," he began. "For many years, you've given me loyalty and love, and I would be remiss if I didn't return the favour. In life, I had your favour, and now in death I give you mine. When I'm brought before my conquering cousin, I will pray, not for my own sake but for yours. I will beg that you be spared from his cruel vengeance, for you gave shelter to an expelled brother in faith. You did what God commanded of you.

You will have my gratitude and my love, on this earth and after. Always."

'May God curse you all to rot in hell if you don't overthrow this tyrant, and may God invent some horrific new anal fungus to afflict all you for your most foul betrayal.'

"I thank you. I love you. Goodbye."

The sipahis bound him in irons and took him to the palace. There was nary a dry eye in the panhandle when he left. Everyone had been shamed by what they perceived to be their own ignorance of the noble spirit that had dwelt among them. Forgotten were the memories of his stubborn arrogance and greed. Forgotten were the daily humiliations and tirades he inflicted on any passers-by. The man's reputation had been thrown in the mud and come out gold.

And the day was only half over.

Chapter Fifty - Afternoon

2:00 pm – 6:00 pm

Constantinople was unrecognizable to Ahmet's eyes. Over the past two months, he'd experienced life in a city wound tighter than a tourniquet. Everyone looked around with worried glances, uttered frightened words in hushed tones and hurried about their daily activities, always worried that they wouldn't have time to finish before the end came. Even through his vice-addled perception, the tension had been palatably thick.

Now, that tightly wound tension was gone. There had been a psychic release, whereby those two months of the siege had just let go. Now was the time to explode into a release of postponed panic. The pressure hadn't begun on April 7, when the Ottoman expedition arrived at the gates. It had been building for twenty years, since the last siege. Even before that, since the Turks first arrived in Anatolia back in 1071. It had been creeping closer to the gates since then.

In August of 1071, what was supposed to have been a skirmish near the village of Manzikert, ended with the capture and ransom of the Emperor for one and a half million gold pieces plus annual tribute. A famous conversation between the then Emperor, Romanos Diogenes, and the Seljuk Sultan, Alp Arslan, was recorded by the emperor in his journal. The victorious sultan asked the captured emperor what he would do, were the situation reversed, to which the emperor answered that he would have had the sultan killed, slowly and painfully, and then his corpse would be paraded around Constantinople for all men to look at, all women to gasp at, and all children to point and laugh at. The sultan laughed at him and said that his punishment was far worse, he would force the emperor to survive and live in shame. Alp died in battle the following November, back home on the other side of the Caspian. When Romanos got back to Constantinople, the nobles of the court blinded him with a rusty dagger and exiled him to the Ionian Islands for the disgrace with which he had burdened the empire. He later died there from an infection resulting from his blinding. Since then, the Byzantines and Turks had been in a zero-sum race to extinction.

Mario and Ahmet had both gone to Constantinople in disgrace as well. While Mario had managed to rise above his own personal weakness, and find a certain footing, Ahmet had not. He'd been devoured by his own demons and left to rot alone on the empty plains.

Ahmet would have preferred a death similar to that of the Great Seljuk, rather than the one Halil had given him. To die alone and disgraced among strangers was hardly an act of mercy as far as the young tribesman was concerned.

When he arrived at the Petrion wall, it appeared that all the fighting had been finished for some time. The district was crawling with the Anatolian tribes, part of Zaganos's command. Guards were posted everywhere, but no one wanted to stay put. Many of the nearby houses were under occupation by guards looking for gold, slaves or just blood. Their tension from the siege had unwound itself.

Since there were no uniforms, name-tags, pyramidal rank structure or standing operation orders, it was by race alone that friend and foe were identified. Ahmet walked into the district, and seemed to know what he was doing. He was hence left alone by the soldiers there. He was obviously a Turk, so there was no point in trying to randomly arrest or extort him, everybody just ignored everybody else and went about their own tasks. Getting lost in the crowd was one of the easiest acts of obfuscation he'd ever performed.

The hospital was a surprising site. The nurses, surgeons and physicians were still running around as they ever had, seemingly undisturbed by the occupation. The army had left them alone, rather than sever the burden of the wounded from the city. It made logical sense. There wasn't much to plunder from the hospital, there was no significant wealth of coin or materials, only their own doctors would know what was worth keeping from the supplies. The abject cruelty of a massacre wasn't carried out, not for any altruistic reasons of civilized warfare, but because it would be time-consuming and get little return in way of plunder. The hospital had found a niche in which it could survive for a few hours, maybe even some days, before the monastery would find itself under the sword of men, hungry for wealth, carving the gold from the ceiling mosaics and pilfering silver crosses. Mehmet had ordered the churches not to be plundered, but until order was restored in the city, everyone knew that it was only wishful thinking.

Ahmet went to the infirmary where his intending murderer, Hectore Pazzi had been kept, and began to look through his belongings. The boot chest that he kept under his bed in the doctor's barracks was easily sprung and its belongings exposed. There were many paper documents that the illiterate Ahmet couldn't understand. They were cast aside. A large main-gauche dagger, meant for parrying, and a collection of crossbow bolts that had been left.

With a shrug, Ahmet left the papers and bolts and took the dagger. One weapon was better than nothing, but this meant that he would have to get in close to the sultan to do his duty, and that would hardly be easy. He closed the case and left the hospital, searching for a spot to lay his ambush.

The Gate of Charisius was hardly the largest gate to the city, but was right next to the palace district. Charisius wasn't large enough for a man mounted on a horse to enter, it was a civilian gate, and not one of the larger military ones. Ahmet looked at the gate and decided that it would be an unlikely place for Mehmet to enter. The sultan would want to be more grand and large scale. He would probably enter the gate of Saint Romanus, the first gate to fall, or Saint Rhegius, or perhaps even the Golden Gate, the largest gate down by the Marmara shore. He might decide to bring his entourage through the mesoteichion, where the city walls fell before his cannons. Mehmet was fond of symbolic gestures.

All of this only served to make the Charisius Gate more appealing as an ambush site. While the probability of it being the original entrance for the Sultan and his party wasn't overwhelming, he would still have to march past the gate on the inside when he turned northward inside the wall to enter the palace compound. One way or another, the sultan would come by this point. It was here that Ahmet would prepare a suicidal final charge.

The twenty-ninth was a glorious spring day, verging on summer. The sun shone down warmly on the faces of all and burned none. Not a single cloud effaced the azure glory of the sky and the only wind was a gentle breeze that gently fluttered the flags of the conquerors. Everyone was so used to the smell of burnt brimstone, dying men and insanitary camp life that those odours were no longer registered by their beholders.

It was a beautiful day for the conquering sultan to enter his beaten down bride.

The assembly of his household took most of the morning. They had planned to enter at noon, but readying flags and military bands took some time, and they were still encountering some resistance in Psarmathia. It was postponed until after the Oghlen prayers, and then postponed again until the sun was far past its zenith.

Halil had wanted the whole event postponed by at least a day, until the city was secured. He would have preferred three days, to let the tribes, levies and the broken headed finish their looting, and only then take on the city as an inviolable possession.

Mehmet, of course, would have none of it. He insisted on entering the first day. He would have been the first through the gate, if he could have been. For two months he had waited and waited in the camp. He had surrounded himself with the divan, and they had been surrounded by the armed camp. With no greenery, no stonework, only mud and tents, Mehmet was pleased to be changing his scenery. The last two months had not been to his liking.

When the time was finally right, he emerged from the capital tents of his makeshift palace and took in the sights before him. Soldiers of the faux Janissary corps marched beside him, carrying the nine horse tail standard of the familial seed of Osman. What was left of his army, the portion that was still in camp, rather than looting the burning house of Constantine, were mostly the reviled but loyal falconers and mastiff trainers, dressed undeservingly in the uniforms of the justly feted corps.

Before him, Mehmet saw the giant walls. The walls that had turned Attila back, and made Mehmet's own esteemed grandfather return home, with his tail between his legs. The first time he'd seen the walls, they were strong, pristine and unassailable. Now they were burnt black, battered by stone, fire and smoke. Their spine had been broken in front of him. At the point where the walls broke, where there was rubble filling the gap, the two towers on either side of that carnage, flew the banner of the Prophet in the light breeze. The city was the enemy capital no more.

Mehmet looked to the south and saw the stretch of the Sea of Marmora where his navy had been humiliated by their Christian rivals. He looked ahead of him and saw the Gate of Saint Romanus, where the Eighth Orta had first taken a part of the wall and been forced back, and northward to the mesotechion, where they breached again but held on.

The procession advanced slowly, with cadence of the music of the *mehter* band, and slowly enough for the collection of Bektashis and dervishes to bless every step of the way. It was a lengthy process that did little but annoy the impatient young sultan.

Once they arrived at the gate of Saint Romanus, the crowd parted for Mehmet, who trotted his horse up to the opened gate. He stopped outside the gate and peered through to the brown hills and grey roads that lay beyond. He raised his hand for attention and addressed his moment of triumph.

"These tribulations have been for God's sake. The sword of Islam is in our hands. If we had not chosen to endure these tribulations, we would not have been worthy to call ourselves gazis. We would be ashamed to stand in God's presence on Judgement Day," he announced. "But now we must carry no such shame. With honour we have comported ourselves, and with valour we've been rewarded. The city belongs to the House of Peace, and will forever more."

After his applause, Mehmet on his white horse walked through the famed gate. As soon as he'd crossed the threshold as a conqueror, he dismounted and lowered his hand to the earth beneath his feet. Mehmet knelt to touch the soil with his hands. It was dry and warm from the sun.

Mehmet looked about and saw some fighting and pillaging going on to the south, he saw empty buildings and unkept roads before him, and more destruction to the north. The city that had once been the capital of the civilized world, was in waste, and not all from the two months of battle.

"Are you alright, Your Majesty?" Halil asked him as he joined his master.

"Have you read much Ferdowsi recently, my teacher?" he asked his Prime Minister, giving him the old address of teacher, for Halil had been tutor to the boy for much of his youth. "You introduced me to his work so long ago."

"He's a great Persian poet. I'm glad you remember."

"Do you recall the words '*The spider spins his webs in the palace of the Caesars. The owl hoots in the tower of Afrasiyab*?"

"It's not that desolate, Majesty."

"It's not really the Constantinople of dreams, is it?"

"It's whatever you make of it, Majesty. With your guidance, it need never be so defrocked again. The future is a new day."

"Hmphf."

"Sire, please stand up. Everyone is staring."

Mehmet came out of a daze.

"Yes, of course," he said as he sprung back onto his horse. The divan followed suit. "We head north, to inspect the breach and honour the soldiers there."

"Yes, Your Majesty."

The parade proceeded northwards towards the palace, but came to a stop at the middle of the land wall, where the flags of the Janissary Corps flew high and proud.

"Congratulations and thank you, Agha!" Mehmet called down at the muster ground of his elite soldiers. You've distinguished yourself, as have your children."

"Thank you, Sultan. Congratulations are due to you and thanks are due to God. I'm but a humble servant," Mesut said with anything but humility. "We haven't been able to find the emperor's body yet, but we will.”

“In time, I’m sure. It’s important, we need that. Which of your soldiers is to be credited with his blood?”

“That would be young Iskender here,” Mesut said with pride. “He’s been a member of the Eighth for less than a year, and he’s shown himself quite well. Speak, Son!”

“It’s an honour to serve you and God, Your Majesty,” Iskender said shyly and in a single breath. He was surprised to see that the sultan, the khan of khans, was not much older than himself.

“It’s an honour to have young men like you in the soldiery, Iskender.”

Mehmet dismounted his horse again, and again everyone in the court hastened to do the same. It was obvious to those around him that the sultan was playing with the formalities of the older men. Musa, the Minister of the Finance fell off his horse and sprained his ankle, but he hid it well enough for the time being.

“Thank you for your service,” Mehmet said and he kissed Mesut on both cheeks.

“You honour me, Sire.”

“And thank you to you, too,” Mehmet added quickly to the blushing Iskender. “What’s to become of the young hero?”

“I was going to speak to him this evening, Sire. It seems that the Eighth finds itself one officer short of a full role, after the death of one of my assistants. I was going to offer the young lad the big coat,” Mesut spoke loudly enough that everyone in the regiment could hear the conversation.

“Tell him if he’d like a court appointment with the devshirme, he’ll have my patronage.”

“I’ll do that, Sire.”

“I’ll see you later then, Agha.”

“Yes, Sire.”

The Sultan’s procession then continued on towards the palace.

“Don’t let it get your head,” Mesut warned the crimson-faced Iskender. “We’ll talk later.”

Neither men could hold back a smile.

Ahmet walked along the inside of the great land walls of Constantinople. There were too many guards at the gates and in the Petrion, but no one was bothering with the void between the gates. He limped as quickly as the wounds on his dreadfully damaged body would allow, to a half a kilometre between the break in the wall and the entrance to the Imperial District. He was all alone, and the imperial procession was marching towards him. He lightly clasped the dagger at his belt.

"That's a lot of men," he said to no one in particular. He wouldn't care to guess how many were following behind the Sultan in his little ride to the palace of Blachernae. Mehmet was at the front, followed by his old master, Halil, and the rest of the Divan.

Ahmet exhaled at the sight of the grand vizier. He bore a grudge against the man for the humiliation he'd suffered, but he'd done so outside of the public eye, and to be fair, Halil had himself been egregiously wronged.

'I don't want to hurt him,' he thought sombrely. *'I just want to get Mehmet. That bastard killed Hussein, or at least ordered it. He ordered my death as well. He ordered my brother and I to kill an infant, and he killed his own brother. He's an offence to God, and by killing him, I'll be able to make some amends for my wasted, sinful life.'*

The Latin words *'Semper sic tyrannus'* are known to the pages of history, but not to the pages of Ahmet's mind as he readied himself on some stairs near the roadway where the procession would soon pass.

'That's a big jump. I've got to make this count because I won't get a second shot,' he thought and counted the imperial bodyguards marching behind the divan. They were the falconers, they were hunters from the barrens of the empire; men more like him than those hateful Janissaries. If Ahmet missed his first chance, those beasts would make short work of him. He might have lived his life in vain, but he had no intention of dying that way.

Ahmet crouched in the shade of the late afternoon sun and prepared his energy to spring as the Sultan's coterie advanced towards their destination. The white horse came into full view, fifteen feet below and ten feet across. In one of fate's ironies, it was a similar proportion to a feat performed by a young Venetian physician fleeing a house of ill repute, barely a year earlier. Like the unlikely physician, Ahmet took a deep breath, muttered a quick prayer of petition and respect to the almighty as he understood him, and leapt out to meet his destiny.

He had no running start, he sprang off the ledge and into the air, propelled by the remaining strength of his wounded legs and he hoped the favour of God. Mehmet's gaze didn't find him in time to do anything about Ahmet's murderous intent.

His horse, however, saw him jump and reared back on her hind legs. A front hoof slammed into Ahmet's airborne chest and broke his sternum, dislocating seven ribs, pushing the air of him and throwing him onto the dusty ground like a broken sack of wet grain.

"Guards!" Mehmet yelled, but there was no need to for they were already sprinting to his side. "Come to me!"

The imperial guards were all over the Sultan. He'd only barely managed to stay in the saddle, and the would-be assassin lay at his feet wheezing in a slump. The guards were all over him, as well.

"Don't kill the assassin!" Halil instructed, trotting up behind the Sultan and the guards. "We'll need him for questioning. He must be an agent of Orhan."

"Give the sultan space," one of the guards demanded.

"Sire, are you alright?" Halil asked earnestly.

"No, I'm not alright!" he swore angrily. "What the hell was that! Why aren't the guards scouting up ahead?"

"You told them to follow behind…"

"Well now I'm commanding them ahead! Let me see this bastard!" Mehmet flew off his horse again, forcing the confused and worried divan to again follow suit. "I want to look at the face of the Christian thief-in-the-night who tried to finish me in my moment of triumph. Look at me, damn you!"

Mehmet forced himself through the guards and looked upon the face of the stranger. He shirked back in recognition. He gritted his teeth and looked up in fury at his prime minister.

"What is this, old man?"

"Sire?"

"Only you would think to do such a thing. So god-damn arrogant! You thought you could do it here! After the triumph! You thought you could have it all! Didn't you?!"

"Sire, I don't understand…"

"Oh, you understand!" the words bubbled from within the poisonous cauldron of Mehmet's youthful frustration and temper. "You though you would have it all! Look at him!"

Mehmet actually kicked one of the guards away to reveal the crippled body of Ahmet, son of Ali, barely capable of breathing independently.

"Your own prided servant, who wasn't able to join us on the campaign! I wondered where he'd gone. You planned a wonderful little surprise for me! You thought that you could kill me, like you killed Sadullah last year!"

"No, Sire," Halil was in a panic now.

"Arrest the prime minister!" Mehmet commanded his guards. "Take him with us to the palace and we'll put him in the prison there!"

"Sire, I had nothing…"

"Silence!" Mehmet screamed. "If Ahmet here lives, he'll testify against you and you'll both be killed on the Stone of Judgement in Adrianople. I try to be merciful in the application of justice, but you deserve no pity or restraint!."

"Sire!"

Halil didn't get to finish that thought, as the guards rather vigorously pulled him from his horse and gagged him.

"We march!" Mehmet proclaimed, refusing to look at either of the now prisoners. "Now!"

The procession continued unmolested to the palace, though Halil was moved to the rear, in honour of his new position as prisoner.

"General, we can't go to the wall and ask DiCastillo to come over and chat! He'd have the Venetians turn on us and kill or arrest us," Olaf stated matter-of-factly as they walked through the forum..

"Right you are, so come with me," Karian directed them up the hill towards the hippodrome. "I can't believe he'd steal from me. If he demanded a piece, I could accept that, but to try and take the whole thing… He just never seemed the type, do you know what I mean?"

"We stole it from the Emperor," Olaf confessed.

"Yes, but that was after he started hallucinating. After he started to lose his grip, and after it became obvious that he wasn't going to hold on much longer. We were just trying to keep a little touch of security for ourselves."

"If you say so, sir," Olaf was unconvinced.

"We would never have taken it if the world wasn't collapsing around us," Adam insisted. "We took this because we knew that once the Turks took the city, we would have to look after our own interests, and that no one would do it for us. Rome might pay the bounty on the city, and buy it from the Turks, western nobles will gladly pay ransom on eastern nobles, Venice will look out for its own, Genoa will look out for its own. Men like us? The Nordic Kings don't care about you rivermen! My homeland is Armenia, it was crushed by the Turks long ago, we now wander the East like homeless Jews! It was security that we put under the altar of Chora! Security!"

"If that makes you happy, Sir, believe that," Olaf insisted. "We did it for the money. We wanted to take the booty back home to Scandinavia, give the jewels to some maids, get drunk and wake up married with a handful of kids and stories that they'd tell their grandchildren about. We're not homeless wanderers, sir. We're warriors. Strong and proud. We've no need to make such rational excuses."

"We're not common thieves!"

"No, Sir. We're far from common. Now how do you intend to summon the Venetian?"

"Here we are."

"What's this?"

"His home," Adam answered flatly.

"It's all boarded up, nobody lives here now!"

"He would have moved most of his things to Galata, and his family as well. But look at how heavily barred and fenced the place is. He's planning on moving back when the war's done."

"So?"

"So we burn it," Adam continued. "He'll come faster than the fire brigade, and he'll try and take anything of any value that he can find."

"And he'll find us waiting for him…"

"That's right. Now hurry up and get that house alight, the sun's starting to go down."

"Yes, Sir!" Olaf said with renewed cheer.

And the Vikings started doing what they were best at: mayhem and destruction. Unbeknownst to their acts, the shadows started to stretch as the waning sun and the long day started to draw to a close.

Chapter Fifty-One - Evening

6:00 pm – 8:30 pm

The Cathedral of Holy Wisdom stands as a monument to Emperor Justinian, as much as to God. The church was built atop a pagan site, where Byzas had sacrificed animals to honour Artemis, and was burnt down during religious riots in the early Fifth Century. A second church replaced it, and a hundred and thirty years later, the second church burnt down in yet more riots. The third Cathedral was the one that stayed. After Justinian had his soldiers crush the rioters who burnt down the second church, he applied the resources of the empire to build a new building to act as the patriarchate and centre for world Christendom. In 1453, it was the largest church in the world, and would remain so until 1520, when the Cathedral of Seville would usurp the title.

Being the centre of Christianity had its advantages and disadvantages. Justinian was hardly the first person to be frustrated by the implacable certainty of the believers, or worry about their numbers. The rioters who wreaked havoc upon the other two would attest to the validity of those concerns.

As the sun started to set on Constantinople, the faithful, both old guard and recently re-devoted, flocked to the Cathedral in hopes that God, the Virgin Mary, the Archangel Michael, a host of saints, apostles, ne'er-do-wells and do-gooders would come to their rescue. The devoted fed off each other, and the giant inner space of the cathedral was filled to standing room only.

Noah, the poor priest who'd been forced into the position of patriarch because of his noted disinterest in people and politics, was saddled with the difficult task of trying to observe the service in the airy spaces of the building. Normally, he'd be able to stand clear of the orchestration of mass like this, but on special days, and today obviously counted in that category, he would have to personally officiate.

Normally a service was a relatively well-behaved event, the people would stand away from the altar, listen to the words of the priest in liturgical Greek, pretend that they understood the obscure dialect and then went home, feeling spiritual ease, knowing that God's demands on behalf of the flock had been attended to. Most people would attend mass on Christmas, Easter and the occasional Saints Days. Only a few people attended the daily masses. Noah hated those people. They were depressing; none of them ever had anything better to do than ready their souls for death.

May 29th was the Festival of Saint Theodosia, a Constantinopolitan nun from the eighth century, and on this particular May 29th, she received more prayers than on any other feast day in her honour; before or since. Her normal patronage over deaf-mutes must have been inspired greatly by the outpouring of devotion.

As Noah went about the normal affairs of a service, trying to keep some semblance of normalcy during the time of crisis, he finished his ablative responsibilities at the front of the altar and turned to face the hysterical mob. He hadn't counted on their being so many. He'd never seen so many people in one place in his life, not even the markets were ever so busy, or so frantic. Even the doors at the back were open, and people were clamouring to enter.

Above the crowd, Cardinal Isaac DiNapoli watched on from the balcony. He'd never seen such an affair either. So many people in such a panic. All down below him, squirming like a bucket full of blind mice. And up on the balcony, he was all alone, save for a few retainers. Normally, Noah would be there to observe the service, but today, this collaborator was taking the service into his own hands. The balcony was theoretically reserved for the Empress, or for visiting dignitaries, but as there was alas no Empress to fill the office, and all dignitaries who could have escaped the city had done so long ago. Isaac had room to breathe.

Noah began to read the benediction. This was the moment he'd been dreading.

The Benediction of Christ, was on the pages before him, and it was in Latin, as agreed upon by the Emperor, the Pope, and he as Patriarch. The old biddies who attended the mass regularly understood that this was the way of things, or it at least they didn't complain. Many of them were old and deaf – they must have been earnest to pray for Saint Theodora's favours. For most of the denizens of the city, this was the first time that they would be hearing Latin spoken from the pulpit of their beloved Church.

"The blessings of the Father, and of the Son, and of the Holy Spirit are with you," he began in the incomprehensible tongue.

The crowd did not approve.

Eruptions of protest came from the crowd, followed by sworn oaths against the anti-Christ, the Pope and Noah personally, began flying around the angry chamber. In a matter of seconds, the un-opinionated cleric became more hated than the conquering Sultan.

"Children! Children!" came the hammer of an angry and

authoritative voice; a voice that could guide lightning if need be. "Listen to me!"

Isaac looked down from his balcony to see what the matter was. There was an old man, a hermit of some kind, clutching a knotted wood staff and surrounded by black cloaked priests. He parted the Red Sea of worshippers and was approaching the altar and the confused occupant of the Patriarchy.

"Who the hell is that?" Isaac asked to one of the attendants on the balcony.

"It-it l-looks to be Gennadios, Your Grace," the attendant stuttered.

"Who?"

"The Patriarch… the old patriarch, sir."

"The one who worked so hard to isolate the house of Christ?"

"That one, yes," the attendant seemed almost pleased that the old man had returned.

"God protect us all."

"Noah!" the returning patriarch accosted the pretender to his throne. "In the name of God, I command you to stop disgracing His house!"

Noah looked blankly at what may well have been a resurrected man. Whereby Saint Thomas refused to believe in the resurrected Christ when he saw Jesus with his own eyes, Noah had no such doubts. Without demanding to see nail-holes in hands, or spear holes in the belly, Noah threw himself off of the altar and onto the hard marble floor before his predecessor's feet.

"Oh, Gennadios, bless you! You're alive, bless you," the priest started blubbering in uncharacteristic devotion.

"Seek not forgiveness from me, but from God, whom you've disgraced here, Noah," the elder priest announced before turning his attention to the gathered mass.

"Christians!" he announced to an instantly quiet room. "Remain calm, for God shall comfort you! We're in the presence of our enemies, and we'll not fear them! Pay them no heed! Worry not for Turks or Italians, Muslims or Papists! Fear only God, and prepare yourself to meet Him, for now is the end time! Now is the first day of the apocalypse! In a week's time none of this will have mattered at all! Devote yourself to prayer, rather than vulgar soldiery! It is only through prayer and devotion to God that you'll be saved when the time comes!"

Thousands of people began prostrating themselves, crying and making devotions, the chaos of the conquest from five minutes ago was transformed into the chaos of the pious and the radical.

"I hate these people," Isaac muttered under his breath and began the long and winding walk down the ramp to the nave of the cathedral.

Foolish old loyalties to the man who'd isolated and near destroyed Christianity in the east might command the souls of these gullible natives, but not his. He was a prince of the church and had no intention of surrendering any devotion or authority to this eastern heretic. It was time that someone explained to that man the true whim of God.

The final chamber of Isodore's labyrinth was a minor reservoir at the end of a long and winding path, wrought with locks and portages that had almost been too much for Mario and his future bride. Isodore's contribution had been only as dead weight for whole of the day, since he'd been shot in the early morning. Mario kept checking on him as he rested in one of the boats, but his ministrations could only postpone the main fable.

"He's gone," Mario announced sadly.

For most of the day, Isodore had lain in one of the boats whilst Mario and Ella followed his maps by lantern to the final egress of their winding journey. They'd arrived at the Saint Barbara Reservoir, where they'd moored the two boats and unlocked the door with the key that the late monk had acquired.

"My brother was always very fond of him," Ella said curiously. "I think that he was one of the only real friends he had. Everyone else, he treated sort of... I don't know how to put it..."

"I understand," Mario wasn't in the mood for a funeral just yet. "We're at the reservoir, so I'm going to take him out of here. We shouldn't leave him in this watery tomb. Open the door, I'll carry him."

They walked out of the iron grated door and emerged on the eastern slope of Acropolis Point. The view was spectacular. They were down below the dramas of the Venetian Quarter, and they were outside of the pontoon bridge of the harbour. From where they were, they could see across to Chalcedon and Bithynia. The Asian hills were catching the last rays of the setting sun. On their little grassy ledge there was fountain and some abandoned houses. The two had found a little island of beauty on the periphery of the chaos above them.

Mario put Isodore's finished body down on the grass near the fountain.

"Thank you, Isodore, God bless you," he said quietly.

Ella was obviously less comfortable around the dead than Mario was, and she seemed perpetually on the verge of losing composure, but she remained strong, and allowed Mario to say goodbye to his friend, a man for whom she'd also shared some friendly affection.

They hardly had leave to give the man a proper burial. They put foliage over his body and weighed it down with heavy stones. Mario prayed in Latin, a ritual of which the spirit of the Italophilic monk would certainly have approved.

"I hope that my brother's alright," she said once Mario had finished.

"Your brother doesn't need anyone to look after him, Ella. We do."

"What now?"

"Come with me, we've got to find a boat to take us to Galata and find your sister."

"She's staying at the Saint Stephen Hospice, near Galata Tower."

"Then that's where we go," Mario continued the thought.

"Do you think the Turk is alive?"

"Isodore's friend? Ahmet?"

"Yes, that's the one!"

"Well, I hope so. He saved our lives."

"He saved my life," she added with a hint of shame. "But he didn't come back."

"Maybe they both died," Mario suggested grimly.

"Oh, this war is ghastly."

"All wars are ghastly, Ella."

"That hardly improves our lot today."

"No it doesn't, but let's hurry and get a boat."

They grabbed a large pouch apiece to care for their immediate amenities and then they secured the sewer door that held their treasure and covered it with loose shrubbery so no one would find the entrance. They left Isodore in the greenery as a repose. They didn't have the time to give him a proper burial, but there would be special brigades organized to clean up the city once order was finally restored. They walked in an awkward silence along the shaded cornice, a coastal road that edged the sea and the cliff of the main hill. It was abandoned. No inhabitants or refugees had nested there for the day.

"I smell smoke," Ella whispered at length. "They're burning the city."

"Come on, walk quickly," Mario urged here. He was less convinced that it was a fire in the city, and was more worried that they'd started fighting in the harbour again, and that their only venue of escape was burning.

When they finally rounded the hill to Phoshorianus Harbour, the first harbour outside of the chain, they saw a terrifying display of the huddled masses of humanity. Everyone had fled down the slope of Acropoline Hill to get to the harbour and try and cross.

"Oh my God!" Ella gasped. "Mario, the city's on fire!"

"It's not the whole city, just a few plumes of smoke."

"Mario, that's where my home is!"

"It's the same area, but I'm sure it's not your home."

"It is, we've got to go!"

"We've got to get ourselves on a ferryboat!"

"No! We have to see if it's my home!"

"Your home is empty!" Mario yelled. "And if it's not, then it's gone by now! We have to get to the other side of the harbour, or we'll all die, your brother's home doesn't matter!"

"But…"

"But nothing! Turn around and let's get on that boat!" Mario didn't like handing Ella so roughly, but he turned her around towards the docks and had to force the first few steps before she was willing to walk on her own movement.

Coming from the direction opposite of the crowd, Mario and Ella managed to get their way ahead of a great many people. Some people were angry about this and voiced their concerns in language not normally heard in polite society, but Mario was past the point of caring about polity. The two managed to get on a ferryboat and sailed for the overflowing town of Galata.

"Shit," Vincent said quietly to himself as he approached the stucco ziggurat that he'd called home for the past decade.

There was no sense in losing control and running around wailing the way so many others would in that situation. Everything that could have been saved had already been put into storehouses in Galata, a service for which he'd paid exorbitantly. The flames threatened nothing but more urban destruction. It was the potential of a living conflagration to demonstrate that his time in the city was indeed at an end.

Still, he hurried to see the flames. He rode out to see the end of what his life had been.

He was surprised when he saw a gang waiting outside the walls, waiting for what they thought would be an hysterical man, charging over after he'd thrown all caution to the wind. Instead, a calm captain of defeated men trotted his horse towards the clot of irregulars.

"What the hell have you done, Adam Karian?" the aloof equestrian demanded.

"We're here for what's owed us, Vincent!"

Vincent looked at the fire behind the Vikings, it hadn't spread through all the house yet, it looked to be confined to the kitchen, but it probably wouldn't stay there for long.

"Very well, you're burning down your city to get what you think is owed. Fine logic. Why don't you tell me what do you think you're owed?"

"We're owed what you stole from us!"

"What have I stolen?"

"You're a liar and a thief!"

"I'm many things, but you'll have to be more specific," Vincent seemed impatient, but he could afford to be. He looked at the Varangians, and they were all armed as infantrymen, with swords and battleaxes, shields, armour and maces. None of them would be able to get close enough to him on horseback unless he chose to allow it.

"You looted the Imperial treasury that was stored under the altar of Chora! You had your agents, the doctor, your sister and the Turk do it. You conspired with the Genoese, Hectore Pazzi to do it!"

"You've gone mad, Adam. My sister is in Galata with my wife, I know of no Turk who's not warring as we speak, and the doctor is hardly my agent. Hectore Pazzi is your friend, not mine," Vincent trotted his horse to the piazza in front of the house while he spoke. To do so, he opened up more avenues of retreat, in the event that Karian and his assembly tried to rush him. "Shouldn't you be trying to escape the city now? You and the Northerners, more than most, don't want to end up as prisoners."

"Shouldn't you be manning a gate somewhere, or have you abandoned that post as well?"

"The boy from Venice signed the surrender a half an hour ago. The Turks won't be allowed to loot the quarter, and we've got a week to withdraw. Only Janissaries will be allowed past the gate tonight to secure the quarter. They'll hopefully put that fire out."

"You really don't know what I'm talking about, do you," Adam made the terrible realization, that he'd started a fire that he couldn't control. Not just in an innocent man's house, but he'd justified the Varangians' greed, and they wanted compensation.

"Sorry friend," Vincent shook his head. He, too, realised what was about to happen to the former general. Unlike Adam, Vincent found cold amusement in this inevitability.

The Vikings started gossiping amongst themselves in their own violently musical language. Words that did not bode well for their commander.

"I smiled when you corrected Stavros about the story of Doubting Thomas," Vincent said while Adam squirmed. "Can you tell me where I can reference the quote about sowing and reaping?"

"Chapter six in Paul's Epistle to the Galatians," Adam answered slowly. "Be not deceived. God is not mocked; for whatever a man reaps, so shall he sow. For he that sows to his flesh, shall of the flesh reap corruption. But he that sows to the spirit, shall of the spirit reap life everlasting."

"You've tried to look out for your own flesh too much here," Vincent continued accusingly. "You'd have done better to have been a priest, Adam. I suppose you could also remember where to find a cheerful idiom about living and dying by the same swords."

Adam Karian's face was drained of emotions by that point. He looked gaunt and his eyes sunk back. The Vikings circled him from behind.

"Goodbye, Vincent, sorry about the misunderstanding."

Vincent had no last words for him. He turned his horse and rode off in search of a fire brigade. He let the Varangians deal with honour among thieves.

The Gokhan Clan was quite proud of itself for its heroism that day. It was one of their own, a twelve-year-old child soldier whose mother had wept rivers of tears when her son went to war, who'd struck down Guistiniano Longo, one of the triumvirs in command of the defence of the city. The child thought that it was grossly unfair how his older brother insisted on trying to take credit for his accomplishment.

The clan had also been at the vanguard of the assault on the rough and tumble Psarmathia neighbourhood at the southern wall. Their reward for credentials earned on the battlefield of Constantinople was the opening of the Venetian Quarter. They charged through an undefended gate in the southern end of the Quarter, near Contoscalion, and began their rights of plunder. Shortly after they'd begun their earned privilege, they received the order to withdraw from a flag-messenger.

"Those bastards," the khan growled to one of his many nephews.

"The imperial district is off limits, as were religious buildings, the panhandle, and now the Venetian quarter! The sun's still out and everything's spoken for! We've given two months to this damn siege, and we'll have nothing to return home with!"

"Khan," the nephew addressed his patriarch reverently. "We have to be out of here by nightfall, so let's make the most of our time. If we attack the giant church, we'll be sure to find enough gold and silver to make this whole thing worth it. There aren't any other clans or soldiers in the quarter. We'd be the first. It'll all be ours. Then we can go back to the rest of the city, and act as though nothing happened."

"Brilliant idea!" the khan conceded immediately. "Everyone, over the hill and towards the big church!"

Finding Holy Wisdom was an easy task, it was the biggest building in the city, and visible from almost everywhere on the lee side of Acropoline Hill. They ran as quickly as they could past the Forum of Constantine and crossed the major intersection which marked the home of Vincent DiCastillo. There was a fire burning, and some sort of scuffle going on, none of which was of any concern to the plundering Gokhans. Their charge was more than enough to scare off the small number of Norse guards who were in the process of beating their former commander to death on the street. The guards disappeared into the chaotic city, and the clan continued on until they reached Holy Wisdom.

While the tribes had no real understanding of what Christianity was, they perceived it to be nothing but a competing religion; a false version of monotheism that incorporated three gods instead of the theological unity of Islam. Trinity had always been a confusing subject for many Christians and non-Christians alike. None of them had ever been inside a church before, and while they'd been told by local sheikhs and imams that the buildings were debauched houses of false gods, idolatry and sinful ways, most of the tribe correctly understood that to be religious posturing on the part of the propagandist. They imagined that churches were very much like mosques, with a religious leader, a community prayer and a sermon, followed by socialising within the group. This perception, held by these illiterate tribesmen, was ironically more accurate than the understandings of many more educated people.

When they saw the sight of Holy Wisdom, it was nothing like what they'd been expecting. There was ecstatic screaming, hooting and hollering, singing and praying, and at the back of the nave, near where the tribe entered, there appeared to be two priests brawling. It was not what they had expected. It wasn't even close. The hate-spitting propagandists were right!

"Traitor! You've damned us all!" Isaac shouted as he grappled with the elderly grey-beard.

"You're the Whore of Babylon and I cast you out!" Gennadios shouted back in his barrel-voiced echo that riled his flock. "You inherit Peter's denial, and his sin! May you rot in the hell of the Antichrist! May you dine on ash! In the name of God I command you to flee from this place, Satan!"

With each fist pounding epithet, the old Patriarch tried with varying success to strike the lean and hungry Italian, who dodged nimbly and did his best to swear in a language in which he was far from fluent.

"You've brought this doom! You've summoned these snakes of hell to torment King Jesus! Better that your heresy be crushed by Nebuchadnezzar than spread to the healthy body of the Christian world!"

"Better the Sultan's turban than the Pope's tiara!"

"What are they talking about, Khan," the confused Turcophone nephew asked his wise elder.

"I don't know," were the only words that could honestly answer such a question. "Get everybody out of here, kill one or two to scare off the rest."

The Gokhans did a fine job of amplifying the spirit of chaos and destruction to what had been a church service gone horribly awry. With a few screams of "God is great!" and few flashing blades, almost a thousand people started a stampede out of the church and into the rest of the quarter. That certainly achieved what the clan had been hoping for.

To the credit of the frightened rioters, only seven people were crushed to death or trampled in the stampede and flight from the now inappropriately named Holy Wisdom. The only two men foolish enough to stay, were the two priests who were hell-bent on finishing what they'd started.

"I wonder what they're fighting about?" the khan asked himself in wonder. "It must be something horrifically important."

He walked over to the brawling priests, took out his dagger, and grabbed the one on top. He pulled Isaac off of Genadios and slit his throat with a shepherd's skill, throwing him to the ground to bleed out the end of his argument on to the marble floor.

"Hey!" the Khan addressed the Patriarch in his own Turkish. "Congratulations, you've won! Now get the fuck out of here!"

Genadios had no idea what the Turk had said, or why he'd done what he'd done, but he was glad it was Isaac who'd died and not him. He couldn't understand the words the man was saying, but he seemed to be pointing, directing the old man out of the church.

"God bless you," he said in thanks for sparing his life and killing the man who'd been trying to dishonour the church he loved so dearly. He ran out of the building and breathed the evening air, full as it was with ash and blood. He looked back into the building he'd just fled and realised that he'd never be allowed back in. He was the last Christian to leave the building. He'd even blessed the looters for raising arms against the Frank.

In shame, he ran off into the tumult of the once great city.

The imperial procession, this time garnered strongly with five hundred heavy foot from the sultan's own guard and the divan, marched triumphantly into the conquered territory of the Venetian Quarter. They were not coming to loot, Zaganos had signed an armistice on the behalf of Mehmet, guaranteeing amnesty for a week, at which point the quarter would officially be surrendered. Mehmet had been furious at first, but the temper died and he insisted on visiting Holy Wisdom himself before the sun set. It was only once he stood under the gigantic dome, and proclaimed the *Shahada*, that he would be able to consider himself truly victorious. No one took the role of Halil and voiced caution. The sultan was long past his willingness to tolerate such a manner of well intentioned advice.

The party traversed the spine road, the great avenue that crested the hills of Byzantium and eventually raised up to the hippodrome. There, they turned into the garden and entered the church through the narthex. Mehmet was pleased to see that the building seemed to have been evacuated already.

"Zaganos!"

"Yes, Sire!"

"I see that there are some men in there now, are they ours or do you think that they may be partisans?"

"They look to be tribesmen, Sire."

"After it was ordered for none to attack the quarter?"

"Yes, Sire."

"Well then, come on. Let's scare some obedience back into them."

The imperial party pushed open the main doors of the narthex and entered the nave, only to find it crawling with over a hundred tribesmen, illegally seeking plunder.

"Attention!" Zaganos called out with the dangerous melody of a howling wolf. "Who is in charge of you honourless thieves?"

"I am! And who are you to say such words to me?" the khan shouted back angrily at the bald convert.

The khan was angry and full of pride. Regardless of who Zaganos was, the petty khan couldn't show deference to anyone now, less his family would rebel and chose a new khan from amongst themselves to replace the ageing elder, whose zest for self-aggrandisement was obviously waning.

"I am Aslan Gokhan, khan and reis of the Gokhans! And who are you?"

Mehmet emerged from the crowd.

"I am the khan of khans. I am the Sword of Osman, and on this day, I take the title of *Kayzar-al-Ruhm* – The Emperor of Rome. I am Caesar and I gave no permission for anyone but my own household to enter this district. I gave standing orders for all churches to be treated as sanctuaries. They are not to be looted, and their inhabitants were to be spared. Where did that blood come from?"

The young sultan pointed at the sullied floor accusingly.

"Sire, I…"

With imperceptibly swift motion, Mehmet cut the Khan's words with a sword that cut his throat. His speed was a shock to all those who witnessed it.

"Everyone who is not supposed to be here, should leave, now," his voice wasn't quite as acidic as that of his newly appointed grand vizier, Zaganos, but the message got across, and what was left of the Gokhan tribe fled through whatever exits they could find.

The sultan spent the following half an hour inspecting the great edifice. He was a little discomforted to know that he'd not in fact been the first Muslim to set foot through the doors, but he'd have to make do. To his great relief, the building hadn't suffered significantly from the depredations of the looters, or the chaos of the former inhabitants.

Once the sun finally dipped below the horizon, and evening gave way to night, Mehmet perked up.

"Gentlemen! It seems that it is now time for prayers."

Aksham Ezani is the fourth of the five daily prayers for observant Muslims, observed when the sun first dips to the horizon.

"Yes, Sire," said Musa, the nervous brother of the recently incarcerated former grand vizier. "Should we return to the imperial district?"

"No," Mehmet said without looking at his exchequer. "We'll call prayer from here."

"In the church, sire?" Zaganos asked. Even the bellicose vizier's bloodthirsty enthusiasm was cut back at the prospect of praying in a church. "Is that a good idea?"

"This is a building, designed by men, and intended for the worship of God. For too long, it has been corrupted away from that purpose by the infidels! Today, we can reclaim it for its original purpose!"

The divan and assembled soldiers all swallowed in unison.

"Compass?" Mehmet asked for a volunteer.

There was silence among the assembled, so Mesut, the new minister of the Janissaries, stepped forward and presented the sultan with the tool in question.

"Thank you."

Mehmet directed himself towards Mecca, brought his hands to his ears, and called the faithful to prayer. The Cathedral of Holy Wisdom, was a church no more. The sun was gone from the eyes of those left in the city.

Chapter Fifty-Two - Night

The harbour of Galata was overflowing with the human explosion that emanated from across the harbour. Innumerable ships packed themselves beyond their natural capacity to carry and bring the miserable last generation of Christian Constantinople to the safety of the Genoese protectorate. The ferries collided into the overflowing docks and forced their cargo ashore, into a crowd that hadn't dissipated, or even moved, since the unsavoury endeavour began.

After an hour of pushing and cajoling, Mario managed to push his way through the crowd and find the alleys of the other side of the harbour district. Once they were away from the disorder of the refugees they could hurry through narrower streets, crowded with humanity that had been forced to pay landowners for the privilege of sleeping on the street outside their homes or places of business.

These streets looped around the hillside colony and the two travellers managed to navigate by directing themselves towards the Galata Tower, the only identifiable building within the over-packed walls. Once they'd poured through the lost souls on the streets, they'd eventually sluiced themselves to the already overcrowded hospice of Saint Stephen.

The hospice was a walled compound without adornment, and with sharp spires along the walls, to deter any extra visitors. There were also signs in Greek and Italian, warning potential pilgrims that there was no room left at this inn.

Mario and Ella banged on the door but the door guard refused to open the gate for any reason whatsoever. His ears were deaf to all pleas.

"Daria!" Ella cried, hoping her voice would penetrate the security.

"Daria!" Mario cried as well. He yelled to morally support Ella. He didn't suspect that their cries would find the proper ears.

"Ella! Oh my! God be praised!" returned an hysterical voice from one of the high windows. Mario and Ella recognised the voice of Vincent's opinionated and emotional wife. "I'm coming down! I see you, stay where you are!"

Ella and Mario embraced in the cool spring night, this was the first reason to celebrate for the two in quite some time. They couldn't see their outremer city through the maze of overhanging buildings between them and the night sky, but they knew it was out there, and they might not be able to see much of it again.

A barred window near the entranceway rumbled, and then opened. Daria's head, enrobed in a white shawl appeared from the darkness and a hand shot out to grab the attention of the two refugees.

"Daria! Sister!" Ella said, running to the window. She grabbed her sister-in-law's outstretched hand and the two embraced through the bars.

"Oh, Ella! I've been praying every day! Where's Vincent?"

"We don't know," Mario answered, but Daria barely noted his presence, she was too overwhelmed with the joy of seeing her sister again.

"How's Alexandra?"

"Wonderful and healthy!" she hurried to say. "I'll see if I can have the doorman let the two of you in."

"Give him this," Mario handed a few gold coins to Daria through the bars.

Daria grabbed the gold thanklessly and disappeared behind the window, closing it behind her. The happy couple moved back down the street to the door, which unethically opened to allow in the bribing guests. A manger had apparently been purchased. On the other side of the door, Daria was waiting for them and hugged her sister tightly, and they both cried with joy. Only once the honest tears of joy were again contained, did she politely welcome Mario and brought the two wayfarers to her small apartment.

Mario was glad nonetheless to be one of the few arrivals to Galata with a roof over his head. The three of them shared a small room, in what had originally been a hospital and was now operating as a refuge and traveller's inn. While the two girls caught up on all the recent events of the past two months, Mario played with Alexandria, now a dazed six-month-old, wrapped in swaddling clothes. Her eyes were the same colour of angry blue as her mother, Mario thought that if Vincent were lucky enough to survive the Fall of Constantinople, he would have tougher battles ahead of him. Mario smiled at that.

"I'm so glad that you managed to escape," Daria said at last. "I hope that my husband did, too."

"Vincent's not the type to dally about once battle's done," Mario said while playing peek-a-boo with the dazzled infant. "I'm sure that Alexandra's father will be here in no time."

"Do you think that the war's going to go on much longer?" the doting mother asked him suspiciously.

"I don't imagine so. The Turks have their city. There's nothing left to fight over. Galata will probably fall to threats rather than swords, now."

"How long will it be until we're allowed back to our homes?"

“I don’t know. The Turks might not let you back. Constantinople’s fallen. It’s their city now, who knows what they’ve got planned.”

“They’ll probably loot it for all its gold and then go back to wherever they came from,” she said confidently.

“Maybe,” Mario wanted to sleep, and he certainly didn’t want to fight with Daria DiCastillo, but he found her prediction to be very doubtful. “But they put a lot of effort into taking the city. It’s hard to believe they’d give it up very easily. I don’t think that Galata’s very safe, either.”

“What do you mean? This city was cowardly neutral”

“I mean that there were Genoese soldiers defending the capital, not to mention their helping with the chain, and Genoa won’t be allowed to keep an armed camp in the middle of the Turk’s conquest. That, alongside neutrality and cowardice prompt aggression, it doesn’t guard against it. At least not for very long.”

“Oh, God protect us!”

“I’m hoping to go back to Venice. I’ve got enough money, or at least I hope I will in the next few days, but that’s another story,” Mario cut himself off. “Ella and I will buy a house and raise a huge family. The East has fallen, and I’m looking forward to getting back home.”

“The world’s going to forget about us here. They’ll abandon us to the Turks.”

“Probably,” Mario agreed. “After five hundred years of crusades, wars of religion and massacre, most of the princes of the west are going to be more than happy to engage in peaceful commerce, and leave the wars to uncivilized men. The time in history where destinies are determined by wars are just about over. There’s a rebirth of humanity going on. A new world is dawning, and no one’s going to want to fight other people’s wars for them.”

“You think?”

“I hope,” Mario tempered his tongue. “The Turks are going to try to turn the city into a Muslim city, but they’ll fail. You can’t force someone to believe in God or Allah or Christ, or Zeus and Athena. The Greeks will always be Christians. The Turks can be there for another millennium, and the mosques will never outnumber the churches, and the Christians will eventually be ruled by their own. There will be a time when all of the blood that’s being shed now will seem like such a horrible waste.”

“You’ll forgive me if I don’t share your optimism, Doctor Mario,” Daria answered sardonically.

“Of course I’ll forgive you, Sister,” Mario’s voice slid over her accusation like velvet. “Time will bear out the history of the city, but I don't think it's anywhere near finished just yet."

"I suppose not," Daria was irritated at how clever Mario though himself to be. "But her glory is tarnished forever now."

"Sister, I don't mean to besmirch your sense of pride and honour in the legacy of your homeland, but that happened long before any of us were born. Today's events just served to put the good silver away. The feast was finished long ago."

"I can't breathe," Ahmet whispered upon waking.

"Then don't," answered Halil's disembodied voice from the darkness. "If you'd stopped breathing years ago, you'd have saved us both untold suffering."

"Halil?" Ahmet whispered, barely recognising the world around him, but identifying the voice of his former patron. "Where are we?"

"We're in the prison of Porphyrogentius. Ironic, for you see, this used to be a palace. Now it's just you, me, horses and guards."

"We're in Constantinople?"

"Yes. We're awaiting execution in the morning. You tried to assassinate the Sultan. Do you remember that? Or was your brain so shaken by opium that you can't understand it all?"

"I remember," Ahmet said slowly. It hurt went he inhaled too deeply. "I remember jumping. I wanted to kill Mehmet. For everything he's done."

"Well, you caught a horse's hoof, and cursed us both. Do you remember that?"

"No, but I sure can feel it."

"I'm getting blamed for organising it. Our glorious sultan is having me executed for planning his murder. He thinks you were my agent."

"No," Ahmet said too loudly for it not to hurt. "I was alone! I'll tell him that, you've got to let me speak to him!"

"Ahmet, you're a fool," Halil said and motioned for him to stall his efforts. "Mehmet doesn't want to speak to you. He doesn't want to speak to me. He probably knows that I had nothing to do with your foolishness. He's wanted to wash his hands of me for a long time. The old should give way for the young. It's the way of things, and I tried to stand in his path too often."

"You were looking out for the empire."

"I was looking out for myself," Halil admitted. "I think that it's probably best that I go now. Can you imagine what would happen to society if the elders managed to hold on for too long? The fire that burns in the heart of people would die alongside its aged leaders. The young are meant to be leaders, not mourners. Tradition can be a great strength. It can even be strong enough to smother itself."

"He should have respected you more."

"I should have retired to live a quiet life, away from court. I should have left the state to younger men."

"Halil…" Ahmet started to try and apologize, for all the things he'd done and hadn't done while in the elder man's service. His apology was cut short by the tumbling of keys in the prison door.

"You two!" came a recognizable voice from the opening door. "You're coming with me."

The voice of Zaganos-pasha drifted away as the bodies of guards came into the room and gathered the two men.

"We were told that this would be done at first light, after morning prayers," Halil insisted.

"It seems that the sultan worries about your brothers trying something heroic, and your opportunity to meet God has been sped up. Rejoice"

Halil didn't resist, he'd comforted himself earlier to the fact that he was not destined to die of old age, but by the blade of an executioner. Ahmet on the other hand, had made no such commitment. He'd warmed himself to the idea of his own mortality, but raged constantly against it. He tried to fight off the guards, but he was not able to stand or fight. The guards carried him by his torso, and his long and notoriously dangerous arms hung off of his trunk as though they were lanyards in the wind.

The two were brought to a clearing in what had once been an atrium for emperors and was now in ruin. The noise from the assembled execution party disturbed an owl that had been treating the palace as home, and he flew once the group gathered. There were torches to light their foul business and stone walls to hide the act from all but God. In the middle of the atrium was a chopping stump and brutal looking two-handed sword. There was also a pool of fresh blood covering the floor. Ahmet derived predictably little comfort when he saw that the sword seemed to be sharp and well cared for. It was more than capable of beheading a man in a single stroke. There shouldn't be a danger of waiting for a second or third blow to finish one's suffering.

"I take it we're not the first guests of honour this night," Halil suggested with mock-offence.

"No, the man calling himself 'emperor' was ahead of you. Imperial prerogative and protocol. I'm sure you understand."

"I'm honoured to take second place."

"Third. The pretender Orhan is now off to argue his legitimacy to a higher power."

"Third, then."

"As you're both aware, the traditional mode of execution for a traitor is to be garrotted with the draw of a bow, but you may both rejoice that you're going to lose your heads in a much less painful manner," Zaganos said without emotion as the executioner levered his sword out of the block.

"God is great," Halil said. "And I fear no earthly hand."

"That sounds suspiciously like a volunteer to go first," The smiling grand vizier replied and pointed at the guards to bring the former occupant of high office to the block.

Halil made no effort to struggle, but instead calmly knelt over the wooden anvil and readied his soul.

"You'll see the world from this position one day, Zaganos. You'll find it seems to put many things into perspective."

"I doubt that, old man. My flag has always flown with the wind, rather than trying to stop it. Everyone knew, even before the death of old Murat, that you'd end this way. Even your brothers knew it! It's an honour for me to be here for the inevitable."

"It's my honour to face death with dignity and without fear. We'll see how death comes for you, when the time comes."

"Soldier," Zaganos indicated the executioner. "Do your duty."

"I'm sorry!" Ahmet blurted out.

Halil looked at his former ward with a faraway glare and it seemed as though he were about to either grant or deny forgiveness, but the executioner's blade was faster than any words. The explosion of blood and bone that flew from the de-capped minister relegated his final words to the prerogative of guesswork.

"Next! Move along," Zaganos said, and the prone body of the tribesman, wracked by guilt and suffering from internal bleeding from the sharp bone fragments of his broken ribs, was placed over the pool of blood that had once been his master.

"I was there, when your brother Hassan died," Zaganos said coldly to his new victim. "He was a tough bastard."

Rage, wrath and guilt took to flame in Ahmet's heart. All of his muscles tensed and he made for one last struggle. While he may die now, he was going to take that bastard with him.

The blade came down before Ahmet could do anything. The grimace on his severed head stayed as a haunting image of the hate that burned in his wasted soul.

"Hmmm," Zaganos hummed, and he looked upon the destruction of lives around him in the blood-stained hollow.

"Thank you, gentlemen," he said to the soldiers. "You've done a good job. Now clean this up and you're done for the day. When you bury Halil, make sure you don't leave a marker or anything to help his family find his body. They're being punished."

"Yes, sir," the executioner said. "And what of the other one?"

"You don't need to bury him. He's nobody. Throw him into the street, let the dogs eat him or something."

"Yes, sir."

"I've seen many strange things in my life," Vincent's voice reflected a concoction of doubt, incredulity and mild amusement when he spoke. "But I've never seen this."

"Do you like my turban?" Ezera asked taking a spin so that everyone in the ambassador's home could admire his accoutrements. "It was a gift from the Emir of Sinope and Kastamonu."

"I'm very happy for you," Vincent said, shaking his head. "So what exactly is your position in the Turkish fleet?"

"I'm the second admiral of the fleet. In a week's time, I'm going back to Gallipoli to oversee the construction of new ships. You'd probably noticed that this fleet had been woefully prepared for the battle. I'm designing the ships myself and overseeing their construction. I enjoy the patronage of Sultan Mehmet, now."

"Congratulations to you then," Balias found it difficult to show any real enthusiasm, as he had no history with the pirate. "What brings you here? Do you want to gloat over your defeated enemy?"

"I have a letter for the ambassador from Zaganos-Pasha, the grand vizier. He's summoning your master to Blachernae for a meeting."

"Regrettably, Don Giovanni won't be able to go anywhere. He hasn't passed yet, but I believe he's haggling with the boatman as we speak," Balias answered. "I'll be taking over the rest of his responsibilities for the time being."

"I never much liked the man, but my prayers go to Giovanni and my congratulations go to you. Here's the message."

Ezera handed the Venetian a scroll, cased in velum and sealed by the crest of the House of Osman. He then let him read, while he focussed his attention to his old friend.

"I'm glad that you've survived, Vincent. I knew that you would, you've never been the kind to fall on your sword for anyone or anything. How is your family?"

"Fine, the girls have been in Galata since all this began. Daria gave birth to a beautiful and healthy daughter about a half a year ago."

"The next one'll be a strong boy, I'm sure."

"We'll hope. So how did you become admiral?"

"Everyone else was incompetent."

"Plague and mercenary rules?"

"These Turks value success more than loyalty. It suits me fine, I don't have to wait for someone with seniority over me to die. Baltaolu, the former admiral, was grotesquely useless, and so the grand Turk exiled him and appointed my patron, Emir Tolga to job. Tolga knew that he had no experience with boats and put me in charge. The grand vizier doesn't like me very much, but he respects my skill and recommended me for the task of building a new navy."

"To fight against Venice?" Vincent asked.

"Could be," he cheerfully replied.

"What did you do to earn that kind of trust?"

"Did you see the whole fleet cross the mountain?"

Vincent nodded.

"That was my idea," Ezera said with pride.

"What?" Balias intervened.

"My idea," Ezera repeated. "My plan, my execution, and my invitation to the table."

"You're actually proud that your ingenuity helped to secure the victory of the Turks here. You're proud that you'll be building their forces to fight against the nations of Christ. You've helped throw dirt into the eyes of your fellow Christians, given the entire Eastern Mediterranean to the Muslims, and now you boast of it? You take pride in your actions?"

"Listen, Balio…"

"Balias!"

"I'm not going to marry you, so I don't care about your office!" Ezera had always been capable of mustering an intimidating fury when the situation called for it. His voice echoed throughout the corridors of the Venetian embassy and even the near-death ambassador upstairs had his torpor disturbed. "I'm an officer in the victorious army, here to instruct you as to what's to happen!"

"No you're not! You're a traitor to Christendom!" the former jailer tried to stand up to the imperious pirate-turned-admiral, but he lacked the sense of aggression and will to fortify that guided Ezera.

"I'll listen to Giovanni and Vincent because they've proven their respectability to me, but you're just some child standing in the shoes of greater men and hoping that no one notices what a flaccid excuse for nobility you are. I'm sure that your family's given you enough property to buy respectability in the senate back home, but in my presence you have no lands, you have no titles, you have nothing! Only what's in your head and heart, and all I see behind those eyes of yours is another effete man of the city! Why don't you go back to Italy, find a nice quorum to sit in and turn away from the East for as long as you can."

"You've allied yourself with the brutal enemies of civilization and Christendom," Balias said as a meek accusation.

"Vincent, I hope you don't find yourself working with this castrato. Listen to me, *Balias,* there are no enemies of civilization among the strong. Civilization is capable only with order, and order is maintained by force. Constantinople had no force or order left. The capital was half-occupied by two competing cities for Christ's sake! The Turks have brought order to the city and to the whole of the East! Sultan Mehmet is the great man of the day. Emperor Constantine never was! He was elected emperor because he was weak and pliable. Everyone knew that! It was the same as that fool on the pulpit, Noah. The decisions were made that co-operation and compromise would take precedence over leadership and strength.

"What a stupid decision that was! Constantine wouldn't upset the court or the Italians, so the competition of factions continued. Noah wouldn't fight for reunification, nor would he fight against it, so the city didn't get help from the Italian west or the loyalist and oppressed easterners! It stood for nothing, and it fell when the winds of war blew too strongly."

"They played the hand they were dealt," Balias answered back.

"And in case you've been sleeping, they lost. They lost badly."

"You may tell your master, that I'll meet with him tomorrow at noon, as per his request…"

"…his instruction," Ezera interrupted.

"At noon. You're excused."

"I leave, because it suits me to do so," Ezera grinned a shockingly aggressive and toothy grin, and then bowed in his most courtly fashion – the same condescending gesture he'd extended to Antonio and Baltaoglu when they'd last met. Politeness could often be the sharpest sword of rudeness. Vincent excused himself as well and escorted Ezera to the foyer, where his bodyguards were waiting to take the admiral back to the fleet.

"You were always good at making friends, Ezera," he said with a morbid chuckle.

"Yeah, sorry about that, that child got me worked up. His type does that, you know that."

"I understand, I don't much care for him myself. He reminds me of that doctor you introduced me to, some years ago."

"Mario? Is he still alive?"

"Oh yes. I think that he conspired with the Genoese to plunder the imperial treasury and ran off with my sister."

"Ha!" Ezera laughed. "You can't be serious."

"When you first introduced me to him, I thought that he was a week little intellectual who'd wandered too far from home, but you assured me that there were surprises in that shell."

"You don't really think…"

"No," Vincent paused, "…but Adam Karian, the Roman general, did. He hunted him down through the city in a murderous rage. Burned my house down in the process."

"You seem very calm about the possibility."

"Well, I didn't approve of him for Ella, because he had no money and status, but I also didn't approve of him as a person. I thought that he was pliable and without character. If he really did what I suspect, then he's solved all of those problems, and I'll wish the two of them a long and happy life together."

"Listen," Ezera said in a hushed tone before he returned to his ship. "This battle is finished, but life goes on. If you need help for you, or your family, to get back to Venice, or anywhere else, I'm staying on the only two-decker bireme in the harbour for now, and next week I'll be off Gallipoli. Contact me, and I'm always there to help. You have to ask for Ayoub-pasha."

"New name?"

Ayoub shrugged.

"I'll do that, thanks."

"And if you have a new brother-in-law, who's recently come into suspicious wealth, tell him this as well. I'm sure that we can work something out."

The two old friends laughed at the idea and hugged goodbye. They each had very different worlds to return to.

"Adam, you look like shit," Guistiniano wheezed when the Armenian General was placed in the bed next to him.

"Look at yourself, Longo," Adam replied through the battered and blue swelling of his face. "Where are we?"

"We're in the hospital in the Venetian quarter. My men brought me here, I don't know how you made it here."

"I don't remember, either," Adam stammered to say. "I feel like I've been run over by a herd of horses."

"No, you've just been beaten up, a horse stampede feels different," Longo joked and allowed his temper to laugh before his body rebelled against his humour. "Ohhh, my belly hurts."

"I'm glad you're alive."

"You, too," the Genoese answered. "Nobody can tell me what's going on, do you know?"

"Constantine's dead, the city's fallen, the quarter's going to be abandoned soon enough. We lost."

"That's too bad," the Genoese said simply. "Well, we fought the good fight."

"That's hardly compensatory. We fought. We lost. Now we've lost everything. A dark shadow's now stretched over the light of the world. How will you answer for this failing, when you stand before God, and He asks you about this?"

"I'm a fair bit closer to that time than I'd care to be," Longo groaned as he felt the pains of his broken bones. "Have you read Paul's second letter to Timothy?"

"Of course."

"He tells Timothy to go out and preach the truth. He says that he's fought the good fight, finished the race and kept the faith," the mercenary's eyes glossed over for a bit. "Towards the end, he knew that the world hadn't been converted to Christianity, but he'd done all he could have. He went on to meet God with a conscience clear. He'd done everything he could have, even if he'd just fought and not actually won the day – even if he'd finished the race rather than won it. We resisted the Turks for two months. They outnumbered us by proportions that would have made any rational man surrender on the first day. They had more men, more ships, more guns, more horses, and they didn't have the same degree of enemies in camp that we did. I wish we'd won, but we didn't. I don't hate myself for that, or you. We did all we could have. I'd hate the Turks for what they did, but I don't have any time or patience for hate anymore. The end of this race is too close. We don't have anything to be ashamed of."

"I do."

"You gave more than anyone could have expected or demanded. It was your stratagem, the whole defence. It was a good plan, if the Turks hadn't opened up the Horne, or if Constantine had listened to you when the gunsmith came, it would have worked out better, but those are the failings of other men."

"I…" Adam wasn't sure how to make his confession. "I broke faith with the emperor."

"How did you do that?"

"I stole from him."

"Everyone stole from him, I'm sure you did less personal profiteering than that bastard Stavros."

"I ordered the Varangians to empty out the treasury. We hid it in a monastery, and planned to plunder it after the city fell. Unfortunately, I was betrayed and someone ran off with the ill-gotten wealth."

There was a moment of silence while Longo pondered his reply.

"Ha ha!" Guistiniano choked on a chortle of laughter. "I knew you were up to something! I didn't think that it was quite so big, but I knew it was something!"

"You knew I was a traitor?"

"I knew you'd look out for yourself, rather than count on the charity of others," he countered. "Thought that seems like a pretty dangerous gamble to make. Whoever plunders that monastery will be a happy looter."

"I think that Hecotre Pazzi stole it from there already."

"What?" Longo seemed genuinely shocked. "That idiot couldn't organise a brawl in a beer-hall. If anyone, it was my damnable brother-in-law, Dominic Trebianno. Pazzi doesn't do anything with his say so."

Adam exhaled in exhaustion.

"I'm tired of suspecting everyone of everything. I wish I'd died in the battle, then I could be remembered fondly as a martyr."

"Hey, don't worry, you can still die from your wounds."

"Thanks," Adam's eyes focussed on his possessions at the foot of the bed. Among them, he would find a sharp dagger that was more than capable of restoring his deflated honour as a last act of dedication. "Why don't you try and sleep. Tomorrow's a new day."

"By God's grace. Sleep well, Adam."

"By God's grace. Sleep well, Guistiniano."

In the hours where no memory of the sun lingers nor encroaches on night's blackness, twelve people gathered in secret ritual. The participants were men of minimal education and women of unqualified virtue. Their names, like the names of so many others who've served importantly, have been either long forgotten or never recorded.

In secret conclave, they gathered quietly outside of the imperial Petrion District, in the Lamb's Pasture, the cemetery next to the Church of Saint Mary among the Mongols. It was a dark and quiet gathering, no one spoke or lit torches, less they lure some plunder-seeking vandals to investigate their actions. They dug a hole in the earth, not deep enough to be a proper grave, for their stealth allowed them little time. When the hole was dug, the eldest among them spoke.

"In the name of the father, the son and the holy spirit, Amen. We commend the body of God's truest servant to the earth. We were made from earth, and to the earth we return. We petition God to accept the soul of our beloved emperor, Constantine Palaeologus, the eleventh emperor to bear the name of the greatest of earthly emperors. May angels guard his soul now, as he surrenders his dominion on earth to serve the dominion of heaven.

"A man such as the emperor deserves a funeral that would last hours, with incense, a procession, and a homily from the patriarch himself. The city should mourn none but him. Alas, that's not going to be allowed tonight. The city mourns itself. Twelve of us gather around the emperor, as twelve apostles gathered around our Lord. We pray that the God of Abraham welcomes you, oh emperor. We pray that your burial spot is never discovered by the heathens, lest they befoul your eternal rest. Your true resting place is everywhere here. Encased in the mighty walls that protected all of our ancestors, the city is now a grave. A grave to priests, soldiers, emperors, artists and philosophers, upon every corner and every street you see the memory of their glory and of yours. May it never be forgotten. Amen."

"Amen," the others mumbled before finishing the task of burying the body.

When the deed was finally done, the unknown labourers dissipated into the darkness, there to lurk until the sun rose again on the city of Constantinople.

Epilogue – August 16, 1460

I t's startling, just how much work goes into the reception of a diplomatic envoy. For months now, chefs, planners, chamberlains and castellans had been making all of the necessary preparations to receive a guest of such import as they were preparing to receive. All over the town of Chora, preparations were made in earnest by the governor's agents. The local inhabitants were less enthused about receiving any such dignitaries from their hated enemies, but that was of little concern to the colonial administration.

The isle of Chios was a sparsely inhabited island in the northern Aegean. The island's main claim to fame since the time of antiquity has been mastic, a resin used in everything from ship tar to perfume to various confections. The only way the islanders had kept their independence from the expanding Turkish hegemony was by the patronage of the merchant city-state of Genoa, which maintained a garrison on the island, and extended enough diplomatic clout to make the island an unappealing conquest.

The flags of Genoa were about Chora, the small town that acted as administrative centre, and the harbour opened wide to accept the arrival of seven three-galleyed triremes, all of which bore the green banner of the Ottoman State, now having left Adrianople and having based itself in the old Roman capital of Constantinople.

The Greek denizens of the island were cheerless about receiving such guests. The Genoese, on the other hand, were pleased to court the friendship of allies such as the Turks. The Turks brought uniform order to a vast swath of eastern Europe, which opened stable markets to the Genoese traders. The opportunities presented by an Ottoman alliance were enough to outweigh the Turk's seizure of the Genoese colony of Galata in the wake of the fall of Constantinople.

The warships bantered about the harbour until they were properly settled into their berths and the official delegation disembarked and approached the main dock, where the Genoese administrator prepared to meet his Turkish counterpart.

One of the interesting things about the two envoys is that the Genoese ambassador was not Genoese, and the Turkish delegate was not Turkish, they were both from eastern Spain.

Ayoub-Pasha, the grand-admiral of the Ottoman navy was a roughly built Catalan seaman who always wore a warm, but aggressive smile on his weather-beaten face. His fine silk clothes and graceful turban did little disguise the nature of a man whose eyes held violent memories and friendly warmth at the same time.

"Peace be with you," he greeted the Genoese governor.

"And unto you be peace," Vincent DiCastillo answered with a bowed head and equally warm smile. The two old friends embraced. "It's been a long time, the beard suits you."

"And the new flag suits you."

"Yes, well," Vincent chuckled, "Genoa was looking for an officer with experience in the area, and they were paying more than Venice."

"You mercenary, you!"

"You're one to talk, *Ayoub-pasha*."

"Yes, I suppose I can't really condemn. Besides, men like you and I don't have countries, Old Friend."

"No, I suppose not. My wife and daughter are looking forward to seeing you. You'll honour our house as a guest."

"And I'm looking forward to seeing them again. Please lead on, old friend," Ayoub had lost none of Ezera's boisterous nature along with his foreskin and religion.

An Ottoman guard stayed in the harbour and the two old comrades took a stroll through the hilly town, leading up to the governor's mansion, atop a crest in the landscape.

"It's not exactly, Constantinople, I know," Vincent said dryly "but it seems better suited to my taste these days.

"It's nice," Ayoub said peacefully. "You wouldn't recognize Constantinople today."

"Is it that bad?"

"It's being rebuilt from the ground up. Old churches and being converted into new mosques. Palaces are becoming stables, fora are becoming caravansaries and the hippodrome's been converted into a quarry. Construction is everywhere. God knows what it'll look like in another seven years."

Vincent had a touch of mirth in his eye when he thought about

"Here we are," Vincent announced as they approached the modest home of the rural governor.

"Is that your family waiting for us?"

"It is," Vincent said proudly. "Come on, our servants have prepared lunch."

The two dignitaries walked up the steps and were met by three figures in dresses, one of whom was carrying an infant.

"Welcome to our home," Deria greeted her guest with a mandatory politeness that was hardly ingratiating. "It's been many years since we last met."

The years hadn't been kind to Vincent's wife. She seemed somewhat shorter, her face was swollen and her skin had dried from age. Her eyes still kept the same coals burning as ever; they didn't seem to have cooled off, despite the passing winters.

"Ah, the lovely Daria," Ayoub said, unperturbed by her obvious disapproval of his presence. "A fiery heart warms the soul. And this must be little Alexandra."

A precocious eight-year-old in a flowery summer dress curtsied to greet the guest. She looked at her mother and tried to match her serious mien, but her heart was far from being as densely fortified against the old pirate's charm.

"You know, the last time I saw you, you were small enough for your mother to hold in one hand," he held out a hand to demonstrate as he spoke. "… and all you did was cry. You don't still cry now, do you?"

"No!" Alexandra insisted. "I'm a young lady, and young ladies don't cry!"

"Good for you!" Ayoub kissed her on the top of her head. "Because I know many young ladies who cry every time I go anywhere."

Vincent guffawed, and Daria obviously didn't share the humour of a debauched reference applying to her young daughter.

"And these are my other two joys, Althea and Hillary."

"They're lovely," Ayoub beamed. "They must make the two of you very happy."

"They do indeed. Now sit down, Ezera. I've missed your company," Vincent motioned to a set table on the veranda of the governor's mansion. "I know that you're forbidden wine, so I've prepared some grape juice for you. It's a little old, I hope nothing's happened to it by way of fermentation."

"Ha! It would be unthinkably rude for me to refuse such an offer, so let's partake. I'm famished for real food. At sea, I've always eaten with the men. And regardless of the flag on the mast, the food is always bad. How's the flag on your mast treating you?"

"Chios isn't Constantinople, as I said earlier, but Genoa's giving me less heartache than Venice used to. I'm the governor here, so I only have to keep a monthly correspondence with the city council. Mostly all we do here is ship agricultural goods out. I track manifests. It's a comfortable retirement."

"I'm glad for you. Few deserve one more than you."

"What about you?" Vincent asked as the four of them sat down to a lunch of bonito stew and candied peaches. "Even out here we hear stories."

"What kind of stories?" Ayoub's face was locked in a grin, but his eyes lost their smile.

"Stories about a big fleet mustering in Gallipoli. Stories about the Black Sea being turned into a Turkish lake. The governor of Kaffa seems to think that the Spanish Admiral..."

"Catalan." Ayoub added ruefully.

"He said Spanish," Vincent continued unabated. "The Spanish Admiral is plotting against Genoa's holdings in the Crimea, and against the Komnenos in Trebizond."

"It's always helpful to know that strangers have such definite opinions as to what I'm thinking about," Ayoub sipped his *grape juice* and enjoyed a not-quite-forgotten flavour. "So, have you heard any news about your brother-in-law?"

"Mario?" Vincent pretended to think, as though thoughts of his sister and her husband were the furthest things from his conscious mind. "I believe that he went back to the Republic for a while."

"Oh really?" Ayoub could see that Vincent was feigning ignorance for his wife's benefit. "I heard that he went back home. Do you know what he's doing?"

"Well, apparently," Vincent laboured to find the facts and words, "He inherited a great amount of wealth from some dying distant relative or some other such scenario."

"Really?"

"Yes," the governor had a mouthful of fish stew and continued. "When the new pope, friendly to the Emperor rather than the Republic, took over in Rome, Venice expropriated several church institutions, including the university. Mario devoted himself to re-establishing the institution as a civic one. Devoted to learning, rather than politics."

"And so Mario is the rector of the school?"

"Not exactly," Vincent said at length. "He then moved to Florence."

"What is he doing in Florence?"

"Do you know the sculptor, Donatello Bardi?"

"No."

"No problem, I hadn't heard of him, either. Mario had enough money to commission some work from some famous artists for the university in Venice."

"So he's living in Venice, surrounding himself with art?"

"For a while," Vincent said. "He then moved on Belgrade, he was an advisor to John Hunyadi."

Ayoub's eyebrow raised. Four years ago, John Hunyadi had led a Hungarian army to victory, routing four Janissary ortas, and turning back the Turkish advance in the Balkans. His name was spoken as anathema in the halls of power.

"Is he in the Balkans now?"

"I don't know for certain. He's a rolling stone now, and not prone to setting down, it seems."

"I can relate," Ezera joked. "But don't worry, that instinct eventually burns itself out in all men."

"We can always hope. I'd heard from a mutual acquaintance that he was travelling west, to Portugal. But I don't know how much stock to place in such rumours," Vincent looked down as his stew and though warmly of absent family. "How's Constantinople?"

"Fine, new administration, new dynasty, same problems. Back-biting, posturing and positioning. Ambassadors and nobles clawing at the sultan's purse-strings. I made sure that your friends, Karian and Cardillo, both had descent burials. Karian was a little difficult, he took his own life, so the church warden wouldn't let him be buried on consecrated ground."

"How did you get around that?"

"I threatened to have my men dig up the whole cemetery and throw the contents into the sea."

"That let him in?"

"Oh yes," Ayoub continued. "The Genoese knight, Longo; we tried to move him to Galata, but he died from infection in Grace of God."

"I think of him every once in a while. He had a practical heroism that seemed to work well for him."

"Of course, you know about the emperor," Ayoub said slyly.

Vincent put his spoon down into his bowl.

"Yes, Ezera. I know about the emperor. I know that he was hidden and buried that no man would ever find him. I also know that your sultan claims to have found him, pickled his head in a jar of honey, and sent it to all the other turbaned kings of the east to show his prowess."

"So the story goes," Ayoub conceded. "It was me that found the body."

"I knew Constantine's face, but I don't think I would recognise the countenance of the remains in that jar that you sent to Egypt and Mesopotamia."

"Oh, I must protest," Ayoub's eyes narrowed in a knowledgeable and vicious condescension. "You'd recognize the face."

Vincent DiCastillo looked into his friend's eyes with disbelief. "Not..."

Ayoub nodded and smiled serenely.

"You're a bastard. You know that, don't you?"

Ayoub shrugged. What else could he say?

"Isodore, Ezera!" Ella called, and the two boys came running. "Quickly, quickly! Get into the carriage, we're going to the port."

"But why do we have to move again, Mama?" Isodore Orsini, the more talkative of the twins, asked. "Why can't we stay here? We don't want to leave!"

"Well, your father has a very important job, in a very faraway place, so we have to go."

"But it sounds terrible! There's nothing there!"

"That's right!" Mario said as he hurried into the foyer of the villa and picked up his two offspring. "And that's why we're going!"

He carried the children to the carriage and his wife followed close behind them. All of their possessions were already loaded onto the good ship '*Constantino*' which was ready to take them away to a new land.

As the carriage rumbled down the cobbled streets of Lisbon on a stiflingly hot August day, Doctor Mario Orsini huddled with his family and explained the ways of the world to his two boys.

"Here in this world, there are many terrible people. There are people that hate each other for no good reason, other than that they've always hated each other. Some people hate because of wars, some people hate because of language, culture or religion. Some people will always have hate in their hearts, and will never be able to walk away from other people's grudges. And we're going to leave this behind because I don't want you two killing or being killed because other people hate each other. That's not going to be for you, okay?"

"Yes, father," the twins said in unison. "Will there be other children where we're going?"

"Not at first," Mario said truthfully. "Some Portuguese sailors found some big islands way off in the Atlantic Ocean, and they're called the Azores. No people had ever been to those islands before, and now we're going there, and we'll be the first to call them home. The king of Portugal has asked me to take five hundred men and start to build a city from nothing. Next year, other families are going to come. We're going to build a new city, with no history. A city that doesn't have any history to live down; a city that's free from blood feuds, racism, religious wars and vendettas.

"Now you know, history is very important, and that's why I'm teaching you two boys about it, so you can know about the past and learn important things. But you can't live in the past, like so many people do. Your mother and I met each other in a place with a glorious past, but no future. It can't have any future because her past is so great and so terrible. Where we're going, there is no past, only mountains, and sea and jungle. The future is what we make of it. It's very exciting."

"Yes, Father," the twins answered mechanically.

Their father had been excited before about new starts for as long as Ella had known him; Constantinople, then back in Venice, then Hungary and now the Azores. Their mother held tightly to a rosary and hoped that this new start would be the last one.

When she first moved to Constantinople after the deaths of her parents in Spain, the permanence and stability of the old city had been a great appeal to making her feel safe. She'd been protected by the walls of her brother's home, surrounded by the walls of the compound, surrounded by the walls of the quarter, surrounded by the walls of the city. That safety was long gone, and stability was not a virtue that her husband valued more than freedom. Their family was now a wind, blowing over all lands.

She wasn't as confident as her husband in humanity's ability to make new starts. Hatred and virulence weren't miasma that hung in the air around stones and trees, nor around the man-made glories of antiquity. They were poisons carried in the heart, and they would travel with us wherever we went.

In the end, she decided to remain silent. There really was no point in trying to stamp down on the possibility of a better world, of a new home. The future is always open, and the promise of a new day never loses its luster. Westward they would sail, chasing the setting sun, chasing a new start and a new world, chasing safety and freedom, chasing history and change, and finding only that new day and a new place to burn the hearth-fires of home.

Appendix A

List of Characters
in the Marching to Byzantium Trilogy

Muslims

Ahmet son of Ali:	Anatolian Tribesman in the personal service of Halil Chandarli
Aynur:	Mehmet's mistress
Fatma:	Most recent wife of the former Sultan
Halil Chandarli:	Prime Minister, opposes the war
Mehmet II:	Eighteen year old Ottoman Sultan
Nulifer:	Mehmet's wife
Mesut:	Janissary commander
Tolga:	Emire of Sinope and Kastamonu, Mehmet's ally and father-in-law
Zaganos:	Second Minister, supports the war

Erkin
Hussein   Three Janissary recruits
Iskender

Western Christians

Balias DiNapoli:	Constable of Venice, part of papal mission
Daria DiCastillo:	Vincent's wife
Dominic Trebianno:	Governor of Galata
Ella DiCastillo:	Vincent's sister
Ezera:	Catalan sea-captain
Giovanni Cardillo:	Governor of Venetian concession
Hectore Pazzi:	Constable of Galata
Isaac DiNapoli:	Bishop of Venice, head of papal mission
Mario Orsini:	Venetian doctor, living in exile
Vincent DiCastillo:	Commander of the Venetian Garrison

Eastern Christians

Adam Karian:	Commander of the armies of Byzantium
Constantine XI:	The last emperor
Gennadios:	Priest opposed to union with Rome
Isodore:	Bulgarian refugee monk, in the employ of Vincent DiCastillo
Noah:	Priest favouring union with Rome
Stavros:	Court noble

Appendix B

Glossary

Things

Akche	A unit of currency based on silver
Anthypatos	Provincial governor or court official
Beylik	A minor Turkish landholding, a barony
Chorbachi	Lit. Soup-maker, Title of the commander of a Janissary Orta
Devshirme	Turkish administrative class
Gazi	An independent holy warrior
Grand Vizier	Prime Minister
Haram	Forbidden to Muslims, i.e. Pork
Harem	Area of the palace forbidden to all but the Sultan's family
Harquebus	An early firearm
Helal	Allowed to Muslims, i.e. fruit
Janissary	Elite Turkish standing army
Khan	Turkic hereditary king
Orta	Division of a Turkish army
Proconsul	Provincial governor
Sanjak	Turkish province
Sipahi	Land-owning gentry who owe military service to the Sultan
Sultan	Literally "Strength" or "Power," it has come to mean a Muslim King
Tagmata	A regiment in the army of the Eastern Roman Empire
Tekke	A lodge for Muslim religious orders

Tugra	A stylised signature or seal of an Ottoman ruler
Ulema	Muslim religious scholars, as a class
Valide Sultan	The formal wife of the sultan, not the equivalent of queen
Vizier	A minister of state

Places

Listed below are the names of cities and countries used in 1453, and their 21st Century equivalent.

Adrianople	Edirne, Turkey
Al-Andalus	Spain
Amaseia	Amasya, Turkey
Araby	Arabia
Bactria	Afghanistan
Brussa	Bursa, Turkey
Chalcedon	Kadiköy, Istanbul
Constantinople	Istanbul, Turkey
Hindustan	India
Iconium	Konya, Turkey
Persia	Iran
Phillipopolis	Plovdiv, Bulgaria
Scutari	Üsküdar, Istanbul
Studion	Bakirköy, Istanbul

Names

Family names were uncommon in Turkish society at this time, common names being distinguished by parentage, for example Ali son of Jenk. Honorifics were added to the end of first names to denote status. For example John

Smith would be John-bey in polite conversation, rather than Mr. Smith. The following suffixes follow that pattern.

Abi: Older brother
Abla: Older sister
Bey: Mister or sir
Hanim: Mrs. or Ma'am
Pasha: To someone of very high status, analogous
               to My Lord